EDWIN ABBOTT
COLLECTION – VOL. 1
THE DISCIPLE'S TRILOGY

PHILOCHRISTUS: Memoirs Of A Disciple Of The Lord

ONESIMUS: Memoirs Of A Disciple Of St. Paul

SILANUS THE CHRISTIAN

THE CHRISTIAN COLLECTION # 690

CONTENTS

BOOK ONE.
PHILOCHRISTUS

MEMOIRS OF A DISCIPLE OF THE LORD

TO THE AUTHOR OF 'ECCE HOMO'

NOT MORE IN ADMIRATION OF HIS WRITINGS THAN IN GRATITUDE FOR THE SUGGESTIVE INFLUENCE OF A LONG AND INTIMATE FRIENDSHIP.

PHILOCHRISTUS THE ELDER TO THE SAINTS OF THE CHURCH IN LONDINIUM, GRACE, MERCY, AND PEACE FROM THE LORD JESUS CHRIST

Forasmuch as almost all those disciples who with me saw the Lord Jesus in the flesh, are now fallen asleep, and I myself am well stricken in years and daily expect the summons of the Lord; it hath therefore seemed good to me to bequeath unto you some memorial of Christ in writing; which, instead of my voice, shall testify to you of him for ever.

All the more need seemeth thereof because the Lord delayeth his coming. For now these ten years Jerusalem hath been trodden down of the Gentiles, and the words of the Lord concerning the destruction of the Holy City have been fulfilled; and yet he cometh not. Yea, and sometimes my mind presageth that his coming may be yet longer delayed, even till all they that knew him in the flesh have fallen asleep.

For this cause I was long ago moved, even from the second or third year after the destruction of the Holy City, to leave some record behind me to testify of the Lord. But when I adventured to write, behold, it was an hard matter and well-nigh impossible, to set forth such an image of the Lord Jesus as should be at once according to the truth, and yet not altogether too bright for mortal eye to look upon and love. Therefore at the last, when I perceived that it was not given unto me to portray any character of the Lord as he was in himself, I determined rather to set forth an history of mine own life; wherein) as in a mirror, might perchance be discerned some lineaments of the countenance of Christ, seen as by reflexion, in the life of one that loved him.

CHAPTER I.

Of my Childhood in Galilee; and how I gave myself wholly to the Study of the Law.

MY former name was Joseph the son of Simeon, and I was born in Sepphoris, the metropolis of Galilee, in the twentieth year of the reign of the Emperor Augustus, about four years before the death of King Herod. In those days Israel was grievously afflicted, and tribulation befell the righteous. Satan put it into the heart of the rulers of the land to move the people to the worship of false gods, and the Lord God had not yet raised up a Redeemer for Israel.

In my fourth year my father's brother, the Rabbi Matthias, was burned alive by Herod for causing his scholars to cast down the golden image of an eagle which the king had set up over the gate of the temple of the Lord. Not many months afterwards, the Romans marched through Sepphoris in order to bring succour to Sabinus, who was hard beset by the men of Jerusalem in the fortress called Antonia; and we fought against them, and my father was taken captive and crucified by Varus. Now as concerning my father and my father's brother, how they were slain, perchance I remember their deaths rather from my mother's often mention of them in after times than from what I heard then: but this thing can I never forget, for I saw it with mine own eyes: namely, how, when my mother brought me forth from the caves of Arbela whither we had been sent for refuge, behold, where Sepphoris had stood, there was not now one house standing; and I saw also the bodies of many of my kinsfolk, which lay unburied and crying unto the Lord for vengeance. Yet the Lord sent no avenger.

After this came tidings that the Parthians, which went with Varus, had laid waste the country in the south far and wide, and had slain our brethren with the sword; and that Varus had taken two thousand of my countrymen in Jerusalem and had crucified them, and among them Eleazar, the youngest and dearest of my mother's brethren. Then my mother led me to a rocky place not far from Sampho. There was a cave there, and only one path led to it, and that so narrow that no multitude of men could force an entrance, if one brave man withstood them. When we were come thither, my mother lifted up her voice and wept, and pointing to the cave she said, "In former times this cave was held by my mother's brother, Hezekiah by name. Six children he had; and he fled from Herod the King with them and with his wife, and here they took refuge. Now when the king could by no means drive Hezekiah hence by force, he offered much gold unto him if he would come forth from the cave quietly. But when Hezekiah refused, the king began to let down armed men by ropes from the top of the hill, with firebrands in their hands, to kindle fires at the mouth of the cave. Then when no hope of safety remained, behold, my mother's brother brought out his children, and slew the youngest with his sword in the sight of the king. Afterwards he laid his hands on his second child., But Herod, perceiving his intent, stretched out his right hand and besought Hezekiah to spare his children and to come forth in peace. But he slew the second also, heaping reproaches on Herod as an usurper and a son of Edom, sitting on David's seat; and he slew the third and the rest likewise, even to the sixth, and last of all his wife; and then he cast himself down the steep place and perished." Then spake my mother unto me and said, "The Lord do so unto thee, my son, and more likewise, if thou avenge not the blood of thy kinsfolk and of thy father." So it came to pass that, even from a child, I hated the very name of a Gentile with an exceeding hatred; insomuch that I should have accounted him blessed who should have taken the children of Borne (according as it is written) and dashed them against the stones.

There stood up at this time divers to lead Israel; but they were no true leaders of the people, and the Lord had not sent them. Athronges the shepherd, a man of great stature, and Simon, one of the servants of Herod the King, rose up in the south of Judah; but they both perished, and their followers were scattered. Again, about the time of the numbering of the people, when the decree went forth from the Emperor Augustus that all Israel should be taxed, there rose up Judas of Gamala. This was about the thirty-third year of the Emperor Augustus. The people came to him from all sides; and Judas taught them that it was not lawful to pay tribute to Caesar, nor to call any man Master, save God alone. At that time I was some thirteen years old; and I saw him when, with a thousand men, he marched into Capernaum and burned down the house of customs there; and as I looked upon his face, and the numbers of his followers, I thought within my heart, "Surely the hand of the Lord is with this man, surely this is the Redeemer of Israel, even the Messiah to whom all the prophets bear witness, that he must arise and judge the land." But five Sabbaths had not passed away before he also had been cut off; and all the men that were with him were either scattered to their homes or slain.

Meanwhile, as I grew up, I was being trained by my mother with all care in the paths of the law of Israel; and according to the custom of my people, at five years old I had begun to learn the Scripture, and, at ten years, Mishnah; and I profited more than my companions in the study of the Traditions. But when I read how great things God had done in times past for His chosen ones, and how He had redeemed Israel by the hand of His servants Gideon and David, then did my heart burn within me; and I besought the Lord that He would repeat His mercies upon His chosen people, and that He would speedily send that Messiah of whom all the prophets spake, for the Redemption of Israel. Afterwards I questioned one of my teachers, by name Abuyah the son of Elishah, and I said unto him, "It is revealed and known before the All-seeing (blessed is He) that our will is to do His will: and what hindereth?" Then he answered and said, "The dough in the leaven" (meaning Gentile customs, which corrupt the customs of Israel even as leaven changeth bread) "and servitude to the Kingdom." Then I said, "Why therefore do we not rise up against the Gentile Kingdom?" But he answered, "Joseph, son of Simeon, busy thyself with the Law. Whosoever is busied in the Law for the Law's sake deserveth many things; and not only so, but he is worth the whole world. He is called friend, beloved; loveth God, loveth mankind; please th God, pleaseth mankind. And it clotheth him with meekness and fear, and fitteth him to become righteous, pious, upright, and faithful; and removeth him from sin, and bringeth him towards the side of merit." Then said I, "But wherefore doth not the God of our Salvation bring freedom to Israel?" But he answered, "It is said, The tables were the work of God, and the writing was the writing of God, graven upon the tables. Read not *charuth*, graven, but *cheruth*, freedom; for thou wilt find none free, save only them which be occupied in the learning of the Law. For whoso is occupied in learning the Law, behold, it magnifieth him and exalteth him over all things."

Then I applied myself more diligently to the study of the Law, and I observed Sabbaths and festivals, and practised ablutions with all scruple; and I became known among my companions as a sin-fearer, instructed in the wisdom of the Law, avoiding those lesser faults which are called the "Descendants," as well as those which are called the "Fathers"; insomuch that I would not even curdle milk on the

Sabbath, because that had been declared by the decisions of the Wise to be a lesser kind of building; neither would I walk upon grass during the Sabbath, because that also had been pronounced by the Rabbis to be a lesser kind of threshing.

Also in the matter of fringes and phylacteries, and in smaller matters, even to the burning of nail-parings, I walked diligently according to the decisions of the Ancients. Thus in all things I strove to bear in mind the saying that "While in the written Law there are light as well as weighty precepts, the precepts of the Scribes are all weighty." I took little sleep, little merriment; I associated myself ever with the wise, and abstained from the company of the people of the land (for by this name the Pharisees were wont to call them that gave not themselves to the study of the Law); I settled my heart to study; I asked, and answered, and whatsoever I received I strove to add thereto. And it came to pass that, because I had a strength of memory more than was usual among my fellow-students, my teacher said to me, "Joseph, son of Simeon, thou art a plastered cistern, which loseth no drop of water"; and by this name of "plastered cistern" I became known among my fellows. And when I perceived that the Traditions said little concerning a Messiah; and that my teachers also said little, and had no hope, nor so much as a desire (for the most part) that a Messiah should ever come, but were wholly given up to the study of the Law; then I endeavoured myself also to do the same, and to put away the thought of a Redeemer.

Nevertheless at times the question would arise within me, "Wherefore do I serve God for naught?" For all around I saw the wicked and the scornful seated, as kings, in high places, and the poor and the humble trampled under foot. There was the name of peace among us, but it was no peace; for Satan was making war upon us under the semblance of peace. Everywhere defilement was taking the land by force or by stealth. Many Greek cities, called by the names of the great ones among the Gentiles, were built in the midst of us, such as Tiberias, and Julias, and Caesarea Stratonis, and Caesarea Philippi; and even in our city of Sepphoris, now rebuilt, we were constrained to admit Greeks to be our fellow-citizens. Theatres and amphitheatres, and games, and alien rites in honour of false gods, had been brought in among us. Images of living things began to be seen on every side, and even our coinage was defiled with the uncleanness of the Gentiles; so that, in place of the vine-clusters and wheat- sheaf and star of Israel, we were forced to handle the semblances of

Thracian shields and helmets, and the winged rod of enchantments, called by the Gentiles the caduceus. Moreover, as each year passed, our fears waxed greater and greater, lest at last the eagles of the Gentiles should be brought from Caesarea into the streets of the Holy City itself, and lest the image of the Emperor should be set up therein. For the former Emperor, even Caesar Augustus, was now dead, and a new Emperor reigned in his stead, whose name was Tiberius. But he attained not unto the former Emperor in wisdom; wherefore the minds of many were unsettled, the common people fearing lest the Romans should take away their religion, and the Scribes fearing lest the common people should incense the Romans by fresh revolt, and so bring destruction on the nation.

So it came to pass that by reason of my continual sorrow for the burdens of Sion, my heart was pressed down with care, and my trouble became too heavy for me to bear; and I found no peace, no, not even in the study of the Law. In vain I repeated to myself the saying of the Wise, "Whoso studieth the Law, he becometh modest and long-suffering and forgiving of insult "; and again, "The Law is acquired by long-suffering, by a good heart, by faith in the Wise, by acceptance of chastisements." I looked upon my countrymen in their servitude, and I could not feel long-suffering; neither could I attain to the wisdom of the acceptance of chastisements.

When I mentioned my trouble to my teacher, Abuyah the son of Elishah, he rebuked me for presumption; for he said that such doubts came of evil, neither would he hearken unto me. Therefore I turned to another of the Scribes, whose name was Jonathan the son of Ezra. Now Jonathan was older than Abuyah the son of Elishah, but not so learned. Howbeit he was of a more gentle and loving disposition. He said to me, "Beware lest thou follow the path of Elishah the son of Solomon." "What path?" I asked. Then Jonathan answered as follows: "It is reported that Elishah the son of Solomon was once studying the Scriptures, and he saw two men taking birds' nests. The one obeyed not the Law, but took the mother with the young; yet he went his way in peace. The other obeyed the Law and took the young only, but let the mother go free; yet as he descended from the tree a serpent stung him and he died. Then said Elishah the son of Solomon, "Is it not written, The young thou mayest take to thyself, but the mother thou shalt surely let go, that it may be well with thee and that thou mayest live many days? Verily the promises of God are naught, for the man that obeyed hath not lived many days, but the man that disobeyed is unhurt." Then said I, "And what answer was made to Elishah the son of Solomon?" And my teacher replied, "Whosoever obeyeth the Law, his days will be long in the world to come." Then was my heart comforted for a while, and I devoted myself even more diligently than before to the study of the Law.

CHAPTER II.

Of my Doubts concerning the Law; and of the Patriots or Galileans; and of the Expectation concerning John the Son of Zachariah.

FOR the space of nine or ten years I was content to give myself wholly to the study of the Law; but when I had now numbered thirty years, my doubts and fears came back to me again. While I sat in the school with the Scribe, and heard. his answers and asked him questions, so long I seemed to myself righteous and on the path of righteousness; but when I came forth into the streets, or back to my mother's house, then seemed my righteousness immediately to have vanished away. At such seasons the learning of the Wise seemed to me not bread, but a stone.

Moreover, my heart was turned from some of the Scribes that lived in Sepphoris, even them that were counted as props and pillars of the Law. To Jonathan the son of Ezra I ceased not to pay honour; but Abuyah the son of Elishah I could not reverence, and others also like unto him: for they had regard unto the praise of men rather than to the love of God. As, for example, Abuyah, whensoever he was delayed by the crowd so that he came not to the synagogue in time for prayer, he would stand where he chanced to be, at the hour of prayer, praying in the middle of the market-place. When he walked, he walked with a mincing gait and with his eyes half closed, feigning to be given up to the meditation of the Law, so that he saw no passer by. On fast days he would ever look pale and worn, as if with watching and hunger; and whensoever he met a woman as he went in the way, he would shiver and turn aside. It came to pass that on a certain day one of his pupils asked him which was the most weighty of precepts. Then Abuyah answered, "The Law of Tassels "; and continued he, "so do I esteem this law that once, because I had chanced to tread upon a portion of the fringe of my garment, going up a ladder, I steadfastly refused to move from the spot where I stood, till such time as the rent had been repaired." Another day, this Abuyah chid my mother because she wore on her dress a ribbon that was not sewn, but only fastened to her vesture. For thus, he said, my mother transgressed the Law by bearing burdens on the Sabbath. But by such teaching Abuyah himself laid upon his pupils burdens grievous to be borne; and among the Rabbis of Israel there were more like unto Abuyah the son of "Elishah than unto Jonathan the son of Ezra.

Many things also in the traditions of the Wise seemed to me not worthy of wise men, nor even of honest men. I had joined myself to a certain brotherhood (who all, or almost all, were Pharisees), such as bound themselves to observe the Law with special strictness, and in particular to pay tithes of all things. The brotherhood was called Chabura, and each of the brethren was called a Chaber. Now it was the custom of us Chaberim to meet on the Sabbath day at one another's houses that we might sup together. But the space between our houses often exceeded two thousand paces, which distance was not to be exceeded by a man journeying on the Sabbath day. Therefore to a plain man it would have seemed that we could not sup with one another on the Sabbath day and at the same time obey the Law. But the Scribes were otherwise minded; and many of them, yea even of the strictest sect, escaped from the Law after this fashion. On the evening before the Sabbath, they would place small pieces of meat, distant two thousand paces one from another, on the road whereon they desired to journey. Where a man's meat is, said they, there is his home. So when they were come in their journeying to the first piece of meat, they would say, "Now I am at my home and may walk yet another two thousand paces." And so, walking from this home to other homes if need were, they walked as far as they listed. This mixing of distances they called *erûbh*, or "mixture;" and the device remaineth unto this day.

Again, if a man's ox were dying on some holy day, and the owner thereof desired to kill it; he was forbidden. But if he slew the beast and then took of the meat and ate thereof, yea, even though it were a piece of flesh no bigger than an olive, and if he said, "I slay the beast to provide a necessary meal," then he was held excused. Likewise, though a man might not buy from a butcher on the Sabbath, yet if he abstained from mentioning the number or weight of the things bought, and the sum of money to be paid, then he might buy as much as his heart desired and be held blameless. Thus he would say, "Give me a portion, or half a portion of meat," and the butcher would give it; and the buyer would go away, paying naught. But next day the money would be paid. And this was called not a sale, but a gift. After the same manner they did away with the Law which remitteth debts in the Sabbatical year. On the day of payment the creditor would come (such was the ordinance of the Scribes) and say, "In accordance with the Sabbatical year I remit thee the debt." Then the debtor was bound to reply, "I nevertheless wish to pay it," and the debt was paid, and the Law was made of none effect.

About the thirteenth year of the Emperor Tiberius, it came to pass that I (being now thirty-three years old or a little more) discoursed with a Greek proselyte concerning the Law. He said to me that it seemed to him better to disannul such ordinances as were not convenient (just as a man might prune a too luxuriant vine); and not to say, "I will obey the ordinance, but I will make my obedience the same as disobedience." His words pleased me; but when I reported this saying to some of the Scribes my friends, they with one consent rejected it. Abuyah the son of Elishah said, scoffing at my doubts, "The Law drowneth them that cannot swim." Then said I (repeating a certain saying of the Greek), "But water groweth bad if it be kept long in one vessel." But he straightway put me to silence saying, "Is this likewise the case with the Law? Nay, it is like unto wine which groweth better as it groweth older." Jonathan the son of Ezra also added in a gentle voice, "My son, thou knowest the saying of the Elders, the first of the sayings of the Wise: Be deliberate in judgment, and raise up many disciples, and make a fence to the Law. But thou, my son, wouldst fain pull down fences. But if we begin to destroy a part of the Law, who shall stay the hand of the destroyer?

And in the end we shall be even as the Gentiles, which have no law. Is it not better to be too careful rather than to be too careless? Is it not better to have too many fences rather than to have too few? For to what is the matter like? Even to a man watching a garden. If he watch it from without, it is all watched. But if he watch it from within, the part in front of him is watched; but the part behind him is not watched. Be thou therefore careful to go in thine obedience even beyond the things which the Law require th at thy hands; and watch the Law not from within, but from without."

There seemed much wisdom in the sayings of Jonathan, and I knew not what answer to make. For if to transgress the Law, even in the smallest matter, was to fall into destruction, then it seemed wise to fence round the Law, even as a man would fence round a pit; and not to suffer the unwary to go near, and peradventure to stumble, and so to be swallowed up. Yet I could not but perceive that it was not well for men thus to resort to the Law and to the Traditions as to a sacred oracle, even on those occasions and in those matters wherein the voice of the Lord speaking unto the heart saith clearly, "This is right, do this. This is wrong, do not this." For thus it must needs come to pass that men would pervert even the Law to the contradicting of the voice of the Lord. And so indeed it was with us. As, for example, the Law forbade fornication, neither did it permit us to marry a woman with intent to divorce her; but one of the Traditions, making the Law of none effect, told us that "If a man first tell her that he is going to marry her for a season, then it is lawful."

Other Traditions sinned yet more grievously in the cloaking of sins and impurities. Hence also the duties of children to parents (albeit upheld indeed by the better part of the Wise) were by many diminished, or even made of none effect.

Now I have heard certain Romans say that in their Law they also use the same devices to observe the letter and to break the spirit. But the mischief was, that our Law was not as the laws of the Gentiles, which concern naught save lands, and houses, and slaves, and the like, and which have not to do with the souls and spirits of men. The Gentiles could break the letter of their laws and sin not: for what sin was it to make a slave free by feigning to sell him, or, in disputing about a farm, to treat of a clod as though it were the farm? But our Law had to do with the supreme God, the Maker of all things, the All-seeing (blessed is He). Therefore to observe the letter and to break the spirit of His Law seemed to be a profaning of His Holy Name. Now I had been trained up from my earliest years to dread the pulling down of the fences, having this precept, as it were, engraved and charactered in my memory, "Whoso pulleth down a hedge a serpent shall sting him:" and I had been taught to prefer Sinai, that is, the teacher of the Law, even to an " uprooter of mountains," that is, to a teacher which hath understanding to remove all manner of offences and stumbling- blocks from the path of the weak ones. Howbeit, at times, after discourse with the Greek proselyte whom I mentioned above, there would arise in my heart this thought, that when the words of the Law seemed to contradict that which was right, then we ought to go into the presence of God and to say, "Thou, God of righteousness, art righteous altogether, neither can it be Thy pleasure that we should be unrighteous "; and again, "Thou art a God of truth, neither can it be Thy will that we should lie with our hands in Thy presence. Therefore permit us in this case to break Thy Law. For Thy righteousness is greater than Thy Law." But the Scribes would not so much as listen to such words as these; for they said that scarce even a prophet durst speak so exceeding boldly. But when I asked them whether it might be that a prophet should arise in Israel, then the most said that it was not possible; for the Shekinah and the Holy Spirit had departed from Israel when the first Temple had been destroyed. Thus my words were an abomination unto my teachers, so that I hid my thoughts in my heart: but it was pain and grief to me.

Yet another trouble was added to me. For as I grew older and understood more of the ways of men and perceived the thoughts of men's hearts, it seemed to me a strange and horrible thing that the Law of the Lord should be cut off from the greater part of the Lord's people: so that it was a current saying with the Rabbis that the common people were an accursed rabble which knew not the Law: insomuch that one of the most pious of our teachers, even Hillel the Great, said that no boor could be a sin-fearer, and that the people of the land (for by that name they called the common people) could not be pious. This, I say, seemed an horrible thing: yet indeed I could not deny that the Scribes must needs be right, and that the people of the land could not be pious, so long as to be pious meant to be obedient to the light precepts of the Law, such as the laws concerning the exact observance of the Sabbath, and concerning purifications, and concerning the consumption of nail-parings, and the like. For the knowledge of all these things was not to be obtained save by men of leisure, that could give their time, and settle their minds to the study of such matters: and how was this possible for them that must needs earn their bread with the sweat of their brow, to wit, the sailors and fishermen, the vine-dressers and ploughmen, the dyers and glassmakers; who all were called of the Scribes "the people of the land"? So it was borne in upon me that our Law was a Law for the schools, but not for the lives of men; and for Scribes, but not for the whole nation. Then my heart sank within me, and I remembered the words of the Prophet, how that a time shall come when men shall no longer teach each one his neighbour, saying, Know the Lord; but all shall know Him from the least even to the greatest; and I wondered if it would please the Lord to bring such a time as that to Israel, and to make His Law clear to all our nation, yea, even to the poor and simple, even to the people of the land.

Others that did not observe the Law so exactly as I did, nor felt the burdens thereof so sorely, were nevertheless ill pleased that the Scribes did naught to free them from the yoke of the Gentiles. Of these some dwelt in Judaea, and a few in Peraea; but the more part dwelt in Galilee, insomuch that the sect of Patriots was known by the name of Galileans. There were also living among us James and John, the two eldest sons of Judas of Galilee, and their youngest brother Manahem. To these, for the sake of their great father, we all had respect. Many also (like myself) were ever in a readiness to avenge upon the Romans the blood of kinsfolk shed in the Galilean wars. Hence it came to pass that in Galilee more than in any region of Syria, the minds of men were ready for revolt against the Romans, and waited but for the ripening of occasion.

Now it came to pass that in the fourteenth year of Tiberius Caesar, there arose a quarrel between the Tetrarch of Galilee and his father-in-law, the King of Arabia; because the Tetrarch had behaved ill to the King's daughter his wife, and sought to divorce her. Then it seemed good to some of my friends to join the army of Antipas the Tetrarch, to the intent that they might thereby gain experience in war; but others spake against it, saying that it was not lawful to take up arms for the unjust against the just.

At this time also a rumour went forth that a new prophet had of late appeared, John by name, the son of Zachariah a priest, who was calling the whole of Israel to repent and to be purified with baptisms, prophesying that the Lord would soon send the Deliverer of Israel, or Messiah: for by this name of Messiah, the Deliverer that was to come (of whom the prophets had prophesied) was commonly known among us. Some said that John himself was the Messiah; others denied it, but said that the Lord had sent down Elias from heaven, and that John was Elias. Many other rumours also were noised abroad, and this rumour prevailed most, that "One from the East would come forth to rule the world," which saying had spread even to Italy and Spain: and we in Galilee thought that this conqueror from the East would be our Messiah. Thus, the hearts of all men everywhere being in expectation, it came to pass that many of my friends (who were the leaders of the sect called the Patriots or Galileans), having purposed these many weeks to hold a council, determined at this time to confer together in a little valley between Sepphoris and Nazareth, there to resolve what should be done.

Most of those present were from the inland parts of Galilee: of these Barabbas, and one other, were from Jotapata. Only Hezekiah, the son of Zachariah (a Scribe, who was thought to be well affected towards the Galileans), came from Jerusalem. And from Capernaum came my cousin Baruch, the son of Manasseh, with three others. There were present also from the region of Gaulonitis James and John and Manahem, sons of the famous Judas of Galilee. James the son of Judas spake first, giving his judgment for war, and saying that Israel had slept too long: "For while we sleep," said he, "the leaven spreadeth; Greek cities cover our land; our own cities are being defiled with Gentile abominations. They are stealing from us even our language. No man may earn a living in Galilee now, unless he speak Greek. With Greek theatres and amphitheatres, and baths, and market-places; with Greek pictures and images, and feasts and games; with Greek songs, and poems, and histories,— they purpose, by easy degrees, to beguile the hearts of our young men from the religion of their forefathers. Our princes are Edomites in the pay of Rome. Our rich men long for the fleshpots of Rome, and call themselves by the name of Herod. Our Scribes, our wise men, cry peace when there is no peace, and wink at the payment of tribute. Publicans and harlots bring down the wrath of God upon the nation, and go unpunished. All these things are as the meshes of the net wherein Borne is encompassing our city. And lo, the fowler layeth the net and the silly bird stayeth still." Then Baruch said: "But is it so indeed that the Romans would blot out our religion? Do they not suffer all religions? The Gauls, the Spaniards, the Numidians, Egyptians and Scythians, all worship divers gods: so have I heard from a Greek merchant at Capernaum; and this, without let or hindrance from the Romans."

"Nay," cried Barabbas, "but thou seest not that the Roman suffereth all false religions and hindereth them not; but he hateth the worship of the true God of Israel. For this alone putteth other gods to shame. The Syrians and the Egyptians scruple not to worship the Roman gods, besides Astarte and Osiris, and to offer incense to the emperor of Rome, to boot. But the children of Israel will bow down to no false god, neither offer they incense before the image of the emperor. Hence cometh it to pass that the Romans hate our religion and would fain destroy it. James therefore speaketh the words of truth; and whoso speaketh otherwise allegeth naught but pretexts of delay and cowardice."

"Peace, Barabbas," said John, the son of Judas; "we meet to hold conference, not to cast reproaches. Nevertheless, my judgment goeth with my brother, that our choice lieth between lingering perdition and speedy deliverance. Hereof this is proof. But lately I was at the Holy City, not many days before the Passover; and there went abroad a rumour that the Procurator Pilate was minded to bring the eagles of the legions from Caesarea to Jerusalem, yea, even into the streets of the Holy City. Then the Priests, even the Chief Priests, yea, even the whole Council, fell down at Pilate's feet, if perchance he would change his purpose. Multitudes ran together round the Praetorium. In vain did they pray and were disquieted. Under the cloak of night the procurator brought in the Abomination. Then all the men of Jerusalem, and all the pilgrims which had come together from the uttermost parts of the earth, clothed themselves in sackcloth, and sat down in the streets about the palace, with ashes on their heads after the manner of suppliants; crying aloud that they would sit there for ever rather than endure the presence of the Abomination. But when Pilate saw all the streets of Jerusalem thronged, so that no one might pass night and day, and all business was at a stand, did he yield from his purpose? Nay, he gave orders that the armed cohorts should beset the streets around us, threatening to smite us with the sword if we should not straightway void the streets. And when we would not, then went the word forth from the captains to draw the swords; and the swords were drawn, and the soldiers were in act to fall upon us. But we uncovered our necks and held them out to the soldiers, crying 'Give us death rather than defilement.' So at the last, but not till blood had been shed, the procurator gave consent that the images should be sent back. Suppose ye that this was a little matter, naught but an error in judgment of the procurator? Would a procurator have dared to risk the peace of the whole province for a little matter? It was no little matter. Pilate did what he did, not of himself, but at the express instance of the emperor; to prove the limits of our slavishness, and to force us into defilement and into the worship of the Abomination."

Hereat there was a general applause; but he, not heeding it, continued, "If ye be of one mind with me that the hour is come to smite with the sword; then how and where? I say, let certain of us join ourselves to the army of the Tetrarch, which even now maketh ready to march against Aretas. Thereby we shall gain experience of war, and, as I hope, win over some of the army to our side. As for the tyrant's guards, the Gauls, Germans, and Thracians, they are bought with his money, so that we have no hope of them; but by far the larger part of the army consisteth of our own countrymen; and many of them may revolt on our side; as they did with Simon against Archelaus, and some also helped Athronges, whom men call a rebel. Meantime, let the rest of us make ready our friends in our several cities to take up arms next Passover. They in Jerusalem will attack the garrison there, others break open the armoury at Sepphoris and in Masada. On the same day our countrymen in Joppa, Caesarea, and Ptolemais will attack and drive out the Greeks. Then will rise a flame of war from one end of Syria to the other. Our rich men, even the Herodians, seeing all the people to be of one mind, will stand with us; and having Israel with us as one man, doing battle for the name of the true God against the gods of the Gentiles, doubt not but we shall have also the sword of the Lord on our side, as in the days of Gideon."

The applause was now yet louder than before; and at first it seemed as though the whole assembly were minded with one consent to obey the words of John the son of Judas of Galilee. But one of the companions of Hezekiah, Levi by name, an old man and grey-bearded, rose up presently and said that the hour had not yet arrived, because, said he, the Sabbath was not yet duly observed, and the wrath of the Lord still weighed upon Israel. Then Barabbas answered with indignation, saying that it was only the rich and delicate, or else they that were enfeebled with old age, who were thus content to be the slaves of idolaters.

Upon this Hezekiah the Scribe stood up to speak: "These young men of Galilee gladly make mention of the old times of Gideon and David, yet do they not themselves imitate the old times in having respect unto old age. For even though Levi were old and enfeebled, yet what saith the Tradition? 'Old age, though it be broken, is yet to be held in reverence, even as the broken tables of the Law were kept in the ark of the Lord.' But what meaneth this youth of Jotapata, when he calleth my friend and companion Levi, the son of Ezra, delicate or enfeebled; and all because the advice of Levi is not the advice of Barabbas? Hear, ye young men of Galilee, the words of Levi are true: the hour hath not yet arrived. 'What hindereth?' ye ask. I answer in the words of the Wise, 'The dough in the leaven.'

"I also, like John the son of Judas, will give proof of my words; but do ye, being Galileans, incline your ears to the saying of a Galilean, according to the proverb, 'A Galilean said When the shepherd is angry with his flock, he appointeth for their leader a blind bell-wether.' Note therefore the leaders of Israel, which have risen up against the Romans of late. Hath God sent them in anger or in mercy? Have they been blind bell-wethers, or endowed with sight? I say naught of Judas of Gamala, in the presence of his sons: but Judas the son of the robber Hezekiah, how went it with him? He thought in his heart that he was a second Joshua, and that the waters of Jordan would part at his word. But who knoweth not his miserable end? As also the end of Athronges: who aimed at the kingdom because, forsooth, he was in stature a second Saul. Simon also, the slave of Herod the king, when he had shown forth his valour by destroying the king's palace at Jericho, became a portion for foxes at Amathus, and his head was cast before the feet of the conqueror. Answer then unto me, ye young men. Hath the Lord sent Simon the slave, and Athronges the shepherd, and Judas the son of the robber, in mercy or in wrath?

"Nay, but since shame hindereth your answering, I, even I, a man of Judaea, will answer for you, according as it is said, 'From Judaea grain, from Galilee straw, from Peraea chaff.' The Lord sent these men in wrath. All these were blind bell-wethers, blinded by the lust of fame or gain. But do ye therefore wait for the true leaders whom the Lord your God will send? Leave it to this young man of Jotapata to follow any knave that may chance to call himself the Redeemer of Israel because, forsooth, he may be a head taller than his neighbours, or may have dreamed a dream, or may perchance have gained some knowledge of herbs or unclean spirits.

"Even now they say there hath appeared in the southern parts (so I heard, coming but now from Jericho) one John the son of Zachariah, concerning whom I judge (if he be indeed a true prophet and no deceiver) that he is either the prophet spoken of by Moses, or else Elias. For that Elias is to come again we all know, because it is so written; and that the prophet like unto Moses must needs appear, this also the Scriptures tell us: but that other prophets should appear is not written, neither is it likely; for the age of prophets is past. But whether this John be Elias or whatever else, meet it is that we go to him; for he may perchance reveal to us what it is our wisdom to do. If ye ask 'What shall be the sign of the true prophet?': I answer, it is written in our traditions, 'A false prophet may show signs on earth and in the deep; but a sign from heaven he cannot Rabbis.' Wait therefore till the sign from heaven shall be vouchsafed, revealing the true Prophet, whom it will be our wisdom to obey, and for whom (during this present) it is our wisdom to wait."

When Hezekiah had made an end of speaking, James the son of Judas was sore displeased at his words, and made as if he would have spoken in answer; but John (who was of a gentler disposition) prevented his brother, and said that Hezekiah gave good counsel. For he, like the rest of us, had been moved by the mention of John the Prophet. So in the end it was determined according to the words of Hezekiah the Scribe; and we brake up without resolving anything further, except that we would go straightway, so many of us as conveniently could, to Bethany beyond Jordan, where the prophet was baptizing. But on the morrow and on the day after, when I spake to my friends and acquaintance concerning John the son of Zachariah, it was a marvel to see how greatly the hearts of all men were stirred at the thought of a new prophet in Israel. For that after so many hundreds of years a prophet should arise in Israel (none having prophesied since the time of Malachi, the last of the prophets, more than four hundred years ago) this seemed a marvellous thing and well nigh impossible, and almost as if a man should rise again from the dead. For the prophets were counted as it were dead and out of mind in Israel, meet to be reverenced for their past words, but not to be hoped for in the time to come. For this cause were we much moved by the mention of the name of John the son of Zachariah. And as the Prophet Elias from the top of Carmel looking out into the Great Sea and discerning a cloud no bigger than a man's hand, foretold the imminent storm, so did all we in Galilee, on the first breath of the rumour of the coming of a prophet, begin to forebode in our hearts of the coming of one that should be no common prophet; but, in all likelihood, Elias from the dead; or else one greater than Moses, to give us perchance a new Law and a new Kingdom.

CHAPTER III

Concerning the Casting out of Unclean Spirits; and of the Nature of the Redemption of Israel; and how I first saw Jesus of Nazareth.

ON the fourth day, I set out in company with Baruch my cousin, the son of Manasseh, my father's brother, intending to go to Capernaum, and thence to take ship for Gamala, where we were to meet James and John the sons of Judas of Galilee; and so to journey all together to Bethany, where the prophet was. When we were come to Capernaum, we tarried two days in the house of Manasseh: and the second day was the Sabbath. Now the house of Manasseh was nigh unto the wharf, so that nothing stood between it and the lake.

It happened that I was sitting on the house-roof and the sun wanted yet an hour or two of setting; and a tumult arose on the beach below, between a Greek merchant and certain of the townsmen. Word had come to the Greek that his son was sick in Bethsaida and nigh unto death: so he had besought certain of the sailors that they would launch their ship and put out to sea, although the sun had not yet set; to the intent that he might pass over with all speed, if perchance he might see his child before he died. The sailors were persuaded by the man's prayers and gifts, and were preparing their vessel to launch it. But the inhabitants, those of the more devout sort, coming together with stones and staves, threatened the sailors, and forced them to cease, declaring that not a boat should leave the strand till the Sabbath should be ended.

The air was calm and still so that the merchant's words came up even to my ears, as he pointed again and again to the coast over against us: "Surely your God will permit you to do this service of kindness. Yonder is my son, mine only son, dying as if within sight of his father. Strangers will receive his last breath, and close his eyes. I beseech you, as ye are fathers, have compassion on a father who must soon be childless." So saying the Greek beat his breast and tore his hair; but in vain. The ruler of the synagogue, who had gathered the multitude together, would not listen to his entreaties; and he departed, weeping and wailing and calling upon his gods in vain.

Then the ruler of the synagogue, seeing the crowd running together, exhorted them to a more strict observing of the Sabbath, declaring that the breaking of the Sabbath was the principal cause of the wrath of God with His people, and of the delay of the Redemption of Sion. He went on to speak of the blessing of the Redemption, and he besought the people to do what lay in them to hasten it forward, by raising up the fences of the Law, and by constant and scrupulous obedience. "Let all repent," he said, "of former slackness and misdoings; for the Lord your God is merciful, long suffering, slow to anger, and of great kindness, and repenteth Him of the evil. To Him belong mercies and forgiveness, though ye have rebelled against Him."

By this time a great multitude was come together, and in the uttermost parts of the throng stood certain tax-gatherers (among whom was the principal receiver of customs in Capernaum, by name Matthew the son of Alpheus), with certain of the looser sort, men and women, outcasts from the synagogue: which had been cast forth, some for weighty offences, but some for light, according to the custom of our Scribes. These had approached, as it seemed to me, because they had heard mention of "mercy," and "forgiveness"; and their faces were somewhat sad, as if they also would fain have drawn near unto the God of Israel, that they might receive forgiveness of sins. But the ruler of the synagogue, catching sight of them, drove them away with reproaches, reviling them as children of Satan. "Even your alms," he cried, "we trample under our feet; away, extortioners and harlots, fit food for fire and worms!"

They departed in haste amid the scoffs and curses of the crowd. But their countenances changed as they went, and there seemed no more thought of repentance in them; for they hardened their faces as flint stones because of the reproaches of the chief ruler. Then it came into my heart that the ruler of the synagogue erred, in that he drove away the sinners that would fain have drawn nigh unto the Lord. And not only he, but all our Rabbis and Scribes seemed to be in the same error, because they drove away instead of bringing nigh. For even the words of the Wise tell us that peace is to be proclaimed to the far-off as well as to the near; and to the far-off first. Moreover the words of the Prophet Ezekiel came to my mind, that if the wicked turned from his wickedness and did that which was lawful and right, he should live. Now the ruler of the synagogue had himself also used words like unto these; yet his acts had not been like unto his words. For after that he had spoken of God as merciful and forgiving, he had driven away the sinners as though God were unmerciful and unforgiving. Therefore he had on his lips the wisdom of the Law; but in the thoughts of his heart and the works of his hand there was no wisdom. Then I repeated to myself the tradition of the Wise, "Whoso hath much wisdom and little works, to what is he like? Even to a tree whereof the branches be abundant but the roots poor and thin: and the wind cometh and uprooteth it and overturneth it." Truly, said I, the wisdom of the Scribes is like unto a tree whereof the roots suffice not for the branches.

Then began I to consider with myself what would be the doctrine of John the son of Zachariah as touching forgiveness and repentance;

and it was borne in upon my mind that we lacked, not the true doctrine of forgiveness (for this we had already in the Law and the Traditions), but somewhat beyond the reach of doctrine; albeit, what it was, I did not yet understand. Also methought we had need of some new kind of wisdom that should avail, not only for Scribes and lawyers but also for the people of the land, for ploughmen and fishermen, yea, perchance even for tax-gatherers and sinners. Then behold, as I mused, methought all the precepts of the Law and of the Traditions lay scattered about on the beach, like so many dry bones (according to the vision of the Prophet Ezekiel), and there they lay, awaiting, till the breath of the Spirit of God should blow upon them and give them life. And, in my musing, I saw One coming, and his face was as bright as the morning star, and the breath of the Lord breathed from his mouth, and he came forward to the bones for to breathe life into them; and I spake aloud and said, "Perchance John the son of Zachariah is the Messiah, and will breathe life into these bones."

But while I thus mused, came Baruch behind me and touched my shoulder, and pointed to the crowd and said, "See, the sun has now just set; and the people are following the exorcist yonder. Shall we not go with them? He is no common exorcist, but by means of certain herbs known only to himself he can draw an evil spirit out of the nostrils of the possessed; and this hath he done many times this week in the presence of certain of the most notable people in Capernaum, insomuch that all men here do hold him in great esteem. And even now he goeth to cast out an evil spirit from Raphael, the son of one of our neighbours: who hath been possessed now these two years."

So lost was I in thought that, while Baruch was speaking, I scarce understood the purport of his words. But shouts and shrieks from below caused me to awake out of my trance. So I looked; and behold, a great multitude below, and in the midst thereof a youth possessed with an evil spirit. The youth was led by three strong men; and as he went, he shrieked aloud and struggled against them that led him. Close after them came one whose sorrowful countenance betokened him to be the father of the youth. Before them all went the exorcist.

Here in Britain it is a rare thing to see a man possessed with a demon. Therefore it is needful to say first, that in the land of Israel (and especially in the lowlands of Galilee along the coast of the Sea of Gennesareth, and also in the valley of Jordan), the unclean spirits prevailed mightily in my days, insomuch that I have noted as many as twelve or even more in a small town, such as Bethsaida. They wandered about the country half clothed or naked, assailing their dearest friends or strangers, or even themselves, with stones or other weapons, such as they could procure. They saw strange sights, demons and flames; their ears were filled with thunderings and roarings of beasts and voices of devils. A stench, as of sulphur and brimstone, was in their nostrils. Their bellies also were beset with worms, toads, snakes, or scorpions; which nevertheless destroyed them not. Two voices, the voice of the demon and the voice of the man, issued from the mouth of the possessed. Verily of all the diseases with which Satan hath been permitted by the Unsearchable (blessed is He) to afflict the children of men, this disease is the worst and cruellest; inasmuch as it poisoneth the very springs of love, causing the son to hate even the father that begot him and the mother that gave him suck.

What were the causes of this evil, wise men have asked, and have given no certain answer. They at Jerusalem said that it was a chastisement because of men's neglect of worship in the Holy Temple; and certain it is, that Gentiles and outcasts from the synagogue were more often possessed than the devout. Nay, I have known some (more especially women) that, having been possessed, were cured by the offering of sacrifice, or by a more constant attending on the worship in the Temple. Others said that it was a punishment for eating swine's flesh; others for dwelling in houses built amid tombs or on ancient burial- places. But others said that they which lived in the lowlands about the Lake of Gennesareth and in the valley of Jordan were more under the unclean demons; for that the demons possessed and ruled over waterish and low-lying regions. And so much is undoubted, that in the inland highlands of Galilee there were few possessed, and in Jerusalem none, or at least no number worthy of mention; but down in Jericho and Capernaum the possessed could be seen at the corner of every street.

Cure there was none, or at least no certain cure. Sometimes sudden terror or sudden joy availed to drive out the unclean spirit. I have heard of one Joachim the son of Levi, that was vexed with a dumb spirit for many years; but seeing some robbers about to kill his father, the string of his tongue was unloosed, and he cried out to them not to kill him. But no physic, nor no diet, was of any certain avail. This uncertainty brought great gain to many vagrant exorcists which wandered here and there throughout Galilee, their scrips full of amulets, charms, drugs, magic roots, and books of incantations. These men, with shouts and shrieks and uncouth gestures and dances, were wont to amaze the demoniacs for a time and to drive them into a kind of torpor; which torpor they called health and peace, and boasted that they had wrought a cure. At other times, by magic arts, they would persuade Satan to go out of the man for a short time, that they might obtain a reward. But in either case, the cure lasted no long time. For in a brief space the demon would awake again out of torpor; or if he had been driven out, he would return, and sometimes bring with him other demons yet more powerful than himself; insomuch that it was a proverb among us that it was better for a possessed person that the unclean spirit should not be driven out at all, than that, having been driven out, he should be allowed to return.

But about the causes and cures of this evil let others consider and dispute: I speak now of the exorcist in Capernaum. Going down straightway with Baruch, I followed him into a house not two hundred paces from the quay. When we entered, there seemed scarce space for the exorcist and the demoniac in the middle of the chamber, so thick stood the people together; but by favour of the master of the house, who was known to Baruch, w^e obtained place in the inner part of the circle. The father of the boy now came up to my cousin. "I have taken Raphael," he said, "to many exorcists before, but never a man of them was to be compared with this learned man. I have described to him the nature of the unclean spirit that possesseth my son, and he protesteth to me that he hath frequently driven out the like kind of demons, and that he is assured of success." Meanwhile Raphael, the boy possessed with the unclean spirit, was seated on the ground in the middle. He no longer struggled nor shrieked, but sat quiet, though sullen withal.

Two slaves now came forth, the first carrying in one hand a bucket of water and in the other a covered basket; but the second bore a chafing-dish. Now all voices were hushed, for the exorcist stepped into the middle of the chamber. "Many," he said, "of my profession pretend to drive out evil spirits, but they do not perform what they promise. But that ye may perceive how far Theudas the son of Eleazar differeth from such common vagrants and impostors, I shall not only cast out this unclean spirit, but I shall also give you proof thereof which ye shall see with your own eyes." He then bade the slaves place the bucket upon a shelf in the room where all could see it; but the basket and chafing-dish were set in the midst of the circle.

Perchance the boy began to understand in part that the exorcist was speaking of him; or it may be that from his father's anxious mien and troubled countenance he conjectured that some new thing was at hand. For he leapt from the ground, and shrieked, and blasphemed God, uttering obscene words, tearing his hair, and marring his cheeks with his nails; and but for the two keepers on either side of him he would assuredly have rent off his garments; and even with all their efforts they had much ado to hinder him.

But the exorcist threw a few leaves and fragments of root on the chafing- dish, muttered a charm, waved his wand, and then waited as though for an answer. Then frowning, he waved his wand a second time, and repeated a louder charm, stamping his foot on the ground, and then waited again. A deep silence fell on all in the chamber, insomuch that no one ventured so much as to draw breath; and even the boy ceased from his struggles and stared amazedly at the exorcist. But he, now standing upright and manifesting in his face that he had received an answer from the unclean spirit, turned from us to the possessed, and fixing his eye full upon his face, he cried in a loud voice, "Thou unclean spirit, thine hour is come. Thy name is revealed unto me, and thy shape likewise. In vain thou wouldst evade my sight, assuming the semblance of a long black worm.

"Lo! by the mysterious power of King Solomon's ring and these strong roots I will draw thee out of the poor boy's nostrils in the presence of this assembly: and when I say the word, thou, obedient to my commands, shalt leave the body which thou defilest, and, in thy passage, thou shalt overturn yonder vessel of water. Dost hear me? Thy name is Ialdabaoth."

Hereat the demoniac shrieked and raved louder than before, and a deep voice, deeper than the voice of a youth, cried out from within him, "I am Ialdabaoth, the worm of darkness; depart from me." The crowd shouted, and the sorcerer, turning to us, "Sirs," said he, "ye see how the evil spirit is already half conquered; for he hath confessed his name and nature to be even as I foretold." Then turning to the boy and applying a ring to his nostrils, he cried aloud, "Come forth, Ialdabaoth;" and with very great quickness, so that the motion could scarce be perceived, (all the time shouting charms and incantations with a loud voice,) he drew forth from the nostrils of the demoniac a shape like unto a long black worm. Now verily the crowd shrieked as if they themselves were possessed; but the boy sat, not struggling, but still and pale, as though no life were in him. But the exorcist, turning himself quickly round to the vessel of water behind him, "Away," he cried, "away, worm of darkness! Back, Ialdabaoth, to the abyss! Back through the air: and dash down yonder bucket as thou fliest!" At the word, the worm vanished, the bucket was dashed down, and the boy fell, as it seemed, lifeless.

We all pressed in upon the youth, wishing to discern whether life were still in him, or no; but the exorcist waived us back, as one having authority; and taking the boy by the hand, he raised him up, speaking kind words to him and to his father. Soon his life returned to the boy, and the exorcist restored him to his father, whole and sound (albeit weak and pale), and, as it appeared, delivered from the unclean spirit. The father, weeping for joy, placed a heavy purse in the hand of the exorcist; who, at first, put it from him, as though he, would have none of it. But afterwards, while he was receiving the salutations and greetings of them that were departing, one of his slaves, being urged by the father, took the purse and placed it in the covered basket.

As for us, it being now late, we stayed not to congratulate with the father of Raphael; but with all speed, made our way through the press; all the people around us praising God and marvelling at the power which the Lord had given to Theudas the son of Eleazar. But we hasted to the house of Manasseh to make ready for our journey; for we were to set forth early on the morrow. But when the morrow came, behold, Baruch was sick of a fever, and could not travel; and I tamed for him for the space of four days. But on the fifth day after the Sabbath, Baruch being now in case to travel, we purposed to take ship for Gamala, which lieth on the southern coast of the lake. For our intent was there to join ourselves to James and John, the sons of Judas, and so to continue our journey with them till we came to Bethany in Peraea where John was baptizing.

Now it came to pass that very early in the morning when we were to set out, the sun being not yet risen, I went to the house of Joazar, the father of Raphael, to inquire concerning the boy's welfare. And when I came to the threshold, behold, another stood at the door; but his back was towards me, so that I knew not who he was. And before I could accost him, the door was opened unto us; and behold, a sound as of shrieking and lamentation. Then we both listened, and lo, a deep voice from an upper chamber, and it cried, "We are Ialdabaoth! We are Ialdabaoth, the worms of darkness!" Then came forth other words of blasphemy and filthiness, so that I loathed to listen to them; and I turned to go back. But at that instant I heard the voice of the father bewailing: and the stranger delayed not, but entered into the house; wherefore I also, albeit against my will, was moved to go in likewise.

So I went in, following the stranger till we both came to the door of the upper room: and there I stood, and durst not enter into the chamber; for my heart was empty of comfort, neither knew I how to console the old man in his affliction. But the stranger that was with me, going forward, spake first of all to Joazar the father, and said some words of kindness to him. Now so it was, that when the stranger first entered into the chamber, the evil spirits ceased not, but raged yet more fiercely than before, crying aloud and saying, "Depart from us; let us alone; let us alone"; and the youth also rent his cheeks so that the blood gushed out; and he would fain have leaped up from his bed. But the stranger (whose face I had not yet seen), hearing the voices of the spirits, turned himself round from the old man to the son: and going up to the bedside he stood there, steadfastly looking at the youth. Now when he thus turned himself, then for the first time I beheld his countenance; and, as I remember, I marvelled thereat, and also at the manner of his dealing with the youth. For, first of all, when he looked upon the youth, his face seemed swallowed up with pity; and then of a sudden it changed again, and he stretched out his arm as one having authority, and as if on the point to bid the evil spirits depart, and this he did twice; but twice again he drew back his arm, as if changing his purpose. Then, at the last, the pity came back upon his face all in an instant, so that his features seemed even melted therewith; and he stooped down and embraced the boy, and kissed him; and, as I thought, he whispered words in his ear. But this I know not for certain; howbeit the boy, in any case, ceased from his raging and no longer struggled, but lay still and quiet, only muttering and moaning a little. Hereat the stranger turned himself to Joazar to take his leave; but I (perchance because my mind misgave me that I had played the eavesdropper, albeit, unwittingly, or for whatever other reason) feared to wait and meet the stranger; so I turned my back, and went forth in haste from the house.

When I was come to Baruch again, I held my peace concerning Raphael, lest I should stir up melancholy in my cousin, since he was freshly recovered from his disease. But, when we went on board the vessel, the sailors were not yet ready to sail. So I lay down on the sleeping-cushion: but no sleep fell upon my eyes. For there appeared ever before me the image of the demoniac Raphael and his sorrowful father; and my heart was weighed down with the thought of their affliction. But I grieved not for them alone, but also for the daughter of Sion; who seemed to be, in a manner, possessed with an evil spirit, and to cry aloud for some one that should cast it out. All the deliverers of old seemed to be even as Theudas the son of Eleazar; and even as the demon had returned into Raphael, so that his last state was worse than the first, even so it seemed with Israel; therefore I besought the Lord to hasten the time of the coming of the true Redeemer of Sion.

As I mused, I began to consider with myself what would be the manner of the true redemption. Beside the demoniac, there appeared unto me the face of Matthew the publican and the faces of the sinners. It was borne in upon my mind that, even though every legionary in Syria were slain or driven out, and though the borders of Israel should be enlarged from the Nile to the Euphrates, yet if we still had amidst us sinners unforgiven, and Priests and Rulers with no power to forgive nor to convert, then of a surety the evil spirit would not depart from us save only for a season.

By this time, as I remember, we were but just putting out into the deep, and the sun was risen. And there came down certain fishermen to the beach to prepare their tackling for fishing: and with them there came one that, as I noted, was no fisherman (for he was not girt as a fisherman): and he walked down to the brink of the waters and looked out steadfastly to the deep. And so it was that, as he looked, the sun even that instant rising above the eastern mountains, shone suddenly upon his face so that I could see it clearly (though we were by this time a full furlong from the shore); and behold, it was the countenance of the stranger that I had seen that same morning in the house of Joazar. So I called to Tobias straightway and asked him who the stranger might be: and Tobias raised himself upon his elbow where he lay on the sleeping- cushion, and he looked, and knew him, and told me his name. And then first I heard the name of Jesus of Nazareth.

Again I lay down to sleep, but still no sleep would come to me: wherefore I took forth from my bosom the book of the prophet Isaiah, which I had with me, and began to read therein. And so it was that as I unrolled it, my eyes fell upon the place where the prophet saith, "To what purpose is the multitude of your sacrifices unto me? saith the Lord: I am full of the burnt offerings of rams, and the fat of fed beasts... Bring no more vain oblations; incense is an abomination unto me; the new moons and sabbaths, the calling of assemblies, I cannot away with; it is iniquity, even the solemn meeting."

Now at that word, "the new moons and sabbaths I cannot away with," I ceased from reading. For I seemed to hear the Greek merchant weeping and crying to the sailors, "Surely your God will permit you to do this service of kindness." Then I called to mind the words of the Lord, "I will have mercy, and not sacrifice;" and behold, it came in upon me all at once, as in a flood, that our exactness in the observing of the Sabbath might haply be an abomination in the eyes of the All-seeing (blessed is He) whensoever it hindereth kindness and mercy. After this my eyes again fell upon the roll, and he read aloud these words wherein the prophet prescribeth the cure for the wounds of Israel. "Cease to do evil; learn to do well; seek judgment, relieve the oppressed, judge the fatherless, plead for the widow." Then I cried aloud, "Is not this a plain and simple path even for the people of the land, that all Israel should walk therein."

Now so it was that Baruch had come up while I was thus reading and speaking aloud; and I knew it not. So he answered and said, "Thou speakest well; notwithstanding I have heard a certain Greek of mine acquaintance in Capernaum say that virtue cannot be taught; for that some men have their hearts inclined by nature to do well, but others to do ill; so that it availeth nothing to say 'Learn to do well.'" Then was I silent for a while, for methought the Greek said well, and indeed we needed, not so much that a new path should be made plain, as that a clean heart and a right spirit should be created anew within us, according as it is written, "Make me a clean heart, God, and renew a right spirit within me." So in the end I concluded to wait till we should understand what new message the prophet John the son of Zachariah might bring to us from the Lord, if perchance he might teach us aught concerning the creating of a right spirit. But by this time our ship was come to Gamala; where we were courteously entertained by James and John the sons of Judas; and we abode with them three days. But on the fourth day we set out for Bethany of Peraea.

CHAPTER IV

Of the Doctrine of John the Prophet, how it suited with the People of the Land; and how I was baptized of the Prophet.

As we drew near to Bethany, we noted many hundreds of travellers on the road, the most part on foot, but many on asses and camels; for rich as well as poor were journeying to the new prophet. A full score of Scribes went past us in the space of an hour; there were also some soldiers going to Machaerus here and there was a tax-gatherer; and Baruch took note of certain that were sinners, outcasts from the synagogue of Capernaum. We had now been journeying for a clay and a half; and toward the end of the second day, we began to see the valley of Jordan right over against us. Going down a little further, we perceived that there was a great multitude gathered together near the bank of the river; and presently we could clearly discern the prophet himself.

Around him stood men in white garments awaiting purification; at a somewhat greater distance, the mixed multitude hearkening to his words. John himself, wearing no tunic, but clad only in a rough mantle of camel's hair with a girdle of untanned leather, was sitting upon a rock, and thence he was speaking to the people in a clear voice, whereof the sound (though not as yet the meaning) was borne up even to our ears. For a while we stood still, with one consent, marvelling at the sight; for there had not been a prophet in Israel for four hundred years and more; but presently, riding down with all speed, we came into the valley, and joined ourselves to the multitude: and, albeit, we could not come very nigh to John, for the press, yet was there such a stillness among all the assembly, that we very soon understood whatsoever he said.

He had been speaking (this I learned afterwards from one of the bystanders) concerning the old wars and troubles which the Lord had sent on Israel; how, according to the saying of the Prophet Isaiah, the Lord had brought the Assyrian against the land as an axe, whereby He had cut down our chosen nobles and princes, even as a woodman felleth the choicest trees. Also how, in the days of the Prophet Jeremiah, the Lord had sent the blast of His wrath upon the people, and had winnowed away the unstable and faithless into captivity, even as a winnower fanneth the chaff from the wheat. The same things were at hand even now, he said: "Now also the axe is laid at the root of the trees; therefore every tree which bringeth not forth good fruit is hewn down and cast into the fire."

Hereat the multitude cried aloud, saying that it was even so; for indeed we all felt in our hearts that the prophet spake the truth. As the Assyrian axe in the days of old, so now the Roman axe was laid at the root of Israel; and unless the Lord turned away His wrath from us, the nation would be destroyed. But then a stillness fell upon the multitude, as we waited till the prophet should tell us what we should do to turn away the Lord's wrath.

Then the prophet set his face toward the men in white garments, and said to them that they should cleanse their hearts and not their bodies merely, and put away the iniquity of their souls, and he called upon them to confess their sins. He bade them also not to trust in their being children of Abraham, nor in the purifications of the Law, nor in the observances of Sabbaths and feast- days. If, said he, the tree was to escape the axe, it must no longer be barren: " bring forth fruits therefore worthy of repentance, and think not to say within yourselves, We have Abraham to our father, for I say unto you that God is able of these stones to raise up children unto Abraham."

Saying these words, he beckoned to the men in white robes that they should follow him. The multitude made way for them; and he led them down to a place by the side of the river where the reeds and thickets of willow-beds had been rooted up, so that there might be free passage into the water. Then he cried in a clear voice, "Receive the baptism of Repentance," and bade them plunge themselves beneath the surface. At the same time he offered up prayers to God; and we upon the higher bank said, Amen. When he had made an end of baptizing the men, he went up again to the rock, and thence he again spoke to the people; and as many as desired purification went up to him there.

Now while the people were going up by courses, I also began to resolve in my heart that I too would go up in the order of my course. Yet had I sore misgivings in my soul; for it seemed as if I were on the verge of a great sea, launching out into the deep I knew not whither. For the teaching of this new prophet in no wise agreed with the teaching of the Scribes and Lawyers, whom I had reverenced; and if I went with him, I perceived that I must needs go away from them. Now it came to pass that a certain Scribe (who was with our company) perceived the reasonings of my heart, and that I was desirous to receive purification at the hands of John. Therefore he took me by the cloak, and held me back, saying, "Behold, if John the son of Zachariah speaketh well, the Scribes have spoken ill, and have taught ill. Yea, and all thy study of the Law, and thy painful meditations therein, and thy nightly watchings and weariness of the flesh have all been in vain. But wilt thou lightly forsake the teaching of the Law and the Traditions of the Fathers, and all for the sake of one new prophet, concerning whom thou knowest not as yet even that he is a prophet? And wherefore shouldst thou thus seek after prophets? Knowest thou not that the Inscrutable (blessed be He) decreed that, after the destruction of the first Temple, there should be no longer with us the Shekinah, nor the Holy Spirit, nor the Urim and Thummim; wherefore it is said, 'From the fourth year of King Darius, the Holy Spirit no longer rested upon the prophets.' But in the place of the prophets' (who were not always with Israel) thou hast now the Scribes always with thee, according as it is said, 'Moses received the Law from Sinai, and the elders delivered it to the prophets, and the prophets to the men of the Great Congregation;' and it is also said, 'from the time that the Temple was destroyed, the gift of prophecy was taken from the prophets and given to the Wise.'"

His words moved me, and I restrained myself for the time. Yet on the other side there rose in my heart a certain Voice, which seemed to come from the Lord, saying, "The words of John are right, and they are simple, converting the soul. Moreover, they arc fit for the people of the land, and not only for Scribes and scholars and pedants. But that he is a prophet, thine own heart convinceth thee; for even when thou hearest him, thou knowest that he speaketh not from himself, but that he is taught from above. And did not also the prophets of old speak like things, saying, 'Rend your hearts, and not your garments,' and bidding Israel not to offer sacrifice, but to Rabbis mercy, and not to observe Sabbaths, but to do judgment and relieve the oppressed?" So between the words of the Scribe and the words of the Voice within me I was in a great strait. Howbeit for the time I restrained myself and did nothing, but remained where I was, giving heed to the words of the Prophet.

Now it came to pass that certain of the soldiers from Machaerus went up: and all we in the crowd waited silently expecting that the Prophet would deny purification to these men, except they should first promise to depart from the army of Herod. But he commanded them only to abstain from robbery and outrage. Upon this certain tax-gatherers (whom the Romans call publicans) took confidence, and they too went up. And now indeed all we that looked on, expected that there should have been a great outburst of wrath and of cursing upon them, as upon traitors and apostates from Israel. But the Prophet received these also, and bade them exact no more than that which was appointed to them. To others he said that they were to observe that saying in the Traditions which enjoineth the doing of kindnesses; that is to say, they were to clothe the naked and to feed the hungry, and the like.

Hereupon arose a murmuring among certain of the Scribes from Jerusalem, who were standing nigh to the place where I was: and I heard the voice of Hezekiah son of Zachariah saying in an austere manner, "It is said, 'On three things the world is stayed; on the Law, and on the Worship, and on the bestowal of Kindnesses:' what meaneth this teacher of strange things therefore, to subvert the Law and the^ Worship, in that he maketh no mention thereof, but he exalteth Kindnesses to the skies?" Then another said, "He allegeth the authority of no teacher; why therefore hearken we to him?" But a third said, "Peradventure he is a prophet, and is taught of God." But Hezekiah made answer, "The time of prophets hath passed. Besides, he hath wrought no sign from Heaven; how know we therefore that he is a true prophet?"

These things spake the Scribes together, as we went back from the river to the place where our tents were pitched; for by this time the sun was setting. But all that night long my thoughts still beat on the doctrine of John; and I marvelled much whence it came that the people so flocked to John as to a prophet; yea, and that my own heart also was so drawn towards him, although he had wrought no sign in heaven, nor so much as driven out any unclean spirit. But the reason seemed to me partly in himself. For his very countenance, yea, even his gesture and carriage, proclaimed him to be, not a student of books, but one that was taught of God; and yet further the hardships that he endured, and the manner of his clothing and food (for he fed on nothing but locusts and wild honey) showed to all men that he did not prophesy for gain. But another reason lay in his doctrine. For the doctrine of John was simple and just, commending itself to the consciences of men; not flattering any nor busying itself with abstruse matters; but fit for the work of life and the paths of busy men, able, as it seemed, to carry purity and righteousness even to the side of the plough, and into the ranks of armed men, and into the shops and offices of tradesmen and tax-gatherers. For this cause the teaching of John won a way into the hearts of men of every degree, save only certain of the Pharisees. So when I thought on all these things, I began to be convinced that he was sent of God.

But when I went forth on the morrow to behold the purification of the disciples and to hear the teaching of the Prophet, my heart was even more drawn unto him. For I compared him with Abuyah the son of Elishah, and with the ruler of the synagogue, that had driven away the tax-gatherers and sinners from the teaching of repentance; and it seemed to me that John was as much better than they, as light is better than darkness. For though he were of a stern countenance and austere in aspect, yet was the austerity of John in no wise as the austerity of Abuyah the son of Elishah. For Abuyah was sour and peevish, for that he ever loved to find fault, and because he desired to obtain occasion for rebuking, to the intent that he might persuade himself that he was better than others: but John seemed to be austere only because he hated sin. So I no more delayed, but went up with the rest, about the second hour of the day; and I confessed my sins and received purification.

After we had been purified, I stood with the rest, clothed in white garments, wholly given up to meditating upon the new life whereto we seemed to have risen out of the waters. But I was aroused by hearing these words spoken with a great vehemency of anger: "Ye serpents, ye generation of vipers, who hath warned you to flee from the wrath to come?" Great indeed was my astonishment when, raising myself to see what they were to whom the Prophet was thus speaking, I discerned the faces of some of the most famous Scribes in Jerusalem. It seemed that they had been questioning him who he was and by what authority he taught these things. But the Prophet rebuked them with exceeding indignation. For he said that they were even as barren trees, full of leaf, but bearing no fruit, * fit for naught but to be cut down and cast into the fire. Then they went backward, being put to utter confusion; but John turned to us that had been purified, and spake to us a second time as follows:

"I am not the Christ. Call not yourselves m} 7 disciples: for I myself am naught but a, herald in the wilderness preparing the way for the Great King. But verily the King cometh. Therefore weep no more for the evils of sin. The rough ways of oppression shall be made smooth; the crooked paths of deceit and violence shall be made straight. Let the daughter of Jerusalem rejoice greatly, for her salvation is nigh. For the glory of the Lord draweth near, and all flesh shall see it together. Notwithstanding think not of me as your deliverer. He that hath the bride is the bridegroom, and the Bridegroom of Sion is the Redeemer, who shall espouse her in the day of salvation. I am but the friend of the Bridegroom. Nay, I am but his servant, not worthy to follow him as slave, nor to loose the latchet of his sandal. Ye ask in your hearts who I am. But think not of me, for I am as one that is no man. I am naught but a voice, even the voice of one crying in the wilderness, 'Prepare ye the way of the Lord, make His paths straight'."

Then he warned us that had been purified not to suppose that we needed no further purification. Speaking of the old days of Joshua the Conqueror, he brought to our minds how our fathers had two kinds of purification; one inferior, with water, wherewith they purified things perishable, such as garments and the like; but a more searching purification, wherewith they purified silver and gold and other imperishable things, and this was with fire. Even so, he said, it was given to him to purify only with the washing of water; but one would come after him, the Messiah and Redeemer; and he would purify us with fire and with the Holy Spirit.

In the evening, when we, that had received the purification, conversed together in the inn at Jericho, there was much questioning whence the Messiah should come, and by what signs he should be known. But most of the Scribes did not believe that John was a true prophet; and Hezekiah protested that he ought not to be called a prophet, for he had wrought no sign, not even on earth, much less in heaven. But this he said not openly, for fear of the multitude; for almost all believed John to be a prophet.

But on the morrow, when we turned ourselves to go northward, heaviness fell upon my heart, and all things seemed flat and unprofitable. All our counsels of action, whether to join ourselves to the army of Herod, or straightway to rise up against the Romans, behold, they now seemed no longer the wisdom of men, but rather the vain talk of children. For what could Barabbas and the sons of Judas do, in comparison with the true Redemption which had been prophesied by the Prophet; or how could they avail to bring about the day of that Redemption? It seemed to be our wisdom to wait for the

Lord, who alone could send the true Redeemer. And yet, on the other hand, how was it possible for one that loved Israel and longed after righteousness, to look patiently upon the servitude of his country? Hence I loathed the thought of living in peace at home.

When I returned to Sepphoris, I applied myself to labour and to study, if perchance I might settle my thoughts; but I could not, for I was divided between two minds. At one time I was minded to obey John and his teaching, and to set no store on the teaching of the Scribes, nor to give heed to what were called the "light precepts" of the Fathers, such as those concerning tassels and fringes, and the purification of vessels, and the observance of the Sabbath for things without life, and the like; and it seemed nobler to cast these things away, and to say that mercy, and judgment, and truth, and kindness, were the great commandments, and whoso observeth these, observeth all. But then at other times, when I considered with myself how frail and fitful a thing is man, how impotent for all good ends, and how easily led aside from the right path by passion and by ignorance, then I trembled at the thought of casting down the fences which had been raised by the generations of the wise; for I feared lest I should be guilty of presumption, and should fall, and be swallowed up with an utter destruction.

But in the minds of other men (and not in me alone) there was at this time much unsettlement and many searchings of heart. For many others in Sepphoris became ill-content with the teaching of the Scribes, and with the performance of the precepts of the Law. Some men even said that, when the Messiah came, there should be no more Law. So, if, even before, men had been expecting the Messiah and looking forward to the Redemption of Sion, much more did they do so now, after the preaching of John the Prophet; insomuch that the whole of Galilee became as dry fuel ready for the flame: and nothing was wanting save a spark of fire from heaven to kindle the whole into a great blaze.

By this time I had numbered thirty-four years, or something more; and it was the fourteenth year of the Emperor Tiberius.

CHAPTER V

Of the Greek Philosophers in Alexandria; and how I had Discourse with Philo the Alexandrine.

Now it came to pass that about this time, at the beginning of the fifteenth year of Tiberius Caesar, very early in the spring, the only son of my mother's eldest brother died in Alexandria; and my mother's brother (whose name was Onias) sent to my mother desiring her that she would suffer me to come to Alexandria to visit him during his affliction. He was a shipwright and a man of great wealth, possessing many corn-ships; and he was desirous to have adopted me for his son. But to this I would not consent, nor did my mother urge me thereto. Howbeit out of love for her brother, and because she thought it would be for my advantage, she desired me to visit my uncle for a time. I had no mind to remain in Alexandria, nor to leave my mother for long. But at my mother's bidding I was willing to go to my uncle for a season, if perchance I might comfort him a little.

Two days I spent at Caesarea Stratonis waiting for the sailing of our vessel; and during that time my heart was moved within me, for that I saw on all sides the signs of the power and prosperity of the Gentiles; for a Gentile city this was, insomuch that, though the wall be on holy ground, yet was the city itself esteemed of our Scribes to be defiled and in a Gentile land. For the region round about was called the land of life; but the city was called the daughter of Edom. A great breakwater here protecteth the ships from the rage of the sea. Each stone therein is thirty cubits long, six cubits deep, and seven cubits broad, let down into water twenty fathom deep. Above the waters the breakwater is of the breadth of one hundred and forty cubits. Over against the mouth of the haven standeth a temple dedicated to Caesar, and thereon two images of marble, very large, the one of Caesar, the other of Rome. There is also in this city a theatre, and an amphitheatre, and a market-place, after the manner of the Greeks; and in all parts of the city there were to be seen baths, and gardens, and palaces, and porticoes, and other public buildings, all adorned, after the Greek fashion, with images of living creatures. When I looked on these things, Satan tempted me and said, "God loveth the Romans more than He loveth the children of Israel; and the wisdom of the Greeks is greater than the wisdom of Sion."

More, yea much more grievously did Satan tempt me when I was come to that great city, even to Alexandria. For here the streets were broader and the public buildings also larger and goodlier than those of Caesarea; and in the streets and public gardens, yea even in the households of the Gentiles to whom my uncle commended me, I perceived the abominations of idolatry. For on every side were to be seen images and pictures of false gods and of demons which they called demigods and heroes; insomuch that the walls of the houses and the chambers, yea even the seats, and couches, and ornaments of dress, and utensils of furniture, and instruments of music were all painted or carven with abominable devices, setting forth the doings of these demons. But when I heard the interpretation of these pictures and graven images, then sometimes indeed my heart loathed them for their lewd and profane spirit; but at other times I was constrained to confess that there was a certain wondrous beauty and delight in the songs of certain of the poets of the Gentiles.

Here also men of all nations and religions, Jews and Greeks, Romans and Egyptians, and strangers from the East, lived all together in peace, making gain, and worshipping after the traditions of their fathers; and no one vexed nor oppressed other. All this troubled me, for I said in my heart, "There is but one God: how then doth the All-powerful (blessed is He) endure that the Gentiles should live thus prosperously in the worship of gods that are no true gods?"

My uncle's house also was a snare unto me and a temptation; for although he himself reverenced the Law, yet did he consort with many of our nation which scoffed at the Scriptures and warred against all sacred things, making it their delight to have the commandments of the Lord in derision, and saying to the faithful among their countrymen, "Do ye still make account of your laws as if they contained the rules of the truth? Yet see, the Holy Scriptures, as ye call them, contain also fables, such as ye are accustomed to laugh at, when ye hear others say the like."

When I rebuked these backsliders and revolters in the presence of my uncle, he spake kindly to me; yet did his words shake my faith. As for the Scribes whose teaching I had once so prized, he described them as meaning well, but not teaching well; and he called them "puzzle-browed sophists," and "those that busy themselves with the letter." The letter of the Law, he said, was full of falsehoods, such as the Greeks call myths, which were intended to warn the wise from cleaving unto the letter of the Law.

Again, he exhorted me not to despise the learning of the Greeks, nor the teaching of the Gentile Scribes, whom they called "Philosophers." "For," said he, "they enlarge and open the mind and help to the right understanding of the Law of Israel." But when I repeated the proverb of my countrymen, "The very air of Palestine maketh wise," and said that the Scribes in Galilee eschewed the Greek learning, warning their pupils against it, as against a net that entangleth the feet, and when I appealed to the Scribes of my uncle's acquaintance, hoping that they should have been on my side, behold, they were with one consent against me and with my uncle. For they all said that the Galilean Scribes spake as unlearned men, and that there was much to be learned from a certain Gentile philosopher called Plato; and one added a line from a Greek play-writer which saith "even from enemies one may win learning." Then was I staggered in my judgment, and bent to their opinion, so that I began to frequent the schools of the philosophers.

But great indeed was my perplexity and bewilderment when I found that these philosophers treated not of such subjects as I had supposed, namely of the nature of the soul, and whether it be mortal or immortal, or whether there be many gods or one God; but they questioned whether the world came together by chance or by design, and whether there be any God or no. Yet howsoever they differed among themselves, they agreed all in believing that our God was not the true God, and that the stories of the mighty works wrought by Him for our forefathers were mere myths and fables; or, if any thought otherwise, they held that our stories were no truer than their stories, and that Aesculapius and Hercules were far more worthy of honour than Elijah and Samson. Now a certain voice within me constantly testified that they were in error; for the righteous teaching of our prophets and our lawyers far exceeded anything that the Gentiles could Rabbis from their philosophers or lawgivers. But I had been taught by the Scribes of Galilee not to trust to this voice within me, namely to my conscience, but only to tradition and authority; and behold, my traditions and the authority whereon I set store were rejected by these Gentiles: wherefore I knew not how to answer them.

It came to pass that, on a certain day, going from lecture-room to lecture-room, I perceived a great multitude passing into a hall in the

Great Library, where there was to be a dispute between two philosophers; so I followed with them. One of the two belonged to the sect called the Stoics, and the other to the sect called the Epicureans; and the dispute was concerning the government of the universe by the gods, which is affirmed by the former sect, but denied by the latter. Now the contention had endured for the space of a whole day already, and yesterday the Stoic had delivered his arguments: but to-day the dispute was to be continued by the other, and so it was that, when I entered the chamber, the Epicurean was at the point to speak.

He began with reckoning up how many unjust acts, how many oppressions and sins, how many diseases and miseries, had been let loose by the gods (if gods there were) to prey upon the children of men. He set forth the diverse gods and goddesses worshipped by diverse nations; the gods of the Grecians and Romans, wrought of marble or ivory; the sword worshipped by the Scythians; the cat and ibis by the Egyptians. What, he asked, had they all done for their servants? Then he said that in a certain region of Syria there lived a nation which professed to reject the gods of other nations and to believe in one only god: but to what end? Their god had allowed their enemies to destroy his own temple with fire, and had given up his chosen people to be the servants of the Romans. He added a story of one of our learned men, whose life had been blameless and whose teaching had been of the One True God. "Yet," said the Epicurean, "what befell this teacher of truth in his old age? His god delivered him into the hands of persecutors, who placed his tongue between the teeth of a dog which had been made exceeding fierce with hunger; and so the dog bit off the tongue of the pious teacher, even that tongue which had ever spoken words of truth. What say we then? If there be a god, then he suffered this wickedness (for without him is naught); and therefore he is wicked. But if there be no god, then at least we are delivered from the constraint to believe that the Supreme Governor of the world is worse than the worst of men."

The people, who had been on the side of the Epicurean from the first, in despite of the interruptions of the Stoic, now loudly applauded; and when it fell to the Stoic to speak, he had little to say. If he discoursed of oracles as proofs of the divine foreknowledge, then the Epicurean asked who had ever been profited by oracles, bringing forward many dark sayings of the gods, which had led men to destruction; and other sayings that savoured of manifest folly; adding thereto jests and flouts of oracles drawn from the plays of the comedians. When the Stoic spake of a life after death, and alleged apparitions of the dead, then his adversary answered that the said apparitions were mere unsubstantial phantasms, such as appear to madmen and drunkards when they see all things two-fold. Lastly, when the Stoic spake of judgment after death, and a final consumption of the world by fire, then the Epicurean demanded proof hereof; and he laughed at the stories of Minos and Rhadamanthus as nursery fables and bugbears to frighten babes withal. He also compared the Supreme Being of the Stoics burning up the world, to an unskilful cook that burneth the cake that he is baking.

Again the people laughed loudly, and shouted applause; but the Stoic, touched with choler, left reasoning with his adversary and began to revile him, calling him atheist and sacrilegious wretch, and other names; which only made the people laugh the more. But I came forth from the theatre sick at heart and saddened, not more by the arguments of the Epicurean than by the faithlessness of the multitude. Then said I, "How know I that there is a life after death? or who hath returned from the grave to bring back word thereof? For it is written, 'Whatsoever thy hand findeth to do, do it with thy might.' But wherefore? 'Even because,' saith the Scripture, 'there is no work, nor device, nor knowledge, nor wisdom in the grave whither thou goest.'" Then again I lamented that I had wasted my years in labour, and much study had been to me a weariness in the flesh, and I said, "It would have been wiser to have preferred mirth, for it is written, 'A man hath no better thing under the sun than to eat and drink, and to be merry: for that shall abide with him of his labour the days of his life, which God giveth him under the sun.'"

From henceforth my days and nights were busied with such questions as these, which crept into my soul against my will, and would not be driven out: After death shall I live no more, and will no one even once think of me, since infinite time burieth all things in forgetfulness! Will it be even as though I had never been born? When was the world created, and what was in the beginning before the world? If the world was from all eternity, then it will always be; but if it had a beginning, then must it likewise have an end. And, after the end of the world, what will be then? What perhaps but the silence of death?

Being constantly given up to such thoughts, I resorted yet more diligently to the schools of the philosophers, hoping to obtain some deliverance from my doubts: but I saw nothing but the contentions of orators, and the *foyning and thrusting* of rhetoricians, fighting not for the truth, but each desiring to prove himself more skilful than his adversaries. So it came to pass that I inclined, now to one, now to another. As, for example, at one time they that taught the immortality of the soul seemed to prevail; then again they that would have the soul to be mortal. When the former doctrine had the upper hand, I rejoiced: when the latter, I was downcast. Thus was I driven to and fro by differing opinions, and was forced to conclude that things appear not as they are in themselves, but as they happen to be presented on this side, or on that. My brain was in a greater whirl than ever, and I sighed from the bottom of my heart.

At the last I went to my uncle in my distress, and poured forth my troubles in his ear. But when he had hearkened to my complaints, he said, "It will be well that thou shouldst have speech with Philo; for he is our principal teacher here, and he will answer thy doubts." But I said in my haste and impatience, "Behold, I have resorted unto the wisest teachers in Galilee, and now, at thy word, I have frequented the lectures of these Gentile philosophers; but they have added nothing to me, for they are as dried-up springs." At this my uncle laughed, and said, "Suppose not, son of my sister, that our Philo is like unto the Scribes of Galilee: for as well might a dog hope to lap up the Nile as that thou shouldst drain dry the wisdom of Philo the Alexandrine." So without more ado I accompanied him to the house of Philo.

When we entered the house of Philo, I admired first of all the homely plainness of his household. For though he were one of the foremost Jews in Alexandria (and there were nigh unto a hundred myriads of our countrymen in the city and the country round about) and kinsman also to Alexander the Alabarch, whose wealth was known to all, yet were there no signs of luxury, nor of pride in his house, nor in his furniture nor in his clothing: and his wife also wore a plain and simple garment without plaiting of the hair, or painting, or adornment with gold and precious stones; and in all the house there was naught whereat the strictest Pharisee could have been offended.

Philo received us courteously; and when I had opened to him at large all my doubts, he. replied fully to them. I cannot at this time set down exactly all that we spake together; but this was the substance.

First, I said that I was loth to be as one of the backsliders among my countrymen, who in effect gave up the Law, deriding it as a heap of fables; yet on the other hand, I confessed that after much study of the Law I had not been able to attain to righteousness nor peace. Thereto Philo made answer that he was not one of them that rejected the Law of Israel; for he diligently observed it, believing that it contained all knowledge and all wisdom; "and," said he, "I consider that Moses was the greatest and most perfect of men, and that he attained unto the very pinnacle of wisdom. But as for the wisdom of the Greeks, it is but as a handmaid in respect of our wisdom; even as the slave Hagar was, in respect of her mistress and queen, Sarah." "Notwithstanding," added he, "when I speak of our Scriptures, I mean that there are two interpretations of every Scripture. There is first the outer meaning, which is as it were the body; but there is, next, the inner spiritual meaning, which is, as it were, the soul. Thus, for example, when thou readest that Eve was made out of the rib of Adam, or that the world was made in six days, or that God talked with Moses in a thorn-bush, the letter of these Scriptures is indeed fable, but the spiritual meaning is truth and life." Then said I, "If the letter be fable why retain the letter?" But he said, "And if the body be unspiritual, why retain the body? As well cast away the body because it is not soul, as cast away the letter because it is not spirit."

Then I asked, "But how shall I attain righteousness?" Philo replied, "All men have in them a certain spiritual nature, in virtue whereof they are allied with the Word of God. Whosoever recogniseth the sins wherewith he is denied, hath the power (if he will use it) of rising above his passions, and conquering his lusts, so that in the end, by repentance and by constant struggling after righteousness, he can follow after the virtues of the Father in heaven who begat him." Then said I, "All this have I done; for I have now these many years observed not only the words of the Law, but also the Traditions of the Elders; yet have I not attained peace." But he said, "Thou puttest first that which should come second; first aim after the virtues that have to do with men; afterward shalt thou attain the virtue that hath to do with God." "It would seem therefore," said I, "that thou dost not advise thy disciples to withdraw themselves from the world, after the manner of hermits." "Yeah but I do advise them," said Philo; "only first men should attain to the lower step before aiming at the higher. For first, they should study truthfulness, striving to love their neighbours, and to be helpful and gentle to all; for man should be gentle, and not savage, being fitted by nature for fellowship and concord. But after that thou hast attained to this lower stage, my counsel is that thou forsake thy home and thy friends, and thy wealth, and all that thou hast, and that thou abstain from business of state, and from all traffic, and that thou give thyself entirely to the contemplation of the divine essence."

Then said I, "Methinks, many of our Scribes in Galilee would not please thee; for they seek after righteousness by other ways, observing the smallest matters of the Law, and afflicting the flesh." "Tell such an one from me," said Philo, "when thou shalt see him perchance abstaining from food or drink at the times of eating, or disdaining the bath and the use of oil, or tormenting himself with a hard couch or with night-watchings, deceiving himself with this show of abstinence, that he is not in the true way to continence, and that all his labour is in vain."

"But what," asked I, "is this highest revelation of the essence of the Supreme (blessed is He) to which the soul shall at last attain?" Philo paused a moment and then answered, "Thou shalt attain to the knowledge of God, as mere being or existence." But I, not understanding him aright, said, "Thou sayest 'existence:' dost thou mean 'holy existence'?" But Philo answered with a smile, "How can we call Him holy who is holier than all holiness? But by 'mere existence' I mean that which is known as existence and in no other way." Then I said, "May we not therefore call Him good? or loving?" "Call Him so," replied Philo, "if thou dost not believe that He is better than all goodness, more loving than all love."

Hereat my heart sank within me; for such a God as this "mere existence" seemed to me not a being able to love me nor to be loved by me, no more than if it had been a triangle or a circle. But presently I called to mind that Moses had named God the Father of the spirits of all flesh: and the prophets also had named God Father. Therefore said I to Philo, "And the name Father also? May we not give this name to God?" "No," said Philo, "except in order to teach the common folk; as when the Scripture saith that God chasteneth those whom He loveth, like as a father chasteneth his son. For God cannot change; neither can He feel anger, nor love, nor joy. But when the Scripture sayeth such words as these, it speaketh for the common multitude, even as when it saith that God spake or heard; or that He smelled a sweet savour; or that He awaked from sleep; or that He repented of that which He had done."

When I heard this, it seemed to me that I had come to Philo for naught; but I said to him, "Thou speakest of that revelation of God, which thou callest mere existence, as being the highest revelation. Is there then a lower revelation?" "Certainly," he replied, "for just as there is, in human life, the thing and the word that revealeth the thing, even so is there also on the one hand God, the true God, THAT WHICH is, and on the other hand the Word of God, which revealeth God to the minds of men." Then I questioned him concerning this Word of God, or Logos (as he called it, using a Greek name): and he answered me fully, yet not so that I could altogether understand him. But this I gathered, that the Word or Logos was a second divine being, inseparable from the Father; and that by the Word was the world made. But sometimes he said that the world, as conceived by the intellect, was the Word, ("for," said he, "as a city, not yet being, is in the mind or reason of the architect thereof, so the world, albeit not being, was in the mind or reason of God";) and with these exact words he made an end of this part of his discourse, for I set them down at the time: "If any one should desire to use still plainer terms, he would not call the world (regarded as perceptible only to the intellect) as anything else but the Reason of God busied with the creation of the world; for neither is a city, while only perceptible to the intellect, anything else except the reason of the architect."

Then said, I "But how do men attain to the revelation of the Word?" "By the exercise of the divine "Word or Reason within them," said Philo; "for all men have in themselves a ray of light from the archetypal Light, the Word of the Supreme Being. For no mortal thing is framed, nor could have been framed, in the similitude of the Supreme Father; but only after the pattern of the second deity, the Word. Now this Word can be received of all them that will live according to it. For the race of mankind is twofold, the one being the race of them that live by the Divine Spirit and reason; the other, of such as live according to the pleasures of the flesh. The universe therefore, apprehended by the reason of man, conveyeth the revelation of the Word. And this revelation, this heavenly food of the soul (which Moses calleth manna), the Word of God meteth out in equal portions among all them which are to use it. For the blessed soul proffereth her own reason as the holy goblet of true joy. But who can pour forth the wine of life, save only the Cup-bearer of God, the

Master of the Feast, the Word? And indeed the Cup-bearer differeth in no wise from the draught. For the Word is the draught itself, pure and unpolluted."

Then it was borne in upon my mind, that in all his discourse (which inforced attention by reason of the beauty of his sayings, and because of his exceeding earnestness) he had left no place for the Messiah 'or Redeemer of Israel, whose coming had been prophesied by John, the son of Zachariah. Therefore I questioned him of this matter. But he smiled and said, "Trouble not thyself on this matter; for it is likely that no Messiah is to come. But it will come to pass, in the day of Redemption, that the children of Israel, which be now scattered over the earth, will be led from all parts back to the Sacred Land, by the light of a great light invisible to all others, but visible only to such as are to be saved." Then, seeing that I was of a sad countenance, he added, "Dost thou not perceive that the revelation of a Messiah would be as much inferior to the revelation of the Word, or Logos, as the revelation of the Logos is itself inferior to the revelation of mere existence, ***το ον*** or THAT WHICH IS? For the revelation of the Logos (that is of God known by creation) is through hope and fear; but the revelation of ***το ον*** (that is God in itself) is through love. And the revelation of a Messiah must needs be a poor and low thing as compared with either of these. But thou shouldst aspire towards the highest revelation of all, even the Father of all, with a divinely inspired passion not inferior to the *enthousiasmos* wherewith the worshippers of the gods of the Gentiles celebrate their inferior rites."

The day was now far spent: so my uncle arose to bid Philo farewell. I thanked him with my whole heart: for righteousness and goodness breathed in his presence; and my spirit was refreshed while I heard him speak.

For the very voice of the Lord seemed to sound from him when he said that to afflict the flesh was of no avail without afflicting the spirit, and that the practice of virtue with men should go before the practice of virtue with God. But when I was departed from him, musing as I returned home, then I saw that the philosophy of Philo could in no wise give me peace. For it was not possible that I should feel that *enthousiasmos*, or divine passion, whereof he made mention, for such a being as Mere Existence: and methought I could feel this*enthousiasmos* for none save a man, or some similitude of a man.

Therefore my heart went back to that lower revelation whereof he spake, to wit, to God revealed through the world; that is, the Word: and this seemed to me more likely to give peace. But as for Mere Existence, albeit Philo called it the Father of all, yet had he plainly told me he meant this only for the unlearned multitude. And whereas he used one word, God, to signify two things, one thing for the learned, and "another for the unlearned; herein, to say truth, his doctrine brought to my mind a certain tale of the poet Homer, which my uncle had but yesternight related unto me; how a certain mighty man o valour, and a wise counsellor among the Greeks, Ulysses by name, deceived the giant Polyphemus, saying that his name was NOMAN. Wherefore, when Polyphemus said that NOMAN had blinded him, his brethren, the giants, thought that he meant to say that not "a man, but a god, had blinded him. And even so Philo seemed to me, when he spake to the wise and learned, to call God no man; but when he spake to the foolish and unlearned, he called Him NOMAN, making them think He was a person.

But what troubled me in this revelation was, that it seemed not to leave any room or place for the Messiah, the Redeemer of Israel. And "Why," thought I, "should the Word reveal himself only through the world, and not through mankind? But if he revealed himself through mankind (which Philo also would allow), why might he not reveal himself through a Messiah?" All that night I lay awake musing on the same thing, and asking whether it might not be that Philo spake truth in proclaiming the revelation of the Word, and yet John the son of Zachariah might also speak truth in proclaiming the revelation of the Messiah. But after long tossing of the matter in my mind I concluded that there was no cause why the one should destroy the other: so I prayed that both might be true.

But as for my former studies, and my old strict observances of the Sabbath and of the precepts concerning the use of purifications and concerning the consumption of nail-parings, and concerning the wearing of tassels, behold, all these matters began to seem unto me things far off, forgotten, and childish. And though I knew not clearly whither to turn, yet I felt at least that to them I could return no more; for I perceived that, even if I became as perfect in these matters as Abuyah the son of Elishah himself, yet should I none the more attain to peace, nor could I find in them that food for want whereof my soul was an-hungered. Wherefore I was now resolved in my mind of this one thing, in any case, namely, that the observance of the smaller precepts of the Law could not gain for me that Banquet, or Manna, or heavenly Draught of the Word of God whereof Philo had made mention. But what the true Manna might be, or how I might attain to it, this I did not as yet perceive. For I was, at that time, even as a little child in a boat without oars or sail, which hath drifted out unawares far into the open sea.

CHAPTER VI

How I found not Salvation in the Worship of the Temple; nor in the Teachers of Galilee; nor in the Essenes; and how I first spake with Jesus of Nazareth.

Not many days after my discourse with Philo the Alexandrine, when I returned from the Great Library to my uncle's house, a messenger was waiting for me, bearing a letter from Rabbi Jonathan. Opening it I read that my mother was suffering under a grievous disease, and being, as she thought, nigh unto death, she would fain see me before she died. So I straightway made all things ready for my journey, and having bidden farewell to my uncle, I set sail on the morrow from Alexandria, and on the fifth day arrived in Jerusalem; where, according to my mother's desire, I purposed to offer sacrifice unto the Lord, and to make vows for my mother's health.

The sun was well nigh set when I came to Jerusalem. But on the morrow, as I went up to the Temple through the narrow ways, amid the throng of them that sold oxen and sheep and doves, new thoughts and doubts rose in my heart, such as I had never felt before when I had gone up to sacrifice during the three great feasts. Methought the Lord must needs turn His face from so much traffic and disorder and defilement of His Holy House. On both sides of the gate Horsea, as far as Solomon's porch, were shops of merchants and stalls of money-changers. Even in the Court of the Gentiles, which is a part of the Temple itself, there were penned flocks of sheep and oxen, with drovers and salesmen. Pilgrims and proselytes from all parts pressed and thronged; buyer reviled seller, and seller buyer; from the stalls of the money-changers one might hear the clink of money mixed with the sounds of contention. The stench also of so many cattle, being increased by reason of the great heat, made the ill-savour of the place almost past bearing. Also I could not but marvel at the greediness of the sellers. For the Chief Priests had let out the right of selling offerings at a great price, to make profit thereof for themselves, insomuch that a single dove was sold for a gold piece.

Then, again, when it came to the offering of the sacrifice, I must needs wait for the space of an hour whilst others were offering up their sacrifices; and the Levites and priests seemed all in haste, and did their work rather as an handicraft than as worship; and many others were sacrificing at the same time, and the cries and struggles of the victims, and the smoke and reek of the fat, and the blood flowing on all sides, caused the place to seem rather like a butcher's shambles than like the House of the Lord. Now all this I had known and seen aforetime, yet had I never taken it to heart. But now there came to my mind certain words of Philo touching the sect called the Essenes, how they worship the Lord with an exceeding carefulness of purity: wherefore they think it not meet to sacrifice the blood of beasts unto the Lord, but they offer up their own hearts, purified so as to be a fit offering for Him. Also at this time (perchance because I was but freshly come from the lecture-rooms of the philosophers of Alexandria, or belike because the Lord would have it so to be, willing by easy degrees to open mine eyes, and to reveal unto me His Messiah) so it was that I could think of naught but the words of Isaiah the Prophet wherein the Lord saith, "I am full of the burnt offerings of rams, and the fat of fed beasts, and I delight not in the blood of bullocks, or of lambs, or of he-goats." These words, I say, so possessed my soul that, even when the victim was being slain, I could not refrain from repeating them to myself again and again; albeit against my will, being fearful to pollute the sacrifice of the Lord, But though I made shift to dissemble my trouble until the sacrifice was ended, for fear of offending the priests, yet when I had returned to my lodging in the city, I could not forbear weeping; for behold, all worship seemed as vanity, and the children of men were in mine eyes as beasts of the field, void of understanding and given over to all folly; and God was He that had made them thus. Therefore I cried aloud in the fervency of my passion and said, "It is written, 'On three things the world is stayed: on the Law, and on the Worship, and on the Bestowal of Kindnesses;' and lo, I know not the interpretation of the Law; and worship is naught but vanity; and as for kindness, my heart is dry and empty of love, so that there is no kindness in me."

On the third day after the sacrifice, I came to Sepphoris. My mother was so far recovered of her sickness that she was no longer despaired of by the physicians. For the time, my joy thereat, and our rejoicing together (because the Lord had suffered us to look on one another again) drove away my former searchings of heart: which notwithstanding presently came back upon me. My mother took a delight in my continual presence, and that I should sit by her bed, expounding unto her passages of the Law; and many a time, while I was doing this, she would make mention of the title wherewith I had been honoured by Rabbi Jonathan, who had called me "the plastered cistern." But oftentimes it was not in my heart to find any words of comfort or hope, and when my mother longed for the draughts of the Law I felt that I was a dried-up cistern, and no longer full.

At the last, on a certain morning, my mother, having (as I suppose) noted my silence before, spake aloud reproving me, albeit gently, and saying, "Why flow not the drops of refreshment from the plastered cistern as in former days?" But I replied in haste, "Call me no longer, my mother, a cistern. For lo, I am become even as a strainer, which letteth out the wine and keepeth in itself nothing but the dregs." Then my mother wept bitterly, thinking that she had angered me, and that I had spoken falsely; and I also wept, partly for that I had made her weep, but still more because my words were true.

Then went I forth hastily into the street; and meeting Jonathan the son of Ezra, and Abuyah the son of Elishah, I accompanied them. And we came to the well that is on the road to Nazareth, about a thousand paces from the town, and there we sat down to rest. For a time we were silent. Then I turned to Rabbi Jonathan and said, "Simeon the Just was of the remnant of the Great Synagogue. He used to say, 'On three things the world is stayed: on the Law, and on the Worship, and on the Bestowal of Kindnesses.' Now there was a certain young man which observed the Law, and worshipped duly in the temple. Also he clothed the naked, and buried them that lay unburied, and fed the hungry: but there was no kindness in his heart. Is such an one, therefore, in the path of righteousness?" Then Abuyah replied at once, "He is righteous. For it is written concerning the statutes and judgments of the Law of the Lord that whosoever doeth them shall live in them; but whether he shall do them easily or with difficulty, or gladly or sorrowfully, concerning this, behold, nothing is written," But Jonathan the son of Ezra was silent for a while, and said at last, "Antigonus of Soko used to say, 'Be not as slaves that minister to their lord with intent to receive recompense; but be ye as slaves that minister to their lord without thought of recompense; and let the fear of Heaven be upon you.'"

Then I replied, "True, oh my Master; but ought not the love of Heaven as well as the fear of Heaven to be upon us? For is it not said, 'Learn for love, and honour will come in the end.'" "Thou speakest well," said Jonathan, "and it is written also as the chief of all the commandments, 'Thou shalt love the Lord thy God, and Him only shalt thou serve.'" Then I said, "But what if a man feel no love of God in his heart? For I have met lately certain of the Gentiles, yea, and some also of our own nation, which have no love of God; whereof some even constantly say that there is no God. Yea, and even in mine own heart arise strange questionings as to whence I came into this world, and whither I am going, and before whom I am to give account and reckoning."

Then Abuyah brake forth again: "Joseph son of Simeon, busy not thyself with questions that are too high for thee: for it is said 'Whosoever shall consider four things, what is above, below, before, behind, it were better for him that he had not come into the world.'" "Yea, but," said I, smiling, "it is said by the Wise, 'Consider three things, and thou wilt not come into transgression, Know whence thou camest; and whither thou art going; and before whom thou art to give account and reckoning.'" Hereat Abuyah arose hastily from his seat in sore displeasure, and he said, "Child, thou hast defiled thyself by going to a city of the Gentiles which is not a place of the Law for it is said, 'Two that sit together without words of the Law are a session of scorners;' and again, 'Betake thyself to a place of the Law, and say not that it shall come after thee, for thine associates will confirm it unto thee: and lean not unto thine own understanding.' Howbeit, I thank thee, Lord my God and God of my fathers, that Thou hast cast my lot among them that do frequent the schools and synagogues, and not among such as frequent the theatre and the circus. For both I and they work and watch: I to inherit eternal life, but they for eternal destruction." So saying he departed, and left me alone with Jonathan the son of Ezra.

Jonathan sat still by my side saying naught, but gazing up into the heaven, or else upon the trees round about us. For all around us were orange- trees and pomegranate-trees; the leaves thereof scarce to be seen for the multitude of white and scarlet blossoms; for the spring was now something worn. The fields also and the gardens and the hedges of cactus, by reason of the rains, were of a marvellous verdure, even above their wont. Behind us, at a little distance, stood a grove of olive-trees, wherein the doves made a pleasant murmuring: and birds of divers colours fluttered to and fro around the well. Nigh over our heads there were passing larger birds, flying in a long train towards the country of the Lake; and far off I could discern an eagle, like a spot, high up in the sky. Then Jonathan spake unto me and said, "My son, dost thou not remember the words of the Psalmist, how he praiseth the name of God because 'He sendeth the springs into the valleys, which run among the hills. They give drink to every beast of the field: the wild asses quench their thirst. By them shall the fowls of the heaven have their habitation, which sing among the branches. He causeth the grass to grow for the cattle and herb for the service of man: that he may bring forth food out of the earth; and wine that maketh glad the heart of man, and oil to make his face to shine, and bread which strengtheneth man's heart.' Doth not the sight of all this glory and beauty cause thee also to say with the Singer of Israel, 'Lord, how manifold are Thy works! in wisdom hast Thou made them all!'"

But I made answer, in the bitterness of my heart, according to the words of the same Psalm, saying, "Thou hidest Thy face, they are troubled: Thou takest away their breath, they die, and return to their dust." Then Jonathan bowed his head and answered nothing, but I continued, "Did not the same hand which made the dove make also yonder eagle to destroy the dove I Did not the God which chose out Israel from among the Gentiles to serve Him, choose out Rome also to rend Israel in pieces? Thou speakest after the manner of Philo the Alexandrine, who saith that God revealeth Himself to us through His Word in the universe. But verily He revealeth Himself not so unto me. Nay rather, unsearchable are the paths of the Creator in the universe, and His ways in the world are past finding out."

Then the old man covered his face with his hands and wept; but soon raising his head he said, "Is it seemly that a son of Abraham should have so little trust in the Lord? Bethink thee of the times when the Holy Temple was burned with fire, and Judah led into captivity: did not all the Gentiles say in those days, 'God hath forsaken them'? Yet did the Lord save Israel out of the hand of the daughter of Babylon, and out of the hand of the Assyrian and the Philistine, as also out of the hand of the Egyptian, in the days of old. Commit thy way therefore unto the Lord, and trust in Him, and He shall bring the word of His prophets to pass.

"Is not the Lord our God perchance even now on the point to stop the mouths of them that complained? Is there not even now, after four hundred years, a prophet again in Israel? But if the Lord sendeth unto us a prophet after so long a time, as it were from the dead, surely it is like that He hath some great redemption in store for Sion. Even during this week have I heard that John the prophet, who hath these six months prophesied of a Deliverer shortly to come, hath of late prophesied that the Redeemer is even now amongst us; and some say that it is a certain Jesus, the son of Joseph, of the town of Nazareth, one famous in word and deed. This Jesus, as they report the matter, being baptized of John, beheld a vision of the Lord; and in that instant the Spirit of the Lord fell upon him; insomuch that, since that time, he both speaketh as a prophet and worketh signs as a man of God. Moreover, I had speech but yesterday with some that say he is come into Galilee, and is even now in these parts. Who knoweth whether this may not be true? But whether it be true or false, trust thou in the Lord God of Abraham and of Isaac and Jacob, whose arm is not shortened, and who is not a man that He should lie."

For an instant, my heart leaped up at the mention of the name of that Jesus whom I had seen in the house of the father of Raphael; but then it seemed not possible that one of so gentle an aspect should be the Redeemer of Israel. Howbeit, I asked Jonathan concerning the vision that had been reported to have been seen of Jesus; and he told me that it had not been a vision of flames of fire, nor of angels, nor of thrones, nor of seraphim, nor any such vision as had been seen of the prophets in times past, but a vision of a dove descending from heaven. Hereat I marvelled and I said, as I remember, in the bitterness and folly of my heart, that the times needed an eagle, and, lo, the new prophet brought a dove.

But Jonathan rose up from his seat to depart, and paying no heed to my last words, he spake kindly unto me and said, "If thy heart inclineth thee, my child, to prove whether there be any avail for thee in a life of contemplation, and whether thou mayest thereby attain peace; wherefore goest thou not unto the village of Jotapata where the Essenes dwell? Menahem the son of Barachiah is their chief ruler, a man that followeth after holiness and seeth things to come; who, being my friend, will for my sake receive thee kindly. Finally my child, offer up prayers unto God and pour forth thy troubles before Him; neither think too evil of thyself nor give place unto dark thoughts; and let not thy prayers be uttered at set times and in set words, but let them express thy heart's desire, according as it is said, 'Make not thy prayer an ordinance, but an entreaty before Him who filleth all space (blessed is He).' Think not also too evil of thine own heart; but remember the saying, 'Be not wicked unto thyself.' And now farewell, for I must needs go back to the city."

Saying these words, the old man departed and left me still sitting by the well. But, as it was not yet the third hour of the day (and the Essene village was distant not much more than a two hours' journey, or three hours' at the most), it came into my mind that I would hearken unto the voice of Jonathan, and visit the village of the Essenes that very day. So I arose straightway and set out on my journey. I rested often during the heat of the day, for I was weary with long watching and fasting; but a little before noontide, I was come to the top of the mountain which looketh down upon the village.

Then I looked, and lo, in the valley the Essenes busy at their labours, even as the ants that move to and fro in an ant-hill; and as near as I could conjecture, they were to the number of three or four hundred thus labouring together. But as I looked, behold, a sound as of one proclaiming the hour of prayer; and lo, the fields were empty, neither was any one anywhere to be seen. Presently they appeared again in white robes thronging to the house of prayer. Then a sound, as of psalms sung by many voices, rose up to my ears, and filled my heart with a deep peace. I waited for the space of nearly an hour, till the assembly had broken up, returning in their white robes to their several cottages. When I had beheld all this, my heart rejoiced, and I said, "If only all Israel could thus return to the Lord, then would the dough be no longer corrupt with leaven, according to the saying; and the wrath of the Lord would be turned from His people." But then came into my mind the saying of Philo, that the virtue towards man must come before the virtue towards God. I remembered also that which I had often before heard of the Essenes, how they neither marry nor give in marriage, but replenish their community by adopting the children of others and by admitting of strangers into their number. Then I bethought myself that if all the children of Israel should become Essenes, Israel would speedily perish; neither could there be any Redemption. For even now, though there had been Essenes these thirty or forty years, or even more, yet did they number no more than three thousand or four thousand men in all Israel; and of these almost all lived in the country, avoiding towns for fear of defilement, and exceeding even the Pharisees in the strictness wherewith they observe Sabbaths and obey the precepts of the Law (save only in the matter of sacrifice). So, as I looked down upon the village, and round upon the hills which shut it in and hid it from the sight of men, the proverb came to my mind which sayeth that "a city that is set upon a hill cannot be hid:" but said I, "the city of the Essenes lieth in a valley." Then I turned my back upon the place and would not go down to see Menahem, but set out to return to Sepphoris.

But as I went, my burden grew heavier than I could bear, and I cried unto the Lord in the sore grief of my heart. For all Israel seemed unto me even as sheep without a shepherd, a nation given over to servitude. For behold, the Scribes, and Lawyers, and all the Pharisees, had set their thought on vanity, and fed the people with chaff and not with wheat. Yea, they despised the poor and simple, and said that the "people of the land" could not attain to the knowledge of the Law. But as for the Priests and Sadducees, they were given over to the pursuit of wealth and to the pleasures of this world. And last of all, these Essenes were as naught save for themselves alone. For they took for their watchword the saying, "Withdraw thyself from an evil neighbour and consort not with the wicked:" therefore were they of no avail to the sinners of my people. For albeit that saying of Hillel was often in their mouths, which saith, "Be of the disciples of Aaron, loving peace and pursuing peace;" yet did they forget the last words of that saying, which bid us also to " love mankind and bring men nigh unto the Law." For the Essenes bring no man nigh unto the Law save themselves only.

But when I came in my journey back to the well where Rabbi Jonathan and I had discoursed together, then did my despair so weigh upon me that I could not so much as cry unto the Lord; for the Lord seemed as one that heard not; and even as I had made a circle in my journey that day, and was now come back to the same place whence I had set forth at the first, and all in vain, even so did I seem to have journeyed these many years in a circle of vain thoughts, searching and groping after God; and all for naught. "For," said I, "I have gone from, the Scribes of Galilee to the teaching of John the Prophet, and from John the Prophet to the wisdom of the Greeks, and from the wisdom of the Greeks to the teaching of Philo the Wise; and yet seem I no nearer to God than before, but even where I was at the first. And they which did profess to guide, have been unto me as no guides. Therefore the foundations of my life are broken up, and the rock of my trust is become as unstable as water. Whithersoever I look, I see no one to avenge, no one to deliver; for the ways of the world are crooked, and sin is stronger than righteousness."

Then a Voice of the Lord spake unto me, and rebuked me in that, albeit I compassed sea and land in search of guides, and had made much of them which explain the Law and the Prophets, yet I had not given myself so zealously to the true guides of Israel, even the Prophets themselves, of whom John the son of Zachariah was one. Now they all with one consent prophesied of a day of Redemption, and of a Redeemer; and without a Redeemer their prophecies seemed maimed and void of fulfilment. Moreover John the son of Zachariah had prophesied that the Redeemer should come speedily, and that the rough places should be made smooth, and the crooked places straight; and Jonathan the son of Ezra had spoken as if the Redeemer were even now among us, yea in our own country of Galilee. So falling on my face before the Lord, I besought the Almighty (blessed is He) to make no long tarrying, but to have mercy upon me and either to take away my life, or else to send the Redeemer unto me, even me, and to grant me His salvation.

But as I arose, there came one behind me unperceived and touched my shoulder; and he said unto me, "Wherefore weepest thou?" I started at his voice, for there was a power in it; but I looked not up for weeping, but made answer and said, "Because of the yoke of the Law; for it is written 'Whoso receiveth upon him the yoke of the Law, THEY remove from him the yoke of oppression and the yoke of the path of the world.' But it is not so with me. For from a child I have settled my heart to study the Law, and to take upon me the yoke thereof, yet have I not attained to the knowledge thereof. But the yoke of the world and the yoke of the oppression of Israel weigheth heavily upon me." Then he that spake said unto me, "Cast away the heavy yoke and take upon thee the light yoke." [1] So I looked up, marvelling at such words, and behold, it was not the face of a stranger, for I knew it; and yet again I knew it not, neither could I bring to mind the name of him that spake to me. But I saw strength in his countenance, and his face was as the morning-star in brightness; and I rejoiced with a great joy, for I knew that the Lord had sent unto me a teacher to guide my feet into the path of life. So I replied, "What yoke, Master?" And he answered and said, "Take my yoke upon thee, and learn of me; for I am meek and lowly of heart." When I heard that, I was speechless and as one astonied to hear such a saying, which seemed in part the words of a king, and in part the words of a child. But when speech came back to me, I said, "My heart is afflicted because of the wonder of the ways of the Lord, and because His paths are past finding out."

But he answered, "They that wonder shall reign, and they that reign shall rest." [1] Now I perceived not all the meaning of his words at the time; but thus much I did most clearly perceive, that here was one that could guide me through all wonderment and perplexity, even unto the haven of rest. But a sudden fear fell upon me that peace would depart from my soul, if my Master should depart; therefore with many entreaties I besought him to tarry that night at my mother's house. So when he had consented we straightway went to the city. But, as we went, my mind still beat upon the thought that I had seen my Master's countenance before; yet could I not call to mind the when and where.

But even as we entered into the house, behold, my mother was crying aloud, being tormented beyond measure by her disease: and when my Master heard it, he asked who cried thus, and I answered and told him concerning my mother's condition. Then straightway he desired to go into the upper chamber where she lay; and having gone in, he looked steadfastly at her, and took her by the hand, and said, as one having authority, "Arise:" and immediately my mother arose and went about as one whole. Now it came to pass, that when he looked steadfastly at my mother, even in that instant I knew his face, that it was the face of the stranger that had looked after the like manner upon Raphael the son of Joazar, even the face of Jesus of Nazareth; and then also in that same instant it was borne to my mind that this was he of whom Jonathan had spoken, concerning whom John the son of Zachariah had prophesied, saying that he was the Messiah of Israel: and I marvelled that I had not known him before; but I perceived that, albeit the same, yet was he not the same; so great a glory and a brightness, as of power from heaven, now reigned in his countenance. All this, I say, I perceived even when he was gazing on my mother; but I durst not for my life speak to him then. But when my mother was made whole and arose from her bed, then straightway I fell down on my knees and bowed before him; and I spake also to my mother all the words of Jonathan the son of Ezra, how that John had affirmed my Master to be the Redeemer of Israel: and I believed, and my mother also, and all our household.

On the morrow, when I would fain have accompanied Jesus to Capernaum (for he was journeying thither), he suffered me not, but said that he must needs go to Capernaum alone; but I was to remain for nine days at Sepphoris with my mother, and on the tenth day I might go down to Capernaum. But he suffered me to go with him about twelve or thirteen furlongs out of the town, and there I was to bid him farewell.

He did not speak many words to me by the way; but what I noted especially in him (as being that wherein he differed from all my former teachers) was that he spake not according to rule, nor out of any books, nor traditions, but as it were out of himself. For he taught as one having authority. There was also yet another difference. For most of the Pharisees were wont to walk with their faces turned up to the sky, or else with their eyes half shut, repeating, as they went, certain passages of the Law, or prayers, or precepts of the Elders; and if they met women they would avoid them; and of children also they took no note, except it were to instruct them or question them in the Law and 'the Traditions; moreover they walked with a sour and austere countenance. But Jesus was in all respects different from these. For he looked on all things, and in all things seemed to see joy and gladness, taking note even of the smallest matters, such as the flowers of the field, and the birds of the air, and also of the trees, and the. cornfields. Moreover, as often as we met women on the way, he saluted them courteously and shunned them not.

But most marvellous of all, in my judgment, was the manner of his dealing with children. For so it was, as I remember, that when we were passing by a hamlet, about six furlongs from Sepphoris, a little child ran out from the door of a house, even under the feet of our asses, insomuch that we had much ado to prevent the asses from trampling down the child. But when I rebuked the child somewhat vehemently, Jesus chid me; and presently, after we had ridden on awhile in silence, he turned to me and bade me always have respect unto little children; "For," said he, "their angels do always behold the face of my Father which is in heaven." Then he added words still stranger and harder for me to understand, that "Except a man were born again and become as a little child, he could in no wise enter into the Kingdom of Heaven."

But I returned, marvelling greatly at his words and pondering them, in my mind. For I could in no wise perceive how we could redeem Israel and drive out the Tetrarch from Tiberias, and the Romans from Jerusalem, and set up the Kingdom of God, and all this by becoming as little children.

CHAPTER VII

Of the Good News; and concerning the Kingdom of God; and how we, desired of Jesus New Laws.

WHEN I drew nigh to Capernaum, it was about the eleventh hour; so I hasted that I might inquire where Jesus of Nazareth abode, before the sun went down: for it was the day before the Sabbath. But as I journeyed down the valley, called the Valley of the Doves, and came to the place where the road turneth round to the right, I could not forbear to draw rein for a while, so beautiful was the sight; and though I had seen it oftentimes before, yet never before, methought, had it seemed so beautiful as now.

On the tops of the hills were walnut-trees; lower down fig-trees; and below them grew luxuriant palms. For the place hath, as it were, several climates suiting several trees and plants; corn also aboundeth in those parts, and flax is not wanting; but the olive-trees (as elsewhere in Galilee) stand so thick together, and so thriving, that it was a common saying, "Thou mayest sooner rear a forest of olive-trees in Galilee than one child in Judaea;" fruit- trees also of all sorts grew there without number, laden with the goodliest fruits, exceeding the fruit-trees of any other part of Galilee; insomuch that the place was justly wont to be called the Garden of Abundance. But the city itself was as a half-circle of pearls, encompassed with gardens as with a circlet of emerald. A multitude of ships and fishing-boats bestrewed the surface of the lake, which was of a deep blue colour, as blue as sapphire; and the waves thereof were very still, because no wind at all was blowing. But as I looked towards Chorazin, the sight in the surface of the waters surpassed the sight of the land. For there, as in a mirror, one might see by reflexion in the water below, all that was on the land above; the walnut-trees and fig-trees and palm-trees, and the oleanders on the border of the waters, and the white pelicans watching for their prey upon the brink thereof, and the hedges of cactus, and the cottages of the husbandmen; all these things were to be clearly seen as if painted on the waters of the lake.

Then came into my mind certain words which my Master had said to me when we went forth from Sepphoris together; how that our Father in heaven provideth for the adornment even of the grass of the fields, and how He hath made the simple flowers of the fields more beautiful than Solomon in his glory. And so it was that, as I thought on these words, I praised the Lord of Hosts, who hath made the world so beautiful; and though I had seen this sight many times before when I had come down from Sepphoris, yet now mine eyes seemed, as it were, to be opened to discern a new beauty therein. But I thought also on Israel and of the blessedness that was in store for this goodly land, if only the Roman could be driven forth. As I thought on these things, an east wind sprang up; and lo, where there had been but a moment ago so fair a sight, naught was now to be seen save troubled waters of many divers colours.

Then I hasted onward, purposing to inquire concerning Jesus of Nazareth first, and afterwards to go to the house of my uncle.

But when I was now at the going down to the city, my cousin Baruch was come forth to meet me, saying I was stayed for at a feast in the house of Manasseh. So I went straightway with him, and the sun set and the Sabbath was begun; and I had not yet seen Jesus of Nazareth. During supper time I would have inquired of Manasseh concerning Jesus; but Baruch had forewarned me that I should be silent. For my uncle, (he was a dyer by trade, and had many slaves and more than one house of merchandise, there and at Magdala, and elsewhere round about the Lake,) being fond of peace and wholly given to traffic, feared Jesus, lest he should beguile the people of Capernaum to take up arms against the Romans. Also he feared for Baruch, lest he too should be led away by Jesus. This I learned from my cousin after supper; howbeit he said not much about Jesus, for my uncle watched us. Only he said that Jesus had been now a full week in Capernaum, and that he was said to be able to work signs, and that certain of the fishermen had joined themselves unto him; but the most part still held with John the Prophet, saying that John was greater than Jesus; neither believed they that Jesus was the Messiah.

On the morrow, about the sixth hour, we went to the synagogue. There was a great throng, so that we were fain to sit in the farthest seats from the Ark of the Law; neither could we discern who sat in the chief seats, nor who read, because a pillar stood between us and the pulpit. . Now first the Law was read and prayers were offered up according to custom; but by reason of my sadness, because I desired to have seen Jesus again, I was even as the parched ground, and no moisture fell upon my soul. But when the Prophets were read, then it was as a shower of heaven on the congregation, and the dew of the

Lord upon our souls; for the voice of him that read was the voice of Jesus of Nazareth.

When he had made an end of reading, Jesus began to exhort the people, saying that he was sent to proclaim good news, to release the captive, give health to the sick, and light to the blind, and to bring Redemption to Israel. God, he said, loved all; not the good alone, but even the bad: yea, God was in very truth our Father in heaven. Therefore how much soever the kindest father on earth may love his children, albeit they transgress against him, much more is the love of God toward us though we be sinners. He did not tell us that we were not sinful; nay rather, he made it clear to us that our sins were as red as blood in the sight of the All-seeing; but none the less, he called us the children of God. As many as would repent should be forgiven; and he spake as if he himself had a certain divine power of forgiveness whereby he might purify the soul and bring us close to God, one family in the presence of our Father. One thing was needful, that we should trust in him and in his message. This day, he said, this very day, are the prophecies of Redemption fulfilled in your ears. Then he cried aloud unto all that were hungering or thirsting for righteousness, all that were weary of the burden of their sins, all that felt themselves utterly hopeless, friendless, and vile, bidding them resort to him as their refuge: "Come unto me all ye that are weary and heavy laden, and I will give you rest."

While he was speaking, methought I was not hearing words, but seeing somewhat that might be seen and touched; so solid seemed the mercies of God, even as a rock whereon one standeth. For Jesus ever testified of the Father as one testifieth that knoweth by experience, and spake of heaven as of that which he had known and felt. Yea, and more than that; a certain strange power was in him to make things invisible to seem visible by his discourse, Wherefore, albeit Moses had called God the Father of the spirits of all flesh, and the Prophets also had taught Israel to say unto God, "Thou art our Father," and all this doctrine was well known and trite among us; yet now, for the first time, the doctrine seemed to be no more a mere dead letter, but a living word. Such a life did Jesus of Nazareth breathe into it, insomuch that his Good News (for so he called it) came upon our hearts as news indeed, never heard before among the children of men.

This long while (since Jesus had first begun to speak), a certain youth whom I had before noted, sitting not far from me, had been muttering and moaning gently to himself; but I was rapt in the words of Jesus, wherefore I had given the less heed to the boy. But now, he stood up, and cried aloud in a deep hollow voice, as of a full-grown man, "What hast thou to do with us? Let us alone, let us alone." Then in his own voice he cried again, "I know thee who thou art, the Holy One of God." Immediately I perceived that it was the demoniac, even Raphael the son of Joazar, whom Theudas the Exorcist had adventured to heal; but a great fear fell on all the congregation, and the women rose up from their places, shrieking for terror. But Jesus, without use of charm or gesture, rebuked the unclean spirits and bade them come forth. Then they tare the youth, so that he shrieked with a piercing shriek; and so they came forth. And Jesus delivered the boy to his father; who would scarce suffer Jesus out of his sight, between joy that the devils were gone forth, and fear lest they might return. Howbeit, now the spirits were driven out so that they returned no more. For the boy lived to be a man; nor did he die (as it hath been reported to me) till he numbered fifty years, dying about twelve years ago, two years before destruction came upon the Holy City.

When Jesus departed from the synagogue, the people thronged him, bringing to him divers requests, some concerning their friends that were diseased or lunatic, or afflicted with devils; others begging him to come and bless their children; others asking him that he would lodge in their houses, or at the least sup with them. For at this time all men, rich and poor, Pharisees, Sadducees, and Galileans, inclined to follow Jesus. But he would go to none of the rich men's houses, but only to the house of Simon the son of Jonah (whom he afterwards called Peter); he was one of the fishermen of the place and had joined himself to Jesus. But Jesus suffered me to accompany him.

But when we were now entering into the house, behold all things were full of disorder and lamentation. For Simon's wife's mother (who abode in the house) had been suddenly afflicted with a grievous sickness, so that, instead of serving the guests, she was laid speechless upon a bed in an upper room. Then they spake to Jesus concerning her. Now I was not myself present when the thing took place; but (as it was reported to me) Jesus healed her after the same manner as he had healed my mother; for he took her by the hand and lifted her up, and she arose whole and free from her disease, and ministered unto the guests.

Jesus straitly charged us that we should tell no man; whereat we marvelled not a little. But howsoever we obeyed him, it could not be hid. And besides this, the fame of the healing of Raphael the son of Joazar had been noised abroad through the whole of the city, insomuch that at sunset, when we went forth, the Sabbath being now ended, we saw great multitudes of demoniacs, lunatics, and some also sick of the palsy and of fever, laid in their beds along the road through which we would have passed. Some also, that were afflicted with incurable diseases, had been brought notwithstanding, because of their entreaties; if perchance Jesus might heal them; and I saw one man that had been blind from his birth.

Now it came to pass that when Jesus came forth from Simon Peter's house, and saw the faces of all these sick people, and the faces of their friends, all waiting if perchance he would help them, his countenance was altered, and the shadow of sorrow fell upon him, and he sighed and said, "Verily for the sorrowful I am sorrowful, and for the sick I am sick." [1] Then he passed along the ranks of the sick people; and wheresoever he perceived that any could be healed, he laid his hands on them, and lo, they were at once freed from their infirmities; and many unclean spirits were driven out from those whom they had possessed. Now most of them that were healed had been possessed with evil spirits; but others were lunatic, or sick of the palsy, or of fever, or had impediment in their speech. But Jesus had a marvellous power to discern, methought, not only them that had faith from them that had not, but also such diseases as were to be cured, from such as were not to be cured, because it was not prepared for him that he should cure them. But when Jesus had made an end of healing, the multitude still followed us; and the friends of such as had not been cured, vexed us with importunities; and others, whose friends had been cured, called down blessings on Jesus, and refused to leave him. Thus, go whither we would, we could not be alone. So Jesus returned to the house, and I went back to the house of Manasseh.

I opened my mind to my uncle that night, and said to him that I purposed to go with Jesus of Nazareth whithersoever he went; and Baruch said the same. But my uncle no longer opposed himself against our wills; only he forewarned us that evil was in store for us; "For," said he, "I have sojourned in Italy among the Romans three years, and I know well that nothing can withstand their power. But whoso gainsayeth them gainsayeth the strength of a king: according as it is written, 'Where the word of a king is, there is power; and who may say unto him, What doest thou?'

All the night long no sleep came to my eyes for musing on all the things that I had seen and heard that day: "For this day," said I, "is, as it were, the birthday of the Redemption of Israel." But when I thought thereon, and considered with myself that I had now joined myself unto Jesus as the Redeemer, and when I compared Jesus with the image of the Redeemer of Sion (such as I had framed it in my mind from the reading of the Prophets, and such as my countrymen expected), then was I as one astonied and amazed to find myself believing in Jesus, and standing on his side. For I had imagined unto myself one that should perchance appear, riding on the clouds of heaven, encompassed by thousands of angels, taking vengeance upon the enemies of Sion, according to the word of the prophet Daniel; or else I had thought to see a royal deliverer, even such another as David himself, mighty with the sword, riding at the head of his ten thousands, ruling the Gentiles with a rod of iron, or breaking them in pieces like a potter's vessel; or else I had fashioned in my mind a Deliverer after the manner of Elias, rebuking kings in their pride, and calling down fire from heaven for a sign, or for the destruction of the Gentiles. Now before this time, I had had no leisure to consider the matter; for, in the presence of Jesus, I had been drawn towards him as by an enchantment: but in the stillness of the night, Jesus being no more before my face, I thought on all the signs and wonders wrought by Moses and Elias aforetime, and doubt fell upon me; and it seemed to me not possible that Jesus of Nazareth could be greater than they, so as to be the Messiah. But when I asked myself, "Could it then be that Jesus is a deceiver?" my heart made answer, "Nay, that could not be. And if thou trust not in Jesus, there is not any one in the world in whom thou canst trust." So I comforted myself in my perplexity, saying to myself, "Perchance the time hath not yet come for Jesus to manifest himself as the son of David, nor as the Son of man spoken of by the prophet Daniel: but doubtless that time will come; and then shalt thou see Jesus, as the Messiah indeed, in power."

But on the morrow, very early, when we went forth to the house of Simon Peter, behold, a mixed multitude had gathered round the doors waiting for the coming of Jesus. And I also waited, standing with them, and heard how they conversed with each other. But it seemed that one had but now come forth from the house of Peter, saying that Jesus could not be found in the house. Then arose a murmur in the crowd; and a certain man from Antioch said that Simon had set a snare for Jesus of Nazareth, and had betrayed him to Herod the Tetrarch. But there was in the press one Gorgias the son of Philip, a man well known to Simon; and he laughed the man of Antioch to scorn. He had been in the army of Herod the King in former times, and his father was a Greek; but he conformed himself to the Law and joined himself to the sect of the Galileans; and his word prevailed greatly with them, because he was versed in warlike matters. This man declared that Jesus had withdrawn himself, that he might not be shut up in prison by the Tetrarch: "And no marvel," said he, "for, seeing that the tyrant hath but now taken John the son of Zachariah, why should he not also adventure to take the new prophet?"

Others, beside myself, had not heard before that John had been cast into prison. So we questioned Gorgias and heard that the prophet had been cast into prison in the Black Castle at Machaerus three days ago. Many of them that were in the crowd had been disciples of John; and they cried aloud that the men of Galilee ought to rise up and deliver the prophet. But Gorgias beckoned with his hand that they should be silent, and when silence was made, he said, "Let us rise up, indeed, but not without a leader. Now the Lord hath sent to us this Jesus of Nazareth: and that he is a prophet sent from God none can deny." The multitude shouted that it was even so, and one or other uttered praises of Jesus; and a certain man said, "Yea, never man spake as this spake." But Gorgias answered and said, "It is known to all that I am a soldier, neither do words prevail with me without deeds. Wherefore I also, until yesterday, did but lightly esteem Jesus of Nazareth. But now he hath shown forth his power in deeds. And he that can do such deeds as Jesus hath wrought in our streets, shall he not do even greater deeds than these when the time shall come for them? Yea, doubtless, all things are possible to him. And what will avail squadrons of horse, or legions of foot, against one that can call down fire from heaven, or cause the walls of a city to fall to the ground? Choose we therefore Jesus to be our leader, and no one shall be able to stand against us."

At this instant Simon Peter came forth, and he confirmed what had been said, to wit, that Jesus of Nazareth was not in the house: but he thought that he was gone forth to be alone. And so it was. For when we had made diligent search for him we found him alone on a mountain, about three miles from the town. We besought him to return; but he answered that he must proclaim the Good News in other villages also, for to that end he had been sent. So Simon Peter and the rest of the disciples accompanied him, and Baruch and I went with them; and for the space of four or five weeks we continued with him, going from town to town in Galilee; and Jesus preached the Good News, and healed the sick; and a great multitude of all sorts was added to our number.

Now the greater part of our band were honest people, hungering and thirsting for the Redemption of Sion: but some were vain men, children of iniquity, seeking the wages of unrighteousness. Especially they that had been formerly soldiers resorted to Jesus, as to a prince or general, like vultures hasting to the prey, supposing that they should gain much spoil if he prevailed against the Romans. And so it was that once when Jesus spake to his disciples, saying that they must be "fishers of men," then Baruch, being offended by the presence of these children of mammon among us, answered and said, "But must the fishers catch vile fish as well as good?"

Hereat Jesus turned and looked sorrowfully on Baruch, and said, "The kingdom of heaven is like unto a net that was cast into the sea, and gathered of every kind: which, when it was full they drew to shore, and sat down, and gathered the good into vessels, but cast the bad away. So shall it be at the end of the age. The messengers of God shall come forth and sever the wicked from among the just, and shall cast them into the furnace of fire. There shall be wailing and. gnashing of teeth."

Another parable spake he to the same effect, that the tares must needs grow with the wheat till the day of harvest, for not till then can the division be made between good and evil. When we heard this, we grieved thereat; for we had supposed that none save the faithful should have been admitted into the Kingdom, and we marvelled why Jesus should first suffer the bad to enter, and then drive them forth. Howbeit, we besought him that he would give us ordinances which we might observe, to the intent that we might not be cast out of the Kingdom. For some of our number had begun to say that Jesus had come to destroy the Law, so that every one might do what he listed; as though Jesus had said that God loveth the wicked as much as the righteous, even though the wicked abide in wickedness. Thus they brought shame upon us, and they set stumbling-blocks in the path of many that had otherwise believed. Moreover the disciples of John the

Baptist compared us with themselves, and asked us concerning our laws and customs and prayers; and, when they found that we had none of these things, then they despised us, saying that our Master was not equal to John. For at this time the fame of John the son of Zachariah overshadowed the fame of Jesus; yea, and for some time after this, even after John had been cast into prison. For this cause we intreated Jesus that he would both teach us how to pray, as John also had taught his disciples, and also that he would lay down laws for the new Kingdom, even as Moses had laid down laws for the kingdom in old times.

Jesus hearkened to our petition in silence. Then he said that he must depart from us for a season and go to the top of a certain mountain; but he appointed the third hour of the following day that we should come to him.

Certain of the Scribes that followed with us murmured at Jesus, because he had appointed that we should come to him on the mountain: and one, finding fault for that Jesus was often wont to spend the whole night praying alone on some mountain, said, "It is written, 'Out of the depths have I cried unto thee, Lord;' therefore it is good to pray from a low place, and not from a high place." But Nathaniel answered and said that Jesus loved to be alone on the mountain by night, to meditate on the greatness of the Lord and how He hath exalted the Son of man, according as it is written, "I will consider thy heavens, even the works of thy fingers, the moon and stars which thou hast ordained:" and "these very words," said Nathanael, "I heard the Prophet but yesterday repeat, when we were upon the top of yonder mountain." Hereat the Scribes murmured the more, saying that it was not written that any prophet in old times thus took counsel with the heavens after the manner of a Chaldean. But Gorgias the son of Philip murmured for another cause, saying that the Prophet ought not thus to mistrust his followers, nor to be so fearful for his own safety, and tHat it behoved the friends of Jesus to take him by force, if need be, and to make him a king. And to this Judas of Kerioth consented and some others.

But to the most of us the words of Gorgias seemed an abomination; for we knew that Jesus did not depart for fear: for indeed fear was not in him. But he desired to be alone because he wished to pray, and because of the burden of his heart. For it grieved him, more than can be told, to see the misery and wretchedness, yea, and the ignorance and the sinfulness of the mixed multitude which pressed round him. All their pains pained him and all their sufferings he suffered, insomuch that more than once I have heard him saying in a low voice to himself, "For them that are hungry I hunger, and for them that are athirst I thirst, and for them that are sick I am sick."

Notwithstanding he was not so much distressed with the pains and diseases of the body as with the pains and diseases of the soul. For the sins of souls seemed to him as real and loathsome as the diseases of the flesh to us; and oftentimes a transgression that would appear slight to us, he counted as a work of Satan; so that whithersoever he moved, he saw sins more than could be seen of common men, yea, a very sea of sinfulness; albeit, underlying the sea of sin and sorrow, he still discerned the Everlasting Arms.

Moreover, because he loved all men with an exceeding great love, for this cause every hour in his life brought unto him a burden passing the power of words to describe. For the sins of men were not unto him as the sins of aliens and strangers, but as the sins of his own brethren: yea, they were even as his own sins; for, although he himself sinned not, neither knew sin, yet what pain cometh from the bearing of a brother's sin, that he knew full well. Wherefore in him was fulfilled the saying of the prophet Isaiah; who prophesied that the Messiah should be a man of sorrows and acquainted with griefs, and that he should carry our sins and bear our iniquities.

CHAPTER VIII

Of The New Laws

ON the morrow, about the second hour, we began to go up the mountain which Jesus had appointed. But having strayed from the path, we knocked at the door of a house which was near the foot of the mountain, and besought the goodman of the house that he would guide us. There opened the door a man of churlish appearance; but he would neither come out, nor so much as speak with us. This delayed us for a time, but we soon found the path, and the way became steep. The sun shone, but not with too fervent a heat, and the north wind blew gently from Hermon, whose top we saw clearly toward the north, clad in snow. On the west was the Mount Carmel, shining with a brightness as of purple; and further off the Great Sea, resembling a blue plain, whereon appeared many sails, almost too small for sight by reason of the distance. We climbed upward through groves of terebinth and oak. As often as we turned round to recover breath, the houses and fields grew smaller, till, at the last, when we drew nigh unto the top, the whole plain of Esdraelon seemed but as a small ground-plat; and large towns appeared as little hamlets, and all the works of man became very small in our eyes, as though we were leaving earth and approaching heaven.

Then said Baruch, "Is not this a second Sinai? For verily Jesus of Nazareth is about to give us a new law." But Eliezer the son of Arak, the principal Scribe of Capernaum (for he at this time followed Jesus and was now with us) rebuked him, saying, "Even though Jesus of Nazareth were the greatest of prophets, yet were he not equal to Moses; for it is said, Sinai is to be preferred even to the uprooter of mountains!" And another said, "Behold, the Word of God, when it went forth from Sinai from the mouth of the Holy One (blessed be His Name), was like sparks, and lightnings, and flames of fire; a torch of flame was on his right hand, and a torch of flame on his left hand: it flew and hovered in the air of the heavens, and returned and graved itself upon the tables of the covenant which were given into the hands of Moses. How then is it possible that the like wonders should be wrought on this mountain?"

Then said Nathanael to Simon Peter that it might perchance please the Lord not always to speak by the whirlwind or by the fire, but, as in the days of Eli as, by the still small voice. And to this Peter agreed, but others did not agree: for though they inclined not to Eliezer the son of Arak, yet it was because they thought that Jesus would of a surety soon work some sign in heaven to prove that he was the Redeemer. But Judas of Kerioth affirmed that Jesus would not, at this present time, lay down laws for the Kingdom, but only ordinances for a season, to instruct the host in the journey towards Jerusalem; but until Jerusalem should be ours, lasting laws would not be made.

While we were disputing among ourselves concerning the saying of Judas, Peter cried "Peace:" for, said he, "yonder is the Prophet:" and looking upward, we saw Jesus on a rock stretching out his hands in prayer. When he had made an end of praying, Peter approached him and besought him a second time to teach us to pray; and Jesus gave us that well-known prayer which is used in all the churches. Afterwards he beckoned to us to follow him, and he came down and stood in the bed of a torrent, which was dry by reason of the drought.

While we were following him, I heard the companion of Eliezer murmuring because there were no words in the prayer concerning the Redemption of Israel; "moreover," said he, "albeit the prayer asketh for bread, yet is there no mention of wine, nor oil, nor even of raiment. But how can a man sit and search the Law and the Traditions, and know not whence he is to drink as well as eat, and whence to be clad and covered?" To this I would have made reply; but Peter again cried to us to hold our peace, for Jesus was beginning to speak.

When he opened his lips, every one was silent for expectation; but, as he proceeded, the silence was a silence as of them that are astonished and disappointed. For he began with setting forth in his discourse a character and image of a citizen of the New Kingdom; and lo, it was not the image of a conqueror, but of one conquered. Also he drew as it were a model of the palace of the Great King, and of the princes and nobles which stand about His throne; and behold, when we compared the model with that which we had imagined in our hearts, and with that which we had read of in histories, the model of Jesus was in all things contrary to the model in our hearts. For in old times men had done reverence unto the valiant, the proud, the strong, the rich and the wise; but Jesus said that the chief places about the throne of God should be given to the hungry and thirsty, and poor; to them, that were innocent and simple; to them that made not war, but peace; yea, even to them which resisted not evil, but rewarded evil with good. Upon all these, as being the nobles and princes of the New Kingdom, Jesus pronounced a blessing; to wit, that all things should work together for good to them, so that they should have all that they needed, according to the words of the prophet, "Behold, my servants shall eat, but ye shall be hungry; behold, my servants shall drink, but ye shall be thirsty; behold, my servants shall rejoice, but ye shall be ashamed." Even so did Jesus ordain that they which hungered should be satisfied, and that the makers of peace should conquer and inherit the earth.

Next, he described the statutes and judgments of the New Kingdom; and, behold, instead of an easier yoke, he seemed to be placing upon us a yoke even heavier than the yoke of the ancient Law, too heavy to be borne. For the old Law forbade us to commit murder; but the new Law forbade us even to hate our enemies. Again, the old Law forbade us to commit adultery; but the new Law forbade us even to entertain a lustful thought in our hearts. In a word, the old Law laid down certain ordinances, which if a man obeyed, he should live therein; but the new Law laid down nothing fixed nor certain for us, so that we might say "I have done this or that, and therefore I have fulfilled the Law of Christ." For the Law of Moses touched the life of man, as it were, in certain points; as for example, in sacrifices, and feasts, and purifications, and Sabbaths, and in the obeying of the Ten Commandments: but the Law of Christ covered the whole of the state of man, the thoughts as well as the deeds; even as the encompassing air, which pierceth into every corner and cavern of the earth, wheresoever human life is. In fine, whereas the Law of Moses commanded us what we should do, the Law of Christ commanded what we should be. For this cause Jesus set himself against all bookishness, and against all worship of Traditions, and even of the precepts of the Scriptures; for he taught that precepts, howsoever they may shape the outward action, shape not the inner man.

Again, as concerning the laws, and the judgments, and the rewards, and the punishments, in the New Kingdom, he spake as if they were not laws of man's device, but rather Laws according to the nature of things, like unto the ordinances of the rain and the sunshine, the harvest and the seed-time. For he said that righteousness was not any such thing as could be attained by a price, nor by the doing of deeds; but that it consisted in a seeing of that which may be seen of God. He also spake of a certain eye of the soul, which, if it were clear, the man would be righteous; but if it were darkened, the man would be unrighteous. Also he spake of a certain law of retributions, which decreeth that whoso judge th shall be judged, whoso forgiveth shall be forgiven, whoso giveth shall receive: adding thereunto this most strange doctrine, that if we would go forth into the world, giving and ready to give, then, from all sides, the world would give to us again; yea, the angels of God, and the elements of the world (which are His ministers) and even the children of men, should make us marvel by reason of their gratitude, giving us back good measure pressed down and running over. Now there is a saying in the Traditions that, "Whenso ever a poor man standeth at thy door, the Holy One (blessed is He) standeth at his right hand. If thou givest him alms, know that thou shalt receive a reward from Him who standeth at his right hand." Jesus therefore added to this doctrine, teaching that God standeth at the right hand not of the poor only, but of every one that is in need of aught, that is to say, of every one of the children of men: wherefore whatsoever is given to men, is given to God, and from God cometh back multiplied to the giver. Howbeit, we were neither to give alms, nor to do aught else, for hope of reward; but only out of love.

Concerning citizenship in the Kingdom and how men should become citizens therein, he spake little to us, as being already citizens therein: save only this, that whoso would come, must come unto him; and through him, as through a door, they should pass into the Kingdom. And behold, the Kingdom was no other than a family, wherein God was at once Father and King, and all men were as children of the Father in Heaven. For the foundation of all was, that the heart and not the hands shaped the goodness and badness of all deeds, and made men to become citizens of the Kingdom: wherefore the heart and not the hands must be purified; nor could any be in truth citizens of the Kingdom except they had the thought of the Kingdom always in their hearts, so that their hopes and treasures were all stored up, not in the banks of money-changers, but in the Kingdom of Heaven.

Then he spake of the exceeding joys of the citizens of the Kingdom of God, and how they are free from all troubles and all disquietudes. But none, he said, could serve God and Mammon at one time; neither was it possible to serve God aright and yet to be distracted and torn asunder by cares concerning meat or raiment. Hereat the companion of Eliezer murmured again, saying that Jesus had before spoken blasphemously in joining the forgiving of sins by God with the forgiving of sins by men, and now he had spoken as a madman, in forbidding us to be careful about food and raiment; "Can a man sit," said he, "and search the Law, and not know whence he is to eat, and drink, and to be clad?" Now whether Jesus perceived his murmuring I know not: but he pointed, first upwards to the birds (for even at that instant there was a flight of pelicans above us) and then downward to the flowers, which bestrewed the side of the brook, and he said that our Father in Heaven fed the birds and clothed the flowers; and should He not much more care for us? Then he bade us seek first the Kingdom of God and His righteousness, and all things else should be added unto us.

Now concerning this Kingdom of God (or Kingdom of Heaven, for he called it by both names) we understood not much at this time: but my judgment now is that Jesus desired that all the Lord's people should be as Prophets, not teaching one the other and saying "Know the Lord," but all knowing the Lord from the least to the greatest. For he perceived that all the tribes of the earth were joined together under one emperor through desire of wealth and ease, and that Israel was joined together through hatred of the Romans and through desire to be rescued from them; but he saw that neither love of ease nor hatred of enemies could bind men together in an enduring Kingdom: but that which bindeth men together is the Spirit of love, which is a Spirit of brotherhood among men and of childhood unto God. For all nations begin with being first families, and then many families together; helping one another by reason of kindred, and not by reason of manhood. Now such a nation as this, and all men of such a nation, Jesus called "born of flesh and blood:" and he said that no nation could leave off to be a tribe and become a nation indeed, except it were born again, not of flesh and blood, but of the Spirit; so as to enter into a certain government of God, which the Greeks called *theocratia*, but Jesus called it the Kingdom of God. Such a *theocratia* Moses had partly established in old times; howbeit the King in the kingdom of Moses was the God of Abraham, but the King in the kingdom of Jesus was the Father of the Son of man.

But now to return to the words of Jesus. He ended his discourse with warning. First he warned us to beware of the common saying, "Give judgment according to the greater number"; for he said that the path to destruction is broad, and many go thereby. He bade us also try teachers and prophets by their works. Last of all, he spake very earnestly against certain which pretended to obey him but obeyed him not. We were the salt of the earth, he said, but if we lost our savour, how could the world be salted, and to what end could we serve, but to be cast out and trampled under foot? Whoso heard him and obeyed him not, such an one he likened unto a foolish shepherd (and even as he spake, there was nigh, within a bow-shot of us, a sheep-cote that had been cast down by the swollen waters of the brook) which built his house upon the sand, so that it fell: but whoso heard and obeyed, he likened him unto a wise shepherd, which built his house upon a rock so that it fell not. This parable Jesus did not at this time interpret to us, but afterwards he made it clear. For even as the Psalmists of Israel spake often of a certain Rock of Salvation, even so was it afterwards a common saying with Jesus both that each citizen of the New Kingdom must build his house upon a Rock, and that the Kingdom itself must be founded on a Rock, so that the gates of Hades or Destruction should not prevail against it. Howbeit what this Rock might be, we did not as yet understand; for he had not at this time revealed it unto us.

CHAPTER IX

How Quartus interpreted the New Law.

WHEN Jesus had ended all these words, he came down from the mountain, and we followed, reasoning much among ourselves. Baruch spake first, complaining that the new Law was full of hard sayings. "For," said he, "when the Prophet proclaimed a blessing on the poor and hungry, that was easy to understand, and I rejoiced thereat: but afterwards, when he bade us bless them that cursed us, and do good to those that injured us, yea, and turn the left cheek to him that had smitten us on the right, and give our coat to him that had taken away our cloak, then indeed his doctrine seemed too wonderful for the mind of man to fathom." Then a certain Essene (who at that time followed with us) made answer and said, "This world is but as a vestibule before the world to come: therefore the Prophet's intent is to instruct us how to prepare ourselves at the vestibule so that we may find grace to come into the King's presence: and his words enjoin on us to abstain from all earthly cares and pleasures, and to withdraw ourselves from the cities of men." But to this Simon Peter made answer that Jesus had taught us to live in the sight of all men, like a city on an hill or like a candle on a candlestick: moreover, he had promised that we should inherit the earth.

But here Eliezer the son of Arak could no longer constrain himself. "I marvel," he said, "that we listen so long without first asking this Prophet by what authority he sayeth these things, or what sign he can work in Heaven to prove his authority. For other teachers received of teachers before them; as, for example, Hillel and Shammai received from Shemaiah and Abtalion; and Shemaiah and Abtalion received from Jehudah the son of Tabai, and Simeon the son of Shatach; and so on successively; but this teacher maketh mention of no teachers from whom he hath received his doctrine: neither worketh he any sign in Heaven. But whence doth he draw his knowledge about the Unapproachable (blessed is He)? Even from the creatures; even from the weeds of the field, and the silly birds that are caught in the snare of the fowler; from the senseless rain and from the shining of the sun; yea, and from the nature of the heart of man, which is evil from his youth! But how much better than all these is the Law, whereby was created all that is; according as it is said, 'Beloved are the children of Israel, in that there was given to them the instrument by which the world was created.'"

No answer was made to the words of Eliezer: but Barabbas took up the words of Baruch, and said, "If we are to turn the left cheek to him which hath smitten the right, and if we are to do good unto them which do us harm, who shall cause injustice to cease in the world! For verily the unjust will wax fat in their injustice and will go on from oppression to oppression." But said Judas of Kerioth, "Listen unto me, foolish ones, and take counsel from me: for is it not even as I foretold? Did not I say unto you that the Prophet would not at this time make laws that should endure for ever, but only ordinances for a season, till we had gained the upper hand. Wherefore ye must know that it is in the mind of the Prophet to draw unto himself the hearts of all people by fair words and gentle dealing: but when the time is come for different policy, then we shall take fresh counsel according to our needs. But now hearken. Did not the Prophet prophesy woe to the rich and the powerful? These are the Romans; and in foretelling woe to them, he foretold woe against the Romans. Again, did he not prophesy blessing for the poor? And we are poor: and in every city of Israel the poor are the greater part, and will fight on our side, and will have a part in our blessing. I grant, he said not that we should be judges and princes: but he promised that we should have that for which we asked; and is not this enough for us? Yea, and albeit he mentioned not expressly money, or lands, or houses, yet he said that our reward should be great. But if persecution or the shedding of some of our blood must needs come before our success, who is so faint-hearted and womanish as to draw back for such a cause? Therefore, I say, be of good heart; and though there be some dark sayings of the Prophet, let us be content to stand fast on those sayings which are plain. But as touching the words of Eliezer, we all know in our hearts that Jesus is not a man as other men, but that he is a leader sent from God; and howsoever he teacheth, and whithersoever he leadeth, it is our wisdom to obey him and to follow him."

The words of Judas pleased us: and we all agreed to them. Only a certain Alexandrine (whose name was Quartus) said to Baruch that he judged not that the words of Jesus were intended to be merely transitory ordinances. Now this Quartus was a man of no common understanding and discernment; and inasmuch as his father had been a Greek and had caused him to be trained in the Greek learning and philosophy, he spake with more art and subtlety than most of my companions. Howbeit he lacked not faith and the love of righteousness; and, his mother being of our nation, he had been circumcised, and had conformed himself to the worship of Israel; but having been bred up in the schools of the Greeks and in the school of Philo, he was at all times desirous to compare the teaching of other philosophers with the teaching of Jesus. He was a merchant, and his business brought him oftentimes to Capernaum, where I had met him; but I had also met him before in the house of my uncle at Alexandria. So when I overheard Quartus saying these words to my cousin, I questioned him how he interpreted the sayings of Jesus, and in particular, that saying concerning the turning of the cheek to the smiter.

Then said Quartus unto me, after some pause, "Be not displeased if I speak in a parable. Many times in Capernaum have I seen mariners (such as know not your waters) grievously tossed by a storm while they strove to enter into the harbour by a straight course, and toiling hard for many hours, but all to no purpose:; but others (which know the secret) leave the straight course on one side, and stand far out to Tarichese. Thence floweth a current toward Capernaum, strong at all times; but in stormy weather it cannot be resisted.

Falling into this current, therefore, the wise mariner needeth but to row softly, or scarce at all, and lo, he entereth into Capernaum as it were upon wings. Now even such a wise mariner doth Jesus seem unto me."

I marvelled at his words. But Quartus perceived that I understood him not; and he continued, "I speak as one groping in the dark. But the meaning of my parable is this: The lake is the world; the vessel is Israel; and Capernaum is redemption. Other pilots have striven to guide Israel to redemption by dint of force, but they have failed: Jesus is the true pilot, and knoweth the currents and streams in the nature of men and things; and by his wisdom he thinketh to guide us aright."

"But what," I asked, "are these streams and currents?" Again Quartus was silent for a while, and longer than before, so that by this time we were almost come down from the mountain; but at last he said unto me, "What seemeth to thee the strongest current in the nature of men?" But, when I held my peace, not knowing what to answer, he spake again very earnestly, "Thou art a student of the sayings of the Wise, Joseph, and canst answer with discerning. Tell me, then, on what standeth the earth?" Then I replied according to the saying, "Upon the pillars; and the pillars upon the waters." "Yea," replied Quartus; "and after these cometh the wind; and what after the wind?" Then I said, "Beneath the wind is the storm, and beneath the storm is the arm of the Holy One; for it is said, 'Underneath are the Everlasting Arms.' Then said Quartus, "It is so; and verily the foundations of earth are the Everlasting Arms of the Father in Heaven: but if the Fatherhood of God be the strongest thing on earth, and if this be the mightiest stream or current in the nature of men, then how may we best sail with that current?" I remembered the words which Jesus had spoken that we were to become as little children; so I answered, "I suppose, by approaching Him as children."

Here Judas interrupted us and said, "Nay, but wisdom is the strongest thing in the world, for it is written of wisdom, 'The Lord possessed me in the beginning of His way, before His works of old. When He appointed the foundations of the earth, then I was by Him as one brought up with Him.'" "Thou sayest well," said Quartus, "but what human wisdom is like unto that wisdom which revealeth God to men? Now as no child can understand his father unless he love his father, so no man can know God (who is our Father in Heaven) unless he love Him; but whoso loveth, understandeth; therefore to love God is the highest wisdom of man." Then Judas scoffed at him and said, "This is nothing but repeating in new words the old saying of the Law, 'Thou shalt love the Lord thy God with all thy heart, and with all thy soul, and with all thy mind, and with all thy strength.' What! do ye then deem our Master to be naught but a merchant that retaileth old wares as if they were new?" So he left us and went on before.

But Quartus continued, "Judas saith truly that the new Law aimeth at the same mark as the old Law. But the means are diverse. For the old Law worketh by purifications and feasts and sabbaths; but the new Law belike worketh in part by these means, but in greater part by other means. And, as I judge, Jesus goeth toward the end of the old Law; but by a path that is new, yea, altogether new. For I have myself heard him say that the redeemers of old were like unto thieves and robbers, using force and violence; but he himself cometh not like a thief over the wall, but like the true shepherd through the door of the fold, that is to say, through the path of Redemption which God hath appointed. Now this path is kindness or love. And Jesus saith that the former redeemers failed of their purpose, for they thought to redeem men by force; but he will not fail, for he purposeth to redeem men by gentleness. And he saith that God ordaineth strength out of babes and sucklings, and that the spirit of childhood is the conquering spirit of the world. Rememberest thou not how our teacher Philo said some things not much unlike to these, teaching that the highest revelation of God is through love? Howbeit, none methinks, save Jesus only, can reveal this revelation. For Philo testifieth of that which is behind the veil; but Jesus of Nazareth hath power to lift up the veil."

By this time we had overtaken the others, whom we found all sitting, and Jesus in the midst of them. By the side of Jesus was a man bearing in his arms a little child. He was come forth from a house nigh to the place where Jesus sat, bringing a cup of water for Jesus to drink. While Jesus was drinking, the father still kept his eyes upon the child in his arms, and his face was full of compassion and tenderness; for the child was very sickly. We soon perceived that it was the same man that had denied to give us guidance in the morning; but at first we knew him not; pity and love had so transformed his countenance. Now it came to pass that when Jesus had given back the cup to the man, he laid his hands on the child and blessed him. And as he blessed him, his face shone as with the glory of the Lord; and the little one also seemed to rejoice and to partake in the brightness of our Master's countenance.

"We both stood still, beholding Jesus. Then said Quartus unto me, "Did not Eliezer the son of Arak say truly, that 'Jesus looketh upon the book of the world as well as upon the book of the Law, and seeth in all things God'? For even as Elias the Prophet loved to commune with God on the tops of mountains, and in deserts, and in caves, and received revelations of the Lord from earthquakes and fires, but most of all from the still small voice; even so doth our Master look upon all things that are, yea even on the smallest things that live or grow, and from all, he heareth a still small voice that speaketh of the Father. Yea, and there is yet more than this. For whithersoever he turneth his face, methinks he giveth of his love to all things, whether they be the flowers of the field, or the birds, or the mountains, or the children of men: and because he thus giveth, it is given to him again; yea, wisdom and joy and peace are given back to him, even from things that have not life; but most of all from the children of men, which are made in the image of God. Therefore said I that Jesus seemeth as the wise mariner of whom we spake but now; for, by the Word of God in himself, he hath haply hit upon a certain current in the nature of created things, whereby he will easily prevail over the blasts of all opposing storms, and be carried into the haven of God, both he and all they that put their trust in him."

"Thy words are fair," I replied, "but they do not persuade me. That the love of children doth bind husband and wife together, and that the bond of families is the bond of nations, this I deny not. Perchance also the love that parents have to their children may have lifted up the hearts of many in Israel, during many generations, to the true God. But how we are to take Jerusalem or thrust forth, the Romans from Syria by becoming as little children, this passeth my understanding. Or dost thou not believe that Jesus will lead us against the Romans in Jerusalem?"

"I know not," replied Quartus (who spoke as one musing, and not giving heed to my question); "but what troubleth me most of all is the fear lest the knowledge of Jesus may haply perish with him; for if he hath (as I judge that he hath) a certain inborn power of winning men over to his will by kindness and gentleness, then, as it seemeth to me, this power may be likened unto the fabled ring of Solomon, which gave unto the owner well nigh whatsoever he desired. But there is this difference. The ring could be delivered from one man to another; but the art or secret of Jesus is, in all likelihood, not able to be delivered to them that shall come after; but it will perish with him. And then what becometh of his Kingdom of God?"

As long as Quartus was speaking I heard him gladly: but when he had ceased, his words seemed like mist in the morning sun; but the words of Judas seemed as the solid ground from which the mist rolleth away. For what Quartus said was hard to understand; but the words of Judas seemed according to reason, and very plain to be understood; to wit, that the ordinances given on the mountain of blessing were transitory, and that we were still to wait for the New Law: and to this I agreed, and not I only, but the most part of the disciples.

CHAPTER X

How some desired Jesus to mix the New Law with the Old Law; and concerning the Legion of Swine; and how Jesus began to teach in Parables.

IT came to pass, not many days afterwards (about a month after the Feast of the Harvest), that we journeyed to Capernaum; and Nathanael, and Gorgias the son of Philip, and I, had been sent on before to prepare a lodging. Now when we were standing at the door of the house where we were to lodge, we heard a sound as of many feet; and, looking up, Gorgias said, "See, hither cometh the Tetrarch's Thracian guard!" I looked and saw a band of about three hundred men, of a wild and savage aspect, bearing targets and girt with scimitars. But Gorgias, noting as I suppose the anger in my countenance, answered, "These dogs (may the Lord destroy them root and branch!) are swift indeed to shed the blood of women and children, but they are as naught compared with the Romans. Could'st thou but see a Roman legion how they march, these would seem unto thee but as jackals at the lion's tail. Mark but how the dogs straggle. But when the Romans march, the spears in their hands all point one way, and the swords by their sides hang all after one fashion, and even their stakes and tools (which they carry behind their backs) do all swing to one time, and their feet, arms, and heads, yea, even to the winking of their eyes, go all together after the manner of a five-banked corn-ship of Alexandria, with her five hundred oars all keeping time; and when they charge, they charge like ten thousand elephants clad in iron. Moreover, they add to their power so much wisdom, that when they halt for the night, each man setteth up his stake in the ground, and taketh his spade, and diggeth his portion of trench before his stake, and behold, the solitary place becometh in a trice a fortified city, with streets and walls and ditches. Verily these Roman swine are all as children of Satan; but a Roman legion is as Satan himself." By this time our Master had arrived; so I was silent. But when he went into the house, I remained without, musing; for the words of Jesus came into my mind again, concerning the entering into the Kingdom; and methought it would be very hard to overthrow these Thracians, and much more the Romans, by becoming as little children.

While I thought on these things there came to the door of the house Jonathan the son of Ezra; for he knew that I was coming to

Capernaum, and he had appointed to meet me there. When he had greeted me in loving terms, he said that he desired to speak with me touching Jesus of Nazareth; "For," said he, "I hear that he turneth from him the minds of many, in that he observeth not the Sabbath." I could not deny this; for indeed Jesus had oftentimes, during our journey in Galilee, broken the Sabbath. Sometimes he had healed the sick on the Sabbath; and but lately on the Sabbath before the Feast of the Harvest, he had healed one that had an impediment in his speech; and when certain of the Pharisees had blamed it, he had said aloud, before all the people, that it was right to do good on the Sabbath, but not to do evil. Moreover, he had not rebuked them that carried the sick to him on the Sabbath, though the bearing of burdens be forbidden. Once, indeed, he had even commanded a sick man to carry with him the bed whereon he lay. I therefore held my peace, but Jonathan added, "Even though he cure the sick on the Sabbath, yet why need he offend the learned and the pious by bidding the sick bear burdens on the day of rest? Moreover, if he desire to go more than a Sabbath day's journey on some errand of mercy, why doth he not use the device of meat, so that he may keep the letter of the Law? Therefore, speak thou unto him, as one that loveth him; and warn him that the Pharisees are wroth."

Then there came into my mind how, on the last Sabbath day, Jesus had passed by a house in a certain village, which was the house of a poor widow; and a great storm of wind and rain, which had arisen in the night, had washed away some part of the wall thereof, so that the rest was in danger to fall. And behold, a man, a mason by trade, was working diligently to repair the breach. When we saw it we were ready to take up stones for to stone him; but Jesus forbade us, and said to the man, "Man, if thou knowest what thou doest, blessed art thou; but if thou knowest not what thou doest, cursed art thou." [1] Thereat we all marvelled, and there was much questioning among us. But when we had considered the matter, we perceived no more but this; that Jesus would not have us to observe the Sabbath as the Scribes observed it.

I therefore replied that I durst not speak to Jesus, nor did I believe that he would give heed to my speech: for that I thought he brake the Sabbath, not out of heedlessness, but of set purpose. Jonathan was astonished at these words, but I continued, "Not that our Master aimeth at breaking the Sabbath: but if a sick man needeth to be healed, he thinketh it right that the Sabbath should be broken for the sick man's sake." Then Jonathan said, "Then what new rule doth he teach? Doth he suffer you to go four thousand paces or even five thousand paces on the Sabbath, instead of two thousand, which the Law alloweth?" But I replied, "Neither four thousand paces, nor five thousand; for our Master maketh no rules. But, as it seemeth to me, there is in him a certain spirit from God which prompteth him to do this or that, and forbiddeth him to do otherwise: and if the spirit of kindness say unto him 'Go,' then he will go and bid us go, though it be ten thousand or twenty thousand paces; and this, even on the Sabbath. For, in fine, he saith that the Sabbath is made for man, and not man for the Sabbath."

Hereat Jonathan was sorely grieved, and said, "If this be so, I fear lest counsel be of no avail." But after that he had weighed the matter, he said, "Even though he be a prophet, and have a message from God, yet are there seasons and ways of delivering a message; and in these matters the experience and counsel of old age may have weight. Therefore I will adventure to speak to him." I was glad that he had thus determined: for many of us had desired to speak with Jesus. Yet I feared lest Jonathan might not prevail. For I had noted that Jesus at first brake the Sabbath, only when a kindness compelled; but when the Scribes and Pharisees were wroth, and strove to place the yoke on his neck, so as to cause him to cease from good works on the Sabbath, then he not only rebelled against it, but made as if he would break the yoke from off the necks of all, especially the poorer sort, to whom the Sabbath was rather a burden than a joy. For the more the Pharisees raged against him, the more he made war against the Sabbath. Therefore I did not forebode well for Jonathan: howbeit, I accompanied him into the presence of Jesus.

When we entered into the house, behold, Barabbas was with Jesus, beseeching him that he would not go into the synagogue on the next Sabbath: " For," said he, "the chief ruler of the synagogue hath a plot against thee, and desireth to question thee touching the Sabbath, that he may raise up a tumult of the people against thee. For all the Pharisees and elders of the synagogue are wroth with thee for the sake of the Sabbath, saying that thou dost both break it and teach others also to break it."

Hereon Jonathan, finding his occasion, spake to the same effect, saying that all the Scribes in the country round about Sepphoris had been turned away from Jesus because it had been noised abroad that he observed not the Sabbath. So he besought Jesus to consider his course well: "Despise not instruction from an elder, my son, even though thou art a prophet. Art thou confident in thine heart that it is a spirit from God, and not a spirit from Satan, that tempteth thee thus to break the Sabbath? Bethink thee also how thou wilt cause the people of the land to go astray. For the simple walk by rules, and straighten their path by ordinances. But lo, thou takest away rules and ordinances; and what dost thou leave in the place thereof? I have heard from Eliezer the son of Arak that a certain man was working even at his handicraft on the Sabbath day, and thou sawest him, and didst not rebuke him: but didst say, that if he had knowledge of that which he did, he was blessed; but if he had not that knowledge, he was accursed. Whence, my son, should the simple and unlearned gain this knowledge whereof thou speakest? But if thou sayest, 'I am a prophet and will give them this knowledge,' then remember that thou too art mortal, and as the grass of the field; and when thou shalt pass away, thy knowledge shall perish with thee, unless it be set forth in rules. But thou givest no rules to thy disciples.

"But come, let us reason together as though thou wert altogether right in this matter, having a message from God to us touching the Sabbath. Notwithstanding, is there not a place and a time for delivering a message, and a place and a time for concealing it? There is a time to go forward; but is there not also a time to make a stand? It is good to set thy face toward the light, that thou mayest advance; but it is good also to turn thy face from the light, that thou mayest see whither thou hast advanced. Moreover, why dost thou cause the Pharisees to stumble, and the rich to take offence at thy doctrine? Art thou not the Redeemer of all Israel? Are not the Pharisees also thy brethren, and the rich also sheep of the flock? Why therefore dost thou drive them from the fold and cast them forth into the wilderness? If thou sayest, 'They are weak,' then take pity, my son, on the weak ones of Israel, yea and perchance on thine own disciples, lest they that may come after thee drink of thy doctrine and die, and the Name of Heaven be profaned."

Now at the first the face of Jesus was not altered toward Jonathan the son of Ezra, and he heard him kindly, yet patiently withal, and as if he knew what the old man would say, before he said it. But when Jonathan begged him for compassion's sake not to cause the weak ones to stumble, then the fashion of his countenance was changed as if he would have wept, and he seemed to us like one in sore straits, for he changed colour and was silent. Judge, therefore, how great was our astonishment when he stood up and rebuked Jonathan as though his words were from Satan.

Perplexity and sore grief fell upon us all, and the old man would have retired abashed. But Jesus took him by the hand and constrained him to stay, and made him sit down by his side and spake kindly unto him. Yet he began to speak again of the words of Jonathan as being a sore temptation, telling us how in former times he had undergone a like temptation from Satan. He had been in the wilderness, he said, and lo, in a moment of time he had been borne to the top of a mountain, whence he saw the kingdoms of the earth and the glory thereof, and Satan said to him, "All these things will I give unto thee, if thou wilt fall down and worship me."

While we marvelled at the words of Jesus, and disputed among ourselves how that temptation in the wilderness could be like unto this temptation, behold, Judas of Kerioth came into the chamber, saying the same things which Barabbas had said, to wit that the Pharisees in Capernaum were laying a snare for Jesus, for to catch him in his teaching, that they might cause the people to stone him. But Jesus gave command that we should pass over on the morrow to the other side of the lake.

On the morrow, while we rowed across the lake, I asked Nathanael what seemed to him the nature of the temptation of Satan whereof Jesus had spoken. Nathanael made answer and said, "Thou perceivest that the heart of our Master overfloweth with pity for the miseries of men; and even to redeem them from these miseries he hath been sent by the Lord. Now as for silver and gold, or fame, .or wisdom, none of these things can in any wise tempt him once to go aside either to the right hand or to the left from the straight path of Redemption. Howbeit, pity and love can tempt him. Wherefore the only temptation that can befall him is from the Voice that saith, Be pitiful, even though thou transgress in pitying; Do evil that thou mayest do good; Gain power by crooked ways, that thou mayest straighten the paths of salvation for them which wander astray; Wink thou at falsehood, that they which err may be guided toward truth." Now this Voice, as it seemeth to me, is to our Master the Voice of Satan; and to listen to it is to bow down to Satan. And Satan, perchance, knowing that in this way alone can our Master be tempted, hath caused Jonathan the son of Ezra to tempt him. But I know no more than thou; only such is my conjecture."

While we thus conversed together the boat drew nigh unto the eastern shore. The mountains came down to the water's edge, so close, and so precipitous withal, that there was scarce space enough to land: and, because the sun still lay low in the east, all was dark before us, though the waters behind us shone fair and bright. But when we were now entering under the shadow of the cliffs, so that we could discern things more clearly, we perceived that there was a margin of shore, but narrow and exceeding rocky, strewn all over with large and small fragments of black rock, which had fallen from the mountain above. Then suddenly there fell on our ears a marvellous strange cry, neither as of a man nor yet as of a wild beast; and while we ceased rowing for to listen, behold, yet another cry, more piercing and strange than the first, and then straightway another: and withal the rocks and cliffs took up the sound and multiplied it, and tossed it this way and that way till all the land seemed alive with the clamour. But Gorgias trembled and said it was an evil spirit, for, said he, "There be burial-places in this part of the coast." Then Peter cried aloud and said, "I see a form as of a man, lank and lean, coming out from the rocks; and it is naked." Then some of us bade steer towards another part of the coast; but Jesus commanded to keep on our course.

Now when we landed, we perceived that it was a man, but he was one possessed with evil spirits. For he had chains about his body; and he had cut and lanced his flesh with grievous wounds. "When he saw us, he took up stones to cast at us, so that we feared to approach him; and certain shepherds from afar off beckoned to us to go back from him. But Jesus went before the rest of us and accosted him. And lo, at the voice of Jesus, the man straightway let the stones fall from his hands; and, for a moment, he stood as one astonied and in a trance. Then he shrieked aloud and made answer to Jesus in two voices, after the manner of those possessed with unclean spirits. For at one time the man spake, and at another the devils. But the devils, speaking in a deep hollow voice, declared that they were swine, and three thousand in number, and that their name was Legion. Moreover they besought Jesus that he would not send them into the abyss (for by this name do the evil spirits use to call that place wherein they must needs wander so long as they have no bodies of men to dwell in), but that he would suffer them to remain in the man's body. But Jesus drove them out, and the Legion went forth into the abyss, to the number of three thousand, and in the shapes of swine. But Jesus did not suffer the man to accompany him, but bade him return to his friends, and to tell them what great things the Lord had done for him.

This mighty work of Jesus I have set down the more exactly, because no such unclean spirit as this was ever cast out by any other exorcist. For other men have been possessed with swine, or toads, or scorpions, or serpents, but not with many in number, seldom with more than seven. But this man was possessed with three thousand swine. For I not only heard him say this to Jesus, but he also repeated it to me; for I conversed with him. He told me also that he himself saw the three thousand swine go forth and run, first upward, and then violently down from the cliff, even to the abyss. Now the man was a Gadarene, a Jew by birth, and a patriot, one of the sect of the Galileans. Howbeit, living in Gadara, which is a Greek city, he had suffered himself to become defiled, and had rejected the Law and the Worship, and had eaten swine's flesh. But it came to pass that on a certain day, even at the hour of prayer, when he thought on these things, a darkness fell, upon his soul, and he saw sights of demons; and sometimes also he saw the sun as though it were red as blood; and he loathed his food as it had been poison. And this continued for the space of six months. But at the end of the six months, on a certain Sabbath, as he stood in the streets of Gadara, so it was that there came a cohort, which is the tenth part of a Roman legion, marching through the town. And he turned and cursed them in the name of the Lord; and lo, as the curse went forth from his mouth, the devils entered into him in the shape of a legion of swine; and they possessed him even to the day when Jesus healed him. All this I heard from the demoniac himself.

When Jesus had worked this miracle we all rejoiced greatly; for we thought that whoso could do so mighty a work, to him all things were possible; and we desired Jesus to go back to the other side of the lake, and there to work miracles that he might convince the Pharisees. But we marvelled that Jesus set so little store on his mighty works, insomuch that he even seemed often- times unwilling to work them. Many also he wrought in private; and many he would fain have kept secret, but he could not. Now when I asked Nathanael (for he was as it were an interpreter unto me to explain such sayings of Jesus as were hard to understand) for what cause Jesus lightly esteemed his own miracles, he asked me whether I had not noted how the common folk resorted to Jesus as a mere worker of wonders, so that sometimes they even interrupted his discourse, being desirous that Jesus should cease to teach that he might begin to work cures. "Now Jesus," he said, "doth not desire that men should come to him merely as the healer of their bodies, but as the healer also of their souls."

"For this cause," said Nathanael, "Jesus often biddeth such as he healeth in Galilee to keep silence, although he suffered the Gadarene in these distant parts to make it known. For he deemeth it his especial work not so much to drive out diseases and evil spirits from the body, as rather to heal the soul, ministering bread to the hungry and wine to them that are athirst, loosing the tongue of the dumb, and causing the deaf to hear, opening the eyes of the blind, and making the lame to leap as a hart in the paths of salvation."

We made no long stay on the eastern side of the lake; but when we came again to Capernaum we found the hearts of the people turned from us. For not only did the chief ruler and the elders of the synagogue watch us, as before, if perchance they could take us at an advantage; but the zeal of the townsmen also seemed to have waxed cold. Scarcely had our boat touched the strand at Capernaum when my uncle Manasseh met me. He took me aside and spake with me very earnestly, saying that he had rebuked his son Baruch for his slackness at business, because poverty was coming upon them as an armed man, by reason of his constant attending on Jesus; and he added, "It is true also of thee as of Baruch, 'He becometh poor that dealeth with a slack hand; but the hand of the diligent maketh rich. He that gathereth in summer is a wise son; but he that sleepeth in harvest is a son that causeth shame.'" "And what said Baruch?" I asked. "He hath consented to my words," said Manasseh, "and hath promised that he will no longer accompany this Jesus of Nazareth in his wanderings: and do thou the like." But this I would not do; so we parted in anger.

Not a few left Jesus at this time, mostly they of the wealthier sort, as were Baruch and Manasseh; some going back to their vineyards, others to their olive-presses, others to the dye-works and glass-furnaces, whereof there were many in Galilee. But the poorer sort joined themselves to Jesus as much as before, being drawn unto him by the fame of his mighty works. Howbeit they also began to wax impatient that Jesus should give the sign for war. Nor did they give now much heed to the words of Jesus; but they paid regard to him as to some great exorcist and sorcerer, who useth his art for good ends.

Therefore the heart of our Master was sad at this time; and he was grieved that the simple folk knew him not: and their words of praise were an abomination to him.

Now it came to pass that on the third day after we had returned to Capernaum, the fame of Jesus, how he had driven out the legion of swine into the abyss, having been now noised abroad on our side of the lake, behold, the common people thronged him more than before; insomuch that, when he began to teach the people on the shore after his manner, during the cool of the evening, they pressed in upon him and interrupted him, so that he was not able to continue his discourse. But Jesus, being grieved thereat, gave command to Peter and to Andrew that they should straightway launch a boat; and he went on board. When the people saw it, they made lamentation; but the boat was stayed at about fifty paces from the land; and Jesus sat in the boat and taught us while we stood on the shore.

When he opened his mouth, we perceived that he taught after a new fashion. For he no longer said "Do this," "Do not that"; but he spake in parables. Now almost all the teaching of the Wise is in parables, and Jesus also had before taught in parables; but these parables had been short, and along with the parables there had been added the interpretation thereof. But it was not so now; for the parable was naught but a tale about a certain sower, how he sowed seed on several kinds of ground: of the seeds, some falling on rock were destroyed by birds; others by heat and the shallowness of the soil; others by weeds; but some brought forth fruit.

Hereat certain murmured, and Gorgias said aloud, "Doth he think to redeem Sion with a tale? Lo, the prophet John is in prison, and the men of Galilee wait but for a nod from Jesus to rescue him; and our Master rescueth him not, but openeth his mouth in dark sayings." But the greater number listened all agape, as though spell-bound; for the very voice of Jesus had power to bind the souls of a multitude. Howbeit, when evening, or at the most when the morrow came, the parable had clean vanished out of the minds of the greater part. Notwithstanding some (but these only a very few) stored up the words of Jesus in their hearts, and diligently pondered them.

In the evening I went with the rest to Jesus; and we besought him to tell us what the parable might mean, and also why he taught thus in parables. When he had answered, I perceived the meaning of the parable, how that Abuyah the son of Elishah, and Eliezer the son of

Arak, were the rocky ground from which the birds picked up the seed; but Baruch, and such as Baruch, were the shallow ground; and Manasseh and the rich merchants and artificers were the fertile ground wherein weeds choked the seed. But still we were fain to know why he spake in parables.

When we again questioned him of this, behold, Jesus cried aloud with an exceeding bitter cry, saying, in the words of the Prophet Isaiah: "I heard the voice of the Lord saying, 'Whom shall I send, and who will go for us?' Then said I, 'Here am I; send me.' And the Lord said, 'Go and tell this people, Hear ye indeed, but understand not; and see ye indeed, but perceive not. Make the heart of this people fat, and make their ears heavy, and shut their eyes; lest they see with their eyes, and hear with their ears, and understand with their heart, and be converted, and be healed.'"

Then were we all sad, and sat silent for a while; for our Master's face was full of sorrow, and this was, as it were, the first shadow of evil that had fallen upon our path. Moreover we began to fear that, as in the days of Isaiah, so it would be now. The Lord had sent his prophet, even Jesus of Nazareth; but the hearts of the people would be hardened against the words of the prophet; yea, the prophet himself would seem to make the hearts of the people hard and not soft, as it was with Abuyah the son of Elishah and Eliezer the son of Arak, whose hearts were made fat and their ears heavy by the words of Jesus of Nazareth.

For we perceived in part his meaning, to wit, not that he desired in truth to shut the eyes of the people, but that he was constrained of the Lord to preach the Gospel, and all pressed to hear it; yet could he in no wise preach it so as to make it plain to all, but only to a few. For behold, he had made trial of the plain way of teaching, and men had thought they had understood him, but they had understood him not; but had esteemed him lightly, as little better than an exorcist. For his words had not pierced into their hearts, but had rested without, as seeds on the wayside; insomuch that they had been carried away by the angels of Satan. Therefore must he now adventure a new path of teaching to the end that, at the least, some few of us might be convinced of our want of understanding, so that we might seek and find the truth; but, to the most, all things should be in darkness, yea, the light itself should be as darkness unto the most.

All this the Lord Jesus spake more clearly afterwards, when he perceived the will of the Father that only a few should be chosen, though many were called: but at this time (perchance because it had been but newly revealed to him) he spake more darkly and with a greater bitterness of sorrow. Howbeit when he had lifted up his head and perceived that we also were weighed down with his affliction, then straightway he made himself to be of a cheerful countenance, and comforted us, saying, "Unto you it is given to know the mysteries of the kingdom of God; but unto them that are without, all things are done in parables." Then he bade us take heed that we taught others even as he had taught us; for, said he, "with what measure ye mete, it shall be measured to you." He said also, "Take heed how ye hear; for whosoever hath, to him shall be given, and whosoever hath not, from him shall be taken even that which he hath." These latter words we understood not then; but, as I take it, the meaning of Jesus was twofold; first, that whoso had not faith nor honesty would receive damage (even as Judas received damage, and not advantage) from the doctrine of Jesus; but, secondly, he seemed to mean that the doctrine was, as it were, lent to each of the disciples, as money upon usury; each being bound to traffic with the doctrine in the commerce of his own thoughts, so as to add thereto. In the same way he told us, at another time, that we were to bring forth out of our treasuries things new as well as old; and he also bade us to "be trustworthy bankers." For of all things Jesus misliked that we should repeat his words by rote; nor did he even bid us copy his actions exactly (but he even said that a time should come when we should do greater works than he had done); and the like also of his words. For this cause perchance, Jesus spake afterwards to us also, even to us his disciples, sometimes in dark sayings; to the intent that we might ponder, and ask and know the truth. For albeit we often feared to ask him questions (because of our folly and our want of faith), yet did he ever desire us to question him; teaching us that only to them that knock, is the door opened; and only to them that hunger, is given of the bread of Life.

When we went forth from the chamber, Gorgias said, "What meaneth the Prophet? Doth he say that whosoever is rich, he shall be made richer? And whosoever is poor, shall he also be made poorer?" Hereat we all smiled; for we knew that our Master spake not of money, but of wisdom: and one made answer to Gorgias to this effect. Then said Judas, "But if Jesus mean wisdom, then how sayeth he

'With what measure ye mete, it shall be measured to you?' But Jonathan the son of Ezra replied, "Is not this even according to the saying of the Wise, 'Man is born to learn in order to teach?' And again, 'He that learneth the Law and doth not teach it, he it is that despiseth the Name of the Lord.' Therefore the meaning of Jesus is, that if a man teach others what he hath learned, the angels give into his bosom a hundredfold reward." To this Nathanael agreed, and he added, "The reward is not as a price that is paid, so many shekels for so much teaching; but it is even as the rain coineth from the cloud, or as heat cometh from the fire. Even so doth wisdom come from teaching. For wisdom is not as a dead block that wasteth with the using, but as a living thing that groweth with exercise. But most of all is this true of that kind of wisdom whereof our Master speaketh."

Then Judas said, "But I would to God that our Master would leave off to speak of wisdom and would do somewhat." And Gorgias said Amen to that. But Simon Peter replied: "It is said, 'Take to thyself a master, and be quit of doubt.' Now my Master is Jesus of Nazareth, and I purpose not to spend the time in doubting, nor to halt between many opinions. For the man that is given to much doubting, to what is he like? He is like unto a ship with many pilots, which attaineth not to the harbour. Therefore have I settled my mind to believe that whatsoever Jesus doeth, that is righteousness, and whatsoever he purposeth, that is wisdom."

To this we agreed, and no more was said. Howbeit many of us could not so far constrain ourselves, but we had some searchings of heart; and passing clouds of trouble sometimes crossed our souls for that the Pharisees were set against us, and because Jesus himself had that day seemed like unto one bearing a burden of the Lord. Notwithstanding on the morrow, when we looked upon his countenance, full of brightness and cheerfulness, and when we heard him speak, after his wont, of the greatness and the glory of the Kingdom that was to come, behold, all our dark thoughts had immediately vanished away.

CHAPTER XI

Concerning the New Power of the Forgiveness of Sins.

AMONG them that came to Jesus, a few were outcasts from the synagogue's, or, as they were called, "sinners "; and it grieved the chief ruler of the synagogue in Capernaum and the elders of that synagogue that Jesus should receive such people. But Jesus received them gladly, and his anger waxed daily hotter against the rulers of the synagogues and against the Scribes, "because," said he, "they kept the key of the Kingdom, and yet they would neither enter in themselves nor suffer others to enter in." He also spake sometimes of a new Key which he must give to his disciples; but this, as yet, he spake not clearly. But as I remember, these words concerning the Scribes were spoken when Jesus first heard of the story of Hannah; which I will set down here, though the matter occurred some days before.

There lived in Capernaum a certain woman whose name was Hannah, sister of the mother of Nathanael. This woman was afflicted by Satan, so that she could not stand upright, but was bowed down to the earth. Now it came to pass that on a certain day when Nathanael visited her in her affliction, behold, the Rabbi Eliezer was in her house, questioning her touching her sins. And Eliezer had persuaded the woman that she was guilty of many sins; for enquiring whether she had visited any of her acquaintance on the Sabbath, he found that one of them, a widow, old and bed-ridden, lived somewhat more than two thousand paces from her house; wherefore he declared that Hannah had broken the Law in visiting this poor widow on the Sabbath. Moreover he reproved Hannah because she had borne burdens on the Sabbath, in that she had worn ribbons upon her garment during the Sabbath, which ribbons were not sewn to her garment; neither had she observed the Law of the Sabbath as touching things that are not living. Many other like sins did Eliezer reprove in Nathanael's kinswoman.

But when she sought how to be forgiven, he said, "Thou hast not sinned against man, but against God. If a man sin against men, the judge shall judge him: but if a man sin against the Lord, who shall entreat for him? But give of thy substance to the treasury of the synagogue, and I will entreat for thee if perchance the Lord will deal mercifully with thee. Howbeit thou must needs wait till the Day of Atonement: for until that day thou mayest not be forgiven. But in the mean season fast, and eat no pleasant food, nor drink wine: but afflict thy soul before the face of the All-merciful (blessed is He) if perchance He may incline His ear unto thy prayer."

Now when Hannah heard these things, her spirit fainted within her, and she knew not what to do, and she cried aloud to Eliezer, "Alas! the Angel of Death is even now upon my threshold, and my sins weigh heavily upon me. I beseech thee therefore, entreat the Lord for me, that He may forgive me immediately, lest I die unforgiven." But he made answer, as before, that she must needs wait till the Day of Atonement; and he made ready to depart. Then she caught him by the garment to entreat him; but he would not stay, but went out.

On the third day after these things, it came to pass that seven evil spirits entered into Hannah and possessed her in the shapes of swine; and Eliezer heard it, and said that it was a judgment of the Lord. Then was Nathanael sorely grieved, and he came to Jesus and told him everything; both that which Eliezer had said, and how Hannah had cried unto him, and afterwards how the evil spirits had entered into her. Rut Jesus (as it was reported to me by Nathanael), being exceeding wroth, arose in haste upon hearing of this story; and he went forth straightway to the house of Hannah and cast out the seven devils, and bade her be of good cheer and live in peace. And then it was that he uttered this saying against the Scribes, whereof I made mention above, namely that they kept the key of the Kingdom of God, but would neither enter in themselves, nor suffer others to enter in.

Now it happened that,, soon after these things, I brought Nathanael to visit the Rabbi Jonathan at his lodging in Capernaum; and we found there the aforesaid Eliezer the son of Arak conversing with him. When Eliezer saw us, he complained sorely of the light-mindedness (so he called it) which our Master manifested in receiving sinners. But Jonathan replied saying that the cause lay in the exceeding gentleness of our Master, because he knew not the evil nature of man.

"For," said he, "from his birth upward, Jesus of Nazareth hath moved in Paradise; and being himself good, pure, and gentle, he believeth that others also are in their thoughts like unto himself, and that they need but a little help to make them in their deeds like unto himself. For he esteemeth of sin as being naught but an infirmity. But time and experience will open his eyes."

Then answered Nathanael and said to Eliezer, "But is it not truly said, son of Arak, that 'The perfection of wisdom is repentance?' and again, 'When a man hath been wholly wicked, and hath repented at last, the Holy One receiveth him'? Nay, it is added that, 'If a sinner repent, all the transgressions which he hath committed are imputed to him as merits,' and that 'Repentance was created before the world.' How then is our Master wrong in receiving them that repent?" But Eliezer answered, with an austere countenance, that repentance availed nothing without works; and he quoted the saying, "No boor is a sin- fearer; nor is the vulgar pious"; and another saying which warneth men "Not to frequent the company of the unlearned." "Moreover," he added, "the All-seeing (blessed is He) alone knoweth the hearts of men, and discerneth the true repentance from the false. Wherefore none can forgive sins but God alone."

Then Nathanael, remembering how great an evil had befallen his kinswoman through the hardness of Eliezer, became exceeding wroth, and brake out into bitter accusations against the Scribes, because they despised the people of the land: "For lo," he said, "more than half of Israel even now goeth down to the pit of destruction, and ye raise no hand to save them. Yea, when the drowning ones lift up their heads from the waters and cry saying, 'We are alive, help us,' then stand ye on the bank and answer, saying, 'Down, down, ye ought not to be alive, ye are not alive.' For ye say that ye make fences to keep in the Law; but ye make fences indeed to keep out the people from the Law. Wherefore your fences are as offences, and ye are guilty of the blood of half the nation of Israel in the sight of the Lord."

Then Eliezer arose in wrath, and as he went to the door, he turned and looked on Nathanael and said, "Like master, like scholar:" and so he went out. But when he was departed, Jonathan said to us, "Eliezer spake unadvisedly and harshly; yet is there truth in his words. For when we shun the 'unlearned' and the 'vulgar,' or the people of the land, we mean such as have not learned their duties toward God and man, which also are wholly given up to the things of earth. Such men are lovers of self, wallowing in carnal lusts: and are they not to be blamed?"

To this Nathanael replied, "True, my father; and if all the teachers of Israel were as thou art, verily Israel would be blessed. But do not the Scribes cast out many from the synagogues for small matters, even though they perform the weightier duties? Yea, I myself have heard Eliezer say many times, 'Hasten to a light precept'; and I have seen him to be more angered for a light transgression than a heavy one. Also many of them say that a 'vulgar' person is one that repeateth not the daily Krishma, or weareth not phylacteries, or fringes, or doth not wait on the learned.

These things do the Scribes exalt, but they pass over justice, mercy, righteousness, and truth."

Jonathan made no answer to this at first; but presently he sighed and said, "Truly we have need of a discerning spirit; and we should pray unto the All-seeing (blessed is He) that we may not make defiled the pure, nor make pure the defiled, and that we may not bind the loosed nor loose the bound." No one spake further about this matter. But Nathanael sat musing, while I conversed with Jonathan concerning his return to Sepphoris and concerning certain messages which I desired that he should deliver to my mother. Presently we bade farewell to Jonathan and departed.

But as we passed through the street together, Nathanael still mused, and, as it seemed to me, was repeating to himself the words of Jonathan, "That we may not bind the loosed nor loose the bound." Then he turned to me and said, "Joseph, is there not a certain saying touching the destroying of the Evil Nature?" "Yes, of a truth is there," replied I; "for it is said that it shall come to pass, in the time to come, that the Holy One will bring the Evil Nature, and slay him in the presence of the righteous and in the presence of the wicked." Then Nathanael smote his hands together for joy, and lifted up his voice and said "Perchance, therefore, in the day of the Redemption of Sion, the Evil Nature shall be utterly destroyed, and we shall no longer pray according to the prayer of Jonathan the son of Ezra, that we may not loose the bound; for all shall be loosed."

While he spake thus, somewhat loudly, behold, a certain Barachiah the son of Zadok heard the last words of Nathanael; and he cried after us and mocked at us and our Nazarene prophet, for so he called Jesus. Now this man was a beggar, crook-backed and lame, and of a malignant disposition, one that took pleasure in slander and mischief: and oftentimes he had thrust himself in the path of Jesus and had besought Jesus to heal him of his deformity. But Jesus would not. So this man called after us, mocking us and imitating the voice of Jesus and saying, "Go in peace, go in peace."

Then I began to question Nathanael why Jesus had not healed this Barachiah.: Nathanael answered and said, "Because he hath not faith. Moreover, as thou knowest, Jesus doth not adventure to heal all afflictions and all diseases. And even if the affliction be such as can be healed, yet he healeth not, except there be .first faith." Then I said, "But how doth he discern such as have faith from such as have not faith?" But Nathanael answered, "I know not; and indeed it is a marvel to me to see how he healeth the sick. But he speaketh of these mighty works as being prepared for him beforehand in heaven. And indeed it seemeth to me that whensoever Jesus doeth a mighty work on earth, he seeth it also done, in that instant, in heaven. For he looketh upon the body of the sick man with his eyes; but with his spirit methinks he looketh on the spirit of the man in heaven; and there he seeth a Hand, even the Hand of the Everlasting Arm; and whatsoever the Hand worketh in heaven, even that doth Jesus work on earth; and if he seeth the Hand unloosing the chain from the spirit of the man in heaven, then Jesus unlooseth the chain on earth. But if he seeth that the Hand in heaven moveth not, then his hand also is stayed on earth."

But I said, "When Jesus hath healed the sick, he biddeth them go in peace, as Barachiah but now cried after us. Now if there be no peace in the man's heart, how can he go in peace? Doth Jesus therefore make peace in the man's heart? Or is it that he merely seeth peace in the man's heart, and speaketh aloud that which he seeth?" "Both," replied Nathanael; "at least, so it seemeth to me. For I judge that Jesus not only discerneth peace, but also maketh peace. Likewise also he seemeth to me to make faith. I know not how it is, but of late a certain Mattathias described to me the manner in which Jesus had dealt with him. Now this Mattathias was afflicted with a disease in his feet, insomuch that he had not walked for these three years: and he was carried by his friends into the presence of Jesus. 'And,' said he, 'before I saw Jesus, I had scarce any hope that he might be able to help me; but when I looked upon Jesus, and saw what a strength shone in his countenance, then I began to have faith, but not much; for still I feared more than I hoped. Yet as Jesus healed first one and then another (for there were many waiting to be healed before me) my faith grew stronger and stronger. But when Jesus was come to the bed whereon I lay, he fixed his eyes steadfastly upon me, so that the brightness thereof passed like purifying fire into my soul; and he looked up unto heaven and then down upon me, and it was as if he had been wrestling with the evil spirit of faithlessness in my heart and had quite driven it out. For now, behold, of a sudden, my doubts and fears and troubles were all clean gone, and my heart was as light as air, and a certain irresistible faith possessed me; insomuch that, though I lay still on my bed, I knew that I had been made whole and that I needed naught save the bidding of Jesus to tell me when to arise. And when the word came, I arose "Now," said Nathanael, "thus spake Mattathias to me. But if he spake aright, then methinks Jesus hath a power to create faith in the heart as well as to heal the diseases of the body."

All that night I meditated upon the words of Nathanael and upon the story of Mattathias: for that a prophet should cure diseases seemed possible, though wonderful; but that any one, yea, even though he were the Redeemer of Israel himself, should have power to create peace and faith, this indeed seemed a marvellous and almost an impossible thing. But it came to pass that on the morning of the very next day, as I remember, we went into the house of a certain rich man with Jesus; and a great company was assembled (some because of the mighty work that Jesus had wrought on the Gadarene, but others, of the richer sort, because they desired to abet the plotting of the Pharisees against him), and Jesus was now on the point to speak to the people, when a noise was heard from the roof above. There had been, no small stir, even before, near the door of the house, and none had taken heed thereof; but now we looked up, and behold, one sick of the palsy in a bed was let down by ropes, until the bed reached the place where Jesus was; for he sat in the gallery that ran round the courtyard, but we stood in the courtyard below. Now many of us thought that Jesus would not heal one that thus thrust himself into the midst of the people, interrupting his exhortation and doctrine; and some cried out to remove the man, but others cried out Nay. Howbeit, when Jesus gave command that there should be silence, there was silence, even such a silence that men feared almost to breathe; so great was the expectation of all to sec what Jesus would do.

Then sounded forth these words above the heads of all the congregation, full of pity, yet like unto the sound of a silver trumpet in clearness: "Thy sins be forgiven thee." I myself was so far off that I heard the words, but could not see the countenance of Jesus. But they that saw him told me that it was even as Nathanael had described unto me the healing of Mattathias. For Jesus fixed his eyes steadfastly on the man, as if he saw, not the man himself, but the man's angel standing in heaven bound before the throne of God, with the chains of Satan round him, and all the host of heaven looking thereon. "His countenance also shone as the sun: pity and sorrow were there, but pity and sorrow swallowed up in the brightness and glory of joy and triumph; and the sick man's face gave back the brightness. But when Jesus perceived that the time had come, and that the word of God had gone forth, and that the chains in heaven had been broken, then Jesus spake and broke the chains on earth." So spake one unto me afterwards, describing the manner of Jesus, how he forgave the palsied man.

But after the first silence there arose a great murmuring and the sound of many voices disputing. The voice of Eliezer was clearly heard saying, "This man blasphemeth; who can forgive sins but God alone?" "Yea," said another, "and sins are forgiven not on earth, but in heaven, at the last day." But others mocking said that the sick man seemed not yet to have gained much profit, albeit his sins had been forgiven. All this noise and stir ceased at once when Jesus began to speak. He said, "Why reason ye these things in your hearts? Whether is it easier to say to the sick of the palsy, 'Thy sins be forgiven thee,' or to say 'Arise, and take up thy bed and walk'? But that ye may know that the Son of Man hath authority even upon earth to forgive sins—" here he paused and stood up, and behold, the whole of the congregation was constrained to stand up with one consent; insomuch that I saw even Eliezer the son of Arak standing up with the rest, and his face was kindling as the faces of the rest, and the silence was even such as could be felt, and the palsied man himself seemed half to raise himself in his bed in expectation: and, like a shock, there fell on us the word "Arise." And lo, the man arose at once, and stood straight up, and Jesus said to him, "Take up thy bed, and go thy way into thy house." And immediately he arose, took up his bed, and went forth whole before them all.

Then were all amazed, and glorified God, and some said, "We never saw it in this fashion." But others praised and magnified the All-merciful because He had given this new authority to men, so as to forgive sins, and this too not hereafter in heaven, but at once and upon earth. But Eliezer and the chief ruler and others of the elders of the synagogue, when they had recovered from their first astonishment, took counsel how they might again catch Jesus in his doctrine. For they said, "None can forgive sins, except God only:

therefore it is certain that this man maketh himself God." Howbeit they veiled their thoughts with a smooth countenance, for fear of the multitude; and going up to Jesus they saluted him before they departed from the synagogue. But Jesus looked wistfully at them, like unto one hoping for good news; for he thought that they would have understood that God had sent him, perceiving the finger of God in the healing of the man that was sick of the palsy. But when he perceived their dissimulation, he was silent until he had come forth from the synagogue: and then I heard him sigh, and he said in a low voice to himself, "For judgment am I come into this world, that those who see may see not."

During the rest of that day Jesus sat musing: and at one time he seemed to be sad, but at another time to rejoice. But even when he was sad, there always appeared a joy beneath the sadness; so that his sadness was but as the cloud that dappleth the side of a mountain, the summit whereof shineth bright in the sunlight. For it was the nature of Jesus always to be cheerful and to rejoice; insomuch that peace and joy seemed to go forth from him to all men and things around him, and from them to come back with increase to him again. But now he was sorrowful, as we gathered, because of the hardness of heart of the Pharisees. For howsoever they might outwardly dissemble, yet did he discern their hearts, that they were inwardly grieved yea, at the goodness of God; wherefore now indeed after this second token of their hardness, it seemed to be indeed the will of God that the Good News should be of no avail unto the Scribes, save only to make their eyes blind, and their hearts fat, and their ears hard of hearing. For this cause our Master sorrowed: but for some other cause he rejoiced, or seemed in expectation of some joy to come.

But as for the rest of us, we disputed among ourselves touching this new power which Jesus had brought into the world; for it seemed more than human, and such as no prophet before him had ever used or so much as sought from God. Only Judas was silent more than was his custom: and he seemed disturbed and doubtful, as one uncertain of his path and not knowing whether to go forward or backward. For when Nathanael spake about our Master's authority to forgive sins, and how in the day of Redemption he would destroy the Evil Nature, then Judas at times heard him gladly, as if he earnestly desired that this should be true; but at another time he scoffed and said that "No forgiveness of sins would drive out Herod from Tiberias, nor the Romans from Jerusalem."

CHAPTER XII

How the Forgiveness of Sins is the Key that openeth the New Kingdom; and how the Old Law and the New Law must not be mixed.

BY this time the autumn was come round, and it wanted but a few days to the tenth day of the month Tisri, which is the Great Day of Atonement. Now so it was that, when we arose on a certain morning (in the first week, as I remember, of the month Tisri), behold, Jesus was not in the house, and when we sought him, we found him on the shore musing; insomuch that at first he was not aware of our presence. But when he saw us, he bade Simon Peter prepare his fishing-boat, for he desired to go out into the deep. So Simon Peter and Andrew launched the boat, and I with them; and Jesus went on board, and there he sat, still musing, while we made ready the tackling and the nets. While we busied ourselves herein, many of the sailors and fishermen of the town came down to the coast and began to launch their vessels; for the day was fair for fishing.

Now there was standing on the beach the hunchback Barachiah, the son of Zadok: for his custom was to beg of the sailors, and to do for them such small services as he was able. But he was hated of the most part of the sailors by reason of his envious and malignant disposition, and because he could not refrain from reproaches and revilings. Moreover they accused him that he had sometimes mislaid or hurt their tackling. Others also said that he had an evil eye and brought evil fortune. Wherefore he fared ill with the sailors, and even when they gave him alms, it was as to a dog or an unclean creature: and oftentimes they struck him when he crossed them. Now it chanced that while we made ready our nets, behold, a certain merchant, coming down to the water, stumbled upon a stone and fell against Barachiah. Then Barachiah cried out in anger, "Wast thou born with a bridle in thy hand that thou should so treat thy brethren as if they were mules or asses?" But the other replied, "Yea, and thou wast born with a saddle on thy back, that I might ride upon thee." So saying, he spurned Barachiah out of his path, so that he fell to the ground: and hereat all the sailors laughed.

Not long after this there came down two sailors, nigh to the place where Barachiah sat wiping the blood from his face; and one of them spake to the hunchback some words, I know not what, but, as it appeared, of kindness. Then straightway Barachiah rose up and went with the man, and willingly helped him to launch his boat and to prepare his tackling. And the man's companion laughed and said, "Whence hast thou the power to soften the heart of that child of Satan?" But when Barachiah was departed, the sailor answered that he had in times past shown kindness to a brother of Barachiah, that was now dead; and he added in jest, "In all men there be two hearts, a heart of stone and a heart of flesh: and Barachiah hath his heart of flesh, even as others, though he be a child of Satan." "Nay," replied the other, "but if there be a heart of flesh in Barachiah, it would need Solomon's ring to find out where it is hid." And so jesting they rowed out into the deep.

Now I perceived that Jesus noted all these words of the two sailors, and likewise that which had befallen Barachiah, and while he listened and looked, the appearance of his countenance was altered; for before, he had seemed in his musing like one waiting for an answer to a question, but now like one that had received an answer. Howbeit still he mused and ceased not, while we rowed out into the deep, and busied ourselves with casting our nets.

But so it was that, as we rowed and drifted hither and thither in our fishing, we were carried very close to the coast, where the rocks came straight down to the sea after the manner of a wall; and suddenly we heard a piteous sound as of bleating. When we looked up, we saw a lamb, which had strayed from the flock, and had come to a stand upon a ledge in the rock, exceeding narrow, so that it could not go forward, neither knew it how to turn back: but there it stood, and bleated often and piteously, so that our hearts were sorry for the creature, and we would fain have helped it, but knew not how; for there was not space to land. But while we hung upon our oars not knowing what to do, Peter cried out, "The shepherd cometh "; and presently we all discerned him, very high up, and clambering from rock to rock for to reach the lamb. And when we all shouted and beckoned to him, he straightway understood us, and coming down, though with much ado, took the lamb on his shoulders and bore it safely away. Hereat we were all well content; but when I looked on Jesus, his face shone with an exceeding joy, too great, methought, for so small a matter, so that I marvelled. For there was no more in his countenance the look of one questioning, but rather of one gazing upon the glory of God. Then when we had hauled in the net, he gave command that we should row back to Capernaum.

No\v the next day Jesus showed forth what he had on his mind. For about noon he went down to the place where one Matthew a tax-gatherer was sitting at the house of customs near the quay. And for a while Jesus beheld him, how he bore himself amid all the concourse and stir of that busy place; then he drew nigh, and called Matthew to be one of his disciples, saying unto him, "Follow me." And Matthew arose and followed him and bade him to a great feast in his house on the same day, and thereto he called many of his acquaintance, both tax- gatherers and sinners, and others of the poorer sort; and Jesus promised that he would come to the feast. But when this was noised about the town, the anger of the Pharisees was great; for they counted it as a sign that Jesus would not join himself to them, nor do anything to gain their favour. But as for the sailors and common people, some rejoiced, others marvelled; insomuch that when we came to Matthew's house, we found a great concourse of people both round the doors and in the feast-chamber.

Now as we entered the chamber, I could not but chafe somewhat for the baseness of the company with whom we were forced to consort. For they were all unlearned men, and given to vain conversation; and many of them had not washed before supper; and the savour of their garments and the heat of the room were scarce to be borne. Moreover I saw at one of the tables Barachiah the son of Zadok, and others with whom I should never have expected to sit at meat. Then the words of Jonathan the son of Ezra came back to my mind, how he had said that Jesus was misled, in that he knew not the evil nature of men; nor could I refrain from imparting these words to Nathanael, who was my companion at the table.

But Nathanael answered that I erred greatly, for that Jesus knew the evil that was in men better than any man, and hated it more than any man: "But," said he, "the evil of unwashed hands and unsavoury garments doth not seem to Jesus the greatest of evils." "But," said I, "these men are given to other sins; and how cometh it to pass that Jesus beareth with the sins of these men, but doth not bear with the Scribes, who do not commit such sins?" Then said Nathanael, "As it seemeth to me, there is a certain light in the hearts of men; and whoso hath this light in him, loveth light, and is drawn towards the light whenever the light is placed near to him, even though he may have turned his back upon the light: and thus these sinners are drawn towards Jesus. But if a man for many years make it his business to quench the light in himself, because he feareth it; then he cannot love the light, nor can he be drawn towards it, even though it be very close to him. Even as the Pharisees fear the light in themselves, and say there is no light save in the Law and the Traditions. Therefore they quench the light in their hearts and cannot see the true light; and they destroy the Word of God in their hearts, and cannot hear the true Word." "But," said I, "if there be stripped off fine-sounding words from thy speech, to what is the matter like? It is as though thou shouldst say, 'it is better that a man should commit murder and adultery and theft (provided that he love righteousness), than that he should abstain from all these sins, but not love righteousness.'" "Thou knowest well," replied Nathanael, "that according to a man's love of righteousness will be his hatred of sin; and whoso really hateth sin, he cannot live therein. Yet what thou sayest is true; there is more hope of the vilest sinner than of the man that hath in his heart no love of righteousness."

I mused for a while, and then I said, "Thou speakest of hope: but doth it seem to thee truthful, looking upon a bad man, to say, this man is good, merely because thou mayest have hopes that he may become good?" But before Nathanael could make answer, there came into my mind the words of the sailor, that "If Barachiah the son of Zadok had a heart of flesh as well as a heart of stone, it would need Solomon's ring to find out where the heart of flesh was hid; "so I told the words to Nathanael. Straightway Nathanael looked toward the place were Barachiah was sitting at table; and then he turned to me and said, "And hath not our Master the ring of Solomon?" Then I also looked at Barachiah; and I marvelled to see what a gentleness there was in his countenance. But Jesus was at that instant beginning a discourse; so we ceased conversing that we might hearken unto it.

The discourse told of a certain son of a kind father, who, taking his patrimony, wandered into a distant city, where he squandered his substance in riotous living, so that he was forced to keep swine like an hireling; but returning to his father he was welcomed. Other like parables he spake: and all the people were marvellously attentive to hear him. Notwithstanding, Jesus would not always discourse himself alone: for he gladly heard others, and by questions led many to speak, questioning them with courtesy in no way akin to condescension (even as a brother meeting brothers after long absence); the merchants concerning foreign countries; the officers of the customs concerning the commerce and wares of the place; the mariners and soldiers concerning the ships and currents and strong places and fortresses whereof they severally had knowledge. With all these common people did Jesus converse, and to each, methought, he added, somewhat of his own nature. And so it was that amid all that concourse of vulgar and unlearned people and boors (as the Scribes would have called them), not one did or said anything unworthy of the presence of our Master. Thus did Jesus give to others, and lo, they gave back to him good measure into his bosom, pressed down and running over, according to his own saying.

But when he rose up to go, behold, Barachiah the son of Zadok also rose up in haste, and coming to Jesus he fell down on his knees before him, and besought him that he would forgive all the slanders and revilings which he had used concerning Jesus and concerning his disciples. And Jesus both forgave him and blessed him. And from that hour even to the day of his death Barachiah was a new creature; insomuch that he was no longer known among them of Capernaum as the viper, or the child of Satan, but they called him "the changed man."

But as Jesus was now going forth, two of the disciples of John the son of Zachariah came unto him. For they had been present in the chamber, though they had not partaken of the feast; and they marvelled at the cheerfulness of Jesus* because he ate bread and drank wine and conversed freely with the common people, not after the manner of their master. So they were offended at Jesus, and said to him, "Master, why do we and the Pharisees fast oft, but thy disciples fast not?" Now John himself had called Jesus the Bridegroom of Israel. Jesus therefore, using these same words, answered and said, "Can the children of the bride chamber mourn as long as the bridegroom is with them?" Then he turned and looked at us, and his face was sorrowful; and he added, "But the days will come when the bridegroom shall be taken from them, and then shall they fast in those days." Then first did Jesus speak concerning his departure from his disciples: and he meant, perchance, that as John the Prophet had been taken from the midst of his disciples, so also, would he himself be taken away from us; for the Lord had revealed unto him that Israel was not to be redeemed easily, nor without much tribulation. But by what power he should be thus taken, whether by imprisonment (as had befallen John), or by death of violence (as was shortly to befall John), or by death in course of nature, concerning these things he said naught at this time. But we neither understood his words, neither took we thought of them.

But as we came forth, we met Eliezer the son of Arak, and the chief ruler of the synagogue, and many of the elders of the synagogue; and they looked at us with sore displeasure. And the chief ruler did not restrain himself, but said to Jesus aloud in the presence of us all, "Is it even so that thou wouldst fain be Ruler over Israel? Behold, on thy side are Matthew the tax-gatherer, and Barachiah the child of Satan, and Mary the sinner; but on my side are Eliezer the son of Arak and all the elders of the synagogue. Is it not better to be the tail of a lion rather than the head of a dog?"

But when Jesus noted how certain of the sinners feared to stand before the faces of Eliezer the son of Arak, and of the ruler of the synagogue, and how they were shaken in their faith and abashed (for that they were accustomed to be despised and to be trampled on, as being without all hope of redemption); then was he exceeding wrath, and he answered and said unto the ruler of the synagogue, "Woe unto the world because of offences: for it must needs be that offences come: but woe to that man by whom the offence cometh." Then he pointed to the sinners behind him (whom he was wont to call "little ones," because they were babes in faith), and he spake again to the chief ruler and his party, saying, "Take heed that ye despise not one of these little ones; for I say unto you that in heaven their angels do always behold the face of my Father which is in heaven. For the Son of Man is come to save that which was lost."

Then Eliezer the son of Arak interrupted him and said, "Why eatest thou, contrary to the Traditions, with tax-gatherers and sinners?" But Jesus answered and said, "How think ye? If a man have an hundred sheep, and one of them be gone astray, doth he not leave the ninety-and-nine, and goeth into the mountains, and seeketh that which is gone astray? And if so be that he find it, verily I say unto you, he rejoiceth more of that sheep than of the ninety-and- nine which went not astray." "But," said another of the Scribes, "why dost thou shun and rebuke the righteous? What evil is it not to be a sinner?" When Jesus heard that, he said unto him, "They that be whole need not a physician, but they that be sick. But go ye and learn what that meaneth, I will have mercy and not sacrifice. For I am not come to call the righteous, but sinners to repentance." So saying, he passed on and left the Pharisees, and we followed him.

Now Andrew and Simon Peter had been disciples of John the son of Zachariah, before they had joined themselves to Jesus. In the evening, therefore, they resorted to Jesus to question him touching the answer he had that day given to John's disciples concerning fasting. I was with them, and also Judas of Kerioth, and a certain Eleazar the son of Azariah, a Scribe of Sepphoris and a friend of Jonathan. Now Eleazar did not venture to advise Jesus to use shifts and subterfuges so as to keep friendship with the Pharisees; but he said that perchance such sinners as might be converted to the path of righteousness might not be able to continue therein, unless the path were fenced in by rules and laws, feasts, fasts, and other like ordinances. He also bade Jesus not separate himself from the congregation; for said he, "Whatsoever is decreed by the congregation below, that is decreed by the congregation above; and what is ratified on earth is ratified in heaven; and with whomsoever the spirit of men is pleased the Spirit of God is pleased."

But Jesus answered that as new wine was not like unto old wine, nor a new garment like an old garment, even so the doctrine of John was not like unto his doctrine; neither could the two be mixed. The doctrine of the Pharisees also, he said, was not like his doctrine, and the two kinds of doctrine needed two several and distinct shapes, even as several kinds of wine need several bottles. When Eleazar heard this, he went out; for these words seemed to him (as he said to John the son of Zebedee) to be a kind of proclaiming of war against the Pharisees; so that there appeared no longer any hope of concord between Jesus and them. Judas also, although he still seemed strangely perturbed, and spake less than was his wont, nevertheless said that a great gulf was opening itself between our Master and the Pharisees; "and," said he, "unless something is speedily done, this gulf will be impassable." Many also that had been disciples of John the Prophet murmured against Jesus, because he had promised to fulfil the Law and had been expected to follow in the course of John, but now he went contrary to the Law and was for choosing a path of his own. For at that time in Galilee they that honoured John the Prophet were more than they that honoured Jesus of Nazareth.

But for my part my soul was given up to thanksgiving and to praise of God, because of this new power which He had sent down to men, of forgiving sins. For if it seemed a divine word to say "Let there be light," and there was light, much more divine a word it seemed to say, "Let there be righteousness," and lo, there was righteousness. And when I remembered the saying of the sailor, how that it needed Solomon's ring to find out the heart of flesh in bad men, and when I called to mind how Jesus had found it out, then it seemed to me that a greater than Solomon was among us. I thought also on the words of Nathanael, how that, in the day of Redemption, the Holy One (blessed is He) will bring the Evil Nature and slay him in the presence of the righteous and of the wicked; and my thoughts were swallowed up in wonder.

CHAPTER XIII

Of the Plotting of the Pharisees against Jesus, how they said he had a Devil; and concerning the Holy Spirit.

THE words of Judas were true, that a great gulf now lay between our Master and the Pharisees; and day by day the gulf grew wider, as I soon perceived. It chanced that Eliezer the son of Arak knew that I was a friend of Jonathan; and desiring to draw me away from Jesus, he wrote a letter to Jonathan begging him to move me that I might return home. This letter of Eliezer therefore" Jonathan sent unto me, and it was to the following effect:

"From Eliezer the son of Arak to Jonathan the son of Ezra: salutation and peace. Be it known unto thee, Jonathan, that this Jesus of Nazareth, concerning whom we once had hopes that he might be a deep well or perchance even an ever- welling spring of the Law, hath proved an empty vessel and a broken cistern. He profaneth the Sabbath and teacheth others to profane it; he eateth without the washing of hands; he teacheth that no man is defiled by that which he toucheth or eateth; in a word, he breaketh the Law and causeth others to profane it. Yet this in part was known unto thee even before, and thou didst deceive thyself, and saidst, 'Perchance he hath a message from God concerning the Sabbath and concerning the Law.' Hear, therefore, son of Ezra, what new thing this blind guide hath taken upon himself to do. He not only teacheth all people everywhere to abstain from sacrifice, wresting to his own destruction that hard saying of the Prophet which saith, 'I will have mercy and not sacrifice.' but he also hath dared to make himself as God, forgiving sins. This he hath done publicly in the synagogue, before the face of the congregation.

"Now would fain deal gently with the young man, because he seemed once to purpose well, and because he hath made unto himself a name for casting out unclean spirits. Moreover he is befriended not only by the rabble that knoweth not the Law, but also by a few of the wise and pious, as, for example, thyself. For this cause we are minded not at once to punish him in accordance with the law for blasphemy, but,to make excuses for him by saying that he is beside himself.

"And this indeed seemeth to be not unlikely, for he is not as other men are; for oft times he sleepeth not, but watcheth (as I am informed) whole nights together; and albeit he seeth no vision (which showeth him to be no prophet), yet he carrieth himself in such strange fashion as if he saw visions daily; also he is wroth at small faults and at no faults (as thou thyself knowest), and yet withal easy to forgive great faults. Moreover of late he most strangely forsweareth the company of all the pious and learned, and consorteth publicly with tax-gatherers and sinners; insomuch that, but now, having called one Matthew a tax-gatherer, to be one of his disciples, afterwards, at a feast in the house of this Matthew, amid mirth and wine-bibbing, he took upon himself to forgive the sins of that Barachiah the son of Zadok, who, as thou knowest, is by all men called the child of Satan.

"Now therefore, for the sake of the young man Jesus himself, it beseemeth thee, Jonathan, to cause this evil to cease, and to warn his friends, if perchance they may see fit to restrain him. Write therefore, I pray thee, to his mother Mary, and to his brethren (but I grieve that his father no longer liveth to restrain him) that they may come and lay hands upon him: for they will listen to thy voice. We desire also that thou wouldst write to the young man, thy pupil and friend, Joseph the son of Simeon, that he may return to Sepphoris, lest he too fall into the pit of destruction along with this blind guide Jesus. If also thou shouldst inform Joanna, the mother of Joseph, concerning all these things, she would peradventure join her voice to thine, that thy pupil might return. But in any case it were well that the certainty of the madness of this Jesus should be noised abroad among all thy friends and acquaintances, to the intent that we may the more easily restrain him.

"Hearken, I pray thee, unto my words, Jonathan, for I will not hide the truth from thee, that certain of us judge the young man Jesus of Nazareth more harshly, saying that he is possessed by Beelzebub. Others also say that hands should be laid upon him without delay, and that he should be delivered to Herod. Now if he hearken unto thee and desist from his consorting with sinners, or if his kinsmen lay gentle hands upon him, then we are willing that he should suffer few stripes; but if not, many stripes will be needful. But if he should be delivered to Herod, or if the people should peradventure take up stones to stone him, who knoweth the end thereof? Peace be with thee!"

Together with the letter of Eliezer was a letter from Jonathan, who besought me to send word unto him about the welfare of Jesus; and I could perceive that, albeit the old man was wroth that any should say that Jesus was possessed with an unclean spirit, yet even he inclined his ear to believe that Jesus was beside himself. For after some words touching the health of my mother, the letter ended thus, "Alas, because of the iniquity of this generation! For verily Jesus was fit to be the Redeemer of Israel; but the generation was unfit. He was as the morning star in his joy, and as the sun in the glory of his brightness; but the night cometh apace, and the sun' must give place to the darkness. Verily, Jesus was of them that have entered into Paradise, and have tasted of the honey of the highest heaven. But perchance he hath seen things not vouchsafed to men to see, even the mystery of the Chariot; and the vision hath been too much for the eye of man, and with much honey the mind hath been demented."

When I received these letters, I purposed at once to inform Jesus concerning the plots of the Pharisees. But he was not at that time at Capernaum, but at Bethsaida Julias; so I hastened thither. When I was come thither, Jesus was exhorting the people; and there was a great concourse to hear him, so that I could not come nigh unto him for the press. But while I stood afar off, behold, Eliezer the son of Arak advanced towards him through the midst of the press; and all men made way for him. But he, making as though he could not advance further, called to Jesus in a loud voice, so that all men should hear: "Behold, thy mother and thy brethren stand without, desiring to see thee."

Now could I see from Eliezer's countenance and from the manner of his speech, and from the faces of some of the Scribes that were sitting in the principal places, yea, and from the faces of some others that were in the outermost part of the crowd (for they nodded and beckoned each to the other) that here was indeed the very plot of the Pharisees whereof Eliezer had made mention in his letter to Jonathan. For the mother and brethren of Jesus had come with intent to lay hands on him, having been persuaded that he was beside himself. And immediately all that were in the chamber seemed to become aware of the plot. For Jesus ceased from his teaching; and many stood on tiptoe gazing toward that quarter of the crowd where the mother of Jesus was waiting, and then they gazed back on Jesus again, marking how he bore himself. So there arose a marvellous great stillness, while every one waited to hear what Jesus would say: and my heart beat so that I could even hear the beating thereof. But Jesus said, "Who is my mother, and who are my brethren?" Then he looked round about on those of his disciples that sat nigh unto him and he said, "Behold my mother and my brethren. For whosoever shall do the will of God, the same is my brother and my sister and mother."

When he had said these words, then the countenance of Eliezer fell. For he had hoped either to have found occasion against Jesus (as though he paid no reverence to his mother, not rising up or going forth to meet her), or else that the brethren of Jesus should have laid hands on him as he went forth, and so all men should ever after have esteemed him as one beside himself. But the words of Jesus manifested that he ceased not to love and honour his mother, howbeit he loved and honoured others also, even as many as were in the Family of God, unto whom he was as a brother or as a son; neither ought he to have forsaken all the Family of God to please the family of Nazareth; for, had he gone forth to meet them that stood without, he had forsaken and caused to stumble all them that sat within. So they perceived what was in the mind of Jesus; and they magnified him the more.

When the Pharisees perceived that they had not prevailed with the common people, they began to adventure a second plot. For they procured a certain Scribe to accuse Jesus in the synagogue, and to say that he cast out devils through Beelzebub the prince of the devils. The name of the Scribe was Hezekiah the son of Zachariah, from Jerusalem; even the same Hezekiah of whom I spake before, when I spake of the meeting of the Galileans in the valley nigh unto Sepphoris. Howbeit, neither did this plot prevail with the common people, For the same accusation had been brought by the Scribes against John the prophet: but in vain. For the people could in no wise be persuaded that such an one as Jesus was possessed with an unclean spirit, nor that sick men could be healed and devils driven out by Beelzebub.

But that which caused most surprise to many of the disciples was to note how great a wrath was kindled in Jesus by this accusation. It chanced, as I remember, that we were in a small synagogue in the town called Jotapata. He had driven out a devil from a young man, and the devil tare the young man as he passed out of him, so that the young man lay on the ground lifeless. Jesus, as his manner was, took the young man by the hand for to help him to arise; and because there seemed no life in him, he stooped down and embraced him for to lift him up. Now the rest of them that were with Hezekiah held their peace, albeit against their will; so great was their marvel at the deed, and so mighty was the presence of Jesus. Only Hezekiah still hardened his heart. Therefore while Jesus was now lifting up the youth, of a sudden was heard the voice of Hezekiah crying aloud, "Thou castest out devils through Beelzebub the prince of the devils: " and all the people were as men amazed, and stood agape, expecting what Jesus would do.

Jesus himself, at first, seemed like unto one in a dream, turning his eyes from the young man (whose life had now returned to him) to the face of Hezekiah, and from Hezekiah again back to the young man; as though either he himself had not heard aright, or else Hezekiah had not seen clearly how great a work had been wrought for the young man. For belike he could scarce believe that any man in Israel could refrain from rejoicing at the young man's deliverance; nor did it seem possible to him that any among the children of men could suppose that a devil could be cast out save by the finger of God. But when he perceived that the face of Hezekiah was set as a rock against him, and that his eyes were as the eyes of one mocking him; and when he looked round also upon the people, and perceived that some of them were abashed and shaken in their faith because he had as yet made no answer, then indeed his countenance was changed against Hezekiah. and he made answer to him after his folly: that, if it was so indeed, and if Satan was divided against himself, then let all men "rejoice, for behold, Satan could not stand. But if not, and if he cast out devils by the hand of God, "Then," said he, "the Kingdom of God hath come upon you unawares."

When he had spoken these words, he stood, as if in pause, and fixed his eyes on the face of Hezekiah. But he looked upon him no more with anger, but with a marvellous pity; and behold, his countenance, which was wont to shine as the sun, became pale and cold to look upon, even as the moon in her brightness, looking down upon a man drowning in deep waters; and he added and said, "All manner of sin and blasphemy shall be forgiven unto men; but the blasphemy against the Holy Spirit shall not be forgiven unto men. And whosoever speaketh a word against the Son of man, it shall be forgiven him: but whosoever speaketh against the Holy Spirit, it shall not be forgiven, neither in this age, nor in the age to come." Never before had we seen Jesus so moved. Hezekiah himself was confounded, and gasped for breath and could not speak, but went out of the synagogue in confusion; neither was there one in the congregation that went out with him.

But when the congregation had departed I went to Nathanael and questioned him concerning this matter.

For even from the first, Nathanael had a discerning spirit, able to discern matters wherein I groped as in darkness; but moreover of late I had noted how he had seemed to grow in wisdom and discernment, so that it was a marvel to see how great a change had come to pass in how short a time: and he was to me, as it were, an interpreter of the words of Jesus. So I asked Nathanael what Jesus meant by the words "blasphemy against the Holy Spirit," and why that sin was above all other sins so that it could not be forgiven.

"For," said I, "Jesus was blasphemed as a gluttonous man and as a wine-bibber, not many days past, in this very place, and I noted well (but thou wast not with us) with what a calmness, yea, even to mirth, Jesus endured the charge. For we chanced to be passing through this very street, and the children were coming forth from the school and sporting after their manner; and Jesus sat him down on the stone yonder and watched them at their sports. And behold, the children had divided themselves into two companies, a small company and a large company; and the small company had pipes and tabors, and were to play thereon; but the others were to conform themselves to the music of their fellows. But when they were now beginning, the larger company could not agree among themselves, and (after the manner of wanton children) they knew not their own minds. So when the pipers piped merry music they would not dance, but cried out for sad music; but when the pipers piped sadly, then they would not beat their breasts, nor make as if they were in the house of mourning, but stopped their ears and called for merry music: whereat the pipers were vexed, and complained of the inconstancy of their fellows. Then do I right well remember how Jesus noted it all, and smiled thereat.

And turning to us, he said, still smiling (though with some touch of sadness), that this generation was like unto those children: for he had come piping merry music, and John the Prophet had come piping sad music, but the men of this generation would listen to neither; for they said that John had a devil, and that he himself was a gluttonous man and a wine-bibber, a friend of publicans and sinners. Now wherefore, thinkest thou, did Jesus endure so lightly to be blasphemed as a gluttonous man and a wine-bibber, but endured not to hear the words of Hezekiah? And what is this sin against the Holy Spirit?"

While I was saying these words, standing beneath the olive-grove on the side of the hill which looketh on Jotapata, Nathanael sat down upon the grass; and I sat down likewise. Then he said to me, "Not many days gone by, I heard Jesus speak concerning the Holy Spirit; and his words were on this wise. As in each man the man's breath or spirit is the life of the body, so in each man there is a certain holy breath or spirit which is the life of his soul; whence also cometh every good thought and deed unto the man. Moreover thou seest that the air which we breathe, and which is the breath of our bodies, is but a part of that great sea of air which embraceth the whole earth so that there is nothing hidden from the touch thereof; insomuch that the same air or breath which is coming towards us from yonder mountain top, making the terebinth-trees to bow, and which even now rustleth in the olive-trees above us, even this is our breath and our life. Now I have heard Jesus say that there is a likeness between this breath of our bodies and the breath or spirit of our souls. For as the wind bloweth where it listeth, and we hear the sound thereof, but know not whence it cometh nor whither it goeth, even so it is with the spirit of our souls, the spirit of goodness, which is the Holy Spirit of God"

Then I said, "But how shall we obtain this Holy Spirit? Or is it indeed needful that we should obtain it, seeing that we have it already? Or do some have it, but others have it not?" Nathanael answered and said, "All have it. But some have little, and none much; and Jesus hath come that we may have it abundantly. But how we shall obtain it, this I know not now. But this I know, that Jesus hath the Holy Spirit in himself, and that he will impart it to us. For I heard him say that no man can enter into the Kingdom of God unless he is born again of the Holy Spirit."

Then he paused, and said, "Is there not, Joseph, a certain saying touching the Shekinah, how that it dwelleth not with one man, but with many?" And I replied, "Yea, but with one also; for it is said, 'When *ten* sit and are occupied in words of the Law, the Shekinah is among them, for it is said, God standeth in the *congregation*of the mighty. And whence dwelleth it even with *two*? Because it is said, 'Then they that feared the Lord spake often *one* to *another*.' And whence even with *one*? Because it is said, 'In all places where I record my name I will come unto *thee* and bless *thee*.'" Nathanael smiled and said, "Our Master also teacheth that the presence of the Holy Spirit is with two or three, whensoever they are gathered together in his name. But this doctrine he foundeth not on words of Scripture; but methinks he seeth that there is a certain Spirit of Goodness or Kindness which passeth from one man to his neighbour and gathereth strength as it passeth. But when a man is alone and without neighbours, it cannot in this way gather strength. For it is a Spirit of Love. Wherefore, as it seemeth to me, our Master teacheth that the Holy Spirit is present, in some sort, in the intercourse between man and man, whensoever men do aught together as the children of God."

"But yet," said I, "I would fain know why Hezekiah the Scribe was thus rebuked, and why the blasphemy against the Holy Spirit is not forgiven." Then said Nathanael, "All men have within themselves some portion of the Spirit of God; even as we now have some portion of that great wind and breath of heaven which here in Jotapata is rustling in the olive-branches, and yonder at Capernaum is driving the fishing-boats, and out in the Great Sea is speeding the ships of Tarshish on their path. Now if thou closest thy mouth and thy nostrils against the winds of heaven and sayest, 'The air is as poison to me, I will not breathe it,' behold, thou perishest. Even so is it with the Holy Spirit. Every man that cometh into the world, hath in him some portion of the Holy Spirit. For the spirit which is in him breatheth of the Holy Spirit, and dependeth and liveth thereon. But if he shall say knowingly in his heart, 'I will not breathe thereof; I will call good evil, and the Holy Spirit I will call unholy'; then lo, his spirit dieth within him, and he can no more enter into the life of God."

Then I said, "Is not the sin of Hezekiah less than the sin of Barachiah the son of Zadok, who cursed Jesus? And Nathanael replied, "No, for Barachiah cursed Jesus in his anger and in his haste, knowing not the truth: but Hezekiah saith in his heart, 'Lo, the truth is not pleasing unto me, therefore I will not look upon it; nay, it is hateful, therefore I will call it evil.'"

Then I mused for a space, and afterwards I questioned Nathanael yet again and said, "Thou hast said that in the Day of Redemption the Holy One (blessed is He) will slay the Evil Nature of men. Therefore at the great day what thinkest thou of them which have blasphemed the Holy Spirit? Will they also perish together with the Evil Nature? Or will there be yet another age after the age that is to come, so that even the wicked may yet be in the end redeemed? For Jesus said that they should not be forgiven, neither in this age nor in the age to come." But Nathanael could not answer this question; and we feared to ask Jesus concerning the matter.

While we thus spake together, behold, Barabbas stood before us: and he saluted us and besought us that we would sup at his house; for he dwelt at Jotapata. But I asked him for what cause he had been absent from us of late, and where he had been, and what the people of Jotapata said touching the words of Hezekiah the Scribe. Touching the cause of his absence he made no answer; but as concerning the people, he said that the men of Jotapata were of one mind, that Hezekiah had spoken for envy. "Nor is it possible," said he, "that a man should believe that Jesus hath a devil, unless he himself should have a devil. For they which have devils say and do all things without forethought and with distraction, as if divided against themselves; but in Jesus there is the contrary from these: for he doth all things with forethought, yea, and perchance" (these words he uttered with some show of anger) "with more than enough of forethought."

Now Barabbas spake with something of austerity, which was not usual with him. Moreover I marvelled at those words which he had said touching "too much of forethought." Therefore I asked him again where he had been of late, and why he had forsaken the disciples. But he answered with still more of passion than before, "Because I am weary of these idle wanderings about Galilee, which bring forth no fruit. Not to sit on stools at the feet of a Scribe did I and my friends join ourselves to Jesus of Nazareth. Why tarrieth he so long idle? Why is his hand so backward to smite the oppressor?" But I bade him be of good cheer, for the hour was not yet come, and Jesus would know better than we the season fit for our uprising.

But he replied, still in great heat, "Thou wouldst fain know where I have tarried these twenty days. Well, I will tell thee. I have but even now come from Machaerus, where I have tarried these two weeks and more, nigh unto the fort called the Black Castle, wherein John the

Prophet is imprisoned. With the Prophet himself I had no speech; for he is kept in close durance, insomuch that he pineth, as I hear, for lack of air and freedom. This I heard from one of the guard, who is a kinsman of mine. Moreover my kinsman told me that had it not been for Chuza the Steward, the Prophet had been slain ten days ago. For the Tetrarch, after supper, being heavy with wine, was moved by the adulteress, even by Herodias, to write letters that John should be beheaded. Howbeit Chuza took order that the letter should be stayed for that time, and won the Tetrarch from his purpose. But what surety have we that the adulterous woman may not win the Tetrarch to write even such another letter to-morrow? And when John shall feel the left hand of the Thracian gripping his hair and the Thracian scimitar (may it be accursed!) hacking at his neck, will he not then cry unto the Lord in his sore agony and say, 'Jesus of Nazareth hath forsaken me: Jesus of Nazareth is guilty of my blood'? For this cause do we Galileans begin no more to trust your Master, because he speaketh many fair words, but we see not from him any doing of deeds."

His words so troubled me that I knew not what to say; Nathanael also was silent. But I besought Barabbas to trust in Jesus because of his mighty works, and because of his Gospel, which surely was a message from God. "Certainly," I began, "Jesus of Nazareth will not suffer the Prophet to die as a dog dieth." But, even while I spake, it came into my mind that the ways of Jesus were not as the ways of other men; neither could I foretell what Jesus would do, or not do, save only I knew that he would do right. So I paused, and added, "or, if otherwise—" But Barabbas, at that word "if," brake away from us, and was departing in fury. Howbeit, remembering himself, he returned and constrained himself, and courteously besought us to tarry with him that night. But we could not; for we were to pass on to another town, and not to tarry at Jotapata. So we bade him farewell.

As we journeyed eastward, I looked back now and then to the high rock whereon the tower of Jotapata is built: for it was exceeding high, being indeed one of the fire-stations whence the new moon was wont to be proclaimed. And as the sun was now sinking towards the west behind the rock, the castle seemed to stand up very clear, and easy to be seen against the red sky. But as often as I looked thereat, the words of Barabbas would come again and again into my mind; and there rose up before me the black castle of Machaerus and the face of the prophet shut up in chains and darkness, and waiting for a deliverer. Then it seemed to me that the shadows of evil were encompassing our own Master also. For the Pharisees had set their faces against him; and though he had avoided their first snares, yet I knew full well that they were even now making others ready. Yea, Eliezer himself had confessed as much; for he had said in his letter to Jonathan that, if other means failed, it was purposed to deliver Jesus over to Herod. And now behold, the Galileans also were like to sever themselves from Jesus and to desert him. So all things seemed full of danger, and there appeared no path of deliverance.

In my dejection there came one upon another into my mind all the dark sayings of Jesus, and especially the words which he had spoken to us in the house of Matthew the tax-gatherer, that "The days should come when the bridegroom should be taken away from the children of the bride chamber, and then should they fast in those days." So I marvelled and pondered what those words might mean, "the bridegroom should be taken away." But they were too deep for me to understand, and I was as one wading in them and out of my depth; nor could I light upon anything solid in them save only this, that they appeared to prophesy some evil.

CHAPTER XIV

How John the Prophet doubted concerning Jesus; and concerning them that are "born of Women;" and of the Beheading of John the Prophet.

ON the third or fourth day after that we had seen Barabbas, we came to Bethsaida. And behold, as Jesus was exhorting the people, there came into the synagogue two disciples of John the Prophet. And the principal Scribe of the place brought the men in, saying that they had a message from the Prophet to Jesus of Nazareth. Then all men held their peace and expected what the message should be; and I remembered the words of Barabbas concerning John, and my mind presaged that the prophet had sent to bid Jesus release him. But the Scribe (for he knew what the message was, and desired to discredit Jesus) said aloud that the message was a strange one, not fit for the ear of the common multitude; therefore it should be reserved for the ear of Jesus alone. But all the people listened the more intently; and Jesus gave command that the messengers should deliver their message aloud, and they did so. Now the words of the message were these, "John the Prophet hath sent us to thee from the prison of

Herod, saying, 'Art thou he that should come, or must we look for another?'"

When we heard these words we all looked that Jesus should either rebuke the Prophet for his want of faith, or else make some comfortable answer, saying that he would come with speed and deliver the Prophet from his bonds. Howbeit Jesus made no answer, but continued his exhortation; and he drove out certain unclean spirits, and forgave sins. But when he had ended these things, he called to the disciples of John, and he repeated to them those passages of the prophets which describe the signs of Redemption, and in particular the prophecy of Isaiah: how the ears of the deaf shall be unstopped to hear the tidings of Redemption, and the eyes of the blind shall be opened to discern the truth of the Lord; and the lame man shall leap as a hart in the paths of salvation; and the tongue of the dumb shall sing the praises of the Lord. And he said unto the two messengers, "Go and show John the things which ye do hear and see: the blind receive their sight, and the lame walk; the lepers are cleansed, and the deaf hear; the dead are raised up, and the poor have the gospel preached to them." Then he added these words, "Blessed is he who shall not be offended in me."

When the messengers were departed, Jesus spake to the people concerning John, saying that John (howbeit he might have changed and fallen from his first estate, seeming to be, for the time, unstable as a reed or pliant as a courtier) was, none the less, truly a prophet, yea, and the greatest of prophets, inasmuch as he was sent by God as the herald of the Redeemer. Then he added thereto a certain saying which filled us all with amazement: yea, and even now after forty years, though I be enlightened with the Holy Spirit, yet can I not choose but be amazed thereat. For the words were these: "Verily I say unto you, among them that are born of women, there hath not risen a greater than John the Baptist: notwithstanding he that is least in the Kingdom of Heaven is greater than he."

When the congregation brake up, many of the people said among themselves that this was an hard saying. Others asked what Jesus meant by dividing them that were "born of women" from them that are in the Kingdom of Heaven; and whether the former meant the living and the latter meant the dead. Now I understood (for Nathanael had instructed me) that Jesus put a difference between them which are born of flesh and blood, and them which are born of the Spirit; wherefore I partly perceived the meaning of his saying, namely, that the kingdom of the Law and of the Prophets now had an end, and that the kingdom of the Spirit of God was at hand; and that the greatest in the former kingdom was less than the least in the latter. Likewise I understood Jesus to say that the sending of this message and the moving of Jesus to take up the arms of the flesh argued in John a certain nature of flesh; as if he thereby showed himself to be born not of the New Kingdom, but of the Old Kingdom of flesh and blood, albeit the greatest therein. Yet for all this, that such an one as Jesus of Nazareth, whose gentleness and meekness (albeit mixed at all times with a certain royal carriage and demeanour) for the most part exceeded the meekness of a little child, should notwithstanding seem to rate so low the greatest of all the prophets of Israel, and exalt so high the meanest of all the citizens in the Kingdom that was to come (which also seemed perforce to include a certain magnifying of himself as being chief in that Kingdom); this, I say, for all my poising and pondering, still perplexed and distracted my mind, as a thing new and strange, and (I had almost said) monstrous to human reason.

I desired to question Nathanael the son of Zebedee concerning these things; but I could not. For having noted the face of one of my mother's household in the congregation, and fearing lest he might have some message touching my mother's health, I hasted to seek the man out: and it proved even as I feared, for my mother was indeed sick, and had sent, desiring that I would come to see her. Therefore I went to Jesus at once, and besought him that he would suffer me to go to my mother. As I went to Jesus, I met Eliezer the son of Arak, and would have passed him. But he, noting that I was somewhat moved, stayed me, and having questioned me, he said, "If thou art wise, thou wilt not go to Jesus: for but now, he forbade one of his disciples to bid farewell to his parents, and another he would not so much as suffer to bury the dead body of his father. For he rageth like a young lion taken in the net of the hunter; and whoso leaveth his side, though it be for an hour, seemeth to him a traitor. Be persuaded, therefore, and quit this Jesus of Nazareth, and his rabble of sinners, and come unto the side of the learned, and thou shalt have eminence among us."

Now I could not indeed deny that Jesus had forbidden certain of his disciples to leave him; but he had done it for their advantage, and because he knew that it would have been ill for them to leave him.

Therefore I answered Eliezer with the same proverb which the ruler of the synagogue had said to Jesus, that it was better to be the tail of the lion than the head of the fox; and so I left him. For he spake out of a malignant heart, and not because he loved me. Moreover, I knew that if Jesus should say, Go not, it would be well said; for I trusted him in all things.

I found Jesus surrounded by many disciples, who had been asking him questions concerning John the Prophet, and concerning the manner of his deliverance. For all we at that time were assured in our minds that John would be delivered: for men counted John the son of Zachariah and Jesus of Nazareth as yoke-fellows in Israel, and the safety of one seemed to depend on the safety of the other, and the salvation of Israel on both. And indeed I myself have often marvelled that Jesus was not moved to adventure to deliver John. But, as I judge, he rejected all such motions as temptations of Satan, because he knew that he had not been sent to smite with the sword but only with the breath of his mouth. Wherefore, if he were tempted at all, it was rather, as I suppose, that he should die with John than that he should fight that John might live. And at this time, methinks, it came into his mind that if indeed it was ordained that John the Prophet should be slain, and perchance he himself also, then was it high time that new labourers should be sent into the harvest of the Lord, to take the places of them that were to pass away. Howbeit, concerning these things I can but conjecture; but, as I remember, when I came to Jesus, he was looking at the young corn in the fields around very intently, and as if he espied in the sight more than others could see. Presently he said to them which sat next to him, "Say ye not, There are yet four months and then cometh the harvest? Behold, I say unto you, Lift up your eyes, and look on the fields, for they are white already to harvest. And he that reapeth receiveth wages and gathereth fruit unto life eternal; that both he that soweth and he that reapeth may rejoice together." Then Judas said to them which sat nigh unto him, that these words signified that John should be delivered at once, and that a levy was to be made throughout all Galilee: and he added aloud, looking to Jesus, that, "The reapers were ready," or words to that effect. But Jesus answered and said, "The harvest truly is plenteous, but the labourers are few: pray ye therefore the Lord of the harvest, that he will send forth labourers into his harvest."

Then I spake to Jesus and told him that I desired to go and see my mother. But I thought perchance that he would have restrained me, if it were so indeed that a levy was to be made throughout all Galilee. But he restrained me not, but bade me go in peace and blessed me, and spake comfortable words to me; and wished me to comfort my mother.

On the next day I came to Sepphoris, and behold my mother was grievously sick and nigh unto death. But when I took her by the hand and delivered to her the message of Jesus, saying that he bade her be of good cheer, even in that instant her strength came back to her, and her disease abated; and on the fourth day it departed, so that she rose from her bed. But when the day came that I should depart, so it was that my mother desired me to go first to Tiberias, there to collect certain debts which were owing to her now many days. To this I agreed, nothing loth, for it seemed to me that by passing through Tiberias to Capernaum I might bring unto Jesus the newest tidings touching the doings of Herod, and perchance also touching the state of John the Prophet. For there were certain of mine acquaintance in the house of Chuza, the king's steward, who lived in Tiberias nigh unto the royal palace. So I set out for Tiberias first. But when I reached the city, it being now about the tenth hour of the day, I found the people gathered together in the Greek quarter by twos and by threes in the streets; and in our part of the city, instead of rejoicings (which I had expected, because the Feast of Purim was at this time), there were everywhere signs of lamentation and mourning. So I saluted one of them that passed by, and asked him what these things might mean. But he glanced at my mule (which I had borrowed, for more speed, of a Greek in Sepphoris; for not many in Galilee, except Gentiles, use to ride on mules), and he said, "I perceive that thou art but a sojourner here, else wouldst thou surely have known these tidings which are in the mouths of all the people, since the eighth hour of the day, touching John the Prophet." Then I said, "What tidings?" He answered "That he is dead, slain with the sword; and they say that his head hath been given to Herodias on a charger. But why speak I of things that concern me not?" So saying he looked at me, as I had been a spy (for the spies of Herod were everywhere in Galilee at this time, and most of all in Tiberias); and so he passed on.

Straightway I hasted on to come to the Greek quarter, seeking the house of Chuza. But on my way thither I passed the royal palace; and at the gate thereof were certain of the Thracian guard keeping watch. Now as I passed them, one of the soldiers called to his companion and said, "But wherefore dost thou keep guard to-day?" And the other said, "I keep guard in the place of Thrasymachus who is gone with three centuries to Capernaum." "And wherefore to Capernaum?" said the first. "There is like to be a tumult in the town," replied the sentinel, "because of the beheading of this John in Machaerus; and they say that the rabble will set some leader at their head, who is to be arrested." "Nay," said the other, "and sayest thou arrested? I would have no arresting, but make quick despatch with these leaders of the rabble. But hath Herod heard of this leader?" "Not so," said the other, "for he is busy in the south with the army; but our general meaneth to take order that Herod shall never hear of him." With that he laughed, and made a sign to signify beheading, drawing his hand across his throat; then he bade his fellow go carry some message for him, for he should be busy that day; "For," said he, "the cohort hath not been gone one full hour yet, and will not be here again these six hours or more, for they mean not to take him by force publicly, but will arrest the man quietly at nightfall."

When I heard these things, my spirit fainted, and there was no strength in me; but when I came to myself, it seemed best to journey forwards at once to Capernaum if perchance I might prevent the coming of the Thracian guard and give the alarm to Jesus.

So I turned the mule's head straightway toward the city gate, and rode on the way that leadeth to Capernaum. But she was sore wearied by reason of the length of the journey, and could scarce carry me. Howbeit after the space of an hour's riding I came up with the rear of the Thracians: but I perceived that I could not pass them. For a certain merchant riding on a fresh mule had passed out from the city gate before me, and behold, they had stayed him, and suffered him not to pass; but he rode behind with the rear. Now when I saw this, I smote my hands together, for I saw that I could be of no avail to my Master. And by this time the houses of Capernaum, that is to say the quay and the houses near the quay, were in sight, and not far off. For one headland only remained between us and the headland whereon the town standeth; and when the Thracians should have passed round that first headland, there were but six furlongs between them and the market-place of Capernaum. But the sun was now nigh setting and the barbarians began to quicken their pace.

Therefore I cried unto the Lord in sore distress and left my mule and climbed up to a rock whence I could watch what befell, and there I offered up prayers to the All-Powerful, who alone is able to save.

Now behold, by this time the Thracians had passed round the first headland, and the last of them were out of my sight, so that I could see nothing but the quay of Capernaum and two or three fishing-boats riding at anchor just off the quay: and there seemed no signs of tumult; for there was no man stirring there. And presently began the helmets of the Thracians to shine again before mine eyes as their front guard drew near unto the town, and still no man perceived them; for the cliff lay between them and the town, and there were still none save two or three sailors on the quay. Then I took off the covering from my head and waved it in the air that the sailors perchance might take note of it: but they took no note.

Now by this time there was but about a space of two furlongs between the front of the column of the Thracians and the quay of Capernaum, and I could hear the captain give the word of command (albeit not in a loud voice) to hasten their march that they might enter the town the more quickly (for darkness was now falling upon the lake); and as the word of command sounded across the water even to my ears in the stillness of the evening, behold, the Thracians hastened their march so that they began to run. Now I held my breath, for I could not so much as pray for very trouble; when lo, a great noise of shouting from the other side of the headland, even from Capernaum; and at the same time a great concourse of people upon the quay, and immediately a long galley appeared, which rowed forth very swiftly toward the eastward side of the lake. Then the barbarians halted, even without the word of command; for they knew that the bird was escaped from the snare of the fowlers: and the noise of their cursing and clamour came up even unto mine ears as I sat upon, my place of watching. But I glorified the God of Israel; and gave thanks to Him whose mercy endureth for ever.

CHAPTER XV.

How Jesus fled from Capernaum, and the Galileans at first fell away from him; and concerning the Levy in Galilee; and of the Visit of Jesus to Nazareth.

WHEN I came into Capernaum, I thought to have heard all men rejoicing for that Jesus had not been taken by the Thracians. But, go where I might, I found it quite contrary; for all men were wroth with him for departing. Barabbas was there, and James the son of Judas of Galilee, and many others of the Galilean sect; but I could not have much speech with them, so hot was their anger against Jesus; but on the morrow, lighting upon my cousin Baruch, I questioned him touching that which had happened, and he said that "the Prophet had turned from him all the hearts of the Galileans because he would not raise up Israel to avenge the death of John." Then I asked how soon they had received tidings of John's death, and he said "Yesterday a little before sunset." I marvelled how the news should have been brought past the Thracians; for, said I, "they stayed all travellers from Tiberias, neither suffered they any to pass them." But Baruch said that James the son of Judas had contrived that lights should be held up each night from Gamala on the other side of the lake, to the intent that the Galileans in Capernaum might know how John fared; and one light should signify that the Prophet lived, but two lights that he lived not. "And," said Baruch, "yestereven before the sun went down, many of the Galileans had gathered together by twos or by threes upon the strand to watch for the signal. And first one light appeared, as was usual; and the men said that it was well, for they had one more day wherein to labour for the Prophet's deliverance. But then Barabbas cried out that there were two lights; and at first no man would believe it, for (because the sun had not yet set) the lights were not plain to see. But presently Judas also saw the second light, and then they all saw it. Hereupon arose a loud lamentation, and the news spread at once through all the city, and the women began to wail, and the men rushed forth into the streets, and there was a great gathering. Presently with one consent the multitude ran together to the door of the house where Jesus lodged; and first Barabbas went in to ask Jesus to be leader of the host, but soon he came forth again, saying that Jesus would not. Then went in James the son of Judas, saying that he would beseech Jesus in the name of his father, who had fought and died for Israel. With James there went in also three others of the eldest and most reverend of the Galileans, and they remained in the house longer, so that the people thought they had prevailed upon Jesus; and there was a great expectation. But when the elders came out, they showed by their countenances that they had not prevailed.

Then there was much clamour; and the greater part cried out that they would not depart from before the threshold of Jesus till they had persuaded Jesus to be leader of the host; and some cried out to draw him forth by violence and to make him leader of the host. But immediately the door opened, and Jesus himself came forth. Then they no more talked of violence; but Barabbas and others of the armed men held out their right hands to him, and promised to give up their lives for his sake if he would be their king. Others fell down on their knees before him; and some caught him by the garment to have stayed him. Only James the son of Judas said nothing; "and it seemed to me," said Baruch, "that at the sight of James, Jesus was more moved than by all the rest. Howbeit he halted not, but moved straight down to the beach.

"Then when the people perceived that he would leave them, they cried out even louder than before, and threw dust in the air and poured it upon their heads; and some threw themselves on the ground in his path for to stay him; and some also spared not threatening. But Jesus took no heed thereof, but went still onward with his eyes fast set upon the ground; till one thrust himself before the rest, crying aloud and saying that they would do more for John dead than for Jesus living, and that it was better for a man to lose his life, as John the Prophet had lost it, than to save his life as Jesus desired to save it. Thereat Jesus stayed for an instant, and lifted his eyes from the ground; howbeit not in anger, but rather as he is wont to do (for thou well knowest his manner) whensoever he heareth a Voice of God. But when all the people shouted again, supposing that he had been bent from his purpose, then Jesus beckoned with the hand, and when he had commanded silence, he spake briefly unto them, and said the hour was not yet come; and so he departed.

"Now," said Baruch, "while Jesus was speaking to the people, and even afterwards while he was in the sight of the people, it was a marvellous thing to see how still they were; for he hath a power over the hearts of the people so that when he is present no one dare move his tongue against him. But as soon as the boat had rowed away and they could see him no more, straightway Barabbas and his friends began to curse and swear; and they said that they would never again ask aught of Jesus, nor place any faith in him. James the son of Judas said little, but his mind seemed to be the same. For this cause therefore all the Galileans are incensed against Jesus; insomuch that, whereas they had begun to rate him far above John, they now esteem the memory of John more than the presence of Jesus."

After this, Baruch began to advise me to sever myself from Jesus and to return to my home at Sepphoris, for, said he, "He hath the Pharisees for his enemies; and the richer sort are also estranged from him; and it is commonly reported that Herod the Tetrarch seeketh to slay him with the sword; and now behold, even the Galileans are turned away from him. Now therefore be persuaded, and come back with me to the house of my father Manasseh, and tarry with us for the night, and refresh thyself, and on the morrow set forth for thy home."

But I made him some fair answer and bade him farewell; for I had determined with myself to take ship that same night, to have sailed over to the other side. But on the morrow, I thought it good (albeit perchance I erred therein) to return first to my mother and to relate to her all that had come to pass, and to bid her farewell: for all men now accounted of Jesus as of one that must either fight or perish: for it could not be that he should live and be honoured of men, and yet not avenge the death of John the Prophet. Wherefore, before I joined myself to a cause that seemed so full of peril, I desired to take leave of my mother.

On the fourth day after I was come to Sepphoris, word was brought that Jesus of Nazareth was gathering the people for battle, and that he was making a levy throughout all Galilee, and for this intent had chosen out twelve of his disciples, whom also he called Apostles; and these he had sent out by two and two through the several villages and towns. Jonathan the son of Ezra brought me these tidings; and I was with him next day, walking on the road between Sepphoris and Capernaum, when we met Simon Peter and Andrew.

They told us that they had been sent forth by Jesus to proclaim the Kingdom of Heaven, and to drive out unclean spirits, and to heal diseases. They came without wallet, or food, or money, trusting to the alms of the people. But when we questioned them as to the Kingdom, and whether indeed it was to be achieved by force of arms (as the rumour went), or by signs such as fire from heaven and the like: concerning this they knew nothing. As for the healing of diseases, we saw with our own eyes that they had this power; for they healed certain that were sick in Sepphoris, and even cast out three or four unclean spirits.

When we had bidden farewell to Simon Peter and Andrew (for they were in haste, passing from place to place like messengers of war) then Jonathan turned to me and said, "Whoso pulleth down his old house and doth not first build for himself a new one, is he wise?" I replied, "Nay." Then said Jonathan, "Lo, Jesus of Nazareth pulleth down the house of the Law; tell me therefore, what buildeth he in the place thereof?" I was silent, for I knew not what to answer; but at last

I said that Jesus spake of a certain new Spirit which would purify the children of men and enable them to attain righteousness without the Law. But Jonathan said, "Nay but, my son, can a Spirit tell each man of the children of men, from day to day, what meat he shall eat and what he shall not eat; and when to fast and when to feast; and what to do on the Sabbath day, and what not to do? Now if the Spirit shall tell each man different things, shall there not be a confusion as of Babel? But if the same things, then why should not these things be written in a law? Moreover who shall tell which man hath the Spirit and which hath not? For all will say they have it." Then I said that I could not answer those questions, but that I trusted in Jesus of Nazareth as in one sent from God, who could not deceive, neither be deceived, for that his deeds and words were those of a prophet. After this manner I answered; but Jonathan said nothing, but only shook his head a little, as one that doubted more than he hoped.

Now on the third day after this discourse (it being, as I remember, the month called Adar, a little after the Feast of Purim), my mother being now completely recovered of her disease, I determined to return to Jesus. For tidings came in daily that all Galilee was ready to rise up when he gave the sign, and I was unwilling to show myself a laggard if matters should come to smiting with the sword. But every day I heard that Jesus was more and more beloved of the people. For all (save only the Pharisees) were now drawn towards him, in that he seemed to be bent upon avenging John the Prophet. And his fame began to be noised abroad through all the country of Galilee and the parts beyond, insomuch that many that had not heard of him before, began to cast in their minds what he could be. And some said that he was Elias. For the common folk, yea, and the Scribes also, were ever expecting that Elias should be sent down to earth, according to the saying of the prophet Malachi. But others said that he was John the Baptist risen from the dead; and this saying was commonly reported, especially among the Gentiles which border on the land of Galilee and in Decapolis, insomuch that Herod himself heard of the rumour, and feared lest it might be even so. But whatsoever men reported about Jesus, in any case his fame waxed very great at this time. For before John was beheaded, the fame of John prevailed over the fame of Jesus in the minds of many; but now all alike, even the disciples of John, looked to Jesus as the avenger of John and as the only Deliverer; insomuch that, at this time, Jesus had both his own fame and also the fame of John the Prophet.

I found Jesus in a village about seven miles to the north of Galilee. But when I had saluted him, I noted that he was marvellously changed; yet not so that he was austere, nor even very sad; yet still changed withal, albeit I knew not how nor why. But I had expected that he should have rebuked me for that I had been so long absent, neither had I come to him with all speed so as to be present when first he made the levy in Galilee. Howbeit, he reproved me not; but questioned me kindly touching my mother's health, and rejoiced when I gave him a good report: but afterwards he gave himself again to meditation. When I was come forth from his presence, I asked the disciples concerning the state of Galilee, and what number of men were ready to fight on our side, and when the levy should be made, and the hour for battle should be at hand. But the rest were silent, and Judas alone made answer, that concerning these things the disciples knew nothing; yea, and from certain signs he conjectured that even to Jesus himself the hour of uprising was not yet known, no, nor yet the manner of it, nor the means for it.

"But," said I, "did not the people in Galilee receive you when ye went forth to proclaim the Redemption?" "Yes truly did they," said Judas, "but all of the baser sort, and the poor folk which have naught of their own; wherefore they be always ready for warfare." "And what answer made Jesus to your report?" asked I. "Truly a marvellous answer," replied Judas, "for when we said that only the poor and simple folk received us, he rejoiced thereat, and thanked God that it was even so." "Nay," said I, "that were hard to believe." "But yea," said Judas; "for his words were these, that he thanked the Father, because He had hidden these things from the wise and the prudent, and revealed them unto babes." Then I looked at Nathanael to know whether it was even so, and Nathanael nodded his head, as if to say that it was so.

But Judas continued: "This also is not the worst. For he hath not only turned from him the Galileans; but besides, since our flight, whereas there is special need to be busy and striving, behold, these ten days, he museth and meditateth, and ceaseth not. Neither are his musings, touching war, nor vengeance, nor military matters; but he broodeth over prophesyings and abstruse matters. And a stranger might go near to think that he had conceived an imagination that, because the Lord hath suffered John the son of Zachariah to die, therefore he must needs die also. But unless he be speedily raised up from this humour of dejection, all is lost."

He said no more at this time, for Jesus came forth into the courtyard where we sat together around the fountain; and straightway we held our peace. Then we fell to discourse of John the son of Zachariah, how great things he had prophesied, and how we had hoped that he should have triumphed with us in the Kingdom of God; and one likened John unto Elias the prophet, saying that he spake in the spirit of Elias, and that many of the common people would have it that this John was indeed Elias risen from the dead. Then another spake of the love in which the disciples of John the son of Zachariah still had their Master, and how, though he were dead, yet did they still cleave to him in their hearts; insomuch that his spirit seemed to rule over them yet more than his living presence. But another said that John the Prophet could not be Elias: for was it possible that the Lord should suffer such an one as Elias to be slain? And to him Nathanael replied that Isaiah the Prophet was sawn asunder, and wherefore not also Elias? Then Thomas, one of the Twelve, lamented for John the son of Zachariah, because he had been thus swallowed up by destruction, neither had he left children to stand in his stead upon the earth; "for they that die, leaving children behind them," said he (quoting a certain proverb of my countrymen) "die not, but only fall asleep: but they that die and leave no children, these die indeed." To this John the son of Zebedee made answer that whoso leaveth behind him children perverse and alien from his own nature, he liveth not, for all his children; but whoso leaveth behind him disciples and followers like unto himself and imbued with his own doctrine, such an one liveth, yea even though he be childless and lie in the grave. Hereat methought Jesus was strangely moved: howbeit he sat still where he was, and spake never a word.

But presently mention was made of Jonah the Prophet, how that he also was an exile and fled from his country, even as our Master had been forced to flee. Then Judas said that Jonah had done ill to flee, for that none could flee from the presence of the All-seeing, the Maker of all things, "for," said he, "the son of man, while he liveth, is like unto a horse tethered by a cord which suffereth him to graze, but resteth still in the hand of his owner." Thereon some one took up the discourse and said, "Nay, but rather the cord is a cord of love, and the owner is not an owner, but a father; "and another disciple quoted the words of the psalmist, "By thee have I been holden up from the womb." Thereat Jesus smiled as if to say that that disciple had spoken well, and he bade John repeat the rest of that same psalm. But when

John came, in his repeating, to the words, "o God, Thou hast taught me from my youth: and hitherto have I declared thy wondrous works," then did Jesus seem somewhat moved. But afterwards when John came unto the words, "Thou, which hast showed me great and sore troubles, shalt give me life again, and shalt bring me up again from the depths of the earth;" then indeed the face of Jesus kindled with a marvellous light, and he bade John cease. But he himself sat, still musing, and his lips moved like unto one repeating the same words over and over again: "Thou shalt bring me up again from the depths of the earth."

It came to pass that, about two or three weeks after these things we came to Nazareth, where Jesus was born. Now Jesus had not gone to the place these many days. Some said that he came thither now for to show unto his mother and his brethren (for his father had been long since dead) that he was sound in health and not possessed nor distraught. Others said that he desired to cause his brethren to believe in him; for at this time they believed not. But others said that he desired to bid farewell to his mother before he went forth to deliver Israel; and to this most people agreed.

But when we came to Nazareth, we marvelled that there was so little faith in the men of that place. For they thronged us, as in the other towns, and they were fain to look on Jesus, and called him by familiar names (some being playmates and school fellows, some his kinsfolk, and almost all of the number of his acquaintances); moreover they were eager that he should do some mighty work before their eyes; yet could they not believe that he was a prophet, much less that he was the Redeemer of Israel. Neither would they believe that he could drive out evil spirits or heal diseases.

Hence it came to pass that Jesus could do no mighty work there. And when they brought unto him many that were sick, and possessed with evil spirits, he looked on them, but perceived that they had not faith to be healed. Wherefore he healed none of them; save only that he laid his hands on a few that were sick of slight diseases and healed them, and even these not without labour. For the same things happened as once in another city, where a man was healed that had been afflicted with a deaf and dumb spirit. For there, because of the man's want of understanding and lack of faith, Jesus took him apart from the people (for there was a great stir of traffic and of men coming and going), and made signs to him, at the same time touching his ears and his tongue; and he also spake very loud in the man's ears, not in Greek, but in the language of the Jews (which is used by the poorer people), saying *Ephphatha*. In this way the man was healed, but only with labour and by degrees. And so it was now, but even worse. Wherefore Jesus himself marvelled at their unbelief.

Now the cause of their unbelief was that they knew him from a child. For, said one of them to Jesus himself in my hearing, "Behold, these thirty years we have known thy goings out and thy comings in; we have also sat by thy side in the school, and whatsoever thou didst learn we also learned; thou didst play with us at our games round the well; we have seen thee a-working in thy father's house; our couches and our seats are made by thy hand; and shall we call thee the Redeemer of Israel?" Moreover another bade him come back to the carpenter's shop; and a third cried out that he had changed trades for the worse, for the Redemption of Israel was a dangerous trade. All these were moved by jealousy, and spake out of the malignity of their hearts.

But a certain old Scribe, Josiah the son of Hezekiah, (which also was the chief Scribe of the place, and had known Jesus and loved him of a child) coming forth from his house, met him and fell upon his neck, and blessed him, and embraced him; and then, when he had looked more narrowly at his countenance, he began to mourn over him as if he were his own son, lamenting for that the bloom of beauty had departed from the countenance of Jesus: "for behold," said he, "sorrow hath driven out the former brightness of thy joy. Thou wast as the dew of the morning, my lamb, but art become as the parched ground at noontide. Behold, my lamb, around thy cradle mercy and righteousness joined hands together; and when thou didst sport amid this valley, lo, truth and peace went ever with thee, and thou didst still hold converse with the angels of God? Unfit art thou, my gentle one, to do battle with the wickedness of wicked men, and with the cunning arts of the adversary. Verily thou wilt be led as a lamb to the slaughter. Hast thou fathomed the depth of the pit of destruction? Or dost thou know by experience the snares of deceit? Return, thou that art the apple of mine eye, while there is yet time, lest evil befall thee. For I know that danger compasseth thee around, and if thou shalt go hence, thou wilt come back to me no more."

Jesus spake comfortably to the old man and consoled him; and while he consoled him, his face shone with joy and love; insomuch that the old man also rejoiced, saying that Jesus appeared now again as he appeared in the days of his youth. But still he besought Jesus to return and to avoid contention with the Pharisees, saying that "no vessel but peace can hold blessing."

But Jesus answered him kindly and bade him farewell. And so we departed from Nazareth.

When we were now come to the top of the hill which looketh down on Nazareth, we rested a little to recover our breath. Now Jesus was sorrowful because of the unbelief of his kinsfolk and acquaintance, and he was silent (as was his wont when sorrow fell upon him), musing and meditating, and, as it seemed to me, praying; even as one striving to unloose the knot of some hard saying or riddle. For the unbelief of his kinsfolk had filled him with astonishment. While he thus mused, we conversed together, and Judas said that it was an error to have come to Nazareth. "For who knoweth not," said he, "that a prophet hath no honour in his own country? For a prophet known is a prophet despised."

But John the son of Zebedee replied that it was a strange thing that the acquaintance and kinsfolk of Jesus should suppose that they knew the mind and spirit of Jesus because they knew his outward shape and mien and manner of speech: "For his mind and spirit pass knowledge; and the more a man knoweth thereof, the more a man must needs wonder thereat." So spake John; but Judas jested at him, and said that John spake as a babe and as a simple clown, knowing nothing of the world. "Yet," added he, looking up at Jesus, "it is strange me thinks that even our Master should also wonder at that which is in no way wonderful." Then John rebuked him and said, "Knowest thou not the saying of our Master, 'They that wonder shall reign, and they that reign shall rest?' Wherefore who knoweth whether it may not be that even our Master day by day learneth some new revelation from God whereat to wonder? For whoso increaseth not diminisheth."

When I heard these words I looked at Jesus, and behold, it was even as John said. For the sorrow that rested upon his countenance because of the unbelief of his kinsfolk seemed to be passing away, and to be revealing beneath it an exceeding joy, as of one learning some hidden mystery, or hearing some glad tidings. And there came into my mind the words of Barabbas (which were contrary to the words of John), how he said that Jesus did everything with forethought; and behold, both the words of John seemed true and also the words of Barabbas; but the words of John seemed the truer. For though Jesus did naught in haste nor in fear nor perturbation; yet was he not like unto one that seeth all things to come, great and small alike, marked out for him as in a chart, nor like unto him which trusteth in the strength of his own unchangeable will. Nay rather, even as a little child hangeth upon the bosom of his mother and hath no will of his own, even so did Jesus continually look upon earth and heaven and on the deeds and words of men; and, look where he might, he discerned in all things some new knowledge, some revelation concerning the will of the Father in heaven; insomuch that no day passed, yea no hour of the day, but Jesus in this wise held communion with his Father.

By this time Jesus was arisen from his seat, and we ceased conversing together when he drew nigh. But Judas, desirous to say somewhat (so as to hide what he had been saying), pointed down to the white houses of Nazareth and to the fields and orchards which compass the city round in the bottom of the valley; and he said to Jesus that the place was exceeding beautiful, like unto a handful of pearls in a goblet of emerald. But Jesus looked narrowly at Judas for an instant, and then down at Nazareth, and then at Judas again; and the sounds of the bleating of the goats and the piping of the shepherds came up to our ears, and the laughter of the children as they sported round the well. When Jesus heard these things, he sighed, and cast his eyes down again on Nazareth, even on the place of his nativity; and he looked at it for a long while very lovingly. Then he turned away his head and departed, and he saw it no more.

CHAPTER XVI

How, after the Death of John the Prophet, Jesus foresaw that he also must be slain: and of the Bread of Life, and the Feeding of the Five Thousand; and concerning the Leaven of the Pharisees and Sadducees.

Now so it was that, at this time, the more the hearts of the people were drawn toward Jesus (for though the people of Nazareth had rejected him, yet was he much honoured in the rest of Galilee), so much the more did Jesus seem to thrust them away. For he began to teach us at this time that he should give us no new law, but a certain manna or bread from heaven. Now if he had said no more than this,

this was not hard to understand; for our Scribes also taught in parables after this fashion: but he added that this manna or bread from heaven should be himself, his flesh and his blood, which should be given for the life of the world. Now albeit I have myself heard the Scribes speak of "the days when Israel shall eat the Messiah," [1] meaning that Israel shall enjoy the presence of the Messiah, yet Jesus seemed to mean somewhat more than this, insomuch that his words were a stumbling-block unto many. And straightway many of them departed from him.

But when I went (according to my wont) to question Nathanael touching these words, he replied that they were hidden from him also. Notwithstanding it seemed to him that at this time our Master was receiving some new revelation, whereof these words might peradventure be a part. For he said that on the day before, when I had been absent, mention had been made of the coming Passover, and how Jesus would not be present thereat; and from mentioning the sacrifice of the Passover they came to speak of other sacrifices; and one said that Jesus had come to take away sacrifice, for that he had said that God desired mercy, and not sacrifice, and that the right sacrifice was that the whole nation should serve the Lord and do His will. Then another, quoting the Scripture, said, "Nay, but the people may perchance stand in the place of the fuel and the fire: but where is the lamb for the burnt-offering?" Then answered another from the same Scripture, and said, "God will provide himself a lamb for the burnt- offering." And at these words, said John, "the countenance of Jesus changed as if he had heard some new word from God." Hereat I marvelled greatly, and wondered what new thing the Lord was preparing for us and for our Master. And the words of Judas came to my mind that, because John the son of Zachariah had been slain, therefore Jesus had begun to imagine that he also must needs be slain. But it was but for an instant; for I durst not so much as entertain the thought of so great an evil.

But, as I now judge, the Lord Jesus began at this time to see clearly that he must needs die for Israel, even as John the son of Zachariah had died, and that he must needs rise again (according to the Prophets); even as the common people spake, saying that John the Baptist was at this very time risen from the dead. For he perceived that the needs of the world, that is to say the will of the Father, required that he should rise again from the dead. Moreover as John the son of Zachariah had gained strength through death, so that all men still loved and honoured John, and were more ready to die for him dead than living; even so Jesus perceived that he also should have more strength to help us after his death than before his death. But touching the manner of his rising again, and the time of it, and whether he should appear in his own shape (as he did indeed), or in some other shape (as did Elias in the shape of John the Baptist), concerning all this, what was revealed unto him I know not; the Lord only knoweth. But that he should of a certainty rise again from the dead, this was without doubt revealed unto him; and, as I conceive, about this time.

For this cause, because he perceived that by the giving of his body and blood to die for men, his spirit would pass into his disciples (even as the spirit of John the son of Zachariah had passed into the disciples of John), for this cause, I say, he spake at this time (as he did also afterwards), saying that he would give himself to be the food of men, even the Bread of Life. For his spirit was a spirit of sonship to God, and of brotherhood to men; and except the world should receive this spirit into itself, the world could not be quickened, and the nations of the earth could not pass into the family or kingdom of God.

From this time also he began to be very careful, even to disquietude, concerning us his disciples, what should be our estate when he should have departed from us; and he desired to impart to us this Bread of Life that we also in turn might impart it to the multitude. Moreover he would fain exercise us already in imparting this Bread of Life, yea, before be had passed away; to the end that, by beginning in his presence, we might learn by degrees to be steadfast in the ministering of the Bread even though he were absent from us. And for this he found occasion not many days afterwards. For about the tenth day before the Passover, Jesus being still on the other side of the lake (but I had been sent with Judas on an errand to Capernaum), it came to pass that much people resorted to him; some from Capernaum, and others from the parts round about the village wherein he had lodged. For, because of the Passover, which was at hand, many were going up to Jerusalem. Also of the Galileans some came; howbeit not James nor Barabbas, nor any of them which had most authority with the Galileans. Now Jesus himself ministered unto certain of them the Bread of Life, and forgave sins, and healed the sick. But afterwards, because of the multitude of them which came unto him (for they were more than five thousand) he caused the disciples to divide them into companies and to minister the Bread unto the people. So they ministered as Jesus bade them, and the grace of the Lord was with them; insomuch that Thomas (who had been at the first loth to minister the Bread, as not being worthy) came afterwards to Jesus saying, "Of a truth the crumbs of thy Banquet which are fallen from the table of the guests do suffice unto them that minister: for the Lord hath increased the Bread of Life within us." So mightily did the Bread of our Master increase in the hands of the Twelve. And Matthew said that Jesus had not only spread a table in the wilderness for the hungry, but that he had also fulfilled his saying, "Give and it shall be given unto you. For," said he, "behold, to each of the disciples there cometh back his basketful of the fragments of the Feast." And the like happened on another occasion, when they ministered the Bread unto another very great multitude— about four thousand in number.

All this I heard when I returned with Judas from Capernaum, bringing word that the Thracians had left the town. So we returned to Capernaum, and there we kept the Passover; for Jesus would not go up to Jerusalem to keep it, though we were very desirous that he should go up; but he said that his hour had not yet come. But scarcely had we been in Capernaum five or six days, and the Feast of the Passover was still not ended, when we fled (upon some new rumour of danger) from Capernaum again to the eastern side of the lake. Now while we were rowing across, some of us murmured (though not so loud methought that Jesus could hear) concerning our many flights and wanderings, and we wondered why our Master would not suffer the common people to make him king.

In the midst of our disputing Jesus called unto us from the hinder part of the boat and said, "Beware of the leaven of the Pharisees and of the leaven of the Sadducees." Then we looked one at another, for we felt that we were guilty; for in the haste of our embarking, because we had come on board before it was well dawn (for fear of the arrival of the Thracians, which was reported to us) we had forgotten to bring with us any unleavened bread; and the feast of the Passover wanted yet two days before it should have an end, and behold, we were going to a Gentile country where our customs were not regarded, so that we could not easily obtain such bread as was needful. Therefore we confessed to Jesus, and said that indeed we were verily guilty of sore neglect.

But when Jesus heard our words, he rebuked us for our want of understanding; and he asked us whether we did not remember how the disciples had ministered the Bread of Life to the four thousand and to the five thousand; and he made mention of the saying of Thomas, one of the Twelve, how the bread had been multiplied in the hands of the Twelve, and also of the saying of Matthew the son of Levi, how the fragments of the Feast had returned to them that ministered, and had satisfied them. So we perceived that he spake not of the leaven that leaveneth bread of corn, but of the leaven which leaveneth and corrupteth the bread of the soul.

Yet forasmuch as the Pharisees agree not with the Sadducees (neither do they teach the same doctrine, nor observe the same customs) I could not understand what this "leaven of the Pharisees and Sadducees" might be. But when I asked Nathanael thereof, he said that perchance Jesus desired to warn us lest we should be led away in our hearts by the desire of this world, and by the haste to be prosperous. "For," said Nathanael, "the Sadducees love place and wealth and ease, and the Pharisees love power with the people, and the salutations of the rich, and the respect of the poor, and the name and reputation for piety; and these sects do both go straight towards their several ends. But, though several in appearance, their ends are really the same. For both the Pharisees and Sadducees serve themselves, and live for their own pleasure. And methinks our Master feareth lest we too in the same way may follow him not out of love and out of faithfulness, but from a desire to be prosperous."

"But are we not," asked I, "to be prosperous in the end?" "Yes, assuredly in the end," replied Nathanael; "but the end may perchance be somewhat farther off than we suppose, and our course may perchance be somewhat slow. For in all works there are two courses, the course of men and the course of God. Now men work visibly and speedily, and with much stir and noise; but the Father in Heaven worketh for the most part invisibly and slowly, and very gently. Now it may be that the slow ways are best. But in any case I begin to perceive that our Master loveth the slow ways best, according to his saying that the Kingdom of Heaven is like unto the wheat, which is sown and watered and resteth long unseen in the earth, and springeth up at last and by degrees, and putteth forth, first the blade, and then the ear and then the full corn; and all this by slow ways, quietly and gently, while the husbandman riseth and sleepeth and goeth in and out, and taketh no heed how great a work the gentle hand of the Lord is working around him."

Thus spake Nathanael, and I gave heed unto his words; for he seemed day by day to grow in the love and knowledge of our Master, and behold, the knowledge of Jesus seemed to bestow upon him knowledge of all spiritual things, so that he was not like the same Nathanael whom I had first known now a year ago. And the other disciples also were greatly changed from their former selves. For we had now been a full year with the Lord Jesus; and it was the sixteenth year of Tiberius Caesar.

CHAPTER XVII

How Xanthias the Alexandrine said that the Philosophy of Jesus aimed at the Taking in of the Gentiles into the Kingdom, and at the Enfranchisement of Slaves; and how he found Fault with Jesus for that he called himself the Son of Man.

BETWEEN the Feast of Passover and the Feast of Weeks I was not much with Jesus; for when I perceived that Jesus was in no instant peril, I returned to Sepphoris for a while, partly by reason of my mother's health, and partly to gather in the harvest. And during this time, when it was perceived that Jesus went not up to the Passover, neither made any levy of the people as had been expected, the Pharisees for a while ceased to lay snares for him: and the common people, though they murmured that he went not up to Jerusalem, nevertheless had him in honour. But the harvest being now over, when I went back to meet Jesus at Capernaum, I found there one of mine acquaintance, a merchant (whom I had known at Alexandria in my uncle's house), a Greek learned in the knowledge of the Greeks. This man was not a proselyte; neither did he in any wise conform himself to the Law of Moses. But he spake of himself, at that time, as a seeker after truth; for he did not join himself to any of the schools of the Gentile philosophers, but chose forth from each whatsoever seemed to him useful or true. He had read our Scriptures, and was greatly given to the study of our psalms and prophecies; and when he had heard me speak of Jesus of Nazareth as being our Messiah, his heart was moved to hear Jesus preach the gospel. So it came to pass, about the first or second Sabbath after the Feast of Weeks, he accompanied me into the synagogue where Jesus was to speak to the people. But as I went, I perceived Abuyah the son of Elishah; and with him were certain of the Sadducees, and some also of the Herodians. And when I saw them, I knew that they had come for no good purpose.

And so it proved. For when we were now assembled in the synagogue, Abuyah came forward and said to Jesus, "Behold, thou art a vessel very full of knowledge, and the people are come together at thy feet for to hear of thee the words of wisdom, according as it is said, 'Powder thyself in the dust of the feet of the wise, and drink their words with thirstiness.' Now therefore, I pray thee, suffer me to ask of thee touching a certain matter." And Jesus said, "Ask." And Abuyah said, "Is it lawful for a man to put away his wife?"

Now when Abuyah spake these words, all the Herodians and Sadducees listened with greedy ears, as though they would devour the words that fell from Jesus, if perchance he should say something against Herod the Tetrarch. For Herod had put away his own wife and had married Herodias, the wife of his brother Herod Philip, which thing was not lawful for him to do. And it was for this cause that Abuyah had asked the question. For the Pharisees considered that in this way they would do one of two things; either they would incense Herod against Jesus (even as they had incensed him against John the son of Zachariah, whose death they had procured), or else they would cause Jesus to appear unto the people a time-server and a prophet of smooth things, a prophet not to be trusted.

But Jesus knew their devices and said to Abuyah, "What did Moses command you?" And Abuyah said, "Moses suffered a man to write a bill of divorcement and to put his wife away." But Jesus answered and said, "For the hardness of your hearts he wrote you this precept. But from the beginning of the creation God made them male and female. For this cause shall a man leave his father and mother, and cleave to his wife: and they twain shall be one flesh. So then they are no more twain, but one flesh. What therefore God hath joined together let not man put asunder." By these words we understood Jesus both to find fault with them that allowed of divorce for every slight cause (as did certain of the Pharisees); and also to disallow of divorce generally, except (as he afterwards said) for adultery; which alone is, of itself, a divorce. But it was quite after the manner of Jesus to found this doctrine not upon the Law, but upon the nature of things, as it was created in the beginning; teaching that woman was not made as an afterthought, nor as a mere pleasure to the man; but that mankind was made, from the first, male and female. And according to this doctrine did Jesus ever behave towards women, showing unto them not only gentleness and kindness, but also a singular reverence.

After these words Jesus began to exhort the people: and he taught them that God require the purity in the inner parts, namely, in the soul, saying, Not that which goeth into a man defile the man, but that which cometh out of a man, evil and impure thoughts and deeds, these, he said, defile a man. Hereat many of the disciples were sore grieved that Jesus should thus openly, as it seemed, trample upon the Law of Moses; and from this time certain Essenes that had hitherto followed with us, now altogether left Jesus. And one of the younger Scribes, interrupting him, cried aloud," He that despiseth the washing of hands shall be rooted out." But Jesus went on to say, Nay, but every plant that the Father in Heaven had not planted, should be rooted out; and as for the teaching of the Pharisees, he likened it to the tares, the end whereof is to be burned. He also likened them and their pupils to blind men leading other blind men; who should all together fall into the pit.

Then he drew, as it were, a model of the New Kingdom; wherein, he said, the only thing needful would be that a man should love God with all the heart, and his neighbours as himself. And when some one asked him who were a man's neighbours, he replied, in parables, that whosoever was sick, or naked, or an-hungered, or in pain or sorrow, whosoever in fine was in need of aught, that man (yea, even though he were a Samaritan), was neighbour unto each citizen in the New Kingdom; and towards every neighbour the citizens were to do whatsoever they would desire that their neighbours should do unto them.

When the people were come forth out of the synagogue, the Greek merchant walked by my side for a while in silence: but Abuyah, who walked behind us, was plainly heard blaming Jesus as one that brake the Law and taught others to break it. Hearing these words, the merchant nodded over his shoulder, and exclaimed, "Yonder pedant, who with his washings would purify the very sun, is altogether void of understanding; else would he perceive that the philosophy of thy Teacher mounteth up to something far higher than the pulling down of the laws of thy nation." Then he questioned me touching Jesus, and of his former doctrine and manner of life since he had begun to teach;

and I replied to all these things and asked of him in turn what he might mean by his words about the philosophy of Jesus. But he seemed rapt for the time in other thoughts, and, instead of answering me, he questioned me further concerning the birth and rearing and childhood of Jesus; and in particular, whether both his parents were of Israel, or whether his mother were not a Greek. But after that I had answered again to all his questioning, when I perceived that he was still musing on his own thoughts, and took no heed of my words, I waxed impatient, and repeated my question somewhat loudly.

Then my friend made answer, howbeit not in the way of a direct reply to my question, but rather as still partly meditating with himself: "Thou describest a gracious, a very gracious nature, ignorant of evil throughout his youth, seeing ever in his mind's eye the Isles of the Blessed, and desiring that same blessedness for all mankind. And lo, whatsoever he desireth that he seeth: for he deceiveth himself, feigning that all things are like unto that beautiful idea which he seeth in his mind." But I said to the merchant, "Nay, friend Xanthias," for that was the man's name, "but when Jesus spake of the Pharisees, did he then seem to thee ignorant of evil?" " Thou didst not give me time," replied the merchant, "to finish my speech: for I was about to say that, as it seemeth to me, thy teacher is even now awakening to the evil that is in the world; and, becoming at last undeceived, he seeth his fair phantasma vanishing away. Thus his gracious nature, yielding to the over great pressure of the evil that surroundeth him, is becoming marred and wounded. Alas for the pitiful change! For behold, his former life, as thou describest it, was like unto a deer sporting gladly in the woods, to whom the flowers of the fields are as friends, and the wind ever bringeth glad tidings. But to what shall I liken the latter end of his life? It is like unto the same deer wounded by the huntsman, who passeth by the same way, and through the same woods; but she is glad no longer, for the dart still cleaveth to her side, and the flowers delight her no longer, and the breezes are messengers of evil."

I was grieved at his words, and all the more because they agreed with certain fears in the depth of my own heart, whereof I had up to this time made no mention even to Nathanael, no, nor yet unto mine own self. But I was grieved also because the Greek knew not the true nature of Jesus. For he spake of him as of one gracious and lovable, but he knew not the might and the power of our Master, how he was like unto a rock immovable, unchangeable; even such another as the Gentiles fable Atlas to have been, who bore up the world by the strength of his shoulders. For I knew that, if heaven and earth had set themselves in league against Jesus, to make him do aught against the will of the Father, Jesus would have stood up alone against earth and heaven, and hell to boot. Moreover, I had noted how there still came forth from Jesus a new strength to bear each new burden, and a new knowledge to discern each new Revelation from the Father, yea, and a new delight to delight therein. For though it were true indeed, as the Greek had said, that Jesus had sometimes marvelled at evil (when it befell him) as though he had been ignorant thereof before, yet was it also true that he seemed to have become greater through the increase of the knowledge of evil. But Xanthias knew naught of this. For he was deceived by the gentleness of Jesus, not perceiving that this same gentleness of Jesus was stronger than the strength of kings. Therefore was I grieved at his words; but I constrained myself and asked him yet again what he might mean by saying that the philosophy of Jesus mounted to somewhat higher than the pulling down of the Law.

Then said the Greek, (t Are there then in this country no slaves?" "Thou knowest," I replied, "that there are slaves: howbeit, not many, nor ill used, nor treated like beasts, as the Gentiles treat them." Then said he to me, "And wouldst thou willingly be a slave in this country?" I said, "Nay." "And if thou wert a slave, wouldst thou wish that thy master should retain thee as a slave, or should enfranchise thee?" I replied, "The latter." Then said the Greek with a smile, "But if ye all became followers of Jesus of Nazareth, would ye not perforce confess that all men were your neighbours, yea, even Greeks and Romans; yea, even Samaritans; yea, even your own slaves?" Then was I silent: for I understood now that his meaning was, that the teaching of Jesus would in the end bring to pass the enfranchising of all slaves, and I knew not what to reply.

But he, still smiling, said, "I perceive that thou understandest my meaning. For the teaching of thy Master aimeth at nothing less than the destroying of all manner of slavery. But without slavery the race of man neither hath existed, nor can exist, as thou knowest very well. For without slaves no work could be performed except the tilling of the land, which alone is fit for free men"I said then to him that in Israel there was not the same disliking of handicrafts as among the Greeks and Romans. But he said, "Dost thou suppose that thy Master's philosophy concerneth only thine own people?" "Yea, of a surety," said I; "our own people, and none else; for he himself proclaimeth the Kingdom to no strangers." He replied, "That may be, for a time: but is not the Samaritan thy neighbour?" Then was I again silent. For there came into my mind that ancient prophecy which saith that in the seed of Abraham, that is to say in the Messiah, all the nations of the earth shall be blessed; and I remembered how oft Jesus had of late taught us that the Samaritans were neighbours to the citizens in the Kingdom. But I put the thought away from me; for the truth was at that time hid from our eyes: neither could I at that time perceive how we could be redeemed or delivered, if we were to treat the Romans as neighbours. But while I mused thereon, Xanthias continued his speech concerning Jesus, and he said that Jesus did wisely in that he seemed to encourage marriage, and to prohibit many wives, and to forbid divorce. "For," said he, "herein I incline rather to Aristotle than to Plato, believing that the state is composed of families; and if the family be rotten, the state cannot be sound.

But to hope to destroy slavery is to hope to pull down the pillar whereon the life of all states is based."

Now was my heart hot within me; and I was fain to speak, and to say that Jesus would indeed pull down slavery in Israel, and make our people to be a nation of priests and princes for the world, and would in the end destroy even the Evil Nature of man. But I abstained from speech; for I knew that my words would be foolishness in his ears, and that he could not understand the Redemption unless he understood Jesus himself. Therefore I made him some courteous answer and accompanied him toward the house where he lay.

But he still continued his discourse of the philosophy of Jesus (as he called it), and he likened Jesus unto the Greek Teacher Socrates, in that neither Socrates nor Jesus would receive teaching upon mere authority, nor because this saying or that precept chanced to have been written in books: but Socrates trusted to a certain power of reason or dialectic, and Jesus to a certain power which he called a Spirit: the two being diverse in appearance, but in truth following one and the same method. Thus Xanthias continued his speech of Jesus; but as he bade me farewell near the threshold, it came to pass that Abuyah, who had been walking behind us, came near, still talking with his companions, and saying in a loud voice that Jesus was as the bramble, whereof Jotham maketh mention in the Scriptures. "Wherefore," said he, "meet it is that we cut down this vile thorn-tree, lest there come forth fire from the bramble and consume the olive-tree, and the fig, and all the fruitful trees of the forest."

When Abuyah had passed by, the merchant said unto me, "Truly I have heard no philosopher whose lectures have so pleased me as the teaching of this thy Teacher; and, though I esteem little of wonders, whereof we have enough and to spare at Alexandria, yet if even the half of that which thou sayest touching the acts of thy Jesus be true, he will deserve worship even better than Aesculapius or Amphiaraus. But as thou knowest, my dear friend, I am one of them which doubt all things; and I incline to the belief that there are no gods, or if there be, that they deal not with human matters. And thereto I incline the more because I see all human things full of misery and oppression. And, unless my fears deceive me, this my belief will be confirmed by the fate of thine own Teacher. For I fear, I greatly fear, lest the friends of Abuyah the Scribe may prevail over the friends of Jesus the philosopher of the New Kingdom and deliverer of the slaves."

So saying he turned himself round to depart. But I was scarce gone ten paces when he called me back, and taking me by the hand very earnestly, "I pray thee," said he, "tell me by what name doth thy Master call himself. A prophet or a teacher? Or doth he say that he is your Messiah? or a lawgiver like unto Moses?" But I made answer that Jesus called himself by none of these names; but, for the most part, only "Son of man." Hereat Xanthias marvelled and said, "But wherefore useth he this title? For thou, and I, and all men, are not we all sons of men? Doth thy Master therefore fear lest his disciples may perchance forget that he is a man and deem him to be a god? For such a title as this, albeit humble in appearance, seemeth in verity too proud for any save such as aspire to be gods. But perchance your prophets have so used this title that it hath some strange meaning, whereof I know naught." Then I said that the word was indeed used by the prophets: for whensoever the Lord speaketh to Ezekiel as to a mortal creature, the Lord calleth him Son of man, as if to set the mortal infirmities of the prophet over against the divine nature of the Lord; but again the prophet Daniel saith that, in the day of Judgment, there shall appear one like unto the Son of man, sitting on the clouds of heaven, and coming in glory to judge the nations of the earth: wherefore the title seemed to signify the weak nature of man, whether infirm or whether exalted. Howbeit, added I, before Jesus, no prophet spake thus of himself as the Son of man.

Hereat Xanthias marvelled the more, saying that this was indeed a strange title, and such as no philosopher had ever before taken upon himself. Then he mused a while, still holding me by the cloak, and would have questioned me farther; but I could tell him no more. So at the last he let me go, shaking his head, and saying that it was strange, it was passing strange, and that there was more in this than he could understand: and as he turned himself to depart, I heard him repeating again to himself that it was a proud title, a very proud title, and such as no wise and sober philosopher should take. And thus he departed, meditating as he went, and so rapt in his study that he forgot to bid me farewell. But when he was departed, so that I had leisure to think on his wonder and on the cause thereof; then I also began to perceive that there was more than I had as yet understood, in this title of the Son of man.

CHAPTER XVIII

Of Signs in Heaven; and concerning the Healing of the Syrophoenician Maiden, how Jesus seemed to gain thereby some new knowledge.

No evil followed on the words which Jesus had spoken concerning divorce; and we remained many days in peace, even till the day of Atonement, which falleth toward the beginning of the autumn in the month called Tisri. But we had friends in Tiberias, who were to send us word by day, or signify to us by lights during the night, if perchance any plot were intended against Jesus.

Now so it was that some of the Galileans did not consent to James the son of Judas, and to Barabbas in forsaking Jesus, neither did they allow the conduct of the Pharisees; but having gathered themselves together they agreed that it was not fit that Israel should so long halt between two opinions; but as it had been in the days of Elias the prophet, so should it be now. "For," said the chief man among them, "Elias gathered the people together and the people promised to be on his side, if he brought down fire from heaven; and he did so. Now perchance this Jesus is even Elias; for many so report of him, and even the Scribes say that Elias must come, and some say that Elias hath come oftentimes before now. But whether he be Elias or no, doubtless, if he be a true prophet, he can work the sign of Elias. For a false prophet can work signs on the earth and in the air, and in the deep; but a sign in heaven or from heaven he cannot work. Therefore meet it is that the Pharisees, instead of setting snares for Jesus, should promise to obey him if he will work a sign in heaven in their presence. My counsel is therefore that we ask Jesus to work a sign in heaven; and if he consent, then that we obey him, even though all the Pharisees speak against him, yea, and though he bid us hold out our throats to be cut by the Romans."

Thus spake the Galileans at their council, not many days after the discourse of Jesus concerning divorce. And the counsel of the Galileans was reported unto the Scribes. But when Abuyah the son of Elishah heard it, he said that this was according to the Scripture and the Traditions, and that it should be so. But Eliezer the son of Arak said that it should not be so; for that it was in no wise certain that a magician could not work a sign in heaven, or at the least, a sign that should appear to be in heaven. But if he could, said Abuyah, then, though the sign should not really be in heaven, yet if it appeared to be therein, all the foolish rabble, even the people of the land, would be drawn after Jesus, and the Pharisees also would be obliged to submit to him. "For," added he, "I have heard of magicians which can make statues walk, and can knead loaves of stones; and of others that can become serpents, and transform themselves into goats, and can open locked gates, and can melt iron in a moment of time; but if they can do things so wonderful, think ye they cannot likewise perform signs which shall appear to be signs in heaven?"

Others also protested to the same effect, and one said that he had been present when a certain magician had been smitten right through his body with the sword, but behold, the sword had passed through him as through smoke, and he had taken no hurt; and another said that he had seen an enchanter at a banquet create all manner of images, and cause dishes to be borne of themselves to wait upon the guests, no bearers being seen. At the last Abuyah himself confessed that he also had once seen a certain magician roll himself on the fire, and yet not burned; and the same man also to fly in the air. "Wherefore," said he, "true it is, as Eliezer saith, that one flying high enough in the air, might seem to fly down from heaven, and so to perform some sign in heaven; and thus might he lead away the common people, which know not the Law." All this I heard from a certain Scribe, a friend of Jonathan the son of Ezra; his name was Eleazar the son of Azariah, and he was present at the meeting of the Scribes.

The same Eleazar also told me that whilst the Scribes were yet debating what they should do, a message was brought, as from one that had spoken with the chosen disciples of Jesus, saying that Jesus would certainly not work a sign in heaven; for that he had refused to do this, though he had been besought by his disciples. When they heard this, they rejoiced greatly; and Eliezer the son of Arak rose up and straightway gave his judgment that they should now change their policy. "For," said he, "the Lord having revealed this new thing unto us, meet it is that we change our path accordingly, neither harden our faces against the will of God. Wherefore my judgment now is, that we ask this Jesus to work a sign in heaven before the face of the whole congregation in the synagogue. For when it shall be perceived that he cannot work a sign in heaven, all men will go from him; for they will know that he is a false prophet." And thereto the rest agreed, and it was so resolved. But I knew not thereof till many days after.

It was the intent of the Scribes to have asked Jesus to work a sign in heaven on the next Sabbath; but in the meantime, lights having been held up by night in Tiberias (on I know not what report or rumour of some danger intended to Jesus by Herod, or some marching forth of the Thracian guard), Jesus gave command to pass over again unto the other side of the lake. We accompanied him, albeit sorely against our will; for there seemed to be no end unto these wanderings or flights; and each new flight was like to turn the hearts of the people more and more from Jesus. Moreover, the manner of Jesus at this time disquieted us, and made some of us to doubt. Not that he seemed to fear; for fear had no part in him, neither did he seem to know what fear meant. But he appeared again (as in former days) like unto one waiting for a message and marvelling somewhat that the message came not.

During these days, and these wanderings to and fro, the words of the prophet Jonah were often in his mouth, and he seemed as if he discerned a certain likeness between that prophet and himself; but what it was we understood not. For sometimes he spake of Nineveh, and how Jonah thought only of his own people, and had no compassion upon that great city of the Gentiles, yea, and fought against the voice of the Lord, who bade him go prophesy unto them; and how he wandered hither and thither, if perchance he could flee from the voice of the Lord. But at other times he spake how Jonah cried unto the Lord even from the belly of hell, and how the Lord inclined His ear unto him, and heard him, and raised him up to prophesy unto the Gentiles; and he quoted oftentimes the words of the prayer of the prophet, "I went down to the bottoms of the mountains; the earth with her bars was about me for ever; yet hast thou brought up my life from corruption, Lord my God." Likewise he made mention of some sign of Jonah, which he said should be manifested to this generation; but whether he meant that he should be sent far away unto the Gentiles, or that he should be cast into the depths, and delivered again, as Jonah was, this we understood not, and the saying was hidden from us.

Now it came to pass, when we had journeyed now many days on the other side of the lake, we came nigh to the mountain of Hermon. Snows cover the top of this mountain both summer and winter; and when the sun in his strength shineth on the snows thereof, it is as though the glory of the Lord had come down from heaven. Towards this mountain Jesus had set his face as though he had an errand thither from the Lord; and as we journeyed towards it, he gazed often thereon and rejoiced greatly. But it came to pass, as we now drew nigh unto the mountain, we journeyed through a certain village of the country; and because we were in haste and Jesus desired that none should know him, we were to have passed quickly through the village before dawn. For the fame of Jesus, how he could cast out unclean spirits, was spread abroad even in that country. But as we passed through the village, we heard sounds as of one calling after us: and some thought they heard shrieks. Howbeit we turned not back, but journeyed forward the more quickly.

Now a certain woman in this village (a worshipper of idols, after the manner of the people of that land) had a daughter possessed with an unclean spirit, which, whensoever it took her, drove her to all manner of wickedness, even to the attempting of her mother's life. So the woman had resolved in her own mind that when Jesus passed by (for he must needs come through that village), she would beseech Jesus to heal her daughter, and she had told her daughter of her purpose, and likewise all her friends and acquaintance; and she had been advised of the approach of Jesus and was watching for us. Therefore seeing us pass quickly through her village, she adventured to bring out her daughter unto Jesus: but her daughter would not come. For even then, at the hearing of the name of Jesus, the devil took her, and she shrieked aloud and strove against her mother, and would have slain her: but her mother ran forth from the house and followed Jesus, calling and crying aloud and piteously lamenting.

Now to us it seemed a strange thing and an unseemly, that a prophet of Israel should thus be beset and importuned by an heathen woman. So we expected that Jesus should have at once sent the woman away. But Jesus uttered never a word, nor so much as turned his face towards her, but journeyed steadfastly forward. And even as one running a race towards a goal settleth his soul upon the prize that is before him, even so seemed Jesus to settle his soul upon the snows of the mountain of Hermon: for they shone in the light of the rising sun, like unto a dove sent from God, whose breast-feathers are as silver, and whose wings like unto fine gold. But the woman ceased not from her following and lamenting, and poured forth before Jesus all the story of her troubles.

At last we adventured to accost Jesus, and we besought him to send her away. But he answered us, still not turning his face, "I am not sent but unto the lost sheep of the house of Israel." Yet as he spake, he slackened his going, and spake, as it were, like unto one doubting somewhat, and willing to have his words amended. Now came the woman in haste up to him, and threw herself before his feet and said, "Lord, help me." Then Jesus stayed. Yet did he still keep his eyes fixed on that which he saw afar off; and for a brief space he was silent; but then he said, as though he were asking a question of his own soul, "It is not meet to take the children's bread, and to cast it unto the dogs?" But the woman answered, "Truth, Master, yet the dogs eat of the crumbs which fall from their master's table."

When Jesus heard these words he turned his face straightway from the glory of the mountain and looked down on the woman; and behold, he rejoiced more because of that which he beheld nigh unto him, than because of the glory that was afar off. For the fashion of his countenance was changed so as I cannot describe it. And immediately he stooped down, and took the woman by the hand and raised her up, and said unto her, "woman, great is thy faith; be it unto thee even as thou wilt."

Now when the woman ran back to her house, she found the child on a bed, struggling, and scarce held of her friends; who stood by, weeping and supposing the child to be possessed, not now with one devil but with many. Then she cried aloud for joy, and told her acquaintance how that Jesus had granted her prayer. And straightway, when the devil heard this saying, even at the mention of the name of Jesus, he tare the child, and departed, leaving her, as it seemed, lifeless. But presently she rose up whole and sound, being delivered from the devil; nor was she ever again afflicted. All this was done by the word of Jesus spoken by the Syrophoenician woman; for he was not present to heal the girl; albeit (as I gathered) the girl had before heard oftentimes of her mother that Jesus was to come to heal her, and how great things he had done for others that were possessed. But when Jesus had heard the words of the Syrophoenician woman, he was no longer minded to journey towards the north, but went back into the village where was the girl afflicted with the unclean spirit. Now the people would fain have constrained him to tarry with them; but he would not, but set his face southward again to go toward the Sea of Galilee. For the faith of the Syrophoenician had strangely moved him, insomuch that he spake as if the Redemption were nearer than it had been before; and, as I judge, he desired to make one more proof of the Pharisees, whether they also would not have faith in him. And straightway he crossed over and came again to Capernaum.

As we rowed across the lake back to Capernaum we rejoiced greatly; for we thought that the time was at hand when the Galileans (for of the intent of the Pharisees we knew naught) would ask Jesus to work a sign in heaven, and Jesus would now grant their request. But when Jesus had done this, we trusted that the whole nation should have believed in him, and that the time should have come that he should redeem Israel. Howbeit certain of the disciples (and more especially Judas of Kerioth) took it ill that Jesus should have listened to the prayer of an heathen woman which was an idolater. For although Esaias saith that the Gentiles are to come to the rising of the Lord, and that the Gentiles shall seek to the Deliverer of Israel, yet had it been always fixed and rooted in our hearts that the deliverance of the Gentiles (if it should come to pass at all) must come by the uprising of the children of Israel, who should be princes and kings, conquering and triumphing over the nations of the earth. And then the Gentiles were to seek to Israel and to become proselytes, entering into the true fold. And this belief Jesus had confirmed in our hearts in that he had bidden us to go not to the Samaritans nor to the Gentiles, but only to the lost sheep of the house of Israel. Which saying Jesus himself now seemed to contradict, having thus healed the Syrophoenician maiden. But whether it had been revealed to our Master, through the words of the Syrophoenician, that the deliverance of the Gentiles should come more speedily than had been supposed, and not by fetching a compass, as it were, round all the borders of Israel, but by a more direct course, concerning this I know nothing: but Quartus judgeth that it was so.

CHAPTER XIX

How Jesus would work no Sign in Heaven; and concerning his Temptation; and wherefore he denied to work Signs in Heaven.

GEORGIAS the son of Philip exceeded the rest of us in his rejoicing at the return of Jesus, and in the largeness of his expectation, saying that it could not be that our Master, when he adventured to work a sign, would suffer himself to be surpassed by any, albeit the most cunning magicians. "Now," said he, "I have heard an Alexandrine say that there are certain magicians which, in the middle of the market-place, in return for a few obols, will drive out demons and diseases, and call up the souls of heroes, and costly banquets, tables, dishes, and dainties, all as though ready for a feast; all which at the magician's wand shall vanish away. If therefore a common magician can do such things for hire, how much more can Jesus do greater things than these for the Redemption of Israel!" Judas also spake after the same manner, and he said that perchance it was well done of Jesus not to work a sign in heaven at first; for had he worked the sign too early, it would have been counted cheap, and would have been despised. "Much wiser," continued he, "to hold the sign back till the people crave for it, and till the Pharisees (supposing forsooth that he cannot do it) venture to promise obedience to Jesus on the condition that he work a sign in heaven. For thus shall they be taken in their own snare." Only John was doubtful, saying to Judas, "Hast thou then forgotten how once in our presence our Master said he should work no sign in heaven?" But Judas replied that our Master had more than once changed his course, suiting it to the needs of the time; "And," said he, "when he shall once perceive that the Redemption of Sion dependeth upon the working of a sign in heaven, then, trust me, the sign will not long be wanting. And so strongly am I assured thereof, that it would even seem to me to be a friendly deed to tell the Pharisees how Jesus hath said that he will never work the sign, and in this way to move them to ask Jesus to work the sign; to the intent that they may dig a pit for Jesus and fall into it themselves."

Now this he spake jesting; but (as I afterwards learned) Judas had indeed moved the Pharisees even, as he said, to ask Jesus to work a sign in heaven. And Judas it was that had sent to Eliezer that message whereof I have before made mention. But these things Judas did, not because he desired (at that time) to harm Jesus, but wishing to help him, and supposing that he should help him by forcing him to do that which, of himself, Jesus would not do. Howbeit of all these things we, at this present, knew nothing; and we took the words of Judas as if spoken in jest. But John shook his head and made no answer.

It was in the winter, in the month called Chisleu, that we returned to Capernaum. But it came to pass, on the first Sabbath day after that we had returned, we went into the synagogue after our custom, and Jesus taught the people; and the hand of the Lord was present among them, and the people were very attentive to hear him. But when he had ended his words there rose up Abuyah the son of Elishah; and he spake after the manner of the Galileans, saying that it was not right that Israel should be any more divided against itself, but that all should confess that Jesus was the Anointed or Christ, if indeed he could show that he was the Christ. "But the proof" said he, "is, as we all know, the working of a sign in heaven. For signs on earth and in the deep, false prophets can work; but not in heaven. Now, therefore, this is the sum of the matter: thou wouldst have us, the Scribes and teachers of Israel, to believe in thee and to follow thee. Our answer is, Work a sign in heaven such as Elias worked, and straightway we follow thee."

While Abuyah was speaking his last words, a hesitation and a gasping overcame him, so that he was almost speechless. For he was abashed by the aspect of Jesus and by the stillness of the multitude. And, to say the truth, when Abuyah spake those words, "such as Elias worked," we held our breath; expecting when the fire of heaven should come down, as in the days of Elias, and should consume Abuyah, and Eliezer, and all the enemies of Jesus; or else we thought that the earth should have opened and swallowed them up, as the earth swallowed up Korah and his fellows. But when Eliezer had ended all his words, and no gulf yawned nor fire came down from heaven, then indeed our hearts sank within us. But Abuyah and Eliezer began to be of good cheer; for they perceived that they had been well advised, and that Jesus would work no sign in heaven.

When Jesus made answer to Abuyah, the people listened to him and were silent; but their hearts no longer inclined unto him as before. For indeed his words were not easy to understand. But he bade the Pharisees note the signs of the times, even as they noted the signs of the weather, and therein, he said, they should find proof enough. Moreover he spake those same strange words which he had spoken before to us privately, to wit, that they should have no sign but the sign of the prophet Jonah. Having said these words he departed from the synagogue; and at sunset, finding that the hearts of all men were turned from him, he gave command once again to launch the boat and to pass over unto the other side.

Never before were the minds of the disciples so troubled as now: for we had all been assured, in the very depth of our hearts, that Jesus had even for this cause returned to Capernaum, because he purposed now at last to work a sign in heaven. Neither could we in any way understand why he should thus suffer the slanderers to triumph, delaying so long the Redemption of Sion. Judas especially inflamed our grief, saying that all was now lost, and that one sign in heaven would have been better worth than a thousand discourses about the Kingdom of Heaven.

But suddenly we were silent; for we heard the voice of Jesus speaking; and he told us that he had formerly been tempted in a like fashion, even as the Pharisee had tempted him; for he had been led by the Spirit into a wilderness, and there in some vision the Evil Spirit had placed him upon the battlements of the Holy Temple, bidding him cast himself down as a sign unto the multitudes of them which were walking in the courts of the Temple; and the Evil One had said unto him, "If thou be the Son of God, cast thyself down: for it is written, He shall give His angels charge concerning thee; and in their hands they shall bear thee up, lest at any time thou dash thy foot against a stone." But Jesus had made answer, saying, "It is written again, Thou shalt not tempt the Lord thy God." Now therefore we all understood (after a dark fashion, and, as it were, obliquely) that Jesus esteemed the temptation to perform a sign in heaven to be a temptation from Satan. But why he so esteemed it, was hid from the most of us, and we feared to ask him thereof.

When Jesus lay down on the sleeping-cushion, I questioned Nathanael why Jesus would work no sign in heaven. "For," said I, "signs on earth and in the bodies of men he daily worketh; as but now, when he raised up the daughter of Jairus (all men supposing her to be dead): and again, at another time, albeit he neither said nor did aught, a woman was healed, though she did but touch him, and that too in a throng: so powerful was the mere garment of our Master to work healing. And when Jesus perceived the woman (discerning the pressure of her hand, albeit in the midst of the throng), then, as thou rememberest, he was neither wroth nor chid the woman for thus, as it were, stealing a miracle; but bade her go in peace, and be healed of her disease. Wherefore then worketh he no sign in heaven? Did not Moses and Elias work signs in heaven? Yet our Master is greater than they." To these words Nathanael made no answer for a while; but at last he said, "Concerning Moses and Elias, and concerning what they did or did not, I am not able to speak. But as touching Jesus of Nazareth, thus much I know, that he lightly esteemeth all signs, both in heaven and in earth, except they reveal the mercifulness of God. For he teacheth that heaven and earth shall pass away, but his words shall remain for ever. And assuredly he seemeth to me to be greater than Moses and Elias, yea, though he should work no sign at all. For he moveth upon the face of the earth like unto the Son of God, and looketh upon all things that are, as being the servants of his Father. But seeing that they are the servants of his Father, he loveth them; yea, he cherisheth even the flowers of the fields; the sky also, and the winds, and the waters seem to him as the ministers of his Father; and the more he loveth the Father, the more he loveth his Father's servants; neither will he check them nor chide them save according to his Father's will, but submitteth himself unto them even more willingly than others submit themselves. For this cause he endure th to be cold, and an-hungered, and athirst, and homeless; neither doth he chide the frost, nor stamp on the ground to make the wheat spring up for him; nor strike waters from the rock; nor bid the stones come together at his word for to build him an house." "But is not this patience," asked I, "the condition of a slave?" "Yes, truly is it," replied Nathanael, "but what saith our Master? He that is to be greatest among men must be as he that is least; he that is to rule must be as he that ministereth; he that is to be king over all must be as the slave of all. Only it is needful that we serve not unwillingly, but willingly. But whoso serveth the Lord in all things willingly, he is no slave, but a son.

"For this cause, in part methinks, Jesus calleth himself the Son of man; as if to show that he is willingly subject to all the fleshly weaknesses wherewith the All-Wise hath encompassed the souls of men to the end that they may depend on Him. For he teacheth that he, being the weakness of man, shall be made strength and exalted to the very throne of God, and we with him; so that we shall reign with God, and the Kingdom of God shall also be a Kingdom of man, according as it is said, 'What is man that thou art mindful of him, and the son of man that thou visitest him? Thou madest him to have dominion over the works of thy hands: thou hast put all things in subjection under his feet.'"

"Yea, but," said I, "the Psalmist speaketh only of the things of the earth, to wit, the 'sheep and oxen and the beasts of the field, the fowl of the air, and the fish of the sea, and whatsoever passeth through the paths of the seas.'"

But to this Nathanael made answer, "In the Kingdom of God the Son of man shall be Lord over all things in heaven and earth, not on earth merely; yea, over death itself, and over the Evil Nature in man. For this cause, even as an earnest of that which is to come, our Master checketh and chideth diseases and devils in them which be possessed. For our Master hateth the devils and diseases even as he hateth the sins of men, esteeming them as the work of Satan, and not as the work of his Father. But the course and appointed order of the world he esteemeth as the vesture of God, whereof he would not disturb one single fold." Now herein Nathanael spake truly. For once only (as I have heard) did Jesus so much as appear to adventure to alter the course of the world. It was on a winter evening, and the disciples were on the lake; but I was not with them. A great storm had suddenly come down on them (as storms are wont to come down from the mountains round about the lake) and the boat was now well-nigh filled with the waves and like to sink. Then the disciples lifted up their voices for fear, and ran to Jesus as he slept upon the cushion, and besought him, saying, "Master, carest thou not that we perish?" Then he arose in grief for them, as it seemed, that they should, after so cowardly a fashion, tremble before the winds; and he opened his mouth to rebuke them. "And all this while," said Matthew (for he was present), "the winds yet raged, and the waves beat in upon the deck, and in another instant, methought, we had been all dead men. But Jesus, noting this, turned himself from us toward the sea, and then (as if it were revealed to him that he, being the safety of the world, could not be wrecked by any turbulence of winds or waves, and therefore that the storm was to cease), behold, he stretched out his hands to the tempest, praying; and straightway the storm seemed to abate a little; and then, perceiving the will of the Father, he stood up like some great king or emperor, and rebuked the storm, bidding it be still; and immediately there was a great calm."

Now on this only occasion did our Master appear to change the course of the world; and methinks, even here, he did it only in appearance. For he spake as he was moved by the Holy Spirit, it being revealed to him that the storm must needs cease lest the fortunes of the world should be shipwrecked, if the Son of man should perish. But if Xanthias findeth fault with this story, saying that on this only occasion our Master spake after the manner of a Maenad, and not worthily of himself, to this I reply that, if Jesus of Nazareth was the Son of God (as I doubt not), then it was fit that he should feel faith, yea, a singular faith in God his Father. And if Caius Caesar, the first Emperor, could be assured that he was not to be drowned, saying to the boatmen that they must be of good cheer because they carried Caesar and his Fortune; how much more might the true Emperor of men be assured that the Fortune of mankind should not be shipwrecked, yea, and rather than this should come to pass, that the storm must cease? For this cause I incline not to the opinion of Xanthias; who saith that Jesus rebuked not the storm, but the disciples, bidding them not be fearful and of little faith. And, though I was not myself present, yet was the matter reported to me afterwards by one that had heard the relation thereof from Matthew the son of Levi, as I said above.

While I spake with Nathanael, there came into my mind certain words of my Greek friend, whom I had met at Capernaum (I mean the Alexandrine merchant), how he had praised Jesus in that he breathed a spirit of soberness and peace, so that, wheresover he might be, he seemed happy and at home; and I told this to Nathanael. But he said, "Thy friend said well; for to Jesus the world is as a great instrument of music giving forth sounds which we hear not, but he both heareth and enjoyeth. And well I remember how once, in the presence of Jesus, there arose a dispute between a musician and another, concerning the sense of hearing and the sense of sight; and the other said, jesting at the musician, 'To believe thee, the sun should have a voice if it is to be perfect.' 'Nay,' said the musician, 'but the sun hath indeed a voice to those which have ears to hearken; for when it riseth in the east, it is not a large round shining shekel, but it is a minister of God and crieth with ten thousand times ten thousand voices, Holy, Holy, Holy is the Lord God Almighty.' And thereat Jesus smiled and said that it was even so, and that in the time to come there would dwell this power of sound not in the lights of heaven alone, but also in the earth, and all that therein is; insomuch that the vine-twigs and grape-clusters should have voices of their own and commune with the children of men."

By this time we had reached the coast, and we went forth from the vessel, and took our way to a little village lying in the road which leadeth unto Caesarea Philippi. And as Nathanael had been sent on before the rest to prepare lodging for us, I could find no more occasion that day to converse with him. But my mind was still beating on the dark saying of Jesus touching the temptation of Satan, and I still assayed to understand why Jesus would not work a sign in heaven: for the words of Nathanael had not sufficed to make the matter clear unto me.

Only concerning the sign in heaven, thus much was revealed unto me, that I myself was not drawn unto Jesus by his signs and wonders, but by reason of my love for him and trust in him; and the same was true also of the other disciples. Moreover Jesus desired that men should be drawn unto him in this way, by love and trust, and by feeling that he was needful to them, and not by being astonished at signs and wonders. Further I questioned myself and said, "If Jesus had caused the sun to stop still, would Abuyah the son of Elishah, and Eliezer the son of Arak, and the chief ruler of the synagogue straightway have loved Jesus and trusted in him, as Jesus desireth his disciples to love and trust in him?" Now I knew that they might have obeyed him and followed him, but they could not have loved him. For Jesus was light: but they loved darkness. Wherefore Jesus could not redeem them nor deliver them, even though he had worked a sign in heaven. For he could not deliver them which loved him not; no, not though he had worked ten thousand signs in heaven.

CHAPTER XX

How Jesus led us, in our Exile, to the Rock of Salvation; and how he founded the Temple of his Congregation thereon; and how he gave the Key thereof to Simon Peter.

As soon as day dawned on the morrow, we left the village where we had lain that night, and journeyed northward; and Jesus set his face once more toward Mount Hermon. We were all very silent, more than was our custom; for we were downcast and dejected by reason of our often fleeing from before the face of our enemies, and because of the delay of the day of Redemption. And though we still loved Jesus and trusted him after a manner, yet we knew not what to think concerning the things that he had done of late. As we journeyed, Jesus spake much concerning faith, and how, without faith, no one could truly believe in him. From time to time he looked at us, as we went by his side; and he seemed as if he were measuring our thoughts by our faces, and reckoning up the sum of our strength: and now he seemed desirous to speak, and now to delay speaking; watching over us as if some great burden were at hand, and as though he feared lest the burden % should be more than we could bear.

But as concerning faith he said some things hard to understand; to wit, that if a man had not faith, there should be taken from him even that which he seemed to have; and yet, at the same time, he said that no man could have faith in him nor come to him unless he were drawn by the Father. Moreover he said that whoso had faith as a grain of mustard-seed, should be able to overthrow trees or mountains. Likewise he added that, if two or three would agree together touching anything that they would ask of the Father in heaven, it should be done for them.

Now as touching the overthrowing of mountains or destruction of trees, some have supposed that Jesus really wrought such wonders as these; and I have heard that stories of this kind are currently reported in the Church. But Jesus did never any such thing. But in our language an "uprooter of mountains" was a name given to any Rabbi that had power by his words to remove great difficulties out of the path of the righteous, and to make smooth the rough places in the ways of the Law. And after the like manner, as I suppose, are to be interpreted the words of Jesus touching the answer to prayer. For it entered not into his mind that his disciples should ask for earthly things as their hearts' desire; but they were to ask for heavenly things, and earthly things should be added to them, sufficient for their needs. Howbeit Quartus explaineth this saying somewhat otherwise, as I shall set forth further on.

As we journeyed, Jesus would not that any should know him: and few took heed of us; for instead of a great multitude, none now went with him, save the Twelve, and three or four others beside myself. But passing by a certain house wherein dwelt one of our countrymen (though we were by this time far beyond the bounds of Galilee) Jesus entered in asking for water; for the weather was exceeding sultry. And so it was that in the house the good folk were making ready to circumcise a child; and (after the manner of the people in Galilee) an empty chair had been set for the prophet Elias, as being the prophet of the covenant of circumcision. But some one of our company (Judas of Kerioth, as I remember) not knowing wherefore the chair was thus set, asked the cause thereof. So the good man of the house said that it was set for Elias the prophet, "who hath ofttimes appeared," said he, "in the guise of a merchant, to one or other of the Scribes in old times; and, three days before the Messiah come, he needs must appear for to anoint the Messiah: but I have heard it said of many, these ten days, that he hath appeared indeed as a prophet, on the other side of the lake, for to avenge the death of John the son of Zachariah."

"When he said these words, we looked each at other but held our peace: and Jesus, after he had courteously thanked the man, came forth and addressed himself again to the journey; but, methought, even more sadly and sorrowfully than before. But still his discourse (as oft as he said anything) was on faith; and presently he began to say in a low voice a certain psalm (which was both at this time and during many days afterwards upon his lips); and in the psalm are these words, first of supplication and then of praise: " Deliver my soul from the sword, my darling from the power of the dog, save me from the lion's mouth, thou hast heard me also from among the horns of the unicorns. I will declare thy Name unto my brethren; in the midst of the congregation will I praise thee." Now when he spake these words touching the "congregation," and also the following words, "my praise is of thee in the great congregation," then so it was that Judas, who had been scarce able, these many days, to restrain himself because of his anger at the tarrying of Jesus, spake aloud and very vehemently, saying that, but one or two months ago, there was indeed a congregation, and a great congregation, which also had been ready with one consent to have risen up against the Romans; "but now," said Judas, "we be scarce a score in all."

Hereat Jesus stayed, and turned round and looked at Judas, methought, to have rebuked him; but when his eyes fell upon our "little flock," as he was wont to call us at this time, not a score in all (for herein had Judas spoken truly), then it seemed as if his thoughts for us drove out the thought of Judas: and he paused as if he would have questioned us: "Do ye also say as Judas saith?" But then he turned again and went before us, beckoning to us to follow a little behind; and so he continued his journey, steadfastly looking toward the north, where the Mount Hermon rose up before us all glorious to behold. But so far as I could gather from some words that I heard, he still spake to himself concerning the "congregation:" and once I thought I heard him praying for us with great passion, and beseeching God that he would bring us out of the horrible pit, out of the mire and clay, and set our feet upon the rock.

When I spake with one of the disciples concerning that which was to come, and how the Kingdom was to be established, now that all Israel was against us, he would fain have kept silence; and when I urged him, he said, "What know I? Sometimes I am lifted up in my soul, and I know and am sure that the Kingdom shall come; but at other times I know not what to think, nor can I understand why Jesus would work no sign in heaven. But then again I say unto myself that whether he be the Redeemer of Israel or no, he is of a surety the Redeemer of my soul. For in his presence I find life: but to be absent from him is death. The sum is, that I trust in him to-day, for I know not what else to do: but as for the morrow and what it may bring forth, behold, all things are uncertain and unshapen in my mind." The like also said others of the disciples, albeit not in such plain terms, for almost all spake unwillingly. Yet could I not but perceive that the most part had been sorely shaken in their faith, because Jesus had denied to work a sign in heaven: and it was even as Jesus had warned us; the leaven of the Pharisees and of the Sadducees had entered into our souls. Wherefore, although we all still called our Master, as before, the Christ or Anointed, and the Redeemer, or at the least, the Prophet, yet inwardly we were wavering in our hearts; and a breath would have moved us this way or that way, towards belief or towards unbelief. For indeed we were being driven down, as it were, from our former faith, whereby we had believed in Jesus as a worker of wonders or fulfiller of prophecy; and we were falling (as it seemed, but in truth we were rising) to another and a new belief in Jesus as a man, full of tenderness, and suffering, and patience, and withal of a goodness that could not be deceived nor disappointed; and this perchance was the very thing whereat Jesus aimed, to wit, that we should believe in him as the Son of man, conquering through weakness. For our former belief was as the mire or shifting sand, because it could give no firm footing: but our new belief in the Son of man was to be as the rock whereon we and all others were to stand immovable for ever. But we, at this present, being, as it were, still on the sand, and not yet aware of the Rock, how nigh it was at hand, we, I say, knowing in our minds that we wavered, were notwithstanding desirous to keep our wavering secret; insomuch that we spake little on this matter one to another, yea, we would scarce confess it each man to himself: so greatly did we tremble at the very thought of severing ourselves from Jesus. Yet, for all our dissembling, Jesus knew our thoughts; even as though he had been seated in our hearts.

By this time the aspect of the country showed that we were leaving the region of the lake. For the thickets of oleander, which but yesterday we had seen blossoming thickly with red blossoms, were here, in these northern and higher parts, still green and in bud. Now also the snows of Hermon seemed very nigh, even over our heads; and we were not far from the town called Caesarea Philippi. The grass was everywhere green under our feet as though the land knew not drought; and trees of diverse foliage shaded us overhead; and as we drew nigh to the town, we heard the sound of many rushing waters.

Yet though all things showed thus fair around us, our hearts were sad, yea, all the sadder for the beauty of the place, which seemed to rejoice while we sorrowed. Jesus himself looked not now (as he was wont to do) on the glories of the mountainous country, but rather on our faces; neither did he take note of the cedars, and the olives, and the groves of oak-trees; nor of the great plains of green grass; nor even of the Mount Hermon, the top whereof, all covered with snow, waxed daily larger and yet larger as we journeyed still northward. Ever and anon he turned to us as if he would have said some new thing to us; but as often, he turned again, as if still perceiving that the hour was not yet come.

"We were now nigh to the outskirts of the town called Caesarea, even at the place where the fountain of the Jordan floweth forth; and here Jesus bade us sit down. If we had had leisure to admire, there was much cause for admiration. Before us, just above the spring, was a cavern wherein the inhabitants worshipped a certain false god of the Greeks, which haunteth thickets and forests, and he is called Pan: whence also the town in former times had been called Paneas. Higher up, on the summit of the cliff, stood a temple of marble, white and fair to look on, built by Herod in honour of Augustus Caesar. Below, from the foot of the same rock, there flowed forth, under cover of poplars and oleanders, many little rills of pure clear water, which, meeting together, made a rushing stream, the noise whereof was exceedingly pleasant. This stream it is which passeth through the lake called Merom, and, flowing southward, becometh our river of Jordan.

But for all these sights we had at that time no leisure; or if we noted them, they brought no delight to our eyes, being unto us but as signs and tokens that we were exiles. Our great river Jordan, the river of Joshua and of Gideon, a river of mighty works and wonders of the Lord, how exceeding small did it appear, even as a mere rivulet, in this land of the Gentiles where it first arose! The cavern of Pan also and the temple of Augustus filled us with sad thoughts, to think how all the world was covered with the worship of false gods as with a net; so that, save in one little corner of Syria, the true God was not known. The name of Augustus also, yea, and the very names of the town whereon we looked, Paneas and Caesarea Philippi, these all but spake aloud, testifying unto us how great was the power not only of the Greek worship, but also of the Roman kingdom, inasmuch as our own princes built these temples and towns, and called them by the names our conquerors. Wherefore it was not possible that a son of Israel, fresh from Galilee, should look on such sights as these and not feel downcast.

Jesus stood a while, steadfastly beholding the temple; then he sat down amid the rest of us. Our speech among ourselves had, even before, become less and less while we waited for that which was to come from Jesus: for we had all perceived these many hours that he purposed to say unto us some new and strange thing. But now, because we knew that the time was at hand, none dared so much as to open his mouth; and a deep silence and a great fear fell on us; and we saw the lips of Jesus moving as if in prayer. But when Jesus at last opened his mouth to speak, he said nothing at first such as we had expected and dreaded. For he neither rebuked us nor prophesied evil, but only asked us touching himself (calling himself by that familiar title whereof I have made mention above) what the common people considered him to be, saying, "Whom do men say that I the Son of man am?" Straightway all the disciples began severally to make answer, saying that most men in that region deemed him to be Elias risen from the dead; but that others supposed him to be the prophet concerning whom Moses had prophesied, and others again called him one of the prophets. These several answers we made to Jesus readily and promptly, for our hearts were lightened because we supposed that this was the question that he had had so long in mind, for which we had all been waiting. But Jesus, as I noted, listened to our speech as a mother listeneth to the prattle of her children. For his lips still moved as if in prayer, and his eyes were fixed upon the temple on the rock before him; and his mind was not with us nor with our words, but with something that still was to come from the depths of the future.

And lo, while we were still reporting this and that, touching the opinions of the common people, Jesus turned himself round and set his eyes full upon us who were sitting before him, but most directly (as it seemed to me) upon Peter, who was face to face with him: and he opened his mouth and said, "But whom say ye that I am?" As he spake these words, he looked at us for an instant as if he could read our inmost hearts, and as if he knew that we could not and would not deceive him. Then he turned from us again, as though to leave us to our own thoughts, because he would not constrain us nor draw forth from us any word that was not our own: and so he remained, gazing steadfastly on the rock and waiting for our answer, for as long, I suppose, as one would take to count ten very slowly.

I have read in a certain story of enchantments how a prince was caused by a magician to plunge his head into a vessel of water and to hold his breath, and behold, while he was holding his breath beneath the water, he seemed to himself to have travelled long journeys and to have been shipwrecked and to have had many other adventures, and to have married a wife and reared up children, and to have passed through a life of many years even till he had reached old age, and all this within the compass of a single breath. Even so was it with us while Jesus was waiting our answer. For we seemed in that moment to be summing up all our past life and all the life that lay before us, in order to answer this question of Jesus aright. For we dared not lie to him nor flatter him; yea, rather we would have displeased him sooner than have flattered him. Such a constraint lay upon us to speak the truth at all times in his presence; and especially now. But what the truth might be we knew not, and searched through all the past and groped in the future, if perchance we might light upon it.

A few Sabbaths, before, we should have been very ready with an answer; for then all men said that Jesus was the Redeemer, the Christ; and we had often said the same thing. But now many stumbling blocks lay in our path. The Scribes and the pious and the learned, all, save a very few, had rejected Jesus. The patriots had joined themselves to him for a long time, but they too had cast him off; yea, and even the rest of the men of Galilee had been led away with them. The poor, as well as the rich, were now against us. In fine, none were now on our side except a few of the lowest of the people, sinners and tax- gatherers and the like. Besides all this, John himself, a prophet, and one whom Jesus had called the greatest of the prophets, even he seemed to have wavered in his faith in Jesus; and when he had besought help in prison, Jesus had helped him not. Yea, and Jesus himself of late seemed to have cast off faith in himself. For when he had been challenged to work a sign in heaven, which seemed an easy thing for a prophet to do, he had refused to do it. Also, he had fled from the face of Herod and from the Pharisees, and seemed to have become a wanderer rather than a deliverer. Else, why were we, children of Abraham and inheritors of the Land of Promise, sitting there like exiles, looking on the temples of false gods in a foreign land? Even in the words wherein he had questioned us, Jesus had spoken of himself as the Son of man. Might it not be indeed that he was, and knew that he was, naught more than one of the common sons of man? When had he called himself the Redeemer? Never.

We seemed in that instant to have been brought by the hand of the Lord into a place where two roads met, and we had to choose one of the two. And if we went by the one, behold we had against us not only Rome and Greece and the whole inhabited world, but also the princes of our own people, and the priests and the patriots, and the traditions also of our forefathers handed down through many hundreds of years, and the Law given unto us by God for which many generations of our countrymen had fought and died; yea, even Moses himself seemed to be as an adversary if we went by that road. But on the other road no one stood against us; only we saw not Jesus there. So the conclusion seemed to be that we had in that instant to choose between Jesus and all the world.

And, as I judge, even for this cause did the Lord lead us into the wilderness together with our Master in sorrow and in exile, to the intent that there, being apart from the world, we might weigh, as it were in a balance, on the one side all the world, and on the other side the Son of man; a man of sufferings and sorrows, a man of wanderings and exiles, acquainted with rejections and contempts; and then that, having weighed the two, we might prefer the Son of man, because of a certain voice in our hearts which cried within us, "Whom have we in heaven but thee? And there is none on earth that we desire in comparison of thee." And this, as I judge, was the faith that Jesus desired of us: and to this faith was the Lord leading our hearts, while Jesus was patiently waiting for our answer. But though it needeth many words to show even a very little of the searchings of our hearts in that sore extremity, yet the time thereof was short, not more (as I said before) than while a man could count nine or ten very slowly.

Then Peter rose up. If it were possible to judge from their countenances, some of the other disciples also were very nigh unto speaking; for their features were as it were in a flux, dissolving in passion, and speech seemed welling upward through them, and the lips of John the son of Zebedee were trembling as if upon the brink of utterance. Notwithstanding it was reserved for Simon Peter to set forth in words and to shape by the force of his soul the thoughts of John and all the rest. He therefore rose up and spake as I never heard man speak before, neither think I ever to hear man speak again, saying, "Thou art the Christ, the Son of the living God."

Twice or thrice at least, before this time, I had heard words like unto these; when either the disciples or the multitude, marvelling at his mighty works, had hailed Jesus as the Son of God. Also many thousands of times have I heard the like confession made in the accustomed worship of the Church. But never till this day, nor ever after, did I hear the words uttered in the same way. For there seemed to come forth from the mouth of Simon Peter no mere airy syllables, unsubstantial beatings of the wind, but a certain solid truth, able as it were to be seen and touched, and not to be destroyed by force of man. What made the difference I know not: nor know I how to explain the difference, except it came from Jesus himself. For indeed it seemed to me that power passed from Jesus into Peter and gave unto him a strength more than his own, and not human. Yea, again and again, pondering that saying of Simon Peter in my mind, I have thought of the words of Nathanael, how he said that Jesus gave a voice to all visible things even though they be voiceless by nature; and, in the same way, it might have been said also that Jesus had power to give a kind of light to sounds: such brightness did he seem to cast upon the words of Simon Peter, insomuch that the words, though old, seemed new, yea quite new, and never heard before. For the tongue and the voice seemed the tongue and the voice of Peter, but the spirit and the light thereof seemed to proceed from Jesus; so that one scarce knew whether it were truer to say that it was Jesus speaking through Peter, or that it was Peter speaking in the spirit of Jesus.

But when Jesus heard the words of Peter, he turned and looked upon all the disciples and upon Peter, and he rejoiced with an exceeding joy, as if in that utterance of faith the first seed had been sown which was to grow up into the Tree of Life; or as if he had seen before his very eyes the laying of the foundations of a great temple, not like unto the marble temple of Augustus built upon the visible rock, but a temple of human souls compacted together by no hands of man, but by the Spirit of God, and destructible by no power in earth or hell. Howbeit he called it not Temple, but rather (using the word which our fathers had used in old days concerning Israel) Congregation. For often-times he had instructed us to believe that the gathering together of the disciples made a temple, wheresoever it might be, even at the ends of the earth: but the Temple could not of itself make disciples: yea, though the Temple itself were destroyed yet he said that God would raise up even in two or three days a new temple not made by hands. So Jesus made answer unto Peter calling him by his two names, first by the name which he had from his father (which name he had as being "born of woman") and then by that name of Peter which he bore in the Kingdom, which name Jesus himself gave unto him: and he signified that Simon the son of Jonah, being changed by faith into Peter (which name meaneth a stone or rock), presented and manifested forth that very Rock upon which the Congregation should be built; and these were his very words: "Blessed art thou, Simon son of Jonah: for flesh and blood hath not revealed it unto thee, but my Father which is in heaven. And I say also unto thee, Thou art Peter, and upon this rock I will build my Congregation; and the gates of hell shall not prevail against it."

Then, as if he already saw the Temple of the New Congregation standing on the Rock, he added yet another blessing upon Simon Peter and his faith, making mention of the key of the New Temple, and promising that he would give this key to Peter, because they which have faith, those alone can forgive: and forgiveness is the key which openeth the Congregation to all the world. Now it is a common prayer with the scholars of the Scribes that "We may not make defiled the pure, nor make pure the defiled; that we may not bind the loosed, nor loose the bound." But Jesus promised unto Peter something better than this, to wit, that the faith which Peter had this day manifested (that is, the faith of the New Congregation) should have power to loose them that else had been bound; and that forgiveness below should go hand in hand with forgiveness above; saying that he would give unto Peter the keys of the kingdom of heaven: and he added, "Whatsoever thou shalt bind on earth shall be bound in heaven, and whatsoever thou shalt loose on earth shall be loosed in heaven."

When he had spoken these words, he arose and went into Caesarea, where we were to tarry that night. We followed him, marvelling much at his words, and especially because of this promise touching binding and loosing. For we did not understand how we could receive such a power; and even though we should receive it, we did not perceive how it would avail us to conquer the Romans nor how it could hasten the Redemption of Sion. Notwithstanding, we rejoiced even more than we marvelled; partly because we dimly understood that the Lord had this day wrought some great work for us; partly because we felt ourselves to be more settled and confirmed in our allegiance to our Master; but most of all because we perceived that Jesus rejoiced with, an exceeding joy, and we could not but rejoice with him.

Only Judas said that he liked not that Jesus should speak of a Congregation and not of a Nation or People. "For," said he, "a Congregation goeth not forth to battle, nor taketh cities, nor setteth up empires and kingdom: but this is the work of a People. Wherefore my mind misgiveth me lest our Master, becoming desperate of his first purpose of setting up a kingdom, should now determine within himself to found a sect such as the sect of the Essenes or Pharisees. For he was not wont before to speak of a Congregation, but he ever spake of a Kingdom of God, or a Kingdom of heaven.' 5 But one made answer and said that it was written, "Let the Congregation of saints praise him; let the saints be joyful with glory; let the praises of God be in their mouth, and a two-edged sword in their hands, to be avenged of the heathen:" wherefore, said he, the meaning of our Master perchance is, that in the time to come, Israel shall be both a nation of conquerors and a congregation of saints. And to this we all agreed.

CHAPTER XXI

How Jesus, having now determined to die, spake of that which was to come, with Moses and Elias, upon the Mount Hermon.

FROM that day forth we noted but seldom in our Master's countenance that look of expectancy which had sometimes perplexed us before. For now, and for many days after, he spake and acted like one that seeth things to come as clear as things past. On the morrow after the blessing of Simon Peter, he called us together, and told us that we must go up to Jerusalem at the next Passover. If we were joyful before, much more did we rejoice now; and Judas smote his hands together for very gladness, esteeming Jerusalem already captured. For he supposed that Jesus could not march up to Jerusalem so as not to raise up the Romans against him, "and when they come against us in battle," he said, "then Jesus will perforce put forth his power against them, and will utterly destroy them."

These words said Judas (but not so loud that Jesus could hear them) during the first stir that followed the saying of Jesus about going up to Jerusalem. But Jesus opened his mouth to speak again, and behold, he prophesied things that passed all understanding; namely, that he should be rejected by the rulers of the people, and delivered over to them, and put to death with insult. But then he added that although this must needs come to pass, yet in a few days afterwards, yea no more than one or two, it should be with him as with Jonah, whose prayer was heard even from the belly of hell, and according to the words of the prophet Hosea, who wrote this saying, "Come and let us return unto the Lord, for he hath torn and he will heal us: he hath smitten and he will bind us up. After two days will he restore us to life; in the third day he will raise us up, and we shall live in his sight."

We stood silent around him, all agape with wonder, and scarce believing our ears. But he spake quietly and cheerfully, like unto one describing what had already been accomplished, or as if he perceived that the thing was as much according to nature as that a stone should fall downwards or a spark fly upwards. For not long afterwards he spake as if this were an ordinance of God, that "Whoso saveth his life shall lose it; but whoso loseth it shall save it:" desiring, as I suppose, to teach us that in death, no less than in life, there prevailed that great Law of God which was ever in his mouth, "Give, and it shall be given unto you:" meaning that whoso gave up his life unto the Father should receive it again abundantly, both now and ever.

Notwithstanding, at this time our ears were deaf and our hearts were hardened against all such words as these, and we feared to ask him concerning them. Only Peter, mindful how Jesus had of late blessed him, and therefore venturing somewhat more than the rest, would fain expostulate. So after he had besought Jesus not to vex the hearts of us his loving followers by prophesying evil things, he spake concerning the death of Jesus, saying, "Be it far from thee, Master; this shall not happen to thee." Then Jesus looked wrathfully upon Simon Peter, even as he had looked before upon Jonathan the son of Ezra, and he rebuked Peter as if he had been the Adversary himself tempting him; and he said, "Get thee behind me, Satan; thou art a stumbling block unto me; for thou savourest not the things that be of God, but those that be of men." Yet was there no hate in his countenance, though he used the name of Satan; but there was grief, and trouble, and many signs of inward perturbation; as if Peter had assailed him where he was weakest, appealing to him in the name of the disciples whom he must needs forsake. Yea, the tears seemed nigh at hand even in the moment of the bitterest rebuking.

After this, Jesus began to speak to us of the journey to Jerusalem, how full of peril, and how desperate it was like to be. For he said that whosoever followed him must be prepared to risk all for his sake. Yea, even as men condemned to die might go forth to their doom with the ropes round their necks or the crosses on their shoulders, even so must we go up to Jerusalem, all prepared for death, if we were fain to go with him. And this he said many times, saying that none might follow him except they would take up the cross; and during all the time of our going up to Jerusalem, the cross was, as it were, the only watch-word that he would appoint for them that went with him: insomuch that some, mocking, called it a journey of the cross, or a journey of the halter. But he added that, if we had courage to go with him, a reward was in store for us: "Whosoever will save his life shall lose it: and whosoever will lose his life for my sake shall find it. For what is a man profited if he shall gain the whole world and lose his own soul? Or what shall a man give in exchange for his soul? For the Son of man shall come in the glory of his Father with his angels; and then shall he reward every man according to his works."

Now at these last words Judas turned away in anger, saying in a low voice, "He speaketh only of what is after the grave" But Jesus straightway added, "Verily I say unto you, there be some standing here which shall not taste of death till they see the Son of man coming in his Kingdom." At these words we all rejoiced again, and Judas with the rest, for, said he, "These words are no dark saying, but such as babes can understand." So we went out from the presence of Jesus marvelling indeed, but rejoicing even more than we marvelled.

Now when we were come forth, and were alone apart from Jesus, we disputed among ourselves what his words might mean. But Judas said (after his wont) that whatsoever was obscure should be interpreted by that part which was clearer. Now Jesus had declared that he would come and reward his followers and take unto himself his Kingdom even in the lifetime of some that were standing by. But as for the rest, concerning the losing of life and finding of it, and as for what Jesus had said concerning his own dying and rising again, it was clear, said Judas, that the words were used poetically and in a figure, as if one should speak of sinking into the pit of the darkness of ruin and then of being raised up therefrom, as it had been described also by Jonah, and as Hosea the prophet had spoken.

But then Thomas said, "Yet methinks, since all men must die, therefore also the Redeemer of Israel must perforce come to the grave at some time; and then what shall befall the disciples that shall remain in the flesh?" To this some one made reply that Jesus would assuredly not depart from life till he had established the kingdom and trampled all our enemies under his feet. Another said that, if Jesus indeed died as a captive according to his own words, then his death would be like unto that of Samson, who destroyed many thousands of the Gentiles in his own destruction. But still Thomas persevered that, whensoever the time came that Jesus should depart from the flesh, then all the brightness of joy would depart from the disciples for ever.

Then John answered and said that Thomas had well spoken, only that the Lord would provide against so great an evil; and he added, "Let us not suppose that the gates of death can separate us from the love of the Lord, neither let our imagination assure us that the grave is a strong place against the hand of the Almighty. For by the Word of God we were framed; and by the Word of God we were born; and by the Word of God we live; and by the Word of God we die; and by the Word of God we are to give account before the King of kings.

Wherefore if even we are in the hand of the Lord though we lie in the grave, how much more is the .Redeemer of Israel, who is in the bosom of the Father! Wherefore my counsel is that we trust in the Lord, and that we rejoice because we see our Master rejoicing."

To this we all agreed. Howbeit, when we tried to understand the meaning of the words of Jesus, the judgment of Judas seemed good to the most part of us. And so it was that when we rejoiced, we rejoiced with John; but when we reasoned we reasoned with Judas. But of this we were all with one consent persuaded, that it could not be that the Lord would permit such an one as Jesus of Nazareth to die a common death; but either he would not die at all, or if he were taken from us, it must be after the manner of Elias, exalted to heaven in a chariot of fire.

But Jesus desired to offer up prayers to the Lord upon Mount Hermon before he set his face to go southward to Jerusalem. For he had long been journeying towards it, and it seemed to be unto him as a goal and limit of his wanderings. Moreover at all times Jesus loved to be alone on the tops of mountains, not as though he counted high places to be more holy than others, but because all visible things testified to him of the Father, and when he looked forth upon the world at sunrise from the summit of a mountain, then the Angels of God which rule over the light and the sky and the earth and the air, seemed to speak unto him with a louder and a fuller voice. Moreover though he spake not of the moon and stars in parables (but only of the flowers of the field and the seed and the smaller things of earth), yet did he oft consider the heavens and the lights therein which are the works of the fingers of God; and for this cause he would sometimes spend a whole night upon a mountain- top alone, meditating on the works of God. So it came to pass that on the morrow after these things we went with Jesus even to the foot of Mount Hermon. There we tarried during the night in a village just below the mountain; but Jesus left us and went up the mountain alone, save that he took with him Simon Peter, and John, and James the brother of John.

Now as for what happened on the mountain, I myself was not present; but the three disciples told us afterwards things that made us to marvel. At first indeed they saw nothing more than common, nor indeed took heed of aught which they saw; for they were wearied with the labour of the long journey, going for many hours up hill, and besides they were faint with hunger; insomuch that, when they were come to that part of the mountain where the snow lieth continually, they were borne down with sleep. Hereat Jesus bade them stay where they were, and pray; but he himself went forward higher up the mountain, as it were a distance of three bowshot; yet not so far but they could hear his voice; for the air was exceeding still, and all sounds came with a marvellous clearness to their ears even from very far off. Now it came to pass that when the three disciples were alone, they strove to pray, sometimes standing up, but at other times kneeling or lying flat upon their faces. Howbeit their eyes were still weighed down and heavy with sleep; but even as they began to slumber, behold, the voice of Jesus, like unto the voice of an angel, fell upon their ears magnifying and praising God. So the night passed, while they lay there betwixt sleeping and waking; sometimes hearing the voice of Jesus and praying with him; anon falling into slumber and dreaming strange dreams and seeing visions; and (betwixt dreaming and waking) scarce able to know what they saw, nor what they heard, nor even whether they slept or waked. But at the last the Lord sent upon them a deep sleep; and how long they slept they knew not, but suddenly with one consent awaking, they perceived that they were on holy ground, and that the presence of the Lord was around them, and the voice of the Lord sounding in their ears. Yet for the instant they knew not what work the Lord had in hand; only they felt that He was very nigh.

But when they came to themselves, they heard the voice of Jesus speaking words as if conversing with men present and face to face. Then for a brief space the disciples lay even where they had been sleeping, still and astonied, supposing that it was a dream and that the voice should have speedily ceased. But it ceased not, but continued. And they heard Jesus plainly speaking both to Moses and to Elias concerning that which was to come to pass in Jerusalem; which, he said, would not be an error, nor a misadventure, but the very fulfilment of the Law and the Prophets, and the fore-ordained will of the Father. (Also Quartus saith (but this I heard not myself from any of the three) that Jesus testified unto Moses, saying that he came not to destroy sacrifice but to fulfil sacrifice.)

But when the disciples perceived that it was no dream, they with one consent started up; and behold, the sun was just risen, and Hermon was all a-fire with the glory of the Lord, and the ice and the snow all around shone like unto burning gold and silver and sapphire, only far brighter, even as the brightness of the Throne of the Majesty on High. But Jesus stood on a rock above them; and when they looked on him, behold, his garments were exceeding white, whiter than snow, and his face was transfigured as the face of an archangel, and his shape was all glorious to behold, shining with a wondrous light; and his eyes were set like unto one looking on the forms of departing friends. For Moses and Elias were now passed away and were no more to be seen.

But Simon Peter, being nigh distraught at the glory of the sight, and scarce knowing whether he were asleep or awake, cried out to Jesus in a loud voice that they would remain on that mountain-top for ever; and he said, "Master, it is good for us to be here; and let us make three tabernacles, one for thee, and one for Moses, and one for Elias." But Jesus took no heed of his words, but kept still gazing upon Moses and Elias. And while they still looked, the Lord sent down on them a cloud, and compassed them round with darkness; and they feared exceedingly when they entered into the cloud; and there came a voice as of thunder out of the cloud, saying that Jesus was the son of God. Then fell the disciples on their faces, and offered up prayers unto the Lord. But presently, when they arose, the cloud had passed away, and Jesus alone was standing by their side.

When Jesus came down from the mountain, all we that were waiting for him in the village below perceived that he had had a vision; for there was still an unwonted brightness on his countenance. Likewise also the people which were with us (for there was a great multitude) marvelled at the brightness of his countenance; and running to Jesus, they saluted him as a prophet. Some also began to beseech him to heal a certain boy which was possessed with an evil spirit. For so it was that, while Jesus was upon the mountain, certain of the Pharisees that dwelt in that village (for there was a synagogue there, and many Jews dwelt round about that country) came to us bringing one possessed with an unclean spirit and bidding us cast him out. So we adventured to drive him out. But we could not do it. Therefore the Pharisees strove against us and declared that we were vagabonds and deceivers, and that our Master was like unto us; and of the multitude part sided with us and part with the Pharisees, insomuch that there was a great uproar and noise of contention. All these things had come to pass while Jesus was coming down from the mountain; but when we saw Jesus near at hand, straightway on both sides we all ceased from our contention.

Now when Jesus understood the cause of the contention, and that the Pharisees were striving against us because we had not been able to drive out the unclean spirit, he looked around both upon us and our adversaries: and behold, we were all heated with disputing, and angered by reproachings, and there was no faith in us. Therefore he was sorely grieved, and he sighed bitterly, and said, "faithless and perverse generation, how long shall I be with you, how long shall I suffer you?" Then he turned to the father of the child (for the man was standing nigh, piteously bewailing his child) and he said, "Bring thy son hither to me." So they brought him.

But Jesus, looking upon the boy and upon the father and upon the Pharisees, and upon all them which were standing nigh, perceived straightway that there was no faith as yet that the boy should be cured. Therefore he asked the father certain questions touching the boy, and the man replied that the boy had been possessed even from a child; "and oftentimes," continued he, weeping as he spake, "it hath cast him into the fire, and into the waters to destroy him; but if thou canst do anything, have compassion on us and help us." When Jesus perceived that the man had not yet faith (but only desire bordering upon faith), he said unto him, repeating the man's words, "*If* thou canst; *if* thou canst. Nay, but believe. All things are possible to him that believeth." And straightway the man cried out for anguish of soul, and said with tears, "Lord, I believe; help thou mine unbelief." Then the face of Jesus was glad, and immediately he rebuked the unclean spirit; and it came forth tearing the boy and leaving him as one dead, insomuch that many said "he is dead." But Jesus took him by the hand and lifted him up, and he arose.

Hereupon the multitude departed, praising God for His goodness; but when we were come to the house, we asked him why we had not been able to cast out the unclean spirit. Jesus answered that it was because of our want of faith; and he repeated the words which he had before spoken, that whosoever had but faith, even as a grain of mustard-seed, should be able to uproot mountains. But such spirits as these, he said, could not be driven out save by much prayer. He did not further rebuke us for our ill success: but our want of faith seemed to engender in him a certain disquietude for our sakes, perchance because he perceived that we were as yet too weak to stand by ourselves; and this, though the hour was nigh when his hand could no longer hold us upright. Howbeit he said no more at that season, but only gave command that we should straightway set out for Capernaum.

CHAPTER XXII

Of our going up to Jerusalem; and of the Division between Parents and Children; and how Jesus testified of a Day of Judgment.

As we passed through the country to Capernaum, we began to tell the people everywhere that Jesus had now determined to go up to Jerusalem at the head of his followers, and that the time of Redemption was at hand. But Jesus forbade us; for he would not that any man should know that he was passing through. Howbeit, even though we were silent, the rumour of his journey was everywhere noised abroad, so that he could not be hid. Many therefore left their ploughs, and their fishing-boats, and their trades, and followed with us: or, if they followed not, they appointed to be with us at the next Passover when we went up to the Holy City. For it was already the month called Adar, so that it wanted no more than four or five weeks to the Passover.

Now certain youths and striplings followed us, not deliberately, nor with forethought, but because they were ever unstable and ever seeking after new things. Them therefore Jesus warned to go back to their homes, telling them that they had not counted the cost of the journey. Others were fain to have come with us; but their friends sought by all means to prevent them, telling them what cruelties the Romans had wrought upon their fathers and kinsfolk in former times; how some had been sold for slaves, some slain with the sword, some crucified; and with many tears sisters besought their brothers, and mothers their children, not to go up to Jerusalem, nor to bring them down with sorrow to the grave. Now Jesus did not call upon such as these to come to him; but if they were minded to come, he bade them remember that they must above all things trust in him and love him; yea, he said that they must love him better than houses, or lands, or kinsfolk.

Hence also it came to pass that in a certain village he spake words which have been a stumbling block to many. For so it was that a certain young man of that village had come forth to meet Jesus; and after he had saluted him, the young man had promised to follow in his army, and to serve him even to the death. Howbeit he besought Jesus that he would suffer him first to go and bid farewell to his father and mother. Now Jesus looked on him, and perceived that he was as a reed that bendeth with the wind. So he said unto him that he must not go: "For," said he, "he that putteth his hand to the plough and looketh back, is not fit for the Kingdom of God." Thereupon the face of the young man fell and he became very sad; yet he obeyed Jesus, for that day, and followed him; but on the morrow he secretly departed for to bid his parents farewell, meaning shortly to return to Jesus. So when Jesus passed through the village wherein the young man abode, behold, the young man was even then coming forth from the door of his home. But his mother ran behind him, and caught him by the cloak, and embracing him besought him again and again not to go with Jesus. Thus she constrained him. But Jesus, looking back on the youth, said, "Verily he that hateth not his father and his mother cannot be my disciple."

Already, even at the beginning of our march, when we first departed from Hermon, there had arisen a questioning among us, who should have the chief places in the New Kingdom. For now, within one month, we looked to see the Romans cast out of Jerusalem, the Holy City and Temple purified, and the throne of the Redeemer established. This done, it seemed to us that Syria would be portioned out to several princes or governors; Galilee to one, Samaria to another, Peraea to a third; after the manner of the Romans, whose custom it is to divide their dominions among many princes. So we disputed among ourselves who should have the best provinces. Judas, as being ever foremost in all actions, claimed a principal share; but the others also were not backward. Thus we disputed as we walked behind Jesus, being now nigh to Capernaum; and so it was that, in the heat of our disputing, we knew not that Jesus was standing still, waiting till we should overtake him. Therefore we walked on, still disputing, with clamour and much anger, till, lo, Jesus was in the midst of us. He looked sorrowfully on us, but said nothing for that time, and we were all straightway silent.

But in the evening, when we were all together in the house, Jesus called us to him, holding a little child by the hand; and when we were gathered round him, he set the little one in the midst of us, and said that we had forgotten his former saying, how that no man could enter the Kingdom unless he became as a little child. Then he added these words, "Whosoever shall humble himself as this little child, the same is greatest in the Kingdom of Heaven." Then said Judas, "Whoso hath wrought much, shall he not receive much? and whoso hath wrought little, shall he not receive little? And is not the Master of the work faithful, who will pay us the wage of our work?"

For an instant Jesus was silent, looking at Judas as though perchance he had not heard his words aright. Then he answered that in the New Kingdom there was no difference of reward; for the least were to be as the greatest. At the same time he placed his hand on the head of the little one and said, "Whoso shall receive one such little child in my name receiveth me, and whosoever shall receive me receiveth not me, but Him that sent me." He also spake a certain parable to us, as if to show that the reward in the kingdom is not by way of price but rather by way of a free gift, coming from the Father, as cometh the rain from heaven, and sufficing for all them which receive it; even as the lord of an estate, out of the kindness of his heart, might give unto all his labourers the same wage (and that sufficing for their needs), even though some of the labourers might perchance be hired later than the rest.

Judas had withdrawn himself before Jesus began this parable. For he was greatly abashed, though Jesus had not rebuked him by name. But Jesus seemed saddened by our disputing, and by our hardness of heart in that we understood him not. Notwithstanding he was still cheerful and gentle according to his wont. For albeit he saw close before his feet the darkness of the valley of death, yet, above and beyond the valley of death was the hill of life, which (at that time) he seemed to see and to describe, even as if he had traversed and measured it out with a measuring reed. Notwithstanding for our sakes he seemed sometimes to be in meditation and sorrow, as though, when he had reached Paradise, he should look back upon us left behind and alone.

When we went forth from before the face of Jesus, we found Judas chafing much at his repulse (for so he termed it), and asking how it was possible that in any kingdom, there should be no degrees of rank or honour? For some, he said, must needs be near 'the throne, others far off; and some courtiers; but others tillers of the land and artificers. To us there seemed much reason in the sayings of Judas, though we liked not that he should pay so little deference to our Master. John also himself confessed that he understood not how it should be otherwise than Judas had said. "Notwithstanding," said he, "if Jesus should see fit not to give us power and wealth in the New Kingdom, we must none the less be content, and not lust after the table of kings;

for our table is greater than their table, and our crown greater than their crown, and faithful is our taskmaster who will pay us the wage of our work."

The words of John did not please the most of the disciples; who said that it would not be fit that Jesus should give power and wealth to other servants and courtiers, and should neglect them that had borne the burden of the first persecutions, who were now to bear the brunt of the conflict at Jerusalem. So they went away still disputing among themselves. Then, when we were alone, I asked Nathanael whether he thought that Jesus had any certain plans how to take Jerusalem or how to drive out the Romans. But Nathanael answered that it seemed to him that Jesus had no such certain plans. Then said I, "Wherefore then goeth he up to Jerusalem 1?" "Because," replied Nathanael, "thus much hath been revealed to him that he must needs go up to Jerusalem, there to be glorified and lifted up. But as to the manner and time thereof, he saith nothing. Yea, and I have heard him speak as if he himself knew not these things, but they are known to the Father alone."

At this time Jesus began to speak more often than before of a certain day of wrath in store for Israel; and, as David on Araunah's threshing-floor saw the sword between heaven and earth, even so did Jesus discern a sword of the Lord; howbeit not stayed, as David saw it, but uplifted and in act to strike. sometimes he spake as if he himself were to wield this flaming sword; but evermore, beyond the fire and the sword, he discerned the glory of the Kingdom of God; and he spake as if the Kingdom could not come except the fire should first be kindled, and he must needs kindle it himself. Therefore once, when Jonathan the son of Ezra said to him that he was accused of his enemies the Pharisees as if he would fain set all Israel on fire, he replied, "The nearer to me the nearer to the fire; but the further from me, the further from the Kingdom." l

Seeing this flaming sword ever before him, Jesus none the less continued to speak of his death. This perplexed us not a little. For at one time he would say that his enemies would be slain with the sword; or destroyed as tares are destroyed with fire; and yet, on the other hand, he repeated again and again that he should die at the hands of his enemies in Jerusalem. Howbeit of the evil prophecy we his disciples took small heed, but gave our minds to the prophecies of good things. For he spake much of being "perfected," and of being "glorified," and how he should be "lifted up" or "raised up" in Jerusalem. Moreover, Jesus was wont to use the word "dead" of them that were in the deep waters of sin; as when he said that "The dead should bury their own dead;" and again, when he said that "The son of man hath power to quicken the dead." Oftentimes also he spake in the same way of raising up the dead, as when he told the disciples of John the son of Zachariah that "the dead are raised up." Hence it came to pass that, if we heeded at all his words touching his death, we were assured that he meant to say only this, that he should be for some days struggling with Satan, and not at once overcoming, but as it were in darkness and in the shadow and depth of death; but that in two or three days he should be raised up and triumph over Satan.

In this belief we were much confirmed by our Master's constancy and stoutness of heart. For on the second day after we had returned to Capernaum, Eliezer the son of Arak, with others of the Pharisees, came to Jesus where he was seated in the midst of his disciples, and making as if they were reconciled to Jesus, they bade him flee from Galilee lest Herod should slay him. But this they did, not out of love to Jesus, but hoping to rid the city of him, and partly desiring to discredit him with the disciples, as if Jesus once more would go into exile for to avoid strife. But Jesus made an exceeding bold answer, and said that the Pharisees were to tell that fox (for so he called Herod) that he would go on his way to Jerusalem not through fear of him, nor in haste, like unto a fugitive, but healing and teaching as he went, both to-day and to-morrow; and on the third day (for the journey was a journey of three days for a strong man, according to the common saying) he said that he should be perfected, even in Jerusalem. Moreover, when Eliezer, nothing abashed, dissembled still further, and bade Jesus take heed lest he should perish even as the Galileans, whom Pilate had slain, Jesus answered that to be slain did not argue that the men slain were sinners above the rest; and then he added that another sword (which they saw not) was near at hand to smite them also themselves, if they repented not.

This gladdened our hearts and made us eager for the journey: and when on the morrow we went up from Capernaum, journeying towards Samaria, there was not one in our band that was fainthearted nor desirous to return. Now at that time there were about three hundred following Jesus. But the greater part of our friends, as we understood, were not to go with us, but to meet us at the going in to Jerusalem, or at some place nigh unto Jerusalem.

When we were come to a certain village in the road (the name of the village is Beth-Gader) where a man journeying towards Jerusalem from Samaria leaveth the Lake of Gennesareth behind him and seeth it no more, then it came to pass that our Master turned him round to look his last upon Capernaum, and Bethsaida, and Chorazin, and upon all the cities of the Lake, wherein he had taught and wrought. And he stood and gazed a long time, and cried out that it should be ill for those cities in the day of Judgment; for if the mighty deeds that had been wrought there, had been wrought in Tyre and Sidon, they would have repented a long while ago in sackcloth and ashes. But when he saw Capernaum, and the fields thereof, and the gardens which compass it round, all bright with the greenness of spring, and the lake, still and peaceful, whereon were fishing-boats and ships innumerable, then he lifted up his voice and prophesied evil against the place, saying, "Thou also, Capernaum, which art exalted to heaven, shalt be brought down to hell; for if the mighty works which have been done in thee had been done in Sodom, it would have remained unto this day." Then spake he to us, saying, that it should be more tolerable for the land of Sodom in the Day of Judgment than for that city. When he had said these words, he turned his back upon Capernaum and upon all the country of the lake; and he departed and saw it no more.

CHAPTER XXIII

Of Covetousness; and of Fleeing from Death into Life; and concerning the Law of Retribution.

WHEN we were now drawing nigh to the borders Ox Samaria, it being (as I remember) about the ninth hour in the second day of our journey, behold, a tumult arose in the front of the band, and shouts as of men contending together. Then those of us that had swords drew them; for we thought surely the hour was now come for battle. But Jesus bade us put up our swords; and going forward he saw a multitude of Samaritans gathered together to oppose us, neither would they suffer us to pass through their country; and they reviled us and began to cast stones at us. When he saw this, Jesus neither reproached them nor persuaded them to let us pass, but straightway commanded that our band should go back a distance of many furlongs on the road whereby we had come, and then to turn eastward; so that we might pass through the country beyond Jordan, thus avoiding Samaria. This seemed to the most part of us a grievous thing and scarce tolerable, that the army of the Redeemer of Sion should be thus turned out of the path by a Samaritan rabble. Therefore we besought Jesus with many entreaties, and some even with tears, that he would suffer us to force a passage; but he would not hear. At the last, when he had now begun to go back, James and John, being filled with wrath because the Redeemer of Israel was thus despised, prayed Jesus that, if he would not suffer them to smite with the sword he would, at the least, suffer them to call upon the Lord that He might send down fire upon our enemies. Hereat we all were in suspense, and hearkened eagerly to what Jesus would say; for in our hearts we had long supposed that Jesus purposed in this way to destroy the bands of the Romans, even as the prophet Elias had destroyed the captains and footmen of Ahaziah. But Jesus looked steadfastly upon James and John and said unto them, "Ye know not what manner of spirit ye are of. For the Son of man is not come to destroy men's lives, but to save them." Then he went back by the way whereby he had come; and we followed him, sorely grieving. Some of us also murmured (and Judas most of all), saying that it was a strange thing that our Master should have threatened to cast the Pharisees into the valley of Hinnom, and notwithstanding would not force a passage through the Cuthite strip (for by this name we termed Samaria), nor call down fire on a rabble of unbelievers. Moreover Judas spared not to say that Jesus must be made perforce to show forth some mighty work against the enemy, or else the Redemption of Sion would not come to pass. And the heart of Judas began from this time to be turned away from Jesus even more than before; and Jesus also, as it seemed to me, began to perceive that Judas was estranged from him. For whensoever his eyes rested upon Judas, then the face of Jesus was as if God had hidden His countenance for a season. After this we went over Jordan and journeyed through the country that lieth eastward of Jordan, which is called Peraea. Here we tarried some days, even till the beginning of Nisan, which is the month of the Passover: and, about this time, were completed two full years during which we had followed Jesus of Nazareth. Now the people and the land of Peraea are not like unto the people and the land of Galilee. For in Galilee the fields are small, and they till corn and vines and olives; and the men are exceeding stubborn and resolute, neither very rich, nor very poor. But in Peraea they have great pastures, and some are rich in flocks and herds, while others have scarce bread to eat; moreover the men are of an unstable disposition, fond also of wealth, and given to ease, and not so steadfast as the men of Galilee.

Therefore it came to pass that in this country and at this season, our Master testified most of all against covetousness, and lifted up his voice against them which had their good things in this world and wanted nothing more. At this time also he spake many parables, which it needeth not to set forth at full length, for that they are well known among the saints. But among other parables, as I remember, he spake one against a certain rich and foolish farmer (the like of whom we saw many in that country) who thought not of others but of himself only, and had promised unto himself many years of plenty and ease, but was cut off by God that night; also another parable against a rich man that suffered the poor to lie at his gate untended; but afterwards the poor man was comforted, but the rich man punished in hell.

About this time also began Jesus to speak less of the Kingdom of God and more of a certain Eternal Life, which, as he said, the righteous and none other should attain. Some would have it that he changed his words, only for fear of the Romans, lest they should suspect his often mention of the Kingdom of God, and lay hands upon him as one aiming to be king; and these men said that Eternal Life signified the Kingdom of God, though in different words. And perchance it did signify the same thing: howbeit Jesus changed not his words for fear, but partly, as I judge, because the covetousness of the people weighed upon him, and because he perceived them to be wholly given up to the lusts of the flesh, insomuch that they were even as dead, and content to lie in the valley of the shadow of death.

For ever as Jesus drew nearer to Jerusalem, the sins of the people seemed to weigh heavier upon his soul, and death and destruction seemed to grow larger in his eyes; insomuch that now he desired to exhort the people not so much to enter into the Kingdom, as rather to flee from death unto life. Yea, so exceedingly did he fear the power of Satan to slay the souls of men, that about this time, when a certain disciple desired to have left him for a season to bury his father, Jesus would have the young man still continue with him, saying that the dead should bury their own dead. Howbeit, though we understood this afterwards, we perceived it not at the time; but whensoever Jesus spake of Eternal Life, then we would interpret the words still to signify the setting up of his Kingdom in Jerusalem.

Notwithstanding, while Jesus spake day by day more earnestly touching them which would not come into the Kingdom of God, and concerning those whose hearts were satisfied with the good things of this world so that they thought they needed nothing, he none the less was tender and gentle to all sinners, and to the afflicted, and to young children, after his wont; yea, and perchance, even exceeding his wont. For albeit he saw daily more and more of the evil nature of men, yet was he not embittered thereby; but whensoever his burden became heavier to bear, then, as it seemed to me, his gentleness appeared greater likewise. Of which gentleness I will here set down one among many instances. When we were come into a certain village, at the end of a day's journey, the hour being now late (for the sun had already set), behold, at the going into the village, stood many women with children in their arms; and they besought Jesus to bless them. Then we (who went before Jesus and the rest to prepare a lodging for him) bade the women take away the children and to bring them on the morrow; for we had walked a long journey and were weary and had fasted long; and, said we, it was not seemly at that hour to trouble the Master. But he was sore displeased at us, and took up the little children in his arms and blessed them and said, "Suffer little children to come unto me, and forbid them not, for of such is the Kingdom of Heaven." He also repeated his former saying, that none should inherit the Kingdom unless they became as little children. These words seemed to some of us well fit for peaceful times and for quiet talk and meditation in Galilee, but not fit now when the hour had come to enter the Kingdom, as we supposed, by smiting with the sword. Howbeit to Jesus these words seemed always fit and seasonable; so gentle was he and so loving, even to the last.

It came to pass that in the throng, listening to these words of Jesus, there was a certain young man whose name was Tobias the son of Zechariah. He also came that same night to the inn, to hearken to the teaching of Jesus: and he said unto certain of his friends in my hearing that he was willing to do anything that Jesus should say, even to the giving of half his wealth: moreover he made many professions as if on the morrow he would join himself unto Jesus and go forth with us to Jerusalem. Howbeit on the morrow, when we assembled early according to our wont to set forth, the young man Tobias was not with us. But we (for it was usual with us to hear many promises and to see few fulfilments) began our journey without him. But we had not gone more than six or seven furlongs when the young man came in haste running after us, and when he had come near to Jesus, he saluted him and knelt before him. For his heart had been inflamed with admiration of the doctrine which Jesus taught concerning the Kingdom of God; howbeit he trusted not in our Master as the Redeemer of Israel, but he loved him as a very pious Scribe, teaching things lovable and excellent. Therefore, willing to gain the favour of Jesus and yet being unwilling to journey forth with Jesus, he was fain to gain our Master's favour and also satisfy his own conscience, if it might be, by doing some other good work in lieu of doing that which he had promised to do. So he called Jesus "Good Teacher," and said unto him, "What shall I do that I may inherit eternal life?"

Now Jesus perceived that the young man was deceiving himself; for he supposed himself to be righteous, but he was not; moreover he trusted in his wealth and thought to buy the mercies of God with a price. Therefore Jesus took compassion on him; and looking upon him, he loved him, and would fain have opened his eyes that he might know himself and be less content with himself. So he desired to show him that he was wrapped up in the love of his possessions. Therefore first of all Jesus answered as a teacher (forasmuch as the young man also had called him a teacher), and he bade the young man obey the Law. But Tobias, like unto a pupil reproaching a teacher for that the task appointed is too easy, replied that he had observed the Law from his childhood upward. Then Jesus, knowing what would come to pass, made mention of the watch-word of our desperate journey, calling it the journey of the cross (or halter, as some people termed it); and he said to the young man, "One thing thou lackest: go thy way, sell whatsoever thou hast, and give to the poor, and thou shalt have treasure in heaven; and come, take up the cross and follow me." Then the countenance of the young man fell, for he had not supposed that the teacher would appoint so great a task; for he had great possessions. So he rose up from his knees, and departed, grieving much, and he went back by the way he had come.

Jesus looked after him as he went; even as a physician regardeth the patient which struggleth against the knife of healing. And he stood still, and marvelled much because of the power of the things of this world over the mind of man, and yet more because of the power of the Lord to deliver the souls of men from the things of this world. For when he considered the weakness of men and the strength of this world, then it seemed to him (as he was wont to say) a harder and a greater work to redeem a rich man's soul than to uproot a tree or a mountain, or what else may be wrought by art of magic. So he turned to us and said, "Children, how hardly shall they that have riches enter into the Kingdom of Heaven. It is easier for a camel to go through the eye of a needle, than for a rich man to enter into the Kingdom of God." Hereat we were astonished out of measure, saying among ourselves, "Who then can be saved?" But Jesus looked upon us and said, "With men it is impossible, but not with God: for with God all things are possible."

Afterwards as we walked behind him, we discoursed further among ourselves concerning these words, and Judas said, "How then? Are we never to be rich!" But another said, "He meaneth that none that are rich can enter into the Kingdom; howbeit when we have attained to the Kingdom, then shall we be rich, though we be poor now; but the rich shall be shut out" But Nathanael said to me privately he thought Jesus meant otherwise; as if he divided the children of men into two parts, the one part having their hopes and treasures in heaven and the other part having their hopes and treasures on earth (according as he had himself commanded us to have our treasure in heaven, saying that where our treasure is, there would our heart be also): now if a man have his treasure in heaven, then though he have five hundred talents on earth, yet they harm him not, for he useth them to good end: but whoso hath his treasure on earth, though he have but five hundred pence on earth, yet they harm him, clogging his soul, and hindering him from looking upwards, because he useth his little wealth to the ends of his own pleasure. "For," said Nathanael, "as often as Jesus speaketh of wealth, he meaneth ever some spiritual meaning, as when he speaketh of bread and corn and wine, and the like."

I doubt not that Nathanael interpreted aright the words of Jesus. Howbeit also true it is that very few whom the world calleth rich, entered either then or afterwards into the Kingdom of God. Therefore I judge that Jesus meant also perchance to warn us how dangerous a thing it is for a man to have more wealth than is needful for simple wants. For the experience of the saints hath been, everywhere and at all times, that fewer men come into the Church with five hundred talents than with five hundred pence.

But after we had discoursed a long time concerning the matter, Judas moved Peter to question Jesus, and to ask whether indeed it was true, that the disciples should never be rewarded with wealth. So Peter went to Jesus and said, "Lo, we have left all and followed thee." He said no more, but Jesus perceived what was in his heart; and he answered and said to us all, "Verily I say unto you, there is no man that hath left house, or brethren, or sisters, or father, or mother, or wife, or children, or lands, for my sake and the Gospel's, but he shall receive an hundredfold now in this time, houses nd brethren and sisters and mothers and children and lands, with persecutions: and in the world to come eternal life." Then he ceased; but when we thought that he had made an end and we were departing, he added, "But many that are first shall be last, and the last first."

These latter words of Jesus troubled us not a little. For of late since we bad left Capernaum, many new disciples had joined themselves to us, and Jesus had suffered them gladly; and now we thought that his intent was that, in the kingdom of Jerusalem, they, even these new disciples, should have equal reward with us, who had followed him through all his wanderings. Moreover we were vexed because in the beginning of our consorting with Jesus he had set much store upon us his followers, saying unto us, "Whosever is not with me is against me," as much as to say that only we, which followed with him, were his friends, but all else were his enemies; but now he seemed to set store upon all them that were not siding with his enemies. For of late when John the son of Zebedee saw a certain man adventuring to cast out evil spirits in the name of Jesus, and yet he followed not with us, John would have forbidden him. But Jesus said ".Forbid him not: for whosoever is not against me is with me." These words were contrary to the words which he had spoken before, insomuch that we knew not what to think.

But as concerning the first words of Jesus, namely, that all our goods, whatsoever we had left for the sake of Jesus, should be multiplied an hundredfold, and that too even in this life, we rejoiced exceedingly. For some that had left small fields, began to reckon that they should have great estates; others that had left houses o1* boats, counted up whole villages and navies that should be theirs when Jesus should be king in Jerusalem. Moreover a certain Scribe, who followed with us, said "This saying of Jesus is also in accordance with the sayings of the Wise; for it is said all things are done according to exact retribution, whether in way of punishment or reward. Even as

Samson (who followed after the desire of his eyes) was blinded by the Philistines; and Absolom (who boasted of his hair) was hanged upon the tree by his hair, so that he died. Moreover also Ham the father of Canaan (who sinned by seeing and by telling, that is with the eyes and with the teeth) was therefore made a slave; as Moses also enacted that whatsoever slave was sinned against by his master in the matter of teeth or eyes, so as to suffer loss thereof, he should be made no longer a slave but free. For this is according to the law of retributions; for with what measure a man measureth, THEY measure to him."

"Nevertheless," said Matthew the Publican, "I would fain know how, when we attain to the Kingdom, the mothers of the faithful should be multiplied an hundred-fold." But some one said, in answer to Matthew, that perchance the meaning of that hard saying was, that as many as were in the Kingdom should be as one family; so that all men, esteeming one another as brethren, should look upon the mothers of their brethren as being their own mothers. Howbeit most of us agreed to the words of Judas, who said that we should take our stand upon the clear sayings of Jesus and leave the dark sayings: now Jesus had said that our houses and lands should be multiplied an hundredfold, and that saying ought to suffice for us.

Thus for that season we gave not much heed to the deep saying of Jesus: but afterwards when I wrote concerning it to Quartus the Alexandrine, of whom I spake before, he explained it after a different fashion. For he said that Jesus had in his mind a law of retribution indeed, but not such a law of retribution as that whereof the Scribes spake, but a far deeper one, a certain retribution of the soul. "For" said he, "the meaning of Jesus is (as I understand it) that whatsoever the mind of man giveth to God, this returneth from God to the mind of man again with increase, in like manner as there returneth from the earth to man whatsoever fruit or produce man trusteth to the earth. For God giveth to man many good gifts, such as food, and houses, and lands, and wealth, and friends, and kinsfolk; and these all are as seed. Now if a man keep these good gifts to himself, and use them for his own pleasure, he is like unto a husbandman that should keep his seeds in a vessel, or closet, feasting himself with .the sight thereof, and not venturing to trust them to the earth; wherefore they grow not nor return him fruits of increase. But whoso trusteth all these seeds *to God, .and useth them according to His will, behold, unto him there ariseth a harvest in heaven.

"For whosoever useth food aright, there springeth up for him cheerfulness and thankfulness and temperance and self-restraint; and whoso useth aright lands and houses and wealth, there springeth up for him liberality and generosity and magnanimity; again, whosoever casteth the seed of friendship into the lap of the divine goodness, behold there springeth up for him a tree of living friendship that knoweth not death. And in the same way, whosoever consecrateth unto God the love of mother and father, he receiveth a new power of love multiplied an hundredfold, and a new feeling of fatherhood, whereby he is drawn nearer unto the Eternal Father. For assuredly, whensoever Jesus speaketh of the increase of houses, and lands, and money, and the like, for them that enter into the Kingdom; he hath not in his mind shekels, and vines of Eschol or Engedi, but he ever seeth a certain spiritual coinage and a spiritual vineyard of the Lord."

After this manner wrote Quartus unto me; making mention at the same time of the words of Jesus, how he had said that whosoever should receive a righteous man, i.e. an observer of the law, in the name of a righteous man, should receive a righteous man's reward; and whosoever should receive a prophet in the name of a prophet, should receive a prophet's reward. "Now by these words." said Quartus, "Jesus signifieth not that a man shall have more or less of shekels, or more or less of food, or raiment, or happiness, for that he receiveth a prophet or a righteous man; but his meaning is this: that whoso by force of fellow-feeling and by the links of faith shall be bound to a righteous man, or shall be bound to a prophet in his heart, he shall become one with the righteous man or one with the prophet, so that he shall receive the like reward with the righteous man or with the prophet, to wit, increase of righteousness, or increase of the knowledge of God's will."

Whether Quartus, or he that made answer to Matthew, be the better interpreter of these words of Jesus, I know not even now: howbeit at that time we gave not much thought to these words, nor to aught else of the doctrine of Jesus. For whatsoever we had learned or whatsoever we thought that we had learned aforetime, while we were in Galilee, concerning the forgiveness of sins, and the not resisting evil, and the becoming as little children, behold, all these lessons now began to seem to us dim and far off, and fit rather for the schools of children than for the stir of the lives of men: because we were now going up to Jerusalem, and because the Day of Decision seemed nigh at hand. For each morning, when we arose, we said unto one another, "Perchance the Romans may this day attack us," and each day, when we lay down to take rest, we reckoned the time and said, "There wanteth now one day less to the day of the Passover: and on that day, if not before, Jesus must of a surety redeem Israel with the strong hand."

CHAPTER XXIV

Of the Falling away of Judas of Kerioth; and of the Times and Seasons; and of the Chief Places in the Kingdom; and how Jesus did and said nothing except it were prepared for him by the Father.

ON the last clay of the mouth Adar, as I remember, we left the young man Tobias behind us: and about three or four days afterwards, to wit on the third or fourth day of the month Nisan (which is the month of the Passover), we came down to the valley of Jordan over against Jericho. Now therefore there wanted but ten days to the fourteenth day of the month, which is the great day of the Passover. As the time drew nigh for our entering into Jerusalem, Judas began to complain very bitterly that Jesus neither strengthened nor encouraged his followers like a wise leader, but kept back some from following, and others, which followed, he made to be of a faint heart. Especially he reproached Jesus for that he did not set forth the Kingdom in clear words; "For," said he, "two or three words would suffice, if Jesus would but tell us plainly the when and the where thereof; but now he speaketh darkly, saying at one time, that it is at hand; at another time, that it is among us; anon, that it is still distant; then, that we must strive to enter into it. "Wherefore, to what is this Kingdom of God like? Even to a mist, which taketh many different shapes, because it hath no substance."

Now Jesus seemed to me to perceive what was in the mind of Judas, and to be grieved thereat; but he took no note thereof in our presence, although Judas had been these many days turning his heart from our Master and inclining himself to leave him. For indeed he had by this time begun to repent that he had ever joined himself to Jesus. Notwithstanding even now, at certain seasons, while Jesus was speaking, Judas was drawn towards him as in old times; but, as it were, perforce, and in spite of himself. Hence it came to pass that he was sorely distracted in his mind, being tossed now this way, now that, like unto a troubled sea. For sometimes, upon no apparent cause, he would break out into protestations of love for Jesus; but at other times, when he thought no one was at hand (yea, and even in our hearing when the passion was on him) he would rage and fume that he had ever left Kerioth for to join such a leader as this, declaring that Jesus would ruin all them that followed him, and saying that he could well-nigh hate him as a blind leader of the blind.

Oftentimes hath it been marvelled how it should come to pass that Jesus should have chosen Judas to be one of his apostles; for he knew what was in men. Why therefore did our Master choose for an apostle one that should afterwards betray him? But the answer which Quartus giveth is this, that, at the first, perchance Jesus did not know that Judas would betray him; yea, and had not Judas hardened himself against Jesus, he might have become a chosen vessel of the Lord.

For, at the first, Judas was no traitor, nor like unto one that should be a traitor; but of a sanguine complexion and disposition, cheerful even to mirthfulness, and frank on a first acquaintance; not given to musing nor premeditating; but active and strenuous, and withal a lover of Israel: albeit perchance somewhat too ambitious and less ready in friendship than in counsel. From a child his mind was ever given to great purposes; and towards these ends he bent all his faculties: for he was of a deep understanding, skilled in the ways of men, and of a discerning spirit, quick to perceive what means were fit to accomplish his ends. But the mischief was that the power to understand was quicker in him than the power to love; for his understanding moved as a flame of fire, but his heart was very cold.

When he first became acquainted with our Master, he straightway clave unto him as unto a great leader of the people, who was like to redeem Sion. Howbeit his heart went not out to Jesus as the heart of John the son of Zebedee, and as the heart of Simon the son of Jonah. For I remember once, when I questioned Simon Peter for what cause he first joined himself to Jesus, Peter said, "Because he had been drawn unto Jesus he knew not how, and by the hand of the Lord "; but Judas said, "Nay, but thou speakest as a sheep or a goat, in whom there is feeling but no understanding: but I applied myself to him with deliberation, as deeming him to be the fittest instrument to do good unto Sion."

Now perchance because Judas gave not so much of his heart unto our Master, for this cause he received not so much back again; wherefore he grew not in spirit like the rest, but went backward rather than forward. And when he found that Jesus of Nazareth was not to be used as an instrument, no not even to do good to Sion; then he began to repent that he had joined himself unto him. Afterwards, when Jesus first took upon him to forgive sins, this was, as it were, the turning-point in the course of Judas. For he was sore disturbed at that time, insomuch that he carried his searchings of heart written even upon his countenance. For he was much moved to have poured himself out before Jesus of Nazareth, beseeching him to take away the coldness of heart, and to give him a heart of flesh. Howbeit Satan hindered it, taking advantage of his pride; for the man was always very proud, and had hitherto been foremost among the apostles; nor could he brook now to step down from his high place and to make himself even as one of the sinners. Wherefore he opened himself not to Jesus, but hardened himself against the voice of the Lord within him.

Yet methinks the conflict was no light one in his heart; and even to the last, he could scarce refrain from giving himself up to Jesus. And, as it seemed to me, for this cause Jesus called him to be one of the Twelve, perceiving how great gifts the Lord had bestowed upon him, and also hoping, by this means, perchance, to have cast out the jealousy and the pride from his heart, and in the end, to have drawn him wholly towards himself. For if Judas could have felt that he was altogether trusted, even as the chief of all the apostles, then belike he would have cast away the pride whereon he clothed himself, and would have opened his heart to our Master; and then verily he would have been a light in Israel, not less than the greatest of the apostles. But it was not so to be; for it was otherwise willed by the Inscrutable.

So it came to pass that, from the time when he was rebuked by Jesus, as I have related above (though in truth the rebuke was not more for Judas than for the rest of the disciples), Judas withdrew himself more and more from Jesus and from the other disciples; neither would he speak freely nor ask questions as before, but he moved the other disciples to question Jesus in his stead. Yet notwithstanding when Jesus exhorted or rebuked us, Judas would ever take the rebuke unto himself above all, and say that Jesus pointed at him, though he did not mention him by name. Then would he fume and rage and depart in anger, and avoid the rest for many hours together. But when he came among the disciples, he would sow strife among us with speech of passion and jealousy; so that he was, as it were, a thorn in the side of the Master.

All this Jesus perceived, and grieved thereat. Yet he said nothing. And, as it seemed to me, his grief for Judas was swallowed up in another and a larger grief; which I understood not then, but now I understand in part. For Jesus at this time began to see more and more clearly that all or almost all in Israel should reject him; and that his disciples should prove faithless, at least for a time; and that he should bring troubles and sorrows and wars upon the earth, as well as joy and peace; and that the day of Deliverance and Redemption was further off than had been supposed. Howbeit, for all this, he turned not to the right hand nor to the left from the going up to Jerusalem: for he knew that the Lord God had an errand for him there; and that his death was to be for the life of men: and that the Lord would in the end give him the victory over all his enemies.

On the fourth day of the month Nisan, being (as I said above) the tenth day before the Passover, we set forth again on our journey to Jerusalem, and much people went with us. And when we came down from the mountains to Jordan, even to the fords of the river, then some expected that Jesus should have stretched out his hand and dried up the river j even as a certain Egyptian false prophet had lately promised to do; and likewise Elias in old times had dried up Jordan, and it had been also dried up at the word of the priests when Joshua passed over. (For both now, and before, and for a long time after, the minds of all in Israel were ready to expect any sign howsoever strange and monstrous, and to follow any that would profess to work such signs; insomuch that, about ten years ago, even on the very day that the Holy Temple was burned with fire by the Romans, even on that last day (as I have heard) a certain false Christ led some six thousand of my countrymen into one of the courtyards of the Temple, expecting a sign from heaven. So strong was faith in Israel; if it be faith indeed, to trust in any that profess to work signs and wonders.) Howbeit Jesus wrought neither this nor any other sign at this season, and we all passed over, even as the other pilgrims, by the fords; but with not a little difficulty and even some peril, for the river was marvellously swollen. Hereat some of the common people that were with us began to murmur, wondering when the time should come that Jesus should put away delays, and work such works as they expected from a Messiah.

When we came unto Gilgal we rested; but Judas made some pretext that he should go on to Jericho before us to prepare the way for Jesus; and, as I afterwards learned, he went to the house of a certain Scribe in Jericho one of his acquaintance, and a principal man among the Pharisees of that city, and he conversed with him a long time. The name of the Scribe was Azariah the son of Simon.

Now while we rested at Gilgal, we looked gladly upon Jericho, gazing at the forest of palm-trees which lay between us and the city. Much did we admire also the four towers of the city, which rose up straight to heaven on the other side of the forest, and the walls high and newly built; surrounded on all sides by thickets of balsam, and gardens of roses, and full of all delights. For the place knoweth not drought, by reason of the perpetual waters; but it is a paradise all the year round. Beyond Jericho, on the other side, we could see, rising up as it were over against us, the mountains that lead up to Jerusalem; insomuch that it was a saying with them of the Holy City that the sounds of the sacred music and the smell of the incense go down even to the men of Jericho. But the ascent is steep and the way bleak and barren, through cliffs and rocks on the right hand and on the left; where no trees are, nor any water; but robbers and murderers lurk at all times in the caves on the sides of the mountains, for to come down unawares upon the pilgrims and travellers which pass by that way. Then said Peter unto John, "Without doubt the Romans will not suffer us to go up; but they will fall upon us by the way. And should not the people be advised thereof, that they may stand upon their guard?" But John said nothing; notwithstanding, he seemed troubled that Jesus took no order for what was to come to pass upon our journey.

When we came unto Jericho, behold, the people had been advised of our coming, and on both sides of the road there was gathered together a great multitude to see Jesus as he passed; and the common people hailed him at this time by the name that was dearest unto the patriots of our nation, calling him a deliverer after the manner of David, and saying, "Hosanna, son of David." But Azariah the son of Simon, who was of the acquaintance of Judas, was come forth also; and he saluted Jesus and besought him to eat bread in his house. Howbeit Jesus would not eat bread in the house of Azariah. For as he passed through the midst of the people, he had espied a certain man, by name Zacchaeus, looking down upon him from a sycamore-tree, into the which he had climbed up, out of the fervency of his desire to see Jesus: and straightway he had called unto the man, and bidden him come down, saying that he must eat bread in the man's house. Now the man was a tax-gatherer, as might have been seen by his dress and tablets, and indeed the crowd shouted aloud that he was a tax-gatherer, when they saw that Jesus had chosen him to eat bread in his house; and they were sore displeased at Jesus. Notwithstanding Jesus was constant in his purpose not to eat bread in the house of Azariah the Rabbi, but in the house of Zacchaeus the publican. So Azariah dissembled his anger and came to the feast in the house of Zacchaeus, and certain other Pharisees with him. Howbeit they themselves feasted not with the common people and the tax-gatherers; but they conversed with Jesus and asked him questions.

Now it came to pass, during the feast, that the heart of Zacchaeus the tax-gatherer was turned unto Jesus (even as the heart of Barachiah the son of Zadok had been turned to Jesus in the house of Matthew the publican, as I related above): and he stood up and repented aloud of his evil deeds, and promised to make restitution, and that also not twofold but fourfold, saying moreover that he would give the half of his goods to the poor. And Jesus rejoiced at his words and said, "This day is salvation come unto this house, forasmuch as he also is a son of Abraham."

Now while Jesus was saying these words, I took note that Judas was making signs unto Azariah; and Jesus had scarce made an end of speaking when Azariah (upon a set plan, as I conjecture, devised with Judas) said to him, "Thou sayest that the Kingdom of Heaven is at hand: tell us therefore when cometh it, and at what hour? So shall we be prepared and ready when it cometh." But Jesus made answer to him and said, "The Kingdom of Heaven cometh not with observation. Neither shall they say, Lo here! or, Lo there! For behold " (and saying these words he pointed to Zacchaeus) "the Kingdom of Heaven is within you." At these words the face of Azariah was clouded with anger; for he had not attained that which he desired: and we also were somewhat sorry, for we had hoped that we should have heard some new thing. But Judas straightway went out of the chamber, not able to contain himself for displeasure.

When the guests and the Pharisees were gone forth, and we were alone with Jesus, we would have questioned him still further concerning this matter; but we were afraid. Howbeit many of the common people, yea and some also of ourselves, expected that on the morrow Jesus should have made an assault on the .barracks of the guard in Jericho and on the king's palace; or, at the least, that he should have suffered us to burn down the house of customs. But Jesus did none of these things: but on the morrow we set forth again to go up to Jerusalem. It was now the sixth day of the month Nisan, and the eighth day before the day of the Passover. After we had journeyed for about an hour, the way being exceeding steep, and the sun (although it was not long risen) beating with an exceeding heat upon us, by reason of the rocks and cliffs around us and before us; it came to pass that we sat down to rest. And Jesus looked down upon Jericho, and on the palm-trees thereof and on the balsam-groves, and on all the gardens of the place, and then he turned and looked to the right hand upon the country where Jordan floweth into the Dead Sea, and he opened his mouth and taught us concerning the Kingdom of God. For he said that, as in old time the cities of Sodom and Gomorrah had been swallowed up in that same sea of destruction which we saw before our eyes, even so should it be hereafter: and the Kingdom of Heaven should come in a flash, even as the lightning which lighteneth out of the one part under heaven and shineth unto the other part under heaven. But first he said that trouble should come upon the disciples; for the Son of man should be rejected, and the days should come when we should desire to see one of the days of the Son of man, and should not see it. Most of all he lamented that in the darkness of that time there should be division in Israel, yea in every household and in every corner of Israel: "I tell you in that night there shall be two men in one bed; the one shall be taken and the other left. Two women shall be grinding together; the one shall be taken and the other left. Two men shall be in the field; the one shall be taken and the other left."

Now this seemed quite contrary to the word which Jesus had spoken yesterday. For then Jesus had said that the Kingdom of God was within us; but now he said that it should come like the lightning. Howbeit, these latter words made us rejoice; for now again we were lifted up in our hearts, supposing that Jesus would work some sudden sign, to destroy our enemies in a moment of time. And Judas was now no longer able to constrain himself (for he had been sore displeased, even before, that the. question of Azariah had not been answered by Jesus): therefore, when Jesus had made an end of speaking these words, how that "the one shall be taken and the other left," supposing that now at last he should obtain to know that secret which he had so long desired to know, he leapt up in the vehemence of his desire, and cried aloud to Jesus, "Where, Master?" But Jesus paused and looked steadfastly at him and said, "Wheresoever the body is, thither will the eagles be gathered together." Saying these words, Jesus arose and turned his face from the Dead Sea and from the pleasant places of Jericho, and bent himself again to ascend the mountainous way which leadeth up to Bethany and thence to Jerusalem. But Judas remained behind standing in the same place, and there I saw him still standing and musing, long after the rest of the disciples had followed Jesus up the mountainous way.

When Judas at last overtook us, lie complained much that Jesus knew in himself what was to come to pass, and yet hid it from his followers. "For," said he, "we risk our lives for him, yet he trusteth us not." Now we were displeased at the words of Judas; for we were assured that Jesus did all things for the best. Notwithstanding we were somewhat moved because Jesus thought not fit to tell us beforehand that which was to befall us in Jerusalem and on our journey to Jerusalem. And so it was that, while we were disputing, there was a great clamour in the front of our band, and a cry went up that the Romans were upon us; and straightway there was much stir of men putting themselves in order of defence (those at least that had arms), and certain of the women cried out for fear. And Peter said it was not unlikely that the Romans should fall upon us here; for this was the very place where they had laid ambush for Athronges and slain him; moreover one came running past us saying that he had seen the glittering of their helmets, and that they were lying in wait for us at the corner of the road. Howbeit the report was false; for there were no Romans, but some one had been deceived by the shining of the sun against the rocks, and so had caused all this stir.

Now Jesus was grieved when he saw that some of the disciples were afraid; and he rebuked us, bidding us not to fear destruction of body, but only destruction of soul. He himself also showed no sign of fear, so that we marvelled at his steadfastness and stoutness of heart. Nevertheless Judas said that it would have been better if Jesus, being a prophet, had forewarned the multitude and had said unto them, "The Romans will not fall upon us save at Bethany, or so many furlongs on this side of Bethany; or, they will not fall upon us to-day, but to-morrow at the seventh hour, naming the place and time exactly:" and this, said Judas, would have been far better than that our band should thus be thrown into a confusion upon a mere rumour.

We said nothing against Judas; for we knew not what to say: neither do I perfectly know even to this day. But Quartus saith that "Jesus knew not all these things exactly, but only generally, and as it were on a large scale; as if a pilot, piloting a vessel into an haven, should know the winds, and the currents, and the shoals, and the aspect and form of the coast, but not all the pebbles upon the strand, nor even the very moment that the ship should come into the harbour. For by certain signs of the times," said Quartus, "Jesus discerned of that which was to come, even as a wise mariner foretelleth the weather by the clouds, and winds, and the other signs in the heavens. Neither was Jesus like unto a magician or common enchanter who pretendeth to change the course of things by his enchantment; but he was even as a Son of God, who can read what is in the book of the future, yea, and can shape the future, because he doeth all things in accordance with the invisible laws of God."

Thus far Quartus; but concerning these things I know not, neither pronounce judgment. But let us return to our journey. Soon after these things, going to John the son of Zebedee, I found him conversing with his mother; and he received me with a constrained countenance not according to his custom. Presently I perceived that his mother desired him to do a certain thing, which he was loth to do. It seemed that Judas had been speaking to her, saying that it was fit that strife should be quenched among the disciples by determination once and for all who should have the first places in the Kingdom; for, said he, until this be settled, there must still be quarrelling among the disciples. For Simon Peter, forsooth, had supposed himself to be chief, because Jesus had blessed him and given unto him a title; but the sons of Zebedee had done no less deeds, and shown no less zeal, than Peter; and they, as well as Peter, had received a title, having been called Sons of Thunder; wherefore then (said Judas) should they not claim the first places? For himself, he said, he had no thoughts about such high matters; for Jesus loved him not as the rest. Howbeit, he desired that the expedition should not fail owing to the strife among the disciples. Now Jesus had promised that if two or three of his disciples agreed touching anything they should ask, it should be done for them. Therefore he bade the mother of John go with her two sons to Jesus and ask of him a certain favour; and if Jesus granted it, then she was to ask that her two sons might be next to Jesus in the place of honour in the New Kingdom.

When James and John had been at last persuaded by their mother, they made their petition unto Jesus. But Jesus refused it, saying that to sit on his right hand and on his left hand was not his to give, save to those for whom it had been prepared by the Father. For he would do nothing unjustly, nor out of respect for persons; but here, as in all things, he desired to conform himself to the unseen ordinances of the Father. And herein Jesus showed himself very different from that which he was supposed to be by Jonathan the son of Ezra. For Jonathan supposed that he was misled by his desires, and that whatsoever things seemed to Jesus desirable, these Jesus fancied to be true: but it was not so; for no one ever saw, more clearly than Jesus, that which must needs be. Only he rebelled not against it, but willingly submitted himself to it and embraced it, as being the will of the Father, and therefore very good. For this cause both now and at other times, he spake of all his words and works as being prepared for him; saying that he could neither do nor say anything of himself, but only that which the Father had prepared. Also I marked, both at this time and often before and after, how Jesus joined together in himself virtues that mix not well together in the minds of most. For with most men a nature that judgeth well and wisely is somewhat cold; and they which love warmly, love neither wisely nor well, but are fond. But with Jesus it was not so: for the more he loved men, the more he loved justice and truth; because, as I suppose, his love of men on earth sprang out of his love of Him in heaven whose name is Truth and Justice.

On this same day Jesus spake much concerning that which was to come; and all his words tended to sadness. For he lamented over the divisions among his disciples, and the divisions that should be in the world, saying that it was as if he had not come to bring peace but a sword; yea, and that he had verily come to kindle a fire upon the earth. Moreover of the day of Redemption he spake as though it were a great way off, and the disciples would need to wait long for it, and to watch, and to pray, and to resist many temptations. Howbeit in every parable he spake confidently of a certain day of Decision or Judgment, when the good should be separated from the evil, and the evil should be cast into the fire, but the good should be preserved for everlasting life.

These things he said to all the disciples; but when the Twelve, and we that were always with him, were come to him in the inn where he rested during the heat of the noontide, he spake privately to us concerning our disputings and contentions among ourselves. For he had noted how sorely the rest of the apostles were displeased at John and James; and also at other times he had perceived that we were jealous one of another. Wherefore he besought us (and as it seemed to me there were even tears in his eyes) to be at peace among ourselves. Moreover he spake about himself, saying that he had a cup of sorrow to drink and a baptism of suffering to be baptized withal, and that he had come to give his life a ransom for the multitude. Therefore if any man among us desired to be chief of all and foremost of all, he desired that man to be foremost in serving, and in ministering, and in suffering; even as he also came to be a sufferer and a minister for the multitude.

Then he besought us with great passion and fervency to suffer nothing to come between us and our entrance into the Kingdom, saying that it were better for us to cut off our right hand or pluck out our right eye and so to enter into life, rather than to enter with two eyes and hands into darkness, into the valley of Hinnom, where the worm ceaseth not and the fire is not quenched. Finally, he lamented over the world, how that it was not fit to be a sacrifice to the Father because it was not salted; and he called us the salt of the world: "But if," said he, "the salt hath lost its savour, wherewith shall the salting be performed?"

Now some of his words were hidden from us, but these last were easy to understand. And we were ashamed of our disputings, and because we were not like unto our Master in singleness of heart. Judas also himself seemed to be moved somewhat at the time: yet, soon after, he spake again as before, saying that it was impossible to obey Jesus, because Jesus said at one time one thing and at another time another; "Wherefore," added Judas, "inasmuch as our Master will neither plan nor perform aught to do good unto himself, methinks it is meet that we his disciples should strive to do him good, even though it be against his own will."

CHAPTER XXV

Concerning the Fire of the Lord; and of the Parables of Watching; and of the Holy Spirit; and how Quartus urgeth that Jesus knew not All Things beforehand.

AFTER Jesus had made an end of this exhortation, he set forth on his journey to go towards Bethany, which lay still far up above us. There was in his countenance even such a brightness as we had noted when he came down from the mountain with Peter and James and John. Whereat we marvelled, because he that had but now spoken to us with such a passion of sorrow concerning a cup of suffering and death, seemed to go towards suffering and death like unto one triumphing in glory. Howbeit we feared to ask him further concerning these things; but we followed after him, questioning among ourselves.

Now Judas ceased not cavilling at the exhortation of Jesus, saying that it was not fit that a leader should make himself like a child, nor that whoso would fain be greatest should make himself least; "For," said Judas, "a leader must lead, not follow; and he must command, not obey; and he must have the forethought of a man to arrange all things orderly, not the afterthought of a child to adventure all things at hazard. Now Jesus, in his former days, when he was like himself, ever took upon himself the part of leader, yea, even a leader greater than Moses; for he was wont to speak in our ears such words as these, It was said to them of old time, Do this, but *I* say unto you, Do that; and again, Come unto *me*, and *I* will give you rest; Take my yoke upon you, and the like. Were not these words the words of a leader? But now what saith he? Even such words as these: 'I am not a leader, but a follower'; 'I am not as the greatest, but as the least'; 'I am not a conqueror, but as one to be vanquished, yea and already vanquished, even as a lamb led to the slaughter.' Nor doth he give command beforehand, nor warn us how to meet the enemy, nor where to expect the onset. But behold it wanteth but a week or less, and there cometh the Passover; and nothing is settled. Verily we are as sheep without a shepherd."

Thus spake Judas in the bitterness of his heart, more freely than he had ever spoken before (at least in our presence), and we marvelled at the bitterness of his speech. But Peter rebuked him and said, "Say not such words as these, Judas, for of a surety Jesus is our leader even unto death; but his ways are not as our ways, and we must have faith in him. Howbeit concerning what is to come to pass on the day after the morrow, somewhat, as I know, is already settled; for he purposeth to enter the Holy City publicly, even before the face of all that dwell in Jerusalem. Now when that cometh to pass, then doubtless he will be moved to perform some mighty work. I say not that he will smite with the sword; for he ever shrinketh from the sword. But perchance he will pray unto the Lord, and the earth will open for our enemies, even as it opened for the children of Korah, or fire will go forth from the presence of our Master himself, and he will consume his enemies with the fervency of his breath. For the mercies of the Lord are manifold, and very many are His paths for the destruction of the wicked."

When Judas heard mention of the going of Jesus into Jerusalem, he held his peace, thinking (as I perceived from his words afterwards) that this was perchance a sign that Jesus was minded to become a leader indeed. But another, taking up the word spoken by Simon Peter touching the fire from the presence of Jesus, said, "And perchance this fire is even what our Master signifieth, when he saith that the adversaries shall be cast into the fire." But another said, "Nay, but it is written, the punishment of malefactors shall be fire and worms. Also it is written in the prophet Isaiah that, when all things are made anew, in that day the righteous shall go up to Jerusalem to worship the Lord, 'and they shall go forth and look upon the carcasses of the men that have transgressed against me; for their worm shall not die, neither shall their fire be quenched.' Therefore it is most certain that, when Jerusalem shall be purified, the adversaries shall be cast forth into the valley of Hinnom, even to the fire and worms; and they shall be an abhorring to all flesh."

To this the most part agreed. Only Nathanael seemed doubtful; but he said nothing in the hearing of the rest. But when I questioned him concerning the meaning of the words of Jesus, he answered that he knew not for certain what they meant; only he felt assured that Jesus had in his mind not a visible but some kind of invisible fire, which preyeth upon wickedness, even as the fire whereon we look preyeth upon fuel. This seemed to me at that time a hard saying, but now I consent unto it.

And to the same effect spake Quartus afterwards, saying, "To Jesus the invisible things were visible, even as those things which are seen with the eyes; yea, they were more visible. Therefore when he looked upon the hearts of men and discerned in them jealousy or malignity or hypocrisy, behold, such men seemed to him as men that are suffering from a sore disease, which disease must be burned away with the fires of God. For as the all-encompassing sunlight bringeth life to them which are whole, but fiery heats to them in whose veins the fever rageth, even so the fire of God (which compasseth all invisible things, so that naught can escape from the flame thereof) purifieth that which will be purified, but consumeth that which is corrupt, according as it is written, 'The jealousy of the Lord burneth like fire for ever.'"

Now Xanthias, the Greek merchant of Alexandria, was wont to say that Jesus would have done well to make distinction between the fire of God and the fires of men; lest his disciples should be led astray by his words, and lest they should suppose that Jesus was speaking of earthly destruction. But if Xanthias had lived unto these days, and had seen how, after the death of our Master, the most part of our nation were given up to darkness and madness, and their city and temple were burned with fire, and they themselves were consumed by hundreds and by thousands, then, as it seemeth to me, he would have perceived that the fire whereof Jesus spake consumeth alike things visible and invisible, and on earth as well as not on earth. Howbeit at this season we understood none of these things, and almost all thought that the Romans and other Gentiles in Jerusalem, and whosoever of our own nation stood up against our Master, should be slain and cast out into the valley of Hinnom to be consumed by fire and worms.

But while we thus disputed among ourselves, behold, we were now come nigh unto the village called Bethany; which lieth high up on the mountain called the Mount of Olives, and looketh, from above, upon the road that goeth down to Jericho. And from Bethany to Jerusalem is but sixteen furlongs or less. Here therefore our journey was at an end; for our Master was to tarry at Bethany, in the house of Mary and Martha, for that night and during the morrow also; for the Sabbath was at hand. But of the rest of our band, some few remained with us; others went forward a little space to Bethphage, which was about a Sabbath day's journey; others, and these the greater part, hasted to pass into Jerusalem before the Sabbath should have begun; for there wanted but one hour of sunset.

During all that night Jesus said not much to us. Only, while speaking to the women after supper, he discoursed concerning the need of patience, and how the disciples in the New Kingdom must be like unto wise virgins going unto a wedding, which take not only lighted lamps, but also good store of oil that they may keep their lamps alight; but the foolish, which take no oil, have not their lamps alight when the bridegroom arriveth suddenly: wherefore they come too late for the feast and are shut out. Thereby, said Peter, Jesus seemed to mean that he was to leave us for a time and to return suddenly; and whoso was not prepared to meet him should be shut out from the Kingdom. Some other parables Jesus spake to the same effect.

Now concerning these parables Quartus judgeth that Jesus spake in them of his resurrection. "For," said he, "the meaning of Jesus was, that if the disciples had not prayed unto the Lord, and watched and waited after his death (but contrariwise had given themselves over to idleness and folly, as men desperate), then Jesus would never have appeared to them; and they would have been shut out from the Kingdom" Others interpret the words, as if Jesus spake of some other coming, which may not perchance be fulfilled in our days. But I incline rather to think that our Master prophesied partly concerning some future coming which is not yet fulfilled; and partly concerning his resurrection and manifestation to us his disciples, soon to be fulfilled; but partly also concerning our nation: how that, after his death, some few should be ready to receive him, but the greater part should be unready; and as for these, darkness should fall upon their hearts, and then the door should be shut, and they should grope around the door, but find no entrance. Which things have indeed come to pass. For at the first, Israel was desirous to enter into the Kingdom, but now the veil is upon their hearts, so that they can no longer have light to enter into the Kingdom, no, not though they desire it.

The morrow, as I have said, was the Sabbath; and all the day, Jesus sat still in the house talking with the women, especially with Mary and Martha the sisters of our host; neither did he go forth all that day, save that he went to the village of Bethphage to see some sick folk. But in the evening he spake to us very kindly, yea, very tenderly, even more than his wont. And though he said not many words, yet all his words were concerning us, not concerning himself; or, if he spake of himself, it was for our sakes, as if he were striving to look into the darkness of that which was to come, so that he might discern what perils awaited us, for to warn us thereof.

As we walked towards Bethphage, it came to pass that Philip said to Jesus (thinking to please him), that certain Greeks which were in Jerusalem desired to see him. Now so it was, that when Philip spake these words, we chanced to be passing through the fields of corn; and the corn was now strong and in ear, for the spring was well advanced. But Jesus stopped at that word Greeks, and looked down at the corn; and then he said that the hour was verily come when he should be glorified: "For," said he, "except a corn of wheat fall into the ground, it abideth alone: but if it die, it bringeth forth much fruit." Then he went on to say that, after his death, we need not fear lest we should be left desolate, for a Spirit should strengthen us; and of this Spirit he spake, at one time as coming from himself, but at another time as coming from his Father; moreover it should come to us, he said, by a certain ordinance, which could not be altered. For just as the ear of wheat cometh not unless the corn of wheat first die, even so his Spirit should not come, except he also should first depart from us.

Hereat Judas brake out in hot anger, "Wherefore, then, go we up to Jerusalem, if our going is to be for naught, and if thou art to depart from us, and if we are to be left as sheep without a shepherd?" Jesus rebuked him not, neither answered as we had expected; but said that it could not be that a prophet should perish out of Jerusalem. Hereat one said, "Nay but, Master, the prophet John perished not in Jerusalem." But to this Jesus made no answer; but only spake a few words touching the difference between the simplicity of the Galileans and the subtlety of the men of Jerusalem; and he condemned the Scribes of Jerusalem and the priests of the temple, for that they made darkness instead of light, causing all Israel, and even the Galileans, to transgress. He also spake as if Satan reigned in the Holy City, and as if he were shortly going down to do battle there with Satan in Jerusalem. So he seemed to signify that Jerusalem was as it were a field of battle, whereon it was meet and right that a true prophet should die. After this he added, that if he were lifted up in the sight of all men, he should draw all men unto him. This joining together of words diverse in nature, of perishing and lifting up, and of departing and drawing all men unto him, filled us with perplexity; insomuch that Judas said in a low voice that the words of Jesus were like unto oil and vinegar, which cannot be mixed. The rest of us also showed, as I suppose, by our countenances that we understood him not; for he looked kindly on us, and rebuked us not, but said that he had yet many things to say unto us, but we could not bear them now. He also added at another time, this promise, that a Spirit of Truth should come, which should guide us into all the truth.

Now so it was that, while Jesus was saying these words, we were now drawing nigh unto Bethphage, and we spake concerning the going into Jerusalem on the morrow. And it came to pass that Matthew, looking upon an ass (which was standing in the village at the back of a house where two ways met), made mention of a certain prophecy which saith that the Messiah shall come into Jerusalem, not as an Egyptian nor as an Assyrian (for they ride in chariots or on horses), but as one of the princes of our nation, who used to ride on asses; and the words were these, "Rejoice greatly, daughter of Sion; shout, daughter of Jerusalem; behold, thy king cometh unto thee. He is meek and having salvation, lowly and riding upon an ass, and a colt, the foal of an ass." Now Jesus overheard these words, but said nothing; yet, as it seemed to me, he took note thereof.

When we returned to the house, Jesus gave command for the morrow, that we should rise early to go down into Jerusalem with him, and that certain of the disciples should go before the rest into Jerusalem, even to our friends and companions there, for to instruct them concerning the time of the going down of Jesus, that they might come forth to meet us. Hereat we rejoiced greatly: and all the teaching of Jesus concerning his death and departure, and concerning the days of trouble and of parting, quite vanished away; and even Judas was glad. And now our minds began to be set once more, and even more than before, upon the Kingdom, and upon our places in the Kingdom. So when we lay down on the supper couches, our tongues still harped thereon; and our disputings were so loud that Jesus could not but hear them. Then was he sore displeased that we should thus think of ourselves when he was to depart from us; and he opened his mouth to speak. But he spake not; for it was as if no words could avail to pierce the hardness of our hearts. Howbeit, when supper was ended and I was gone forth from the chamber, then, as it was reported to me by some (but others say that it happened on another evening), he arose from the table, and girded himself as a servant, and would wash the feet of all the disciples; and when they would have resisted, he constrained them; but when he had made an end, he said, "I have given you an example that ye should do as I have done to you."

After this manner therefore that Sabbath ended; but throughout the whole of the Sabbath and all the evening after, yea and on the morrow, and during all the days before his suffering, Jesus, as it now appeareth unto me, was wholly bent upon serving us, and upon helping us, thinking ever of our needs and our weaknesses, and how we should fare without him, and how he could strengthen us so that we might be ready when he suddenly came back to us. For our sakes also, as I judge, he made entry after that public and solemn fashion into Jerusalem, to the intent that no man might hereafter reproach any of us and say, "Thy master was no Messiah; for he dared not show himself as Messiah before the face of the people; neither did he claim allegiance, but only professed himself a servant; nor did he manifest bravery, but hid himself from his enemies even to the last."

For this cause do I in no wise assent to the saying of Xanthias, that the going in of Jesus into Jerusalem was not worthy of him. For, as I judge, he did it for our sakes, and not for his own; yea, and for the sake of the whole world; that it might be on record for ever how that the Son of man, though he were the humblest of men, did nevertheless claim for himself the allegiance of all them that were in the city, yea, and of all that were in the inhabited world; as if he were at once the king and the servant of mankind.

But as touching that other saying (not of Xanthias, but of the Scribe Hezekiah) that, "If Jesus had been a prophet indeed, he should have prophesied unto his disciples the whole manner of his death, and the manner of his resurrection, and the manner of the giving of the Holy Spirit," concerning this I say nothing, as one doubtful and waiting for the truth. But Quartus is perchance herein too bold (though he speak out of his great love for the Lord Jesus) in saying that our Master "knew not little matters that were to come, but only great matters. And so he knew that the fire of heaven would fall on Jerusalem, but when it would fall, this was hidden from him. Likewise, he knew that he must die; for unless he died his Spirit would not come; but when the Spirit should come, this too was hidden from him.

"Yea and even as touching his own death and rising again; that he should go unto the Father he knew, and that he should come again he knew; but on what day he should come again, and at what hour he should manifest himself to his disciples, this he knew not. And even for this cause, perchance," saith Quartus (who was not present in

Jerusalem when the Lord suffered and rose again), "he was so earnest with you that ye should give your minds to watching and praying in the hour when he should be taken from you; to the intent that, when he came suddenly back to you from the grave (manifesting himself to you in the night, whether in the first watch, or at midnight, or at cockcrow, or whensoever it might be) he might not find you given over to surfeit and drunkenness, and to the thoughts and cares of this present world; and so your hearts should be closed against the sight of him, and he should not be able to reveal himself unto you. For if, when Jesus died, ye had given yourselves over to despair and recklessness, then though Jesus himself had stood before you, coming from his grave, yet would ye none the more have seen him."

Against these words of Quartus there standeth, as it were, in opposition, a certain prophecy of Jesus, wherein he was wont to declare to us that he should be raised from the dead in three days, limiting the time exactly. And true it is that Jesus made often mention of certain words of the prophet Hosea which speak thus about being revived in three days: "Come and let us return unto the Lord: for he hath torn and he will heal us; he hath smitten, and he will bind us up. After two days will he revive us: in the third day he will raise us up, and we shall live in his sight." Now because of this prophecy, which was very often in the mouth of Jesus, it hath been supposed by many that Jesus knew for certain that he should die on the day of the Passover, and that he should lie in the grave two days, and be raised up on the third day.

But to this Quartus yieldeth not. For he saith that the words "two days" and "three days" were used by the prophet Hosea to signify only "a short time," even as the Romans also, and men of other nations, speak of "the day after the morrow," or "in a day or two," when they mean "a short time hence "; or even as the Hebrew tongue, speaking of past time, useth "the third day" to signify "some time ago." Moreover Quartus urgeth that, if Jesus had known of the day and hour, he would assuredly not have harrowed our souls with a needless sorrow, but would have told them to us; and he thinketh that Jesus spake concerning his coming from the grave, when he said that the day of the coming of the Son of man was not known to any, neither to the angels, nor even to the Son himself, but only to the Father.

"Therefore in my judgment," saith Quartus, "when Jesus spake about the fire which should consume his enemies, and concerning his death and lifting up or glorifying, and concerning his departing and coming again, and concerning the giving of the Holy Spirit, he knew indeed that all these things must needs come to pass, because they were according to the pattern and ordinance of things invisible; but when, and where, and how they should come to pass, he knew not. Neither did he hide that which he knew, cloaking it from you his disciples, for to keep you in ignorance and in suspense; but he spake as he knew, and all that he knew, so far as ye could understand it."

Thus wrote Quartus to me; and sometimes I incline to his words, but at other times I do not. Howbeit, to whichsoever opinion I incline, it mattereth little; for whether Jesus knew little or much of that which was to come (and he himself told us that he knew not all), my love for him is the same: save that sometimes it seemeth to me as if he were almost more lovable and more divine, going forth into the darkness of death in trust and faith, and knowing not everything that was to betide him, than if he had had the descents and ascents and all the paths of Hades marked out for him exactly beforehand as in a chart.

CHAPTER XXVI

How Jesus went down to Jerusalem, as a King, to wage war against Satan in the Temple,; and how he foresaw that the Temple must be cast down; and of the Parable of the Withered Fig-Tree.

ON the morrow (which was the first day of the week), some of us rose earlier than the rest, and went down to Jerusalem to carry word to the other disciples and to such as were friendly among the Galileans (for many of them favoured us at this time, and a great number of them had come up to the Feast) that they might come forth from the city to meet Jesus and to welcome him. But the rest of us stayed with Jesus in Bethany. About the second hour of the day, when we were now about to set forth, Jesus sent Matthew the tax-gatherer, and another, to the village over against us, bidding them bring the ass whereof we had taken note yesterday; and if any man said aught, Matthew was to make answer that "the Master hath need of him." When the ass was brought, Jesus mounted thereon, and we set forth at once; and it was now about the third hour of the day.

When Bethany was by this time out of our sight, as we went by the road that lieth between the Tombs of the Prophets and the Mount of

Offence, suddenly we heard a shouting as of a mixed multitude, and presently we discerned a great crowd of the disciples coming over the brow of the hill towards us, with many hundreds of the Galileans, all waving palm-branches in their hands, and hailing Jesus as the son of David. Now Jesus was riding before our band, upon the ass; but when the two bands met, there was a great shouting for joy; and the former band turned round and went on as vanguard, but our band marched on behind. Presently, as we drew near to the descent of the Mount of Olives, when we began to descry that quarter of the Holy City which men called the City of David, the shouting became louder, and so it continued, even there where the road descendeth so that the Holy City is no longer seen.

But when at last we attained unto the summit of the Mount Olivet, so that the whole of the city was seen at once spread out before our eyes, with all the roofs, and towers, and pinnacles thereof, and the gilded battlements of the temple, shining like fire in the sun, then indeed the splendour of the sight so lifted up our hearts that we were even beside ourselves for admiration; and looking unto Jesus as the King of all this glory, we cried even louder than before unto him as our King and Conqueror, like unto David of old. But Jesus neither now nor at any time during the entering into Jerusalem seemed at all lifted up by our salutations and praises; nor yet, on the other hand, was he of a gloomy or sad countenance as though he foreboded evil and ruin. Rather he was as one waiting and expecting, looking perchance for some sign of the will of the Lord, in case it might yet please Him to turn the hearts of the Pharisees, that they might be converted and live. Therefore also when he looked on the glory of Jerusalem below his feet, he was neither astonished at the beauty thereof, nor did he (at least at this time) weep or lament over it: but he gazed at it, as it were in suspense and questioning his own spirit; if perchance it might be the Lord's pleasure to manifest Himself to the daughter of Sion, and to stay His hand from destroying the beautiful city; or whether that could not be, but evil must take his course.

But we, at this time, perceived naught of that which was in our Master's mind; but we lifted up our voices and shouted amain, hailing him as Son of David, and crying, "Hosanna to the Son of David! Blessed is He that cometh in the name of the Lord! Blessed is the kingdom that cometh of our father David!" Some also cast their palm-branches down in the road before him, and others strewed their garments in the path to do him honour. After this fashion therefore, shouting, and singing, and praising God, the whole multitude of us came down from the mountain into the valley below.

When we drew nigh unto the gate of the city, we saw that only some few of the citizens were come forth to welcome us. For the most part feared Jesus, lest he should bring down the wrath of the Romans upon the Holy City; neither knew they him as the Galileans knew him. But instead of the citizens, there stood a great throng of children gathered together before the gate; and when they heard the voices of the disciples and the voices of the Galileans, immediately they also took up the cry, and sang "Hosanna, Hosanna," in a clear shrill voice, after the manner of children, so that their song sounded forth quite distinctly, and above all the noise and shouting of the multitude. Now of the Pharisees, none had gone forth from the city to welcome Jesus; but certain of the younger among them, desirous to look on the coming in of Jesus, as on a show in a theatre (and perchance willing, by the manifesting of their contempt of him, to overawe and to control the multitude of pilgrims), were come as far as the gate; and there they stood, over against the children, waiting the coming of Jesus, and with many gestures and beckonings signifying their displeasure. When therefore they heard the sound of the singing, they straightway rebuked the children, and would have them to hold their peace: but when the children would not, then turned the Pharisees in sore displeasure to Jesus, and bade him constrain them. .

Now Jesus all this while had seemed rapt in other matters; even as if he heard not the shouting nor the singing, neither understood the meaning thereof; but as if he heard other voices which we could not hear, and which, even for him, were not easy to understand. And when he drew nigh unto the gate of the city, and beheld the Pharisees, how they stood all together, and made no sign of welcome; then he looked up (methinks as I now remember it) with a wistful countenance to the gate, as though he partly expected that the very stones should cry out from the wall (according to the saying of the prophet Habakkuk), as if bearing-witness against the unbelief of the Pharisees. Even thus looked Jesus, as he drew nigh to the gate, and there seemed as it were a shadow of doubt and expectancy upon his face; and just then it was that the Pharisees thrust themselves in his way and bade him stop the brawling of the children, for so they termed it.

Now for an instant Jesus seemed scarce to understand the intent of the Pharisees, nor even the meaning of their words. But when he perceived it, and when he turned his face toward the children (who all this time ceased not from their singing, but cried Hosanna, Hosanna, even louder than before), then his mind seemed to come back to earth, and his countenance became clearer, and he smiled for joy; for methought in the voices of those simple children he acknowledged the very voice of the Father in Heaven speaking by His little ones on earth, and showing unto him how that there must be no sign of fire from Heaven, nor no mighty work of any visible sort; but only strength through weakness, and wisdom through simplicity, and the Kingdom of God through little children, according to the eternal ordinance.

This behaviour of Jesus, though we understood it not then, yet was it partly interpreted to us, even at that time, by the answer which he made unto the Pharisees, saying unto them, "Verily I say unto you, if these should hold their peace, the very stones should cry out." Moreover, afterwards, when they would have had him rebuke them in the Temple, and when they said unto him, "Hearest thou what these say?" then Jesus spake unto them yet more clearly, and said, "Yea, have ye never read, 'Out of the mouths of babes and sucklings Thou hast perfected praise'?"

When we came to the foot of Mount Moriab, we arrayed ourselves to enter into the temple, and we went in by the gate called Shush an. But lo, the courts of the temple and all the ways which lead into the courts were crowded with oxen and doves, and drovers and money-changers; and it was more like unto a market-place or shambles than to a temple of the Lord: even as I had beheld it two years before, when I came to offer sacrifice during my mother's sickness, yea, and worse also. For during the week before the Passover, almost the whole of the Jewish nation was wont to assemble in Jerusalem for to offer sacrifice, even as many (so it hath been reported to me, but it is well nigh past belief) as three hundred myriads; wherefore, though there should be but one lamb slain for a score of pilgrims, yet the number of beasts to be sacrificed at one time must needs be many thousands, not less than one hundred and fifty thousand. When Jesus looked around on all this stir and traffic, he was sore displeased, and his anger was very hot, yea, such as I had seldom noted the like in him before; and he bade the merchants and money-changers take their wares hence. But when they would not, he made unto himself a scourge of cords and drove them before him; and the disciples and the people did the same, and overthrew the tables of the money-changers, and thrust out them which sold doves. And Jesus said unto the Pharisees, "It is written, My house shall be called the House of Prayer; but ye have made it a den of thieves."

When Jesus spake these words, the Pharisees were exceeding wrath, and certain of their servants ran forward as if they would have laid hands on Jesus. Howbeit, Hezekiah the Scribe (the same of whom I have often made mention above) checked them, lest there should have been a tumult of the people. But it was plain to all men that they would fain have destroyed Jesus, only they feared the people. Therefore Jesus made no long stay for that day in the temple, but gave commandment to return to Bethany (for he would not tarry in Jerusalem by night lest the chief priests and Pharisees should lay hands upon him); and certain of the disciples accompanied us to the gate of the city, but not many.

While we were going through the streets of the city toward the gate, we conversed concerning that which had happened, and especially concerning the driving out of the merchants and the money-lenders; and most said that it was well done, for the presence of them that bought and sold denied the House of the Lord. But a certain Greek, of Philip's acquaintance (one of them that had desired Philip that they might see Jesus), said that it was not well done of our Master, thus with his own hand to drive out them that bought and sold: " For," said he, "it is not the part of a philosopher to use violence, nor to be moved by passion to anything that is against seemliness and dignity, nor to take upon himself the part of a common door-keeper." Not much was said in answer at that time, for other thoughts possessed our minds; only John said that our Master did well to be angry, because he saw his Father's House defiled. Nevertheless oftentimes, since that day, the words of the Greek have come into my mind, and also other like words of Xanthias, how that "towards the end of his life, Jesus of Nazareth was driven out of the bounds of his patience by the persecution of enemies; so that he became bitter and somewhat austere."

But my judgment is not so. For to me it seemeth that all through those days of tarrying in Jerusalem and in Bethany, our Master was neither bitter nor austere. But he had ever before his eyes the thought of us his disciples; and he was ever musing on our desolation, (which, should fall upon us when he should be parted from us), and how we should fare, contending without him against the Pharisees and against all other evil. Therefore he desired to leave it, as it were, on record, that the worst kind of sacrilege is the sacrilege of them which handle sacred things without the feeling thereof. And, as he had entered into Jerusalem like one having authority, so he desired perchance (for our sakes) to manifest himself, in the temple also, as one to whom obedience was due. Again, whereas Xanthias saith that Jesus, ever before in Galilee, taught us to endure evil) and not to put down evil by force, as now in Jerusalem; "The former rule," saith Quartus, "applieth only to the brethren that live in the midst of them that know not the truth. But wheresoever a nation or a congregation, shall recognise a certain law" (as our nation did in the worship of the temple), "there perchance the breaking of the law is not to be suffered, and the law is to be maintained, even by force. For it is one thing to avenge oneself, but another to avenge a law." After this manner wrote Quartus; but, in any case, Xanthias was assuredly wrong in saying that Jesus was "embittered by persecution;" unless it be bitter to call Satan Satan. For he was gentle and tender and very loving even to the last.

Howbeit at this time our thoughts were full of other matters, so that we were the less bent on defending our Master against the friend of Philip. For we were something downcast, and Judas even more than the rest, because nothing had come of our entering into Jerusalem; but, as Judas phrased it, all our great purposes had ended in naught. "For," said Judas, "the Lord hath given occasions, but we have used them not. For first, when we entered in at this same gate this morning, then I looked that Jesus should have given the word to disarm the guard that kept watch therein. But afterwards, when we had entered into the city and all the citizens were gathered to us, then at least I hoped to have heard him give commandment to assail the Fort of Antonia; or else I expected that he would have worked some sign in heaven, to have turned every one to our side, and so to have driven out the Gentiles without shedding of blood. But now we have gained nothing. Nay, we have lost everything. For we shall not again gather the multitude thus round us. And as for the Pharisees, he hath now so angered them that, even were he to work an hundred signs in heaven, I doubt they would not now accept him." Hereupon John said that we must have patience and trust in Jesus; but Judas made answer that the time had passed for patience, and that other courses must be tried.

For the space of two days, namely, the second day of the week, and likewise the third day, Jesus resorted to the temple daily, and taught the people there: but the more he saw of the temple, and of the priests therein, and likewise of the Pharisees and Sadducees (who disputed with him daily in the temple), so much the more his heart loathed the abominations which he discerned, insomuch that he seemed like unto one contending against Satan himself, enthroned in the Holy Place; and his words against the Pharisees in those days were as if he desired that they should be engraven in fiery letters upon the hearts of all that heard him, for ever. So hot was the vehemency of his passion against them; yet not against them, but against the Satan in their hearts, who through them reigned over Israel. For whatsoever Jesus had noted of evil in the teaching of the Scribes in Galilee, and whatsoever of blindness and narrowness, yea, and of persecution and malignity; all this, and much more did he note in the Scribes of Jerusalem; insomuch that the Holy City and the temple itself now seemed to him to have become a very source of evil, poisoning the waters of life for the whole of the people.

At the first, the Pharisees began to lay snares to take him at an advantage before the face of all the people; but he answered them according to their folly, proving to all the people that they knew not the foundations of truth. When they asked him by what authority he did that which he did, he would not tell them; but they must first tell him whether the baptism of John were from heaven or no; which question they feared to answer. As to the giving of tribute, he said that the denarius (which had on it the image of Caesar) spake, of itself, that they that used it should give Caesar his due. But when he gave back unto the Pharisee the denarius, saying these words, "Render therefore to Caesar the things which are Caesar's," then he paused for an instant, and afterwards added, "and to God the things that are God's." This he said, not as though some things belonged to Caesar and not to God; but as though each man, in giving unto Caesar his dues, must bear in mind that he was thereby giving to God his dues also; for a time might come when it might be a defrauding of God to give Caesar tribute; but, at that time, to have refused tribute to Caesar, would have been to refuse God His dues. So he bade them obey the signs of the times, yet so as never to defraud God; nor would he lay down any rule, as they had desired, but pointed to the foundations of righteousness, which lie in the heart and not in the hands. The like also he did in saying that the love of God and of man was the chief commandment of the Law. But concerning the Sadducees and their doctrine, that there is no resurrection, he said that the second life differeth from the first as much as angels differ from men; so that the bands whereby we are bound together here, will not be the same as will bind us together there. Howbeit he said not that there should be no bands hereafter, nor that these present bands should vanish; but only that they should be different, and not carnal, but spiritual. Moreover he questioned the Pharisees concerning their expectations of the Messiah and their interpretations of the Scriptures; and they could not make answer to his questions.

But all these were only as the beginnings of the conflict. For presently the Pharisees began to wax more vehement in their disputations and to reveal their hatred of him more clearly. And when Jesus looked upon their faces, he discerned his own death instant therein. So he turned and spake to the people in parables, likening Israel to an estate let out to greedy husbandmen, which killed the servants of their lord, and last of all slew his son also, when he came to receive of the fruits of the land. Again, he likened the Kingdom of Heaven to a wedding feast, and the Pharisees to murderous people, subjects of a king; who would not come to the wedding of the king's son, but slew his servants that invited them. Then one in the crowd, a Galilean by birth, and a man of loose life, cried aloud, "That is well said, prophet; for we, that are poor, shall enter into the Kingdom; but the rich shall not enter." But Jesus straightway continued his parable and described an unworthy guest, admitted indeed to the feast, but soon cast out, because he had come in not having on a wedding garment.

Thus all the day was spent in contention; but in the evening, at Bethany, Jesus spake unto us very tenderly concerning the Holy Spirit (the mention whereof was at this time daily more and more upon his lips), and how this Spirit should abide with us for ever and be always our guide and helper. Moreover he encouraged us to be of good cheer, saying that, though the world were against us, yet he had overcome the world: and that he could give us a peace that should last for ever, Likewise he began at this time to say more oft and more clearly (for he had said the like before once or twice in dark sayings) that, besides his little flock (for so he was wont lovingly to call us), there should be yet other flocks gathered unto him, and there should be one fold, and one shepherd. Now of all this we understood not much at that season; for our hearts were not yet opened to it. Howbeit his words were sweet to the ear, yea, and they reached to our very souls; insomuch that we were drawn unto him even more than before, and loved him with an exceeding love: but still it was hidden from us that our Master was shortly to depart.

But as concerning the Pharisees, Jesus told us that the wrath of the Lord must needs fall upon them. And he likened them unto a fig-tree which (after the manner of fig-trees) should, by course of nature, put forth fruit first and leaves afterwards; but this fig-tree, he said, putteth forth leaves but no fruits. Therefore the Lord, seeking fruit, goeth unto the tree, rising up early in the morning; and he looketh on it, and behold there are leaves, but no fruits. Then was the Lord wroth, and breathed upon the tree, and said unto it, "No man eat fruit of thee hereafter for ever:" and lo, when He returned and came by the same path again in the evening, the tree had withered away. When we heard these things, straightway there came into our minds another parable which our Master had spoken in former times concerning a barren tree; how the owner thereof cometh to the gardener and saith, "Lo, these two years I come seeking fruit and find none. Cut it down." But the gardener besought the Lord that it might not be cut down till another year should pass, if perchance it might in the meantime bear fruit. Thence we perceived, comparing the two parables together, that Jesus discerned the wrath of God now nearer at hand. For before, there was mention of hope and of a respite of two years; but now there was to be no hope and no respite.

But most strange it was to us to note how the worship and splendour of the temple, caused him no pleasure, but rather displeasure. Yet so it was. For on the second day of the week, when he was going forth from the city in the evening, a certain citizen of Jerusalem besought the disciples that they would show him the buildings of the temple; "For," said he, "it were a shame that Jesus of Nazareth should have been now two whole days in Jerusalem and not to have seen these sights." But when the disciples moved him to see these things, he seemed like unto one constraining himself to look upon them that he might do us a pleasure: and when he had looked round upon them all, then he was silent for a while, and we perceived that they pleased him not. At last he opened his mouth and said unto us, "See ye not all these things? verily I say unto you there shall not be left here one stone upon another that shall not be thrown down."

But when another spake of the many years during which the temple had been a-building, Jesus answered that, even though the temple were destroyed to-day, the Lord could raise up the true temple in three days. Now whether by "three days," he meant three days exactly, or "two or three days," according to the common phrase, concerning this matter, it has been disputed sufficiently above. But when he spake of the true temple, assuredly he meant, not the temple of Herod, but that invisible temple set upon a rock, whereof he had before spoken to Simon Peter; and this temple seemed to him at all times one with himself: therefore said he that the true temple would be raised up, meaning the Son of man, and, in himself, the Church or Congregation of mankind.

But all this was hid from us at that time, save that we understood Jesus to set no store by the temple of Herod, in that he discerned the fire of God's wrath impending over it. And to us, as I remember, yea even to us that had daily converse with Jesus, it seemed strange that he should so set at naught that same temple which he had himself cleansed. For throughout all the land of Israel, the temple, being but one (and not many, as in Gentile countries), and very full of most ancient memories, because it presented and signified to us the former temple of Solomon and the tabernacle of Moses, this temple, I say, albeit Herod the Idumaean had built it, nevertheless seemed to us, in Israel, very holy, and well nigh one with Israel itself. And for this cause Xanthias blameth the saying of Jesus touching the temple, how that it should be thrown down: for saith Xanthias, the casting down of the temple must needs have seemed to the common folk in Israel all one with the casting down of Israel itself even as the Romans took it ill when, in after days, Gaius Caesar desired of his gods that the Roman people might have had but one neck that he might have destroyed it at a blow. Wherefore Xanthias findeth fault with this saying of Jesus, as not politic, nor discreet.

But, in my judgment, Jesus spake herein not truthfully only, but also expediently; yea and expediently for all time; bearing witness, as it were, even now to all the churches, lest perchance the service of the Lord become the service of Satan: as it was in the temple of Herod. For all things therein seemed unto him to savour of hypocrisy, being done to obtain praise and admiration of men, but not to lift up the heart unto the Lord; so that the very splendour and brightness hid, instead of revealing, Him whose name is the Truth. Therefore when he was led to the treasury and bidden to mark how great gifts the rich men cast therein, he stood awhile watching; then turning round to us, he pointed to a certain poor widow (who had cast in no more than two mites, or a farthing), and he said, "This poor widow hath cast in more than all they which have cast into the treasury." Many other like words he said at this time: and, in fine, he ceased after the first day to speak concerning the purifying of the temple, nor would he any more call it his Father's house; for he perceived that it was become a den of thieves and that the purifying must be by fire. But that which most of all made us at that time to marvel, was, that he spake of the Chief Priests and Pharisees as murderers. But hereby he meant, as I judge, not only that they desired to slay him, but also that they were slaying the souls of all Israel by giving unto the people a doctrine and a worship, that were as poison to the hearts of mankind. Wherefore, as a man might discern with the eye the spots of blood upon the hand of a murderer, even so (but with much more clearness) did our Master discern the blood of Israel upon the souls of the Priests and Scribes in the temple; insomuch that the temple itself appeared even as a great slaughterhouse, and the worshippers as murdered men, and the priests as butchers girt for the slaughter of Truth.

Therefore on the last day, even on the third day of the week, when the sun was nigh setting, and the time was now at hand that Jesus should depart from the temple, and he knew he should enter it no more; behold, he stood up in the presence of all the people, and poured forth denunciation against the Pharisees as being verily the children of Satan. Some of them he charged with love of gain; and he bade the multitude especially to beware of those Scribes who devour widows' houses and wring forth gifts for the synagogues, and for a pretence make long prayers. These, he said, should receive even greater condemnation than the rest.

But even against them that cared not for money, yea even against all the Pharisees, he brought grievous accusations.

For he said they had quenched the spirit of life within their hearts, so that Satan had taken possession of them and used them as his tools. For this cause they could not distinguish between small things and great, between the purifying of the outside and the inside, between that which sanctifieth and that which is sanctified; and they esteemed the tithing of mint and anise and cummin of more avail than mercy, judgment, and truth. Also he said they had made the interpretation of the Law into a gainful profession, doing whatsoever they did for to be honoured and admired of men. Therefore he spared not to call them, not only fools and blind, but also hypocrites. For he said that they knew in their own hearts that they had no sight and no knowledge, yet they professed to see and to know; and they had cast out their own consciences, yet would they fain appear able to judge between right and wrong. Thus they presented one appearance to men, which look only on the outside; but another appearance to God, who discerneth the inside; and therefore he called them actors in masks, or hypocrites; he likened them also unto whited sepulchres, hiding death within them. For they hated the Spirit of life, and they lived by rules and precepts which work death; and they would neither enter into life themselves, nor suffer the people of the land to enter in; and they feared and hated prophets and prophecies, and would fain destroy them; and they had hated John the prophet while he lived, and now they hated Jesus, even to the death: and this, while they professed to repent of the persecutions of the prophets by our forefathers, and to build monuments to their memory, saying, "If we had been in the days of our fathers, we would not have been partakers with them in the blood of the prophets."

After this, he turned round, to go forth for the last time from the temple. But as he came to the steps, he looked back upon all the Pharisees, and upon all their friends (who stood all gathered together behind him, watching him depart), and he pronounced a curse upon them; as though it needs must be that they must yet continue their course; and Satan must accomplish his purpose in them, and must be revealed in all his wickedness working through the Pharisees his bondsmen; and the judgment of the Lord must needs fall upon these servants of Satan: "Fill ye up the measure of your fathers. Ye serpents, ye generation of vipers, how can ye escape the damnation of hell? Wherefore behold, I send unto you prophets and wise men and scribes: and some of them ye shall kill and crucify and some of them shall ye scourge in your synagogues and persecute from city to city. That upon you may come all the righteous blood shed upon the earth, from the blood of righteous Abel unto the blood of Zachariah son of Barachiah, whom ye slew between the temple and the altar. Verily I say unto you, all these things shall come upon this generation."

CHAPTER XXVII

How Jesus prophesied of Troubles, and of a Great Battle against Satan; and in the End the Victory of the Son of Man; but, first of all, his Death.

WHEN Jesus had made an end of denouncing the Pharisees, many of the young men with them and their servants were desirous to have laid hands on him; and they came near as if for that intent, but the older sort checked them. Yet was their wrath clearly to be read in their faces: and when I came out of the temple, being a little space behind the rest, Hezekiah the Scribe overtook me and said, "Young man, I warn thee that thou mayest with speed sever thyself from this blind shepherd: for lo, he hath to-day provoked war, and war shall fall upon him; for unless he perish we shall perish." But I made answer, that I should follow Jesus constantly even to the end. Then he spake again of the evil which, he said, had befallen that rash young man Barabbas; how that he had been taken ten days ago by the Romans on the road that goeth down to Jericho, while he was riding at the head of a band of Galileans that were raising sedition: and, said Hezekiah to me, "Thy friend of Jotapata is to be crucified, as I hear, two or three days hence. Take heed therefore unto thine own steps, lest thou also fall into the same destruction." I made him no further answer, but departed, sorrowing not a little for the sake of Barabbas: for I had not before heard how great an evil had befallen him.

When I overtook the rest, I heard the disciples conversing earnestly one with another; and the Greek, even the friend of Philip, bade us take note that we were beset with spies and watched; for "When ye issued from the temple," said he, "I perceived that the servants of the chief priests and the Pharisees watched you whithersoever ye turned; and, meseemeth, it is their intent to lay hands on your Master this night. But I marvel why your Master so inveighed against the Pharisees, transgressing the bounds of seemliness and decorum, at least in my judgment." So spake he, after his Greek fashion; but Judas also spake to the same effect, and said that we had come up to Jerusalem to destroy enemies, and lo, we had destroyed none, but made many.

The rest knew not what answer to make to these words; neither did I myself at that time. Howbeit, now I know well that Jesus came not to prophesy smooth things, but to teach us the truth. Therefore was it most needful that he should speak the truth, and nothing less than the truth, concerning the Pharisees; to the intent that the eyes of all mankind might be opened, even to the generations of generations, that they might discern that the sin of sins is hypocrisy. For other sins wound, but this sin slayeth, the conscience. Peradventure also Jesus foresaw that a time might come when certain, even among his own disciples, would err as the Pharisees had erred, shutting their eyes against the truth, as being unfit for use and not convenient. And he that came to make a spiritual Israel, a nation of priests and ministers for mankind, was it not most needful that he should thus as it were mark out and brand with censure the special sin of priests? He also that came to redeem all the children of men from all evil, was it not most necessary that he should make clear in the sight of all men what was the greatest evil? For if men knew it not, how could he redeem them from it? And well I know that, if he had not assailed the Pharisees as he did, then these same Greeks who now say that "Jesus transgressed the bounds of seemliness," would in that case have said (even as Jonathan the son of Ezra said) that "Jesus knew not the evil in human nature." Notwithstanding at this season we thought not of these things; but we feared what should betide to our Master if the Pharisees took him and cast him into bonds.

But a certain man of the Pharisees, Joseph by name, of the town of Arimathaea, clave unto Jesus; and although he dared not openly consort with us, he sent a servant after us, when we came forth from the Temple, to bid Jesus not abide in the same house this night as last night, because, said he, "the Pharisees purpose to take thee." He also warned Jesus not to come into Jerusalem on the morrow. But if Jesus desired to have some chamber in the city wherein to keep the Passover, Joseph promised that he would provide one. So much I heard myself; for I was nigh to Jesus when the servant of Joseph brought the message; but the answer of Jesus I heard not, save that he thanked the messenger courteously.

In the meantime we had passed out of the gate of the city, and had begun to climb up the side of the hill called Olivet; and by reason that we were in the depth of the valley, the sun had by this time set for us. But when we had gone some space up the side of the hill, as we turned round to take breath and rest, behold, the sun had not yet set, but was just beginning to sink; and the western quarter of the heaven was lit up with a light exceeding red and fiery, and the roofs of the temple and the towers of the castle of Herod shone as with a blood-red flame;

and though our hearts were heavy with many thoughts, yet could we not choose but look. But when Jesus saw the city and the temple, whence he had but now come and wherein he was never to set foot again; his eyes were filled with tears, and he changed colour and could go no further, but sat down upon a stone and covered his face with his hands: and then he looked again upon the city and wept, mourning over it and saying, "O Jerusalem, Jerusalem, thou that killest the prophets and stonest them which are sent unto thee, how often would I have gathered thy children together, even as a hen gathereth her chickens under her wings, and ye would not! Behold, your house is left unto you desolate. For I say unto you, ye shall not see me henceforth, till ye shall say, Blessed is he that cometh in the name of the Lord."

Having said these words, he arose and went on his way, going up the hill. And we followed him, as men in the Valley of the Shadow of Death, that follow an angel of deliverance, but fear while they follow, lest at any time their guide should vanish out of their sight, and they should be left alone. Even so followed we Jesus up the Mount of Olives, and we feared much to question him concerning his words, but we feared even more to remain silent and so to be ignorant concerning the approaching peril. Therefore presently Simon Peter, with two other disciples, went to him and questioned him, saying, "Tell us when shall these things be." Jesus turned and looked upon our faces, and he perceived that we were all desirous to question him. So he beckoned to us to sit down, and he himself sat down upon a stone, and we also sat down upon the ground around him.

Then began Jesus to pour forth many prophecies of troubles near at hand and troubles far off; and he seemed like unto one upon the shore of a stormy sea covered with mists and darkness, who peereth into the night if perchance he may descry the ship wherein his friends sail tempest-tossed; even so did Jesus look forward into that which was to come, for our sakes. For though his own end was at hand, his thoughts and words were all for us. But he also had in his mind the prophecies of the prophet Daniel; who had prophesied, many generations before, that a time should come when the worship of God should fail, and a king of evil set himself up to be worshipped, and the daily sacrifice should be taken away, and the abomination of desolation set in the place thereof. Daniel likewise prophesieth that those of the nation who were of understanding should remain upright; yet even these should fall for a time, to try them and to purify them. But because the prophecies of Daniel were like unto the words of our Master, I will here set them down; for Daniel saith, "They shall pollute the sanctuary of strength, and shall take away the daily sacrifice, and they shall place the abomination that maketh desolate.

And such as do wickedly against the covenant shall he corrupt by flatteries; but the people that do know their God shall be strong and do exploits. And they that understand among the people shall instruct many; yet they shall fall by the sword, and by flame, by captivity, and by spoil many days. Now when they shall fall they shall be holpen with a little help; but many shall cleave to them with flatteries. And some of them of understanding shall fall, to try them, and to purge, and to make them white, even to the time of the end, because it is yet for a time appointed."

Now these prophecies of Daniel were fulfilled, in part, in the days of that wicked king Antiochus who is called Epiphanes, or Illustrious; but Jesus prophesied that they, or others like unto them, should still be fulfilled. Howbeit, in my judgment, he did not prophesy that these things should come to pass merely because Daniel had prophesied the like; but because, looking upon the present, he discerned the signs of the times (according to his own saying), and hence he perceived that which was yet to come. For his words were the words of Daniel; but his thoughts were the thoughts that came to him from that which he saw in the world. For when he looked upon the world, he saw love of self, and love of ease, and all manner of baseness and servility; and all the empire was given up to the worship of a man, even the Emperor Tiberius, and that man a tyrant and a man of sin, a slave to all abominations of the flesh. Wherefore death was reigning: over the whole of the world. But when he looked to Israel, which was appointed to redeem the world and to lead the world to the knowledge of the true God, behold, Israel himself was blind; and they which should have been priests unto the Gentiles were as naught but pedants; and these too, given over unto all sin, hypocrites, and murderers in their hearts, and children of Satan.

Therefore it was discerned clearly by Jesus (having his eyes open to things future even as our eyes are open to things present), that a great conflict was at hand between evil and good, evil rearing itself aloft in the world to receive the worship of all mankind and driving out the true worship of God; and for a time evil must prevail. For if he looked upon us his apostles or disciples, then he perceived even too easily in our hearts the signs of weakness and instability; and for this cause he prophesied that we should all desert him and fall away for a time. Moreover, because he saw how the men of Israel thirsted for redemption, yea, and how all the children of men desired some deliverance from their present evils, therefore he knew and prophesied that, when he had departed, his place would not be left empty, neither at once nor in after generations; but in every time and in every nation false deliverers and false redeemers should arise, saying that men should obey them, and that they would deliver men. For this cause he warned us against false Christs, yea, even though they should work signs and wonders.

But as concerning the times and seasons when these several troubles should arise, he said naught; nor did he describe the manner of the wars, nor the nations, nor the armies that should make war. Now Quartus judgeth that Jesus knew not these matters; and true it is that Jesus himself spake concerning the time of his coining, saying, "But of that day and hour knoweth no man, no, not the angels of heaven, neither the Son, but the Father." Only, concerning one part of the prophecy, he said, for certain, that this generation should not pass away till all had been fulfilled. But this, saith Quartus, he knew because of the signs of the times: for as to that which he said, "Ye shall not see me henceforth, till ye shall say, Blessed is he that cometh in the name of the Lord," Quartus supposeth that Jesus himself knew not the time thereof, but only this, that it was not possible that Sion could behold him until Sion desired him: for the beholding of Jesus after his death was not to be with the bodily eye, but with the spiritual, through love and desire. Now concerning the foreknowledge of Jesus, what things he knew, and what things he knew not, I have said above that I pronounce no judgment. But true it is that at this time he spake unto us a third parable concerning the fig-tree, and said that we were to discern the coming of these evils from the signs of the times, even as men discern the coming of the summer from the fig-tree, when it putteth forth leaves. For, like as the summer causeth the fig-tree to put forth her leaves, or like as the scent of the carcass guideth the vultures to the prey, even so he taught us that the sins of men, and especially of Israel, would bring after them miseries and judgments, not by chance, but of necessity.

Therefore he prophesied that great tribulation should fall on the land of Israel, such as was not since the beginning of the world to this time, no, nor yet ever shall be. And except those days should be shortened, there should no flesh be saved; but for the elect's sake those days should be shortened. But after the tribulation of Israel, he prophesied that all the empire should be shaken, and the thrones and princedoms thereof should be cast down, and the throne of the Son of man should be set up on high in the sight of all men, and the tribes of the earth should mourn, and the Gentiles should see the Son of man coming on the clouds of heaven with power and great glory, and the elect should be gathered together by an angel as with the sound of a trumpet from all the corners of the earth. Finally he exhorted us to watch in patience, for we knew not at what hour our Master would come.

Now as concerning these prophecies, part were perchance fulfilled when our Master came to us from the grave; for then to them that watched and waited he appeared. But part also, in my judgment, yea, and a great part, were fulfilled ten years ago, when Jerusalem was trodden down by the Gentiles, and the temple was burned with fire, and Israel was scattered over the face of the earth, and many were slain, and many more sold for slaves, and such tribulation befell them as never before. But part remaineth to be fulfilled, when men's hearts shall fail them because the empire shall be shaken, and the thrones of this world shall be cast down, and the worship of the Son of man shall be set up. For albeit the empire fell not in the days of Nero, when all men expected that the end of all things was at hand; yet must the empire needs be cast down. And it is like that this shall come to pass in my days, even in the days of me Philochristus, the writer of this book. And when Israel shall turn unto the Lord Jesus and shall call them blessed that come in his name, then shall Israel see him, according to his saying. Howbeit concerning the day and the hour we have no knowledge thereof; only we know that in the end the Son of man must come with glory; and until the Son of man shall reign over the world, peace cannot be; that is to say, cannot be so as to be settled and firm. For all things move violently to their place, but easily in their place. Wherefore the ways of the world cannot be smooth, nor can the children of men and the tribes of men move smoothly and easily in the world, until the Son of man be in his place as King of the world over all men and over all nations, and until all men and all nations be in their places as his servants; and then there shall be peace for ever; but not till then.

But all this I write, having been enlightened by the Spirit. But at the time when we were sitting thus round about Jesus, listening to his prophecies, we were not yet enlightened; for the Spirit of Jesus was not yet in the world, because Jesus was yet with us. Therefore were we all greatly dismayed by his words, and our hearts quite failed us; and when he had made an end of speaking, we sat still silent; and the shadow of night, stretching over the face of the earth, seemed unto us like to a shadow of Satan encompassing both us and all the world and our Redeemer himself, in whom we had trusted that he should have redeemed Sion. Thomas at last brake silence, and said, "Alas, Master, dost thou not remember thine own words on that other mount in Galilee, where thou didst pour blessings on us, and didst strengthen us with comfortable sayings, telling us that the meek should inherit the earth? Verily the prophecies of the Mount of Olives do not accord with the prophecies of the Mount of Blessing." By this time it was become dark, so that we could not clearly discern the features of Jesus, for the moon had not yet risen; but he seemed to turn his face suddenly to Thomas as though his words had grieved him. Howbeit, he said nothing, but arose from his place, and we followed him up the mountain even unto Bethany.

When we had been a full hour in Bethany, our Master called for Judas, that he should bear some message to Joseph of Arimathea in Jerusalem; for Judas was oftentimes employed by Jesus about such matters, being a man of understanding, and of a ready wit, and having a knowledge of the ways of men. more than the rest of the disciples. But search being made for Judas, he was not to be found; and this seemed not a little to disquiet Jesus. Howbeit, he bade me go in his stead, and bear a certain letter to Joseph of Arimathea. So I went down straightway and delivered the letter; and having received an answer written and sealed, I set forth to return to Bethany. Now the moon was by this time risen, and shining very brightly. So, because I was minded not to be seen of any of the servants of the chief priests, I kept myself in the shadow of the street as I went forth to the gate of Kidron; and it being now late, even in the second watch of the night, there were few people stirring.

But as I was now near to the street called Straight, whereby one turneth to the right hand to go unto the gate, methought I heard the sound of the voice of the night-watch going their rounds. So I drew near to the wall, and remained in a corner where I could not be seen. And straightway Hezekiah the Scribe came by, and Judas with him, walking very near the place where I was (but they discerned me not) and talking in a low voice together. And as they passed, I clearly heard

Judas say to Hezekiah, "But if he should call down fire upon the guards?" And Hezekiah made answer, "Then thou wouldst have done him good service," or words to that effect: but the exact words of Hezekiah I heard not, because they were by this time gone somewhat past me. Neither could I hear what Judas said in answer to the words of Hezekiah. Only I noted, even afar off, that after they had conversed some while longer, Judas held out his right hand to Hezekiah, and Hezekiah seemed to take it as a pledge.

When I saw this, my mind misgave me that all was not well; yet did it not so much as enter into my mind, at that time, that one of the Twelve could purpose treachery against our Master; and, because of my message and my haste, I gave no thought to the words that I had heard. But I sped away to the gate, and passing through unquestioned, I went up the mountain in haste; and when I came to the top, I found John, the son of Zebedee, waiting for me, to take me to the house where Jesus lay that night; for he was not to abide in the same house as before, for fear of the Pharisees. So I came to Jesus and delivered my letter; and I found with him a certain Nicodemus, a great teacher among the Pharisees. He had come to converse with Jesus, but secretly, for fear of the chief priests. Then I delivered my letter to Jesus, and I told him how I had seen Judas discoursing with Hezekiah. But the old man, even Nicodemus, was troubled when he heard me make mention of Judas, and he turned to Jesus and said that from friends came sometimes even more dangers than from enemies; and as he had before warned Jesus against the plotting of the Chief Priests, so now again he besought Jesus not to adventure himself in Jerusalem on the morrow. Then he gave thanks to Jesus for his doctrine, and departed. But when the letter of Joseph of Arimathea was opened, it confirmed the words of Nicodemus; for he also bade Jesus not come to Jerusalem on the morrow, but to tarry till the next day. He also added (but these words Jesus read not aloud, so that I knew not of them till afterwards) that Jesus should keep the Passover on the day after the morrow; howbeit not at his house, but at another house which his servants should prepare. He also gave Jesus a sign whereby he might be guided to the house. Likewise the letter bade him beware of false friends.

When Jesus had made an end of reading aloud those last words bidding him beware of false friends, his heart was sorely troubled, and the burden seemed more than he could bear; and he went out for a while to be alone and to pray. But presently he returned and spake comfortable words to us, and cheered us with his kindness; and so for that night he lay down to rest; and some of us slept while others watched. Howbeit that night no enemy came.

On the morrow (which was the fourth day of the week) Jesus neither went down to Jerusalem, nor sent any down to make preparation for the Passover. But he remained with us in Bethany, part of the time in the house, and part in the fields round about, going with us hither and thither, and speaking more and more to us of that same Holy Spirit whereof he had spoken before; which should guide us, he said, into all truth, and teach us what to reply unto our enemies, and be unto us a comforter and a friend, yea, the source of all happiness and good. And more and more he spake concerning his departure; insomuch that, though we were unwilling, yet by this time we were constrained to suppose that our Master must be severed from us for a season, and that we must watch for his return. Yet how or in what way he should be taken from us we could not conjecture: only that he should be slain by his enemies we had no manner of belief, no, nor so much as a fear thereof, although he had so many times prophesied it to us. For the thing was hidden from us of the Lord, that we should neither believe it nor conceive it.

But the women were otherwise minded, and were very full of fears. To them it seemed that, if Jesus was indeed about to be taken from them, then it mattered not whether he were taken in a chariot of fire or by whatever other means: and they lamented over him as over one already dead. Many times did we rebuke them for their faithlessness (for so it seemed to us), but they would not cease. Judas also rebuked them even more bitterly than we: for he had come to us on the morning of that day, saying that he had been with certain of his acquaintance in Jerusalem that he might be informed concerning the plots of the Pharisees. Jesus received him kindly, even more methought than was usual; and when we sat together at meat that night, he placed Judas next unto himself, John being on one side of him and Judas on the other, in the seat of honour.

Now so it was that, while we were at meat, behold, one of the women came behind Jesus, having an alabaster box of very precious ointment, and poured it on his head, at the same time uttering most piteous cries and lamentations. Then Judas changed colour; for his heart misgave him, as I judge, that the lamentations of the women might prove true; and besides, he was wrath perchance because the love wherewith this woman loved Jesus put his semblance of love utterly to shame. Therefore he rose up from his seat in indignation and said, "To what purpose is this waste? for this ointment might have been sold for three hundred pence and given to the poor." We also ourselves in like manner murmured against the woman. But Jesus said, "Why trouble ye the woman? for she hath wrought a good work upon me. For ye have the poor always with you; but me ye have not always. For in that she hath poured this ointment on my body she did it for my burial." Then he paused, and mused for an instant, and added a prophecy, that wheresoever his good tidings of Redemption should be proclaimed in the whole world, there also should this that this woman had done be told for a memorial of her.

Now before these words, while we had sat at meat listening to the discourse of Jesus, Judas seemed as if his heart were enlarged towards Jesus; and albeit at times he fell to pondering and musing (like unto a man doubting of two courses which to take), yet anon he would be aroused by some word that Jesus spake; and then his countenance would kindle, and he would stoop forward, as in old times, with his eyes all a-glow, listening as if he would fain devour each syllable with his ears. But now his countenance fell, and he was filled with rage because he had been rebuked by Jesus; and he went forth from the chamber, and we saw him that night no more. But as for us that remained, our hearts became exceeding sorrowful; for now indeed it pressed upon us that the departure of Jesus must needs be sad and grievous and full of sorrow, like unto death. But still, that he should die indeed, and be buried: this, even now, we could in no wise believe.

CHAPTER XXVIII

How Jesus, by his Testament, bequeathed himself to his Disciples forever; and how he bare the Sins of Men in Gethsemane.

WHEN the morrow came (which was the fifth day of the week) Jesus abode still in Bethany, and went not forth to Jerusalem. Now so it was that the Passover that year fell on the Sabbath day; and because of the multitude of the sacrifices that were to be slain between the two evenings in the temple, it was a custom that certain of the pilgrims should keep the Passover on a day before the Sabbath. For it was said (though I can scarce believe it) that there were nigh upon three hundred myriads of souls in Jerusalem during the Passover week; and even though the women partook not of the feast, yet the number of lambs to be slaughtered must needs be very great. Therefore we expected that he should have gone down to Jerusalem that day, for so it had been determined with Joseph of Arimathea; and we marvelled that he did not go. But he continued speaking unto Mary and Martha and other of the women. And by this time it was noon, and yet nothing had been done.

But at the last Peter went to him and reminded him that after two days would be the feast of the Passover; and he asked Jesus where he desired that we should prepare for the feast. Then Jesus bade Peter and John go to a certain street in Jerusalem and to stand there during the ninth hour of the day; and they should meet there a certain slave of Joseph of Arimathea bearing a pitcher of water upon his head; and they were to say, as a sign to the man, "The Master saith, my time is at hand; I will keep the Passover at thy house with my disciples;" and the slave would show them an upper room prepared; and there they were to make ready. For the space of an hour after Peter and John were departed, Jesus continued still speaking unto the women: then he arose and bade them farewell, and set his face to go down to Jerusalem.

When it was now late, the sun having set two hours or more, we sat down to keep the feast; and Judas also was with us. While we sat at meat, we spake, according to the custom, concerning the ancient deliverance of Israel in the days of Moses: but our hearts were very heavy, for we said within ourselves, "We need not a past, but a present deliverance; and, behold, it is not to be." Jesus alone was of good cheer, and rejoiced with a marvellous joy; and he spake very cheerfully and tenderly to us, and said that his heart had yearned to eat this Passover with us, for he should not eat with us again till the Kingdom of God should be established. Now at this we marvelled, but we rejoiced not; for we had learned by much experience not to rejoice at the promises of Jesus as if they were the promises of common men. Moreover we were sore disturbed by a certain saying of Jesus. For in the midst of his comfortable discourse to us, he suddenly brake off, saying that one of us, that sat there at meat with him, should betray him. And he said, "The Son of man goeth as it is written of him; but woe unto that man by whom the Son of man is betrayed! It had been good for that man if he had not been born." And hereat we sat a while dumb and looking each at other, wondering whom Jesus might mean, and afterwards we brake out into many and passionate questionings, each asking whether he himself was to be the traitor: but Jesus made no certain answer, none at least that I heard. At the last, before rising from the table, Jesus looked earnestly upon us all, as if his heart went out to us: and he pitied us, and said that he would now give us his last gift; for this feast was as a funeral feast, and he was to die and leave us alone; therefore, before he died, he desired to bequeath to us somewhat by his last will and testament.

While we marvelled what this gift or legacy might be, behold, Jesus took bread and blessed God, and brake it and gave it to each of us, saying, "Take, eat, this is my body." After this he took wine and blessed that likewise, and bade us drink of it, saying, "This is my blood of the New Testament, which is shed for many." So we ate and drank as we were bidden, even like children that have no understanding; nor did we then discern the meaning of his words. Howbeit, even at that time we understood somewhat of his purpose; for we perceived that Jesus was pouring his love, yea, and his life, into our hearts; and our souls stretched out as it were toward the truth, namely, that Jesus, in this testament of his, was bequeathing himself to us his disciples, to be our possession for ever.

Now all the other disciples were strangely moved, insomuch that their hearts were melted with the fervency of their love; but Judas alone was unmoved. Yea, rather he was moved indeed, but in a manner quite contrary to the rest. For when Jesus reached unto him the bread, all eyes were upon him, for we could not now refrain from suspecting him: but he ate it against his will, and as though he ate it with difficulty; and when he had eaten it, he looked angrily at us that gazed still upon him, and then he rose up in haste from the table, like unto one possessed with Satan. Now while he was eating, Jesus beheld him with a marvellous love and pity, yea, and, as it seemed to me, with a great struggle and conflict of soul, as if he were wrestling for the last time against Satan for the soul of Judas. But, when he perceived that Judas had hardened his heart against him, he sighed, and said some word unto him, but what it was I heard not: and hereupon Judas went hastily forth, and left Jesus still sitting with us. Then did our hearts misgive us yet more. For none could any longer doubt that Judas was indeed a traitor; and we bethought ourselves for what cause he had gone forth, and when he would return.

But Jesus neither stayed him, nor lamented when he had departed; but he seemed like unto one in whom all tears and sorrow had been swallowed up in a certain unfathomable depth of joy. For he looked up to heaven and offered up praise unto the Lord, the Deliverer of Israel, and he bade us join him in singing a portion of the great Hallel; for the singing of these psalms was according to the custom of the Passover. Now so it was that, in the singing, Jesus must needs utter certain words that tell how the Lord giveth life out of death: "The snares of death compassed me round about, and the pains of hell gat hold upon me. I shall find trouble and heaviness, and I will call upon the name of the Lord, Lord I beseech thee, deliver my soul:" and then, "Turn again then unto thy rest, my soul, for the Lord hath rewarded thee. And why? Thou hast delivered my soul from death, mine eyes from tears, and my feet from falling. I will walk before the Lord in the land of the living." While he sang these words, it was a wonder to see the face of Jesus, with what a brightness he looked up to heaven, and how great a trust shone from his countenance; insomuch that, as we gazed upon him, our hearts also seemed lifted up with his. But Jesus went on, until he came to those following words of the Hallel which say how "The right hand of the Lord hath the pre-eminence: the right hand of the Lord bringeth mighty things to pass. I shall not die but live, and declare the works of the Lord. The Lord hath chastened and corrected me, but he hath not given me over unto death. Open me the gates of righteousness, that I may go into them and give thanks unto the Lord."

At the last, when we sang of the stone refused of the builders but become the head stone of the corner, he sang with an exceeding clear voice, not loud, but very piercing, so that it seemed to cleave us to the very heart; and behold, our voices became lower, even as his became clearer; and we feared to sing the same words as he sang; but we were rapt with wonder as we looked upon his countenance; for it was as the countenance of an angel seeing the very glory of the Most High and gazing upon Him face to face. And when he sang the last words of all, "God is the Lord who hath showed us light, bind the sacrifice with cords, yea even unto the horns of the altar. Thou art my God, and I will thank thee; thou art my God, and I will praise thee"; then indeed it came to pass that all we that listened to him were lifted up in spirit with him in an ecstasy, being delivered from all our doubts and cares and fears, looking down on them as petty things; and it was even as if Jesus were holding us by the hand and carrying us up with himself above the firmament, to the seventh heaven and beyond, yea even to the Throne of the Blessed.

That instant, a knocking was heard at the door, and one entered in haste and as if in terror; and he went up to Jesus and whispered in his ear. Then the glory faded from the face of Jesus, and he became sad, and straightway gave commandment to depart. But as we went forth from the chamber to the roof (for the guest-chamber was an upper chamber and upon the roof, as was the custom in my country), we heard from the slave that a guard had been sent forth by Annas to seek Jesus, and that Judas of Kerioth was thought to be with them, to guide them to the place where Jesus was. So we went down immediately from the upper chamber where we had been at meat; and behold, as we passed from the brightness of the moonlight, which shone upon the roof, down into the darkness of the shadow of the street, we seemed to have passed out of life into death, and to have been cast down from Paradise to the depths beneath the earth.

Now when we were all come down from the house into the street, Jesus stood for a while in the midst of his disciples looking up to the sky; and he seemed for an instant like unto one doubting whither he should go. For first he made two or three steps toward the temple and the tower of Antonia, as if to go thither (but this would have been certain death, for the guard was coming thence, and we should have met them); but then he looked at us and seemed to change his purpose. For he turned towards the gate that leadeth to the vale of Kidron. Now why he did this we knew not at that time; but afterwards we judged that he was moved at first to go to meet the guard that he might give himself up at once unto death; but when he had thought thereon, it seemed better for our sakes that he should still remain with us a few hours longer. Perchance also he wished to commune with God alone upon the mountain of Olivet; for he ever loved the loneliness of mountainous places and nightly prayers. Moreover Quartus writeth to this effect, that "though Jesus knew that he was to die, yet the manner of his dying, and how he should be taken, was not known to him: therefore he would not prevent the hand of the Lord, but would avoid the peril by all honourable means even till the last, leaving the decision with the Lord."

As we drew nigh to the gate of Kidron I was near him, and I heard him repeating some saying of Scripture to himself; and at the last, he spake aloud and said, "All ye shall be offended because of me this night, for it is written, I will smite the shepherd, and the sheep shall be scattered." But when he marked us, how exceedingly we sorrowed at these words of his, then he began to encourage us again; and he spake some words how that he would return to us, or guide us hereafter. Now what he said exactly I know not, for I was a little behind the rest. But he looked around him in the narrow street, as though that were no place for him to abide in: and then he added some words concerning Galilee, which I did not clearly hear. Howbeit, it seemed to me that he said he should manifest himself to us hereafter, not in Jerusalem but in Galilee. And so also most of the disciples interpreted his words. But we all with one consent cried out that we would never desert him nor go from his side; and he listened to us gently, even as a mother listeneth to the prattle of a little child which prattleth concerning the things which he will do when he cometh to man's estate. Even so listened Jesus to our speech; but when Peter was vehement, even above the rest, in protestations, Jesus interrupted him, and said that before the morrow's sun had risen, yea, before cockcrow, Simon Peter should have denied him.

By this time we were come to the gate of the Kidron valley; and methought certain of the servants of the chief priests, which stood together at the gate, were advised of the intent to arrest Jesus, and were fain to lay hands on him. Howbeit, many were coming in and going out, and we that were going with Jesus joined ourselves together around him, insomuch that the guards suffered us to pass; for they could not then have taken him quietly, nor without a tumult; which thing they purposed to avoid. And so it was that, as we closed ourselves together for to encompass Jesus, and to guard him, my place was very nigh unto Jesus, even next upon his left hand; and as we went down the steep path which leadeth across the brook Kidron, I chanced to stumble; and Jesus took me by the right hand to stay me from falling. And the touch thereof remaineth with me unto this day; for his hand was not again to touch my hand upon earth.

When we were now going up the hill on the other side of the brook (being by this time quite out of the shadow of the city walls, so that we could see all things in the moonlight very clearly), we perceived that Jesus was still meditating on prophecies; and ever and anon he looked upon us, as though his care for us were a burden on his soul. And perchance he desired to prepare us to live without him in the world; and not to depend upon the exact words of his precepts, nor to make therefrom a rule nor a law unto ourselves, but to obey the Spirit only; making new rules and laws for ourselves if need were, even as the times might suggest and the Spirit might bid us. For he said unto us, "When I sent you without purse, and scrip, and shoes, lacked ye anything?" And we said "Nothing." Then said he unto us, "But now he that hath a purse let him take it, and likewise his scrip." Here he paused awhile, and then he added these words: "And he that hath no sword let him sell his garment and buy one. For I say unto you that this that is written, must yet be accomplished in me: 'And he was reckoned among the transgressors.' For the things concerning me have an end." Hereat we wondered, that Jesus (who had ever spoken against smiting with the sword) should bid us buy swords. Howbeit, we answered that we had two swords with us. Straightway Jesus ceased from walking, and stood quite still for an instant; and it seemed as if he marvelled at our want of understanding, but yet perceived that he must needs be content, for he could do no more to help us. Therefore he said nothing, but presently continued to walk on as before. But, as I now suppose, his meaning was to prepare us for much tribulation, and that we should, in the days to come, use all means and all faculties in his service. Howbeit, even to this day, I understand not altogether that saying about the buying of a sword. But as I judge, Jesus had invisible things in his mind, and he spake of the stores and treasures, and of the weapons also, that were like to be needed in the great and terrible war which we were to wage against Satan in the days to come.

Against this, Xanthias urgeth (and methinks not without show of reason) that the scrip and purse whereof Jesus made mention in Galilee were not invisible things, but visible: but, if they were visible, so also must the sword needs be, whereof Jesus made mention in the same saying. But Quartus replieth that when Jesus, being still with us in the flesh, sent the disciples forth in Galilee without purse and scrip, he would have them to go forth not only without visible purse and scrip (which indeed they did), but also without the spirit of the purse and the spirit of the scrip, that is to say without forethought and provision, the better to awaken them to whom they were to preach the Good News: and this, saith Quartus, was the main part of the precept of Jesus. But now that he was to be no longer with us in the flesh, he changed his precept, bidding us use the spirit of the purse and the spirit of the scrip: and "after those words," saith Quartus, "that ye might the better understand them, Jesus paused" (which indeed he did, for I took note of it) "in the midst of his saying, and bade you buy a sword, supposing that ye would know assuredly that he (who ever hated the sword) could not mean a visible sword, but an invisible: even that two-edged sword which Jesus brought into the world to do battle against evil withal. And belike," saith Quartus, "Jesus meant that, after he should be taken away, we were never to be content to defend ourselves against evil, nor to lead harmless lives in peace and quiet (as the Essenes are wont to do); but that we were evermore to do battle against evil, and to assail it, and to give up all things sooner than cease to make war against it."

At this, time came down one from Bethany to tell us that the servants of the chief priests had beset the house of Mary and Martha, and others were watching on the road for to take Jesus if he should come up the hill. Therefore Jesus turned aside from the road and went unto a place whither he had also beforetime gone with us: it was a small vale, wherein grew many olive-trees, insomuch that it was hence called the Press of Olive Oil, or Gethsemane. When Jesus came to this place, we would fain have still accompanied him; but he suffered us not, but bade us stay where we were, and there to watch and pray, lest we entered into temptation: for these were his very words to us. But taking John and Peter and James, he himself went forward about a stone's cast; and we noted that, after a short while, he parted from them, though they were fain to stay him (for we could hear all things as well as see, because the night was very calm, and no less still than bright); and he went on yet another stone's cast or somewhat less, and the three disciples sat down where they were. Then Jesus stretched out his hands unto the Lord and prayed with exceeding earnestness; and to us, where we stood, he seemed as one in a sore agony; for at one time we could discern him standing erect, but at another time kneeling or prostrate upon the ground; and though he spake not loud, yet could I hear words that made my very flesh to shiver and creep; for he cried unto the Lord and said, "Father, if it be possible, let this cup pass from me." These words he said more than once, so that I could not but hear them; and a sickness of heart and an horror fell on me that such an one as Jesus of Nazareth should come to such a pass, and should ever need to say, "if it be possible."

Now so it was, that in spite of our sorrow and anguish of heart, all we that watched with Jesus at this time were so pressed down with a strange slumber that it was not possible for us to resist the burden thereof upon our eyelids; and oftentimes we would walk up and down and speak each to other for to shake off the leaden weight from our eyes; but we could not, no, though we were angered, and reproached ourselves aloud. For we had not slept much during three nights past or more, because of the need of watching for Jesus; and besides, the very unexpectedness of all that sorrow which had of late encompassed us round on every side, caused us to feel like unto them which wander in the wilderness of a dream or vision of the night, insomuch that we scarce knew whether we were asleep or awake: and the anguish of Jesus itself was unto us as it were but a part of a bad dream. For we could not attain to understand his sorrow, nor to share in his burden. Only we knew that he sorrowed not for fear of death. But we knew not at that time the secret of his agony, how he was at that instant wrestling with Satan for the salvation of all the children of men. Yet so indeed it was. And though the suffering of Jesus was seen of men when his body hung upon the cross, yet meseemeth it was seen of God when he was prostrate upon the ground in Gethsemane, and his soul was crying unto the Lord and saying, "if it be possible."

Loth am I to write many words concerning that which is above all reach of words, yea, and above all reach of the thoughts of men; yet will I here set down that which was said unto me concerning this matter by a certain Alexandrine, a friend of Quartus, who was a man of an understanding spirit and of discernment above the common. This man, when I once marvelled aloud, in his presence, as to the cause of the agony of Jesus, made answer to me and said, "What was it, thinkest thou, that caused Jesus more pain and sorrow than aught else?" So I replied, "Without doubt, the sins of men: for he often spake as if it were a pain to him, even to forgive the sins of men." But the Alexandrine replied, "As it seemeth to me, Jesus did not merely forgive sins twice or thrice in a week, nor in a day, no, nor even in an hour: but his whole life was a state of forgiving, and a state of bearing sins and of carrying iniquities, and of making himself one with sinners. For this end it was needful that Jesus should have strength to trust in men and to hope for men: for without trust and hope thou knowest it is impossible for thee to lift up a sinful man in forgiveness, howsoever great may be thy love for the sinful.

"Therefore, even as the Gentiles fable that Atlas doth bear up the pillars of the earth, even so, methinks, Jesus of Nazareth knew in himself that he bare up the pillars of the invisible Jerusalem, the city of the souls of men; and so long as he had strength to trust and hope, so long he knew that the invisible city stood and was to stand; but, if he should fail in trust and hope so that he should fall (even for a single instant), then behold, in that same fall of the Son of man fell all the world, yea, all the souls of men, and all the Temple of the Congregation of the children of God; and so the universe became the hunting-ground of Satan, and the children of men his prey, and God was not. Peradventure, therefore, the burden of Jesus was this bearing of the sins of men, and especially of the sin of Judas and the infirmities of you his disciples, and the thought of the impotence of good to conquer evil. Moreover perchance there rose up before him the image of the morrow, when he should hang upon the cross, and when the strength and force of life should leave him, and there should be no one to succour, no one to comfort; and a vision from Satan stood before him, and he heard a voice that whispered evil things: 'If now thou shouldest lose thy trust for an instant? and the pillar should be snapped? and the invisible city should fall? and the gates of hell should prevail over the gates of heaven?' This then is what the Alexandrine said unto me concerning the suffering of Jesus: but it needeth not to say that at this time we understood naught of these things: only we perceived that some terrible thing was at hand. But about the space of an hour or more, as I judge, had passed since we first heard Jesus say, "if it be possible "; and now methought Jesus was less disturbed in praying. And presently we saw him standing upright, very clearly to be seen in the light of the moon, which streamed upon him through the olive branches; and these words were borne to our ears through the stillness of the night, "my Father, if this cup may not pass away from me, except I drink it, thy will be be done." But some of the disciples told me afterwards that at this time they saw a shape, as of an angel clothed in white, ministering unto him. But I saw it not, for it may be that I was at that time slumbering: for soon after I had heard Jesus speak these last words, there fell a deep sleep upon me and upon the rest of the disciples that were nearest to me.

Afterwards they all slumbered and slept, even the sons of Zebedee and Peter also; and perchance this thing was from the Lord, to the intent that Jesus might bear all his burden alone.

After this, I remember no more, save that I had a vision of the night in my slumber, wherein I saw Jesus of Nazareth clothed in bright raiment, glorious to behold. He stood and prayed upon the summit of a mountain. Howbeit in my dream it seemed to be not Mount Olivet, but the Mount of the Law in Galilee. And as I looked upon him, his stature grew larger and his raiment brighter, till the brightness thereof filled the sky, and set it all in a flame. "With that I awoke on a sudden, and opening mine eyes, I perceived that there were flames indeed around me; then, leaping up, I found myself in the midst of torches, and armed men compassing me round. Yet could I discern, through the midst of them all, Jesus, with a calm countenance, stooping over John and Peter and James, and arousing them from sleep.

Now all that came to pass thereafter was finished in a few moments, though it take long to tell. For Judas, who was the guide of the armed men, ran swiftly before the rest up to Jesus and said, "Hail, Master," and saluted him. And, as I was told by them that were nigh to see, Judas seemed as if he knew not, even at the last, what would come to pass, nor scarce what he himself was doing. For he embraced Jesus and pointed to the soldiers that followed behind him, as if half expecting that Jesus would call down fire upon them. But Jesus looked upon him as if looking upon a stranger, and made him such answer as to show that he perceived his treachery; whereat Judas drew back, they said, as one distraught. Then Simon Peter drew a sword and struck a blow at one of the soldiers; and the rest of us ran up to have joined in the fray. But Jesus straightway rebuked us, and bidding Peter put up his sword, he yielded himself up to the soldiers. Yet even to the last he was as a son obeying the will of the Father, and not like unto one acting from constraint; for I myself heard him say unto Simon Peter, "Thinkest thou that I cannot pray to my Father and He shall presently give me more than twelve legions of angels? But how then shall the Scriptures be fulfilled, that thus it must be?"

Now up to this moment we had not yet fled; for we could not even then believe that our Redeemer, the Messiah, the Son of the Living God, would be led captive; yea, even though he resisted not, yet were we assured that the Lord God of Israel would stretch out His hand to deliver His Holy One. So we still waited and were in expectation. But when at last the servants of the high priests laid their hands on him, and the soldiers bound him and dragged him roughly away, and yet no fire from heaven came down upon them, neither did the earth open her mouth to swallow them up; then we all forsook him and fled.

CHAPTER XXIX

Of the Crucifixion of Jesus; and of his Last Words upon the Cross.

THOUGH we had so basely fled from our Master, yet away from him we were not able to rest. Therefore we followed after the guard down the mountain, even into Jerusalem, and mingled with the concourse that was gathered together before the doors of the High Priest's house. Near me was John the son of Zebedee; who, having some acquaintance in the household of the High Priest, gained access into the house; and Peter also with him. But I remained without; and I conversed with the people, making as if I were no Galilean, but a citizen of Jerusalem. For I perceived that the most part of the multitude were men of Jerusalem, some indeed citizens, but the greater part servants of the chief priests, and money-changers, and cattle-dealers; who had been gathered together of set purpose by the enemies of Jesus.

But when I asked one why he hated Jesus (for the man had declared aloud that he trusted that day to see Jesus on the cross), he replied, "Because this Galilean marreth our trade, and taketh away our living; for behold, these three days men buy no beasts for sacrifice from my stalls in the temple." And another said, "Yea, and he maketh no secret that he purposeth to destroy our religion, and change our customs which Moses appointed: for he saith that he will destroy this temple, and boasteth, forsooth, that he will raise up another equal to this in three days." Now this saying of Jesus (which indeed he had not said, for I have set down his words exactly above) had been carried from mouth to mouth throughout Jerusalem; and the chief priests had everywhere caused it to be rumoured that the intent of Jesus was to destroy the temple with fire during that Passover. Therefore the hearts of many of the devout and sober people were turned away from Jesus.

After we had waited about two hours or something less, a certain Scribe came up to a servant of the chief priests, who was conversing with me; and the Scribe asked the man concerning the multitude, for what cause it was gathered together: and the man said, "To see the false prophet, named Jesus of Nazareth, who is to be condemned to death." "Nay," said the other, "then thou losest thy labour. For if a man be tried for his life, he may not be tried on the day before the Sabbath; for the Law alloweth appeal on the morrow. Therefore if, as thou sayest, Jesus of Nazareth is yonder being tried, it cannot be that he is tried for his life." Hereat I rejoiced greatly, for I bethought myself that it was even so as the Scribe had said, wherefore it could not be that Jesus was to be tried for his life. But when I drew nigh unto them (for the press had parted us for an instant): "I give thee a yea for thy nay," said the other, "for thou knowest the Law, but I know my master Annas; and he is not the man to allow a little matter of a day to stand in his way; nor to permit the booths and shops in the temple (whence cometh profit to the priests) to be destroyed by false prophets and Galileans to boot." Then indeed my heart misgave me that it was to be no trial, but only a murder.

Just then one came down the steps leading from the High Priest's house, and the people ran together towards him to know what had been done. He stood still, and made a gesture that they should keep silence; and then in a clear voice he spake to the multitude and said, "The council hath pronounced that Jesus of Nazareth is a man of death." Hereupon there was a general shout, for all knew that to be "a man of death" meant to be condemned to die: and straightway a cry arose, "Stone him, stone him; bring him out that we may stone him." But the man checked them that shouted, saying that the accused must first be led to the judgment seat of the procurator, Pontius Pilate, for without his judgment it was not lawful that any should be put to death.

Then my heart revived a little again; for it seemed there was still some hope. But seeing Simon Peter come forth from the High Priest's house, I pressed through the throng if perchance I might come at him, to ask him touching the trial, and what the witnesses had testified, and how Jesus had borne himself. But Peter seemed not to see me; and even when I called him by name he would not hear me. At last, by dint of striving, I came near him in the throng and caught hold of his garment, and stayed him by force. Then, indeed, he stayed; but as he turned round and his face looked upon my face, behold, I saw in his countenance shame, and remorse, and despair; and he assayed to speak, but could not, and wrung my hand in silence. Then waving me off that I should not any more stay him, he hasted away, and I durst not follow him; for it was evident to me that the prophecy of Jesus had been fulfilled, and that Simon Peter had denied our Master.

I turned back into the throng, for my intent was to have remained standing without, till such time as Jesus came forth. But I heard the servant of the High Priest say to one of his acquaintance that the procurator was not one to have his sleep broken by business at so early an hour; "Therefore," said he to his companion, "go home to thy house, and warm thee, if thou wilt; for there will be naught to see these three hours." Then it came into my mind that the mother of Jesus, and likewise Mary Magdalene, and the other women, were all this while in Bethany, neither knew they aught of that which had befallen Jesus; and it was fit they should be told. Therefore I went forth by the gate of Kidron and up the Mount of Olives even to Bethany; and there I writ a few words, telling what had befallen, and left it in the hand of one of the servants of the house; for to go in myself and to tell the tale, and to look upon their sorrow, I durst not do it. This done, I hasted back for to go down to the house of the procurator, making sure to have arrived thither long before they had made an end of the trial. But when I was gone but two or three hundred paces from Bethany, one of the women ran after me with tears and lamentations, beseeching me to return and to tell them all; and she constrained me. So I returned and told them all; and the memory of their lamenting remaineth with me unto this day.

Thus passed a long time, a very long time as it seemed to me; but at last I withdrew myself from them perforce, and hasted down the mountain. But when I was come to the palace, behold the trial was over; and I saw the rear part of a moving throng, and one told me that they were taking the prisoner to be crucified at Golgotha. Then my heart within me seemed to burst; but though I was faint before with long watching and weariness, I was not faint now, but sped after the throng. Many times did I strive to press in amidst them, if perchance Jesus might look but once upon me, or I might see his face, or so much as catch a sight of his garment as he walked; and I wept and was ready to curse myself that I had gone from the High Priest's door before I had seen my Master's face. For now I could not see him, no, nor anything of him, save now and then the cross, which, as they told me, he was carrying upon his shoulders; but I heard the men in the crowd saying what insults had been offered to him, and how he had been scourged and mocked, and spit upon, decked with a crown of thorns and a sceptre of reed; and I was as one distracted, in whom there is no power of thought.

By this time we had passed out of the city through the western gate, and the fore part of the multitude was come to the place of execution; and they that went before me came now to a stand; and I saw the cross lifted up for an instant, to the intent, as it seemed, that it might be laid upon the ground; and one near me said, "Now they are making ready." Then I gnashed my teeth, for I could do naught else; but I was ready to curse God (blessed is He), for I knew right well what that "making ready" meant; and a deep silence fell on all the crowd; and I could hear the blows of the hammer upon the nails; and every man held his breath, if perchance there might come the sound of a shriek or a groan. But no such sound came to the place where we stood.

Presently arose a very loud shouting from the multitude that stood before me, and behold, the cross was reared up so that the top thereof was a little above the heads of the people; and from afar off I could just discern Jesus. But I saw not his face; for his head was bowed forward and his hair, hanging over his forehead, hid his eyes. But when I thrust myself forward to have approached nearer, I could not for the press. At the same time there rang in upon mine ears a very storm of mocking and reviling and cursing against Jesus from all the bystanders, yea, even from the women and little children (with such a venom of slander had the Chief Priests poisoned the minds of the people); insomuch that I seemed to stand alone among a host of the children of Satan; neither could I endure any longer to behold such a sight, amid such beholders, and to be of no avail. Wherefore I became as one possessed; and I turned my back upon the cross and forced my way out of the crowd; the people calling after me and mocking me, and plucking me back by the cloak as I fled.

But even as my body fled away, my soul was drawn back unto the cross; and I feared to go back lest I should see Jesus, and I feared to go forward lest I should never see him. And these two fears were as two devils that possessed me, driving me hither and thither about all the hills and valleys of that neighbourhood for the space of two hours or more; and during all that time the fear to go back was the stronger. But about the eighth hour of the day, as I wandered like unto one dreaming, not knowing whither I went, behold, I stood on the top of a certain hill; and thereon was a flock of sheep quietly pasturing, and the shepherd-boy piping to them, and sunlight was all around. But casting mine eyes downward, I saw very far off, under a dark cloud, the multitude still standing round Jesus, and three crosses in the midst (for other two were crucified with him); and all in so small a space that it seemed no larger than a man's hand.

Then came my misery back to me with a shock; and it seemed a wonderful and an horrible thing that in a little corner of the earth the Almighty should suffer such a one as Jesus of Nazareth to be slain on the cross: and yet, behold, the sun shone and the shepherds piped to their sheep, and there was peace upon the mountains, and all as if nothing strange were happening below. But soon these and all other thoughts were swallowed up in one remembrance, namely, that if I would see Jesus alive, not many minutes now remained unto me; for the sun was sinking towards the west, and I knew that he could not be suffered to remain upon the cross when the Sabbath began; for that had been against our customs. Therefore I ran down with exceeding speed, and came again to Golgotha about the tenth hour.

When I was now within two or three furlongs of the place, I perceived that some of the people were already coming away; for the Passover was near at hand, so that they must needs go to their homes. So I ran on, and came to the place where the multitude was standing. And because the throng was diminished, I was now able to come very much nearer to the midst of the multitude, not more than a stone's cast from the cross. But alas for the sight I saw! For though I was so close, I could not discern anything of Jesus as he once had been; because his head was bowed forward even more than before, and moreover there was an unwonted darkness over all the place. The people were very still, nor was there now any more sound of cursing or mocking; for of them that still remained round the cross some were the friends of Jesus, and others had been greatly moved (so it was told me afterwards) by the manner in which he had borne himself upon the cross; insomuch that even the soldiers which kept guard mocked him no more, but stood watching in silence. But I came forward to the furthest that I might, and placed myself where haply he might see me; and I would fain have called unto him; but I durst not, lest I should trouble him, for he was very still. But when I was now come so close unto him that I might almost discern his features in spite of the darkness, behold it was as if a trembling ran through all his limbs, and he raised his head a little, and a voice came forth, which, whoso heard, could not forget for ever: "My God, my God, why hast thou forsaken me?" Then there was another cry exceeding long and loud, and a second trembling running through all the limbs even to the neck and face; and then a stiffness as of death.

Now up to the very last I had not given up all hope that Jesus might yet come down from the cross, showing forth some mighty work worthy of a Messiah; nor did I indeed know how much hope I had had, till this moment wherein all hope perished. But now, when I turned myself to go away from the cross and to leave Jesus for ever, all things seemed ended, and I felt as one alone in the world; yea, I knew not whether there were a God, or whether I myself lived, or all life were not a dream. Thus I went forward, as one in a trance; when on a sudden I heard the voice of Hezekiah the Scribe: "Art thou not yet convinced of thy folly? Behold, it is written that thou shouldest not put thy trust in any child of man. For when the breath of man goeth forth, he shall turn again to his earth, and then all his thoughts perish; even as this thy master, the false prophet, hath perished. But blessed is he that hath the God of Jacob for his help, who keepeth His promises for ever. But thy master, how keepeth he his promises? Unless perchance," and here he lowered his voice and looked jealously at me, "unless (as is reported to us) ye Galileans hope to steal his body from the grave and so to feign that he is risen; but that shall not be. For though your patron Joseph of Arimathea may have his will to-day, yet will we take good order that we have our will to-morrow. For the body of a false prophet deserve th not honourable burial."

I could endure his words no longer, but ran past him as one mad. But, when I was now rid of his presence, passing back into the city by the western gate, my mind ran on all such things as I had done with Jesus on the day before, and my feet turned of themselves toward the house where we had kept the Passover together. Thence, but still as one in a dream, scarce knowing what I did, I bent my way towards the gate of the valley of Kidron. Here I was musing how, but yesterday, in this very place, I had walked by the side of Jesus, even at his right hand, and how the touch of his arm had held me up in my stumbling; when behold, I started back as if I had seen a spirit. For the voice of one close to me in the twilight whispered with an hissing sound, "He is not dead." I looked, and behold, Judas stood before me. His face was pale and his eyes glared, and passion so wrought his features that they moved and quivered, as if against his will, like unto the features of one possessed by Satan. When I drew back from him, at first he would have stayed me; but seeing that I loathed him, he also drew back and said, "Nay, be not afraid, I cannot betray another. But he is not dead. Hast thou not seen him?" I marvelled at him, but said nothing, only shaking my head. Then Judas replied, "Think not that I have slain him; he liveth: he hunteth me to death; these three times have I seen him. I have not slain him. Why then doth he yet hunt me? But thou, thou didst love him, be thou at peace with me." Saying these words, he came forward again to have taken me by the hand; but I could not. Then he turned away and laughed such a laugh as I pray God I may never hear again. But as he departed, he cried aloud, "Thou rememberest his words, 'It were better for him that he had never been born': verily he was a prophet." Then he laughed again, even such another laugh as before; and he cursed the God that had made him. With that he went his way, and I saw him no more.

For a while I stood where I was, as if in a trance, almost expecting that the words of Judas should prove true, and that Jesus should come forth to me out of the air around me. Then I passed through the gate of Kidron; and, crossing the brook, I began to go out by the way which leadeth to Bethany. But ever as I went up the mountain, I pondered over the words of Judas, "He is not dead, I have seen him:" for I could not forget them, nor put them 'away from my mind. And behold, whithersoever I looked in the twilight, all things bore witness unto Jesus and seemed to say the same words, "We have seen him. He is not dead." For if I looked back at the city gates, then I remembered how Jesus had lately passed through them in triumph; and if I looked on the road before me, then every tree and rock seemed to testify that Jesus had but now been there again and again, in his passing between Bethany and the city; and at one place he had spoken a certain parable: at another, he had sat down and rested; or at a third, we had asked him certain questions and he had answered them. Thus the whole of the mountain and all things thereon seemed to cry aloud with one consent, "He is not dead "; but my heart cried back again, "Nay, but he is dead indeed."

When at last I came in my wanderings nigh to the top of the mount, even to the stone whereon Jesus had sat down in the midst of the disciples and had prophesied of his coming, then could I no longer refrain myself; but I threw myself on the ground in a passion of tears and sobbings, beating my breast and rending my garments. And when

I desired to cry unto the Lord in my agony, behold, the words of Jesus on the cross came into my mouth; and if I tried to fashion some other prayer, no other words would come to me, but I could do naught but repeat them over and over again, crying unto the Lord and saying, "Why hast Thou forsaken him? Why hast Thou forsaken him?" So speaking, I scarce refrained from doing even as Judas had done, so as to curse the day wherein I was born; and I became again as one distraught. But after a time (but how long a time I know not) a darkness came down upon mine eyes, and all things swam around me, and I fell to the ground as one without life.

When I came to myself, behold, I lay upon my back and looked upward, and the moon was shining high in the heavens above me. So I thought how the same moon had shone down with the same brightness yesternight upon my Master in Gethsemane. "And now where is he?" I ceased from that thought, and went back in my mind to thoughts of the past. Then I remembered what a splendour, even such as I now saw, had shone upon our Master's face when he came down from Mount Hermon, and when he came up from Jericho to Bethany, and also when of late he gave us the bread and wine at our last supper together. Also there came into my mind the words that he had spoken, when this brightness had been upon his countenance: how he had then prophesied, and more than once, that he should be slain; but we had never believed him. Yet his words had come to pass. Then I asked within myself how it was that Jesus had foreseen his own death and prophesied it so oft, yet had never been dismayed nor even disturbed by the thought thereof; and I remembered that whensoever he had spoken of his death, he had spoken also of a certain rising again, or coming: and I said aloud, "If Jesus prophesied his death truly, why might he not also prophesy truly concerning his coming again?"

But against this hope there set themselves those last words which had come from the mouth of Jesus on the cross, "My God, my God, why hast thou forsaken me?" Now these words are the first words, and as it were the prelude, of one of our psalms. So I began to repeat to myself the words of the 'psalm; which beginneth with sadness, yea even from the depths of sorrow, but these words follow afterwards: "I will declare thy name unto my brethren: in the midst of the congregation will I praise thee. For he hath not despised nor abhorred the affliction of the afflicted; neither hath he hid his face from him, but when he cried unto him he heard." So I wondered whether Jesus, in speaking those last words, had in his mind all the words of the psalm, and "Perchance," I said, "in saying the first words, he signified (in his sore weakness when the breath was departing from him) that he desired to say the whole; for the first words are but as a title to the whole. Wherefore, perchance, beneath the sense of the forsaking, there was a deeper sense that God did not despise the affliction of the afflicted." Then I mused again concerning the words of the Psalm, and especially on these, "When he cried unto him, he heard" And I looked up to the moon and the stars in heaven, which are the work of the hand of God, and I asked whether it was possible that the Maker of so beautiful an order in heaven should suffer disorder to prevail upon the earth; and my heart said that it could not prevail for ever. "Therefore," said I, "God must needs have heard Jesus of Nazareth when he cried unto Him. Yea, though He seemed not to hear, yet must He have heard indeed. Yea, even though Jesus be dead, yea, even though Jesus be not the Messiah, yet surely the Lord must have heard Jesus; for not to have heard him, would have been not to be God"

Then rose I up and stood and stretched out my hands in prayer unto the Lord with whom all things are possible, that He would show forth His mercy upon me; and behold, when I tried to pray, my lips would shape forth no other prayer, but that He would bring back Jesus unto us, even though it were for a moment of time, that we might look upon him and know that he still lived. And at one moment I rebuked myself because the thing seemed impossible; but the next moment that prayer rose up again, and no other. But when I had prayed, I lay down again, for I was very weary; and because I was now more at peace within myself, there came upon me a sweet sleep.

In my sleep I dreamed; and the Lord sent unto me a vision of the night, whereof the former part was like unto the vision which I had had the night before, but the latter part was different. For again, methought, I saw Jesus standing on the top of a mountain in great glory; and albeit his face was like the face of him that hath passed through much tribulation, yet did the glory prevail over the sorrow, and he rejoiced as one triumphing over Satan and Death. As I looked, methought Jesus was lifted up in a chariot from the mountain towards the clouds, and angels accompanied him as he rode upward; and a sound of solemn music came down from above to greet him. The heavens opened, yea, even to the seventh heaven, and there appeared the likeness of a throne on the right hand of the Majesty on high; and ten thousands of thousands of saints were about the throne, with palms in their hands, singing hosannas unto the Son of David. But even as the chariot rose higher and higher, the music waxed louder and fuller; till at the last, when the chariot was now nigh unto the throne, behold all the harps in heaven rang out hosannas with such a peal of praise as made me start out of my vision; and I awoke, and it was a dream.

CHAPTER XXX

How the Holy Spirit, through much Sorrow, prepared the Disciples to behold Jesus risen from the Dead; and of the Vision of Angels, which appeared first of all unto the Women.

WHEN I awoke, it was now hard upon the third hour of the day, and the sun from behind Mount Olivet was shining brightly down upon the city. All things below were full of beauty and glory, nor would a stranger have known that the stain of innocent blood was upon the place; so fair shone all the city rejoicing in the Sabbath sun. When I looked thereon, the memory of my dream vanished, even as the mists which I saw rolling upward from the side of the mountain and vanishing into the pure air. My misery returned upon me again; and I felt once more alone and without God in the world. But I resolved to go up straightway to Bethany, if perchance I might there find the apostles in the house of Mary and Martha. When I was come thither, I found them all, save Judas; and I entered in and sat with them in silence; and for a long time we neither prayed nor spake together, nor so much as lamented aloud; but there we sat speechless and comfortless; for the hand of the Lord was heavy upon us.

At the last spake certain of the women, saying that they had brought spices, such as are used in the embalming of bodies, and that they purposed to go early on the morrow for to embalm the body of Jesus. Then I asked where he was buried; and they told me, "in a garden of Joseph of Arimathea, nigh unto the place of crucifixion." After that, I asked whether any had stood near, and in view of the cross while he was suffering; for I had been thrust away by the crowd. Then John the son of Zebedee answered and said that he had been nigh, and that Jesus had borne all the anguish with a marvellous constancy. He told me also of certain other words which Jesus had spoken while he was on the cross, and that a soldier, after his death, had wounded his side with a spear; but when I asked him whether he had heard Jesus speak also those words which I had myself heard, namely that God had forsaken him, then John said nothing, but only moved his head as if to say that it was so; and the rest also were silent, for we feared to think on those words.

After we had all thus sat silent for a while, one of the women began to speak again and to say that all things had happened according to the words of Jesus; for he had said that he should be slain; and he had blessed Mary, in that she had anointed his body for the burial. Then another of the women began to bring to our mind how Jesus had long ago prophesied that the time should come when we should desire to see one of the days of the Son of man, and should not find it. And another spake how, at another time, when we were in the country round about Hermon, he had prophesied that he should be slain; therefore, said she, he was a true prophet. But Thomas made mention of the saying of Hosea, whereof Jesus had oftentimes been used to speak, "Come and let us return unto the Lord, for he hath torn and he will heal us; he hath smitten, and he will bind us up. After two days will he revive us; in the third day he will raise us up, and we shall live in his sight." Then said Thomas, "A part of the sayings of Jesus hath indeed come to pass "; and he added no more. But all we that were in that chamber sitting together, knew what Thomas had in his mind to say (for it 'was in our minds also), namely, that the rest of the words of Jesus were not to be fulfilled. So again we sat silent; for indeed our souls were wholly given up to meditating on those words of Jesus, "after two days he will revive us "; and each knew that the others were meditating on the same; yet durst none of us say so much as a word, nor so much as confess to himself that the words could import anything now; for about that matter we feared even to hope.

But by degrees our tongues were loosed, and we began to speak more freely concerning the goodness of Jesus, how exceeding gentle he was at all times to the young and simple, and to the poor and oppressed; how full of peace and cheerfulness; how thoughtful for others, how forgetful of himself. Then we spake of his marvellous power in the forgiving of sins, and in the healing of diseases, and in the casting out of unclean spirits. And one said that with all these faculties he joined a marvellous grace of modesty and humility, so that no child could carry himself with less of pride or ostentation. "Yea," said another, "and yet withal, though he were never so simple and humble, he ever spake of himself, none the less, as the haven and refuge for men, saying such words as these unto us, 'Come unto me, and I will give you rest,' and again, 'Take my yoke upon you:' moreover he bade us take his voice as our Law in the stead of the Law of Moses, saying, 'It was said to them of old, do this, but I say unto you, do that.' Therefore are we of all men most miserable in that, having received from God the very source of light and life, now we are deprived thereof." Then Peter said, "Yea, verily we have none else to whom we can go, for Jesus alone hath the words of eternal life; and without him we have no life." But said another, "If God be good, how could it be that He should have forsaken Jesus, so that he cried aloud, 'My God, my God, why hast thou forsaken me?' Then Nathanael spake and said (the very thought that was in my heart also) that perchance Jesus used those words, desiring briefly to pour forth all the trouble and all the trust of his heart; for, said he, "These words are as it were the title of the psalm, and the psalm beginneth with trouble, but it endeth with trust." To this the rest agreed that it might be so; but we all felt within ourselves that this was small comfort: for we needed not only to think that it might be so, but to know that it was so.

Then one said that the Kingdom of God and the Redemption of Sion were now as far off as ever. But Mary of Magdala said with great vehemency, "that she mourned not for the Redemption of Sion, but because the breath of life was taken out of the world, for without Jesus there was no more truth nor righteousness. He trusted in God, would not God deliver him? Was he not the Son of the living God? If, therefore, the Father live, how can the Son be dead?" She added yet other words still more passionate, as if God were no God unless Jesus were restored to life. We chid her, and would have stayed her speech: for, though she did indeed express the very feelings of our hearts, yet were we afraid to see them put into plain words, and besides, we dreaded the pain of new hopes. For to hope that we should look again on Jesus, and afterwards to fail of that hope, had been to have had Jesus snatched from us a second time.

By this time the sun had set, and the women began to make ready the spices for the embalming. But I (because it had been reported to certain of the disciples that the chief priests purposed to set a guard round the tomb) determined to go down that I might see whether the tomb were beset with guards or no, and whether the women could have easy access to it. I easily found the place in the light of the moon, and it was even as the women had said; for the garden of Joseph lay not more than three stones' cast from the place where Jesus had been crucified. So I stood for a while looking on the stone, which was at the mouth of the tomb, and no man else was in the garden. But while I stood near the tomb, very nigh unto the mouth thereof, I heard a sound on my right hand; and when I turned round, behold, a light; and the lights grew many as I looked, and I perceived that there were torches approaching. So I went back some distance, and still the torches came nearer; and the men were, as it seemed to me, servants of the chief priests, but I discerned also the face of Hezekiah the Scribe; and they all stood round the tomb, and I also stood and watched them from afar off, to see what they would do. But I could not remain; for they sent out watchers on all sides calling to one another in a circle, like unto men keeping sentinel, for to spy whether any one were near.

Then I fled perforce and in haste; and though I fled straightway, yet could I not contrive but the watchers perceived me and chased after me and went near to take me. But I escaped out of their hands, and went up to Bethany to bear word unto the women. And when the women heard these things they were sore distressed. Howbeit they resolved that in any case they would go forth to the tomb very early on the morrow.

But before we lay down to rest that night, we spake again of Jesus, and concerning all that he had said and done; and we continued our discourse late into the night, and were loth to break off; for while we discoursed together of former times, we seemed to have Jesus again in the midst of us. But at the end, when we were now ceasing, the Spirit of the Lord fell upon Mary of Magdala, and she lifted up her voice and sang as the Lord moved her, and the words were even from, the psalm whereof we had been but now speaking, while discoursing concerning the forsaking of Jesus by God. Now the song describeth the suffering of the Messiah. Therefore when she came in her singing to these words, "They pierced my hands and my feet; I may tell all my bones; they stand staring and looking upon me. They part my garments among them, and cast lots upon my vesture ": then we wept, remembering the sufferings of Jesus. But when she sang the next words, "But be not thou far from me, Lord. Thou art my succour, haste thee to help me. Deliver my soul from the sword, my darling also from the power of the dog. Save me from the lion's mouth: Thou hast heard me from among the horns of the unicorns. I will declare thy name unto my brethren; in the midst of the congregation will I raise thee. For he hath not despised, nor abhorred the low estate of the poor; he hath not hid his face from him; but when he called unto him he heard him": then we wept no longer, but we marvelled while we looked on her, and while we hearkened to the words of her singing: for she sang as one taught of God, so that we durst not stay her; yet we thought in our hearts, "Notwithstanding when Jesus called unto Him, He heard him not." And when we thought on this we besought her that she would cease.

Howbeit she ceased not, but began to sing yet another psalm, a part of the great Hallel; even the very words that Jesus himself had sung to us on the night before he suffered. And the other women joined with her, and they sang so that the sound thereof pierced to our very souls. Then could we endure it no longer, but covered our faces with our hands. But they continued singing, "I shall not die, but live, and declare the works of the Lord. The Lord hath chastened and corrected me, but he hath not given me over unto death. Thou art my God, and I will thank thee; thou art my God, and I will praise thee."

Now while they were singing, I had closed mine eyes; and lo, there rose up before me a vision of the upper room where we had supped together with Jesus on the night that he was betrayed: and I seemed to see the face of Jesus himself; yea, though I was not asleep nor in a trance, yet did I see Jesus himself sitting again as if at meat with us. Therefore was I loth to open mine eyes; for I feared that, when I opened them, J should no longer see what I saw. But when the women had made an end of singing, then opened I mine eyes, half expecting that it might prove no vision, and that Jesus would be sitting before me in the midst of us. But I saw nothing;, nor were the women any longer with us, for they were gone forth into another chamber to finish their preparations for the embalming. For they desired to visit the sepulchre very early in the morning, and it was by this time the third watch of the night. About the space of an hour, I remained in the chamber with the rest: then I heard the footsteps of the women as they passed forth from the house. I tried to sleep, but could not; for ever in my mind was present the thought of Jesus in the tomb, waiting the approach of the women to embalm him. So my heart went forth with the women upon their errand, and I reckoned over the time and said ever and anon, "Now they are come down from the mountain; by this time they are nigh to Golgotha; now they are in the garden; now they are at the tomb." Then I saw before mine eyes the women embracing the dead limbs of our Master. "And now," said I, "the stone is rolled away and they have entered in: they weep, but he answereth not, neither heareth; his eyes move not nor make any answer to their eyes; they clasp his hands, but his hands clasp not theirs again."

When I thought on these things I arose in sore extremity nigh unto despair, and went up to the house-top. Above the mountains of Moab, to the east, there was a faint token of dawn. I thought of the coming day, and I loathed it; for without Jesus the light seemed unto me as darkness. Moreover when I strove to pray, Satan tempted me very sorely, so that I could not pray: for I said, "Behold I am without Jesus: but God without Jesus is to me as no God." Then fell I flat upon my face and wrestled with Satan in prayer, and I besought the Lord again and again that He would give Jesus back to us, yea, though it were but to look on him for one moment, that we might be assured that all was well with him. How long I prayed I know not, but it seemed to me many hours; and sometimes I stood in my praying and watched the dawn growing brighter; and even as the dawn grew, my fears and doubts grew with it; but at other times I lay prostrate and shut out the light. So at last the sky began to brighten towards sunrise; and still I was crying unto the Lord from the depths, according as it is written, "I wait for the Lord; my soul doth wait, and in his word do I hope. My soul waiteth for the Lord more than they that watch for the morning, more, I say, than they that watch for the morning."

Now while I lay grovelling in the very deepest of the depths, beseeching the Lord to destroy me if I might not have peace, behold, a sound as of many feet below, without the house, and then a knocking, exceeding loud; and one asked from within, "Who is there?" And the answer came piercing the air, "HE IS RISEN! HE IS RISEN! JESUS IS RISEN FROM THE DEAD!" Now at first I thought that the voice was the voice of an angel; but when I considered, and heard how answer was made, and the door forthwith opened, and a sound as of feet entering, then straightway I knew that it was the voice of one of the women come back from the sepulchre. Immediately, therefore, going down, I found all the household stirring, and the women returned, and all the disciples gathered together, and standing round the women, questioning them, and listening to their words.

Then the women told us how they had gone down to Golgotha, even to the tomb; and when Mary of Magdala was now nigh, even at the mouth of the tomb (for she walked somewhat before the rest), behold, the great stone at the mouth of the tomb was rolled away.

Then she called aloud for despair, and her companions hasted to her; but when they were now come to her, as she was even now adventuring to enter into the tomb, of a sudden Mary cried out again, saying, "Behold, an angel of the Lord!" And lo, there appeared to them (even to all the women and not to Mary only) an angel clothed in white; and they all heard a voice which said, "He is not here, but is risen." And, said Mary Magdalene, the voice added that we were to return to Galilee, and there we should see him; but another of the women said that the voice seemed to her also to speak of Galilee, but she heard not those other words which Mary heard. Also some of the women had seen two angels, but others only one. But as concerning this at least, all the women were agreed, namely, that they had seen a vision of angels, and that they had heard a voice which cried out, "He is not here, he is risen;" but, for the rest they spake diversely, and as if they scarce knew what they said for very fear; for they were sore afraid and...[text missing; see Note V].

Now when we had spent much time in questioning and hearing the women, I desired to go down forthwith to the sepulchre, for to see it with mine own eyes: but the women stayed me, and said, "It were better to wait; for Peter and John are already gone down." So I waited, but in sore trouble of mind; for at one time I believed, but at another time I doubted. For as concerning the tomb, it came into my mind that it was like enough that the servants of the chief priests (whom I had seen in the garden during the night) might haply have broken open the tomb and stolen away the body; but then on the other side there was the vision of the angels and the voice; and besides, it was being borne in upon my mind, and upon the minds of most of us, that Jesus must indeed arise from the dead, for thus should both the words of the prophets be fulfilled, and his own words also; but otherwise they could not be fulfilled. So I waited till John and Peter should return. But while I was still waiting and marvelling that they tarried so long, there came in certain of the disciples; these were not Galileans, but abode in Jerusalem, and they asked us whether we had seen aught that night. We said "No." Then said one of them to us, "Last night, in returning from beholding that which came to pass at Golgotha, about two hours after sunset, Miriam, my sister's daughter, saw her father (who hath now been buried these six weeks) risen from the grave and standing wrapped in the grave- clothes near her bed; moreover two other women of mine acquaintance saw the bodies of their little children, fresh and blooming as if they were verily alive;

and another, a certain young man named Mattathias (but he is not known to me), is said to have seen his brother, who hath been buried more than a year, standing as if alive, so that he even approached him and called him by name. And other wonderful sights have appeared to very many." And his companions confirmed all his words, saying, "The like also we ourselves have heard."

While we marvelled at their words, the two disciples, Peter and John, came into the chamber. But they had seen nothing; only the stone rolled away, even as the women had said, and the tomb void of the body. Then one of the disciples brought again to our minds how that Jesus, even before his death, had bidden us go into Galilee, saying that he would there manifest himself unto us; and when we questioned Mary of Magdala, she constantly affirmed that the voice of the angels was to the same effect. Therefore I resolved that I would set forth that very day to go to Capernaum. For a hope was now waxing strong within me that I should after all see Jesus again. So I set out without delay, with certain other of the disciples; howbeit the greater part would stay in Jerusalem yet a few days.

CHAPTER XXXI

How Jesus appeared ofttimes to his Disciples; and how, after many Days, he ascended up to Heaven.

WHEN we came to Capernaum, on the evening of the third day, we spent the rest of that day in praying and praising God; and we fasted and besought the Lord that we might see Jesus according to His promise. And so we spent the next day likewise. But on the morrow, which was the fifth day of the week, it being now a full week from the time when Jesus had broken bread with us on the night when he was betrayed, we determined that we also would break bread together, even as he had commanded us, in memory of him. And about the sixth hour of the day, when we were seated together in an upper room praying to the Lord, there came in Peter and James and other of the disciples, but now returned from Jerusalem. And Peter related how the Lord Jesus himself had appeared to him; and James said that he also had seen the Lord Jesus. Now at first I feared lest it might be the will of the Lord that Jesus should reveal himself to none save the Twelve; but I understood that Mary of Magdala also had seen him.

Then two other of the disciples, and they not of the number of the Twelve, related to me how Jesus had appeared to them also, at the breaking of bread. For they had walked forth together conversing much about Jesus of Nazareth, and about the hopes which they had had that he should have redeemed Israel. "And so it was," said one of them (for I will set down the story as it was told me by one of the disciples, whose name was Cleophas), "that we had just made mention between ourselves of the voice and the vision of angels; making mention thereof as of an idle tale. And it was the hour of prayer. And because of the extremity of our sorrow we both fell on our faces, and poured out all our desire before the Lord, beseeching Him for the Redemption of Israel. Then the Lord Jesus had compassion on us and came to us. For when we rose up from praying, we heard a voice from the Lord Jesus himself, chiding us for our folly and slowness of heart in not believing all that the prophets had spoken; for that it was needful that Christ should have suffered these things, and thus to enter into his glory: and lo, at an instant the whole of the truth of the Scriptures lay before our eyes, and all the meaning of the words of the Lord Jesus withal.

"As we went forward, our hearts burned within us while the Lord revealed unto us the Scriptures and all the meaning of his prophecies; but still our eyes were not opened to discern that he himself was present with us; yet we perceived that there was a divine presence near us. But when the sun was setting and we drew nigh unto the village whither we were going, our hearts became faint and dull, as if the presence were departing from us. Therefore we knelt down once more and besought the Lord that he would continue to us the strength of his presence. Notwithstanding even now our eyes were not opened that we should discern him.

"But in the evening, it being now late, when we were sat down to eat bread together, our hearts being full of the presence of Jesus, we brake the bread and blessed it, even as Jesus had broken and blessed, and then we said aloud, according to his word, 'Behold, the body of the Lord;' and lo, at that word the cloud was removed from our eyes, and first my companion, and then I also, discerned Jesus on the other side of the table, reclining as if at meat (even as he reclined when he last brake bread with us), and with his hands stretched out as if in the breaking and blessing of bread. Now for a while (but I knew not how long, except that it was not very long), Jesus remained with his hands still outstretched as at the first, looking at us with a very loving countenance, but saying naught; and we sat upright as men astonied and speechless, and not able to move for astonishment; but when we rose up for to have embraced him, straightway Jesus vanished out of our sight."

All we that were in the chamber rejoiced when we heard Cleophas saying these things. Only Thomas believed not; for the thing seemed unto him too beautiful to be verily true, and he said, "If I believe that Jesus is risen from the dead, and afterwards find that it is not so, then shall my misery be increased twofold: therefore will I believe not." And he added moreover, "Except I shall see in his hands the print of the nails and put my finger in the print of the nails and thrust my hand into his side, I will not believe." We were grieved at the words of Thomas: howbeit none rebuked him, for we knew that he spake out of his exceeding love of Jesus. But we besought him to break bread with us that evening, according to the commandment of Jesus.

So about one hour after sunset, we were assembled all together in the upper room (it was a room in the house of Peter, wherein Jesus was wont to sit at meat with us in past times), and Thomas also was with us. But the door was shut and made fast for fear of spies; whom the Scribes in Capernaum had begun to set over us for to watch us. When all things were now ready, first we sang a psalm, even the same psalm that Jesus had sung on the same night in the week before, when we kept the Passover together. Then Simon Peter offered up prayers and praises to God, and made mention of the comfortable words of the Lord Jesus, how he had said that he would never leave us nor forsake us, but that wheresoever two or three were gathered together in his name, there would he be present among them. Last of all he spake of the testament of the Lord Jesus, how he had bidden us break bread and drink wine in memory of him, that we might partake of his body and his blood. Then began Simon Peter to break bread and to reach it to each of us, and at the same time he said, "This is the body of the Lord." But behold, in the midst of his giving of the bread, Peter made a sudden pause and was silent, and his eyes were fixed, and he gazed steadfastly upon the place which had been left empty at the table; for Jesus had been wont to sit there in times past, wherefore in that place durst no man sit. Then I turned round hastily to look, and behold, Jesus was there; as clear to view as ever I had seen him in this life, only very pale, and there were the nail- prints in his hands, and methought there was a wound in his side; and the brightness of his love and compassion passed sensibly forth from his eyes to mine, and all my soul went out to him as I looked; but I could in no wise speak, nor did I desire to speak; for I had thoughts deeper than all words.

Now not a hand moved, not a word was spoken: and there was such a silence as if one could hear and count the footsteps of time; neither could I turn mine eyes from Jesus till I heard Thomas weeping beside me; but he threw himself on the ground, stretching out his hands to Jesus, and reproaching himself for his faithlessness; and at the same time, pressing the bread, even the body of the Lord which he held in his hand, he cried out saying, "My hand hath touched; yea I have touched; I believe, I believe." But neither he nor any of us durst adventure to go to that part of the table where Jesus sat; but when I looked again, behold his hand was stretched out (even as the two disciples had described their vision of Jesus) as if he brake and blessed the bread that was his body; and Thomas also heard a voice (but I heard not the voice) saying that he was to touch with his hand, according to his own saying, and to be no more faithless, but believing. After this Jesus vanished from our eyes, and neither in his coming nor in his departing was the door opened, but it remained shut fast; whereat we all marvelled.

From henceforth old things seemed to pass away, and all things became new unto us. For whithersoever we went, and whatsoever we did, we knew that we had the presence of Jesus with us, even when we saw him not. But oftentimes he revealed himself to us, and we saw him plainly; and this too not only in the house and sitting at meat (albeit he oftentimes, and methinks most times, revealed himself to us in the house), but sometimes also abroad in the fields, or even on the lake. Yea I myself was once present when a storm came down upon us on the lake, and the winds sent up such waves as were like to have covered our boat, and we cried unto Jesus in our terror; and behold, the storm ceased, and the clouds parted asunder, and we saw Jesus walking on the waves and stilling them under his feet. And to others of the disciples he appeared at another time, when they had been toiling the night long at fishing, and had caught nothing; and he gave unto them a draught of fishes exceeding any that they had ever before taken.

But the most of the manifestations of Jesus were vouchsafed to us when we brake bread together; after which manner also he revealed himself unto James, as I have heard. For James had taken an oath that he would neither eat nor drink until he had seen Jesus risen from the dead. Therefore on the night after the vision of angels which had been seen by the women, James was in the house at Bethany with Simon Peter and John, and the table was spread for supper; but James would not eat. Then suddenly Jesus was seen sitting in the midst of them, breaking bread and blessing it, and bidding James to partake thereof. But, as I have said, Jesus appeared to us at other times and in other places, and not merely in the breaking of bread; and sometimes in visions without a voice, but at other times in a voice without any vision, and sometimes also, as it has been reported unto me, by signs and tokens (without either voice or vision), and even in the guise of strangers; and all this for the space of little less than a year, insomuch that, if any one should adventure to set forth all the manifestations of Jesus, and the time and place and manner of each, I suppose that the world itself could not contain the books that should be written. Therefore passing over these, I will relate how Jesus appeared in Galilee on a certain mountain to more than five hundred of the brethren at one time.

It was on this wise. A year, or not much less, had passed away since the rising of Jesus from the. dead; and we were still tarrying in Galilee, and the Passover was at hand. Now during that year the number of the disciples had been increasing, but not much; for we had not at that time been moved to proclaim the Resurrection of Jesus. But as the Passover drew nigh, Jesus began to manifest himself less often to us; and he made known to us by the mouth of Peter and of other of the disciples that the time was at hand when he should ascend up to heaven. Then there arose a questioning among us whether we should go up to the Passover or not; for some said that Jerusalem was an accursed city (because the doom of our Lord had gone forth upon it), and that we should not go up; but others said that we should go up; for the Lord would there reveal his will to us. Then it seemed good that the disciples should meet together on a certain mountain in Galilee, whereto Jesus had often resorted aforetime; and there we were to consider of these matters and to ask counsel of the Lord. Now when we were assembled to the number of five hundred in all, women and men together, behold, as we were all offering up prayers with one consent in the name of the Lord Jesus, there was a cry, "Behold him." And Jesus appeared unto us, of the same aspect as before, but fainter, and as it seemed standing at a distance from us; insomuch that some that had not before seen Jesus risen from the dead, were in doubt; and others said they saw nothing. But when we prayed more earnestly, behold, Jesus came closer to us, so that all, or almost all, could discern him; and he waved with the hand as if bidding us go southward. Afterwards the Lord spake by the mouth of Peter, saying that we were verily to go to Jerusalem. And so it was determined.

Now in the meantime, while we were waiting till the Feast of the Passover should come round, our hearts began to burn within us as if something great must surely come to pass, and the time must be at hand when we should go forth to preach Jesus to the world. For words may not describe with how great a joy we lived during those days one with another, and what a passion of love knit our hearts together; and it seemed a sin that so much joy and happiness should not be imparted to others besides ourselves only. For at this time we, the disciples of Jesus, were as it were in Paradise, and joy went ever with us. For if we sailed upon the lake in our fishing-boats, Jesus was there; or if we remained in Capernaum, working in the gardens, or on the quay, or about the booths, or went out into the fields, Jesus was there; and when we met together in the evenings to break bread in memory of him, or in the early dawn on the first day of the week, to renew the remembrance of his rising again, then verily Jesus was not only there, but also often visibly there; insomuch that while we touched his body with our hands, and while.we drank of the blood from his side, we were able at the same time to feast our eyes upon the brightness of his countenance. Yet with all our joy we were not yet moved to go forth to preach the Good News. For it seemed sufficient for that present time that we should take delight in the presence of Jesus, and suck in strength from often beholding him visibly present among us.

Howbeit, though we were still as children clinging to the mother, and not yet able to walk alone, notwithstanding day by day we were learning some new thing concerning the will of the Lord: and the teaching of Jesus, which had in times past been hid from us, began now to appear more clear, and our eyes were being opened also to understand the Law and the prophets; and we all now understood that it had been the will of God from the first that Jesus should die upon the cross and give his life as a ransom for many. Moreover, we began to perceive that a time might be at hand when the Lord Jesus would depart from us, and seem to leave us alone upon the earth to preach the Kingdom of God: and we no longer feared to be alone, for we knew now that the Lord Jesus could never really leave us.

So we came up to Jerusalem. And it came to pass on the day of the Feast of the Passover, Jesus once more revealed himself visibly to us; and by the mouth of Peter he spake concerning that which was to come, and said that he must now be lifted up from among us: howbeit his Spirit should abide with us, and thence we should receive the power of forgiving sins. Some also said that they saw Jesus open his lips like unto one breathing forth breath upon another; as if he then breathed upon us the spirit of forgiveness: but this I saw not, nor anything that Jesus did, save that he blessed and brake bread, after his wont.

Now after the Passover we waited patiently at Jerusalem for nigh forty days; and all that time Jesus revealed himself not to any one of us, neither by sight nor by voice: and we questioned much among ourselves whether we ought to delay longer, for our hearts were desirous to preach Jesus. But when the feast of Pentecost was now at hand the word of the Lord Jesus came to us, saying that we should go forth to Mount Olivet, even to Bethany. And we went forth even as the Lord led us: yet he spake no word more to us; and it was now the tenth hour of the day. And after that we had walked for some while this way and that way upon the uplands of that mountain (even where our Master had walked in times past), and when we had spoken much together concerning all that he had said and done in these same places, behold, we came unto a hollow cleft in the mountain, whither no path led. nor was any habitation of men nigh unto it. Now by this time it wanted but a little of sunset: yet were we loth to go back to Jerusalem till we should have understood what the will of the Lord might be. So Peter said, "Sit we down here, and let us pray that the Lord may reveal his will unto us."

So we sat down and prayed; but we saw nothing, neither did the Lord speak by the voice of any of us. So we waited yet longer; but nothing came, vision nor voice nor sign; and by this time the sun had set. Notwithstanding it was not yet dark, for there was a wondrous brightness in the west, and behold, all the clouds and air above us were filled with a glorious appearance as of amber, and sapphire, and gold, and flames of fire. Then Peter stood up and stretched out his hands unto the Lord Jesus, and looked up to the heaven and said, "Thou, Lord, didst promise that wheresoever two or three were gathered together in thy name, there wouldst thou be in the midst of them. Therefore, Lord, be present now, we entreat thee." Now before the words had well passed from his lips, he ceased on a sudden, and his eyes were fixed, and his hand pointed to the sky, and John also cried out, saying, "He goeth up: lo, I see the Lord Jesus going up to heaven." Then I looked where John pointed, and lo, I also saw the Lord. But his face was no longer pale as before, nor were the prints of nails any more to be seen in his hands and feet, neither could I now discern his features so clearly as was usual: for his whole form seemed robed in a vesture of glory, and a crown of light about his head, and he sat upon a throne of sapphire. For the space of a minute or more we all gazed fixed in wonder; but then the throne rose slowly upwards, and with it rose likewise the angels, like unto flames of fire, round the sapphire throne; and so the glory grew fainter and more distant, and at the last a cloud or a darkness passed over it, and received it out of our sight.

But when the glory had now quite departed, we remained a long while steadfastly looking up to heaven, yea, even to the darkness of heaven, if perchance the glory might yet return to us. For we knew that we were now bidding farewell to the Lord Jesus for ever. But at the last Peter spake to us and said, "Be not sad, brethren, because Jesus is gone from us: for I heard the word of the Lord coming unto me, even from the angels about the throne of Jesus, and the message of the Lord unto us is this, 'Why stand ye gazing up unto heaven? This same Jesus which is taken up from you into heaven shall so come in like manner as ye have seen him go into heaven.'"

Then we returned thanks to God, praising and magnifying Him whose mercy endureth for ever; and we returned to Jerusalem rejoicing and singing songs of praise. But in the evening, when we sat together at meat, Simon Peter said that it behoved us, while we returned thanks to God for the gift of the Law (for it is a custom of our nation to do this on the evening before the morning of Pentecost), to return thanks yet more for the gift of the grace of Jesus; and he also besought the Lord to give us his grace even more abundantly, that the law of Jesus might be written on our hearts. So we sat late into that night conversing together and praying and singing praises unto God.

On the morrow we rose up very early and assembled ourselves together again to pray: and there were with us many disciples of several nations, devout men; not Galileans only, but also Alexandrines, and men of Cyrene, and some of Mesopotamia and Cappadocia, who all believed in Jesus. When we were now all assembled together and the door had been made fast, then Peter stood up, and thanked the Lord for that He had given to us His Holy One, Jesus of Nazareth, whom He had now taken to Himself; and he besought the Lord that, as He had taken up Jesus to heaven after the manner of Elias, so, after the same manner, He would send down some portion of His power upon us (even as Elias had sent down power upon his disciples) to the intent that all the people might know that the Lord had sent us to preach His word to Israel.

Then did the Lord hear us and answer us from heaven, even as He answered Elias by fire in the former days. For behold the Spirit from above fell upon us, and there was a sound as of many voices, even as the roar of many waters; and as the Lord touched the mouth of the prophet Esaias with fire, even so did He give unto us the Spirit of fire upon us, according to the saying of John the son of Zachariah, so that our hearts were all a-glow, and our faces kindling; and we prophesied as the Spirit gave us utterance, according to the saying of the prophet Jeremiah, "Behold I will make my words in thy mouth as fire." But herein was a great marvel; for we sang no psalms, nor did we speak in Scriptures, nor even in any articulate words; but we uttered strange sounds, whereof we felt the sense, but knew not of what language they were; for our tongues moved as the Spirit bade us. But behold, certain of the disciples that had not been moved by the Spirit to speak in tongues, were moved by the same Spirit to understand the meaning of our words; and one came up to me and said, "Thou speakest the language of Mesopotamia, even as I heard it in my childhood; and I verily understand thee, for thou speakest the very thoughts of my heart, thanking God for that He hath chosen us forth to be the servants of His son and to proclaim His Gospel to all the world." Then came another, a man of Cyrene, and he said the like, namely, that I spake in his own language, which was not the language of Mesopotamia, but the Punic tongue. Now while we all marvelled hereat, and knew not what to think, Peter stood up and said that the purpose of the Lord was that, in the times to come, all men upon the face of the earth should be of one language and of one family. "And to this end," said he, "God hath this day sent unto you this sign and token. For this day is fulfilled among you the saying of the prophets: And it shall come to pass that I will pour out my Spirit upon all flesh. For the time is at hand when all men shall know the Lord from the least to the greatest. For men shall no longer be taught of priests saying, Know the Lord; nor shall the knowledge of Him be given only to the rich and to them that have leisure; but upon the servants and upon the handmaids in those days will the Lord pour out His Spirit,"

Then did we all rejoice with an exceeding joy, and we went forth openly into the temple for to magnify the Lord therein. And as I went, my heart leaping up and dancing within me for the fervour of my gladness, there came into my mind how, about three years ago, Philo the Alexandrine had spoken to me of a certain*enthousiasmos* that should fall upon the righteous: but his *enthousiasmos* was I knew not what, a passion for "mere existence," or for " that which is "; and I could not attain to apprehend so much as the meaning of it. But now I had indeed attained to the true *enthousiasmos*, which uplifteth and ennobleth and comforteth the soul, and stirreth to action, and purifieth the thought, and pervadeth every corner of the life of man, and includeth all things create and uncreate; so that my heart went out in love to all the creatures of God, and to all men without distinction, Gentiles as well as Jews, tax-gatherers as well as Scribes; yea, even to the Romans did my heart now go forth in love.

But when we were come together to the temple, the Pharisees and the chief priests and all the people marvelled at our boldness. For we were as changed men in their sight; because we no longer feared them as of old; neither, on the other hand, did we hate them, nor desire to revenge ourselves on them for that they had slain Jesus. But we pitied them; yea, we felt an exceeding compassion and love for them, as for them that wandered in darkness, while we sat in a great light. Therefore were we exceeding bold; and as for fear, we had forgotten what it meant: but we desired to pour out the good news of Christ before all men. For our hearts could not contain themselves for the abundance of joy and gladness and peace which the Lord had vouchsafed to us. So the people gathered themselves together around us. But when the Holy Spirit fell upon us, some men mocked, and called us drunkards; but the more part gave heed when Peter spake to them.

So Simon Peter spake in the ears of all the people, and said to them, even as he had said to us, that this outpouring was for a sign to men, because the Lord was to pour out His Spirit upon the face of the earth. Moreover he added that Jesus was indeed the Christ, and that the Lord had raised him from the dead (whereof we were witnesses), to the intent that he should come again to judge the world in power; for he should assuredly prevail, and cast down all his enemies beneath his feet. When the people heard these words, they believed in Jesus; for a power went forth from the mouth of Peter and from the mouths of the other disciples, so that their words pierced into the very souls of such as should be saved. And we purified them (for we also baptized, even as John the son of Zachariah had baptized his disciples) and baptized them in the brook of Kidron. Then was fulfilled the word of Jesus of Nazareth, which he spake unto the apostles, saying that he would make them "fishers of men;" for on that day the net of the Gospel was indeed cast, and great was the draught of the fishes, so that there were added unto the Lord three thousand of them that believed.

CHAPTER XXXII

How Jesus now ruleth the World, sitting on the Right Hand of the Father in Heaven.

HERE must this history have an end. But I marvel how smoothly and easily the relation seemeth to have ascended from Jesus on earth to Jesus in heaven, as if by some ladder of easy ascent, and as though there were not seven heavens between. And perchance men would marvel the more, if I had been able to set down exactly the image of Jesus as he appeared to me at the first in my mother's house at Sepphoris, or when he sat with us in the fishing-boat on the lake; so that the image of Jesus as he seemed then, might be compared with the image of Jesus as he seemeth now. But I know that I have not been able to do this. For my pen hath still outrun the story: and in adventuring to describe Jesus as he appeared to me on earth, I have often failed of my intent, and have described him, not as he appeared to me on earth, but as he was hereafter to appear to me from heaven.

Oftentimes, musing on the difference between Jesus, as he was in deed and in truth, and Jesus, as we in Galilee supposed him to be, I have questioned myself and said, "Whence this waste of the life of the Lord Jesus? For if it be good for us to know him, and if the knowledge of him be eternal life, as we believe; then how much better bad it been that we should have known him while he was alive, and not to have tarried for the knowledge till death had taken him from us?"

Now, looking back, I seem to discern a reason for our ignorance, or, at the least, a certain wholesome fruit springing therefrom. For methinks, had we known the Lord Jesus as he was, and all his greatness and glory, and all that was to betide him, and his resurrection, and his ascension, even then when he sat with us at meat, and went in and out with us throughout the villages of Galilee; I say, had we known even then that Jesus was to be raised from the dead, and to sit at the right hand of God, methinks we could not have loved him so dearly, nor have spoken with him so familiarly, nor have questioned him so freely, revealing unto him all our infirmities, and trusting him as a friend, yea, loving him as a very son of man, even one of ourselves.

But the Lord so ordained it that we should come to Jesus as to a great and good man, becoming infected with his spirit and imbued with the love of him as of a mortal being; and then, when he had caught our hearts as it were by guile, so that he had made himself now needful unto us even as the very breath of our lives, then began he to say unto us, "Whom say ye that I, the Son of man, am?" And lo, trying our hearts, we began to perceive that this same Son of man, who had so given life to our souls, could be none other than the very Son of the Living God.

Hence it came to pass that, when he departed from us, and when we felt a void in our hearts, and when we questioned ourselves what it was that we had lost, and what it was that we most loved and trusted and revered, yea also, and what it was that we must worshipped as divine; then behold, searching our hearts, we found that there was nothing in heaven above nor in the earth beneath, nor in the waters under the earth, no, nor in the host above the heavens, that could compare with Jesus of Nazareth. And so it was that, when we worshipped him as the Son, it seemed not unto us as if we were honouring him by calling him God; but (if I may speak as a child) it seemed rather as though we were striving to honour God by saying that God was one with Jesus. For saying this, seemed all one with saying that God was Love.

Therefore if any put this question unto me, "Why believest thou not that Romulus is God, and Liber, and Amphiaraus, and Elias, and Enoch (who all are said to have escaped death), and yet thou believest that Jesus of Nazareth is God?": my answer is this, that I believe Jesus to be God, first, because God is Love, and Jesus is Love; secondly, because God is Might and Jesus is Might; and lastly, because, if Jesus was not indeed divine, then must he needs have been a poor deluded creature, unfit and unable to do any great work for the children of men. For certainly, albeit he was the most humble and lowly of men, yet did he ever speak of himself, not as one of many redeemers, but as the redeemer of men, the refuge of the wretched, the forgiver of sins, the source of life and truth.

"But," say some, "Jesus was of a surety not Might; for he came not as a conqueror, but as one conquered." Now, methinks, concerning them that say such things, it was well said by Xanthias that "they are like unto the foolish giant Polyphemus, who could not think that Ulysses could be Ulysses indeed, for that he was not a giant like unto himself. In the same way certain persons of gross understanding" (even of such an understanding as I myself had, before that I had been enlightened by the spirit of Christ) "suppose that Jesus could not have been the Messiah, for that he did not come into the world as they themselves would have come, nor do the works which they themselves would have done, had they been Messiahs. For they would have come into the world, forsooth, riding on the clouds, or borne on chariots of fire, or working signs in heaven or portents upon earth. Now this is even such a Messiah as Polyphemus would have devised for himself. But it was surely a much more divine thing that the Word of God should come into the world as a poor man, and the child of the poor (as if to show that no estate of man is too low to be sanctified by the Divine Word); and that he should subdue all men unto himself, not by force nor portents, but by love, patience, and suffering; submitting himself patiently to all the laws of the world, yea even to the law of death, and yet triumphing over them all through the force of righteousness."

Thus spake Xanthias, and I assent unto his words. But furthermore, if I believed Jesus to be the Son of God when mine eyes were opened to discern him after his resurrection, much more do I believe it now; because all the years as they pass by, yea, and all the seventy nations of the earth, are as so many angels of God, which do cry aloud with a clear voice and say, "Jesus of Nazareth is our King; Jesus of Nazareth, though he be in heaven, is ruling on earth." For whithersoever I look throughout the Empire, I behold the love of Christ beginning already to rule over the tribes of the earth, though as yet it be in small beginnings. In Britain, where I now write, in Gaul, in Spain, in Italy, in Greece, in all the parts of Asia Minor, in Carthage and Egypt, yea even unto Babylon and the parts far beyond the River, the Lord Jesus now hath his worshippers.

Too long were it now to recount what I beheld in Alexandria and in Rome concerning the power of Christ and how the churches in those cities increased and are still increasing. But thus much have I noted concerning the law of Christ, that it differeth from all other laws, in that it is fitted for all nations and climates and times. It is as useful for the poor as for the rich. It loveth order and concord, and hateth disorder and tumult. It loveth truth, righteousness, and happiness; it hateth deceits and unrighteousness and misery. It doth not say unto all nations, "Take unto yourselves the customs of the Greeks," nor yet "Take unto yourselves the laws of the Romans," neither doth it prescribe any pattern of government as the best: but what saith it? It saith, "Love God and thy neighbour; and I, even I, will give thee strength to love them." For our law is none other than the Lord Jesus himself, dwelling with us again, and abiding in our hearts for ever, through faith.

Therefore is the law of Jesus in the end to prevail over other laws. For other laws are laws of fear, and they rule by constraint and hinder growth; but the law of Jesus is a law of love, and ruleth through freedom, causing all good things to grow, and making the heart to leap up with joy. Other laws need addition of rewards and punishments; but the law of Jesus assigneth fit reward, and executeth needful punishment, of itself, without help of king or lawgiver. The laws of other lawgivers will pass away with the passing of those needs for which the laws were made: but the law of love will abide for ever, for the need thereof passeth not away. And when that law shall be established, then, and not till then, shall wars cease from the earth, and all nations shall be as one: for as Moses gave Israel a~ law to knit the ten tribes into one nation, even so hath the Lord Jesus given us a law to knit the seventy nations of the earth into one family of God.

In this hope I rejoice, even in the midst of tribulations, for I trust that Jesus of Nazareth reigneth. Therefore shall my heart not fail, albeit the signs and mighty works of the Church seem now to be passing away, and devils be not now cast out as of old; nor are the sick so often healed; and the saints speak less oft with tongues. For if the signs of righteousness and mercy and truth abide in the Church, those other signs may perchance be suffered to pass away. But that which sometimes troubleth me more, is that, as I hear in some of the churches, the saints are overmuch given to the governing of the congregations, and the arranging of the worship of the saints, and the observing of feasts and fasts, more than to the waging of the war against unrighteousness. For though it be well to follow after peace, yet can I not forget that the Lord Jesus studied not to lead a quiet life, but spake unto us saying that he must needs send a sword on earth. And who knoweth not how he stood up with the sword of his mouth against the Pharisees in the Temple of the Lord? The like of which contests and protestations against evil we hear not so oft, methinks, as in old times: howbeit, perchance even herein the Holy Spirit guideth us. But be this as it may, I still trust in the Lord Jesus; yea, even though there be (as I hear there be) divisions in certain of the churches, yet trust I in him. For I perceive that the Lord's ways are not as our ways; but the last are made first; and the weak become strong; and the foolish are exalted above the wise. Therefore, even as from the fall of Sion there seemeth to have come uprising to the Gentiles, even so perhaps out of the divisions of the churches may arise truth for all the world.

But as concerning the hour of the coming of the Lord, I deny not that he tarrieth long, even past all expectation. But inasmuch as the Lord Jesus himself said that he knew not that hour, for this cause I judge that no man shall know it. Only this is revealed unto me, that when the Lord shall come, it shall not be after such manner as we expect and shape forth in our minds, but the manner thereof shall be unexpected and new: better, I doubt not, than ever we hope or imagine, yet none the less, strange; yea, and perchance, at the first, full of disappointment. For I perceive that all the dealings of the Lord with men are after this fashion. He ever prepareth some good thing for us, exceeding all that we had expected; notwithstanding, with the good, there cometh also some wholesome pain or temptation that we expect not. For thus the Lord dealt with Adam in Paradise, and thus with Israel in the Promised Land; and thus also dealt the Lord Jesus with his disciples on earth. Wherefore thus also, I doubt not, the Lord Jesus will deal still with his disciples now that he reigneth in heaven.

But why speak I in conjectures concerning these unknown matters, or why yearn I thus impatiently for the hour of the Lord's coming, seeing that the Lord vouchsafeth to me, even on earth, his perpetual presence in mine heart, and the signs of his presence compass me everywhere around, so that even to live is joy? For verily to thee, Lord, and to thy Kingdom, all things in heaven and earth do bear witness.

The faces of all children, whom thou didst call thy little ones, give, back the brightness of thy countenance; the goodness of all good men testifieth unto thee, the supreme pattern of all good; yea even the bad and the weak proclaim their need of thee, Lord our Redeemer, in whom alone is power to create goodness in the worst, and to make the weakest strong. To thy word the seed-time and harvests bear witness; the flowers also do sing of thy trustfulness and hope. If I look unto the earth, thou hast trodden and sanctified it; if to the heaven, thou hast gone up into it and dost possess it; if I think of the terrors of the depths beneath the earth, behold, thou knowest them, and hast passed through them, and overcome them, and hast broken the bars thereof; that they may no more keep captive them that shall follow in thy footsteps, passing through the darkness of the grave. Thus hast thou, Eternal Word (by whom in ages past the worlds were created) now in these last times created the universe anew for them that love thee; so that all things do serve thee and proclaim thy Good Tidings, and the world is become unto thee as a vesture, and the elements are become thy servants: yea death itself thou hast subdued to be thy minister, and sin thou shalt subdue to be thy bond-slave.

Who is like unto thee, most mighty Lord, for verily thy truth is on every side. Whither shall I go from thy Spirit, or whither shall I flee from thy presence? If I climb up into heaven, thou art there. If I go down unto the dead, thou art there also. If I take the wings of the morning and remain in the uttermost parts of the sea, even there also shall thy hand lead me and thy right hand shall hold me. Therefore when I sleep in the grave, I am in thy cradle; and when I shall arise up and awake, behold around me are thy everlasting arms.

THE END OF THE HISTORY OF PHILOCHRISTUS

POSTSCRIPT

It had been my purpose, beloved brethren, to have continued this history from the year after the Lord Jesus suffered (in which year I left Syria and came to Alexandria) even to this present year, the tenth year after the destruction of the Holy City. Herein I was minded to have set forth how great things the Lord wrought for us in the Church of Alexandria, and the troubles that befell us there; even to the time of my going on the embassage unto Gaius Caesar along with Philo the Alexandrine. Next it was my intent to have spoken of the Church of Rome, how it grew and prospered, and how in those days the Spirit of the Lord began to lead the saints towards wisdom in the governing and administering of the Church; lastly, the history would have told how I accompanied Julius Plautius the legate hither, even to Londinium, where now I write, where the Lord had prepared a work for me to do in building up the Church in Britain. For in this way methinks it might have been possible for you, my brethren, more clearly to discern how the Lord Jesus, though he be now in heaven, still guideth his Church upon earth.

Notwithstanding, because I am now stricken in years (being now fourscore and six years of age), and forasmuch as I know not whether I may have life to complete so great a work, it seemeth best (although I have in part already written these matters of my later life) first to make an end of this former history, especially considering the troubles now imminent in Britain from the barbarous people, and to defer the rest to a more convenient season.

Farewell.

SCHOLIA

I

These words of the Lord Jesus are not indeed found in our Gospels; but they have been handed down by tradition.[1] Nor have I been able to find in the history of Philochristus any sayings of the

[1] They belong to the twenty traditional sayings "which seem to contain, in a mere or less altered form, traces of words of our Lord."—(Westcott's *Introduction To The Study Of The Gospels*, p.453.

Lord Jesus, save such as have been either handed down by tradition or else recorded in our Gospels.

Moreover, the writer (as it seemeth to me, having diligently compared this history with the Gospels of the holy Evangelists Matthew and Marie and Luke) maketh mention of all such miracles as are found in all the three Gospels (though the raising of Jairus daughter and the healing of the woman with the issue be but briefly mentioned) but if any miracle is found in one or in two Gospels only, concerning that he is silent. And this he seemeth to do not by chance, but of set purpose, as if he were minded to speak of those miracles only which are common to the first three Gospels. But Anchinous the son of Alethes maketh conjecture that Philochristus had in his mind a certain Original Gospel (whether it were a book or tradition) of exceeding antiquity; whence also the holy Evangelists drew that part of their several relations which is common to the first three Gospels.

II

Here again the writer of this history addeth nothing to our knowledge: for of oil the words that Philo the Alexandrine uttereth to Philochristus, there is scarce one that may not be found in the writings of Philo, suck as we now possess. The like observation also is to be made concerning that which Philochristus reporteth of the sayings of the Scribes: whereof there is scarce one but I have found it (or the like of it) among these sayings of the Teachers of Israel which have been handed down to us even to this day.[2]

III

Whereas Philochristus reporteth that a certain Scribe in his days spake of "eating the Messiah," I find no such saying current in those days. But true it is that, many years afterwards, Rabbi Hillel (but this is not the same as Hillel the Great, who lived in the generation before Philochristus) said these words: "There is no Messiah for Israel, since they have already eaten him in the days of Hezekiah."[3] Moreover the saying of Moses, how that the nobles of Israel "saw God and did eat and drink," is, without doubt, explained by some of the Teachers

---

[2] *Sayings Of The Jewish Fathers* by C. Taylor, M.A., published by the Cambridge University Press.

[3] *Sayings Of The Jewish Fathers*, p.74.

among the Jews to mean that the Shekinah was as meat and drink to the nobles. But whether this saying was current in those days, or whether Philochristus erreth here also (as elsewhere), certain it is that many of the sayings of the Scribes reported by Philochristus were not made known nor published till very long after; and meseemeth he hath perverted the doctrine of the Scribes with intent to cause the reader to have them in derision.

But Anchinous live son of Alethes saith that, howsoever the sayings of the Scribes (whereof Philochristus maketh mention) have not been handed down to us as spoken in those times; yet the cause is, saith Anchinous, that few sayings of those times have been preserved. But if they had been preserved, then, saith he, we should have found that Philochristus described the teaching of the Scribes with exactness; even as the Gospels also bear witness that the Scribes in those days strained at gnats but swallowed camels; and overmuch esteemed the tithing of mint and anise and cummin, and the purification of pots and platters; and counted an oath that was sworn by the gold of the Temple, as being weightier than an oath that was sworn by the Temple itself.

IV

Herein it is marvellous to see with what a persistence Philochristus cleaveth only unto that part of the first three Gospels which is common to all the three; so that one might go near to suppose that Anchinous was right, in that he conjectured that Philochristus doth this not by chance, but of set purpose; having before him, perchance, some book or tradition which contained no more than this. For whereas Philochristus saith that the women heard some mention made of Galilee, but what it was, they agreed not exactly among themselves: I will here set down, in order, the three relations:—

1 (*Saint Matthew*, xxviii. 7) "And behold HE GOETH BEFORE YOU INTO GALILEE; there shall ye see him: lo I HAVE TOLD YOU."

2 (*Saint Mark*, xvi. 7) "HE GOETH BEFORE YOU INTO GALILEE: there shall ye see him, as HE SAID unto you."

3 (*Saint Luke*, xxiv. 6) "Remember how HE SPAKE unto you WHILE HE WAS YET IN GALILEE."

But as to the Gospel of the holy Apostle John, I have not been able to find out whether any part of it were known to Philochristus. Albeit

Anchinous saith that Philochristus, although he make no mention of any of the acts, nor of the long discourses, nor set dialogues of that Gospel, nevertheless useth the doctrine of that Gospel as the foundation of the whole of his history. Notwithstanding, saith Anchinous, Philochristus seemeth not to attribute this doctrine to John the son of Zebedee (who ever speaketh after a different manner, and rather as one of the Sons of Thunder, or as the writer of the book of Revelation, than as the writer of the Fourth Gospel), but to Nathanael and Quartus.

V

After these words, "for they were sore afraid," cometh a blank in the Manuscript. And it is worthy of note that in the Gospel of the Holy Evangelist Mark, at the selfsame place, occurreth a blank, namely, after the words, "for they were afraid," in the eighth verse of the sixteenth chapter. And Anchinous saith that at this point the Original Gospel came to an end.

VI

Here Philochristus is unlike himself. For whereas he is wont for the most part to omit miracles, albeit the Gospels relate them, here on the other hand he inserteth one, albeit the Gospels omit it. Howbeit, true it is that the holy Apostle Paul seemeth, in his first epistle to the Corinthians, to make mention of some manifestation of the Lord Jesus to the holy Apostle James. And the same is mentioned in certain traditions.

But it is to be noted that, in the whole relation of the Resurrection of Jesus, Philochristus departeth from his usual course. For he reporteth many manifestations whereof mention is not made in all the three Gospels, nor even in two, but in one only; and he speaketh of others also innumerable. Howbeit he maketh no mention of that manifestation wherein the Lord partook of fish and honey with the Disciples.

THE END

BOOK TWO. ONESIMUS. MEMOIRS OF A DISCIPLE OF ST. PAUL

ONESIMUS TO THE READER

Art thou a slave, as I was? Or an orphan, as I was? Or wanderest thou still, as I long wandered, in the wilderness of doubt and sin? Then for thee is written this story of one that was made free in Christ, and adopted to be the child of God, and in the end brought safe out of the deep darkness of Satan into the Light of the Eternal Truth.

THE FIRST BOOK

§ 1. OF MY CHILDHOOD

In the last year of the Emperor Tiberius I and my twin- brother Chrestus were found lying in one cradle, exposed with a great number of other babes upon the steps of the temple of Asclepius, in Pergamus, a city of Bithynia. Sign or token of our parents, whether they were free-born or slave, there was none; but only a little silver seal hung round my neck, and on the seal these words in Greek characters, I LOVE THEE, and on my brother Chrestus another of the same fashion, bearing the inscription, TRUST ME. Many a time during the days of my wandering have I spoken reproachfully in my heart, saying that our parents gave us small cause for trust, and that it was poor love to send out into the rough world two innocent babes with no other equipment against evil than these slight toys. But the hand of the Lord was in it, to turn this evil into good in the end.

Ammiane the wife of Menneas was the name of our new mother. Her own son Ammias was but lately dead; and that which drew her kind heart to us more than to any other among so large a multitude of poor babes there pitifully lying on the temple steps, was that in my brother Chrestus she seemed to discern a likeness to her lost one.

Menneas took us, together with Ammiane, to his house in Lystra, a city of Lycaonia, where was the better part of his estate; and soon afterwards he died. But his widow, the good Ammiane, to whom old Menneas had left all his possessions, treated us as if we had been her own children, and taught us to call her mother; and we had no thought but she was our mother indeed. Yet as there had been no formal adoption of us according to law, we were still in the eyes of the law not free, but slaves; for so runs the law, that whosoever is exposed as a child and saved and reared, becomes the slave of them that rear him. For our enfranchisement had been first delayed, and then forgotten in the sickness and death of Menneas; and by that time we were so established in the household that none questioned but we had been enfranchised, and all thought of it was laid aside. Therefore according to the law we were still Ammiane's slaves, and not her sons, and in danger to be sold whenever our dear foster- mother might dic. But of all this neither I nor my brother Chrestus knew anything; but we rejoiced in the love of her whom we called mother; and all the household loved us for her sake, and some for our own. And so the days rolled on in happiness till I had come to my tenth year.

§ 2. HOW I FIRST SAW THE HOLY APOSTLE PAULUS

It was in the spring, as I remember, of the fifth year of the emperor Claudius that I first saw the Holy Apostle, whom I saw not again till many years had passed away; and though I was at that time but a child of ten years or thereabouts, yet every circumstance of it is imprinted upon my memory. It was the cool of the evening, and I was without the wall, hard by the Iconian gate, on one of the smaller hills that look down upon the town, a little to the north of the Iconian road. Hermas, our herdsman, was playing upon his pipe some song to the god Pan, and the goats were gambolling around him. But I—being wholly taken up with teaching a little kid to dance to the sound of the music—paid no heed to the chidings of our nurse Trophime, who would have had me go back with her to the city because it was now near sun-down. So lifting up her eyes and seeing some dromedaries and a dust on the Iconian road, "Look, dear child," said she, "yonder come merchants from Iconium; if therefore thou wilt go with me without delay, thou wilt see their stores of pretty things, and perchance Ammiane will buy thee somewhat."

Hearing this, I willingly ran down with her to the city gate; and arriving thither before the travellers, I waited till they should enter. But when they were now nigh, I perceived that they were no merchants, and I would have turned away. Yet I did not, for somewhat in the face of one of the travellers held me fast, I know not how, so that I fixed my gaze on him perforce, even as a bird fascinated by a serpent; and indeed I thought myself to be bewitched and spat thrice; but yet I stood still gazing upon him. At that time he was not yet bald, he had a clear complexion, a nose hooked and somewhat large; he was short of stature, and as he walked he bent his head a little forward, as if not able to discern things clearly; his eyebrows were shaggy and met together; but what most moved me was the glance of his eyes which were of a penetrating brightness, as though they would pierce through the outside of things even to the innermost substance.

When the travellers were entered into the city, I stood still in wonder, as one who had seen a dream betwixt sleeping and waking. But soon, coming to myself again, I chid my nurse that she had drawn me away from the flocks by stratagem and I persuaded her to return for some short space, that I might continue my sport. But my heart was no longer in it, and presently, it being now sunset, I came down with Trophime to go into the town. Scarce were we come within the gates when we perceived a great concourse of the people near to the market; and running thither we entered with the rest into a courtyard and there found a great multitude assembled, and the travellers, in the gallery above, discoursing to them. What touched me (as being a child) more than all the words that were spoken, was the marvellous stillness of the multitude, who all listened as if the speech were about matters of life or death, so that herdsmen and ploughmen and litter-bearers and water-carriers and others of the lowest and meanest sort, coming into the courtyard with shouts and scoffings, no sooner passed into the circle of the hearers than they were at once subdued and tamed like the rest; among whom, most earnestly listening, as I noted, was a poor creature, part demented and part buffoon, whom, having been lame for thirty years and more, we were wont to call "lame Xanthias." This man, when the traveller had made an end of his discourse, said some words that I could not clearly understand; whereupon he that had been speaking came straightway down from the gallery and drew nigh to the lame man, and fixing his eyes upon him he took him by the hand. If there had been a silence before, there was a tenfold silence now, even such a silence as one seemed to feel in one's flesh. But the stranger first lifted up his eyes to heaven and then gazing fixedly on the lame man he cried in a loud voice, "In the name of Jesus of Nazareth, rise up and walk;" and behold, Xanthias,—this man who had been thirty years lame,—rose and walked and leaped, and wept aloud praising and magnifying God. Then there was a great shouting, and all rushed forth into the market place, some crying "a miracle," "a miracle," others holding up Xanthias in their arms to show him unto the people, others magnifying the new god whom the strangers had revealed to us, others crying out that the strangers themselves were gods, namely Zeus and Hermes, come down from heaven as they had come down in the old days; and saying these things, some sped away to the priest wishing to offer sacrifice to the strangers. But suddenly there was a deep silence again, and we perceived that the traveller, he I mean who had healed Xanthias, was once more speaking to the people. What he said I could not clearly understand, being more busy with noting his countenance than the meaning of his words; but I gathered so much, that he said that he and his companion were not gods but men, and that indeed there was One God above (not many gods) who gave all good gifts to mankind and who now called all men to come unto him. When he had made an end of speaking, the women pressed close to him with their babes and children that he might touch them; and so it was that Trophime pushed me forward with the rest. Then he laid his hands on me and looking kindly on me asked Trophime whether I was a native of these parts and who was my father. What Trophime replied I did not hear, except that my father was now dead; but the stranger looked on me more lovingly than before and said, "The Lord be unto thee as a Father, little one"; and laying his hands on me a second time he blessed me.

§ 3. OF THE STRANGER, AND OF DIOSDOTUS THE PRIEST OF ZEUS

When we were come home to Ammiane, I spoke freely to her as I was wont, concerning all that I had heard and seen; and I asked her which of the two she judged to be the wiser and the mightier, the hook-nosed prophet—for so I called the stranger—or Diosdotus. Now Diosdotus was the priest of the city, a man of noble birth and very wealthy, having rebuilt the baths at his own expense after the earthquake, as also his father before him had rebuilt the amphitheatre. He was also tall of stature and of a gracious and commanding carriage. Yet now I could not help making comparison between him and the stranger of mean presence and short stature; bethinking myself that Diosdotus had lived for thirty years in the same city as poor lame Xanthias and yet had suffered him to be still lame, whereas the strange prophet had healed him on the very day of his first coming in. However Ammiane laughed and chid me for my question, saying that I did ill to compare an obscure vagrant soothsayer with the high priest of Zeus; for that there were many travelling priests of Cybele and Sabazius and jugglers and necromancers that would work signs and wonders in the eyes of the common people, and all for a drachma or two; but Diosdotus was none of these, nor to be mentioned along with them. Nevertheless, when the report came in from all sides that the lame man was wholly cured, she said she would send for Xanthias, as soon as might be, that she might see him and learn the truth of the matter, and what charms or herbs the stranger had used. But about the fourth or fifth day afterwards—my foster-mother having in the meanwhile, upon one cause or other, delayed to send for Xanthias, but many rumours coming daily to our ears of the great wonders which the magician was working—word was brought that the stranger had been slain; others said that he had ascended to the sky, others that he had been swallowed up in the earth; but all agreed that he was not now in the city. Then we found that there had been a great conflict in the Jews' quarter; for certain Jews had come over from Lystra to Iconium pursuing after the enchanter (so they called him) and accusing him of many grievous crimes. Now it happened to be a time of drought, and the rain, which had begun to fall on the day that the stranger came to Lystra, ceased on that same day, about the time of his entering in, and fell no more for six or seven days, though all the crops were perishing for want of it. So the Jews said that this plague was fallen upon the city of Lystra because we gave shelter to an accursed necromancer; and having persuaded the people they stoned him. But his body could not be found; wherefore the people were the more persuaded that he was a necromancer, insomuch that all now (except Xanthias and a very few others) believed him to be no prophet but an evil-doer and a deceiver of the people.

But on the very day after these things the sun was darkened, and still no rain fell; and on the third day after the stoning of the stranger, came a great plague of locusts so thick together that they lay two inches deep in the race- course; and not many days after that, came the shock of an earthquake; and ten houses in the Jews' quarter were wholly thrown down (besides others sorely shaken and shattered), insomuch that some fourscore of the Jews were slain, and their synagogue was utterly destroyed. Upon this the people began to change their minds again, and some made bold to say that the god of the new prophet had sent these evils; and so the city was divided, and part held that the stranger was a deceiver and an enchanter, but part that he was a teacher of the true God and a prophet. At last when the customary sacrifices seemed of no avail, but the drought still endured, and by intervals there came ever and anon shocks of earthquake, it seemed good that there should be a solemn procession of all the city to avert the wrath of the gods, one for Pessinuntian Cybele, the other for Asphalian Poseidon and the third for Zeus Panhemerius. This last far surpassed the other two in splendour, and amidst the whole procession most of all to be admired was Diosdotus the chief priest, himself most like to a god, clad in white linen with a purple border, and a garland on his head, and attended by the inferior priests, and by ministers bearing incense and scattering flowers and perfumes; and after them, the white oxen with their horns gilt for the sacrifice, and then the choir of boys, with laurel branches in their hands, singing, to the accompaniment of the lyre, the hymn which had been chosen by Onomarchus the secretary of the senate. Beholding all this splendour (exceeding anything I had ever before witnessed) I inclined now to prefer Diosdotus to the strange prophet; and all the more because Ammiane was clearly on the side of the former. Moreover on the second day after the procession there fell rain in abundance. So all the people now turned to magnify Zeus Panhemerius; and the drought and the earthquake were forgotten, and with them the memory of the stranger faded away.

Yet in my dreams sometimes, both then and for many months afterwards, methought I saw the strange prophet who had healed Xanthias, standing over against Diosdotus and contending against him; and I heard his voice again and again in the darkness, saying, "The Lord be unto thee as a father."

§ 4. HOW WE GREW UP AT LYSTRA

Six or seven years passed smoothly away for me and my brother Chrestus. Our dear mother Ammiane caused us to be taught singing and dancing, as well as riding and the exercises of the gymnasium; and partly because of our beauty and partly because we were regarded as the adopted children of one whom all the citizens loved and honoured (for there are still extant inscriptions in Lystra praising our benefactress and calling her the MOTHER OF THE CITY, on account of her many gifts and benefactions to the people of Lystra) we were chosen among the choir of boys who were to sing songs year by year in honour of Apollo and Ephesian Artemis in accordance with the recent decree of the senate; and in all our riding-lessons and wrestling-lessons we took part with the well-born youth of the city; for all knew that Ammiane intended us to be her heirs after her death. But in my fourteenth year it happened that, while seeking for a goat that had strayed in the mountains, I missed my footing and fell down a steep place, where I was taken up for dead; and Hermas brought me home wounded well- nigh to death with two deep gashes on my forehead and left cheek. In a short space I was recovered of my wounds; but I was grievously disfigured with the scars upon my face, and when I went with my brother, as I was wont, to the choir-master, he plainly told me that I was no longer fit to dance nor sing with the choir, for the god required comely youths to minister to him. Hereat I was sore vexed, and yet more when I perceived (or thought that I perceived) that in the palaestra also and in the riding-school I was no longer so welcome as of old; for some openly jested at my disfigurement, and others, who had before courted my company, now avoided me; at least so I thought, misconstruing perhaps and aggravating little slights, in my discontent. However it was, I became morose and lost my former cheerfulness; for the world seemed changed and turned against me. But the kind Ammiane, discerning what was amiss with me, persuaded me to apply myself to letters; and she bought for us one Zeno, a Greek, to be our tutor. Now Chrestus, being the leader of the choir and the favourite in the palaestra, by reason of these distractions cared less for learning; but I, withdrawing myself from my former pursuits and devoting myself to letters, made good progress in my new studies, so that I soon became skilful at transcribing Greek characters; and I took a great delight in the reading of Euripides and others of the Greek play-writers, but most of all in the poetry of Homer. And in these pursuits I continued till my sixteenth year, finding pleasure in many things but most of all in the love of my beautiful brother Chrestus.

§ 5. HOW AMMIANE DIED AND MY BROTHER AND I WERE SOLD FOR SLAVES

But now indeed our trouble was at hand. For to ward the end of my sixteenth year, our dear foster-mother died, and whether it was that she had made no will, or that the will had been stolen or lost, certain it was that no will could be found. It was commonly said, in the household, that a will had been made and deposited with one Tertullus, a banker of Iconium, but that he had destroyed the will, being persuaded by Nicander of Tyana the heir-at-law, and the two witnesses being both dead. Diosdotus the high-priest of Zeus affirmed that Ammiane had deposited a will with him fourteen years ago in the presence of two witnesses, immediately after the death of her husband, but that she had received it back in the presence of the same witnesses, two years afterwards, and had deposited no other will in its place. Whatever the truth may have been, when Nicander arrived on the second day from Tyana, there was none to dispute his claim; so, though he was known by all to be hateful to Ammiane and had not set foot on her threshold for fifteen years, he now took upon himself to give orders for the funeral and to dispose all things according to his pleasure. Hereupon arose a great wailing and lamentation among the household, that is to say all that were old enough to know what it was to be a slave. For many of them had looked to be made free by Ammiane's will; and to some she had in express terms promised freedom: and others, who had not been long with us, knowing the kindness of their mistress, expected that they should not be sold, or that after four or five years of service they should be made free. For so much as this was customary with all the wealthy townspeople of Lystra, those at least that had large possessions in land and many household slaves; and how much more might have been expected from one who had been publicly praised as the "mother of the city"! But now all these hopes were dashed to the ground; and all were at the mercy of a new master, of whom we knew nothing by hearsay except that he hated our dear mistress, and from our own knowledge we had begun to suspect that he was greedy, cruel, violent and tyrannous.

For a few hours Chrestus and I remained weeping bitterly in the room where we were wont to sit with Zeno; but when Nicander entered and, in answer to his question why we wept, we made answer that we were weeping for our mother, he reviled us as beggarly brats, slaves seeking to escape from our condition; and spurning us from the chamber bade us be gone at once to the slaves' apartments. Going thither we found all faces full of sorrow; yet none so sorrowful as not to be able to spare some little further sorrow for our case; all pointing to us and exclaiming at our ill fortune because yesterday we had been free and heirs to great possessions, but now we were slaves and a second time motherless.

I suppose that our cruel master foresaw that some of the friends of Ammiane would, in all likelihood, interfere in our behalf, if not by appeal to the courts of law, at all events by offering to purchase us from him; for he gave command that on that very day, immediately after the performance of the funeral rites, we should be sent to his estate at Tyana. A miserable procession was that, wherein Chrestus and I walked for the last time together, following our dear Ammiane to the grave! The whole household filled the air with lamentations, for themselves even more than for their mistress, so that there was little need of the hired mourners.

But when all was over, and the funeral line moved back homeward, Chrestus and I for a short space turned quietly aside and betook ourselves to a new-made tomb cut in the side of one of the hills that look down upon the city; and there we sat down and wept and poured forth all our sorrows in one another's arms, beseeching the gods to have mercy upon us. For we began to see that we could expect no pity from Nicander, and that he would not hesitate to sell us and to part us asunder if he could thereby make more profit from us; and our hearts swelled to bursting at the thought that we, who had never been divided, should now perchance be parted, each to live lonely and desolate till our life's end. As we wept, we looked down upon our dear home. The fields beneath us had been the fields of Ammiane; we could call by name the sheep and goats that were leaping and bleating in the valley at our feet; the temples in which we had worshipped, the shining roofs of the houses of many well-known friends—all reminded us of past happy days, happy most of all because we had enjoyed them together. At last we rose up to go down to our new life of slavery. But because our minds misgave us that we should be parted on the morrow, we determined to take our last farewell there alone, and not in the presence of Nicander nor before the eyes of the household slaves. And Chrestus said that we should interchange some token, whereby we might recognize each other in days to come, if ever the gods should bring us together again. So we took from off our necks the charms which we had always worn from our infancy and I received from Chrestus his seal with the inscription TRUST ME, and he mine with the words I LOVE THEE. Then we bade one another farewell, no longer able to constrain ourselves, but with piercing cries falling each on the other's neck and weeping and calling on Ammiane to help us because the gods helped us not; and then, drying our tears, without another word we went down into Lystra. Here Nicander, rating us for our delay, gave command that we should be at once placed on separate camels and set out for Tyana.

§ 6. OF THE DEATH OF CHRESTUS

On the third day after we were come to Tyana, being summoned to the presence of Nicander, we found with him certain of Ammiane's household slaves, and by the side of our master a smooth-faced Greek from Delos who seemed to be inspecting and appraising the slaves; who, looking at my scar, laughed and said that he should not need to ask Nicander to name a price for me; but he praised the beauty of Chrestus and caused him to be stripped and to walk up and down the room, and to sing and to go through the steps of two or three dancing-measures; and finally he declared with an oath that he was more beautiful than Nireus and that he would buy him at Nicander's price. When we heard this, we both of us fell down at the feet of Nicander and of the slave-dealer, beseeching them in the name of their parents and their brothers also, if they had any, that at least they would not part us, but that the Greek might buy us both; and at the same time I told the slave-dealer that I could read and write Greek easily and rapidly, so that I might fetch a good price as an amanuensis; and even the rest of the slaves of Ammiane fell on their faces before our master and joined in our petition.

But Nicander angrily spurned us, and the Greek said to Chrestus that he must go to Rome where he would fetch ten times as much as a paltry amanuensis or grammarian because he was as lovely as Ganymede and sure to please some great nobleman or perchance the Emperor himself; but added he, "Your brother is of no worth to me, for I deal in none but pretty boys; and therefore, any beautiful one, thou must needs make ready to be my companion at once, for I should be by this time well on the road to Tarsus." Hereat Chrestus arose and following the Greek his master he would have gone forth without a word more from the chamber. Nicander, scoffing at his misery, called him back to say farewell to me, "for," said he, "it may be some time before you see your brother again." But Chrestus remained silent; only, as he went out at the door, he turned round to me and held up the little token round his neck. But that silence was better than many words, and the memory of it abides with me unto this day.

So long as Chrestus was in the chamber I restrained myself for his sake lest I should break his heart with my weeping and passion; but when he was gone forth I again attempted to bend Nicander with prayers and entreaties. But finding all in vain, I leaped up from the ground in fury, and invoked curses upon him threatening that I would slay him if ever I found occasion. At the word he clapped his hands and calling in the slaves of his household, "Take this young rebel," he said, "to the upper quarries, and put him to hard labour with the lowest class, till the brat understand his condition, and learn to be a slave and to submit himself to his betters." So while Chrestus was being carried away to Tarsus, I was dragged to the quarries, which were in a wild place, void for miles round of all human habitation, about twenty miles north of Tyana. In these quarries there laboured a large gang of slaves, with scant food and scanter clothing, forced to work in chains under the burning sun all day, and at night locked up like sheep in a foul den underground; and if any died, little heed was taken of it, for it was cheaper to buy new slaves than to treat the old slaves well. But I doubt not that Nicander, who had good reasons for wishing to be rid of my brother and me, did what he did wittingly and with forethought, supposing that I should soon have succumbed to the hardships of the place and the life, and that the quarries should have been my grave and his deliverance.

On the morrow I began my labours amid a new sort of companions, creatures to all outward appearance resembling apes and dogs rather than human beings, some stamped and branded on their foreheads with T for "thief," or M for "murderer"; others having their backs discoloured with the weals of the lash or torn and bleeding with the marks of fresh punishment; others with collars round their necks, or clogs and fetters shackling their legs and feet; others labouring beastlike under a kind of fork or yoke; all were chained in some fashion, and all had one side of the head shorn, so that they might be recognized at once if they should break away and escape any distance. Speech was not allowed among us; and as we toiled on from sunrise to sunset amid the heated rocks, the only sounds that could be heard (beside the clinking of the tools upon the stone) were the threats and curses of the overseers and the crack of the whip followed by the scream of some stricken slave. All the more leisure was there for thought of Chrestus, whose fate was infinitely worse than mine, because he was to go to Rome and there to be sold for his beauty; and I knew well the saying of the philosopher that "What is counted impurity in the free-born must be counted a necessity in slaves." Thinking on these things I felt such an agony that neither the heat nor the parching thirst could be compared with it; and even the first feeling of the slave-whip upon my shoulders, though it maddened me for the moment, could not drive out the thought of Chrestus. But hatred and thirst for revenge and distrust of the Gods began to blend themselves with my love of my brother; and whereas at first I had prayed to Ephesian Artemis to preserve him, now I began to doubt whether prayers availed anything.

I had been scarce a week in the ergastulum when, as we came forth in the morning to be marshalled and numbered, according to our wont, before going to our several places in the quarries, I heard the voice of Hernias behind me giving some message to Syrus our overseer. But when I leaped forward to embrace him, he spoke roughly to me, calling me a fool and a rebel, and saying that he would have no speech with me till I had submitted myself to the worthy Nicander. I shrank back quickly to my place, feeling myself friendless indeed now that Hernias had turned against me. By this time we were on our way from the ergastulum to the quarries, and I with the rest in my place in the rear. But when the crack of Syrus's whip showed that he was at some distance in the front of the long column, I heard my name called in a low voice and Hermas was by my side. He told me in few words that he had accompanied the slave-dealer to Tarsus, but that on the way Chrestus, either slipping or casting himself down in a narrow and precipitous part of the road, had fallen down a high cliff and had been taken up sorely gashed and wounded, and within two or three hours afterwards he had died. In my heart I knew that Hermas spoke the truth, but I refused to believe his tale, saying that he was in league with Nicander to deceive me; else, why had not he brought some token? But the old man with tears in his eyes, declared that he would have brought me the charm that hung round my brother's neck, but one of the slaves had stolen it; however, in his last moments Chrestus had written some message on his tablets for me; and so saying he produced the tablets which I knew to be indeed my brother's. Now all my hopes fell, and I knew that I was alone in the world; yet could I neither speak nor weep but walked on without a sign; but the old man looking anxiously in my face bade me trust in him, and seeing Syrus approach, he pressed my hand and departed. For almost all that day the overseer—perchance because he suspected something amiss, having caught sight of Hermas stealing away—would not depart from my neighbourhood but kept his eyes so fixed on me that I dared not stop my work for an instant to pluck the tablets from my bosom where I had thrust them; and what I did I knew not, but I could neither think, nor weep, nor do anything but toil on, like some machine. But toward sun-down, a little before we were marshalled that we might go down into the ergastulum, seizing my occasion I plucked out the tablets and upon the first leaf of them I found traced in faint characters, as if by a feeble hand, the words on the token which I had given him, I LOVE THEE; and when I read them, the tears delayed no longer. [4]

§ 7. OF MY LIFE IN THE ERGASTULUM

If it was a marvel that my body held out against the hardships of the quarries, it was much more marvellous that my soul perished not. Nor do I speak now merely of the words and deeds of darkness wrought by the slavish herd in their underground den, from which the grace of the Lord preserved me; but I speak of the trust in any divine governance of the world which seemed at this time to be in danger to be utterly extinguished, or even to be replaced by a belief in evil. For not only was I becoming day by day more like a brute beast in mind and soul as well as in body, listening with less horror to the obscene jests and tales of my companions and learning to take all evil as matter of course and to expect no good in the world; but also I began to think that, if there were gods indeed, they could not be such as the Epicureans would have us believe, "idle gods that take no thought for mortals," but they must be bad gods to have made, and to endure, so bad a world.

Now I knew that Ammiane had believed in witches and necromancers and the like; yea, and even Zeno our tutor, though he were a philosopher and of the Stoic sect, had freely confessed that he himself would be unwilling to be persecuted with the charms and incantations of witches. As often therefore as my companions turning from their obscenities and filthy tales, began to tell of witchcraft (which they were wont to do more especially after earthquakes, when they were under some influence of fear) and stories about Empousae and blood- sucking monsters, and the raising of spectres and the drawing out of the hearts of living men, at such times I would give an eager ear to all their sayings; and although Zeno had taught me to believe that these superstitions of the common people were no better than old wives' fables, yet now I began to incline to the opinion that these stories were true. And in my present condition the gods of darkness, such as Hecate and Gorgo and the like, seemed to have more substance and real power than the greater gods Zeus and Poseidon, who were worshipped in processions by noble priests in fine raiment with perfumes and flowers and offerings of fat victims,

4 This description of the slaves in the ergastulum is from Apuleius.

but did nothing for their worshippers. When therefore I heard how one witch had drawn forth oracles from a little babe whose throat she had cut and enslaved its spirit; and how another had obtained vengeance over her enemies by means of the marrow of a child whom she had buried up to the midst in the ground and then left to starve in sight of abundance of food; and others had caused their enemies to pine away by making waxen images to be pierced with needles or melted at slow fires, and the like; then came the thought of Nicander in my mind, thus caused to waste away and to live without a heart and suddenly to drop down dead, and I prayed that I too might learn these mysteries.

One evening more especially I call to mind, when we had been driven earlier than usual into our dungeon because of a great storm and earthquake, and all the earth seemed in a flux the crags from the hill sides falling on this side and on that, and whole cliffs swaying to right and left as if we were on sea and not on solid earth and nine or ten of my companions had been already crushed by the rocks or by the falling in of the sides of the quarries. When we were thrust into our dungeon, sitting in darkness, we could still feel the ground moving beneath us and ever and anon such rockings and rumblings as made the more timid cry out that some gulf would open and swallow us up alive, others, that the sides and roof were falling in upon us. But, of a sudden, amidst the din and tumult of so many voices, a few weeping, but the most part shouting and yelling and blaspheming and cursing the gods, we heard one of the slaves speaking out clearly above all the rest and commanding silence. His name was Nannias, a Colchian by birth; and he bade us desist from our fears and take heart, "for," said he, "I myself have brought about this storm and earthquake, and as I hope, we shall soon learn that our master has miserably perished in it."

Then all held their peace and listened to the Colchian who continued thus. "From my earliest years I was instructed by an old witch (who bought me as a babe) in all the arts of magic; and from her I learned how to raise the winds and how to lull them, and how to make away with a man though he be miles distant, in such wise that none may know the causer of the mischief. From my infancy I have ever taken a delight in all evil. For why not? The cross has been the tomb of all my brothers, my father and my grandfather; nor will I degenerate from my ancestors. The world is against us; let us also be against the world."[5] At this all shouted in assent; but the Colchian impatiently continued, "My first master in Laodicea I destroyed by placing bones and blood, and nails from a cross, together with certain herbs which I will not now mention, beneath the floor of his bedchamber, so that he wasted away and died in less than a month to the astonishment of the physician. And what was best and sweetest of all, I caused the suspicion of the deed to fall on the overseer of the slaves, a tyrannical wretch like Syrus, who was condemned to the wild beasts on the charge of having made away with our master by slow poisons." Hereat all shouted and applauded even louder than before; and then though the earth still rocked and groaned beneath us, and the sides of the ergastulum swayed in and out more violently than ever, yet every one sat silent in the darkness waiting to hear what project the Colchian might have in hand so as to take vengeance on Nicander.

While we all held our breath he cried aloud on Hecate the goddess of darkness and hater of light, who delighteth in blood, to come and seize Nicander, at the same time appealing to other horrible-sounding and unknown gods, and invoking on Nicander the most direful curses. When he ceased, behold, up from the ground (as it seemed) there came a thin voice, not loud but very piercing and such as made my very flesh to creep, saying, "I come, master, I come, I come." Hereat we all leaped to our feet and some shrieked aloud that the demon was upon them, and then all rushed this way and that, and many fell in a heap wallowing together on the floor, and such a hubbub as if hell itself were let loose; and methought if the uproar had continued but a few moments longer, many of us would have been made mad; but at the instant the guard came in with one bearing a lamp, and nothing could anywhere be seen; and they smote on all sides with their whips till the clamour had well nigh abated; and then they went out leaving us in the darkness as before.

Now during all these many years I had had few or no thoughts of Him in whose name Xanthias had been healed; but on this same evening of the earthquake, while I was musing whether there were gods or no, it came into my mind that besides invoking Hecate and Gorgo and the rest, it might be wise to offer up prayers to the God of

---

[5] A quotation from Plautus.

the strange prophet whom I remembered in my childhood, that He also might join in destroying Nicander. But blessed be the Lord, He hindered me from thus blaspheming His Holy Name; for whether it was that I remembered that the prophet had said that this God was a God of mercy and would be as a Father to me, or whether it was the memory of the pure and holy face of the prophet which seemed not to agree with my impure and unholy prayers, certain it is that the Lord closed my lips and restrained my tongue that I should not take His name in vain. But when all the rest were at last asleep I lay a long while awake and musing upon the words "the Lord be unto thee as a Father" and wondering what manner of god this "Lord" might be.

§ 8. HOW I WAS SOLD TO PHILEMON OF COLOSSI

Not more than three or four days had passed since the prophecy of the Colchian, and it was the 8th month or thereabouts from the time of my first being brought to the quarries, when behold, one morning, coming out of the ergastulum to our work according to custom, we found, in the place of the usual overseers, a band of soldiers; and instead of being drafted off to our several stations in the quarries, we were caused to march in one column through Tyana. As we passed through the town, we heard the reason of our journey. Nicander was dead. However he had not perished, as the Colchian had prophesied, in the earthquake; but having committed an outrage on the wife of one of his slaves, he had been mortally wounded by the man in a fit of passion. Yet had he lived long enough to revenge himself by causing the whole of his household to be put to death, three hundred in all, including those who had been of the household of Ammiane, among whom perished our faithful Hermas, and our old nurse Trophime. On the morrow he died, and the heir, entering on the estate, had ordered all the slaves that were in the quarries to be sent to Tarsus and there sold. So brutal had I become and so hard of heart during my stay in the ergastulum, that even the news of the death of Hermas and Trophime did not greatly move me, and the pain of it was not so great as the pleasure I took in hearing of the death of Nicander.

When we were come to Tarsus and set up on the slave-platform, and there caused to leap and dance and carry weights and to proclaim aloud what arts and accomplishments we knew, I felt little shame, but only some faint desire to know who would be my master, and at the same time a rebellious hatred against gods and men, as being all alike unjust, and a determination to be avenged on mankind. At this time my knowledge of letters and my skill in transcribing stood me in good stead. For when one of the slave-dealers had seen me give proof of my skill upon tablets, he bought me at a higher price than the rest, and after taking me to the baths and using medicaments to remove or lessen the marks of my stripes, he clothed me decently, and placed me with a Greek teacher to increase my skill in letters; and after two or three months thus spent in Tarsus, I was sold to one Philemon, whose step-son Archippus had been studying rhetoric in the schools. My new master was a wealthy citizen of Colossae and a man of learning, devoted at that time to Greek literature, and he had come to Tarsus to take note of his son's progress in the schools there and to conduct him home; and by reason of a growing infirmity of sight he desired to buy some slave who could read Greek with understanding and take short notes of such things as he dictated. So he bought me for four minae, and I accompanied him to Colossae.

I was now in my eighteenth year, being the last year of the emperor Claudius; but though young I was not so pliant or supple of nature as might have been expected from a youth. For I was, as it were, old and stiffened with suffering; and however the kind Philemon might show me favour and allowance, yet would my mind still harp on this, that, if I had my rights, I should be free, and whosoever was my master possessed me unjustly. Moreover the terror of my recent life in the quarries never forsook me; and each night I said to myself, "I am pampered and made a plaything to-day, but I may be cast into the ergastulum to-morrow." This bitterness of distrust spoiled all the pleasures with which the good Philemon would have gladdened my new life at Colossae and indeed my present freedom from oppression and my very leisure, giving me increased occasions for brooding over my loneliness, made me more morose than ever. Sometimes when I looked at the little token which my brother had given me and bethought myself of the token that I had interchanged with him, I would declare that I had not only bestowed on my poor Chrestus the legend I LOVE THEE but at the same time I had parted with my very faculty of love—so barren and dry of all affection did my heart now seem—and as for the other legend TRUST ME, I would inveigh against it as idle and deceiving. For whom had I on earth to trust? My parents, who had forsaken me"? Or Chrestus or

Hermas or Trophime, who were now but dust and ashes? But if I looked elsewhere, to the gods in heaven above, or to the gods beneath the earth, behold, I saw none save beings that either rejoiced in evil or at least had not power to destroy evil; which therefore were either too bad or too weak to claim trust from men.

But herein is thy hand manifest, Lord Jesus; for through the loss of earthly love and trust thou wast leading me to thyself, the fountain of all goodness, thou whom to love is to trust, and to trust is to love, and in the loving and trusting of whom is Life Eternal. Blessed art thou, who dost free the oppressed and guide the wanderer! Blessed art thou, Lord of all Love, who didst take from me unto thyself the earthly love of my dear brother that thereby thou mightest guide me to a better and higher Love, even to thyself, in whom, long afterwards, I found my brother once again.

THE END OF THE FIRST BOOK

THE SECOND BOOK

§ 1. HOW I RETURNED TO THE WORSHIP OF FALSE GODS

PERCEIVING that my mind was under some trouble or disturbance, my master often turned the discourse to matters of morals and philosophy, and especially to the belief in the gods and the divine government of the world; and I told him plainly that I had no such belief, for that the world seemed to me governed by chance, or by fate, or by evil gods, but in no case by good gods, seeing that ill-doing prevailed in the world. Upon this Philemon, being grieved because of my unbelief, asked me whether I had had much discourse with his friend Artemidorus, the Epicurean, on these matters. When I said no, not much, but that my unbelief arose from my own experience of things, because I had seemed to discern more proof of the power of evil than of good, he bade me take comfort; for he would in due course emancipate me, and meantime I should be to him as a friend. After this he advised me to study the books of Plato and of Chrysippus, if perchance I might thus frame myself to a better mind. But when I urged (which indeed was not my own argument but I had heard it lately from Artemidorus) that the stories concerning the gods were full of all manner of myths, and fables containing portents, and metamorphoses, such as no sane man could believe, to this he replied that the whole world was full of no less wonders, if a man rightly considered it; for that summer should follow spring, and autumn summer, that storm should follow calm, and calm storm, and that the whole world should be so orderly and evenly governed as it was, this, he said, was a far greater wonder than the metamorphoses of which the poets speak. In particular he pointed out the wonderful things past all common course of nature, which were to be seen in that very neighbourhood of Colossae and Laodicea; and taking me with him up and down the valley of the river, called Lycus, which flows through, that region, he showed me how the water is there changed into stone of a dazzling brightness, so that the hills are in many parts covered with the appearance of snow, and cataracts abound of the same substance, and how other mountains vomit forth smoke and fire, and others have wells and springs bubbling upward hot from the earth. Again on another day he brought me to a certain pool sacred to the goddess Cybele, and bade me mark how sheep and goats and cattle, driven into this pool, straightway fell down and perished, but the priests of Cybele, entering into the same waters, stood upright and unhurt in the presence of many spectators; and upon this he asked me what more proof was wanting of the power of the goddess to protect her votaries? When I could make no reply, he affirmed that all these wonders were placed at hand to convince them that disbelieved in the gods; for if we were forced to believe in these wonders, being as they were before our eyes, why should we be so loth to believe other wonders that our eyes had not seen?

In course of time the words of Philemon and still more his kind deeds and the kindness of his wife Apphia, had power to quench that rancorous spirit which had inflamed my heart. Other friends also, both at Colossae and in Hierapolis, moved me in the same direction, I mean towards a belief in the gods. Among these was the good Epictetus (a slave like myself and at that time a very young man) concerning whom I shall have much to say hereafter; and a certain Nicostratus of Laodicea, full of zeal for learning, but devout and liberal, and of a gracious nature. Nor must I forget Heracleas, a great reader of the works of the ancient poets as well as of the philosophers, who had studied for some time in Alexandria. These three, being of the acquaintance of Philemon, treated me with exceeding courtesy, seeking my society and willingly conversing with me; and I soon perceived that almost all the rest of our acquaintance though in no respect given to superstitions, nevertheless agreed in believing that the world was governed by good and divine powers.

§ 2. HOW SOME OF PHILEMON'S FRIENDS AVOWED A BELIEF IN ONE GOD

I soon found that, although the philosophers whom I have mentioned above, believed in gods, yet their belief differed much from that of the common people; for the latter believe in many gods, but the former inclined to acknowledge one god under many names. It was at a symposium, during a public festival in honour of Artemis, that I first heard this opinion broached by Nicostratus who said that "there was in reality but one Power, however He may manifest Himself to mortals by many different shapes and names in several lands and nations, speaking also through different prophets, a Delphic woman in Pytho, a Thesprotian man in Dodona, a Libyan in the Temple of Ammon, an Ionian in Claros, a Lycian in Xanthias, and a Boeotian in Ismenus." I looked that he should have been reproved and put to silence by my master; but Philemon said nothing except that this doctrine was not fit to be taught in that shape to the common people; and the rest seemed to assent to Nicostratus. Heracleas, in particular, said that "though the number of gods and demons, or demoniacal essences, be far more than the 30,000 whereof Hesiod makes mention, yet the mighty King of all this multitude, seated on his stable throne as if He were Law, imparts unto the obedient that health and safety which He contains in Himself." To me also, in our private and familiar discourse, the young Epictetus would always speak, not of many, but of One, who guides all things and to whose will we must conform ourselves. As for idols and statues of the gods, of which I had always been wont at Lystra to speak as being themselves gods, so that I could scarce think of the gods apart from them Nicostratus said openly at this same feast, that it was no marvel if the immortal powers preferred to inhabit beautiful shapes of gold and stone and ivory; which nevertheless were of course to be distinguished from the gods themselves, as being but the integuments of the divine senses; but Heracleas went yet further (and Epictetus with him) saying that one should no more accost an image than a house (instead of the householder); and that images were not needful but only helpful for the forgetful souls of men.

When Heracleas avowed his belief in the myths and metamorphoses and fables about the gods I said to him, "Why, Heracleas, are there no metamorphoses in our days?" "Because," replied he, "men have degenerated from their progenitors of ancient date. Therefore it is no marvel that the gods refuse to perform such wonders as of old for mankind upon earth. But in the former days the pious were naturally changed from men into gods, and these are even now honoured, such as Aristaeus, Heracles, Amphiaraus, Asclepius, and the like. Having regard to these facts, any one may reasonably be persuaded that Lycaon was changed into a wolf, Procne into a swallow, and Niobe into a stone. At present, however, now that vice has spread itself through every part of the earth, the divine nature is no longer produced out of the human, or, in other words, men are no longer made gods but only dignified with the title thereof through excess of flattery, as some among us call the emperors gods even while they yet live." To this Nicostratus assented, but added that "the lies of the multitude are sometimes to blame, pouring contempt upon undoubted facts in the attempt to adorn and exaggerate them, as for example, asserting not only that Niobe was changed into a stone, which is true, but also that Niobe on Sipylus still weeps, which is not true." More passed between them; but this I discerned clearly that both they and many others, while acknowledging one god under many names, agreed with Philemon (and not with Artemidorus the Epicurean) in believing without doubt the myths and fables about the gods.

§ 3. HOW NICOSTRATUS URGED THAT, WITHOUT THE BELIEF IN THE GODS, THE LIFE OF MAN WOULD BE VOID OF PLEASURE

It happened about this time that there was a great feast in honour of Artemis, and the customary processions and dances, and games also and chariot- races and plays exhibited in the theatre. Being sick at this time and not able to go abroad, Philemon besought Nicostratus to take me with him to the theatre, and to show me the pomps and shows of the festival, which far exceeded anything that I had ever seen in our little town of Lystra. So on the morning of the festival, early before sunrise, I went to the house of Nicostratus; who had no sooner saluted me than he began at once, after his manner, to take occasion of the festival to commend, in a long discourse, the belief in the immortal gods. "For seest thou not," said he, "how to all men, poor as well as rich, slaves as well as masters, the festivals of the gods bring round brightness and gladness?" Methinks he noted that my countenance was altered when he spoke of" slaves," for he hesitated and was silent for a moment; but anon, collecting himself, he continued cheerfully thus: "When I speak of slaves, I mean not such as thou art, being already half emancipated and rather thy master's friend than his servant; but I mean rather the poor wretches toiling in chains or grinding at the mill, to all of whom the festival brings relief and some gleam of joy. For five days ago, before the feast began, sawest thou not how even at the approach of the holiday all was astir within the city, yea and without too; food and wine and fruits and oxen and sheep for sacrifice being brought in from the country; old garments purified and freshly decked out, new ones bought or borrowed from friends; the statues of the gods taken down and carefully cleansed and polished till they glitter." At this point he was interrupted by a slave who had been waiting to tell him that it was time to go forth to the temple. Descending to the court-yard we found all the household awaiting us, clothed in their best attire, the little children bearing frankincense in their hands and the victims adorned for sacrifice. Regarding them all with a glad countenance and saluting many of them by name, Nicostratus bade me remember that at this same moment every householder in Colossae, however austere or miserly by nature, was constrained by the observance of the gods to go forth in like manner to offer sacrifice. "And now," continued he in an unbroken discourse, "we shall all go to the great temple. Prayers will be offered up; none but words of good omen will be uttered; no sound of quarrel or abuse or even of ribald mirth will be heard in the whole of the vast assemblage. After this, some offer sacrifice; the rest stand by as spectators. Then begins the feasting, some feasting in the temples, others at home where you and I will make merry together. And as for the rest of the day and the days following, thou shalt see how pleasantly they will pass. Yet all this is but a copy of that which happens at every festival in every city where the gods are rightly reverenced. For during the feasting, the whole city resounds with singing, some chanting hymns in honour of the god, others odes and songs, serious or merry, according to each one's pleasure. I omit to speak of the processions and shows, all full of beauty and delight, but not more beautiful here than in a thousand other cities of Asia and Europe."

Here he broke off, to salute some of his acquaintance. "Hail, Charicles! and you too, Charidemus! I rejoice to see you in the city, and forget not that to-morrow you are bespoke to dine with me." Then turning again to me, "Note, I pray you," said he, "how all the people, both citizens and country-folk, are knit together in concord on such days as these. For there is scarce one citizen in Colossae but has invited some stranger or some acquaintance from the country to partake of his good cheer. Amid the drinking old friendships are drawn closer, new friendships are begun. After dinner some show strangers about the city; others sit down in the market-place and talk pleasantly together. Throughout the day no law courts are open, no execution is allowed, no debtor need fear arrest, no slave dreads the lash; all quarrel, all strife receives at least a cessation, which sometimes brings about a permanent peace. In the evening the feasting begins again, and all sit down to sup; so many are the torches that the whole city is filled with light; each street resounds with the flutes and the joyful songs of the revellers. Austere sobriety is laid aside for once, and to drink a little to excess in honour of the gods is esteemed no great disgrace. Thus for three days the feast continues; and when it is over we part with vows of friendship, in peace and good will, praying that we may live long enough to see such another feast come round again. Now," concluded Nicostratus, "take away the gods from out of the world and what cause remains why men should thus meet and rejoice together? For where there are no gods, there are none to be thanked, and therefore no thanksgiving; but thankfulness is the salt of life. Whosoever therefore takes away the gods from the life of man takes away the prime cause of human joy, and must be esteemed the enemy of all mankind."

I felt in my inmost mind that a keen and subtle disputant, such as Artemidorus, might have had much to urge against these arguments of Nicostratus; yet at that time many things joined together to incline me to accept his reasonings. For having been now nearly a year at Colossae I had received on all sides such tokens of goodwill, and I may almost say of affection, as had already well nigh won me out of my first condition of distrust; and although it were not according to reason to argue that whatsoever things are pleasant must needs be also true, yet did it appear beyond doubt that life without the gods would be full of dullness and gloom, all men being everywhere wholly given up to cares and self-searchings. And I reasoned thus with myself, "If indeed there be gods, then it were wrong not to acknowledge them; but if there be no gods, why even then it seems happier to believe that gods exist, and, in that case, how can 'no gods' deem belief in gods to be a sin?" So for my part, being at that time recovered from my melancholy, and young, and in good health, and taking pleasure in the pride of life and the pleasure of the flesh, I concluded to take the happier side and to believe that there were gods ruling the world to good ends.

§ 4. HOW PHILEMON, FALLING SICK, INCLINED TO SUPERSTITION

About this time Philemon falling sick, turned to a melancholy, and becoming wholly changed from his former disposition, gave himself up to all manner of superstitions. Resorting in vain to all the physicians of the place, he was led at first to try charms and amulets, and then to consult soothsayers and astrologers and the priests of strange gods; and thus, little by little, partly by the burden of his disease enfeebling his understanding, and partly by reason of the company which he now frequented, he became daily more timorous and superstitious. He offered sacrifice almost every day, and anxiously awaited the report as to the entrails; he resorted often to the priests of all kinds of gods more especially Isis, Serapis, and Sabazius, and sometimes he would invite them to his own house, so that our house became a kind of temple in Colossae; he purified himself many times a day both with the lustral waters and with other strange purifications; he would wear naught but linen, and abstained from many kinds of flesh, and in the end from all flesh; if he saw a sacred stone he would fall down on his knees before it and anoint it with oil. Nay, once, during this melancholy fit of his, when we had set out after much preparation upon a journey to Ephesus, the sight of a weasel—though we were now fully a mile past the city gate—made him turn back and give up the journey altogether. At last, when no remedies and no charms availed anything, supposing himself to be under the special displeasure of some unknown god, he took to his bed and could not be persuaded to leave it.

My master having been about a month in this case, growing daily weaker, there came to him one Oneirocritus of Ephesus (the same to whom he himself had been intending to journey) who also himself had been sick of some disease insomuch that the physicians had despaired of him; but he was now quite recovered. This man coming into Philemon's chamber questioned him concerning his condition and symptoms, and the sacrifices he had offered, and the gods he had propitiated. Then he spoke concerning himself and his own deliverance, how after he had been sick nearly twenty years, he had been healed by Asclepius at the famous temple in Pergamus; and he very earnestly exhorted Philemon to go thither with all speed. At the same time he described the wonders wrought by the god on those that believed in him, and the punishments he had inflicted on the impious and unbelieving. Upon this Artemidorus the Epicurean whom, because of his exact knowledge of medicine and his skilfulness in noting symptoms, Philemon would never exclude from his bed-chamber, even in his most superstitious moods—once more recommended Philemon to try the baths of the neighbouring city of Hierapolis, saying that it was not wise to despise remedies merely because they were near and easy and familiar. "For this disease," said he, "arises from no anger of the gods or any such matter, but from some disorder of the liver which may not improbably be removed by the hot baths of Hierapolis." "But if the liver be disordered," replied Oneirocritus, "truth compels me to speak of the virtues of a certain sacred well in the precincts of the temple at Pergamus, availing for the healing not of one disease, but of all; for great multitudes of the blind, washing therein, have obtained their sight; others have recovered from lameness; others from asthma and pleurisy; nay, to some even the mere drawing of the water with their own hands, (it being so prescribed by the god) has restored soundness and health."

Then others of the companions of Oneirocritus added other stories all tending to the honour of Asclepius; some indeed possible and deserving of attention, but others absurd and fit only to move laughter; how, for example, a sculptor in Pergamus had been punished with immediate disease for making a statue of the god with inferior marble, but having atoned for his fault by making a second statue of fit material, he straightway recovered; also how a fighting-cock, wounded in one leg, chancing to take part in the procession of song in honour of the god, extended his leg, no longer wounded but whole, and hopping onwards crowed in harmony with the songs of the choir; and lastly how a certain rich Epicurean having had a dream in the temple of the god, forthwith obeying the heavenly vision, burned the books of Epicurus, and having made a paste of their ashes applied a poultice to his stomach and thus was perfectly healed. This last story seemed to touch Artemidorus (because of the contempt, as I suppose, which it cast upon the doctrine of -his master Epicurus) and he was on the point of making some rejoinder, when Oneirocritus, like one inspired with a divine enthusiasm, broke out into a long and passionate discourse concerning the benefits that he himself had received from the god Asclepius: "For seventeen years," he said, "I had kept my bed through disease, and for many more years I had been ailing and infirm, troubled with the falling sickness; yet such hath been the favour of the god toward me, manifested by continual tokens of his presence during my sickness as well as at my recovery, that I would not exchange my state for all the health and strength of Heracles. For I am one of those who have been blessed, not once only but many times, with a new life, and who, for this cause, esteem sickness a blessing. Many a time, half awake, half asleep, have I found myself not indeed seeing the god but conscious of his presence, my eyes full of tears, my hair erect, and a savour of divine odour in my nostrils. Thus have I received the most helpful manifestations. It was thus

Apamea, the day before the great earthquake; it was thus, half in a dream half in a vision, that he also showed me how Philoumene the daughter of my foster mother had devoted her life for mine; and behold on the eighth day she died and I recovered from my disease. Moreover at one time the god appeared to me in no dream but in a vision, having three heads, and his body wreathed in flames; and at another time not Asclepius only but Athene herself also appeared to me and held converse with me. A sweet odour exhaled from the aegis of the goddess and she bore the shape of the statue of Phidias. My nurse and two other friends, who happened to be sitting by my couch, stared and were astonished, and at first they deemed me to be beside myself; but presently they also understood the discourse and were aware of the divine presence."

While Oneirocritus was saying these words, his eyes kindled and his voice trembled, and he seemed ready to weep for joy and gratefulness; and there was not one present except the Epicurean who was not somewhat moved to sympathy. But after a pause Artemidorus praised the priests of Asclepius, saying that it was well known that they were wise physicians and prescribed wise remedies, but that their cures might well be believed to be according to nature. To which Oneirocritus replied with exceeding vehemence: "Nay, but let any one consider how strange and past all natural invention, yea, how contrary oftentimes to all the rules of art are the prescriptions of the god, some being bidden to swallow gypsum, others hemlock, others to strip naked and to bathe in cold water, (and these so weak and puling that their own physician durst not prescribe to them to bathe even in warm water) and assuredly, when all this is considered and the great multitude of them that are healed, beholding the sides of the temple all covered with the votive tablets of them that have given thanks for their recovery, surely the veriest atheist will cry out 'Great is Asclepius, and holy is his temple.' Therefore, most excellent Philemon, my counsel is that you also, despising all other waters, whether they be of Cydnus, or Peneus, or Hierapolis should resort to the sacred well in Pergamus; and, if you do this and the god so will, you shall assuredly return healed of your disease."

To this the greater part of those present gave assent. Only Artemidorus, when mention was made of the votive tablets of those that had recovered, whispered to me: "But where, Onesimus, are the votive tablets of those that have not recovered? Or perchance the temple could not find room for so many?" And when Oneirocritus had departed, he did not conceal his judgment that of the things that he had related, some were according to nature, but others only the dreams and imaginations of one that was scarce master of himself. But the rest were entirely against the Epicurean and on the side of Oneirocritus. And so I found it both then and afterwards in most places whereof I had experience, not only in Asia but also in Greece and Italy: those that believed in the gods were many; and those that believed not were men of culture and learning, but very few. And with the multitude in some places to be an Epicurean or an Atheist (for it was all one with the common people) was deemed a crime sufficient to bring down the wrath of the gods in shipwreck, famine, pestilence, or earthquake. The magistrates also everywhere dissembled, even though they were atheists; and they not only offered sacrifice and kept holidays, but also of their own free will, and at their own cost, they built and repaired temples, and set up statues to gods in whom they disbelieved, esteeming this kind of dissimulation to be a sort of piety. But as for myself at this time, I was in a strait between two opinions; for on the one hand I had begun to despise the excessive and unreasonable superstitions of Philemon, but on the other hand while I respected Artemidorus as an honourable man and a seeker after truth, I shrank from his philosophy as void of hope and happiness. So with my mind I inclined towards Artemidorus, but with my heart not indeed towards Philemon as he now was, but as he had been; and I believed in the gods with my wishes, but I disbelieved in them with my reason and understanding.

§ 5. HOW I ACCOMPANIED PHILEMON TO PERGAMUS

On the morrow Artemidorus came again and would have dissuaded Philemon from going to Pergamus, maintaining more fully than before that he had spoken with many to whom the god had revealed prescriptions and that there was nothing divine in them: "for to some " said he " being of a melancholic temperament the god prescribes the hearing of odes, hymns and other music, or sometimes even farces; to others riding on horses; to others bathing in cold water; to others walking or leaping; to others frequent rubbing and careful diet; thus the god gives in each case wise and exact prescriptions such as a skilful physician would use; but in all these, and in the cures that issue, there is nothing of the power of a god." Philemon listened patiently enough, but replied (not without sense as it appeared to me) that if this were so, or were not so, in either case one of two good results might be expected; for if it were a god that prescribed, then he should receive benefit from a god's prescriptions, but if it were not a god but only the priests, even then he should have the prescriptions of physicians so skilful that they obtained the praises of Artemidorus and were esteemed by the multitude to have the wisdom of a god. So it was settled that to Pergamus we should go, and in the autumn of that year we came thither. There was much in the place to delight a youth such as I was then; first the town itself fenced in on two sides by rushing streams and on the north side by rocks scarcely to be scaled; also the stately buildings and especially the library; and as I had the charge of Philemon's books I took pleasure in learning here the art of preparing parchments and smoothing and adorning them; for the place is very full of transcribers of books and the banks of the river (which is called Selinus) are covered with the shops of those who tan skins and prepare them for the use of booksellers. Thus passed seven days, pleasantly enough;

and all this time I saw not Philemon, for he spent almost every hour apart from his friends in the temple, engaged in processions and purifications and the like.

But on the eighth day he came to me with a cheerful countenance saying that after he had thrice gone in the sacred processions, and had daily heard solemn music and been present at the thanksgivings of those who each day had departed whole from the temple, a sweet sleep had fallen upon him wherein he had seen a vision, namely, a chasm round and not very large, about five or six cubits in diameter, and himself on the point of going down into it, and behold, one prevented him and went down in his stead. When he recounted the vision to the priests, they bade him be of good cheer, saying that the interpretation of the dream was this, that he himself should not die nor go down to Hades (which was signified by the round pit) but that he should recover and some other should die in his place; and for the rest they bade him bathe daily in cold water, and walk often and hear cheerful music and abstain from overmuch study. So we returned to Colossae with lightened hearts; and already Philemon began to shake off his melancholy and to recover apace. But in the second month after we were come back, Apphia fell sick and was nigh unto death. And hereupon Philemon's distemper returned on him worse than before; and as his wife became better, he became worse, insomuch that he began to despair of his life. Then Oneirocritus of Ephesus came a second time to visit him; and he, when he had heard the account of Philemon's vision, how he had seen a round chasm and one descending into it, affirmed that the meaning of the god was that Philemon should go to the cave of Trophonius in Lebadea in Greece, where there is even such a chasm, the same in shape and dimensions also, and men go down to it to learn things to come, and this, he said, was without doubt the intention of the vision; but the ministers of the temple had interpreted it amiss. Now therefore nothing would serve but we must needs go to Lebadea.

§ 6. HOW I WENT DOWN INTO THE CAVE OF TROPHONIUS

As soon as the season of the year came round for a sea voyage, we sailed across to Athens, and thence to Lebadea, where we were to make ready for descending beneath the earth. When the day approached, Philemon was advised by some of his friends (and also by the ministers of the god) not himself to go down, because of his age and infirmities, lest the suddenness of some voice or apparition in the darkness beneath the earth, should affright him and drive him out of his wits or even slay him outright. For although no one that had at any time consulted the oracle had ever suffered anything fatal (save only one Macedonian of the body-guard of Antigonus who had descended for sacrilegious purpose, and in despite of the sacred ministers, with intent to seek for hid treasure, and he had been cast forth dead by some other passage and not by the way he went down) yet did all, whether strangers or natives, look upon the descent as a matter of some peril not to be lightly taken in hand. So when I perceived that Philemon desired me to go down in his place but would not urge nor so much as ask me, lest I should think myself enforced to consent, I willingly adventured to descend.

But I found it was no such short and simple matter as I had supposed. For on presenting my petition to the priests I was caused to wait many days, first of all in a kind of House of Purification, which was dedicated to Good Fortune, and during all these days I offered up several sacrifices, not only to Trophonius, and to his children, but also to Apollo and to Cronus, and to Zeus the King, and to Hera the Driver of Chariots, and to Demeter called Europa; and even when all these sacrifices had been inspected by the priests and pronounced propitious, yet my good fortune must needs still depend upon one last sacrifice of all. This was to be a ram offered on the last night, whose blood was caused to flow into a trench while invocation was made to Agamedes; which, if it had been unpropitious, would have made all the other sacrifices of no effect, and all my master's money and my pains would have been spent for naught. Although I was in no humour for scoffing at that time, yet on that last evening, while I awaited the report concerning the entrails, I could not but marvel that any god should desire mortals to approach him by paths so costly and so tedious. For had I been a poor man, I had long ago spent all and more than all my substance in the sacrifices which I had offered, and the purifications I had undergone, and the fees I had paid to the ministers of the god. During the period of purification I had abstained from warm baths, and had bathed only in the cold waters of the stream called Hercyna; but on the last night of all, I was bathed with a special solemnity in the same stream by two priests called Hermae. Then I was made to drink of two fountains flowing forth, one on either hand, whereof the former was called the fountain of Forgetfulness, the other the fountain of Remembrance. All this was done, they told me, that I might forget the past and remember the future and in particular the response of the god. Last of all they took out of a veil a certain very ancient image of the god, said to have been wrought by Daedalus; and on this they bade me look very reverently and intently even till my eyes were weary. This done, I was clad in a white linen tunic, curiously girt round with garlands, and led towards the cavern.

This was a pit, round at the top, but inside in shape not so much like a cylinder as rather a cone whereof the summit has been cut off; for the base was somewhat larger than the opening, the circumference at the top being about a score of cubits, and the depth, as I should judge, fifteen cubits; but of the circumference at the bottom I cannot speak exactly. The way to go down into the pit was by a ladder. Before I went down the priest told me that when I had touched the bottom I was to feel about for two small round holes in the side, a handsbreadth or so from the bottom and near the foot of the ladder, each large enough to hold the foot and the lower part of the leg. Laying myself on my back I was to place my feet in these two holes, "and thereon," said the priest, "though the openings be never so small, yet through these will the god draw inwards the whole of your body, as with the irresistible force of some whirlpool, and then in an inner recess, if he be so pleased, he will hold converse with you either by voice or by apparition, or perchance by both. But be of good cheer, bearing in mind that, except that sacrilegious Macedonian of whom I spoke to you, there was never any one yet that was harmed by the god."

When I lay down, and the lights above had been taken away, my mind was all astir, not dizzy nor faint, nor disposed to torpor, but more active than my wont, tossing a multitude of thoughts to this side and that, neither believing nor disbelieving in the god. Then it came into my thoughts that Artemidorus had explained the wondrous pool of Cybele, fatal to cattle, by saying that some kind of creeping vapours adhered to the surface of the water, and he bade me take note at Lebadea, whether any kind of vapour could be seen or felt in the pit. So I drew a long breath or two but could neither feel aught nor taste aught, save only that my mind seemed still busier than before, tossing and retossing thoughts without end. Next, falling on a different course of thinking, I considered with myself whether perchance I was playing a sacrilegious part in thus coming into the midst of the god's mysteries in order to spy them out and reveal them to Artemidorus;

and I resolved that I would submit myself to the god and think only of the image of Daedalus, even as the priest had bidden me. Now all this takes indeed some time to set down, but to think the thoughts needed scarce a moment, and countless other fancies and imaginations and resolutions passed through my mind; but the last determination of all was that I would rebel against the god and not suffer myself to be drawn through the crevices; and scarce had I conceived this rebellious fancy, when lo, my chest began to heave and my heart to beat more and more violently, and I felt the throbbing of the veins in my temples; and then whether my body was indeed carried into an inner recess, or whether my spirit alone was carried, being separated from the body, or whatever else happened, I. know not for certain; but there was as it were the clapping-to of a great door shut with a loud jar, parting me off from all things, and then a singing in mine ears, and a bright light that grew brighter, and then methought I lay as it were living, and yet beyond life, and not able to move hand or foot, yet able to think and hear; and there was a voice from the depths of the cave in the Boeotian dialect "Philemon must go first"; and presently I felt myself drawn upwards and heard the voices of the priests saying that "the man will soon come to himself," and behold I was being carried to a throne called the throne of Recollection; whereon they placed me and straightway questioned me concerning the things that I had seen or heard while I was still staring and groping about me like one distraught. When I had made reply according to my ability, they wrote down my words on a tablet and gave me back to my friends who led me away, being still unable to guide myself and ignorant both of myself and them. But not many minutes had passed before I recovered my mind; and then a spirit of lightness and mirth possessed me, insomuch that I laughed loud and long and this without cause, and could not restrain myself from laughing; but when I was ashamed thereat and even Philemon was fain to rebuke me, one of the priests that stood by, said that there was no cause either for my shame or for his rebuke, for laughter after this fashion was ever wont to seize those with whom Trophonius had held converse.

§ 7. HOW ARTEMIDORUS SPOKE AGAINST THE BELIEF IN GODS

That I had received a vision none doubted; but concerning the meaning of the vision there was much dispute. For the priests of Trophonius (though it was not their special duty to interpret the visions vouchsafed by the god, but only to prepare the way for them by introducing those that desired to consult the god) interpreted the words of the voice and the shutting of the gates as meaning evil for my master, namely, that he should enter Hades first, and that the gates should then be shut, so that I should not follow him till afterwards. But I thought, and so did some others, friends of my master that were with us, that the meaning rather was, that Philemon should enter into happiness first, but that I should be shut out; and even now methinks that was the truer interpretation; for Philemon indeed entered first into the Kingdom of Light, and I followed after. Notwithstanding at this time, between these two interpretations, we knew not what to think; and my master returned to Colossae even more melancholy than before. Artemidorus said, scoffing, that we had a goodly time with the gods, only that they were slow of speech or fond of circuits; for Oneirocritus had sent us to Asclepius, and behold, that god had given us a dream but not the interpretation of the dream; and afterwards we had gone to Trophonius, and he had given us a vision, and an oracle in broad Boeotian to be the interpretation of the dream; and now nothing remained but we should go to Delphi to obtain some oracle that might serve as the interpretation of the dream; or last of all, if the son of Zeus should answer, like the rest, doubtfully and darkly, then must we go to Zeus himself in Dodona that the Father might enlighten for us whatever the Son might have left too obscure. I was not greatly moved by the gibes of Artemidorus; for the vision that I had seen, or seemed to have seen, weighed with me more than his mockery; nor did I then believe the word of the Epicurean, who constantly affirmed that the fit which had befallen me had arisen from the vapour of the cave, aided by the trickery of the priests and the force of imagination. But another scruple (so the Lord willed it) troubled me much more, coming into my mind again and again; I mean that all these rites and ceremonies, purifications, sacrifices, and the like were only possible for the rich, not for the poor; wherefore the religion that required these things was for the few and for the free-born and not for the many, and the miserable and the oppressed.

Yet can I not deny that Artemidorus also had a great share in loosening me by degrees from the worship of false gods. For as Philemon grew more and more melancholy, and I may almost say morose, he shunned all company and mine with the rest, and so left Artemidorus and myself to hold discourse together. At such times, when our speech naturally fell on the metamorphosis (for we could not call it otherwise) of my master, Artemidorus would speak at great length concerning the miseries of religion, and how great evils it had wrought on mankind, leading them to wicked sacrifices, and orgies, and to self- torturings and agonies of soul, and all to no purpose; and how much more beautiful it was to believe that all the universe is bound together by one fixed and unchangeable order which gives life and decay to all things according to law. And oftentimes he quoted to me the verses of the Latin poet Lucretius, praising those who with a discerning eye can look upon all apparent wonders in heaven and earth, perceiving that there is a cause of each. When I alleged on the other side such wonders as Philemon had spoken of, as being abundant in our own land—the burning mountains, hot wells, fatal vapours, and rivers and cataracts that changed into stone,—concerning all these he had causes and explanations to set forth, as also concerning the thunder and the lightning and many other supernatural things; and when he perceived that some of his explanations convinced me, then he would always add that there was no place left for the gods in the Universe, but that when men had learnt entirely to give up all thought of gods and Elysium and Tartarus, and had attained to seek and expect happiness in naught save a life of virtue upon earth, then all things would go well with us on earth, or at least much better than at present.

Now as for the immortality of the soul and the life beyond the grave, to these things I adhered, mainly because I loved to think of Chrestus as still existing; and as touching the existence of a god also, Artemidorus himself could not make it clear to me how the beginnings of the world came to pass without some Mind; so that as to these matters, though I was somewhat moved by him, I was not greatly shaken. But as for the myths and fables of the wondrous deeds and transformations of the gods he quite overthrew all my faith in any such things; urging that the order of the world testified against them, and that our often experience of the invention and refutation of like marvels showed that they were necessary for the vacant truth-contemning minds of the multitude, but none the less false and to be discarded by seekers after truth.

Even to this day do I call to mind the time and place of that particular discourse of Artemidorus which most moved me. We were walking near the city of Hierapolis (which lies close upon Colossae) amid the hills covered with the snow-like marble made out of water, whereof I wrote above, and I had taken him to see some of the vaporous springs which Philemon had shown me, inferring from such wonders the existence of the gods. Then Artemidorus spoke his mind to me freely, after his cynical manner, concerning these and other so called metamorphoses and miracles. For after he had with, very great clearness and not a little cogency of words and reasons set forth his theory concerning the marble cataracts, finding me obstinate against his conclusion that all things are according to order and that all the stories of the metamorphoses are false, he suddenly changed his humour and said mirthfully, "But come now, most devout of mankind, lest perchance I should seem to you unfair, pressing unduly the argument on the "one side but neglecting what might be said on the other side, see, I will take the part of Socrates and will maintain the truth of the ancient stories. At Philemon's supper last night, you heard how stoutly the pious Nicostratus supported our most excellent host in affirming that it was possible that the loving Haley one was translated into the sea-bird of that name, which is said ever to mourn for her husband. Now mark how far inferior is the devout Nicostratus to the more devout Artemidorus." Then, adjusting his cloak and speaking in a pompous fashion with a sonorous voice after the manner of some philosophers of our acquaintance, "Alas," he said, "blind creatures that we mortals are! Alas, purblind judges of the possible and impossible! For we, deluded ones, pronounce according to the ignorant and dull abilities of faithless men. And therefore many things, in themselves easy, seem to us difficult, and many things in themselves attainable seem to us not to be attained. And this befalls us sometimes through our inexperience, sometimes through the infancy of our minds. For, as compared with the First Cause of all, every man, be he never so old, is but a child; and human life, when compared with eternity, is but a childhood's span. Who therefore shall decide what is likely? For which, think you is the harder or the more unlikely? To raise a stillness out of a blustering tempest, and to spread a cloudless sky over the whole of Europe and of Asia, or to change the shape of one woman into the form of a bird? We see even children every day shape distinct forms and figures from wax and clay. Then certainly God, who is too excellent in greatness and wisdom to be brought into comparison with the wisest of human beings, can effect more wonderful actions than these which are easy and familiar. Nature, we see, finding in a comb of wax a shapeless worm without legs or feathers, bestows on it wings and feet, and enamelling it with great diversity of fair colours produceth a bee, the wise artificer of divine honey! Seeing therefore this marvellous transformation, why doubt we of thy lesser wonder, Halcyone, most dutiful of birds? Nay, but from henceforth I will not cease to scoff at the folly of poor puny mortals, who can neither comprehend great matters nor small, but doubt of most things, even of those which concern ourselves, and yet dare to deny the power of the immortal gods to transform halcyons or aught else. And for my part, even as the fame of the fable hath been conveyed to me from my ancestors, so will I extol the praise of thy songs, thou bird of mourning, conveying it to my children and to their posterity after them; nor will I cease to repeat the story of thy virtuous love for thy husband, thy constancy and thy patience, to my wives Xanthippe and Myrto." Then, putting aside all mirth, "Do you not see, my dear Onesimus," said he, "that, upon such reasoning as this, any impostor can palm off any portent upon the credulity of mankind. Nay, so eagerly does the multitude seek after portents that they will oftentimes refuse to pay homage even to the truth, unless it come accompanied with portents: and indeed such is the nature of our Phrygians in this region (and the Paphlagonians are no better) that if a juggler will but play his tricks before them, taking with him a player on the flute or tambourine or cymbals, straightway they will gape upon him as on a messenger from heaven, and believe as he instructs and do as he commands. But it is not the part of a philosopher, my dear friend, to accept falsehoods through laziness, or credulity, or enthusiasm, but rather to esteem sobriety and incredulity to be the very sinews of the soul, remembering the words of him who said, 'I love Socrates well and Plato well, but Truth best of all.' And surely, if there be a god indeed, as you and your philosophers will have it, and this god a good god, then to such a god that man must be most pleasing who most honours truth; but the man who serves falsehood must be unpleasing, whether folly or knavery be the cause of such a servitude."

His words moved me not a little; for I seemed forced at least to this conclusion that whether there were an Elysium or not, whether gods or no gods, in any case truth must needs be better than falsehood; and when he spoke of falsehood as a "servitude" his words galled me all the more because I was a slave;' and I confessed in my heart that I had been acting slavishly in resolving to believe what was pleasant, merely because it was pleasant, and without much regard to the truth of it.

So I vowed within myself that howsoever Philemon might enforce my limbs to his service, he should not constrain my mind to this or that opinion contrary to what I believed to be the truth; for though my body might be the body of a slave, in my mind and thoughts I would be free.

§ 8. HOW I JOURNEYED WITH PHILEMON TO ANTIOCH IN SYRIA

Now began my old fit of doubt and trouble and moroseness to return upon me. I had long misliked the excessive and, as it seemed to me, pusillanimous superstition of Philemon; and the more because, although he spared no pains nor cost in resorting to oracles and practising new superstitions, he had not yet bethought himself of his promise that he would emancipate me. Lately also he had built for himself a tomb at a very great expense, saying that it was unreasonable to prepare for oneself a sumptuous house wherein we should spend threescore years at the most, and yet to take no thought of that other abode wherein a man needs spend all his time hereafter for many years. But while he made this so costly and careful provision for his bones, he made none for his family nor for his slaves; for it was known that he had some months since destroyed his former will and he had not as yet made another; so that both I and all the rest of the household were now in danger to be sold to we knew not what master, if anything evil should suddenly befall Philemon. Yet when Artemidorus urged him to the making of a will, he resented it as if it were done upon some expectation of his death. For at times, in his melancholy, he came to such a point of suspicion as to imagine that all men, even his household, were set against him and wished to murder him. So I began to rebel once more against the worship of the gods, partly (as before) because it seemed to be a religion for the rich and not for the poor, but partly also because it seemed possible to be religious and yet to be swallowed up with thoughts of self, having no regard unto others. Notwithstanding I gave not up as yet all belief in divine things; but I became a seeker after some religion which should afford redemption not for the few but for the many. Now it chanced that one Eriopolus, a wool-merchant of Antioch in Syria, coming to Colossae about this time to buy wool, and finding Philemon well-nigh despaired of, spoke to him concerning a certain sect of the Jews who, said he, were marvellously skilled in exorcising evil spirits and in the healing of certain diseases, adding, however, that not all the Jews possessed this power, but only those who worshipped a certain Chrestus or Christus, in whose name they adjured the demons. Then another, a dyer from Ephesus, confirmed his report, saying that the Jews which worship not this Christus, persecute the others, calling them "magicians;" and said he, "not many weeks ago, at Ephesus, when some of the Jews which worship not Christus, had v assayed to drive out evil spirits in this name, the man that was possessed leaped upon them, and overcame them, and drove them away grievously wounded." " By what name then," asked my master, "are these Jewish magicians known?" " At first," replied Eriopolus, "they were called Nazarenes or Galileans, but, of late, they go by the name of Christians (so at least the common people call them), and there are certain of them scattered up and down in several cities of Asia, and one of more than common note among them, Paulus by name } is at this time tarrying at Ephesus. But for the most part they congregate now in Antioch, although, as I have heard, the root and origin of the sect is at Jerusalem, the chief city of Judaea."

Hearing this my master determined to journey to Antioch to make inquiry of this new sect; and Artemidorus also himself now encouraged him in his purpose, judging that anything was better than thus to remain at home brooding over his ill health and imagining evil. Apphia also assented. So in the spring of that year (it was the second year of the emperor Nero, and I was at that time in the twenty-first year of my age) we made ready for our journey. Though I loved to see new sights and faces, after the manner of youth, I was nevertheless loth to go on so superstitious an errand; and besides, I despised the Jews, so far as I knew them, as being a gain-loving people, full of pernicious superstitions, and so inhospitable as not even to eat with strangers. However, I would not willingly have suffered Philemon in his melancholy to go alone, even had I been his friend and not his slave. When we were to set forth, Artemidorus bade me write to him, as often as I had occasion, concerning the Jews at Antioch, and especially concerning this new sect; " for," said he, "to those who have taken their stand upon the hill of Truth, it is sweet to look down upon the wanderings of them that stray in error, wherefore I ever take pleasure in the hearing of some new superstition or error among men." So I promised that I would send him letters as often as messengers went to Asia from Philemon.

Our journey was first by land to Ephesus through a very fertile country; and thence by sea to Seleucia, a city which lies at the mouth of the river Orontes, and it is as it were the harbour of Antioch; which lies higher up the river, about forty miles by reason of the wanderings of the stream, but by the road distant no more than a score of miles or less. If I admired the country between Colossae and Ephesus, the fruitfulness of the s.oil, the greatness of the mountains, and the beauty of Ephesus itself and the far-famed temple of Ephesian Artemis, much more did I admire the city of Antioch, which is the third city of the empire for greatness, coming next after Rome and Alexandria; and it lies along the river Orontes, for the space of four or five miles, stretching between the clear waters of the river and the high mountain called Silpius, surrounded by a wall not less than five and thirty cubits high and ten cubits in thickness. Being very spacious and indeed equal to three or four large cities in amplitude, it is divided into four wards or demes; and it has royal streets, built by kings desiring to do favour to the citizens of so goodly a city, and called after the names of the sovereigns that built them, namely, the street of Herod, the street of Seleucus, and others. Through the midst there runs a broad street adorned with four ranks of columns forming two covered colonnades with a wide road between, and along the whole street (which is more than thirty-six furlongs in length) there are statues and busts beautifully wrought of white marble. Greek names have been given to all the region round about, such as Pieria, Peneus, Tempe, Castalia, insomuch that to hear the names of the villages one might fancy oneself in the haunts of the Muses; and not two hours distant from the city there lies a fair large garden or *paradise* (as the people in these parts call it) Daphne by name, which the citizens of Antioch often frequent, and it is full of all manner of flowers and goodly trees and watered with a great abundance of streams, and noted for the worship of Adonis. Such and so full of all manner of delight was the place in which I now found myself, a city no less populous than spacious (for it numbered as many as five hundred thousand souls) and no less full of mirth than of beauty; for the people of Antioch are known throughout the world for their gaiety. Here therefore I laid aside the austerity of my recent thoughts, and forgetting questions of religion and philosophy I disposed myself to be merry with the multitude of those who were making merry around me, so far at least as I could be permitted to do so by the duty of constant attendance on Philemon; and, if I had had my own desire, I should never have set foot in any synagogue of Jews or Christians.

But blessed be thou, Guide of the misguided, who didst not suffer me for ever to stray in the paths of false pleasure and in the ways which lead to delusion, but in due course thou didst bring me to the door of thy fold; and though I stumbled at the threshold, yet didst thou not suffer me to fall for ever, but didst still uphold me and step by step didst turn me back again to the pastures of eternal peace.

THE END OF THE SECOND BOOK

THE THIRD BOOK

§ 1. OF MY FIRST THOUGHTS CONCERNING THE CHRISTIANS

I AM now to describe how I first came to the knowledge of the brethren in Antioch, though I attained not yet to the truth. For I stumbled at questions of philosophy and of tradition, and therefore I entered not into the fold of Christ. But the main reason for my failure was (as I now think), first, that I came not in faith, and secondly that I came not to Christ and the teaching of Christ himself, but rather to a sort of doubtful disputations about Christ, which, whether a man believe or disbelieve in them, do not contain the revelation of the Lord Jesus.

Concerning this part of my life I am in a strait what to set down and what to pass over. For if I should endeavour to call to mind and repeat all the evil things that, in the days of my ignorance, I said and thought about the Saints, then I fear lest I should seem profane and almost blasphemous, thus a second time reviling the Lord Jesus in speaking evil of his church. But if on the other hand I gloss over the truth, blanching and extenuating my error and presumptuousness, then I seem to be dealing falsely and hypocritically, making myself to be better than I was, instead of magnifying the mercies of the Lord shown forth upon one that was perverse and obstinate in error. In this perplexity having chanced to light upon certain letters which I sent at this time to Artemidorus by his request (but he, long afterwards, not many days before his death, delivered them to me and bade me keep them), these same letters (which till of late I had altogether forgotten) it now seems good to me to set down faithfully word for word, neither altering nor extenuating anything. The first letter shows how I was unwilling at the beginning to go into the synagogue, and what slanders the common people falsely reported about the brethren; which I in my folly supposed at that time to be true. The next (after the reply of Artemidorus, rebuking me for my proneness to believe the rumours of the common people) shows how I went for the first time into the congregation of the faithful, and how the Lord began even at that time to draw me towards himself.

"ONESIMUS TO ARTEMIDORUS, HEALTH.

"Concerning Antioch and all the pleasures of this delightful city I wrote to you in my former letter; but whereas you marvel because I have as yet written nothing touching the Jews; you must know that up to this time we have found no occasion to be present at their worship. For we find that there is a greater discord than we had supposed between this new sect of the Jews and the rest, insomuch that the latter will scarce own the new sect to be Jews, nor do they frequent the same temples nor practise the same kind of worship. Hence it happens that these new Jews, out of fear to be persecuted, do all things in secret, having no public processions nor sacrifices, and allowing none to see the statue of their god (if indeed any of the Jews have any god at all) and celebrating their mysteries in great privacy. However, all the philosophers with whom I have spoken, as well as the men of rank in the city (such as are among Philemon's acquaintance), agree that it is a vile and execrable superstition, which would fain subvert all laws and all the dignity and peace of the empire. It is also commonly reported that none are admitted to their sacred rites until they have committed some monstrous crime; so that, whereas in other religions the priests of the several mysteries say, 'Let none approach but the pure,' the priests of this sect on the other hand say, 'Whosoever is a murderer, whoso a thief, whoso an adulterer, let him draw near that he may be initiated; for all such does our god invite.' Likewise the common folk say that at their sacred rites a most shameful sacrifice is made of a little child, on whose flesh and blood these wretches feast as if they were the choicest dainties, and also that brothers and sisters among them commonly practise incest. But all this I write, not of my own knowledge, but from the general report, which notwithstanding comes from so many different witnesses, that I cannot doubt but it is mainly true. However, I will write no more concerning these people till I have somewhat to say of my own seeing or hearing. But for my part I could be well pleased if the good Philemon would be persuaded not to seek further into this superstition.

"In my last letter I omitted, in so great a multitude of new things, to make mention of a garden belonging to one Onias, a citizen here, which contains not only many goodly flowers, but also runlets and fountains of water quaintly devised, and many apes and peacocks for show and for amusement, and above all several parrots, of which one has been so excellently trained to speak, that it surpasses by far any starling or any other talking bird that I have ever heard before; and the common people say it is possessed. But even you would marvel to see with what aptness and semblance of understanding it collects and most seasonably utters the sayings of those around it, reminding me not a little of the saying which I have often heard from your lips that the reason of some inferior animals borders upon the reason of man himself. Farewell."

" ARTEMIDORUS TO ONESIMUS, HEALTH.

"Whereas you write that you have resolved to make no further mention of these innovating Jews until you find out something of your own knowledge concerning them, more weighty than such old wives' fables as are reported by the common rabble, by lazy philosophers, and by pompous town-councillors, all of them indifferent to truth and accuracy, so I beseech you for the future to carry out this resolution; for, believe me, knowledge is not to be thus cheaply and painlessly acquired without judgment and labour. But I hope that before very long you may have discovered something certain of this sect, no less worthy of reporting than your experiences of the parrot of Onias. Farewell."

§ 2. OF THE DOCTRINE OF THE CHRISTIANS

"ONESIMUS TO ARTEMIDORUS, HEALTH.

"Having been now twice present in their temple or synagogue I have much to say of these Christians.

"It happened that, about ten days ago, the friend with whom my master lodges, introduced to us a certain merchant of Cyrene who had some slight acquaintance with one Lucius, a man of Cyrene, and a notable teacher among this sect. So by his means we were. invited to be present at their synagogue on a day when the uninitiated are called together, as many as desire to make a trial of the new religion or to learn the truth about it. When we were all assembled to the number of four or five hundred, there stood up one Simeon, surnamed Niger, who delivered a speech by no means so foolish as I had thought likely, and it was to this effect: There was but one God, he said, who had made no distinctions of nations, as Greeks, barbarians, Scythians and the rest, but all men of one blood, intending them to be one brotherhood. This God sent unto mankind signs and testimonies of his good will, giving unto all nations the sun and moon and stars to be for signs and seasons; moreover to the Jews he sent special messengers, or prophets, to proclaim his will. But when, notwithstanding all these testimonies, mankind still disobeyed the divine will, it seemed good to the superior god to send down to them no longer a prophet or common messenger, but a son, as if the time had arrived when they should no longer grope after God, but apprehend the divine nature.

"Then this Simeon went on to affirm that this son of god had verily come into the world about threescore years ago, during the reign of the Emperor Augustus, in the shape of a man, one Jesus (called also the Nazarene, because he was of the city of Nazareth in the north of Palestine), who had proclaimed a Gospel or Good News, namely, that God is the Father of men, not merely their Maker, but their Father, loving all men as parents love their children. Moreover the Son had manifested the Father's nature by many works, especially by healing the souls of men, not only taking away sins, but also giving unto his disciples the power to take away sins. In a word the Son had done for the Father, if one might trust Simeon, much the same deeds as Apollo is said to have done in early times for Zeus, introducing into the world purifications of the soul. Then also (quoting, as I was told, from some of the ancient books of the Jews) Simeon declared that this Jesus of Nazareth was the Redeemer of whom those books had prophesied; for, said he, 'to them that sat in darkness Jesus hath shown forth the light of truth, he hath opened the eyes of them that were blinded by sin and ignorance and caused those whose souls were maimed and were crippled with vice to walk straight in the paths of virtue, and he hath raised up them that were dead in sin.'

"Now followed a marvellous paradox, or rather what our friend Evagoras the rhetorician would call a*bathos*.

For it was actually confessed before us all by this same Simeon that this son of god, who had wrought all these marvellous works, was slain in the sixteenth year of the Emperor Tiberius, and this, not in battle nor in a tumult, but by command of the governor Pontius Pilatus, dying the death of the vilest criminal, being actually crucified! And, not content with this ignominy, they confess also that he was most shamefully insulted and scourged before his death, and that he was rescued neither from insult nor from death by the superior god whom they call the Father. But to compensate for all these disgraces, the speaker affirmed in the first place that this death constituted some kind of sacrifice or expiation, wherein this Christus played at once the part of priest and victim, offering himself up for the sins of the whole world (he having been no unwilling sacrifice but having surrendered himself to death and having indeed predicted his own death as a prophet); and in the second place, as the crowning marvel of all, he affirmed that the superior god had raised up the inferior, that is the Son, after the latter had lain for several days in the tomb, insomuch that, long after his death, he appeared to many of his disciples, of whom some are still living as witnesses.

"'Nursery tales'—replies my wise preceptor, nor do I say otherwise. But what filled me with astonishment, almost more than was fitting, was to note the gravity, earnestness and sobriety and yet at the same time the enthusiasm wherewith Simeon delivered himself, especially when he bore witness to the rising again of Christus (for by this name Jesus is commonly known among them); speaking as if at that very moment he were standing in the presence of him that was risen from the dead, and yet enjoining chastity, truthfulness, honesty, and all other virtue, with such a calmness that not a few of those present, and Philemon among the rest, were well-nigh carried away with the force of the man's belief, and themselves persuaded to believe the like. Nor could I altogether marvel; for it was not possible to suppose that the man was a knave or cheat; yet neither did he appear to be a madman, and certainly he spake not as a fool.

"But I omit too long the main matter for which Philemon came hither, the healing of diseases. concerning this, Simeon said little; rather taking it for granted, as I judged, than arguing of it or dwelling upon it at any length. But he said that signs had been wrought both by Christus and by his disciples, in the casting out of devils and in the healing of sickness; and he appealed to some of those present, as if they knew this of their own knowledge. Afterwards I spoke with many of them on this matter. Almost all told me that they knew others who had been healed of divers diseases, and some few (not more than three) affirmed that they themselves had been healed of palsy, two of them by one Paulus, of whom I made mention above, and the other by this same Simeon. Of the rest whom they averred to have been healed, some were said to have been healed by Paulus, others by one Petrus, a man of great repute among them, others by this Simeon and not a few by one Philippus, who is even now (as they tell me) sojourning in Hierapolis. Of these sick folk some have been wholly healed and immediately; others partly and only by degrees; but for the most part more completely and suddenly than any cures wrought by Asclepius. The diseases are mostly palsies (which abound here) and also fevers, and partial dumbness or lameness, and the more severe kind of ophthalmia; but the most common is that kind of insanity which by the common people is termed 'possession.'

"Of this latter kind one instance I myself witnessed on the very day on which I heard Simeon thus discourse; and it was wrought by Simeon himself in the synagogue. For after he had made an end of the first part of his discourse, he began to call upon all the people to repent, saying that the superior god whom he named the Father, would speedily judge all the world in righteousness, punishing the bad and rewarding the good, and in that day the Son,—namely, that very Christus whom Pontius had crucified,—should come again with great glory. Hereon one cried out in the assembly after the manner of demented people, saying 'Avaunt! Away! Away from me!' adding loud exclamations against the name of Jesus. Simeon forthwith ceased from speaking, and looking very intently on the man's countenance caused him to be brought near, and stretching out his hand as with authority in a loud voice adjured I know not what evil spirit to go forth from the man. The demented man immediately fell to the ground as one dead; but Simeon took him by the hand, and raised him up and restored him to his friends; and he went forth from the building delivered from his disease.

"The man happened to be the brother of our host's door-keeper; and his madness was confirmed to me by many witnesses, as being of long continuance, yea, and I myself had seen him in a pitiable plight, gibbering and gaping as one mad in our courtyard a full month before; and our host himself (who is no friend to the Christians) constantly affirmed that he had been mad for the space of at least fourteen years. Wherefore thus much is certain and not to be denied, that a man who was demented for fourteen years, up till the seventh day of this month, is now on the fourteenth day of this month in his sound mind and to all appearance likely to remain therein; and this has been wrought by certain words uttered by this Simeon Niger. Now if this effect proceeds from natural causes, as the great Epicurus would doubtless assert, the causes (none the less) seem worthy to be sought out and examined.

"When the madman was led forth delivered from his disease, I had much ado to prevent the worthy Philemon from standing up publicly and praying that he also might be initiated into the sacred rites of this new religion by means of purification with water; which they practise not many times, as with us, but once for all, and with more than usual solemnity; and I suppose that Christus himself instituted this purification; at all events no one is admitted without it. But I besought the excellent man not to do so rash a thing with such precipitate haste, and at least to wait till he should have discovered whether those who are initiated into the Christian rites, are also to submit themselves to the whole of the law which the more ancient religion of the Jews enjoins upon that nation. For the time I succeeded and kept him from his purpose. But I could wish that Archippus or Apphia were here present with him, and not I alone. For I greatly fear that, if he be so violently moved a second time, I may no longer be able to restrain him. Concerning the second visit to the synagogue, having many things to write, and the messenger of Philemon being already on the point to depart, I must defer what I would further say to another occasion.

"One matter had almost slipped my memory; and it is perhaps hardly worth setting down. Going this day to the garden of Adonis I saw the youths and maidens passing in procession through the golden gate of Daphne; and there calling to my mind other processions such as I had seen in my youth (but this far surpassed them all) I remembered how I was wont as a child to make comparisons between a certain Diosdotus, a priest of Zeus of a goodly presence and lofty stature, and a certain unknown wandering priest or juggler, mean of aspect, bald-headed and hook-nosed, who in my presence had healed one that was lame and known to have been lame for thirty years. This happened when I was a mere child scarcely (as I think) past my tenth year; but to-day it came into my mind that both that wandering priest and this Simeon—albeit differing greatly in countenance and appearance, Simeon being tall and the other short or inclining to shortness—nevertheless agreed in this one point, that they spoke of things invisible not only as if they saw them, but also in such wise as to make others fancy that they saw them. And, if I err not, that prophet also spoke, as did Simeon, concerning a certain son of god whom the superior god had sent into the world. Wherefore I now conjecture that that same wandering prophet belonged to no gods of the Greeks, but was, even as this Simeon, a Jew, and one of this sect that believes in Christus.

"One other matter also I omitted to mention, that this new religion makes no distinction between those of different nations, nor between rich and poor, slaves and free; for all that belong to the sect are esteemed citizens of one nation, or rather brothers of one family; and certainly I noted in the synagogue that there were observed no distinctions of wealth or rank; for whether a man were a town-councillor or a water-carrier, it was all one; we all sat together. Farewell."

§ 3. HOW ARTEMIDORUS QUESTIONED ME FURTHER CONCERNING THE CHRISTIANS

"ARTEMIDORUS TO ONESIMUS, HEALTH.

"Your letter was acceptable to me, my dear Onesimus, because it contained no longer mere hearsay concerning these Jews, but the things that you yourself had seen and heard. Now you will do well to make inquiry more particularly on the following points: 1st, Does this sect of Jews, (or Christians if they are to be so called) possess any sacred books? 2nd, As touching this son of the Divine Being, of whom you speak, was he (according to their saying) begotten by the superior god from some human mother; or came he into the world as the child of some divine mother? or in what other way? For I assume, of course, that his followers do not believe him to have been born of a human father. But if he was also not born of a human mother, then what certainty is there that he had human flesh and blood; and in that case, how could he be subject to death? But perhaps they say that he did not really die? In that case, however, he did not really rise from the dead; so that both his death and life would seem to have been a make-believe, the death a not dying, and the life a not existing; yet it is not easy to see why even an inferior god should come into the world for the purpose of not existing; 3rd, Touching the wonderful works said to have been wrought by this Christus, were they all acts of healing such as you describe? Or were there not also some such tricks and portents as wizards and enchanters and jugglers profess to perform, such as the breathing of fire from the nostrils, and the changing of earth into bread, and of water into blood, and the producing of sudden banquets and then causing them to vanish again, and the summoning up of apparitions, and drawing down of the moon from the sky, and other such vulgar marvels? 4th, This rising again of Christus from the grave, was it seen and attested by enemies as well as by friends? And, if so, did the enemies turn to his side, being convinced by the marvel? Or, if not by enemies, was it at least seen (according to what the Christians themselves affirm) by impartial witnesses? And did these, by reason of what they saw, believe in him and follow him? And after his rising from the grave, did he eat and drink and bathe and lecture and sleep as before? Or, if not, in what respects was his manner of life changed, and in what guise did he appear, and moving with what motion? Also if he was, as you say, executed like a slave upon the cross, did his limbs manifest, to all that saw him, the marks of his execution? Or did these scars appear to some, but not to others? Lastly, forget not to inquire (for this is of the greatest importance) whether any touched him, and also how he came among his followers, after his rising again; whether by opening the doors in the usual way and ascending stairs, or whether the doors being shut, he showed himself in the midst of his friends. My fifth and last question is, what laws has this leader laid down for his followers? and on this point I would have you inform me as fully and exactly as you can.

"Because I have asked you so many questions, my dear Onesimus, you will probably infer (and you will not be wrong) that the subject attracts me and that I set much value on your information: which indeed comes to me all the more seasonably because here, in this very neighbourhood, these Jews, or Christians, have been of late making no small stir; especially at Ephesus, where that same Paulus of whom you speak, has been these many months, openly teaching the philosophy of your Christus, and his lectures, (or as some say his portents) have drawn away many pupils to hear him, who also have accepted that purification by water which gives admission to this sect. And from what I have heard I gather that their philosophy—for religion it can scarce be called having no gods except perchance one, nor scarce any rites or sacrifices, nor any processions, nor feasts, nor holidays—after the manner of the doctrine which is ever in the mouth of our young friend Epictetus, deals mainly with the practice and not much with the theories and speculations of life. For many that were before noted for thieves or drunkards or loose livers are reported to have been turned from their swinish living by Paulus, so as to live lives well nigh worthy of philosophers. Moreover, strange to relate, this magician, for so they call him, sets himself against all magic in others; and many of his followers, turning from their so-called magic arts, have brought their Ephesian charms and their books of magic, yea, and even their lawful silver shrines of Ephesian Artemis herself, to-be burned or melted down. So great indeed is the diminution of the purchase of the shrines that by this time the silversmiths begin to cry out; and I heard but yesterday that complaints are coming in from the graziers who fatten the victims for the temples, that their business is diminished and like to slip away from them altogether if this new superstition be not checked.

"As to exorcism, you did not amiss to remind me that attested cases of sudden healing are not to be put aside merely because the illiterate multitude calls them by absurd names and explains them by absurd causes; but perhaps I also shall not do amiss to remind you (surrounded as you are by all manner of superstitious and credulous people) that every such case is assuredly to be explained, if not by deceit and fraud, then by some moving of the imagination (for imagination is a powerful causer of many undreamed effects), or else by some other cause or causes of which we may for the time be ignorant.

"Take for example the following instance of one reported to have been raised from the dead; which I myself have with great expense of time and labour but recently search e.d out and for the truth of which

I can vouch. About a month ago our friend Nicostratus came to me in that state of frenzy which, as you know, is customary with him when he has anything to relate which he cannot himself explain saying that a nobleman in some part of Phrygia or Cilicia had been raised from the dead after being a month or more entombed, and that he had spoken with a Laodicean, one who had either seen it done or at least knew all the facts, and could attest their truth; but Nicostratus himself knew no more about the matter, and, as I found on questioning him, he proposed to inquire no further about it, but to spread the rumour throughout all Colossae, just as he had imparted it to me. With much ado I obtained from him the name of the Laodicean (for the futile creature had well-nigh forgotten even that), and on the first occasion that offered itself I went to Laodicea to see him. The story of the Laodicean was to this effect, that the dead man had died of a fever, and had been buried so long that the body must needs have become corrupt; and behold, a magician came to the door of the sepulchre and pronounced charms and incantations, and straightway the door flew open and the dead man came forth alive, wrapped in his grave-clothes; but what was the name of the deceased, and who it was that raised him up, and when and where it was done concerning all these points he neither knew anything, nor had he himself seen it, nor heard anything from any eye-witness. Tracing the matter backward I learned at last the name of the man supposed to have been raised from the dead, no nobleman at all, but an honest dyer of Hierapolis, Tatias by name, and my informant told me that the said Tatias, though he had indeed died from a fever, had not yet been buried at the time when he was restored to life; he added the name of the physician who had seen Tatias laid out for burial; but who had raised him from the dead he did not know. So to the physician I went; and here at last I gained some glimpse of the truth. For I understood from him that Tatias had not died of fever, but of a sudden flux of blood to the head, such as is commonly called syncope. Notwithstanding, the physician stoutly affirmed that Tatias was really dead; not unnaturally, because his own credit was else like to have been diminished, if he had suffered one that was still living to be laid out for burial. Thence going to Tatias himself—a man of sense and understanding and, in spite of his superstition, able to discern truth from falsehood—I heard the whole story according to the exact truth, and here it is, set down exactly from his lips.

"It seems that he had been a pupil or hearer of one Philippus, a Christian (who, as I take it, is the same Philippus as he of whom you made mention in your last letter to me), and having embraced this new religion, he had been desirous for some days of receiving the purification customary for the initiated; but some accident still delaying it, he grew perturbed, lest it should be more than accident, and lest the gods were against his being purified. At last, on the appointed day, purposing to go with others of the uninitiated to the pool where the rite was to take place, he was suddenly called away to see his mother, who being seized with a violent fever was said by the messenger to be on the point of death. But finding her sickness to be only slight, and no danger at all of death, he determined to hasten with all speed to the mysteries, hoping that he might after all not be too late, for the day was not yet far spent. So coming at last into the place of assembly in great heat and fatigue of body and still greater trepidation of mind lest it should be all in vain, and he a second time 'disappointed of salvation'—for these were his very words—in this condition of mind and body he was called upon in the midst of a great multitude already assembled to stand up on some kind of platform and there to make profession of his new religion. So mounting up he adventured to speak in due form; but behold some demon (to use the man's own words, for he spoke as one of the ignorant) had wholly possessed him, depriving him of the power of speech and causing all things to appear to turn round before him; and anon he fell to the ground, and was taken up for dead, and brought back to his own house? and being given over by the physician as dead, he was washed, laid out, and all things made ready for his entombment.

"But during all this time, though the man was lying on his back not able to move hand or foot, yet was he not wholly dead. For though he could not so much as stir an eyelid, yet was he aware, he says, of the presence and words of the physician, and of the wailing of the women and the mourners, and able to understand the speech of those who stood around him; and a deep horror fell upon him lest he should be carried out and entombed alive, and die miserably before he had attained to salvation; 'but,' continued he, 'the more my horror grew upon me, the less seemed my power to move, being bound fast by the fetters of Satan.' However he took some comfort because he heard his friends say that they had sent for Philippus (who was at that time absent from Hierapolis) to come and offer up prayers. What followed I will now recount in the words of Tatias himself. "When," said he, "the man of God entered the chamber, I was at once aware of his presence, all standing up to salute him, and I also desired to stand up but could not; then I was aware that he drew nigh to me, and I felt that he looked on my face though I saw him not; and he said aloud that it was not well that I should die till I had made confession of my faith and been washed in the living water; then the sound of the mourners ceased and there was a deep silence, and I knew that he was looking on me again, and a certainty began to possess me that I should be delivered; and he spoke a second time saying that he did not believe that I was dead, but that I slept, and that it was the Lord's will that I should be awakened; and at the word he took me by the hand, and I felt a thrill through my body, as if the bands of Satan began to be loosened; and then calling me by name he adjured me in the name of Jesus of Nazareth, who arose from the dead, to rise up and walk. And straightway strength seemed to flow into every part of my body, and my limbs no longer refused to obey me, and I sat up and spoke and magnified God."

"My reason, dear Onesimus, for describing to you thus fully this matter of Tatias, is two-fold; first, that you may perceive that no truth is to be rejected or passed over; secondly, that you may be encouraged to remember that many things which at first seem false or fabulous, or else contrary to nature, will, when sifted and examined, appear to be neither false nor unnatural, but true and in accordance with nature. Therefore I beseech you, as long as you are in Syria, and in condition to find out anything new about these Jews, search with all zeal; and trust not to hearsay but test all things yourself as far as you may, seeking the truth with a just sobriety and incredulity. Spare not pains nor labour: for without doubt some great cause must needs be at work to produce so great effects as are wrought by these Christians; men for the most part illiterate and inexperienced in philosophy j who notwithstanding appear to have attained a remarkable skill not only in the healing of certain diseases but also in turning many of the viler sort towards courses of honesty and virtue. Search therefore and with all diligence; but forget not the proverb:—

Sober incredulity

Is the wise man's security.

§ 4. HOW THE CHRISTIANS HONOURED THE PROPHETS OF THE JEWS

"ONESIMUS TO ARTEMIDORUS, HEALTH.

"To proceed with the answers to your questions. These Christian Jews have no sacred books of their own; but they use in their worship the sacred books of their countrymen. For although they (or at least many of them) reject the sacrifices and festivals and laws ordained by their ancient lawgiver Moses, yet do they by no means reject the books of oracles or prophecies which they commonly call 'the Prophets.'

Now many of these prophecies predict that there shall come a great ruler of the nation of the Jews, who shall deliver them from all their enemies and make them to be conquerors of the world; and this their future Ruler or Redeemer they use to call 'Messiah' (which word means 'sent' because he is to be 'sent' from God). So far therefore both the older Jews and the new Jews agree; but the great difference is this; the former still look forward to the coming of their 'Messiah,' the latter say he is already come, and that he is no other than he whom they call Christus. Now because it is a great stumbling- block to the older Jews to suppose that their conquering Messiah was not only himself conquered but also slain with insults and with the death of a slave, for this cause the Christians spare no pains to show that the oracles of the older Jews themselves predicted that he should be so slain; and they also labour to show that the same books of prophecy foretold how the Messiah should be born, and the manner of his life; and that all these predictions are fulfilled in the birth and life of their Christus. Hence it comes that they think it of little account to say that Christus did this or that, or that he was born and died at such a place and at such a time, unless they can also add that 'all this was done that the words of this or that prophet might be fulfilled.' And more than this; as often as they have read one of the passages of the prophecies appointed to be read in their worship, first one arises and then another, water-carriers and tent-makers and leather-cutters and the like, all attempting to show that this sentence and that sentence point to none other than Christus; and n this fashion not only do they strain the words of their prophets and enforce them to receive all manner of meanings which they could not naturally have, but also they unwittingly encourage and, as it were, vying with one another, provoke their own and one another's imaginations to remember some new things that Christus did, or said, that perchance fulfil the words of the prophecy.

"Hence proceeds already a manifest alteration of the doctrine of the Christians, and more is likely to proceed. For you may already perceive different shapes of teaching among them, and each later shape departs further from the truth in order to come nearer to the ancient prophecies. Thus, for example, there was read in our presence in the synagogue an ancient dirge which is commonly interpreted to predict the death of the Messiah, wherein it was said that his hands and feet were pierced, and that gall and vinegar were given him to drink, and that his enemies divided his raiment and cast lots for it, and that the passers-by wagged their heads at him and mocked him for his trust in God, saying, 'He trusted in God, let God therefore deliver him, if He will have him.' Now, after this had been read and after the principal speaker, who was a man of some discretion, had pointed out that this prophecy was fulfilled by Christus, I took occasion, when we left the synagogue, to question the man thus:

Onesimus. Say you then that in all points this prophecy was fulfilled by Christus?

The Speaker. In these points that his hands and feet were pierced, and that his enemies derided him, and that vinegar was given him to drink.

Onesimus. You say well, for a draught is wont to be given to those who are condemned to death; but tell me further, did any cast lots for his raiment, and did the bystanders say these precise words 'He trusted in God' and the like? And is it so handed down in your Tradition?

The Speaker. It is not indeed so handed down in our tradition; but it may have been so.

When I had thanked him for his courtesy I hastened forwards to an honest and illiterate leather-cutter to whom I put precisely the same questions; but now mark the different replies in this, which I call the second, shape of the Christian doctrine.

Onesimus. Tell me, good friend, was this prophecy, whereof we heard but now, fulfilled in all points by Christus?

Leather-cutter. Assuredly.

Onesimus. And did his enemies cast lots for his raiment?

Leather-cutter. Assuredly.

Onesimus. And did the bystanders say 'He trusted in God' and use these exact words?

Leather-cutter. Assuredly.

Onesimus. And are these things taught in the Tradition concerning the acts and deeds of Christus?

Leather-cutter. Not that I remember.

Onesimus. Then did Simeon, or Lucius, or Petrus, or Paulus or any other ever teach thee these things in the synagogue?

Leather-cutter. Not that I remember.

Onesimus. Then prithee, how knowest thou that these things are so?

Leather-cutter. Because it must needs be that all things that are written in the Law and the Prophets should be fulfilled in Christus.

"Behold, my dear Artemidorus, the second shape of the Christian doctrine; which, if it be not speedily committed to writing, what third or fourth shapes it may assume, the wit of man cannot conjecture. But one thing is certain, that in every case the leather cutter will carry the day against the learned man, and the man who believes everything against the man of discretion who believes some things and rejects others. Thus, although Christus died not a generation ago, and was born (as is thought) scarce more than two generations ago, yet already are there current many fables and stories which overshadow the things that he really did, and the doctrine that he really taught, and all this because of the ancient prophecies of his nation; so that, for my part, whensoever I hear one of their teachers say that Christus said or did this or that, and make no mention of any prophecy, then I incline to believe him; but when he adds that Christus said or did anything 'that a prophecy might be fulfilled,' then I shut my ears against the man's words, knowing that they are, in all likelihood, imaginations and fancies.

"A second noteworthy point is, that they make frequent use of figures of speech, and these sometimes so mixed up with facts and histories that it is hard to understand whether they are to be taken according to the letter or not. Thus, for example, whereas they assert that their ancient Lawgiver gave them bread called manna and water from the rock, this they mean literally; but whereas they say that Christus was in no way inferior to him, for that he also gave them 'bread from heaven' and 'living water,' yea, also and (as some add) 'wine instead of water,'— all these phrases are to be taken, not according to the letter but (most say) spiritually. Yet even some of these relations my friend the leather-cutter accepts as literally true, and his opinion will soon prevail; such confusion is there between the figures of speech and facts of history in the minds of the illiterate. Again, when the teachers speak of being 'delivered from death,' they mean (for the most part) not that which we call death but rather the decay and corruption of the soul; and in the same way, when they speak of the unclosing of the ears of the deaf, and of the eyes of the blind, and of making the lame to walk in the straight path, in all these cases their meaning (and the meaning of the prophets) is not to speak of the things of the body, but of the things of the soul. Yet even these the common sort have begun to interpret not of the soul but of the body, and hence have arisen already many perversions of the history of the acts of Christus.

"From this cause have proceeded, I doubt not, many of the false accusations which are commonly reported against these Christians and which I myself once ignorantly believed. For example, whereas they are commonly charged with slaying and eating a little child (and many also add that the Christians cover the child with meal, and then cause those who would fain be initiated, to cut the meal with their knives so that they may be unwittingly led to perpetrate murder), the charge arises, as I am persuaded, from the misunderstanding of certain words used by the Christians in their mysteries. For in these secret rites, offering up no sacrifice of their own, they commemorate (as I am informed) the sacrifice of Christus; calling by that name his miserable death, and affirming that it was voluntary and that he thereby offered up his life for the world; and for this cause they not only call him the Son of God but also the Lamb of God, and just as those who offer up a victim partake of the flesh of a victim, even so do these Christians, partaking of bread and wine, profess solemnly that they eat the body and drink the blood of the Son or Child of God; and hence has sprung the belief of the common people that the Christians slay and eat a little child. As touching the charge of incest commonly brought against them, I am persuaded that this also is groundless; but it is possible that the Christians calling one another brethren and sisters (as being members of one brotherhood) have caused those who love them not, to suppose that brothers and sisters are permitted in their sect to unite in marriage. But another cause might be alleged, for they are wont to speak of their state or republic sometimes as the New Jerusalem, but sometimes as a living person, the Mother of the Faithful, and, speaking of the parentage of Christus, they say that this Mother gave birth to him, describing her (in poetic figures and with numbers that are customary in their sacred books) as a Woman clothed with the sun, and the moon under her feet, and upon her head a crown of twelve stars, and they say that she brought forth a man-child who should rule all nations with a rod of iron, which man-child is no other than the 'Messiah,' or Christus. But again, others using a different figure describe the republic not as a Mother, but as a Bride, chaste and spotless, being betrothed to Christus, whom they praise as the Bridegroom; and this manner of speech, strange as it may seem to us Greeks, is familiar to them, being commonly used in their books of prophecies, which often speak of their nation as a Bride, and the superior god as the Bridegroom. Now it is possible that some, hearing that, among the Christians, the Son is betrothed to the Mother, and not staying to consider whether this betrothal be a figure of speech or true according to the letter, have affirmed that incest is allowed among them. But whatever may be the cause of the error, an error it is beyond all question. For these Christians, however they may fall short in understanding, are not inferior to philosophers in the purity of their lives. Much more I have to write about the traditions of these people, which I must defer till my next letter."

§ 5. OF THE ANCIENT HISTORIES OF THE JEWS

"ONESIMUS TO ARTEMIDORUS, HEALTH.

"The further I proceed, my dear Artemidorus, searching into the history of this strange sect, and always bearing in mind your proverb that 'incredulity is the philosopher's security,' the more I perceive the difficulty of the task you have laid upon me. For I now find that these very people who profess to worship Christus and who recognise in him the fulfilment of ancient prophecies, nevertheless neglect, and I might almost say, despise all modern writings and records, insomuch that even at this present time no account of his words and deeds is committed to paper. Of this strange neglect there are several strange causes, and the first the strangest of all. You must know then that these people commonly believe (even the wisest or least foolish of them) that Christus will speedily return enthroned upon the clouds to make himself governor over the whole world; so that it is needless to write the words of one who himself will soon be speaking upon earth. The second cause is, that there is a tradition among the Jews, current now for many hundreds of years, not to write new sacred books, but to hand down by word of mouth from teacher to pupil, through many generations, such traditions as may be needful. A third cause is, that, Christus having given unto them no clear and definite law nor even many distinct precepts, his followers stand not upon his exact commandments; and indeed some fear not to say openly that they care little for the letter of his commandments, for that he himself promised to send them a certain good demon or Spirit (even such a one as Socrates had) which should prompt and warn them what to do and what to avoid, and teach them how to defend themselves against their persecutors and before their judges. I have omitted a fourth and last cause which is not the least important; namely, that most of the followers of Christus have been, from the first beginning of the sect, men of no education, but illiterate and scarce able to write at all, so that they naturally preferred speaking to writing.

"So much for the books or no books of the Christians. But there is yet another obstacle in the way of my search. You have been wont to hold up to me Thucydides the historian as a pattern of the truth-loving disposition and as the model to all that desire to record that which has happened. But in this nation there neither are, nor ever were, any such historians; nor is it their nature to relate things according to the exact truth. Not that they love falsehood better than truth; but the minds of their writers seem ever on the poise between poetry and prose, between figures of speech and plain sense, between hyperbole and fact; and as in all their histories of their nation they discern evermore (as Homer has it) the 'accomplishment of the will of Zeus,' even so their pens lead them ever to speak of their God rather than men, and of things invisible rather than visible, and of the purpose and object of each event, rather than the how, and when, and where of it. Hence it has come to pass that all manner of poetic tales and legends having been embodied and as it were interlaced in their relations, it is impossible to tell where the poem ends and the history begins; and the constant reading of these ancient poems or histories, or history-poems (if you so please to call them) has made them careless of truth, and I might almost say contemptuous of it, unless it abound with marvel. Of which disposition, though I might set down many proofs, take these two only, as patterns of the rest. To this day it is commonly believed among them that, during a certain great victory wherein they gained possession of Palestine, the sun and the moon stood still at the bidding of one of their ancient generals; and that, about the same time, the whole of the wall of a fortified city fell to the ground at the sound of the trumpets of their army.

"Some of these relations of portents have come into their histories from errors. For example, one of their poets speaking, in all likelihood poetically, of a drought which dried up the waters of the river Jordanus so that the ancient Jews passed over easily to the conquest of Palestine, and addressing himself in apostrophe to their God who guided their nation across, uses these words, 'The waters saw thee, God, the waters saw thee and were afraid'; which words the historians straightway take up and interpret literally, and behold, a relation, incredible and portentous, how the waters of the river rose up like a wall on this side and on that, so that the whole nation might pass through dry- shod, as if through a defile. I deny not that, in this and some other cases, error may excuse their exaggeration; but my complaint is that all this nation (and the older Jews much more than the Christians) are so given up to hyperbole that there is no trusting anything that they say, that is at all marvellous, without a careful testing of it. For example, among the older Jews, I have heard a certain teacher say that the city of Jerusalem is situate on a river of clear water many furlongs in length, though there be, in truth, no river at all nearer to the city than Jordan, which is one hundred and eighty furlongs distant; and the same man said that the smell of the sacrifices and the sound of the music in Jerusalem goes down to the men of Jericho, which city is distant a full day's journey; and another affirmed that the twanging of the bow- strings of the multitude of enemies caused the walls of Apamea to fall; and also that a certain Rabbi (for by that title they honour their teachers) was so pious that he emitted from his body flames of fire, insomuch that the beholders marvelled at the splendour, and whatsoever insect approached him, was straightway consumed.

"Judge therefore what kind of history the unwritten traditions of the life of Christus are like to contain when I have sought them out for you. However I will do my best to collect them, and to send you such information as I can obtain about them, together with the answers to your former questions. Having taken brief notes of the discourse of one Lucius of Cyrene, the chief speaker in the synagogue, I purposed to send it to you; but not having yet written it out fully, I will send it at my first leisure; and when you read it, you will more easily understand how much the traditions concerning Christus are in danger to be conformed to the ancient prophecies of the Jews.[6]

"This letter I see deals with naught but 'obstacles' and 'difficulties' and 'burdens'; yet I beg of you, my dear Artemidorus, not to suppose that I murmur at the task you have imposed on me or that I count the labour wasted. For indeed the more I muse on the matter, the more I judge that this Christus must have been endowed with a truly divine genius, or force of character (or whatever faculty else you may please to call it) to have produced so vast an influence on a nation so perverse and morose as these Jews, not to speak of many thousands of the viler sort of Greeks who after attaching themselves to his sect have turned from vice to virtue. Philemon is well, but still unquiet and hardly to be controlled. Farewell."

§6. HOW ARTEMIDORUS QUESTIONED ME FURTHER, AND OF HIS RELATION CONCERNING THE CASTING OUT OF THE SWINE

"ARTEMIDORUS TO ONESIMUS, HEALTH.

"Although I could have wished, my dear Onesimus, that you had been able to answer my first questions, point by point, yet your account of the discourse spoken by the Christian priest Lucius was not without interest for me; confirming, as it did, an opinion that I have ever entertained, namely, that no portents how incredible soever, and no absurdities however palpable, can ever deter the multitude from embracing a new belief, if there be somewhat in it of a nature to fascinate the soul and feed the imagination. But still my desire is that you should do your utmost to discover what this superstition contains, of a nature thus to fascinate the multitude; for it is not apparent to me from anything that you have hitherto written, since you describe a religion that has no sacred books, no feasts, no

---

[6] This discourse (which should have found place here) was missing from the collection of the papers of Artemidorus, at the time when I was transcribing them; but having chanced upon it some months afterwards, I purpose to set it down at the end of the book

processions, no code of laws that might unite and regulate a disorderly mass of men.

"In addition to this I would gladly receive answers to these two further questions, on the first of which you yourself touched in your first letter but so as to suggest rather than explain: 1st, Does this sect require that all, as many as join themselves to it, Greeks as well as Jews (for I understand that Greeks also are admitted by them), shall observe the laws of the Jews? Or does it remit the laws for those who are not Jews? Or are they remitted for all, Jews as well as Greeks? 2nd, I cannot understand from the discourse of Lucius whether he supposes Christus to be born of man and woman in a natural way, or in a divine way born of woman only. This question I believe I asked before; but now I repeat it, partly lest you should suppose it to have been already answered by the priest's discourse, partly because (in conversation with certain Christians of Hierapolis) I have heard that there is some diversity of opinion concerning this matter among the Christians themselves.

"Here might I well make an end; but because I have especially charged you to report to me concerning any portents related of the life of Christus, I will briefly explain to you my meaning and purpose herein. A thousand times, as you know well, I have wearied you with repeating that no religion can ever commend itself to the multitude unless it be first clothed, as it were, in a vesture, whereby the eyes of the many may be drawn towards it. For it is not given to the multitude to love the naked truth; but they must needs clothe her in their purple and set on her brow diadems of their own giving. Well, my friend, even such a clothing, adorning and crowning of religion, are you methinks now witnessing. For it is beyond all question that in a few years, if not already, the believers in this new faith will have clothed or embellished the life of their Leader with all manner of wonders, which in itself it had not. And already I discern this process of clothing, in the beginning and first endeavour. For whereas your Lucius preaches about 'the Star of Judah' shining, and the 'preparing of the table in the wilderness,' and the stilling of the storm by him whose 'path is on the deep waters,' and the testimony of Moses and Elias on the right hand and on the left of Christus, and the giving of the 'Bread of Life' and the 'living Water,' and 'the Wine of the Lord's Blood.'—I doubt not but both these and many other figures and metaphors either are, or speedily will be, so interlaced with the tradition of the life of Christus, that his followers will soon believe (even though they believe not already) that he did really and actually walk upon the waves and bestow upon them miraculous water, and miraculous wine and bread, yes, and that a special Star shone forth at his birth, and that saints rose from their graves along with him, and that Moses and Elias did really appear on his right hand and on his left bearing testimony to him, and a thousand other portents which it would be easier for you to enumerate than for me, but equally tedious for both of us. Wherefore, since you assure me that these people have as yet no sacred books, but only an unwritten tradition, I would have you inquire diligently concerning this tradition whether it contain any such wonders as these; and if not, then whether their common talk (which must needs in the end insinuate itself into their tradition, unless there come some let or unforeseen hindrance) have not already begun to imbue itself with miracles and marvels of this sort.

"As touching the transmutation—so let us call it—of things metaphorical into things literal I myself have of late obtained one instance which I will contribute to our common store. Upon receipt of your first letter, discoursing with a certain acquaintance of mine—one Evander, a physician and an educated man, not I think unknown to you—concerning the causes and symptoms of 'possession,' he made this observation, that it is the custom of the patient in such cases (his stomach, as well as his mind, being altogether corrupted and diseased) to suppose that he has within his belly all manner of filthy and foul creatures, such as toads, serpents, dragons, scorpions, adders, dogs, swine and the like, which creatures, when the possessed man is suddenly healed, he often sees (or rather imagines and fancies himself to see) going forth from his mouth into banishment or destruction. And he added that among the Phrygians the possessed were wont to suppose that hooded snakes or scorpions were within them, but among the Jews (who have a special abhorrence of certain animals considering them to be unclean) it was more common to imagine the presence of swine; and not unnaturally, said he, because these animals (having no real existence but being the mere offspring of the imagination) necessarily vary with the imagination that gives them birth. Then he went on to relate how a Jew being (as all Jews are) a great hater of the Romans, and also considering swine to be unclean, had imagined himself to be possessed by a Legion, not however of soldiers but of swine; which swine, when they were cast forth into the deep or 'abyss' (for by this name they are wont to call the void place wherein bodiless spirits or demons are supposed to roam) were seen by the Jew, the possessed man, to go forth from his mouth and run violently down to the said abyss. This tradition, he said, he had heard some years ago from another physician who lived at Tiberias, not far from the place where the man had been healed; and he that had healed him was, according to the saying of the physician of Tiberias, no other than this very same Christus, who is now worshipped by your friends, the Christians, as a god.

"When I heard this, considering with myself that in all likelihood, if this were so, some story of it would even now be current among the followers of Christus, I went on the morrow to Hierapolis, to that same Tatias of whom I made mention in my previous letter, and questioning him about them that are possessed, whether he knew of many that had been healed by Christus, I recounted to him my story concerning the man possessed with a Legion and asked him whether that was the true account of the matter. To which he replied that in his youth he had heard that account, or somewhat like unto it, but it was not exact; for how, said he, could a legion of creatures of the size of swine, be shut in within the compass of one human belly? But, according to him, the true story was, that the Legion of evil spirits having been cast out of the man, assumed the shapes of swine, and were then cast into the abyss. Then another of the same sect who happened to be present, said that neither was that version of the story altogether exact; for why should demons, having shapes already, perchance of gnats or flies or whatever else, assume fresh shapes of swine? But the truth was, that the legion of demons being two thousand in number—for the latest narrator of all, mark you, is assured of the exact number, which was not known in the earliest traditions—finding themselves on the point to be cast out of the man's body, and fearing to be without bodies and so to be cast into the abyss, besought Christus that it might be permitted to them to pass into the bodies of two thousand swine; which swine happened to be at that instant pasturing—conveniently indeed for the demons but contrary to the laws of the Jews—near to the demoniac. 'Then,' said he (for it is worth while to recount his exact words) 'when the Lord suffered them, behold, the whole legion of demons rushed into the two thousand swine; but they gained nothing thereby. For the swine rushed violently down a steep place into the sea of Tiberias' (no longer you will observe into the abyss) 'and were there drowned.' To this account another companion of Tatias assented, as being the latest and truest tradition; but he added yet a new fact, namely, that those who were feeding the swine being terrified (as how should they not be?) by so great a destruction, tied away into the city, and that the citizens coming together in much fear, besought Jesus that he would depart out of their coasts.

"Meditate much, my dear Onesimus, upon this story; and may it be profitable to you in your search after the truth. But why do I speak of truth in such a case as this, where so few grains of truth are inclosed in so great a mass of falsehood? Sometimes, indeed, I repent of having imposed on you so barren a task; nevertheless persevere, for there must be some powerful cause to produce so great an effect upon the lives of these Christians, even though they be unlearned and superstitious. Farewell."

§ 7. OF THE TRADITIONS OF THE CHRISTIANS AND OF THE NATURE OF CHRISTUS

"ONESIMUS TO ARTEMIDORUS, HEALTH.

"Having long delayed to answer your questions I will now do my endeavour to explain more fully, 1st, What are the traditions of these Christians; 2nd, What is their belief about Christus, whether born according to nature or otherwise; 3rd, What portents are reported to have been wrought by Christus.

"1st. The tradition about the words and deeds of Christus begins from the time when he first took upon himself to profess teaching publicly and ends with the record of a certain vision of angels, after his death, wherein it was declared to some that had followed him to the last, that he was not in the tomb but was risen from the dead. There is also another tradition as I am informed, of the longer discourses and prophecies of Christus; but this not having as yet been translated into Greek, is not circulated in all the churches; but the shorter sayings and the acts of Christus are already known in Rome and Ephesus and Alexandria, as well as in Jerusalem and Antioch; and there are two or three versions of this Tradition already, and like to be more, unless these are shortly committed to writing, for in different churches different forms of the tradition spring up. Also besides these versions of the Tradition (which are for the most part the same among all their churches) there are many additions or supplements concerning the birth and childhood and death of

Christus, and concerning his manifestations to his disciples after his death; but these have not yet attained to be considered parts of the Tradition itself.

"Some of these relations many of the Christians now desire to have set down in books and to cause to be read in the synagogues. But the Jewish part of the brethren are against it, saying that it is not the custom thus to commit doctrine to writing; however the Greeks are mainly for it, and within a few years I doubt not but that it will be done. But for the present (as I told you before) the Christians use no sacred books save the ancient books of the Jews.

"2nd. As to the nature of Christus, and what he is supposed to be by his followers, I conversed with Simeon himself, and I found that there was diversity of opinion. 'There are', said he, 'some of our sect who, while they admit that he is the Christ',—for that is their manner of speech, meaning by 'Christ' the 'Anointed,' that is, the future Ruler, as I think I wrote to you before,—yet hold him to be a man and born of men. With whom I do not agree, nor would I, even though most of those who believe as I believe, were to say so; since we are enjoined by our Master to put no trust in human doctrines but only in such things as are proclaimed by the blessed prophets and taught by himself. Further he added that some, on the other hand, believing Christus to be a god, would not admit that he was born of woman, but supposed him to be begotten of the Supreme God without aid of humanity at all, and so to have come into the world, a man in appearance, but in reality a spirit or angel. 'And seems it not to you,' said I, 'that such a belief does more honour to your leader than to suppose him to be born of woman?' But he replied 'No, for under appearance of doing him honour, this heresy makes the life of our Master to be feigned and false; for we believe that for our sakes he hungered and thirsted, and felt pain and sorrow, and that for our sakes also he died; none of which sufferings could he have veritably endured, if he had not been really a man born of woman, but had only appeared to be a man, being in truth a spirit.' Then I said to him, 'But what hinders that your leader should have been born both of man and woman and yet be a god? Might not the superior god, if he chose to send his son into the world as a man, send him thus into the world; conforming him in all things, and in his birth no less than in his death, to the nature of mankind?' Hereat he mused, and for some while made no answer; but afterwards he said that it was not so believed in any of the churches, and that it did not seem to him possible that the common people should believe any man to be god, unless he were begotten of some god, as the story went even about the inferior gods of the Greeks, such as Heracles, Asclepius, Amphiaraus, Romulus, and the like.

"3rd. Your third question is concerning the wonders said to have been wrought by Christus, whether they are portents, or such as may be explained according to nature. To this I reply that, in the Tradition, almost all the works are works of healing, and all to be explained according to nature, saving some four or five; and these four or five relations seem to me to have arisen from figures of speech, or prophecies or hyperbole even as I wrote to you before. For example, the Tradition contains already that story of the casting out of the swine from the demoniac, whereof you wrote to me; but diversely reported, some saying that the matter happened at a place called Gerasa, but others at Gadara, and some affirming that one demoniac was thus healed, but others two.

"The other portents in the Tradition may be briefly mentioned, and some of them you yourself have already mentioned, by anticipation, in your letter; 1st. A certain testimony of Moses and Elias to Christus which is now said to have been delivered upon a 'holy mountain,' and it is added also that Christus conversing with them was suffused with a celestial splendour, and that there was a voice from heaven proclaiming Christus to be the Son of God. But as for this, and another case of a voice from above and a vision of the heavens opened and a dove descending, I know not whether it is not fitter to set it down as a vision or waking dream, rather than an error springing from a figure of speech; 2nd. The second is some story of a storm stilled by Christus wherein he walked upon the waves; as to which again I know not whether it has sprung from metaphor misunderstood, or may not also in part have sprung from some phantasm apparent to the first followers of Christus (for they were fishermen) while fishing in the lake in Galilee either before or after the death of Christus; 3rd. The third is, a relation how Christus fed many thousands of his followers with bread in the wilderness, and this on two occasions. Now this, as I judge, springs altogether from error of metaphor. For as I wrote before, Christus himself taught his followers to call him the Bread of Life, meaning that his doctrine must be the sustenance of their souls, and this manner of speech appears to be common with the Jewish Rabbis also, who say that in a certain ancient book all 'feasting' is to be understood of the feeding upon the

Law, yea, and one even speaks of 'eating' the Messiah; and to this day the disciples of Christus use such language as this, which I myself heard but of late spoken by the priest of the Christians; 'thou who didst come down from heaven to be the Eternal Bread, and didst refresh the race of men, sojourning in the wilderness of the world, with the Bread from heaven, even with thine own body.'

"Now it might have been supposed that such figures as these would bear upon themselves clear token that they are but figures; but that which has persuaded men most of all to interpret them according to the letter, is that all the Jews alike, both those who observe the Law and also the Christians, believe that Moses gave real bread from heaven unto the ancient nation of the Jews, when wandering in a barren wilderness. And to increase the wonder they add that on every seventh day (which, as you know, is to them a day of rest whereon no work is done) no bread came down, but a, double supply on the sixth day; and they say also that each was to gather no more than a prescribed measure according to the number of his household, and if any gathered more, it stank and became corrupt. Nay, and among these Christians (who are firmly persuaded of the exact truth of all this ancient fable) I have heard it said that this bread of Moses—or manna, as they call it—had this marvellous virtue, that to several people it had several tastes, according to that which each desired, so that to one it became as it were flesh of kids, to another of sheep, to another grapes, to others figs, and so on. Now believing that Moses wrought so great a portent, these Christians are well nigh constrained to believe also that Christus wrought no less; else were their Christus inferior to Moses.

"And indeed having of late turned over the histories of the Jews—for they have been translated into Greek, though of a very barbarous and corrupt dialect—and having there read of innumerable portents; the sun and the moon stayed by human voice; asses made to speak with the voices of men; rivers dried up by being smitten with a rod; city walls cast down by the sound of trumpets; iron made to float; water brought out from a rock; chasms caused to open in the earth; chariots of fire wherein prophets ride aloft; pillars of fire to give light to the faithful by night if there were no moon; flames of fire called down from heaven by the word of a prophet to light his sacrificial fire or to consume his enemies; I have been filled with amazement that there are so few marvellous relations in the Tradition about Christus. For example, the ancient books of the Jews contain two accounts how prophets raised up them that were dead; but the Tradition has no such relation except one concerning a little child who had but a few minutes been pronounced dead, and in whom (doubtless) the life was not extinct. Concerning; this matter I myself heard a dispute between a Jewish Rabbi and certain Christians; to whom the Rabbi affirmed that Christus must needs be inferior to the prophet Elisha because Christus had only raised up a little child whose breath had scarce departed from her body, whereas Elisha, even when dead, by the mere holiness of his tomb had given life unto a man that had been many hours dead, when he was now being carried out for burial. Hereat the Christian was manifestly at a stand. However, he made shift to reply that it was reported in the church at Ephesus, that Christus had raised up a man that was dead, and carried out to burial. But the Rabbi rejoined that, 'even if that were true, it would but prove that Christus was equal to Elisha, not that he was superior; for if he had been superior he would have gone beyond Elisha and have raised up some one that had been dead and buried three or four clays; for during three days the angel of life is still present with a man, but on the fourth day he fleeth away.' To this the Christian had naught to reply, but growing angry he declared that Moses and the Prophets testified concerning Christus that he was indeed the Messiah; and 'if the Jews would not believe Moses and the Prophets, neither would they believe though one were raised from the dead.' Thus the conference broke up, but methinks the Christians were somewhat perturbed in their inmost hearts that they had no relation to bring forward of some dead man who had been raised from the tomb by Christus, after he had been some days buried; and methinks, before many years, some such relation as this is like to find a place in the traditions of the sect, and I marvel that it has been delayed so long.

"Many other relations of portents (especially concerning the birth and the manifestation of Christus) are current in the supplement—if I may so term it—which is made by the talk and common speech of the Christians, and diversely in diverse churches; but I know not if any other portent be contained in the Tradition, except it be one, which is as it were half way between the Tradition and the Supplement, not of equal weight with the former, but more commonly reported than the latter; and it is clearly a misunderstanding of an allegory. You must know then that in the sacred books of the Jews it is customary to speak of both men and nations as trees, either a vine, or a cedar, or an oak, or an olive, or bramble, as the intent may be, to represent severally fruitfulness, or protection, or strength, or prosperity, or peace, or a malign disposition. It seems therefore that Christus was wont to compare his own nation to a barren fruit-tree, and especially to a fig-tree making a great show of leaves but bearing no fruit; and on this theme he was wont to utter divers allegories; one, how the gardener prayed the Lord of the orchard to spare the tree for three years, but after the third year, if it were still barren, then to cut it down; and a second allegory in a higher strain, how the Lord looked down from heaven upon the tree which he had planted, and behold, it had abundance of leaves, and he came to it seeking fruit and there was none; and then he sent a spirit of destruction on the tree, commanding that no fruit should henceforth grow on it, and the tree withered beneath the breath of the Lord, and on the morrow it was dead even to the roots. This allegory therefore, as it seems to me, the Christians, misconstruing and supposing the Lord to be Christus himself (for they commonly call him 'Master,' 'Lord'), have imagined to be no allegory, but fact, wrought by Christus himself upon an actual fig- tree; and some even add the place where the deed was done, and other minute matters, after the manner of the growth of such relations.

"I would gladly have added some words concerning the rising of Christus from the dead, but the merchant by whom you will receive this, being now about to set forth, and the messenger no longer able to wait, I must defer what more I have to say to a second letter. Farewell."

§ 8. OF THE RISING OF CHRISTUS FROM THE DEAD

"ONESIMUS TO ARTEMIDORUS, HEALTH.

"The Tradition, as I have said before, is silent concerning the rising of Christus from the dead; but in divers churches divers manifestations are reported; concerning which I questioned Simeon, asking him whether he himself had spoken with any that had seen Christus risen from the dead. He said, 'Yes, assuredly, with at least ten persons, of whom one was Paulus, to whom Christus appeared ten years after his death.' Then I questioned him whether these men had touched Christus, or only seen him. He made reply that they had seen him but not touched him. Then I asked him how they that saw him knew that it was he indeed, and no phantom, or perchance some evil spirit deceiving them. He made reply that Christus had showed unto them his hands and feet, bearing the wounds of the cross; and further, that phantoms appear not to many assembled in one place, but only to solitary persons, whereas Christus had appeared oftentimes to large numbers of his disciples. He said also that it was currently reported that Christus had suffered one of his followers, who doubted, to touch his side; and that he had eaten in the presence of many; and that he had said 'Handle me and see that I am not a bodiless demon'; but all these things, he confessed, were not in the Tradition. Also, in answer to my further questioning, he said that no enemy of Christus had seen him after death, nor had any save those that loved him most dearly; nor had any been converted to the side of Christus by thus seeing him, save only one, namely that same Paulus, about whom I have more than once made mention, who, about ten years after the death of Christus, while grievously persecuting the church, and after he had slain many of the Christians, had suddenly been changed from an enemy to a friend, by seeing Christus and hearing words from him.

"The sum of all seems to be that the body of Christus was not indeed raised from the grave—for that were against all course of nature; and besides, if it had been so, why was the Tradition silent on the proofs of so great a wonder?—but that some kind of image or phantasm of the mind represented him to his followers after his decease. And musing often on the matter I have called to mind how many relations are current of the apparitions of the deceased, and how they may be explained according to nature. For after looking intently on the sun, the eye, being closed, sees an image of the sun floating through the air; and methinks in somewhat the same fashion those followers of Christus who best loved him, and to whom he was as the sun and brightness of life, suddenly finding themselves bereft of him and in the darkness of sorrow, might perchance—even in the course of nature— receive an image of him so imprinted on their minds that even the eye itself might be enslaved to the mind's desire, and be impressed with the same image. Still the marvel is that it appeared not only to many at once—which, if the influence were more than commonly powerful, might possibly come to pass—but even to an enemy, namely Paulus, which cannot be so easily explained. However, I have no other answer to this riddle; and yet of late I have pondered for hours together on the answer, wandering as it were in a labyrinth of questions and riddles and problems, and sometimes catching a clue, and then losing it, and as far as ever from the truth.

"But whatever be the answer, these Christians are of a certainty rather deceived than deceiving others; for no one can have had to do with them, as I have, without perceiving that they are altogether devoted to virtue. And this indeed is the marvel of marvels, how this Christus should have had the power to turn so many thousands of souls to virtue, being many of them base and vile and given to all vice, and most of thorn of the common sort with no natural magnanimity or nobleness, and all, with few exceptions, unlearned and illiterate. Yet even this ill-ordered and confused rabble, Christus hath been able so to transmute and temper and purify that, out of so many thousands, there is scarce one that would not be willing to lay down his life, I say not merely for the name of Christus himself, but even for his 'brethren,' as he calls them, that is to say, the cobblers and water-carriers and camel-drivers who sit beside him in the synagogue.

"And this brings me to your last question, what it is in this religion of Christus which naturally draws the common people to it? Now were I to reply that it is the hope of blessedness or the dread of punishment after death, you would reasonably rejoin that these hopes and fears are held out by other religions, yet have little strength to prevent evil doing. And were I to give as reason the great concord which binds all these Christians together, you would no less reasonably ask me whence comes this same concord? Lastly, were I to add (for this is indeed one reason) that the common people are drawn by the power which these Christians possess (although it is but in the course of nature) to cure certain diseases suddenly by working on the imaginations of men, still Artemidorus would be dissatisfied and would inquire, whence came this power?

"Wherefore, although sorely perplexed and more perturbed than might perhaps become a student of philosophy, I confess that I can allege no other cause for the power of this Christian religion than Christus himself, that is to say, some kind of influence arising from the memory of Christus which he seems to have transmitted to his first disciples, and they to others, and so on till at last a very great multitude is infected .with it, and seems likely to. infect many more. Now if you ask me what plan of philosophy I have discovered in the Tradition, or what sayings of Christ lead me to attribute so great a power to his influence, I must answer that as the Tradition is not written, I have not been able to write down more than a few sentences of it, nor indeed have I had leisure for this till now, for I gave all my mind at first to the inquiry concerning the general ten our of the doctrine of the Christians. Nevertheless some few sayings of Christus which I have set down, ring again and again in my ears like some spell or incantation not to be forgotten, as if they would almost persuade me contrary to sense and reason that he was indeed a purifier of the human race.

"How greatly is the mind perplexed when it compares Christus with other philosophers! Must we not suppose Socrates, must we not deem Pythagoras, superior by far to this Christus? And yet who would die for the name of Pythagoras or Socrates? Or perhaps the merit is not in the man himself, but in some secret art which he has discovered, or happened on, by chance, of uniting men together and implanting in them the love of well-doing. Of such an art I sometimes think I have discovered signs in those sayings of Christus which have come to my knowledge. But when I have studied them more fully I will write to you further on this matter. Farewell."

§ 9. HOW ARTEMIDORUS BADE ME CEASE FROM FURTHER INQUIRY

Being somewhat alarmed by my last letter (so he confessed to me afterwards) lest I should not only permit Philemon to join himself to the Christians, but also become a Christian myself, Artemidorus wrote to me as follows, more vehemently than became a philosopher.

" ARTEMIDORUS TO ONESIMUS, HEALTH.

"If I bade you make further inquiry concerning the mad doctrines of this mad leader of madmen, I do so no longer. He who converses with lunatics more than is fit is in danger to become himself infected with their insane delusions.

"Besides, what possibility is there that you should attain to the truth? What aids have you, what instruments? There are none. No witnesses, no written documents, no regard for truth, no power of reasoning, no faculty of distinguishing things in the course of nature from things against nature. Amid such a chaos you are fighting against error with your hands tied. Cease then, I beseech you, from your vain attempt to build where there is no foundation. But do your utmost to induce the worthy Philemon to return home with all speed, lest he be entangled in the cobweb of this imbecile superstition; and lest perchance even Onesimus at last, by frequent converse with these miracle- mongers and forgers, suffer his regard for truth to be so far blunted that he himself may be tempted to gloss over and excuse their impostures."

§ 10. HOW I STUMBLED AT THE THRESHOLD OF THE DOOR AND WENT NOT IN

I take shame to myself that I was not in any such danger as Artemidorus supposed, of becoming a Christian at this time. Had I, indeed, been enabled to pursue the study of the words of the Lord Jesus, perchance having been thus led to know him I might have entered into the fold at once and so have been spared much misery. But it was not so to be. For, on the very day that I wrote the last letter to Artemidorus, it pleased Philemon to set out suddenly for Jerusalem, nothing contenting him but that we should visit the Christians, as he said, in the place which was the centre and source of the sect. Now those disciples with whom we conversed in the Holy City were of the straiter sect of the Jewish Christians, all of them maintaining that it was fit to come into the Church by first accepting the Law of Moses, and that the uncircumcised, albeit Christians of a certain sort, were inferior in righteousness to them that had received circumcision. And they spoke against Paulus and all others that denied the need of circumcision, saying that Paulus was no safe guide but a teacher of heresy.

In part the narrowness of these brethren, in part the newness of the sights which I saw in Jerusalem, and in part also the fear that I had, lest by becoming superstitious I should fall below the rank of a philosopher and lose the esteem of Artemidorus, caused me to harden my heart against the promptings of the Holy Spirit which would fain have led me to the Lord Jesus. But, in spite of all my efforts, certain of the words of the Lord (both then and for many months afterwards) kept coming to my mind, and in particular these: 'There is more joy in heaven over one sinner that repenteth than over ninety and nine persons that need no repentance," and again, "Come unto me all ye that are weary and heavy-laden and I will give you rest"; and there were times when these last words so fascinated me, and I felt so weary of myself and such a longing for the peace which he could give me, that I went near to calling aloud unto him " Verily I am weary and heavy-laden, I will come unto thee, Lord." But the cares and pleasures of this world choked the good seed so that I could hear no more of the sayings of the Lord, and strove to forget such as I had heard. Hence it came to pass that my next letter to Artemidorus (though I had not yet received his message of warning) breathed not a syllable of any desire to become a Christian.

"ONESIMUS TO ARTEMIDORUS, HEALTH.

"O for an hour of Antioch or Colossae! Never before had I understood how much of the joy of life we owe to the Muses till I came hither, where the Muses are despised. Here are no temples (save one) no processions, no dances, no games, no chariot-races, no plays, no pictures, no statues, no libraries; the very air breathes dullness and superstition. If one brings a statue into these streets it is sacrilege; and they shrink from our poems and songs, our literature and our very language, as if it were a sin to be a Greek. And then the hideousness of their temple, which during their festivals so reeks with the multitude of slaughtered sheep and oxen that it resembles a kind of shambles! Never may I again see a whole nation offering sacrifice as it were wholesale! Even now I cannot forget the shrieks of so many ten thousands of victims, and the reek of the burning fat and all the ill savour of so many worshippers thus pressed together—and all this in a barbaric building, with not so much as a single statue to adorn it, nothing but eternal grape-clusters and stars and the like, all bedaubed with gold in true eastern fashion for ostentation's sake. Ostentation everywhere, beauty nowhere! for an hour of Colossae or the pettiest Greek town in Asia, to relieve the staleness of this Jerusalem, surely the weariest and dullest of dull places!

"But I am like to forget the occasion which caused me to take up my pen, and which indeed (together with the suddenness of the journey hither) has for the time driven out of my mind all thought of the Christians. You must know then that, ten days ago, I beheld for the first time a battle, if battle it is to be called, where one side kills and the other is killed. It was after this manner. Coming to Jerusalem and having now accomplished about half of the journey between the city and Jericho, we, being mounted on dromedaries, overtook a great multitude of mixed folk journeying on foot, four or five thousand or more, as I should judge, some with swords, some with spears, some with bows, but not a few unarmed or bearing nothing save pruning-hooks and mattocks. Making our way with much ado through this motley multitude (who would not have suffered us to pass, being Greeks, had there not been with us certain priests that were going up to the Temple) we found that this rabble called itself an army, and that they were following a certain prophet, whom I saw, but I did not rightly understand his name; only thus much, that he was from Egypt, and that, being able to work all wonders, he had promised them that he would take Jerusalem and destroy the Romans in one day. And what think you was the prophet's plan? There is a mountain called Olivet on the eastern side of Jerusalem. Hither the multitude was to journey, and here to take their stand. Thereupon the prophet was to lift up his hands in prayer; the walls of Jerusalem (even as the walls of Jericho in old days were east down by the sound of trumpets) were in like manner to fall to the ground; and the faithful would rush in and slay every Roman with the sword. Heard you ever the like, for simple credulity and self-conceit? And then to listen to the babbling and boasting of these illiterate peasants! What great things they would do when they had smitten the Romans! How the prophecies should be fulfilled, and how they would rule over the Gentiles and break them in pieces like a potter's vessel! How they would cut the throats of every Samaritan, and destroy the temple in Gerizim, and be avenged on Edom! Never, never before have I felt better content that the whole world is under the firm and just dominion of Rome!

"However you shall hear how the Romans despatched this business without much delay. Having gladly left these dangerous companions, and hastening up the steep road, we had not gone twenty furlongs before we met a squadron of Roman horse, blocking the road; but after questioning us, they suffered us to pass up to a village named Bethany. We soon came to a winding place in the road, which, being very high up, commanded a view of all the road below. Thence looking down we saw the helmets of the horsemen in an ambush, in a valley on the northern side of the road, and we could hear the multitude (though we saw them not by reason of the winding of the road) with psalms and shouts, and without any order or discipline, coming up the hill; and soon their vanguard (if vanguard it could be called where all was unguarded) would have passed by the mouth of the valley so that the Romans could cleave the rabble in two parts whenever it pleased them. Soon afterwards the trumpet rang echoing through the hills, and anon we saw the helmets and swords all flash together, and then such a crying for mercy, such a shrieking and clamour, as made me stop my ears for horror; and we hastily turned away towards Bethany. But we were still some furlongs distant from the village when the Romans overtook us, their arms and armour all dripping with blood, goading before them many hundreds of captives fettered together; and on the morrow, near the western gate as I went out of the city I counted no less than a hundred crosses.

"Most gladly do I again open this letter to add that we purpose with all speed to leave Jerusalem, and to come to Ephesus. Hereto Philemon is moved, not so much by the unquiet times here, as by a letter announcing that Apphia is sick; for whose sake I am truly sorry, and I beg you to join with the worthy Evagoras (whose zeal is greater methinks than his knowledge in medicine) that she may be restored to health; but for Philemon's sake I rejoice, for assuredly a month's sojourning in Jerusalem would no less draw him to the Jews than it would drive me from them."

On the morrow we left Jerusalem and came to Caesarea Stratonis; and then to Sidon and so home, as I shall recount hereafter. And all this while I remained still an unbeliever, outside the fold of the faithful.

But even so must it needs have been, Lord. For to thee none draweth nigh through weighing of probabilities, no, nor through belief in thy mighty works, nor through trust in traditions concerning thy birth and rising again; but it is through Love of thee and Trust in thee alone that thou art embraced; for thou art Love, and by thee alone is the heart of man made capable of thee. Wherefore it pleased thee in thy mercy that I, in seeking to find thee should not find thee, to the intent that afterwards in not finding thee I should find thee. For now, I reasoned, I examined, I sought; yet I found not. But afterwards, I reasoned not, I examined not, I sought not; yea, I fled from thee that I might wander in the wilderness of sin; but even there didst thou meet me and through thy love mine eyes were opened; and I could not choose but know thee to be my true Shepherd, and when thou didst call me by name I could not choose but come. THE END OF THE THIRD BOOK

THE FOURTH BOOK

§ 1. HOW WE CAME TO ATHENS

LOOSING from Sidon we were driven by violent winds to the Chelidonian isles. There the Pamphylian sea divides itself from the Lycian; and the floods, meeting several ways and breaking against the promontory, swell into terrible billows rising higher than the cliffs. But when we were now in great peril of our lives, the Lord had mercy on us. For he sent a star which, seeming to settle upon our top-sail, by a left-hand course directed our vessel again into the sea, just when it was ready to be dashed upon the cliffs. I had often before heard speak of these marvellous stars, but never yet had seen them; and although Artemidorus had taught me that they were no gods but mere effects of causes according to nature, yet, in such extreme peril, being filled with thankfulness for our deliverance, I could not but join myself with the mariners and the rest of the crew in doing worship to the twin-gods. That very night—having often before of late had visions of a man seated on the clouds and encompassed with brightness—there came to me another such vision, but of more than usual splendour, and he beckoned to me and said that the stars had been sent by him, and not by these twin-gods whom I had ignorantly worshipped. But I shook off the dream as being a mere phantasm of the night, not knowing that it was from the Lord.

Escaping from the peril of the seas, we sailed through the Arches, and thence were driven onwards, not however to Ephesus, whither we desired to have come, but to Piraeus. There, owing to the sickness of Philemon, we spent some days, during which I lodged in the house of Molon the rhetorician; and when at last my master returned to Colossae, I persuaded him to suffer me to remain at Athens for a while, that I might study rhetoric and attain the true Attic pronunciation and idiom, so that I might be the more useful to him as amanuensis and secretary. But I had other reasons for desiring to remain. For besides the delights and novelties of the city—which were all new to me because I had not been able to persuade Philemon to spend more than two days there when we last came to Greece to visit Lebadea—I had already conceived a love for Eucharis, Melon's only daughter. But, of this, more hereafter. Meantime it chanced that Philemon, returning to Colossae, much infected with the superstition of the Christians (as Artemidorus termed it), had caused the latter to suppose that I also was in the same condition of mind; which (to my shame be it spoken) was far from the truth. However, Artemidorus taking it to be true, and being sorely incensed against me, wrote the following letter which I will here set down, being the last I received from him on this matter.

§ 2. HOW ARTEMIDORUS REBUKED ME, SUPPOSING THAT I WAS IN DANGER OF BECOMING A CHRISTIAN

"ARTEMIDORUS TO ONESIMUS, HEALTH.

"So Onesimus thinks it possible to reconcile philosophy with the vilest and falsest of superstitions. Come now and let me demonstrate to you, if your ears are not yet altogether stopped against the truth, 1st, the blasphemy and absurdity of your new religion, 2nd, the uselessness of it, 3rd, the self- conceit of it, 4th, the uncertainty of it, 5th, the folly and puerility and degradation of the man who stoops his neck to the yoke of it.

"To begin, then, it is blasphemous. For it teaches that the Supreme God has sent down his only son in the shape of a man to deliver men from sin. What! are we to suppose that the Son of the Supreme can be made like unto a mortal? As if a convention of frogs around a puddle should croak among themselves debating which is the greater sin, and should say, 'Behold, the Supreme God has sent down his only son, in the shape of a frog, verily born of a frog, to deliver all the race of frogs from their iniquities'; or as if a number of worms should examine their souls and say, 'Alas, alas, we are fallen away from the divine image of the Supreme; and therefore our Father in heaven hath sent unto us his son made in the image of a worm.' Away with this impiety of likening the Architect of the universe to sinful frogs and self-introspective worms! For if there be a God—which I do not myself believe, but if there be one—doubtless he is as little like a man as like a frog or a worm; but infinitely superior to all his creatures, and transcending all their knowledge.

"But sin forsooth is a terrible evil, and the usefulness of this new religion consists in this, that it is to 'take away sins'! Which of the Greek or Roman philosophers, of any note, has recognised this absurd fiction of*sin*? It is a mere Jewish phantasy, unknown among other nations, except where it may have been insinuated by these vagrant proselytisers into the minds of a few women and children or imbecile dotards. Error there may be; but sin cannot be, whether there be gods or not. For if there be no gods there can be no sin; and if there be gods, who made all things, it is inconceivable that they should have made sin. Nor, if sin had any existence, could it be increased or diminished. For all rational people know that there neither were formerly, nor are there now, nor will there be again, more or fewer evils in the world than have always existed; the nature of all things, and the generation of all things, being always one and the same. And whereas these Christians profess, 'We were sinners by nature, but the All-Merciful hath changed us'—they ought to be taught that no one even by chastisement, much less by merciful treatment, can effect a complete change in those who are sinners by nature as well as by custom. Hence this boast of removing sins is an imposture, and the religion that makes the boast is useless. Moreover what an insult is it to their superior god that these men should admit that he made them after a certain pattern and then changed his mind and desired to remake them! Or else they are forced to introduce a certain Satan, who by his devices, perverted men forsooth from the divine image, and so for a time overcame the superior god. But it is clear, even to a blind man, that a superior god, overcome, though but for a time, by an inferior god, is for that time, no longer superior, much less Supreme and All-Powerful. Therefore your religion is proved to be not only useless, but also blasphemous.

"In the third place, mark the impudence of it and the self-conceit. For admitting that the superior god could send his son as a man, can we possibly believe that he would send him as a Jew, and not as a Greek, or as a Roman, or as a man of no particular nation? I have heard you laugh at Zeus in the comedy when he wakes up after his day's debauch and despatches Hermes to the Athenians and Lacedaemonians to complain that they curtail his sacrifices and keep him on short commons. But why do you not laugh at your own superior god who, awakening after the slumber of many thousands of years, despatches his son to one single nation, and that the smallest and vilest and most contemptible upon earth? Moreover consider how exacting and impudent is your religion beyond all others. Heracles, Asclepius, and Romulus, claim not to be the only children of god, but leave room for others also. And how many others! Worship, if you will, him who was put to death upon the cross, but set not yourselves up above the Getae who worship Zamolxis, or the Cilicians who worship Mopsus, or the Acarnanians who pay divine honours to Amphilochus, or the Thebans who do the same to Amphiaraus, or the Lebedians who (in company with you yourself) pay reverence to Trophonius. For how is your Syrian saviour better than the Theban, or the Cilician, or any other of the host of his rival saviours? Nay, he is inferior, if we are to trust that which is reported concerning him and them by the followers of each. For Christus did but show himself to men in times past, whereas these others, if you are to believe those who worship them, are still to be seen in human form in their temples, appearing with all distinctness.

"Next, as to the uncertainty of your new religion. Consider that just such another as your Christus, might come into the world to-morrow, and indeed such are continually coming forward in the market-place of every town in Asia, who are wont to say, 'I am God, or I am the Son of God, or I am the Divine Spirit. I am come to save you because ye, men, are perishing for your iniquities;' and they persuade their dupes by promises or threats: 'Blessed is he who does me homage; on all the rest I will send down eternal fire.' And then the followers of such an one in a confident voice call on us saying, 'Believe that he whom we preach is the Son of God, although indeed he died the death of a slave; yea, believe it the more on this very account.' If these people bring forward a Christus every year, what is to be done by those who 'seek salvation'? Must they cast dice to decide to which of all these saviours they should pay homage?

"But lest you should imagine that I am entirely dependent upon you for my knowledge of this sect, understand that both here, and in Hierapolis, and in Ephesus, I have made search concerning it; and I am become an adept in their ridiculous jargon which speaks of 'the narrow way' and 'the gates that open of themselves'; and 'those who are being slaughtered that they may live'; and about 'death made to cease in the world; and how 'the Lord doth reign from the tree'; and of 'the tree of life' and 'the resurrection of life by the tree.' All this talk of timber, forsooth, because their ringleader was not only slain on the cross of wood but also a maker of crosses, being a carpenter by trade! And I suppose if, instead of being crucified, he had been cast down a precipice, or into a pit, or hanged by the neck, or if, instead of being a carpenter by trade, he had been a leather-cutter, or a stonemason or a worker in iron, then these absurd people would have exalted to the skies a 'precipice of life,' or a 'pit of resurrection,' or a 'cord of immortality,' or a 'stone of blessing,' or a 'sacred leather.' What child would not be ashamed of such babble as this!

"And this brings me to my last point, the shame and disgrace that any philosopher must needs bring both upon himself and upon philosophy, in stooping to so puerile a superstition. If you know not this, at least your new friends know it; for like the hyena, they seldom attack a full-grown man, but for the most part children or imbeciles; and to the best of their power they would destroy reason saying (like so many Metragurtae, or Mithrae, or Sabbadii) 'Do not examine, but believe,' 'Your faith will save you.' The wisdom of the world is evil, foolishness is good.' For this cause, because they distrust the wise and sober, they prefer to decoy the young, saying to them, 'If ye would attain to the knowledge of the truth, ye must leave your fathers and tutors and go with the women to the women's apartments, or to the leather shop, or to the fuller's shop, that ye may there attain perfection.' And they retail the sayings of these illiterate creatures as if they were repeating the precepts of a Socrates: 'Simon the fuller, or Eleazar the leather-cutter, or John the fisherman affirmed this, or that.' I say nothing also of the immorality of a religion, which asserts that God will receive the unrighteous, if he humble himself, because of his unrighteousness, but he will not receive the righteous man who approaches him adorned with righteousness from the first. All these immoral theories, these lies, and myths, and vile superstitions, are taught by the Christians; and taught in the name of whom? Of one who died as a slave after being deserted (according to their own confession) by his most devoted followers. And taught for what cause? Simply because a phantom of him was seen after his death by a half frantic woman and some dozen of his other companions who conspired together for the purpose of deception. For my part, if I must needs give a reason why this most absurd religion attracts the multitude, I should say that it is because the multitude in their inmost heart, prefer falsehood to truth; and if I desired a new proof that the world is governed by chance, or by fate, and not by gods, I should discern it in the growth of this pernicious superstition. Farewell and return speedily to thyself."

§ 3. OF MY REPLY TO ARTEMIDORUS

I was astonished at the passion of his letter; and though I was at this time neither a Christian nor likely to become one, the injustice of my friend moved me to say somewhat on the other side. My reply was to this effect:

"ONESIMUS TO ARTEMIDORUS, HEALTH.

"Your vehemence surprises me. That I am not, and shall not be, a Christian, must be clear from my previous letters; and that which I saw in Jerusalem has set me, even more than before, against the Jews and all things Jewish, Nevertheless, Artemidorus, I am for from agreeing with you in all your condemnation of this sect, which you seem to me, of set purpose to misunderstand.

"And why do you vent dogmas on me? How know you that God is unknowable? Were it not more seemly for a philosopher to conjecture, and not to know, where knowledge is impossible? Why therefore should a man be ashamed of conjecturing (in Plato's company, I think) that the most perfect image of the Supreme God is neither a frog, nor a worm, but a righteous man? And if man be at all like unto the Supreme Goodness, then to be virtuous, I suppose is to be most like Him; and to be sinful is to be most unlike Him, a calamity from which the Supreme Being Himself might naturally desire to deliver mankind. However, I purpose not to argue with you, for I cannot think that you yourself believe in your own arguments, you who say that there is no difference between sin and error; or else I suppose you will be consistent and blame your slaves equally if Glaucus to-morrow commits theft or murder, and little Chresimus says that five and six make ten.

"But one word concerning Christus himself. It is but a few weeks ago that I heard you praise some Roman or other for saying that we ought to choose out some noble life, to be as it were a carpenter's rule, by which we might straighten our own crooked life; why will you not praise me then, if upon finding this Christus to be a truly great and' noble man, I make his life the rule of mine? But you reply, 'What do you know that is noble and heroic in him?'I will answer this question when we meet. Meantime let me say that though I know but little, it is more than enough to assure me (for your letter proves it) that you know nothing of him. Do not again suppose that I am likely to be a Christian. I am prevented from this by arguments, and by feelings still more powerful than arguments. Yet I have at least this advantage, Artemidorus, over you, that I have not yet allowed prejudice unphilosophically to blind my eyes to the truth, and that, after studying the life of Christus, the store of the examples of great men, which you yourself have exhorted me to treasure up in my heart, is now enriched by the example of one more man, both good and great, who has been able, according to your own avowal (perchance by the mere memory of his goodness), to convert fullers and leather-cutters and thieves and adulterers into decent citizens. Farewell and be thyself."

Although I spoke thus in defence of the Lord Jesus against the unjust reproaches of Artemidorus, yet was I very far from following the Lord, yea and perhaps all the farther that I had learned to talk admiringly of him as of a man on a level with Socrates and Pythagoras and others. For this kind of admiration took up that place in my heart which should have been filled by faith or trust, and left no room for them. Nor indeed was I fit at that time to come to the Saviour because my eyes were not yet opened to discern my own sins so as to desire forgiveness; for the Saviour calls unto himself the " weary and heavy-laden," but I was not yet weary enough nor felt as yet the burden of my sinfulness. And as for all those questionings of words, and traditions, and proofs, on which Artemidorus had set me, they had taught me indeed many new things about the Lord Jesus, and what other people believed concerning him, but they had not taught me the Lord himself, so that I might know him and love him and believe in him. And when at last I began to draw nigh unto him and to listen to his words and to meditate on them, behold, I was called away from my instructors in Antioch, and found afterwards no one like-minded who was willing to set forth before me the very words of the Lord; but, on the contrary, those of the brethren whom I met in Jerusalem, cared not so much for the Lord as for the Law of Moses, and drove me back from him when I was desirous to draw near.

But why do I blame others when I was myself mainly to blame? For I erred in the pride of my heart, because I preferred the wisdom of the Greeks to the wisdom of the Lord Jesus. Therefore didst thou, O All-Wise, permit me to have my heart's desire, and to serve the Greek Philosophy and to take that yoke upon my neck, that I might prove it and know it, whether that service were freedom indeed; and then didst thou make me to pass through the dark valley of affliction and didst suffer my wandering steps to stumble and sink in the mire of wickedness, to the intent that I might understand at last that the Wisdom of the Greeks, for all the beauty of it and the pleasant sound of it, has no power to lift up a drowning soul from the deep waters of sin.

§ 4. OF EUCHARIS AND OF MY LIFE AT ATHENS

Partly perhaps because Eucharis had lived with her father some years in Rome (where women lead not so sequestered a life as in Asia and at Athens) and partly for want of slaves, and because her mother had died when she was still in tender years, but also in great measure because of the ability of her mind and the depth and extent of her knowledge, Eucharis was rather as a pupil and companion to Molon than as a daughter and housewife. Her grace and beauty were more than equal to her learning; but that by which she drew my heart to herself was the gentleness of her disposition and the singular modesty with which she bore her many accomplishments. For though she was the flower of the house and the delight of her old father, yet did she never in any wise strain or try his affection by caprice or humours; yea rather, by reason of his poverty, and because he had scarce a slave whom he could call his own, she, to whom all should have ministered, was content and glad to minister both to the old man and to his friends, and this with all willingness and aptness, and yet so modestly and quietly that her coming was as noiseless as the sunshine, and we only knew that she had departed because the brightness seemed to have passed out of the chamber. When I became the old man's pupil, and in no long time the most intimate of all his pupils, I obtained also a share in the pleasure of her constant and familiar society; and, by degrees, gaining the liking of my old tutor, I was helped to the friendship of his daughter as well; and conceiving for her an affection more intimate than friendship, I was blessed at last, in return, with the certainty of her undivided love.

The time had now come for me to put the kindness of Philemon to the proof. From the first, he had treated me rather as a son than as a slave; and, whithersoever I had accompanied him, his carriage towards me had always been such as to lead even those who knew that I had once been a slave, to suppose that I had been long ago emancipated. So I straightway wrote to him, telling him of my affection for Eucharis, and how I had obtained the consent of Molon; and although I did not venture to express the hope that he would make me free at once, yet I besought him to make some promissory emancipation (after the custom common in Asia) that I might be free, on condition of serving him faithfully for such period as he might please to name. This limited request I made, rather for form's sake than as supposing that he would stand upon conditions; for, remembering his constant kindness, I looked for nothing less than that he should wholly emancipate me at once. So having sent off this letter I confidently waited for an answer. Meanwhile I spent the time pleasantly in the society of Eucharis, and Molon, and my companions in learning; and I also took a great delight in the beauties and antiquities of Athens.

The dreams and visions with which I had been visited in Syria, and still more while I was tempest-tossed sailing to Peiraeus, soon ceased after I had been some few days in the house of Molon. Each day brought with it some new thing to see or hear. Though the streets of Athens were not to be compared with those of Antioch, being small and mean and narrow and not evenly built, yet the public buildings and temples and theatres far surpassed anything I had seen in any city of Asia; and as for the statues of the gods, they fairly ravished the heart with their beauty. Moreover an edge was given to every pleasure of sight by the hearing of some history or legend; how Demosthenes spoke in yonder place of assembly, and in these groves and porches walked Aristotle amid his disciples, or Plato taught, or Socrates conversed, and here the tyrant was slain by Aristogeiton, and there Pericles pronounced the funeral oration over them that fell in the wars. Also, it so chanced that, besides the daily sight of the palaestra and the attendance at the lectures, the Dionysian festival with its customary plays came round while I was still at Athens. I had seen plays before in Asia, yet these so enchanted me with the beauty of the masks and choruses and the marvellous skill of the actors that I was well-nigh swallowed up with the glory of the drama; and finding occasion to be introduced to some of the actors, I frequented their society and heard them rehearse, and sometimes myself practised recitations in their presence, endeavouring to gain some knowledge of their art. Amid all these engaging pursuits and delights, the time passed as if upon wings; and in the evening the greatest delight of all, after the thousand pleasant distractions of the day, was to talk with Eucharis and her father concerning all that I had seen and heard.

We conversed together of all matters of art and letters and philosophy, and not seldom about my own life, the sorrows of the past, and what remained in the future; and, as was natural, my travels in Syria were not forgotten. Yet about these I spoke seldom and sparingly, lest I should be forced to make mention of the Christians;

concerning whom at that time I was loth, I scarce know why, to say aught either for good or evil. But on the last day of our being together, some fate (as I then called it) decreed that I should no longer keep silence concerning them. It was after this manner. We had been conversing together, Molon and I, touching the Pythagoreans, by what bond of fellowship their society was in former times bound together, and by what cause that bond was broken. And thereupon I all unwittingly let fall some words (and repented as soon as they had been spoken) how a certain Christus, a Syrian, had founded a society, somewhat akin to the Pythagorean sect. Then Eucharis straightway would have me give some account of this Christus and his society; and when I made as if I had not heard her, and afterwards would have put her off on some pretext saying that the matter was not worth her hearing, or that I knew not much of it for certain, and the like she looking steadfastly upon me and perceiving (I suppose) that I was in some confusion, besought me not to hide from her anything that I knew. So I, not finding any escape, began to describe to her the new Brotherhood or Commonwealth of Christus, as I conceived it; and being carried onward I spoke more freely than I had intended, and summing up all that I had heard and some things that I had imagined, I described how wealth and violence were to have no more power in the world, and there was to be no more oppression, and sin was to be taken away by forgiveness; and those that the world counted great were to be cast down, and he that was humblest and made himself least was to be lifted up and, in a word, the most willing servant of all was to be king of all; and all the nations of the earth were to be as one Family, wherein Christus was to be the Elder Brother, and the Father was none other than the Supreme God; and how (as his followers averred) he had foretold that he should be slain, yea, and declared that he would willingly die, but that, overcoming death, he should manifest himself to his disciples after death, and be constantly with them; and how his disciples alleged that somewhat of this kind had indeed come to pass, for that many of them had seen him in apparitions by day or dreams by night; and lastly how (whatever error else there might be among this sect) this Christus of a truth appeared to have a marvellous power to turn the vile and wicked to lives of virtue and purity.

All this time Eucharis was rapt in thought; but I was so intent on the matter of my discourse that I noted not her countenance till I had well-nigh made an end of speaking; but when I perceived it, I broke off, saying that after all, it was but a Jewish superstition, and that as for these apparitions of Christus, they were but according to nature, if there were indeed any apparitions at all. But Eucharis, still musing and pondering, made no answer for a while, and at last asked my opinion concerning all dreams and visions, whether they came from the gods or no. I said, "No, but from natural causes." Then replied Eucharis, "Yes, but if, as your Artemidorus says, the twin -stars that bring mariners help, come to us from natural causes, and yet you worship the gods that send them; may it not also be that some dreams and some visions, though coming to us—like air and light and the fruits of the earth—in the common course of nature, may nevertheless be sent to us by the immortal gods?" Then after a' pause she added, "And you too, Onesimus, while studying the life of this Teacher, have you too been visited by him in your dreams?"

Fearing to be engaged in any further discourse concerning this matter I rose up to bid Molon farewell, alleging the lateness of the hour; but at that moment there came a knocking at the door, and presently appeared Chresimus, a slave of Philemon, bearing a letter for me, and with the letter this message by word of mouth, that the old man desired my most speedy return. I broke the seal at once, fearing that Philemon might be sick and nigh unto death. But the letter said not a word touching his health, nor did it give any answer to my request for freedom, neither 'yes' nor 'no,' only bidding me use all expedition to return because " something of great import" had taken place, concerning which he would gladly have speech with me before resolving further in the matter on which I had written to him. I wished to have tarried yet a few days in Athens, but Philemon's command was express that I should return on the next day, and that Molon should excuse me to my friends; and, so saying, Chresimus went forth to make ready for our departure on the morrow. My heart sank within me as I turned to bid farewell to Eucharis, foreboding that I should henceforth live without her, and that life without her would be death. But she comforted me, saying that her memory must always live with me, as mine with her; and that we must take hope as our common friend; and clasping round my neck a little amulet which, I was ever to guard with the token of my brother Chrestus, "On thy brother's gift," she said, "there is written TRUST, and on mine there is HOPE; and with trust and hope we must needs do well; for as to love we need no assurance ": and with these words she bade me her last farewell.

§ 5. HOW I RETURNED TO COLOSSI, AND OF MY NEW LIFE WITH PHILEMON

Even while Philemon embraced me on my return to Colossae, I perceived that he was marvellously changed. Whereas he had been wont to wear on his countenance an anxious and restless expression, now he was calm and composed, with a cheerfulness that seemed to spring (not as in the former days of his settled health when I first knew him) from easiness and good temper, but from some deep change in his nature. The suspicion that came into my mind on beholding him was confirmed by the first words he uttered thanking the Lord for my safe return; and he immediately avowed that he had become a Christian. Had he then, I asked, submitted himself to the Jewish law? No, he replied: Paulus (the same of whom we had heard so much while we were in Syria) who had admitted my master into the sect of the Christians, had taught him that it was neither needful nor fitting that he, being a Gentile, should observe the laws of the Jews. When I asked him what Artemidorus said, he bade me no more mention the name of the Epicurean, whose society, said he, I have for some time renounced. Of others of my best friends he spoke in the same way, especially of Epictetus, and Heracleas; but he made mention of other persons, mostly bearing Jewish names, and men either not known to me or known to be illiterate and of the common sort, with whom he hoped I should soon be better acquainted; "for they," said he, "belong to us—as will you also, my dear Onesimus, in due time, I hope and earnestly believe—and the brethren of Colossae are wont to meet at worship at my house." My thoughts being in a maze" I thought to turn the discourse by questioning him concerning friends and kinsfolk, and I inadvertently asked whether his sister's son—who was wont to come in from the country to visit him each year—was intending to come to the city at the forthcoming feast of Zeus; but Philemon, making some hasty sign to deprecate my speech about the festival, added gravely and with authority that he was assured I should no longer wish to take part in the procession nor to go to any of the games or public spectacles; " for," said he, "it is not gods but demons that preside over such shows." Much more he said on this topic; and I found that my last letter to Artemidorus (as the Epicurean had reported it, misconstruing it, I suppose, in his passion) had caused Philemon to think that I was already a Christian in heart.

But, concerning Eucharis and emancipation, not one word.

After waiting a long while to see whether he would be the first to speak, I reminded him of my request. He replied that he had a good will, yea and a sincere affection for me, and that he fully intended to emancipate me; but he did not think it fit that I should take to wife the daughter of a rhetorician and declaimer such as Molon, one who was by pursuit, as well as by disposition and nature, devoted to the worship of false gods. He had therefore arranged for me a marriage with the daughter of a very worthy citizen, Pheidippides the wool-seller, who, though not as yet one of the brethren, was most favourably inclined towards them, and who was quite willing to give me Prepousa to be my wife, if Philemon would emancipate me and give me a sufficient estate; and this, said he, I shall willingly do.

I was speechless with anger. But Philemon supposed my silence to be caused by excess of gratitude unable to find vent in speech. So looking affectionately on me he said there was no need of thanks, for that he was willing to do much more than this rather than suffer my soul to be ensnared at Athens. Then, in the same tone of authority in which he had spoken throughout (unusual in him and to me most unexpected and distasteful) he said that I was wearied with travel and had need of rest; wherefore he desired that I should consider myself excused from my attendance and retire to my chamber. When I went forth from his presence, a great gulf seemed to divide me from Eucharis, and from freedom, and from all hopes of a happy future.

As to the religion of the Christians I was no longer drawn to it even so much as before. Had I not in former time restrained Philemon from joining himself to it? Had he not in those days acknowledged that my understanding was superior to his, deferring readily to my advice? And now was I to confess myself in the wrong? Was I, slave-like, to bow to one inferior to me in mind, because he chanced to be the master of my body? How could I meet Artemidorus or Epictetus after so great a disgrace? On the morrow therefore, when I attended Philemon in the library and he asked me what I thought of his proposals, adding that he trusted I should soon be willing to receive baptism, I with difficulty restrained myself so far as to answer merely that at present I was unwilling, and that in any case I did not wish to marry Prepousa. He was silent for a while and evidently displeased. Then he exclaimed, "If only Paulus were in Asia at this time, my hopes of thee would be speedily fulfilled." But as I had been often present willingly at the Christian meetings in Antioch, he said that I could make no objection to be present at the meetings of the brethren in his house where I should receive instruction which, he hoped, would soon induce me to be baptized. About manumission as before, not a word; but I perceived that it was hopeless to ask for it.

That some day I was summoned to attend one of the meetings of the brethren, at which were present all the slaves of Philemon, and not a few belonging to other citizens, and many freedmen also, and some that were free- born; but these, few, and for the most part Jews, and not men of any breeding or education. And I, being wilful at that time, and contemptuous of others, and given to think far too highly of myself, looked down upon these unlearned brethren, and stopped my ears against the truth and hardened my heart, scoffing within myself at their faults of speech and solecisms, and at the barbarous dialect of their Greek; and besides, to speak the truth, the discourses of Archippus, the son of Philemon, were too much upon the prophets and too little upon him to whom the prophets bear witness. So they moved me no more than the discourses of Lucius at Antioch, or even less. Yet once when Tatias—the man whom Philippus had raised from the dead—stood up and testified how all things had become new for him since he had believed in the Lord, and how darkness had passed away and all was full of light and joy and peace, and how the Lord Jesus was a friend that never failed in the hour of need; then for the time, spite of myself, my heart was touched and I seemed ready to stretch out my hands to the Saviour; but at that instant methought I saw Philemon watching me narrowly to see whether I was moved by the discourse, and thereon my heart rebelled again and I could think of nothing but the great gulf which my master placed between me and Eucharis. Thus was my heart still hardened against the truth.

Being in this condition of mind, I found my new life full of dullness and melancholy. Each day passed like the day before, and prepared for a morrow that should be still the same. The images of the gods had been removed from the hall and from the court-yard; no pictures, no songs, no garlands, no feasts, nor meetings of friends; our old acquaintance seemed to have disowned us, and there were no longer any occasions for discourse on arts, or letters, or philosophy. Even the library had been despoiled of many of the best and choicest books; the busts of most of the great poets and authors had been removed; and Philemon employed me during many hours of the day in transcribing, no longer Euripides or Menander, but the Greek translations of the books of the Jewish prophets. The only diversity in the circle of our daily life was that on certain days the household met for worship; but if I profited little from the first day of meeting, I gained even less from those that followed; for then a certain Pistus, a Paphlagonian slave, took a great part in the prayers and discourses, especially when Archippus was absent , and one might as well have hoped to gather grapes from brambles as good from the words of Pistus. If such was our life at home, it was vain to look for change in life abroad. For I was no longer permitted to go to any public spectacle: and the society of every friend and acquaintance for whom I had any affection was proscribed. In this solitude and dejection I looked for counsel, but could find none. To Artemidorus, being so near a neighbour, I durst not resort, for fear lest Philemon should be informed that I had disobeyed his prohibition, but I resolved that I would use the first occasion to go to Hierapolis that I might there ask the advice of the young Epictetus.

§ 6. CONCERNING MY VISIT TO EPICTETUS

When I came to Hierapolis I found Epictetus keeping his bed and scarce able to move a limb. His master, he told me, had tortured him most cruelly, twisting his leg so as to force the bone from the socket; and the physician had declared that he would be lame for life. In answer to my execrations against all masters of slaves and Epaphroditus his master in particular, "Peace, my friend," said Epictetus, "our masters are becoming better and not worse; and besides, ever since the sixth year of Claudius, we have a law in our favour. For before, if we were turned out to die in the streets, and then were impudent enough to recover, our masters could claim us back again; but now the divine Claudius has decreed that if Death spare us, our masters shall spare us also. However my chief consolation lies not in the laws of Claudius, but in philosophy; for since you and I were last together, you must know I have become a philosopher. "Prithee," said I, "if slaves can indeed become philosophers, let me have some benefit of your philosophy; for assuredly I have need of it. Did not your philosophy fail you when that cruel wretch so wantonly injured you?" "Pardon me," replied Epictetus, "he did not injure me, as indeed I explained to him at the time." " Explain then to me," said I, "this most mysterious riddle." "I told him that he could not injure me though he would injure himself. Hereon he retorted that he would break my leg. I replied, 'In that case my leg would be broken, but what of that?' At this he stared like a bull, and said that he would cut off my head. To that I rejoined, 'And when did I ever tell you that I had a head of such a kind that it could not be cut off?' Upon that he burst into a passion, threw me down, kicked me, and began to twist my leg. As he proceeded, I warned him and said, 'If you continue, you will certainly break it.' He continued; and then I said to him, 'There, now my leg is broken; but you have not injured me, but only my leg, and perhaps yourself.'"

All this seemed to me new and yet not new. Sitting down on the bench beside his pallet, I said, "Well, but, Epictetus, this differs not much from the philosophy of the Stoics or the Cynics." "I did not maintain," replied he, "that my philosophy was new. Nevertheless I do not perceive that it is very common in these parts," "You mistake," said I, "a great many in Hierapolis read Chrysippus, and not a few even in Colossae." "Read Chrysippus," exclaimed my friend with a laugh. "Yes, read Chrysippus, but how many act Chrysippus? Much as if we were to go to a wrestler, and say to him, 'Come, Milo, show us how you can give your adversary a fall,' and Milo should reply, 'Nay, rather step into the next room, and feel the weight of my dumb-bells.'" Then he turned affectionately to me and said, "It is not the object of life, my dearest Onesimus, to have read the hundred and forty volumes of Chrysippus, but to put the precepts of Chrysippus in use, and to set them before men in a brief form fit for use; and this is what I am endeavouring to do." "Set them before me then," said I, "for Zeus knows that if you have any philosophy fit for use, I can find use for it. What therefore is the foundation of your philosophy?"

"The foundation," replied my friend, "consists in the distinguishing of things in our power from things not in our power. The things that are needful are in our power, viz. justice, temperance, truthfulness, courage and the like; but the things that are not in our power are not needful, such as wealth, beauty, reputation, health, pleasure, life, and the rest. Many philosophers admit this in word, but do not carry it out in deed, partly because they talk much and do little, and being immersed in speculations are not ready for actions, when the hour for action is at hand. But if a man have this foundation once solidly built within his heart so as to be able to base all his actions on it, from that time he will be perfectly free and do all things according to his own will. Therefore make up your mind once for all what is your object in life; what it is you want. A dinner? or to escape a whipping?

Well, then, you will do your master's bidding to gain your dinner, or to escape a whipping. But a philosopher will not do this, because he does not fear hunger, nor a whipping, nor any master. 'What,' you say, 'must not a philosopher fear Caesar?' No, for he does not fear the things that Caesar can bring. For, mark you, no one fears Caesar in himself, but only the things that Caesar brings with him, such as the sword, banishment, poverty, torture, disgrace. But fetch me Caesar here without his thunders and lightnings, and see how bold the veriest coward will be. Why then should a philosopher fear Caesar, since he has no fear of Caesar's thunder and lightning?

"Distinguish therefore between what you can and what you cannot do, and in that knowledge you will find freedom. If you are thoroughly persuaded in your inmost mind that those things only are yours which are really yours and which are needful to you, then you will aim at nothing which you will not attain; you will never attempt anything with any kind of violence to yourself; you will blame no one, you will accuse no one; nobody will ever hinder you from the accomplishment of your desires; in fine, you will never be subject to the least regret. Take an instance. My leg, you will observe, is inflamed, and it has certain sensations which are called painful. Good: that is the popular manner of speaking. But it is a mere imagination. My inflamed leg does not hinder me from being honest, just, and courageous; in other words from attaining the objects of existence and the aim of all my desires. Consequently I have, accustomed myself to bear always in mind that pain of this kind does not concern me and is no real evil. For it is of the nature of things that have no dependence on me. 'But you will be lame for life,' say you. That is very probable, and indeed our physician tells me it is certain. But what then? When I am lame, my lameness will be an obstruction to my feet in walking, but not to my will in doing what it is inclined to do. It follows that sorrow and the signs of sorrow such as weeping and groaning, are all the mere results of false conceptions and imaginations. What is misfortune? Prejudice. What is weeping? Prejudice. What are complaints, discontents, repining, fretfulness, restlessness? All so many forms of prejudice, and prejudice moreover concerning things uncontrollable by the will.

He paused. "You have defined sorrow," said I, "and how do you define death?" "A mere mask," he replied. "It has no teeth. Turn it on the other side and you will find it does not bite you. It is a mere going away. Life is as it were a feast. At birth God opens the door to you, and says, 'Enter.' At death, the feast being now ended, God opens the door to you once again and says 'Depart.' Whither? To nothing terrible. Only to the source whence you came forth. To that which is friendly and congenial: to the elements. What in you was fire, goes away to the fire; what earth, to earth; what air, to air, what water, to water. There is no Hades, nor Acheron, nor Cocytus, nor Pyriphlegethon; but all is full of gods and divine beings. He who can think of the whole universe as his home, and can look upon the sun, moon and stars as his friends, and enjoy the companionship of the earth and sea, he is no more solitary nor helpless exile. Let death come to you when he will. Can death banish you from the Universe? You know he cannot. Go where you may, there will be still a sun, moon, and stars, dreams and auguries and communications with the Gods."

I interrupted him. "You say there is no Hades; are there then no Elysian fields?" " I do not know," replied he; " but why seek any greater reward for a good man than the doing of what is good? After being thought worthy by God to be introduced into His great City, the Universe, so that you may discharge for Him the duties of a man, do you still cry for something more, like a baby for its food? Do you need coaxing and sweetmeats to induce you to do what is right? Be not like a bad actor that forgets the part assigned to him, when he steps upon the stage. 'I was sent into this world to play a part.' Well said, Mr. Actor; and what part? 'The part of a witness for God.' Good: repeat your part. 'I am miserable, Lord; I am undone; no mortal cares for me; no mortal gives me what I want.' What babble is this! Away with the fool. He has forgotten his part; hiss him off the stage.

"Or take another of my metaphors. God is your general, and you must be to him a loyal, obedient soldier, having sworn an oath of obedience, which you will sooner die than break. Dost Thou wish me to live? I live. To die? Then farewell. How wouldst Thou have me serve Thee? As a soldier? Then I go cheerfully to the wars. As a slave? I obey. Whatever post Thou shalt assign to me, I will die a thousand times rather than desert it. Where wouldst Thou that I should serve Thee? In Rome, or in Athens, or in Thebes? Thou art not absent from populous cities. Or on the rock of Gyarus? Thou wilt be with me even there. Only if Thou shouldst send me to live where it is no longer possible to live conformably with nature, then, but not till then, should I depart, accepting as it were Thy signal of recall."

Here he made an end, and I sat for some time silent. His words were to me as a trumpet-blast arousing within me a host of virtuous resolutions, which I at that time mistook for virtuous acts, and thought myself already an athlete or a hero; even as a drunken man supposes himself Heracles, or as the reader of the hundred and forty-three volumes of Chrysippus believes himself to be a man of virtue. Presently I arose and thanked him, saying that I went forth as it were to the Olympian contest, to put in use the precepts of Epictetus my trainer. He smiled, and as I went forth from his chamber, he called after me, "Yes, but Onesimus, for this contest you need not wait four years."

§ 7. HOW I TRIED THE PHILOSOPHY OF EPICTETUS

Epictetus was right; I had not long to wait for the contest of which he spoke. It began on the morrow, and continued without intermission; for day by day I was constrained to be present at the meetings of the Christians, and day by day Philemon questioned me whether I had not now at last been persuaded, and whether I was not willing now to be baptized. However, I followed the advice of Epictetus, and said to myself, "Truthfulness is in my power, but the goodwill of Philemon is not in my power, therefore it does not concern me, and I will not trouble myself about it." But, in the evening of each day, when I perceived that the breach was widening between me and my master, and when I called to mind that it depended on him whether I should be free or a slave, and united to Eucharis or parted from her for ever, then my mind misgave me that I could not honestly say, "His goodwill concerns me not." Oftentimes I checked myself, saying that I was placed in the Universe as a sentinel by God, and that I must not neglect my post wherever it might be; but as often as these words came to my memory, there came others also, namely that "if we were placed by him where we could not live conformably to nature, then we might accept this as the voice of a trumpet, sounding recall and bidding us quit this life for another." And said I to myself, can it be considered living according to nature, that I should live in subjection to such a servitude as this? Or is it living according to nature, to be removed from all learning, just when I have been trained to use and enjoy it? and to live apart from all friends, consorting with none but slavish dispositions? and, in a word, having many faculties trained to noble uses, to be placed in a position where all those faculties must needs rust unused?

Meanwhile the conduct of Pistus widened the breach between my master and me and altogether envenomed my very soul against the faith. This man had been Philemon's secretary during my absence at Athens; and now, finding himself like to be supplanted, he began to alienate Philemon from me by sly insinuations, hints, letters unsigned in a strange hand, and sometimes by open questions cunningly asked of me in Philemon's presence. As, for example, on the day when I had visited Epictetus, he asked me, in my master's hearing, whether Epaphroditus was in good health, he being the master of Epictetus, and a very dissolute man. When I said "Yes, as far as I knew," I could see from Philemon's countenance that he greatly disliked my going thither; and I at once explained that I had not gone to see, nor had I seen, Epaphroditus himself, but only his slave Epictetus, who was sick. Yet the cloud on my master's brow did not altogether vanish; and he did not forget it. For that same evening he took me aside, saying that it was time to have clone with youthful passions and caprices, and had I considered his proposal—not about baptism, for he would not at that season make mention of higher matters—but concerning marriage, and was I willing to marry Prepousa? I said " No." Hereat he became very grave, saying that it was a very suitable match for me, and well fitted to keep me from evil courses, such as young men were liable to; and he bade me think further of it and meantime to be more discreet what company I kept, for he disliked that I should so much as enter the house of such a one as Epaphroditus, though it were but to visit a sick slave. It was all in vain that I attempted (perhaps too obscurely, for I could not now speak freely with Philemon as in old days) to explain that I stood in need of counsel and that I had gone to Epictetus for it. "That is settled " was all he had to say, before he dismissed me to my chamber. Only, as I was departing, he called me back, and asked me whether I had at least given up the thought of Eucharis. I said " No." To which he replied that he was very sorry for that, for he could not consent that my soul should be ensnared by such a marriage, and so long as I entertained that foolish passion it was not possible for him to entertain the project of emancipating me. So saying, he dismissed me to my chamber, speechless with passion. In this mood I took up my pen and wrote thus to Epictetus:

"ONESIMUS TO EPICTETUS, HEALTH.

"I leaned on your philosophy, and it has proved a broken reed. No longer can I live under the insupportable yoke of my slavery here. Yet what am I to do? I cannot live conformably to nature. "Then die" say you. And what then becomes of Eucharis, who would break her heart for my departure? Your philosophy takes no account of wife, or children, or those dear friends who are second selves. Their happiness is not in your control; and yet how can you be tranquil in their unhappiness? Answer me that.

"One question more. A fellow here, a Paphlagonian, one Pistus, is poisoning Philemon's mind against me, drops notes, in a strange hand and nameless, accusing me of deceit, theft, frequenting brothels and all manner of impurity. His last stroke has been to persuade Philemon to forbid me from visiting you. I hate him, and intend to hate him. Does your philosophy allow of hate?

"A third question. You say, We are soldiers and must die sooner than desert our post. But who shall go bail for our General, that he is not a fool or a knave, or anything but a name? Looking on the battle-field of the Universe I see a conflict but the issue doubtful; no signs of generalship, or at least of victory; in one place joy, in three places sorrow; pleasure here, pain there; virtue sometimes prevailing, more often vice; one master, twenty slaves; animals preying (by necessity) on other animals; men (by necessity or choice?) oppressing other men; everywhere conflict, the General nowhere. Read me these riddles, or be no Oedipus for me.

"Pardon me, dearest friend and guide, but I am beside myself with passion, anxious, not for myself but for one beyond the seas, who sits awaiting tidings from me and feels her life. to be bound up with mine. Strong in your presence, absent from you I am most weak. Impart, I beseech you, some of your strength to one who sorely needs it."

§ 8. HOW I WAS ACCUSED OF THEFT BY THE DEVICES OF PISTUS

At this time, and before I had heard from Epictetus, I received a letter from Eucharis. After some delay, vainly hoping to be able to impart more joyful tidings, I had written to her putting as bright a colour on the future as I could, but not concealing Philemon's strong objections and present refusal; and now I received her answer. It was inclosed in a letter from Molon, in which he spoke of his class and his pupils, and hoped that I was continuing my studies at Colossae, entering also into details about his recent lectures; at the close of his letter he added that Eucharis was not in good health, and that he feared she was troubled in her mind, being infected with superstition. Her old nurse Thallousa affirmed that she had been fascinated by the evil eye; but he thought the mischief had been in part caused by certain women of her acquaintance, Christians from Corinth, who had brought to Athens some strange rites and doctrines of one Paulus, and who seemed to have disturbed her mind. However he trusted that her trouble would pass away when better tidings came from Colossae. The letter of Eucharis was to this effect.

"Do not cease to hope, dearest Onesimus. If I grieve, it is because I seem to see thee grieving. Could I but know that thou wert hopeful, I also could be both hopeful and happy. Thallousa would fain console me, when I weep, by telling me sad stories of others who have loved and have been made sad by separation, but I am not so cruel as to be made happy because others are sad; so I seek comfort elsewhere. Dearest, when we were last together, some doubtful words fell from thy lips, questioning, methought, whether there be any Elysian fields such as the poets sing of. Yet does it not seem (this present world being so very full of sadness) that there must needs be some Isles of the Blessed, called by whatever name, where those whom hard fate has divided here, but whom the good gods must surely destine to be some day united, shall meet again never to be parted? Dearest Onesimus, dearer to me than my own life, what if we meet not again on this earth? May it not be that we shall meet elsewhere? Yet, even for this life, I still trust and hope; and do thou the like for my sake. To think of thee hopeless kills me. dearest friend, sweet cause of my heart's most bitter sorrow, think not that I reproach thee because thy love is cruel. Sweeter, far sweeter, to mourn as I mourn for thy absence, than never to have known and loved thee. Farewell and hope on; and believe me faithful to thy love, whether I live or die."

At the end of the letter were added these words: "I see I have ended my letter with a word of evil omen. Onesimus laughs at omens; but for my own pleasure I will avert the evil by repeating a former question. The visions concerning Christus that thou didst speak of, have they ever appeared to thee too in thy dreams? Because thou didst forget to answer this same question when I first asked it of thee, let this violet, which I now kiss, be my ambassador that thou forget not a second time."

While I sat with the withered flower in my hand, musing on Athens, seeing, as if before mine eyes, the little chamber in which even at that instant perchance Eucharis sat spinning, and Molon reading by her side, a message was brought to me by Pistus that Philemon desired to see me in the library; " and," said the Paphlagonian in a malicious tone, "you were best think of some subtle defence, for the old man knows what you have done. But you will probably prefer to appease him by confessing." The man's malice angered me, and I entered the room in some heat. It soon appeared that a copy of the plays of Aristophanes was missing from the library. Philemon was at that time reviewing his books with great exactness, destroying such as seemed unfit for a Christian household; and he had expressly enjoined on me not to take any of the works of the poets of the Old Comedy out of the library, and I had obeyed him. But when this book was missed, Pistus had affirmed that he had seen me reading it in my chamber. Understanding this I replied roundly that the Paphlagonian lied. But Philemon bade me bethink myself whether unwittingly I might not have taken it from the library, being always fond of the works of that poet, and having in former times been accustomed to take freely from any part of the library such books as I desired; and he added that, of the rest of the household, very few could understand the book, being illiterate, and those who could have read it would not do so, because they had received the seal in Christ and belonged to the saints. I could but repeat that I had not taken the book. On this Pistus said, with a sneer, that, if that were so, the worthy Onesimus would probably be quite willing that his room should be searched. I at once assented; but scarcely had two slaves quitted the room on their quest, when the villainy of Pistus was revealed to me; and I turned and took him by the throat saying that, if the books were found in my chamber, the Paphlagonian had hidden them there. Hereat Pistus fell on his knees, making as if he were terror-stricken by my violence, and calling the Lord to witness his innocence. Philemon indignantly bade me desist; but his indignation became still greater when the two slaves returned bearing the missing volumes, which they had found it seemed, hidden under my couch. In the presence of all the slaves he ordered me to return to my chamber, saying that at first he had never thought to accuse me of stealing the books, but only of thoughtlessly or wilfully borrowing them, but now he knew not what to think. So I went back to my chamber under suspicion of being a thief; and entering I found on my table this letter from Epictetus.

§ 9. HOW EPICTETUS FURTHER EXPLAINED HIS PHILOSOPHY

"EPICTETUS TO ONESIMUS, HEALTH.

"A bad performer cannot sing alone but only in a chorus. In the same way some weak-kneed folk cannot walk the path of life alone, but must needs hold somebody's hand. But if you intend to be ever anything better than an infant, you must learn to walk alone. It angers me to hear a young man say to his tutor, 'I wish to have you with me.' Has not the fellow God with him? But, Onesimus, you are not willing to take God as your guide in practice, though you profess to do so in theory. For with your lips you say, 'Lord, suffer me to go straight on for twenty-five furlongs and a half, and then to take the first turning to the left.' However, let me attempt to answer your questions; but not in order, for first I must show you that whether there be a good God or no, you must needs act as though there were a good God or else you must die. First then, that there is Demeter, is it not clear to all those who eat of bread? And that there is a Helios or Apollo, is not that also clear to all who enjoy the sunlight? Call the former Bread, and the latter Sunlight, if you will; still there they are, and you must partake of them and acknowledge them, as long as you partake of the Feast of Life.

"But you complain that the Host of the Feast is unkind or foolish, not making proper provision for his guests. Foolish man! Then why remain a guest? Do not be more foolish than children. When the game ceases to please them, they say 'I will play no more.' So do you, if the feast please you not, say 'I will feast no more;' and go. For remember the door is always open. But if you remain at the Feast, do not complain of the Host; for that is silly. Remember therefore that if the Host intends you to remain as His guest, in that case He has made all needful provision for you; but if He has not, that is a token that your way lies towards the door.

"Apply this rule to yourself and her whom you love. As it is better that you should die of hunger and preserve your tranquillity of mind to the last gasp, than that you should live in abundance with a soul full of all disturbance and torment, so is it better that Eucharis should die and you be in peace, rather than that your betrothed (or any else the nearest and dearest to you) should live and you be in perturbation of mind. Nay, a father ought rather to suffer his son to become undutiful and wicked rather than himself to become unhappy. You are not to say, 'If I chastise not my son, he will prove undutiful;' but you are to prefer your own serenity of mind to the dutifulness of a son and to all other objects; and the same rule holds as regards Eucharis. Thus and thus only will you be always at peace, and able to despise the worst of omens."

After this Epictetus fell to speaking in a more general way about philosophy and philosophers, and of their duty to the multitude; of which some part I omit, but the rest was to this effect:

"But perhaps you say, ' The multitude has not this knowledge of the folly of sorrow; and if we bewail not with them when they bewail, we shall seem to them brutish, and be hated. Or how shall we explain our theory to the multitude?' For what purpose should you desire to explain it to them? Is it not enough that you are convinced yourself? When I was a boy at Home, as I remember, and when my master's children came to me clapping their hands and saying, 'To-morrow is the good feast of Saturn, did I tell them (think you?) that good does not consist in sweetmeats nor such things as they desired? Nay, but I clapped my hands too. In the same way, when you are unable to convince any one, treat him as a child, and clap your hands with him; or if you will not do that, at least hold your tongue. When therefore you see a man groaning because he, or his betrothed, is likely to be given in marriage to another, first do your best to recover him from his evil and mistaken opinion. But if he will not be persuaded, nothing hinders but you may pretend some sadness and a certain fellow-feeling of his affliction. Only have a care that grief do not effectually seize your heart while you think only to personate it.

"You see then that I forbid you sorrow either for yourself or for others. No less do I forbid you hate. For why should you hate, or even be angry, with a wicked man, a thief, say, or an adulterer? 'Because,' reply you, 'they take from me that which I most dearly value, my wealth or my reputation or the affection of my wife.' In other words they take from you those objects which you love, and desire to excess, though they do not depend on you. But the remedy is to abstain from loving these things to excess. Always remember also when any one injures you, as it is called, that the cause of the injury is ignorance or erroneous opinion. For no one would commit a crime if he knew that he was thereby destroying his own soul. Through erroneous opinions Medea slew her children and Clytemnestra her husband. Why therefore hate a man merely because the poor wretch is terrribly ignorant and is doing himself the greatest of all injuries, while he falsely supposes he is injuring you?

"Bear in mind further that everything has two faces, whereof one is endurable the other unendurable. For example, when your brother is injuring you, look not upon him as an injurer but rather as a brother. Even if you cannot do this for your brother's sake, you must do it for your own. For in all things you must consider not your brother nor your brother's interests first, but yourself and your own serenity of mind. 'My brother'—perhaps you say—'ought not to have treated me so shamefully.' Very true; so much the worse for him. But that is his business, not yours, and you are not to injure yourself on his account. However he treats you, you must treat him rightly. For your treatment of him is in your power, and therefore is your concern; but how he treats you, is not in your power, and therefore concerns you not. If therefore your enemy reviles you, try to think well of him for not having struck you. 'But he has struck me.' Then think well of him for not having wounded you. 'But he has wounded me,' Then think well of him for not having slain you. 'But I am dying of the wound he gave me.' Then think well of him for having opened unto you that door which the Master of the Feast has appointed as your exit from His banquet. Apply this rule to Pistus, and if he has poisoned Philemon's mind against you, think well of him that he, has not yet poisoned your body itself.

"But the former rule is the more important, that you are not to set a value on the things that are beyond your own control. Does Fortune take things away? Laugh at her then. When Philemon and his friends deprive you of your wonted freedom, and take away your books, your reputation, your prospect of marriage, you must consider yourself before a tribunal of boys who are mulcting you of knuckle-bones and nuts. 'So Epictetus makes light of love and marriage and the bands of family affection.' Not so; he recognizes them for the common people but not for Onesimus and Epictetus, nor for other philosophers in the present war of good against evil. For as the state of things now is, the philosopher should hear the trumpet sounding for all good men to make ready, like an army drawn up for battle in the face of an enemy;

and he should be without all distraction, entirely attending to the service of God.

"Finally, whatever betide, be not a slave. 'I must go to the ergastulum,' says Onesimus. And must you go groaning too"? 'I must be fettered like a slave.' Must you lament like a slave too? 'Marry Prepousa,' says Philemon, 'and become a Christian.' 'I will not.' 'Then I will slay you.' 'Did I ever assert that I could not be slain?' That is the language that befits my Onesimus; not to look at the spectacle of life like a runaway slave in the theatre, who shivers whenever any one touches him on the shoulder or mentions his master's name. Instead of swearing allegiance to Christus to conciliate Philemon, swear rather never to dishonour God who loves truth, nor to murmur at anything that betides; for all things betide according to His will. At all times endeavour to listen to His voice; for He accosts you and speaks to you thus: 'Onesimus, when you were at your lectures in Athens, what did you call death and imprisonment and all other such external things?' 'I? Things indifferent.' 'And what do you call them now?' 'The same.' 'What is the aim and object of thy life?' 'To follow Thee.' 'Go on then, boldly.'"

§ 10. OF METRODORUS AND HIS ADVICE

I read and re-read the letter of Epictetus; but it could no longer settle my doubts nor quiet my mind. What was true in it seemed to be stale and useless, namely, that each man was able to do whatsoever he wished, provided that he wished only for those things that he was able to do. And again, what might have been useful, if true, seemed not true, or at all events not certain, I mean that the Master of the Feast was good. For all that Epictetus had said came to this, that if we remained as a guest at the Feast, each one was bound to act as if the Master was good, or else to depart from the Feast. But why was a philosopher bound to suppose something that might be false, or else to slay himself? For, all the while, there might be no Master of the Feast at all, but only a talk about Masters, and in reality neither Master nor Feast, but only a kind of scramble for sweetmeats. Or else there might be not one Master, but many, some good and kind, others bad and unkind. Or what if the Master were Himself good but thwarted by His wicked servants so that the guests were starved and not fed? In that case might not the guests fairly complain? And to make believe that the Master was perfectly good and wise (and all for the purpose of attaining for oneself calmness and tranquillity of mind) this seemed a kind of flattering of the Master and deceiving of oneself, that was scarcely worthy of a philosopher.

This peace and tranquillity of Epictetus, the more I thought of it, the less I admired it. For, in spite of his denial, it seemed to loosen all love and friendship, as well as hate. How could I "preserve my serenity of mind " while I was reading the letter of Eucharis? Ought I to say to myself, "Whatever may betide Eucharis, I at all events shall be completely happy"? That seemed to me not possible; no, nor desirable. If Eucharis sorrowed, I felt that it would be sweeter for me too to sorrow than rejoice. Then again, as to hating, Epictetus would have me not hate Pistus for being bad, but speak well of him because he was not worse. Now this perchance might tend to tranquillity, but how could it be consistent with truth? For if a man steal from me one mina, am I to thank him for not stealing two? As well, when a man gives me one mina, abuse him for not giving me two! It is the duty of a philosopher neither to speak better of a man, nor to speak worse of a man than he deserves. Besides, Epictetus seemed to err in speaking of all wickedness and crime as merely caused by erroneous opinions, for to me such faults as slander, cruelty, and baseness, seemed altogether different, and fit to be differently regarded, from such a fault as an unskilful reckoner might commit in saying that six and seven make twelve. In all these matters Epictetus seemed to me (and indeed still seems) to go astray because he had wholly set his mind upon the attainment of an object which perchance the Master of the Feast does not intend His guests to attain in this world, I mean perfect and unchangeable serenity of mind.

Being in a great perturbation with all this conflict of thoughts, and inclining now more than ever to believe that there were no gods, I determined to disobey the command of Philemon and to resort to my friend Artemidorus that I might ask counsel of him. So I went to him on the morrow, when both Philemon and Pistus chanced to be absent from the city. But he had gone on some business of law to Laodicea. However I found in the courtyard of his house a certain friend of Artemidorus, known also to me, one Metrodorus, whom I believed (but did not for certain know) to hold the same opinions as Artemidorus. I saluted him gladly; and, because the sight of a friendly face was now rare for me, I took pleasure in conversing with him (although I had not been greatly inclined towards him in former days) walking up and down in the portico and discoursing about divers matters and in the end about matters of philosophy and religion. And to be brief, not having any other counsellor to go to, I imparted to this man (although I knew but little of him) some of my troubles and perplexities, asking what would philosophy advise me to do in my sore strait?

When I had made an end of speaking, Metrodorus ceased walking and stood still, near a broken slab of pavement in the portico, where some ants had built a nest and were passing busily to and from the crevice. So here Metrodorus coming to a stand, and looking down upon the ants and then up at me, said, "If there be gods indeed, as perchance there are, I will now show you what it is likely that they think of us mortals. Certain people say that the gods being infinitely wiser and nobler, as well as stronger, than we are, must needs have a care for us, and rule our actions aright. Now, my young friend, here stand we two upon this pavement, two human beings as much (T suppose) superior to these myriads of little busy insects at our feet, as the gods are superior to us. Well, my friend, do we have a care for these ants? Surely not. Do we sorrow for their sins and compassionate their errors? I think not. Do we rule their actions aright? Do we stir a finger to help them in the storing of their food or to avert the destruction of the whole republic of them? Nay, but we take not a single thought for all their doings and misdoings, their virtues and their vices (for doubtless these creatures have their virtues and their vices even as we have) except it may be to amuse ourselves withal, or to rid ourselves of them if they become inconvenient. But you say, men are so vastly superior to ants. Not more, I take it, than the gods (if any) are superior to men. But in men, you urge, there is so much more of diversity in character and in action. Who knows? Only stoop down and look at these diminutive beings more closely. Mark what a bustle they are in; all working, but not all doing the same work; some, look you, are the scavengers, carrying out the ordure, others the marketers carrying in vast fragments of bean-shell or hastening onwards along with pieces of barleycorn in their mouths; some also, as it seems to me, standing still and ruling or instructing the rest. And who knows also but, besides their architects and masons, they have their demagogues and counsellors, cooks also and musicians, yes and philosophers too after their manner, philosophising perhaps about us two at this very moment, and very prettily demonstrating the truth of the theories of thc priest-ants, saying that 'Man being a noble Being, infinitely powerful, and wise, and good, must needs take thought for us, poor mortal ants, and rule our actions aright, and in the end conform us to Himself'— whereas, my dear Onesimus, so far is this from being the case that on the contrary"—and here he stamped heavily upon the ant- hill—"I thus with one little movement of my foot, subvert the whole ant-universe, for no other cause but my own particular pleasure.

"O my dear Onesimus, is not belief in the gods by this time almost too antiquated? If there were some new fashion of it, I might recommend you to try it; but every fashion has been tried and has become stale. Your young friend Epictetus shows a preference for one god; but to the true philosophers his theories are like the rest, quite musty and past discussing. However, if you are resolved to deal in such wares, it is good to have a choice; and the choice is large. Perhaps you prefer a legion of gods and demons? Or, aiming at the golden mean, what say you to choosing a moderate few, an oligarchy of gods? Then there are in the market for you some gods that speak, and others that are mutes; some that are still active and vigorous, such as Isis, Serapis, and Sabazius; others that are past work and cashiered, such as old Ares, Enuo, and Hephaestus; or if you are curious about rank and precedence, you can have gods of different ranks, first class, second class, third class; some with bodies, some, if you prefer it, bodiless. Last of all in the market come the atheists, who will sell you a vacuum, if you will give them many years of your life for it. But is not the best course after all to keep your time and pains and money and avoid the market altogether: neither believing nor disbelieving, but never giving a thought to the matter?"

"And does Artemidorus hold these opinions?" said I, after a pause. "I think so," he replied, "At least he never mentions the gods to me; and you best know whether he has often spoken of them to you; but from what you say yourself, I infer that he has not. However, even Artemidorus is not so consistent as I am. For he is ever fretting himself about the sun, and the moon, and the planets, and their motions, and about the tides and their courses, and sometimes he busies himself with noting the diverse superstitions of men; whereas to my mind the best kind of life is to vex oneself with none of these trifles, but to be content with myself and with all things around me, believing that they cannot be better, and so to eat and drink like Sardanapalus and to—

Sleep soundly stretched at ease—

as Homer sings of Ulysses sailing sweetly homeward. Therefore my advice to you is to take the goods which the gods (if there be gods) at this instant clearly destine for you. Make friends with Philemon. Become a rich man and obtain your freedom. Marry Prepousa and be happy with her, and, if need be, with others. And as for this Jewish purification, if, to obtain Philemon's good will and a fortune to boot, it be necessary to endure a washing, why not wash? You can be as dirty as you like when you are rich and free. However time presses, and I must go. But in fine, I would have you take as your Mentor my sepulchre, for you cannot have a better precept than that inscription." "What inscription?" said I. "You must surely have seen it," answered he; "it was the talk of all Colossae three months ago, and they cannot have quite forgotten it so soon. However, you have not been much out of doors of late. You must know then, that some months ago, when my poor wife departed this life, she ordered these words to be engraved upon her tombstone:—

THOUGH MY SOUL DWELLETH IN EARTH

MY SOUL DWELLETH IN HEAVEN.

Now I could not gainsay the poor woman's last wish, and therefore I permitted the inscription. Yet I felt, as a philosopher, that it was due to my philosophy that my epitaph should be of a very different character, consistent with my life. So considering with myself that my executors might possibly not carry out my instructions if I gave orders for an inscription over my body, in opposition to that of my lamented wife, I therefore caused these words to be cut in my lifetime, beneath my wife's inscription, over the place where my body will in due time be laid:

ENJOY THE PRESENT,

FOR WHEN THE SPIRIT HAS LEFT THE BODY,

DESCENDING TO LETHE,

IT WILL NEVER AGAIN LOOK ON THE WORLD ABOVE.

"And you have not seen it? You will find it on the Laodicean road, on the right-hand side, about three furlongs from the gate. But I must be going. Farewell, my young friend, and take my advice. As for the wise people who profess to know everything and to teach everybody, no two of them agreeing together, pay no attention to them. Snap your fingers at all their philosophies and controversies. Take in a substantial cargo of good things. Trim your sails for a pleasant voyage through life, making up your mind to be often merry, seldom serious, and never sad." So saying, he departed, and I returned to the house of Philemon.

§ 11. OF THE DEATH OF EUCHARIS AND HOW I WAS AGAIN ACCUSED OF THEFT

The words of Metrodorus himself had not much weight with me. But the image of that ant-hill came again and again into my mind, making me ask, "Is it so indeed that men are but as insects in the eyes of the immortal gods?" And as day after day went on, and still no letter nor message from Molon, my nights being sleepless and my days given up to expectation and suspense, I resolved (even as a weak mariner yielding to wind and tide) that I would suffer myself to drift with the event: if the gods led me to good then I would believe in them, but if to ill, then I would not. So for the space of ten days my mind swayed this way and that, tossed with a very tempest of increasing troubles, and still no tidings from Athens, although nearly a month had passed since Molon's former letter. At last I began to suspect that Pistus might have intercepted some letters from Eucharis; and if this suspicion had rankled long in my mind, it would have gone nigh to make me mad.

But toward the end of the month one of the slaves who was well affected to me brought me a letter bearing the familiar seal of Molon, which, when I had in all haste opened it, contained no letter from Eucharis, no, not so much as a little piece of paper, nor any words written in her hand, nor even a flower or aught else by way of token; and I shook it again, but still nothing fell out. So I sat down holding the letter in my hand, unread, foreboding the worst; and how long I sat I know not, but in those minutes (if they were minutes) there seemed to have passed over me years, yea ages of misery; and I had reckoned over my life even to the grave, and beyond the grave, into a darkness that was without end.

"Eucharis is dead"—so the letter began. The rest was very long and full of lamentations, telling how the Christians had caused her death, or else perchance her sorrow for my sake; how the followers of one Paulus had persuaded her to be baptized; how her father, though he had foreseen and noted the mischief, could not stay the progress of the disease, and how, for the rest of his life he must live alone in the world. But my eyes travelled idly over this to return again and again to the first words: "Eucharis is dead." So suddenly had she passed away that at the last she could not so much as write me one word of farewell, nor do more than bid her father send me this message, that Onesimus must always keep the token she had given him and not forget her last words.

During my torpor, while I sat in a kind of trance of misery, the letter had fallen to the ground. Stooping to pick it up I unwittingly took in its stead the letter of Epictetus, and began to read it. "A bad performer cannot sing alone, but only in a chorus: in the same way some people cannot walk the path of life alone."

Most true! And I was one of those " bad performers," one of those who "cannot walk the path of life alone." But what then? Were there not "bad performers" as well as perfect actors, and was there no place for them in the world? I was not meant nor made to walk alone. But why had the gods made me of a nature to walk in dependence on some guide, and then, after mocking me with the semblance of the gift of so precious a guide as my beloved one, snatched her away that they might see me stumble and fall? Even so they had given me Chrestus, and snatched him away. So it had been with all their gifts to me. They had given me a love of learning; but now they forbade me to learn; they had given me a thirst for truth, but had driven the truth far away; they had given me the breeding and habits of a free man, but had condemned me to be a slave. Each gift had been a curse in disguise.

Now came back into my mind the image of the ant-hill of Metrodorus, and then there rose up from the depths of darkness the lessons I had learned in the ergastulum, which I had thought I had forgotten, but now they seemed as fresh as yesterday, and more real than any other memory of my life. And now once more I inclined to believe that some bad demon or demons possessed and governed the world, exulting in our miseries and mocking at our foolish prayers and silly gratitude. Either they, or chance, ruled over the Universe. In either case, no good God; no one to love, no one to trust, no one to whom in some invisible world I could intrust my darling Eucharis and my brother Chrestus, feeling confident that all was well with them. Eucharis and Chrestus! Say rather Dust and Ashes. Then Satan filled my heart and I lifted up my voice in blasphemy and cursed the Master of the Feast who had given command that I should depart, yet would open no door for my departure, and I looked about me for means to destroy myself. But the hand of the Lord delivered me. For when I had made a noose with the thongs of my sandals, and having fixed the end to a beam was now in the act of placing it round my neck, behold, Philemon entered the chamber with a stern countenance, and two or three slaves behind him. He at once accused me of taking many precious volumes from the library with intent to steal them. I denied it, but he affirmed that it must needs be so, for they had been found yonder, pointing to a hole beneath the floor in my apartment, and, said he, "your attempt to slay yourself convicts you; for having perceived that the books have been recovered, you desire to prevent the punishment of your theft."

Perceiving that I was speechless—as indeed I was, marvelling at the iniquity of Pistus, or whoever else was my enemy—Philemon bade all the slaves depart the chamber, and then taking me by the hand, with tears in his eyes, he besought me to confess the truth, saying that he had noted, now these many days, how Satan had taken advantage of me because I had hardened my heart against the word of the Lord; and he implored me to repent and to wash away my sins. Now if I had shown him the letter of Molon describing the death of Eucharis, I might perhaps have persuaded him that I was not guilty of theft, and that other causes drove me to attempt my life. But I could not do it; for in my madness I regarded him as her murderer. Therefore I in no way endeavoured to persuade him, but merely answered with much vehemence that in truth I was not guilty, and that either Pistus or some enemy had devised this plot against me. Upon this, Philemon clapped his hands and called in the slaves, saying, in their presence, that it was useless to argue with me or to beseech me, and that I was fascinated by some woman who had ensnared my soul, adding withal some words not indeed gross nor unseemly, but very bitter to me at that season, knowing poor Eucharis to be but lately dead. So in that instant I leaped upon him and seizing the stylus which he held in his hand I attacked him with it, and assuredly, had not the slaves run together and stayed me, I should have slain him outright; but as it was, the Lord had mercy on me, and I did but wound him very slightly. But I foamed at the mouth as one mad; yea, and indeed I thank the Lord that I was verily mad at that time, and that I spoke not, but Satan spoke within me. For I seemed to see Christus as an evil demon pursuing me without ceasing, setting Philemon against me and inspiring Pistus with malice, and now last of all slaying my beloved Eucharis; wherefore I uttered such terrible execrations against the Lord Jesus, as even now fill me with horror so much as to think of; and write them down I durst not. But Philemon, stopping his ears, rushed in haste from the room, wringing his hands as if all hope were now lost, and leaving me struggling in the hands of Pistus and the rest of the household who were binding me.

That evening I heard what had been resolved concerning me. Philemon's brother, a decurion of Smyrna, who had not yet been converted to the faith was very earnest that I should be crucified according to the custom; but Philemon was constant against it, partly out of his affection for me, even then not wholly destroyed; but partly because the brethren have been from the first always unwilling that any should be punished with that death whereby the Lord Jesus was slain. So it was determined that I should be sent into the country to an ergastulum about one hundred and twenty furlongs north of Laodicea.

But here must I needs pause. For now begins my pen to describe the deepest of the depths of my most sinful life; whereof, whensoever my mind unwillingly goes back to that black darkness, I can say no more than this: "All things are possible with thee; thy blood, Lord Jesus, can cleanse from every sin."

THE END OF THE FOURTH BOOK

THE FIFTH BOOK

§ 1. HOW I ESCAPED FROM THE HOUSE OF PHILEMON

REMEMBERING the ergastulum of Nicander I determined not to endure that manner of life a second time. My.bonds had not been very firmly fastened, and the same good friend who had brought me word what was resolved concerning me, had loosened them still more. So when it was past midnight, as near as I could judge, creeping out from my chamber I found the porter sleeping, and without difficulty obtained possession of the key. I was opening the door to depart, when I suddenly bethought myself that I was going forth into the world without an obol in my purse, so that I must needs beg my food; in doing which I should surely be discovered and at once apprehended. So I went into a small chamber next to the library, wherein Philemon was wont to keep money, and I took out a purse. I extenuate nothing, I excuse nothing. Yet the truth may fairly be set down; and it is true that I purposed not to take so much, but as I opened it, I heard, or thought I heard, a noise from Philemon's study, and straightway fled as I was, having the purse in my hand; and so in great haste and trepidation, being now thief as well as fugitive, I opened the house-door and ran for my life. For an hour or more I wandered about the street avoiding the watch, and as soon as the gates were opened, I went forth on the Ephesian road.

Then for the first time taking thought whither I should go, I determined to break all ties of friendship and acquaintance and to betake myself to some large city such as Corinth or Alexandria where I might be easily unknown. Meantime I must needs hide somewhere in the upland country; for in the port of Ephesus constant watch was kept for runaway slaves, and the crier was soon likely to make my escape known in the streets of Laodicea and Hierapolis. So, leaving the Ephesian road, I made my way as best I could straight towards the mountain called Cadmus, which rises up in these parts very high and precipitous and containing many spacious caverns fit for fugitives to hide in. As I went, I found myself amid several tombs cut in the sides of the hill a little away from the road, and the sun now shining from the east lit up the inscription on the face of one of the tombs nearest to me so that I could read each word of it plainly, and it was the very inscription which Metrodorus had mentioned. "Enjoy the present, for when the spirit has left the body, descending to Lethe, it will never again look on the world above." Then began I to mock bitterly at that philosophy which could bid me, a slave and an outcast and one of the most wretched upon earth, to "enjoy the present." But at that very moment methought I heard the sound of pursuers, and putting my ear to the ground (which is all of pumice-stone in that region, very porous and hollow, and resonant almost after the manner of a drum) I plainly heard the hoofs of horses approaching. So I pressed on over rough and smooth making for the mountain. As the sun rose higher, I came to one of the spurs of Cadmus. High up in the sides of that mountain are many holes wherein eagles build their nests; and many of them were even now soaring in the air with choughs and crows screaming below them, but all so high that the eye could scarce discern them. The sounds of these birds together with the bleating of the flocks pasturing on the mountains, the scent of the flowers, the freshness of the morning air, and the beauty and the brightness of all things around, seeming to rejoice in the sunrise, constrained me in despite of myself to feel some pleasure in them, and I rested there for a while. But anon fear (and by this time hunger) forced me to hasten away.

Coming now to a building I desired to ask food; but I found that it was a temple, as could be perceived from the notice set up at the entrance to the precincts; which, even after the lapse of so many years, I am not able to forget, because at that time it seemed to me a type and pattern of all the religion and worship of the gods. For there were written up these words: " Let no man enter these sacred precincts who shall have tasted goat's flesh nor lentils for these three days, or fresh cheese for one day. But whoso shall have touched a dead body let him delay entrance for forty days. Likewise, whoever will enter, let him bring with him the highest purity, namely, a healthy mind in a healthy body, free from a guilty conscience." Then there came into my mind once again, only with much more force, the thoughts that I had had at Lebedea, namely, that the gods are helpful only to those who need no help, being happy and virtuous; or else only to the rich who can pay for many sacrifices and purifications; but as for the poor man who cannot give them fat bullocks and lambs, they have never a word to say for him; and if a poor man be a sinner and an outcast to boot, then a temple is no place for him. With such thoughts as these, sorely dejected in mind and beginning to be very weary in body as well as hungry, and the heat of the sun becoming now more than I could well endure, I betook myself to some kind of shepherd's cot which I found open and empty; and there I lay down and slept.

I was awakened by the sound of music, ill played, as though by a beginner; and for a time, betwixt asleep and awake, I lay still without moving, not knowing what had become of me, or where I was. But presently the music came to a sudden stand, and a voice cried, "May the all-powerful Syrian Goddess, Parent of all things, and the holy Sabazius and the Idsean mother strike thee dead, thou dolt whom a week's labour has not sufficed to teach thy notes. A pretty flute-player art thou. I am a ruined man with thee." With that, I started up and beheld an old man, very fat and with a smooth face and having a cast in his eye; and by his side a youth, whom he was attempting to teach to play on the flute; but neither could the pupil learn, nor had the teacher skill to teach. I soon perceived from his attire and language, as well as from the ass bearing the image of the goddess, and the company of dancing girls who were with him, that he was one of the begging priests of Cybele; and it seemed that his flute-player had deserted him so that he could gain no money from the people by his sacred dances, for want of the music. After watching them for a short time (unknown to them, for the corner wherein I had been lying was very dark) I lost patience to see how ill the old priest taught and the youth learned; and coming forward I took the flute from the hands of the youth and showed him how he was to use it. At first the old man stood speechless with astonishment at the suddenness of my coming in upon them; but when he perceived that I had some skill in music, he asked whether I could make shift to play for him. I told him that I knew not that kind of music, and would have gone forth from the cot without more words; but he stayed me and begged me to give some proof of my skill; saying I must at least eat and drink with him and his company, for the village people had given them two kids and a cask of wine. So I was overpersuaded by my hunger, and after we had eaten our fill, he gave me to drink of unmixed wine, because, said he, there was no water nigh; and my thirst con~ strained me to drink. Then he began again to ply me with importunities to go with him at least as far as Pergamus, adding that if I wished to escape notice (and here he looked at me as if he knew that I had some secret) I could take no better course than this, but if I left him, who knew but questions might be asked, and I might be noticed more than I desired? And hereon, when he saw me wavering, and inflamed with wine, he put the flute once more into my hands, and called out that the dance should begin; and thus saying he led the ass into the midst of the chamber, bearing the image of the goddess which was covered with a silver veil. Then I began to play and the women to dance, and the priest applauded and cried that the music should go faster. At first I played against my will and my heart was not in it; but as I looked upon the women dancing in their many-coloured tunics with their eyebrows darkened, and their Phrygian caps on their heads, and their saffron shawls streaming in the air, all dancing, at first slowly and then more quickly round the image, by degrees it was given to Satan to have power over me because I had not resisted him. So I began to take a pleasure in it, and I said, Surely now is the time to cast aside all virtue and to forget the name of goodness and to begin a new life, wallowing in all sin, And even as Satan thus moved me, I began to play the music more furiously, as if possessed by some demon, and the women, after their manner, brandishing their swords and battle-axes, began to leap more furiously to the sound of cymbal and tambourine, and they bared their arms and shoulders scourging themselves with whips wrought of pieces of bone till the blood flowed out; and because it flowed not fast enough, they scourged themselves harder, yea, and in their leaping they bit their own flesh and screamed like wild beasts; and then the old priest stopped the music and clapping me on the shoulder bade me pledge him in another cup of wine, for I must needs go with him to Pergamus and be his flute-player; and I like a dumb beast could not say No, but drank of his wine and so consented.

§ 2. OF MY LIFE AT PERGAMUS

Let it be permitted me to pass over the story of my wanderings until I came to Pergamus. Not that I would conceal or gloss over any of the sins I committed at this time. Yet although thou, Lord, hast forgiven all things, methinks I could not set down those deeds of darkness, without seeming to pass through a second course of sin. Suffice it that in all the acts of my companions, in all their thieving and lying, their blasphemings, revellings and impurities, I was not behind any, the vilest of the vile. But it pleased the Lord, after three months of thus wallowing in the mire, to hold out the hand to me, though it were but for a season; and it was after this manner. When we came to Pergamus, going on a certain day to visit a priest of Asclepius I chanced to speak of the children that were daily exposed upon the Temple steps, and I showed him (but not as from myself) the token of my brother Chrestus, saying that it had been given to me by one of my acquaintance to whom it had belonged, who was now dead. When the priest read the inscription TRUST, he started and changed colour, and very earnestly questioned me whether my acquaintance had ever spoken to me touching a brother exposed at the. same time, and wearing a token with another inscription, mentioning at the same time the words of it. I LOVE THEE. Then it was my turn to start, and I confessed that I had heard mention of it, but that this brother also was long since dead. "Truly then," said the priest, "I sorrow greatly for their poor mother's sake, who came to the Temple not more than six or seven months ago, to make inquiry concerning two children who had been exposed in the first year of the emperor Claudius, twins, and wearing two such tokens as you have described." So then, comparing the date, as well as the other circumstances, I knew that the children could be no other than myself and my brother Chrestus.

Now all my dissimulation was swallowed up in the eagerness of my desires, and I gave the priest no peace, questioning him again and again about the lady of whom he spoke; insomuch that I doubt not he suspected the truth. But all my questioning was vain; for he said that the lady would tell neither him nor his fellow-priests whence she came nor whither she was going; but she had declared in parting that she should come again to the Temple before long, if she lived. She was of tall stature, with brown hair and grey eyes, of fair complexion and somewhat pale, with a slight scar on the left cheek, and of a sad expression, and she spoke Greek with the Attic accent;. moreover she informed the priests that she had sought in vain for her children for many years. Straightway from his words I conceived the image of one who could not have been guilty of any cruel or unnatural deed, and I became assured in my mind that some foul play or irresistible constraint, but not her own will, must have separated us from our mother. And a new feeling possessed me that, if I could find her, I might still have some one who would love me. But when I seemed to see her coming again to the Temple, and myself meeting her and telling her all my story, and the story of Chrestus, and showing her my token, and falling on her neck and embracing my mother, and how she also would embrace me as a SOD, then it came into my mind, "And how could such a mother own such a son as Onesimus is now"?"

In that moment, thou, Lord, didst show me unto myself that I might hate myself; and on that same day I left the priest of Cybele and cast off my old companions, and having found a lodging with one who prepared skins for the covering of books, I determined to earn my living if possible as a transcriber. For the space of three or four months I lived after this manner, forswearing my former dissolute life and letting no day pass but I visited the Temple; for the sun never rose but I said to myself 'this day perchance she may come'; and I ruled all my life by the thought of her, and the hope of her, if perchance I might yet find one that would love me. But the Lord had ordained otherwise. For on a certain day (about the beginning of the fifth month after I had first come to Pergamus) taking my work to the shop of a bookseller with whom I had dealings, I found there two or three men of learning standing together conversing of books and parchments and the like; and taking up a parchment, one said to a companion that he had seen even such a book as this, so transcribed and adorned, in the library of Philemon of Colossae. Then a terror fell upon me lest I should be discovered, and without so much as waiting to be paid for my labour, I made shift to leave the shop, upon some slight pretext, and returning to my lodging for a few minutes I went forth thence to the city gates, and ceased not travelling till I came to Ephesus, where I went on board a ship bound for the city of Corinth.

§ 3. HOW I CAME TO CORINTH AND SAW THE TOMB OF EUCHARIS

At Corinth I found no man to employ me as a transcriber. But because of the number of rich people in that city (some living there but many more resorting thither for pleasure) and many spending their whole lives in continual revelling, there was a great demand for such buffoons, and mimes, and inferior actors, as attend at great men's feasts to make them merry; and to this occupation I was now forced to stoop. And so being cut off from all hope of finding my mother, I fell again into my old ways of reprobate living. Besides the baseness of my mode of life, I was weighed down by a perpetual slavish dread. Whithersoever I went, or whatever company I frequented, I was never secure, fearing always lest some one should take me by the throat and claim me as Philemon's slave, a thief, and a would-be murderer; and whenever I saw a slave's body hanging on the cross, with the crows fluttering round it, or a gang of branded wretches with shaven heads dragged in manacles through the streets, at such a time I would say, "Sooner or later this will be thy fate, Onesimus." This took all the heart and spirit out of my resolve to lead a virtuous life. Sometimes I determined at all hazards to go back to Pergamus; for it made my heart sick to think of her who had been seeking me there many years, perhaps even at that instant standing on those steps of the Temple which I had been wont day by day to frequent in the hope of seeing her. But at first I durst not, and after some days when I had at last determined and made ready to depart, I remembered how I had told the priest of Asclepius that both Chrestus and Onesimus were dead; which he belike had by this time conveyed to my mother, so that she would now give over seeking in despair, and come to Pergamus no more. The thought of her new sorrow was heavier than I could bear, and thus that image of her which had been but of late so precious and helpful, became unto me now so full of sadness that I sought to flee from it in revellings and drunkenness.

The end of all was that the hand which seemed to have raised me for a breathing-space out of the deep gulf of destruction now plunged me down again; and I fell once more to a life not worse perhaps, but assuredly not much better, than that which I had led with the priest of Cybele. Yea, such a wretch was I now become that I began to be content with wretchedness, preferring darkness and fearing any glimpse of light lest it should make my darkness more visible; insomuch that once or twice at this season, as I remember, I took off the little tokens from my neck, the gifts of Eucharis and Chrestus, and thought to cast them away, because when I felt them upon my breast they troubled me at nights, suggesting visions of the past and hopes not possible. But, base and vile though I was, my courage failed me, and I could not do it.

One day, after late revelling, when thoughts like these had been disquieting my soul, I found myself wandering through the streets near the quays where the ferry takes passengers across to Peirseus; and scarce knowing what I did I stepped with the rest into the boat, and presently I had disembarked and was walking up toward the city of Athens, yet all the while cursing my folly in coming whither I should not have come. For I feared lest I might be recognised, and still more lest I should rouse up memories that were best forgotten. Yet on I went, for all my self-reproaches, as if I were a lifeless engine impelled by some power outside me, till I came to a little garden hard by the wall, wherein was a tomb of Charidemus, a brother of Eucharis, who had died these many years; and entering in I read the words over the grave, which oftentimes I had read with my beloved by my side:

GOLDEN YOUTH, READ HERE THINE END:
I SPRANG FROM DUST, TO DUST DESCEND.

Eucharis had always been wont to find fault with this inscription as being too sad, and she would protest that, when she died, she would have somewhat more hopeful inscribed upon her tomb. This saying of hers coming to my memory reminded me of that which in my lethargy had all this while escaped me, that her tomb also would in all likelihood be in this same garden; and as I turned round my eye fell at once on a new-made sepulchre and on it this inscription:

TWENTY YEARS OF FLEETING BREATH
THEN EUCHARIS WENT DOWN TO DEATH
WHOM I FONDLY CALLED MY OWN,
NOT KNOWING SHE WAS BUT A LOAN
LENT BY DEATH, WHO FROM BELOW
SENDS SHORT DELIGHTS TO MAKE LONG WOE.
TOO SHORT A LOAN, POOR TWENTY YEARS,
FOR SUCH VAST INTEREST OF TEARS
WHICH HE MUST WEEP, WHO NOW REMAINS
TO FEEL A LONELY FATHER'S PAINS.
DEAR DREAM, SWEET BUBBLE, PAINTED AIR,
BREAK, LEAVE POOR MOLON TO DESPAIR.

When I read these words I could not but feel some touch of pity for the poor old man mourning alone in his chamber where we three had been wont to sit so happily together; and looking on the wreaths and garlands that were on the sepulchre and perceiving that they were all very old and faded, I remembered that Eucharis was born as on that very day, and I marvelled that the old man had not come forth to do honour to the tomb and to deck it with fresh flowers, and methought some strong cause must have hindered him; for it was now nigh upon sun-down. So though I durst not have looked him in the face, I arose and went into the city again, even to the street where he lived, in case I might see him coming forth from his door; and up and down I walked till sunset, my head muffled in my cloak, and all that time I saw him not. Nor was I like to see him. For when I inquired of one that came forth from a neighbouring house whether Molon yet lived in that street, he looked on me as if pitying me for my ignorance and said that the old man had died but two days ago and was to be buried on the morrow.

Now I would fain have persuaded myself that it was well with me, because not a single friend remained to reproach me, nor any one whose love or good opinion might deter me from leading a life according to my own desires, or the drift of fortune: yet at night when I lay down in Corinth, the thought of Eucharis would force its way into my soul, and when I shut my eyes I could see nothing and think of nothing but the inscription on her tomb; and at the last the memory of my beloved one prevailed, and tears fell from my eyes for the first time since I had read her last farewell. But on the morrow all was forgotten. I went forth to my task of buffoonery as usual; and the day and the night passed according to custom, in jesting, and drinking, and revelling, and sin.

What shall I say unto thee, Lord, concerning these things? Shall I say, Blessed be Thou, Lord, who didst suffer Thy servant to sin much, that he might be forgiven much, and that he might love much? Nay, but Thou art a righteous Lord and hatest unrighteousness. Lord, this only can I say, Thou knowest all, and yet Thou hast forgiven.

§ 4. HOW I SAW THE HOLY APOSTLE PAULUS, BUT KNEW HIM NOT

Though I had at this time no lack of employment, yet I began to be in debt as well as in want. For by continual revelling and gaming and drinking, I had spent all the money that I had brought with me from Pergamus, I mean the money of Philemon. Therefore about this time (it was the ninth year of the Emperor Nero) certain of my companions, who were in the same case as myself, persuaded .me to accompany them to Rome, where they would obtain no less employment, they said, and better pay. At any other time I should have been not a little moved, coming thus for the first time to the chief city of the world; but such a lethargy had fallen on me that I took little or no note of all the greatness and splendour of the place, save only that I well remember the day when I first saw the Emperor presiding at the games in the Circus Maximus. For on that day seeing one that was a matricide, and a murderer, and an abuser of nature, thus enthroned in the chief seat of empire, and worshipped as God with the applause of such a concourse as would have gone nigh to make up a great city, and beholding also what vile sights were there exhibited—things detestable and not to be mentioned, with which the deaths of thousands of gladiators cannot be compared for horror—then it was borne in upon my mind that there need be no more dispute as to whether Good or Evil reigned over the world; for here before mine eyes was Evil visibly reigning, and called God by all. Wherefore, though I went to no greater excesses than before at Corinth, yet was I hardened and confirmed in evil, drowning my shame in wine and striving to banish all distinction between evil and good.

Yet even at Rome there were seasons when, in my heart of hearts, I was weary of my sinful and desolate condition, and longed for the touch of a friend's hand; and at times I yearned to be a fool and to believe in something, cursing the wranglings and disputations of the philosophers who had taken from me all faith in the gods, so that I could no longer put trust in anything; yea, at such moments I would fain have been a peasant in the poorest village of Asia (such a one as poor old Hermas or lame Xanthias whom I remembered in my childhood), worshipping Zeus, or Pan, or aught else, so that I might only be not myself. Life wearied me, yet I feared death, yea, I feared even sleep; for the darkness was full of terrors, and my couch brought me no rest, but only horrible phantasms of dread abysses, and visions of falling down for ever, and of hands stretched out to stay me and then drawn back, and of sad faces veiled or turned away. The daylight which chased away the terrors of sleep, brought ever back with it shame and remorse. Thus all things, both by night and by day, seemed set in array against me. But indeed (albeit I knew it not) my miseries were of the Lord; for by these means, didst thou, Judge that judgest rightly, even by these righteous torments and just retributions, prepare me to be delivered from unrighteousness and to be made free in the Lord Jesus.

After I had been in Rome a few weeks, I was admitted into a club or collegium of actors; where I made acquaintance with the actor Aliturius, a Jew by birth, one that was in great favour with Poppaea who had that same year been married to the Emperor. Now the lady Poppaea, like many others of rank and quality at that time, was given to the observance of the Jewish law; at least so far as concerned Sabbaths and abstinence from meats and the use of certain purifications; and she had with her a certain Ishmael, who had been high priest among the Jews. Hence it came to pass that, by help of Aliturius and through favour of Poppaea, I was admitted to perform and recite at several feasts and drinking parties in the palace, and sometimes even in the presence of the Emperor himself, but more especially before the officers of the Praetorian guard.

One evening, as I came from a feast where I had been making mirth for some of the officers, returning through that part of the palace which looks towards the Circus Maximus, there passed by me a guard of soldiers having a prisoner in chains, whom they led into an adjoining chamber, and I understood from them that the man was to lie there for that night, that he might be ready on the morrow; when the Emperor himself proposed to hear his cause in the temple of Apollo, which was near at hand. "And who," said I, "is this prisoner whom the divine Emperor thus deigns to honour?" The man, they said, was one of the Christian superstition. Now at that time, being in favour with Poppaea and the Jew Aliturius, and it being my occupation to be a jester for the officers and soldiers, I was wont to make the Christians matter for jest and scoffing, not sparing sometimes (may the Lord forgive me) to assail even the Crucified One in my jesting. So being inflamed with wine, I thrust myself unbidden into the chamber, telling the guard that we would examine the prisoner at once, "Wherefore," said I, "be ye *judices* or jury, and I, for the nonce, will be the divine Emperor himself."

Having therefore made for myself a kind of tribunal, I sat down on it, taking a centurion to be my assessor, and the rest of the soldiers, joining in the jest, sat down upon the floor; and when I bade the soldiers " produce the prisoner," he sat up, but not so that I could see his face clearly, the lamp being behind him. Then I accosted the man in derision, saying that from his aspect I discerned him to be Heraclitus the crying philosopher, and I asked him whether he also, like Heraclitus, taught that "men are mortal gods, and gods immortal men." To this he replied, as if willing to enter into the jest, that he was a teacher of joy and not of sorrow, but that indeed he taught that God and men were at one. After this, mocking at his baldness, I asked him whether he were Pythagoras risen from the dead, or whether he could teach us to be something more than men and to be in harmony with the Universe. He laughed gently at this, replying that, though indeed he could teach these things, yet was he no philosopher but rather a soldier; and Saying this, he raised his head and looked at me very intently as if he were weak of sight; and at this moment the light of the lamp, just then falling on his face, perplexed me, because I felt sure that I had seen this man before; but where or when I could not tell. However, recovering myself, I asked him in what legion he had served and under what Imperator, and he replied, still preserving a calm temper and smiling, that he served in the Legio Victrix and under the auspices of the Imperator Soter, or Salvator. Hereat the soldiers applauded, and I perceived that I was being beaten on my own ground. So thinking to catch the old man by some slip, or to drive him into an inability to answer, I asked him what were his weapons. But he replied that he used the shield of faith, and the breastplate of righteousness, and the belt of truthfulness, and the sword of the word of God; and, said he, I fight the good fight of righteousness against unrighteousness, wherein the victory must needs be in the end upon my side, as your own hearts also testify; for which cause is our legion rightly called Victrix. He added some words which I cannot now recall, about the nobleness of such a battle, and the glory of it, which moved even the drowsy soldiers; insomuch that they said with one consent that the man had reason on his side and that they wished him well. "Then," said I, making one last adventure to have the laugh on my side, "where then is thy Imperator that he does not bear witness unto thee?" At once he replied, "He will bear witness for me, and he is with me at this instant"; and these words he uttered with such a force of confidence and with a look so fixed and steady, gazing methought on some one whom he discerned behind me, that I leaped up and looked over my shoulder, trembling and quaking lest there were some phantom in the room. The soldiers also were, for the moment, somewhat moved, howbeit less than I was; and thinking perchance to shift the shame of their fear from themselves, they called out that I was not worthy to sit on a tribunal, nor to represent the divine Emperor. So, to put the best face I could upon my discomfiture, I concluded briefly with a mock-oration, saying that the prisoner appeared to be a valiant soldier, and that he seemed worthy to be allowed the privilege of abstaining from swine's flesh, and of worshipping an ass's head, if it so pleased him, and with that, I proclaimed the meeting dissolved.

§ 5. HOW I LEARNED THAT PAULUS WAS THE PROPHET THAT I HAD SEEN IN MY CHILDHOOD, THE SAME THAT HAD CURED LAME XANTHIAS

As I was going forth from the chamber with the rest, he that was guarding the prisoner stayed me, questioning me concerning the Emperor's health, and asking me whether it was likely that the Emperor would hear his case in person to-morrow. I said that it was not unlikely; for though he had not been in good health, yet now that he was wedded to Poppaea, she made him give heed to all Jewish matters. "Yea but," said the guard, "this fellow is no Jew, such as the other Jews, but of a different faction, which they call seditious; and the rest of his people hate him." "I understand that," said I, "but whether the Jews love him or hate him, in either case Poppaea will be for him or against him; and of that he is like to have experience to-morrow." Then the soldier began to explain to me the nature of this sect; but I interrupted him, saying that I knew everything concerning them, "having learned their customs at Antioch"; and whereas I was always wont to preserve silence about my life in Asia and about everything and every one that had to do therewith, now on the other hand, something I know not what, made me add the words "and at Colossae;" and as soon as I had said it I repented of it and hastened to go forth from the chamber. But the prisoner rose up from his couch and, catching me by the cloak, asked whether I had been lately at Colossae and whether I knew one Philemon, who was a citizen of that place. I said "no; " and he sat down with a sigh, keeping his eyes fixed upon me; and then, as I was going forth, the expression of his features came back to my mind on a sudden and I remembered the hook-nosed prophet who had healed lame Xanthias in years gone by at Lystra, and I could not forbear asking him whether he had ever been in the region of Pamphylia; and he answered "yes," and when I mentioned Lystra, he said he knew that city and had been there. Then I asked in what year, and he answered in the fourth year, or thereabouts, of the Emperor Claudius. So perceiving that the times agreed, I questioned him further whether he had healed a sick man there, and to make sure, I said one sick of the palsy; but he replied " No, but a lame man, that had been lame many years," and with that he leaned forward to me as if still desirous to answer and ask further questions.

But at this point the soldier, he I mean to whom the prisoner was chained (for the rest were gone forth) having now laid himself down upon the pallet to sleep, smote the prisoner upon the face with the palm of his hand, saying that it was bad enough that he should lose his seat for the games in the Circus Maximus to-morrow, where the people were even now gathering (and indeed we could hear the noise and shouting of the multitude outside) and that he would not further be cheated of his slumbers by a miserly Jew, who refused to give a single denarius to the soldier that was at the pains of guarding him. Hereat the prisoner began with a cheerful countenance to compose himself to lie down by the side of his keeper, only saying that his friends had been very willing to fee the keeper; but the guard having been that day changed, and he himself being (as it chanced) without money, it was not possible for him to give any fee at that time. But the soldier, nothing moved, struck him twice, yet harder than before, with his fist, bidding him hold his peace and saying, with a curse, that excuses were not denarii.

I know not whether it was the patience and constancy of the prisoner that moved me; or because his presence seemed to carry back my mind to the days of my childhood, reminding me of the pleasant fields and flocks round Lystra, and my brother Chrestus and my old nurse Trophime, and the shepherd Hermas; but, be the cause what it may, certain it is that I was drawn to the man as if bewitched or fascinated, and taking out such money as I had (which was but very little) I gave it to the soldier. At the same time I asked the prisoner whether he had made any attempt to gain the intercession of Titus Annaeus Seneca, a great philosopher in those days and the former tutor of the Emperor. "Nay, but the old bookworm has no power in these days with our Emperor," said the soldier taking my money, "and could no more rein him in now than a butterfly could rein in the dragons of Hecate; besides, if he could, think you that a man of quality, such as the Emperor's tutor, would regard such scum of the earth as these Christian wretches? However, whatever he be is no business of mine, and money should have money's worth; so I give you five minutes with the prisoner; but, mark me, no more."

I felt as one caught in a trap. Twice had I endeavoured to depart from the chamber because I desired to avoid speech with this stranger, who knew Colossae and my master Philemon; and now of my own motion I had so wrought that I must needs have speech with him. So I sat down, and asked the prisoner his name. "My name was once Saul," he answered, "but I am now called Paulus and I was born in Tarsus." Hereat I stood up to go at once, but my limbs refused to obey me and I went not, but stood where I was, gaping and staring like one mad; for I seemed to see before me, next to Christus, the bitterest foe of my life; because this Paulus had caused Philemon to be my enemy and by his superstitions had slain my beloved Eucharis. Yet on the other hand it was borne in upon me that here was one that had seen Christus risen from the dead, and I remembered as if it were but fresh in mine ears, his invocation over me in the days of my childhood, "The Lord be unto thee as a Father"; and I felt that however I might endeavour, it was not possible for me to hate this man, nor easy to resist the spirit that was in him, for I was in his presence as one under a spell. So, though my fears bade me depart, the hand of the Lord constrained me to remain. While I thus stood stammering, uttering something perchance but meaning nothing, Paulus interrupted me, taking me by the hand and saying, "I perceive that there is to be more discourse between us; wherefore I will only say this, that this night my prayers shall ascend to the Father of our Lord Jesus Christ in thy behalf. For the Lord hath need of thee, and verily thou shalt be saved and redeemed from all thy sins. To-morrow, as thou hast heard, I stand before the Emperor; but if (as I doubt not) I receive deliverance from the mouth of the lion, I am to discourse at sun-down concerning the mercies of the Lord Jesus in the house of Tryphsena and Tryphosa, hard by the Capenian gate. Prithee, my benefactor, bestow on me yet another benefit, and promise that thou wilt be there." " No " was in my heart, but " yes " came from my lips before I knew that I had framed an answer, and I left the chamber as one in a trance.

§ 6. HOW I WAS LED INTO THE NET OF THE GOSPEL

As soon as I was come forth from the presence of Paulus I resolved one thing for certain, that, go whither I might to-morrow, I would by no means go to the house of Tryphsena; for, in spite of all my former disbelief in witchcraft, I began to believe that verily some kind of fascination was being used against me to make me a Christian against my will. For a long time I dared not lie down to rest, but sat reasoning with myself and endeavouring to call to mind the arguments of Artemidorus against the Christians; yet ever and anon the face of Paulus would appear before mine eyes, and I seemed to hear him saying that the gods are immortal men, and it came into my mind that, if indeed there were but such a god as my beloved Eucharis or Chrestus, only immortal instead of mortal, how willingly would I trust in him, how gladly face all peril and endure all hardship for his sake I And then I bethought myself of the saying of Paulus about his leader Christus whom he mentioned as still living and bearing witness to him, and how he seemed to see Christus behind me; and with that I leaped up crying for help and screaming like one distraught; and so timorous was I that I lit a second lamp and sat down again resolving not to sleep that night at all. But presently sleep, whether I would or not, fell upon my eyelids, and a confused mixture of many visions passed before me, Paulus and Pythagoras and Heraclitus, all beckoning to me, and speaking about an "immortal man" and a "mortal god"; and then such a chaos of words and sights that I grew dizzy, till at last I saw a small white cloud which grew larger and opened itself and inclosed all the former chaos, and on it was written "Chrestus"; but as I approached, it was not "Chrestus" but "Christus," and then "Chrestus" again, till the cloud burst with a loud sound as of thunder and disclosed my brother, bright and smiling as in old days, and on his breast he bore the token I LOVE THEE and he stretched out his arms to me. But when I ran to embrace him, behold, on his hands and feet the marks of grievous wounds, and the expression of his countenance was the same and yet not the same; so that I stood and drew back, and, though he beckoned to me, I fled. But he pursued after me and I still fled from him, and all around there were voices and faces of good and evil, the good helping my pursuer, the bad helping me; but, as he gained fast upon me, the priest of Cybele smote the ground, and, behold, a great yawning chasm, wherein was a multitude of skeletons with open arms waiting for me, and I leaped into the chasm, and the arms of the skeletons were clasping me round; when suddenly I awoke and found myself upon the ground, shrieking and struggling and my limbs all shivering and bathed in sweat; and by this time the night was well nigh past, and the first light of dawn was to be seen in the east.

So great was my terror that my first resolve was to depart at once from Rome. But then I bethought myself that, whithersoever I might travel, I could not avoid bad dreams; and, if I desired to avoid Paulus, no place was so convenient for me as the most populous of all cities. So I concluded to remain where I was, but to spend that day in Tusculum; whither I accordingly set out a little before noon. But I had not gone a few paces from the door of my lodging, before the slaves of a certain rich Octavius, one of my patrons, came suddenly behind me and, catching fast both my arms, bade me return with them, saying their master entertained company that day unexpectedly, and much desired my presence to make them merry. When I would have excused myself, they replied that they were under constraint to take no refusal; for Octavius had threatened them with a whipping if by fair means or foul they brought me not. Moreover, as they were to dine very early, I must come with them at once, though it was but the seventh hour, and thus they would be sure of me.

So I went with them under a kind of friendly violence and entertained the company after my power. But what I said and did I know not, save only that at the beginning of the entertainment I overheard one of the guests say to his neighbour that Tychicus (by which name I was known in those days) was that day in admirable fooling; and his neighbour replied that truly Tychicus would be the most wittily obscene buffoon in the whole of the city, but for a certain unevenness in his jesting, as if he were possessed with two spirits, a lewd spirit and a surly spirit, "for," said he, "after keeping all the table in a roar of mirth for two or three hours, if you watch the fellow for a minute or so when he thinks none are looking at him, he falls into a moroseness, or else a kind of vacancy, as if he were a soothsayer and saw visions." When I heard this, I drank even more recklessly than my wont, saying to myself that I would drive out that spirit of vision-seeing and give myself wholly to the evil spirit. And noting that it was near sun-down, so that I was free from the snares of the enchanter Paulus, I grew more and more furious in my revelry, exceeding all bounds in grossness and blasphemy so that the guests applauded amain and covered my head with crowns of roses.

When I was at last dismissed, the guests now retiring to prepare for a second banquet, it was full two hours after sunset. Now the house of Octavius was on the Coelian hill (where now stands the Colosseum) so that I was in no way constrained to go near the Capenian gate in order to return to my lodging. But the Lord constrained me and it was as if my feet took me thither against my will. Again and again did I repeat to myself, "Fool, why goest thou into the snare with thine eyes open?" But I replied, "What harm in merely going through the street, since it is certain that I shall not enter the house?" Yet, as I drew near to the street, I perceived the folly of going whither I desired not to go, and I drew back and turned aside going towards the Praetorium. when of a sudden a fear fell upon me, and I felt a hand laid on my shoulder from behind, and I trembled from head to foot hearing the voice of Paulus: "My son, thou art not in the right way." Fain would I have made some excuse, or have fled at once without excuse; but neither could my tongue avail for words, nor my feet for flight. So I went on with Paulus even as a captive, and he took me by the hand and led me unresisting into a house where was a large congregation of the Christians already assembled and expecting his presence; through the midst of whom I walked, crowned as I was with roses, and dripping with unguents and staggering in my gait, so that all gazed at me with wonder and some perchance in anger. However they all made way reverently for Paulus, and for me with Paulus, he still holding me by the hand. Then Paulus ascended a bema or platform and began to speak to the people. At first I sat still, as one hearing and yet not hearing, content to listen but not knowing why I listened; like a brute beast not capable of understanding. By degrees my senses returned, and his words seemed to come nearer and nearer to me till they penetrated my very soul; but I cannot recollect them so as to set them down, except a few of the last sentences, and these not exactly.

When I came to myself, he was speaking of the mercies of the Lord, describing how he himself had persecuted the faith yet had obtained mercy. Who therefore, said he, could not be pardoned, since he had been counted worthy of pardon? Who was so vile and sinful that must needs say 'I am not worthy to draw nigh unto the Lord' since he, Paulus, the sinner and persecutor, had been embraced by the arms of his mercy?" Therefore, say not within yourselves 'What new sacrifice shall I bring"?' For the Lord Jesus Himself is your sacrifice; neither say in your hearts

'With what new purification shall I draw nigh unto him?' for the blood of the Lord Jesus is your purification; neither say 'What new deeds must I do?' or 'What new life must I lead?' for the Lord himself hath prepared thy deeds that thou shalt do; and as for thy life, it is no longer thine own; for behold thou art dead; and the life that thou shalt hereafter live, is the life that Christ shall live in thee. Come therefore unto thy Lord and trust in him.

"Stumble not, ye Jews, at the cross, neither say within yourselves, 'The Crucified cannot be the Christ; he that died the death of a slave cannot be our King.' Nay, but I say unto you, because of the cross, and not in spite of the cross, the Lord Jesus is the Christ; and because he made himself to be the servant of all, therefore is he now exalted to be King over all. Also, ye Gentiles, stumble not at the sepulchre of Christ, saying, 'It is not possible that one that is dead should rise again'; for verily these eyes have seen him, and your own consciences bear witness for me that I speak not as one deceiving you, but that I verily saw the Lord Jesus. And as many of you as believe, have, as a testimony, the presence of his Spirit in your hearts; and as many as shall believe shall have that same Spirit dwelling among you, as earnest of the glory that is to come, bringing with it love towards God and good-will towards all men. Come therefore unto the Lord Jesus, and behold, the grave hath no power to make a gulf between you and him. Say not 'He is in the heaven far above us,' nor 'He is in Hades far beneath us'; for I declare unto you that neither heaven, nor earth, nor that which is beneath the earth, can part you from him; fear not the gods nor the Gentiles, nor the reproach of men; fear not the thrones nor powers of this world; if Christ be for us who shall be against us? Fear ye not therefore the fears of this world; for behold, for them that are called of Christ, all things work together for good; for I am persuaded that neither death nor life, nor angels nor principalities, nor things present nor things to come, nor height nor depth, nor any other creature shall be able to separate us from the love of God which is in Christ Jesus our Lord."

Now at first as I came to myself, and heard the voice of the Apostle discoursing of Jesus and of the life in Him, and of the joy and peace of it, being made conscious of my inward darkness and of the unattainable Light, I felt the burden of my miseries too great for me to bear. A shape of evil seemed to sit pressing down my soul, stifling her groanings and exulting over her unavailing struggles; bidding me stop my ears against the voice lest it should disquiet my heart in vain, because having taken side with evil and having wilfully blasphemed, I was now his lawful slave, and regrets were unavailing; and because I would not obey him, methought he was encompassing me all around with thick walls of an impenetrable dungeon, wherein I lay as in a sepulchre beneath the earth, fast bound, not able either to see or to hear. But suddenly, as if a great way off, I seemed to perceive a sound, though very faint, that "if Christ were for us none would be against us," and with that, a shaking of the walls of my dungeon; and after that, came the other words of the Apostle each after each, battering at my prison, so that wall after wall fell with a great crashing noise; and last of all there came that thunderous proclamation roaring around mine ears, that neither things present nor things to come, nor height nor depth nor any other creature should separate us from the love of God which is in Christ Jesus our Lord; and heareat my whole dungeon straightway parted, like a curtain rent asunder, and brightness burst in upon me as a flood, and the Lord Jesus revealed Himself unto me as the Light and Life of men.

THE END OF THE FIFTH BOOK

THE SIXTH BOOK

§ 1. OF THE TEACHING OF PAULUS

WHO shall describe the marvels of the change when from the sea of sin a human soul is caught up into the life above, and lifted into the blessed brotherhood of the saints of God? No fears, no doubts, no remorse; but only a certain purifying fire of repentance within me, stimulating me to a life of virtue and to the helping of others, even as I had myself been helped. In addition to the delight of continual communion with my beloved teacher Paulus, my spirit was also refreshed by all the brethren of the church. For in them I found such a joy of fellowship as I had never before known, not like a common collegium where men meet merely to eat and drink and to be merry and to pay for the funeral of some deceased companion, and to give help to those of the collegium who may chance to be in need; but the Christian collegium, if I may so call it, was far above all these, being bound together with a tie not to be loosened by death and so strong and passionate as I had never experienced nor even conceived, a veritable enthusiasm and insatiate desire for well-doing.

Marvellously great therefore was the change for one who had been but yesterday friendless, an outcast, despised of all men, now to find himself encompassed round with friends or rather brothers and bathed as it were in a flood of friendship. But the greatest help of all was the Lord Jesus himself, present in my heart by day and night, a constant fountain of inexpressible peace. Now also I heard once more and learned these words of the Lord which had first drawn my soul towards him at Antioch; and other words I learned beside these, full of grace and healing. Many a time in Colossae, and sometimes even in Pergamus and Corinth during the days of my darkness, I had caught myself unwittingly repeating to myself that most precious exhortation of the Lord Jesus to the weary and heavy laden, that they should come unto him and he would give them rest; but then I had repeated these words as an unbeliever or as a doubter, striving to harden myself in unbelief; now I repeated them with understanding, knowing them by experience to be true, and acknowledging that in him alone was rest. Notwithstanding the Spirit of the Lord, and the manifestations of the Spirit, came not unto me from the learning of the sayings of Jesus, but from the preaching of Paulus, who first revealed to me the power of the Lord unto salvation.

At this time I told Paulus the whole story of my life, and although I supposed that matters of love were scarcely fit for his hearing (as Epictetus had spoken of them slightingly, as beneath the attention of a philosopher) yet I concealed not either my former love for Eucharis or the bitterness of my sorrow for her death. He was moved by it more than I had thought possible, nor did he rebuke me as I had expected. Hereon I described to him the doctrine of Epictetus, who forbade me to sorrow for her or for anything, or any person, because it was necessary to preserve serenity of mind. But Paulus shook his head, and said that it was not right that we should in this way seek to escape from the troubles of life by separating ourselves from others; but that we ought to rejoice with them that rejoice and sorrow with them that sorrow, and that we should fulfil the law of Christ by bearing one another's burdens. Yet he bade me think of Eucharis as of one not dead but sleeping, and not in the hand of Death but in the hand of the Lord, "for " said he, "whether we live, or die, we are the Lord's."

Again, when I spoke to him of my former doubts concerning the ruling of the world, whether it were for good or ill, he said that men had been placed in the world as if in twilight, to seek and grope after God; but that now the day had dawned in the manifestation of the Lord Jesus and in his rising again from the dead; " for " said he " this, and nothing else, is the salvation of the world, resolving all doubts and showing forth the triumph of good over evil and of life over death." And in all his doctrine he made mention of the Resurrection of the Lord Jesus as being the foundation of the whole Gospel and the seal of its truth.

As to the objections of Artemidorus (for I hid none of them nor aught else, because of the perfect trust I had in Paulus) namely, that the Lord Jesus had not been sent into the world till after so many centuries, and then to a most despised nation the Apostle lightened these doubts by teaching me more fully concerning Israel; how the seed of Abraham, though lightly esteemed of men, had been chosen of God to proclaim his will; and how all things from the beginning, both the questionings of the Gentiles, and the Law, and the Prophets of Israel, had prepared the way for the coming of the Lord. But whereas Artemidorus had said that there was no sin, and Epictetus also had taught me that sin and crime were no more than " erroneous opinion," Paulus now taught me quite otherwise, that an Evil Nature was in the world from the first, contending against the Good, and that the Evil is the cause of all our sins and miseries; howbeit, he bade me believe that out of our very sins the Love of God worketh a higher righteousness, making evil itself to be a kind of step of ascent to a greater good; which belief I do still, and ever shall, hold fast. Touching any signs and wonders wrought by the Lord (whereon certain of the brethren were wont to set great store) he said but little, although he himself wrought no small signs in the healing of diseases; for that which drew him to the Lord was not signs nor wonders but a love of him, and a trust in him, as being the spiritual power of God manifested to the saving of the souls of men. In the same way I also believed, and do still believe, in the Lord Jesus, worshipping him not as the worker of wonders and portents, but as the Eternal Love of God, governing the world from the first, and in these last days made flesh for us, that in him we might know God, and love God, and be at one with God.

§ 2. HOW I RETURNED TO PHILEMON AT COLOSSAE

Even before I had been baptized (which took place on the seventh day after I had first heard the preaching of Paulus) I had resolved that I must at once return to Philemon. However, by the advice of Paulus, I went not straightway to Colossae, but abode some days with him at his lodging, that I might be strengthened in the faith of Christ; and each day drew me closer to my new teacher. Those who knew him not might perchance have accused him of inconstancy; for his manner of speech and the features of his countenance changed every moment; and he was skilful as an actor to suit himself (in all honourable fashion) to them with whom from time to time he had to do, whether Jews or Greeks, bond or free, soldiers or courtiers, or whatever else. But the cause of his thus conforming himself to others in things indifferent was not inconstancy nor dissimulation, but a sincere love for all men and a power of feeling as others felt, so that his own nature disposed him without constraint to carry out that precept which was always on his lips, "Rejoice with them that do rejoice, and sorrow with them that sorrow." And beneath all this appearance of inconstancy there was a firm and solid resolution, the depth of which could not be known but by those who knew the depth of the love of the Lord Jesus.

From Paulus (who knew Philemon well) I heard that my former enemy Pistus had fled from Colossae some months ago, being convicted of theft, and after his departure his devices against me had been discovered and my innocence proved; hearing which I was the more willing to return. Nor did the Apostle longer delay me, saying that he doubted not but Philemon would do what was right; but to make assurance surer he would write a letter to him whereof I should be the bearer.

I had not been an hour in Colossae before Philemon signified his desire to emancipate me without conditions, at the same time lamenting that he had been led by the practice of Pistus to suspect me without cause; and for the brief remnant of his life, he (no less than Apphia) bestowed on me a truly parental affection; which I for my part endeavoured to requite with something of the care and attention due from a son. Soon afterwards I was appointed to the ministry, and I laboured in the church at Colossae to supply the old man's place, inasmuch as he became daily more infirm and less able to preside over the congregation. Many difficulties in the work began at this time to perplex me, because there appeared in our little congregations divisions of opinion. Some of the brethren were plain simple folk (slaves most of them) delighting in wonders; and these, besides believing other portents, supposed that, after their death, they would reign on earth with Christ for many years wearing the same flesh and blood which now they wore. Others (but of these only a few) coming to the knowledge of Christ from the study of philosophy, denied that there was any further resurrection, after the human soul had once been raised up from the death of sin to life in Christ. Again, others maintained Christ to be not very God, but only the greatest of a great train of angels created by God; and some of these affirmed that Christ was not a man at all (save in appearance only) but that he merely went through the form of appearing to be born and to suffer and to die. Many also attacked the Law of Moses and the ancient Scriptures of the Jews; and these (not understanding the doctrine of the Apostle concerning the progress of all things, and how the Law was but as a slave to bring us to Christ) taking it for granted that I must needs maintain the Law to be perfect, and the doings of the Patriarchs to be perfect, yea, and the letter of the Law to be perfect, endeavoured to bring the Scriptures into derision, by asking whether the true God had nails and hair and teeth and the like, as well as hand and voice and nostrils; because, said they, the Scriptures declared that he had the latter; and if the latter, why not the former?

Against all these opinions it seemed needful to contend, not so much inveighing against that which was false, as rather pleading for that which was true. Many times did I now desire that* my teacher, the blessed Apostle, had been present to direct and guide me. But then there came into my mind the saying of Epictetus that "it is only a bad performer who is afraid to sing alone," and how One greater than Epictetus had promised that he "would be ever with us." Yet I began to lament (as did others also) that we had no writings of the words and deeds of the Lord which might have served as a lamp and guide to our feet. However, in spite of these contrarieties, it was still a great refreshment to note the work of the Spirit among all such as believed in the Lord Jesus, yea, even among some that erred in opinions. For not only did all alike abstain from magic arts, and festivals, and sacrifices to demons, and the like, but a wonderful change came also upon their whole lives: the thief no longer stole; the lewd became chaste; the cruel merciful; the timorous and servile no longer feared aught save sin. To crucify slaves had become a thing hateful and abominable; to expose children was to sin against God; wealth and pleasure were despised; and, in a word, such temperance, constancy and benevolence as are recommended by philosophers in their lectures to a small circle of pupils, these very virtues were practised by the whole multitude of the saints; and this, not out of ostentation, nor "to preserve one's own serenity of mind" (as Epictetus would have had me think) but simply out of an insatiate desire to serve the Lord Jesus by loving and serving men. Nor could I fail to perceive how fruitful and blessed was the service of the Lord; for that very peace and freedom of mind which Epictetus had held up to me as the chief object of life, and which I had found impossible to obtain by aiming at it, behold, now that I no longer aimed at it, but only desired to serve the Lord, this same peace of mind came as it were unasked into my bosom, peace deep, and calm, and past all power of tongue to utter or mind to understand.

§ 3. OF MY DISCOURSE WITH ARTEMIDORUS CONCERNING THE FAITH

About this time died Artemidorus. Of late the old man had become infirm and bedridden, and I visited him often, and spoke much with him touching the faith of Christ; and he received me the more willingly because he had a great love for Epictetus (who was now absent with his master in Rome), and he was wont to say that I was now become a second Epictetus, setting my superstition aside. He retained all his force of mind and keenness of understanding; and still, as in old times, he would fain have judged the Faith of Christ by the weakness of the weakest of the brethren, and not by the strength which made them strong. For example, because certain of our church (living from day to clay in expectation of the coming of the Lord) were wont to catch up, perhaps too greedily, every light rumour of war or famine or earthquake, as signs of the Last Day, on this account he would call the Christians *misanthropi*, enemies of Caesar, and haters of the empire. Again, because others among us gave much time to fasting and prayer, and in that condition discerned (or in some cases perchance seemed to discern) visions of the Lord; or because a few, more superstitious than the rest, abstained from eating flesh; for this cause he mocked at all the saints as dreamers of dreams and given to foolish austerity and unprofitable abstinence.

None the less, he willingly heard me speak of the Lord Jesus, and sometimes himself questioned me concerning him. One such conversation I remember, a few weeks before his death, when, upon my entering his chamber, I found him in a deep study: and, as soon as he saw me, scarcely giving me time to salute him, "You Christians," he said, "believe in a good God, who is all-powerful; whence then comes evil into the world?" "I will explain that," replied I, "when you can explain whence arose the atoms which, as you say, made the Universe." He said, "Nay, my friend, I have no theories to maintain on this subject; but evil is opposed to your supposition of a good and powerful God." "Not more," I replied, "than atoms, existing from the beginning, are opposed to your supposition of no effect without a cause." Then he was silent, and said no more on that point. But producing my letters which I had written to him from Antioch (and it was at that time that he gave into my hands those papers the substance of which I have set down above) he urged against me more especially that which I had myself said, that the religion of Jesus was narrow, giving precedence to Jews, and compelling all men to be Jews in the observing of the Law; and he added that, however Paulus might affirm the contrary, this and nothing else was clearly the intent of Christus himself. But it was not difficult for me to show that, howsoever Jesus had purposed that the Gospel should be preached to the Greeks through the Jews, yet his doctrine and kingdom had, from the first, been intended to include all mankind, without observance of the Law. I also repeated to him as many of the sayings of the Lord as I had been able to collect and to commit to memory; and hence I proved to him that he at whom Artemidorus had been wont to scoff, was neither juggler, nor magician, nor impostor, but a great Conqueror of the minds of men, and one whose doctrine and practice went down to the roots of life, and to the foundations of all things. And this indeed, when he had heard the account of his life and doctrine, Artemidorus did not deny, admitting himself to have misjudged in former times, and professing now to revere Christus as he would revere Socrates, or Epicurus, or Pythagoras; "but still," said he, "the acknowledgment of one great and good man more in the world, proves not that the world is divinely governed." Then I urged him again with a ne\v argument, saying that it was very credulous to suppose that this wonderful Universe had come together by chance and without a Mind, whether the Mind had wrought through atoms or otherwise, and that if there were such a Mind, then those things that were done and said in accordance with that Mind would prevail (being in harmony with the universe) but those things that were not in accordance with it would come to nought; wherefore, since the words and deeds of Jesus of Nazareth had been already so very powerful (and that too without aid of force or cunning or any customary aids of great conquerors) it seemed certain that they were indeed in harmony with that Mind of the Universe to which Jesus had taught us to give the name of Father. To all this he listened patiently and attentively; and that he pondered these matters in his heart may be judged from the following rough notes which I found among his papers in his handwriting, dated about the time of our discourse together, that is to say a month or thereabouts before his death.

§ 4. OF THE DOUBTINGS OF ARTEMIDORUS

"THE PROBLEM OF THE CHRISTIANS.

"This Christus lived in Syria less than forty years, and, after doing nothing worthy of mention, was put to death upon the cross by Pontius Pilatus, governor of Judea. He made no conquests, no laws, and few disciples; and of these few one betrayed him. He wrought, it may be, some cures of a kind to startle the multitude (doubtless in accordance with nature, by working on the imaginations of men); but in any case none marvellous enough to persuade men that he was a prophet; for it is not denied that his own countrymen delivered him to execution. After his death, his disciples constantly affirmed that he had appeared to them, and in one case this was confessed by an enemy; but (saving this belief in his resurrection, and some kind of expectation that he would always be present with them as an ally) he bequeathed to his followers nothing except a policy that was no policy, but rather a dream, somewhat after this fashion:—

"THE DREAM OF CHRISTUS"

"The world is to be a commonwealth wherein the Supreme God is to be King, and all mankind the citizens. But God being the Father of men, mankind are to be to him as children, and to one another as brethren. Of this commonwealth the laws are to be as follows:—

"1. *The Law of Love.* Love (and not Force nor Cunning) is the strongest power in the world; and as little children take captive the hearts of their parents by force of love, so are the Christians to take captive the world by becoming as little children, loving all men and thereby constraining all men to love them in return. [Surely the vainest of vain dreams! In the fulfilment of which I will then believe when I see the sheep loving the wolf and thereby constraining the wolf to love them in return.]

"2. *The Law of Giving and Receiving*. As by giving to Nature the husbandman receives a manifold return, so by giving to the Unseen Nature and Spiritual Harmony which Christus believed to exist men shall receive an abundant harvest in return. Thus, by giving love, a man is to receive a return of love; or giving pity, a return of pity; or service, a return of service. [All this may be, and yet there may be no God. For doubtless, if a man give love to his fellow men, even though they love him not in return, yet he thereby enlarges his imagination of the Divine Love, and warms his heart with the fancy that he is now more perfectly loved by that Divine Person whom he has painted for himself out of the colours of his own mind. This dream may make some men happy, and more women; but though a dream may give pleasure, it does not cease to be a dream.]

"3. *The Law of Sacrificing*. All sacrifices of beasts are to be done away, the only true sacrifice being the sacrifice of the will, whereof the sacrifices of beasts are but as emblems. In the life and death of Christus (being a perfect sacrifice of the will) these Christians suppose the perfect sacrifice to have been offered up. Hence they regard Christus as the High Priest of mankind offering himself up for all men; supposing that by force of sympathy with him, which they call 'faith,' they are able to be united with him and so to take unto themselves his sacrifice. [I deny not this doctrine of sacrifice to be less ignoble and superstitious than the notions of the common sort; who vainly imagine that they can bribe the Supreme by sheep and oxen. But, even were it true, it seems too high and unsubstantial for the minds of the common people. Besides, as there is no God, there can be no sacrifice, so that this also is a dream, like all the rest.]

"4. *The Law of Forgiving*. It is supposed that, by force of sympathy, every disciple of Christus has a power of raising up men beneath him in goodness, whom they call sinners. This 'sympathy' they call bearing the sins of others, and the result of it is forgiveness; and Christus is said by them to have brought this power into the world and to have bequeathed it to his disciples. It differs, they say, from our 'forgiveness,' in that it means not the mere remission of punishment, but the putting away of sin itself. [All this is simply natural, and may be seen in any family or assembly of human beings; wherein the better always have a power of raising up the worse, and those who are injured have power to set at rest the minds of their injurers by forgiving them. Therefore all that they can claim for Christus is, that he possessed this power perchance in a singular degree, and discerned how great a force it had over the minds of men; and perhaps also that he (by some special and peculiar influence) imparted it to his disciples.]

"5. *The Law of Faith and Trust*. No man, said Christus, could be forgiven sins by him, except he had 'faith;' and in the same way his followers maintain that without 'faith' it is impossible to obtain the forgiveness of sins, but by faith the worst of sinners can be forgiven." [This again, so far as it is true, is merely natural; because no offender can so much as imagine himself freed from the consciousness of his wrong-doing by the forgiveness of the man injured, if he distrust the latter and esteem him as an hypocrite. And without doubt this "faith" as one may see even in a dog that has faith or trust in his master has not a little power to confer magnanimity on men by raising their minds to the level of a high idea of God, even though that idea be but an empty imagination. But here, as elsewhere, there is a deficiency of proof; for what is wanted is, not superstructure, but foundation; for I will not dispute the power of faith, if these Christians will first give me somewhat certain to have faith in.]

"ANSWER TO THE PROBLEM.

"This being the commonwealth and these the Laws of Christus, the problem is, whence comes it that so many thousands of men are drawn towards him, and thereby led out of evil and vile courses into lives of virtue? For other religions (and Onesimus justly urges this argument) hold out similar hopes of Elysian fields, and terrors of Hades, and purifications from sin; and some also, like the religion of Pythagoras, pretend to join men into brotherhoods; and almost all afford portents sufficient to satisfy the natural credulity of men; yet do they not succeed in persuading their votaries to lead virtuous lives.

"The answer is, in my judgment, two-fold; first that the Laws of Christus are in accordance with the Harmony of things—by which however I am far from meaning that there are gods, or any such things as sin, forgiveness and the like, for all these things are probably mere imaginations—but I mean that human nature is so framed as to be turned from the imagination of sin by the imagination of forgiveness and these other imaginations which Christus has devised; secondly, Christus himself appears to have been of a nature to imprint himself upon others to a degree much above the common; and his power over the minds of his disciples (as has been sometimes seen in the case of others, both teachers and law-givers and private men) instead of being diminished after death, was greatly increased.

"A third cause may be alleged by some, namely, that his disciples believed and cause others to believe, that he rose from the dead. But is this a cause, and not rather an effect? For we must surely ask, what caused his first disciples to believe that he had risen from the dead? Perhaps they did not believe it, but pretended to believe it, and deceived others. But this I do not think to be true in the case of Paulus; who was changed from an enemy to a friend by an apparition of

Christus at the time when he was persecuting his followers. For this reason, and for others, I incline to believe that the first disciples did not deceive others, but were themselves deceived by apparitions, naturally arising from affection and imagination. Yet can I not deny that, on this supposition, the influence of Christus, being supposed to be so powerful over the minds of men as to force even an enemy to become a friend by the apparition of him whom he had persecuted, far exceeds anything that I have witnessed, or heard, or read; and it raises Christus to something almost above the nature of man.

"The sum of all is, that this commonwealth of Christus appears to me but a dream, though, I deny not, a noble dream. And even were it to prosper beyond expectation in the future, as it has already prospered in the past, yet could I not entertain it, having no belief in a god or gods. Yet thus much I admit, that, if I were able to believe in gods of any kind, I know not where among gods or men I could find anything more worthy of worship than this Christus, reasonably worshipped, without violence to nature; for if Plato was right in saying that 'there is nothing more like god than the man who is as just as man may be,' then certainly Artemidorus may say that 'if there were a god, there would be nothing more like god than Christus.'"

§ 5. OF THE LAST WORDS AND DEATH OF ARTEMIDORUS

Thus wrote Artemidorus three or four weeks before his death; and from certain words that fell from his lips afterwards, I have hope that he came yet nearer to the Truth than this. However in his case I perceived (not indeed for the first time, but more clearly now than ever before) that it is not argument nor force of philosophy that brings into the Church of Christ them that are without, but it is rather the Spirit of Christ in the Church. For this Spirit, the Spirit of loving-kindness, and justice, and purity, and patience, not only binds us that are in the Church close together, but also causes them that are without to desire to enter in, while they wonder and admire at the concord of the brethren. In this way the common people of Colossae—rich as well as poor, though more often the poor—coming by twos and by threes to our assembly, were daily converted; but Artemidorus, being (as I have said) bedridden, could neither know how great a change had been wrought by Christ in the lives of the brethren, nor what a spirit of power reigned over us in the meetings of the congregation, with which perchance he himself might have been imbued had he been present among us. Therefore when I urged him a few days before his death, to believe and to be baptized, though he was neither amazed nor indignant, as of old, yet he shook his head, saying that he was now too old and too sick to leap, at so short notice, into a new philosophy. "Nor," said he, "could the gods themselves, if there be gods, take it in good part that I, who have been, all my life through, a perfect Mezentius, not merely offering no libations to them but even denying their existence, should now present to them as it were the dregs of the cup of this life." In this mood he continued even till his death. Some of the brethren rebuked me afterwards because I had not warned him of the fiery wrath that awaits them that harden their hearts against the Lord. But I was not unmoved by the old man's answer to Archippus, who had made some mention to him of the terrors of hell. To which Artemidorus replied that if Christus were indeed a lover of truth, then he would of a surety make some allowance for one who, all his life long, had sought such truth as he could find, however imperfectly, and who now, in his old age, was loth for shame to say, "I will believe Christus to be god because, if there be no gods, I thereby lose nothing; and if he be god, I thereby gain much." These words the old man spoke to Archippus in my presence, when he was now in extreme weakness, so that he could scarce move his hand to bid me farewell; and on the morrow he died, without making any sign at all of faith; only he whispered to his secretary, a few minutes before his death, to tell me this as his last message, that, whereas he had charged me always to bear in mind the proverb that "incredulity is security," now he perceived that there was room for trust as well as distrust in the life of man.

THE END OF THE SIXTH BOOK

THE SEVENTH BOOK

§ 1. HOW I CAME TO ROME TO SEE THE BLESSED APOSTLE

ABOUT six months after the death of Philemon, which took place in the same week as the Great Fire in Rome, word came to us that our brethren in the city were being called in question for their faith, having been falsely accused of many monstrous crimes and especially of having set the city on fire. Soon afterwards, in the month of January, we received most grievous tidings concerning them, how some had been cast into prison, and others slain with all manner of insults and tortures. The infection of this suspicion soon spread to Asia, first indeed to Ephesus, where it was soon allayed, but afterwards even to Colossae, so that tumults were raised against us; the more because of the earthquake which, in the summer of that same year, utterly destroyed Laodicea , and in Hierapolis also and Colossae many houses were cast down and many slain; which calamities the common people imputed to us, the Christians, as if the gods had sent this plague on them because sacrifices had been withheld by our impiety. All that year I remained at Colossae striving to confirm the brethren in the faith and to encourage the weak; for though the magistrates were not against us but rather for us (knowing that we obeyed the laws) yet could they not altogether resist the vehemence of the common people, especially now that the fury of the multitude had some pretext in the example of the Emperor. Wherefore even against the will of the governors of the city, ten or twelve of the brethren, having violent hands laid on them by the rabble, bore witness to the Lord with their blood. But, towards the end of the year, the cooler weather setting in, and the memory of the earthquake a little abating, the multitude began to cease from the first heat of their fury; when, behold, we received of the brethren of Rome a truly piteous report, how the Emperor was more incensed against us than ever, causing such as were citizens to be beheaded; but as to the rest, crucifying some, burying others alive, casting others to the wild beasts, or burning them, besmeared with pitch, like torches. While we were all mourning for their tribulation, there fell on us two blows of heavy tidings, first that the blessed Apostle Petrus had been taken and crucified, and then that Paulus also had been put in bonds and was under accusation, and like to be put to death. Then I could no longer restrain myself; so finding that all things in Colossae now tended towards peace, I left Apphia with Archippus (who had come to lodge with us for a season, his house in Hierapolis being quite cast down by the earthquake while ours was standing and not greatly damaged), and I made all haste to Rome, hoping to find Paulus still alive, and at least to have some speech with him before he died.

When I came to Rome, I went first to the house where the Apostle had been wont to lodge in times past, to make inquiry concerning him; but it was not to be found, nor any of the houses near it, having been burned down in the Great Fire. Then I turned my steps to that part of the palace wherein I had first had speech with him; but that also was burned down. For the whole of the former palace had been consumed by the fire; and the Emperor was even then building for himself his new Golden Palace (as it is now called) on the Coelian and Esquiline hills. Then I made endeavour to find the house of Tryphoena and Tryphosa where the church had been wont to meet; but that also was not to be found. For indeed the fire had been far greater than I had conceived, and greater also (as I should judge) than any other fire within the memory of man, having wholly consumed four of the city wards, and partly destroyed seven more, leaving only three of the fourteen altogether untouched. So, what with the fire and the informers, the brethren had been driven out of the city; and among these, Clemens and Linus. But, meeting at last with Asyncritus, I understood from him that the holy Apostle was in close keeping, in one of the dungeons of the New Palace. But whether his cause had been heard or not, and (if tried) what the issue had been, of this he was altogether ignorant. To the palace therefore I straightway betook myself, and finding there my old friend the actor Aliturius I frankly avowed to him that I was a Christian and that I was ready to die if I could but have speech with one of their number, named Paulus; who then lay in one of the dungeons of the New Palace. He chid me for my rashness saying that, if he himself had been such as he was when we were last together, I had been a dead man; for what prevented him from informing against me and gaining a great reward?" But now," said he, "I also have known something of this Paulus and (albeit I am myself no Christian) I would fain do what may be done to aid him and do you a pleasure." Then he took me to the chief jailer, and by fair words, and large gifts, and promises of close secrecy, I won him to consent that if I would come thither on the morrow in the dress of an actor as in old times, I should have speech with Paulus.

§ 2. HOW I SAW PAULUS IN PRISON

On the morrow, having gone to the palace, I was straightway led down to the dungeon, and thence from the outer prison into the innermost of all— rather a *barathrum*, or pit, than fit to be called prison. As we went down the steps, I questioned the jailer touching the other Christians, whether any had been of late condemned to the beasts, and whether the Apostle stood in this peril. He replied that the prisoner was a Roman citizen so that he was free from that death; " and besides," said he, "the Roman people will not have any presented before them to do battle with beasts, except they be proper men and able to fight for their lives, but this man was from the first lean and sorry-looking, and now belike he is so worn with imprisonment in the inner dungeon, and scant food to boot, that I doubt we shall not find him alive." By this time the man had descended the lowest step and stood on the floor of the pit, turning his lamp on every side, but making visible naught save pools of water, and filth, and mire, and darkness without end. But presently, stumbling against something, I called to the jailer, "Paulus is here"; and he, bringing the lamp, turned it so as to see more clearly, and said. "There is no life in him."

Then I cried unto the Lord in my soul for mercy; for indeed, when the* light of the lamp shone upon his face, he neither spoke nor moved hand nor foot, and his eyes were fast closed. But when I raised up his head, and called him by his name, he opened his eyes and looked on me, and I perceived he knew me. Then I persuaded the jailer to take him out of this horrible pit into the outer dungeon; and we brought him out into the court-yard, and the jailer departed, leaving us alone, saying only to Paulus as he went forth, that it was the last watch of the. night and that the tenth day was at hand; which words I could not then understand. When we were together, I took out bread and wine mixed with water, which I had brought with me, and besought him to eat and drink. He seemed loth at first, but afterwards tasted a little, and his spirit was revived, and strength came back to him, and he praised God that he had vouchsafed to refresh him with the sight of me once again. And turning to me with a smile he said—playing on my name Onesimus, which being interpreted means "profitable"—"Truly thou hast been a profitable child unto me, and by this thy kindness thou hast repaid him who begot thee in Christ; and yet I know not whether I should thank thee or blame thee; for I was in the spirit when thou earnest, and the Lord had sent unto me a vision full of delight in which methinks my soul would have passed away but for thy coming, so that by this time I had been with Christ. Yet doubtless it is the will of the Lord that I should be with thee a little longer."

Then he ate again of the bread which I had brought and drank also; and being now somewhat stronger, he sat upright, and laying his right hand lovingly on my head, he said with a smile, "Hast thou a grudge, my child, against the headsman, that thou wilt give him the trouble of taking off my head? for he and the jailer methinks had planned together that the prison should have spared them their pains; but now thou hast marred their counsel." "Surely," said I, "thou art not yet condemned by the Emperor." "Not by the Emperor himself," replied Paulus, "for he, as they told me, is on a journey to Greece; but by his freedman Helius, from whose lips 'Guilty' is a word of no less weight than from the Emperor's. In fine, it is now the ninth day since sentence was given that I should be beheaded; but the custom is, that the prisoner shall not suffer death till the tenth day, which", as the jailer but now said in thy hearing, is nigh at hand, or perchance already begun.

Hereat my eyes filled with tears, for pity of myself rather than of the Apostle, because I had come this long journey from Colossae and would gladly have come ten times that distance to have speech with him, and to seek comfort and help and guidance from his lips, as from an oracle, yea, rather as from the Lord himself; and now, behold, all my labour was for naught, and he, my guide and deliverer, and father in Christ, was to pass away from me at the season when my need of him was sorest. But Paulus comforted me, saying that he was glad, since the Lord so willed it, that he should die in the sight of men and not in yonder pit, and that he accepted me as an angel from the Lord bringing a message that he should bear public witness with his blood to the name of the Lord Jesus. Then he bade me tell him such tidings as I had to tell of the brethren at Colossae and at Ephesus; and when I told him that both there, and in all Asia, the Lord was day by day adding to the number of the elect, he broke out into thanksgiving and praising of God, declaring that now he was well pleased to be offered up, for the work of his life was accomplished.

§ 3. HOW PAULUS RELATED TO ME THE STORY OF HIS LIFE

After this he sat silent, but as it seemed to me praising God in his heart, and there was a wondrous light upon his countenance; and so he continued for some space musing and saying nothing. But I was in a great strait between two wishes, being on the one hand fearful to trouble or disturb him, and this too on the eve of his departure; and yet having a fervent desire to receive from him some last precepts for the guidance of the church. Presently however the Apostle himself broke silence thus: "Onesimus, my child, the hour approacheth when I shall bid thee farewell. If therefore thou wouldst ask aught of me, ask now; for the time is short." Then I betwixt the suddenness of the granting of my desire, and the multitude of the questions in my mind, could not find what to ask; but I exclaimed for sorrow, "Alas, my father, Petrus being now slain and thou also on the point to leave us, we shall be as sheep—" At this he interrupted my words, putting his hand upon my mouth; "Nay, say not so, my child, that ye will be as sheep without a shepherd; for there is one Shepherd that hath promised that he will never leave thee nor forsake thee." I was silent, being abashed because of my want of faith; and he also sat for a while, musing and saying nothing. But at last he said, "The story of my life, and how the Lord guided me, yea, and constrained me against my will to follow him, this, having never yet related unto thee, I will now relate, or as much of it as the time may permit, that thou also mayst take courage, believing that even so will the Lord be a shepherd unto thee, guiding thee safe unto the end. Perchance also what thou shalt hear may enable thee the better to understand the mystery of mysteries, namely, how the kingdom of heaven is to be opened to all men, and how the Jews are for a time cast away that the Gentiles may be brought in, and so all mankind may be saved, even as the Lord ordained before the foundation of the world."

After a pause he began as follows: "Thou hast often heard those who wish not well to me, jest at my carriage and presence as being contemptible; and they say right, for so it is, and so it hath been with me from my childhood even to this day. For it pleased the Lord to chasten me in my tender years, making me weak of vision, and well nigh blind. But it was turned to good for me. For because of the infirmity of my eyes, not being able to see such things as others saw, nor to take pleasure in the pride of the. eye, and in the glory of this world, and because also, whenever I went abroad, I was despised and mocked at, for this cause I began very early to bend my mind to take pleasure in knowledge and learning, and to think on the beauties of things unseen, and on the strength of things that are esteemed weak; and I said often to myself 'Truth is stronger than all things visible and shall prevail over all.' When I grew older, this mind remained in me. The love of women moved me not, nor gold, nor any desire of pleasure; but I had a fervent zeal for the truth and for the Lord whose name is Truth, that his name should be hallowed on earth, and that the people of the Lord (for so I then deemed my nation, even Israel after the flesh) should reign over the inhabited world.

"The troubles and humiliations of Israel discouraged me not, yea, rather they confirmed me; for methought the Scriptures showed clearly that ever, in times past, greatness sprang out of small beginnings, and triumph out of humbleness. I perceived also that the Lord wrought all his deliverances by means and ways unexpected and strange to men; not by force of arms, nor by wisdom or cunning, nor by wealth, but for the most part by faith contending against all these things, even as David was caused to prevail by faith against Goliath, and by faith Abraham was made to be the father of the Lord's people. Therefore it disquieted me not that the Lord's inheritance; for even thus Egypt and Assyria and Babylon and Persia and Syria had ruled over us, each in turn; yet all these great empires had passed away, but the people of the Lord and the Law of the Lord still remained, and, said I, if we still have faith, we shall still remain and shall in the end be saved. Likewise I perceived that in every great deliverance there cometh first a transitory shadow of the deliverer, which is not the truth itself, but is of this present world; and afterwards there cometh the true deliverer, which is of God; and the will of this world is ever set against the will of God. For after this manner the world would have had Ishmael to be heir, but the Lord appointed Isaac; and again, the world would have had Esau, but the Lord, Jacob; and the world chose Eliab, but the Lord, David; and even so, said I to myself, the world would have had in times past Egypt, Nineveh or Babylon, and, in these present times, Rome; but the will of the Lord standeth fast, that he will have none other but Jerusalem to be his chosen City. With these thoughts did I comfort myself during my youth, saying, 'Though we be now under the yoke, we shall not always be thus.' Howbeit I perceived not that I should have gone yet further in my reasonings and I should have said, 'Israel after the flesh cometh first, but there is an Israel according to the spirit that shall come after; and the world chooseth Jerusalem as it now is, but the Lord chooseth a new Jerusalem, even a city in heaven.' But this was not yet revealed unto me.

"As I grew up, when I looked around me to discern what it should be 'that should deliver Israel, I could perceive nothing except the Law. Men, as it seemed to me, might pass away, yea, prophets could not be always with us; but the Law remained, and would remain, a safe guide for ever. Therefore I gave all my mind and my labour and leisure both by night and by day to the study of the Law and the Traditions; wherein if aught seemed to me unfit for the times, or imperfect, I would stifle all such whisperings and murmurings of my soul with such words as these, 'Doubtless the Law is perfect; for if it be imperfect and in error, we must needs be without a guide; and without a guide the people goeth astray, and Israel is lost, and the promises of the Lord are made of none effect; but this cannot be.' Therefore it seemed to be the mark of a wise man and one that loved Israel to see no blemish in the Law, yea, to see perfection, though my understanding discerned imperfection. So by degrees the Law took such a hold upon me that it seemed all one with truth itself, and instead of saying, 'Truth is great and shall prevail,' I began to say, 'The Law is great and shall prevail.' Then my parents, perceiving that I was wholly given to the study of the Law, determined to send me from Tarsus to Jerusalem, there to be brought up at the feet of Gamaliel, one of the most learned of the Scribes. And there in Jerusalem I remained many years, perfecting myself in the knowledge of the Law, and endeavouring thereby to gain righteousness.

"As I grew more learned in the Law, so did I grow in contempt for them that were unlearned. I perceived that there were many, both men and women, that had not leisure nor opportunity for the observance of the more minute Traditions of the Law; and some of these were troubled in their souls, full of doubts and questionings, desiring forgiveness and deliverance from sin, but not attaining to it; others were even cast out of the synagogue for light offences; and this unlearned and ignorant multitude was despised by the teachers of the people, as if they were brute beasts to be restrained by bit and bridle; and I also despised them likewise. Yet sometimes when I saw a rich man that had leisure, highly honoured in the synagogue, and a poor man shut out for neglect of some lighter matter of the Traditions, which perchance he had no leisure to observe, my heart would say, 'Surely these ways are not God's ways. Surely to trust thus in the Law is not faith.' But then I would still quench all these questionings, as before in Tarsus, saying, 'If these ways be uneven, which is the even way? And if we are not to obey and trust the Law, what shall we obey, and in what shall we put our trust?' By such answers as these I hardened my heart; and as an ox struggles against the goad of his master, even so did I resist the Lord, who would have goaded me into the path of truth.

"When I came to have to do with the followers of the Lord Jesus, or Nazarenes as I then termed them, I hardened my heart still more, and esteemed them accursed because of the cross. For I said 'Whosoever is crucified is under a curse. Wherefore this Jesus, whom the Nazarenes call Messiah, is accursed, and his followers also. Moreover if this sect prevail, the Teachers of the people will be despised, and the unlearned will have the upper hand, and the Law (which is the Truth) will be trampled under foot; wherefore the Truth itself as it were proclaimeth that these Nazarenes are. liars and deceivers.' So I hardened myself like a flint against them.

Yet by degrees as I learned more and more of the life and manners of the saints, their zeal in well doing, their long-suffering and patience, their purity and justice, and above all, the steadfastness of their faith in God through the Lord Jesus Christ, then, even in the midst of my course of persecuting them, I could not forbear sometimes from reproaching myself in such words as these: 'This man whom thou art dragging away to prison hath attained to a righteousness beyond thy compass; this woman, whom thou threatenest with death, hath a faith in God surpassing thine.' With such self-chidings did the Lord still goad me toward the right road; but I still kicked against the goads and hardened my heart against him."

§ 4. HOW PAULUS CONSENTED TO THE DEATH OF THE BLESSED MARTYR STEPHANUS

Here the Apostle ceased for a space, as if he were unwilling to make mention of somewhat that came next to speak of; but anon, as though all thought of bitterness was swallowed up in the remembrance of the marvellous mercies of the Lord, he continued with a kindling countenance and speaking more quickly than before. Now, although I treasured up each word that fell from his lips, yet because of his manner of speech p~ being as much Hebrew as Greek, and very brief, abrupt, and vehement at all times, and now more than ever, I was not able to set down his words exactly, though indeed I wrote them on my tablets a few hours afterwards. Wherefore it must be understood that the exact words, both before and in that which follows, are not his. But the substance I will set down with all faithfulness, and it was to this effect.

"The more closely I joined myself to the Pharisees against the Nazarenes, and the more I saw of the cunning, and baseness, and hardness of heart of those inferior instruments by whose aid our chief priests and elders were wont to execute their designs, the more was I troubled with doubts. Sometimes when I lay down to rest at night, after a day spent in persecutions in the company of these base companions, the words of the Prophet Isaiah would rise up against me in the darkness, 'Wash you, make you clean; cease to do evil, learn to do good; your hands are full of blood;' and once, when I was sitting down to meat, methought I saw blood upon my hands. All the more did I frequent the temple and offer up many sacrifices and purify myself with daily purifications that I might wash away all sinfulness if perchance there were any stain of guilt upon me. But still I was not at ease, neither had my soul rest. By degrees, the Temple itself, and the sacrifices in the Temple, instead of taking away my burden, began to acid thereto. For of the multitude who came together thither, very few appeared to come worthily; some being strangers come from afar to see strange sights; others desiring to expiate evil deeds or to pay vows, but not with any sincere love of righteousness; and many more because it was the custom, and not because they loved the worship of the Lord; not a few also with purpose to make gain, trafficking in beasts for victims or serving as money- changers. All this I noted daily, and it troubled me more and more, because I perceived that many were hardened in ill-doing by their worship and by their sacrifices, and their feet stood in the Temple of the Most High, but their hearts drew nigh unto Satan; and again the words of the Prophet rose up to my mind, 'Sacrifice is an abomination to me; bring no more vain oblations.'

"But when I said to one of the elders that it were well if the money-changers and sellers of victims could be put away from the holy place, and if the stir and tumult of the Courts of the Temple could be diminished, he said that I was of too tender a conscience, and that it would not be possible to obtain such a temple as I desired, clean, and pure, and spotless in all points, unless I wished to join myself to the Nazarenes who dreamed of some magic temple not made with hands, wherein some invisible sacrifice of the imagination was to be offered up, and not the blood of bulls and goats. These words (although I knew it not at that time) sank deep into my heart. For though I abhorred all thought of imitating the Nazarenes in any matter, yet could I not refrain from pondering in my mind the thought of some new Temple, not made with hands, nor liable to be polluted nor destroyed by the hand of an enemy, but imperishable, incorruptible, undefiled. Being in this perplexity, I thirsted for some new revelation from the Lord, and besought him that he would send some prophet or deliverer who should make all things clear. But then the word of the Lord brought back to me that which had been revealed to me even in my childhood, namely, how each deliverer of Israel was wont at first to be despised and rejected; and fear fell upon me lest, even if the Messiah himself should come before our generation had passed away, the Pharisees should not acknowledge nor receive him. But, all this while, it never so much as entered into my heart that the Messiah was already sent, and already despised, and already rejected by the rulers of the people; but I had my eyes fixed on some deliverance yet to come.

"None the less, yea, rather the more, did I persecute the Church of Christ, giving my voice ever in favour of violent courses and advising that the common sort among them should be less regarded, but the leaders sought out with all diligence and slain. So it came to pass that by my advice the servants of the chief priests laid hands on the blessed Stephanus (concerning whom I have often spoken unto thee in times past) and set him before the Council, and accusation of blasphemy was brought against him; and I sat with the Council when he made his defence. The words of his speech were as a two-edged sword cleaving my heart asunder and strengthening all my former doubts against me. For he declared unto us how, even as Israel had rejected other deliverers, so had they rejected Jesus the Messiah, and that this was fore-ordained by God; as also that the Temple of the Lord was not to stand for ever, but that there was to be a new Temple not made with hands. So he showed how Joseph and Moses had saved the people, albeit they had been at first rejected; and how Israel had made a calf and turned to idolatry; and how Moses, being permitted to make the earthly tabernacle for the hardness of their hearts, had, none the less, made it after the pattern of a better tabernacle not made with hands; and how the Temple itself had not been made by David, but only by Solomon (who in his old age went after other gods); and with that he cried aloud that no earthly Temple was fit for the Most High, using the words of the prophet, 'Heaven is my throne, and earth is my footstool; what house will ye build me, saith the Lord?'

"Hereat the men of my faction, and especially those from Cilicia and Asia, cried out that Stephanus blasphemed, and they rent their garments and would have stopped his mouth with their uproar; but he rebuked us, saying that as we had persecuted the prophets, so had we murdered the Holy One. Hereat the uproar waxed still louder; but I sitting speechless all this time, and not able to take my eyes off his countenance, perceived that, of a sudden, as if one had plucked him by the sleeve, he turned round and ceased from rebuking the multitude, and stood still, looking upward very intently as if he saw somewhat. Then a great splendour shone upon his face, and he stretched out his hand towards heaven saying, 'Behold I see the heavens opened and the Son of Man standing on the right hand of God!' At this I could not forbear turning round also, and gazing upward to the heaven above me, if perchance I also should see somewhat there. But I saw naught (for my eyes were not yet opened) and anon arose another general shout that the prisoner was worthy of death, and all cast dust in the air and rent their garments again. So the whole multitude arose, and I with them, not knowing whither I went, nor do I remember what further happened, till I saw Stephanus on the ground, covered with blood, in a loud voice beseeching the Lord that this sin might not 'be laid to the charge of us his murderers; and, behold, the clothes of them that stoned him were lying at my feet, in token that I was the chief doer of this deed."

§ 5. HOW THE LORD APPEARED TO PAULUS

"On the night after the blessed Stephanus died, I had no rest, nor for many nights after. Dreams and visions visited me in my sleep. Sacrifices and ablutions I made without ceasing, but they brought me no peace; neither did my prayers find answer from the Lord. They that were rich praised me, and I was held in honour by the rulers of the people, but I said in my own heart, 'Doth not the Lord, the God of

Israel, cast down the wisdom and power and riches of this world and raise up the lowly and meek?' By night methought I saw the face of Stephanus covered with blood and praying for me; and the hand of the Lord was heavy on my soul filling me with fears and thoughts of evil. Yet still, like the stubborn ox, kicking against the goads of the Lord, I resolved that I would not think on idle dreams, as I called them, but that I would give myself with a single heart to the persecution of the Nazarenes. So I. gladly obeyed the High Priest who besought me at this time to go to Damascus, bearing letters to the chief men of that place, that I might have power to imprison such of the Nazarenes as I could find there.

"We journeyed slowly; for the burden of the Lord was grievous upon me, and my eyes (which were infirm by nature) were now, more than ever, dimmed and dazzled, so that I could scarcely endure the light of day. Likewise by night evil dreams departed not from me. Now also, methought (which had not been so before), I began to hear a strange voice (yet as it were in my heart and not in my ears) as if some one reasoned with me, accusing me that I had slain Stephanus without cause; insomuch that sometimes I could endure no longer to listen in silence, but made answer to the voice aloud; but presently, it was as if no voice had spoken, and one of my companions overhearing me, reproached me in jest, because, said he, I discoursed aloud with myself, preferring my own speech to theirs. Therefore that I might not hear these voices, I ceased not speaking with my companions, reasoning with them (though none reasoned against me) and proving to them from the Scriptures again and again (though none denied it) that the Law must not be set aside and that the Temple must abide for ever, and that this Jesus was a deceiver of the people. But ever and anon there would come into my ears (yea, even in the midst of my speaking) such words as these: 'What if the Law were indeed foreordained to prepare the way for Faith? What if there should be indeed a new Temple, prepared of God, not made with hands?' Then would I weary my companions with the superfluity of my reasonings and disputings, waxing fiercer and louder than before in defence of the Law and against the Nazarenes. They that went with me, falling in with my humour, ceased not to revile the deceivers of the people as they termed them; and one among them speaking of Stephanus (of whom all this time I had made no mention) said that he had been a hypocrite and a deceiver even in his death, gazing up to heaven as if to persuade us that he saw a vision, and framing his face to assume a divine appearance of gentleness and peace, and all to delude the people.

"Hereat my heart was stirred within me and I was moved to say that I did not feel assured that Stephanus (however deceived) was acting deceitfully at that moment when he was on the point of death; but as I feared lest this might cause my companions to suspect that I favoured the Nazarenes, I restrained myself and assented (against my conscience) to the man that had spoken thus. So I answered, 'Thou sayest well; this Stephanus was a deceiver.' Then, because I felt that I had lied, straightway there swelled up within me a violent desire to cry aloud 'Stephanus was no deceiver;' but still. I rejected it as a voice from Satan, and strove to turn the discourse to other matters. But in vain; for now, even as if they were desirous of set purpose to thwart me, my companions would speak of naught else but Stephanus, and how he bore himself, and what he said, and of the manner of his death, and of his vision.

"By this time we were come unawares within sight of Damascus; and I looking afar off upon the pleasant gardens that encompassed the city, rejoiced greatly because here, I said, I shall have rest from my weariness, and here these voices of Satan will cease from troubling me. But even as I spake thus within my soul, the Voice came to me much louder than before, and not once but many times: 'Wilt thou yet continue this course of blood? Wilt thou again shed innocent blood? Wilt thou yet kick against the goad of the truth?' Then I made answer 'Yes I will continue;' and these words I repeated again and again. Then suddenly the hand of the Lord fell on me, my body seeming on fire as well as my soul, and my eyes not knowing whither to turn for pain, and at last I could no longer contain myself for the sore agony of my doubting, but said aloud (yet not so that my companions could hear), 'If now that deceiver Stephanus were no deceiver, if—and behold, I looked up to heaven as Stephanus had looked, and lo, a brightness indeed, as of the glory of God; and a voice no longer in my soul but in my ears also, penetrating to my soul, and saying, 'Saul, Saul, why persecutest thou me?' Then I fell upon my face, knowing who it was that spoke, yet constrained to ask as though I knew not, and I said,'Who art thou, Lord?' And he said 'I am Jesus of Nazareth whom thou persecutest. It is hard for thee to kick against the goad. Then said I 'Lord, what wilt thou have me to do?' And he made answer saying, 'Arise, go into the city, and there it shall be told thee what thou shalt do.'

"So I arose: but behold, I was wholly blind. Being led into the city by my companions I lay some days still under the heavy hand of the Lord, pondering many thoughts and doubting whether it -would please the Lord to restore to me my sight; and during all this time I spoke many things not according to my own knowledge, for I was no longer master of myself. Among other matters the Lord caused me to make mention of one Ananias, one of the chief among the Saints in Damascus (whom I had purposed to have slain) saying that it was the Lord's will that he should come to me and make me whole. Whereof when the rumour came to the ears of Ananias, he, being also moved by a vision of the Lord which he himself received, came to me and laid his hands upon me, and straightway my senses returned to me, and presently I began to see a little, and in no very long space I was made whole and received my sight as before."

§ 6. HOW PAULUS WAS PREPARED FOR THE PREACHING OF THE GOSPEL

"When I was recovered of my blindness, some of the brethren in Damascus would have had me go up to Jerusalem that I might be instructed in the faith by those that had been disciples before me. But the Lord suffered it not, but bade me go into Arabia; where, for the space of two years, I remained, giving myself wholly to prayer, and to the reading of the Scriptures, and pondering the purposes of God. And here it pleased the Lord to reveal many mysteries unto me and more especially the mystery of the New Temple and the heavenly Jerusalem. And the grace of the Lord was poured out upon me very abundantly, working for me good out of evil, enabling me to discern the truth the more clearly perchance because I had once fought against it. For as I had ever been wont to say, 'If the Nazarenes be right, then are the Jews wrong, and if Jesus be the Messiah, then are the Law and the Temple destined to pass away,' so now, believing that Jesus was indeed the Messiah, I had the less difficulty in believing that the Law must needs pass away, and all things must be changed.

"At the same time it was revealed to me in the spirit that the outward fashion of all things must change but the will of God abideth for ever; for in spite of death, and sin, and all the devices of Satan, the purposes of the Highest are unchangeable; which have been, and shall be, fulfilled, in many diverse shapes, yet ever remain the same; and how the redemption of the world through Christ and the casting away (in part and for a time) of Israel, together with the bringing in of the Gentiles, were not by chance—as if the purposes of the Unchangeable were changed—but fore-ordained before the foundation of the world; even as it was also fore-ordained that Adam should fall, and Abel should be slain, and that Ishmael and Esau should be rejected to the intent that Isaac and Jacob might be chosen; in all these things I now discerned the unchanging purpose of the Lord triumphing over Satan from the first, and out of sin and death drawing forth life and righteousness. Also, as regards the death of the Lord Jesus upon the cross, I no longer felt shame at it, nor passed lightly over it in my doctrine (as some do still, my Onesimus); for I perceived that it was a sacrifice fore-ordained, yea, the only true sacrifice and oblation for the sins of men, whereof all former sacrifices had been but shadows.

"Likewise it was revealed to me that mankind must rise from the death of the flesh and be born to the life of the spirit. For as man was first made and sinned in Adam, so man was afterwards made again and born to righteousness in the Lord Jesus; the first Adam was the shadow, the second, the truth; the first Adam was of the earth and of this world, the second Adam was of the spirit and of heaven. And as all men are bound to Adam by the bonds of flesh, so must they be bound to the true Adam by the bonds of the spirit, that is by trust or faith and by love, whereby men must be so knit to the Lord Jesus that whatsoever hath befallen him must also befall them. For all flesh, being redeemed in Christ, is made one with Christ. As therefore the Lord Jesus suffered and died and rose again and reigneth in heaven, so must the children of men, even all the nations of the earth, suffer and die according to the flesh, but rise again according to the spirit, and reign in spiritual places, perfected with him. And this hath been the eternal purpose of God from the foundation of the world.

"Moreover, lest I should despise the past, and reject the Scriptures, or lightly esteem the Gentiles, or stumble because of the many generations of darkness which have been since the world was created, all of which knew not the Lord Jesus, for this cause the Lord revealed unto me that he for the most part worketh by slow means, and teacheth by slow degrees; first the elements, or teaching for babes, then for youths, then for full-grown men; and this is true for every soul of mankind, yea, and for every nation also. Wherefore I no longer despised the Gentiles, albeit the Lord had suffered them for many generations to go astray after idols; nor did I begin to despise the Law of Israel, although I no longer esteemed it as before. For it was revealed to me that, though the Law had been ordained only for a time, and because of the hardness of our hearts, and could make nothing perfect, yet did it prepare the way for perfection in Christ. For by the grace of the Lord it was given to me to understand that all things in heaven and earth, whether past or present, whether among the Jews or the Gentiles, yea, even the beasts of the field and the very dust of the earth beneath our feet, were all created for the glory of God, to testify that he, the Highest, is the Father of men, and that men must be conformed to his divine image.

"Wherefore, since the will of the Lord standeth fast, take comfort, dear Onesimus, child of my bonds and heir of my labours, and overcome evil with good. Shut not thine eyes against evil, but fight against it with a stout heart. Whensoever thou lookest upon it triumphing in high places; or setting itself up as having dominion over the earth; or creeping into the Church, causing therein errors, schisms, and deceits; yea, and when also thou lookest upon it in thine own heart, prompting thee to despair because of thine own ill courses in old days—then do thou contend against it in the name of the Lord Jesus, and in his name thou shalt surely overcome it. Say not in thine heart, 'Rome is against us,' but say rather, 'Rome that now is, shall be like unto Babylon and Nineveh, which once were, but now are passed away.' Look not upon the outward things which are but for a moment, but upon the things which are not seen, which are eternal; even as I also look not upon these my manacles and fetters, and upon this poor wasted flesh nigh unto destruction, nor upon the filth and foulness of yonder pit; but instead of this earthly flesh, I see the heavenly body wherewith my Lord shall shortly clothe me, and instead of this visible darkness, mine eyes behold the invisible glory of the Eternal Majesty on High, wherein enfolded, amid the blessed company of the saints above, I shall for ever magnify the unsearchable riches of the mercies of God.

"And now, since thou knowest whither I go, why wouldst thou, dearest Onesimus, that I should longer delay my departure? For I have been these many years like unto a servant making all things ready for a journey, that, when the master shall knock, he may be prepared to go forth to a pleasant land. And behold, the Master knocketh, and the door is now open, and shall I not gladly go?"

§ 7. THE LAST WORDS OF PAULUS

When the Holy Apostle had made an end of speaking, I was ashamed of all the questionings which had disturbed me at Colossae; and in his presence I felt myself lifted up above all doubts. Yet again, looking to the future when I should be alone, I said, "One other question I would gladly ask of thee," and he bade me " Ask on," and I proceeded thus: "Thou saidst, but now, that all men and all nations, yea, and all created things, are made subject to ignorance, and error, and death, and sin, to the intent that they may be raised from the lower to the higher; even as children are led up from the restraint of nurses and guardians to the freedom and knowledge of manhood, and as Israel also was led from the law to Christ. Now therefore I would that thou shouldst resolve me this doubt: As it is the nature of every child of man to pass through error to the truth, and as Israel also hath erred, may not we also "err, even we the Saints of God? And certain of the saints who say that they have seen the Lord Jesus in dreams and visions or other ways, may not they also sometimes err? Yea and in the Traditions of the Acts and Words of the Lord, amid much that is true, may there not also be somewhat that is false?"

Hereat he smiled and said, "Thou hast well questioned me. Assuredly we, even the Saints, may be, nay, must needs be, in some error. For whereas hereafter we shall discern all things as they are, seeing God face to face in heaven, on earth we can but see them darkly, as it were through a mirror. Yet be thou ever prompt, my dear Onesimus, to make distinction between those cases where to err is to lie, and hurtful to the soul, and those where to err is not to lie, and therefore not in the same way hurtful. For I also, not many months ago, was in error concerning the time of the coming of the Lord. For as a peevish child is impatient till the day shall dawn, though the sun be not risen nor like to rise, even so I desired that my Lord should come before his time, while I still lived, and that I should be snatched up into the clouds to him, before this generation had passed away. But now I perceive that the day of the Lord is not yet, nor will be perchance during this generation nor the next, nor perhaps for many generations yet to come. Herein therefore I erred, but inasmuch as this error was not against my soul, to err in such a matter was not to sin.

"But now let me tell thee what kind of error corrupteth the soul, and warreth against righteousness. Whoso supposeth that to abstain from swine's flesh maketh expiation for impure thoughts, or that a man may be envious and a slanderer if he do but observe Sabbaths, I say unto thee that such a one walketh in the darkness of error that wholly cloudeth the soul and shutteth out the light of God. For these opinions or beliefs are against the perfect Law of Love; against which whatsoever opposeth itself is not of God but of Satan. From such errors as these flee thou, and fight thou, with all thy power; but the other errors none can altogether avoid, nor be thou overmuch troubled concerning them. As I myself was in error touching the day of the Lord, so doubtless art thou touching some other matters, and so are and so will be, many others of the saints, liable severally perchance to several errors. Yea, all earthly knowledge of heavenly things must needs be, in some sort, error, because they are seen as it were by reflection through an imperfect glass; for the perfect God none hath seen nor can see in the flesh. Wherefore doubt not but thou art assuredly in error; yet be not on that account disquieted, provided that thou strive to attain more and more of the truth. Neither forget thou that the Spirit of the Lord Jesus Christ shall be with thee to guide thee into all truth, and to turn darkness into Light before the feet of the Saints, from generation to generation, that all men may grow in the knowledge of the Lord, and in the understanding of his unsearchable ways.

"Be not thou therefore, my son, shaken in thy faith, if in the Traditions of the Acts and Words of the Lord some things be diversely or inexactly reported; only strive thou earnestly to keep pure and undefiled that truth which is the source and foundation of the rest; I mean, that Jesus of Nazareth the Son of God hath manifested to us the love of the Father through himself, and that he, having verily risen from the dead, reigneth in heaven and helpeth his saints on earth, purposing to conform all nations of men to the Father and to destroy death and sin through his cross. Believe this, my son, and cause others to believe this; and then thou needest to concern thyself little with genealogies and minute disputings of words and diversities of traditions, nor even about sundry visions and dreams, whether they be of the Lord or no; for the foundation of the faith consisteth not in knowing how, or to whom, or when, or in what places, the Lord hath manifested himself or shall manifest himself, but in believing that he is verily not dead, but liveth. All this I say, not as if thou shouldst be careless or slothful about the attainment of the exactness of the truth, so far as lieth in thee; but place not letters before words, nor words before things, nor any kind of knowledge of things, no nor even prophecies nor visions themselves, before Love. For verily I say unto thee, the time shall come when prophecies shall fail, tongues cease, and knowledge vanish away, but Faith, Hope, and Love shall never pass away but shall abide for ever, and the greatest of these is Love."

The sound of the unloosing of the prison-bars now fell upon my ears, and presently the jailer entered saying, "The night is spent, and the guard ready." I besought him that I might accompany Paulus to his death, but the jailer would not allow it, saying that I must remain with him in the prison, for he should lose his place were it known that I had been with the prisoner. When I would have urged him further, the Apostle suffered it not, saying to me with a cheerful countenance, "Nay, my son, tarry thou with our friend here; for thinkest thou that thy father cannot walk alone, or fearest thou lest he stumble in the darkness? Nay, but if the night be spent, the day must needs be at hand; therefore fear not." The man marvelled, not understanding that the Apostle spoke of the day beyond the grave; but he said, "Thou goest to death bravely; however, there is no need of haste if thou wouldst have meat and drink to be thy *viaticum*." "I thank thee," replied Paulus, "but I have other *viaticum*, whereof, since there is no need of haste, I would gladly partake with my son; suffer us, therefore, if it may be, to be alone yet a brief space longer." Then when the man had retired, Paulus said to me, "Now, my son, because the time is short, let us make haste to be with Christ a while, and with all the company of saints, both the blessed ones that have gone to rest before us and those that have remained below." Then he took of the bread and wine which I had brought; and when he had broken and blessed, we ate and drank, and the Apostle called on the Lord in prayer. What words he uttered I know not; for I was as one in a vision, and the walls of the dungeon seemed to have fled away, and as he continued speaking of the Lord in heaven, who is above all thrones and powers, and of the glory that is to come to us with him above, I seemed to pass beyond earth, and upwards from the lower heaven, even till the highest of all, even to the region of everlasting joy, where thou, Eternal, dost feed Israel for ever.

When I had come to myself, I was still kneeling, but the holy Apostle standing before me, with his hands upon my head, blessing me; and he touched me on the shoulder saying, "I go, Onesimus."— "

Nay, my father," replied I, "let us abide here evermore in heaven." But he made answer, and these were his last words—" Thou hast a work yet to do, Onesimus, and a battle yet to fight for the Lord; yet be assured of this, my child, that wheresoever thou mayst be on earth, thou shalt verily abide with me in heaven, for I am Christ's and Christ is thine."

THE END OF THE SEVENTH BOOK

THE EIGHTH BOOK

§ 1. OF THE DEATH OF NERO, AND HOW ROME WAS DIVIDED AGAINST ITSELF

AT thy bidding, dearest Epaphras, I once more take up the pen; having been minded before to have concluded this book with the end of the life of the blessed Apostle Paulus upon earth. But indeed thou sayest well that all unwittingly I have been writing, not so much the story of mine own life (which had a fit end methinks when I was first brought to the knowledge of the Lord Jesus and began a new life in Christ) nor yet the life of the blessed Apostle, but rather the history of the manifestation of the power of Christ; wherefore thou biddest me continue this history, passing over smaller matters in my own life, and speaking of such greater matters as concern the Church of God; and this, by God's grace, I will now endeavour to do.

When I returned to Colossae and to my labours in the church there, endeavouring to keep the brethren in the right path, in accordance with the doctrine of the blessed Apostle, at first I had small success. For whereas even before, the Jewish brethren had been bitter against me, now, after my return, their bitterness had increased, yea, and was daily increasing. Hereof the main cause was the troubles of their brethren which were in Syria. For now of late the fires of those discontents which had been as it were smouldering, even from the time of Cumanus the Proconsul, nearly twenty years ago, and then in the time of Felix, about ten years ago, broke forth into flame. During the same year in which I had gone to Rome to see the Apostle, the Emperor Nero had sent Titus Flavius Vespasianus to have command over the legions in Syria; and from that year onward for nearly five years, even to the time when the Holy City was destroyed, naught but wars and rumours of wars ran all through the world, and more especially through Syria. Throughout all that time the Jews were shamefully oppressed, thousands, yea, tens of thousands, being sold (even before the siege of the Holy City) to be slaves in Rome, or scattered through the cities of Asia. These and countless other injuries set the whole nation—yea, even many of those that believed—against all Gentiles, whether belonging to the saints or not; and more especially did they rage against the memory of the beloved Apostle Paulus, some saying that he was no true Jew, others that he was not really an Apostle as the rest of the Apostles, and others even calling him " the -enemy." So there was for five years and more a great battle raging in the Church, whether the saints should observe the Law of Moses or no; and for some time it seemed not unlikely that the Jewish faction would prevail and that the Gentiles would be compelled to submit to the Law.

During all these five years the minds of all men were marvellously moved, and the empire was divided against itself, and many among the saints thought that the Lord would daily appear. At first indeed the Church began to rejoice because their chief adversary, the Emperor Nero, was taken away. I was in Corinth, as I remember, in that year, ministering to certain of the saints (whom I had known formerly in Rome), who had been sent by the Emperor to work at the great canal, which he desired to have made between the two seas near that city; and while I was with the prisoners, a trireme came sailing past within bowshot, decked with flags and garlands. One of the guard, that kept the prisoners, cried aloud, “What tidings from Rome?" And answer came back across the water, "Nero is no more." Then all held their breath because none could believe such happy tidings, and when the voice came again from the trireme, "Nero is dead," then all the prisoners, yea, and the guards too, raised a shout for joy, and within a very few hours, they all were free and the business of the canal at an end. Not unlike the joy of these prisoners was the gladness of the whole Church of Christ when he whom they called the Beast was taken out of their path.

But anon came divisions, nation against nation and army against army fighting who should be emperor; and first one and then another rose up and passed away, and all was chaos, nothing solid or sure. But there was heard again the old prophecy that "One from the East" should come forth and rule over the empire. Some said that this was

Vespasianus; others (and this began to be commonly believed more especially among the Jews and the Jewish faction of the saints) that Nero, being raised from the dead, would come again from the East across Euphrates with all the kings of the East, to make the rivers run with the blood of his enemies; and this even from the first, straightway after the death of Nero, was commonly believed in Rome by the baser sort, insomuch that many deceivers arose pretending to be Nero, and his effigies were set by unknown hands in the public places, and the rostra were crowned, and sacrifices offered in his name; and thence this belief spread quickly through the empire, and it is commonly believed even to this day, namely, the fourth year of the Emperor Domitian wherein I now write. So it came to pass that even after the death of Nero, the minds of men were still in division and discord; and the Jews of Syria, yea, and certain of the Jews also among the faithful, had expectation that still their nation would prevail, because Rome seemed divided against itself; and as long as this opinion held, so long the Jewish faction had the upper hand in the Church.

§ 2. OF THE JEWISH FACTION

But presently came tidings that the legions were gathered together against Judea, and then that they were encompassing Jerusalem round about, and afterwards that the Holy City was closely beset, and that the brethren had fled forth, but that the Jews that stayed therein were at discord among themselves, and in great straits, insomuch that they were driven to feed one on the other for lack of food. But still not many of the Jews among the faithful believed that the Holy City would be taken; for they supposed that the Lord from Heaven would stretch out his hand to save the place which he had chosen. So when the tidings came at last that the Holy City had been indeed taken and burned, and the Temple also, and that all the sacred furniture of the Temple had fallen into the hands of the Romans, at first none would believe it; but when it was no longer possible to doubt, many began to believe that the end of the world was now at hand, and to some it seemed as if, with the passing away of the Holy City and the Temple, the old world were passed away and a new world already begun.

From this time forth began the Jews to sever themselves into two distinct parties. Some on the one hand, seeing the will of the Lord in the taking away of the Old Jerusalem began to fix their thoughts on Jerusalem that is above, even the spiritual city, the Bride of Christ; and as they could no more fulfil the Law according to the letter by offering sacrifice in the Temple, they now began to turn themselves more from the letter to the spirit, and from the sacrifice of bulls and goats to the sacrifice of the Lord Jesus; and so it came to pass that this party joined themselves more closely to the Gentiles that were in the Church. But upon the other and larger faction of the Jews the destruction of the Holy City had an effect altogether contrary; for being embittered against the Gentiles even before, now, in the extremity of their rage, they made no distinction of Roman or Greek, believer or unbeliever, but hated all alike. Hereat none could marvel, that knew how great had been their sufferings and oppressions; thousands slain with the sword, thousands on the cross, thousands with famine, tens of thousands sold for slaves or condemned to the mines and quarries; those that were suffered to live, burdened with taxes, often dispossessed of their lands, and their lives made miserable with penalties and insults, so that to be a Jew seemed now the same thing as to be an outcast and laughingstock for mankind.

Hence, among some even of the more honourable of the Jews, now to cease to be a Jew seemed all one with beginning to be a coward and a renegade; wherefore they preferred to be more Jewish than before; and, because they could not now observe the Law in such matters as appertained to the Temple, on this very account they observed all other matters of the Law more diligently than before; and, in a word, the Temple being gone, the Law became unto them both Law and Temple also. In former times the unbelieving Jews had spoken against the Church of Christ and blasphemed the brethren, but only on certain occasions; but now they began to make a rule and habit of cursing us with formal curses, so that it became a part of their worship in the synagogue. Of Nero, the deceased Emperor, they ceased now to speak reproachfully, because they esteemed him as an enemy to Vespasianus, or at least, to the saints; and Poppaea, his concubine or wife (a woman of no virtue nor purity) they praised; but the Emperors Vespasianus and Titus were in their eyes as monsters, to be smitten with the plagues of God. Such a spirit of blindness fell upon the greater part of the Jewish nation at this time; wherefore seeing they saw not, and hearing they could not understand, nor be converted to the Lord. Such of the Jews as took a middle course—who were commonly called Ebionites—neither wholly separating themselves from the Church of Christ, nor yet desiring to cast in their lot with the Gentiles, were sorely exercised at this time; and many were the defections and apostasies among them; and the Gospel with them was a Gospel of sorrow rather than of joy. Hereof some judgment may be formed, and some knowledge of the history of the Church in Syria from a certain letter written to me in the seventh year of the Emperor Vespasianus by one Menahem, a foremost teacher among the Ebionites, of which letter I will now set down some parts.

§ 3. OF MENAHEM, THE EBIONITE

After many lamentations for the evils of Israel, and especially because the Holy City had been destroyed by " Babylon " (meaning Rome) whereby the sacrifice had been made to cease, the letter turns aside to describe the manner of the worship of the Temple in times past and especially the presence and glory of the High Priest: (t Alas, how was he honoured in the midst of the people in his coming forth from the sanctuary! He was as the morning star before the sun hath risen, and as the moon at the full, yea as the sun shining upon the Temple of the Most High, and as the rainbow giving light in the bright clouds. When he took the portions of the priests' hands, he himself stood by the altar compassed round with his brethren, even as a cedar of Lebanon compassed round with palm-trees. He stretched out his hand to the cup and poured out the blood of the grape, a sweet smelling savour unto the Most High King. Then shouted the sons of Aaron, then sounded the silver trumpets, to be heard for a remembrance before the Most High. And the people besought the Most High by prayer before him that is merciful, till the solemnity of the Lord was ended. Lord, if thou didst so much hate thy people that thou must needs cast them down, yet shouldst thou at the least destroy them with thine own hands and not give them over to Babylon. For what are they that inherit Babylon? Are their deeds more righteous than ours that they should have the dominion over Sion?"

After this Menahem reproached me in his letter that I had made myself one with " him " (meaning Paulus) " who professed to be a Jew and was no Jew; " and he affirmed that Jesus had not come to destroy the Law but to confirm it, and that we blasphemed God because we made Jesus to be even as God, whereas he was a man and of the sons of men, howbeit the deliverer and Messiah. Thence, passing again to the condition of his nation he added this hope that "the hand which now had power" meaning the Emperor Vespasianus should be wasted suddenly, and that "Babylon" (that is to say Rome) should be cast down, and that the spoils that she had taken from the nations should be carried back to the cities of the East in the day of vengeance of the Lord. After these things, said he, a time should come when men should hope much but obtain naught, and labour, but not prosper; for the world should be turned back again into the old silence for seven days, even as in the first beginning, so that no man should remain; and, after that, the Judgment should come, and the Lord Jesus should judge the earth and reward his brethren in Israel. But still the strain of trust died away in sorrow, and the thought of the Deliverer was lost in the thought of Israel, and the letter came to an end in these words: "Our psaltery is laid in the ground, our song is put to silence, our rejoicing is at an end; the light of our candlestick is put out, and the ark of our covenant is defiled; our priests are burned with fire, our Levites led captive, our virgins and wives defiled and ravished, our righteous men are carried away, our little ones destroyed, our young men brought into bondage, and our strong men become weak; and the seat of Sion hath now lost her honour, for she is delivered into the hands of them that hate us."

After this manner wrote Menahem the Ebionite, a good man and devout, and one that loved the Lord Jesus and was himself of a gentle and meek disposition. Wherefore if even in so gentle a nature the thought of Jesus was swallowed up in the thought of the Holy City, much more was this likely to happen with others of his countrymen. And so indeed it was. For each year of troubles now seemed to cast a new veil of ignorance on the hearts of the Jews so that they might not understand the Scriptures, nor discern the will of God, nor be brought into the Church of Christ.

§ 4. HOW THE CHURCH WAS GUIDED AT THIS TIME BY THE SPIRIT OF GOD

Out of all these evils and troubles one good at least was gained, that there was no longer any danger lest the Church of Christ should become a mere sect of the Jews. For now to all the believers of the uncircumcision, the destruction of the City of Jerusalem seemed to be a sign sent from God that the Law was at an end, and that all things were to be made new in Christ, yea, and wholly new: and it became a common saying that the vesture of the Church was not to be made up out of the rags of the vesture of the Law, patched and botched up to serve new needs; but that it was to be a wholly new garment, woven afresh in one piece, without seam or rent. As for the Jews, they that stayed in the Church, finding themselves now constrained to choose between the old garment and the new, gave themselves with a more single mind to the Gospel; but the greater part went out from us, as I have said. They also that were called Ebionites, who had once had much power in the Church so that they had persuaded many, began now to be lightly esteemed; and whereas in former times they alone seemed to be the Church, and the rest heretics; now the contrary came to pass, and the Ebionites themselves came to be thought heretics insomuch that the name Ebionite became a reproach among the faithful—and the doctrine of Paulus the Apostle was considered to be the doctrine of all the Churches. From this time forth therefore there was no more fear lest the Lord Jesus should be regarded as a mere prince or prophet in Israel. In old days many had said that he was but as John the Baptist and some (more especially in Ephesus) had been baptized with John's baptism and no other; but now all men believed that John was far inferior to Jesus, and the traditions of the Church began to teach this more clearly and fully than before. Also because men now perceived that the Kingdom of the Lord Jesus was to include all nations of the earth, and indeed to consist of Gentiles rather than Jews, for this reason there were sought out such parables and discourses of the Lord as taught and explained the calling of the Gentiles into the Church. And all through the Church it was everywhere believed that Jesus was not a mere prophet, but King of kings and Lord of lords.

When great multitudes of Greeks and many other nations had now been brought into the Kingdom of Christ, they began, as was likely and reasonable, to seek out traditions concerning the nature, birth, and parentage of the King and Prophet in so great a Kingdom. The common people among the Gentile brethren believed as a thing of course, that he was divine and of divine parentage. "For if," said they, "Trophonius and Heracles have been called gods, and if we have been wont to give the name of gods to the Emperors, even such as Caius and Claudius and Nero, how shall we deny it the Lord Jesus the King of kings"?" Herein the minds of the unlearned were doubtless led to a right conclusion, though a philosopher might justly find fault with the method of it, and might understand differently the " divine parentage " of which they spoke. Nevertheless, from this desire to do honour to the Lord Jesus, there crept into the Church some error. For some began to deny that he was man at all, or born as men are born, affirming: it to be monstrous and incredible that a divine being should pass through a mortal womb. Others—but these were but very few in the Gentile churches—favoured the old opinion of the Ebionites that Jesus was merely human, although superior to any other of the children of men.

Between these two errors, some denying that the Lord Jesus was divine, and others denying that he was human, the Church was marvellously guided by the hand of the Lord, so that the greater part of the brethren held fast the true belief, namely, that he was both human and divine. For as the most part of the Gentiles revolted against the doctrine of the Ebionites, who would have had Jesus to be a mere prince or prophet of the Jews, so did the common sense of almost all the brethren perceive, as by a heaven-sent instinct, that, howsoever he might be divine, he must also needs be human and able to suffer human-like, or else be of no avail to bear the sins and sorrows of the children of men. Thus by the Spirit it was revealed even to the simplest and meanest of the brethren that in Christ Jesus God and man are joined together.

About this time also began the Churches to commit to writing the traditions of the acts of the Lord; and, not long afterwards, certain of the longer discourses of the Lord, having been written down in Greek, were joined to the other tradition and came to be commonly read in the churches; but this happened for the most part toward the end of the reign of Vespasianus, or not much before. For as long as the disciples and apostles of the Lord themselves lived, it had seemed to the saints that there was no need of books, having as it were the living words of the Lord Jesus among them. Moreover before the destruction of Jerusalem, the saints for the most part lived in continual expectation of the coming of the Lord, wherefore, hoping soon to have heard his voice from heaven, they were the less careful to record exactly the words he had spoken on earth. But now, during the reign of Vespasianus. when the Church had rest, and peace was everywhere, and the Lord seemed to delay his coming, and one by one the disciples of the Lord fell asleep, and the accounts and traditions of the words and deeds and especially of the birth and rising again of the Lord began to be multiplied with great diversities and not without many errors, then it was revealed to certain of the saints that the time was come when the traditions must be set forth in writing. But all this came to pass at a time when I was far away in Britain; whereof the reason will be set forth in the next chapter.

§ 5. HOW I CAME TO PHILOCHRISTUS, A DISCIPLE OF THE LORD IN BRITAIN

About the seventh year of the Emperor Vespasianus, it pleased the Lord, in a manner altogether unexpected and marvellous, to reveal to me the names of my parents. There was a certain Philochristus, a Jew by birth but not one of the Jewish faction, a man of some learning, who had studied Greek letters at Alexandria; and he had been a disciple of the Lord Jesus, having himself seen the Lord in the flesh. This man I had met many years ago at Antioch, and, being drawn to him by his love of truth and the simplicity of his nature, I had recounted to him the story of my life, telling him the place and exact time wherein I had been found as a child at Pergamus, and withal showing him (for so the Lord would have it) the very token that had been hung round the neck of my brother Chrestus, which I then wore. About this time therefore I received a letter from Philochristus (who was then in Britain at Londinium), telling me that he had found my former nurse, one Stratonice, who had come to Britain as a slave in the household of Pomponia the wife of Aulus Plautius the legate, and who now belonged to the saints that were in Londinium. This Stratonice, it seemed, had chanced to speak to Philochristus about her former mistress, how her twin sons were taken from her by the guile of some runaway slave, she being then in Asia, in the last year of the Emperor Tiberius (mentioning the exact year when my brother and I had been found); and when Philochristus further questioned her whether any sign or token had been on the children, she replied that one bore round his neck just such a token, and with the same inscription, as I had shown to Philochristus. She added that the slave, who had been persuaded thereto by one that desired to make a way to an inheritance through our death, had confessed his guilt three or four years after the deed, and that my mother (whose name was Euelpis the daughter of Nicomachus, an Athenian by birth) had, since that time, made continual search for us, at Pergamus and elsewhere, even till the day of her death, which had happened in the first year of the Emperor Vespasianus; but my father (whose name was Clinias the son of Aristodemus, also an Athenian by birth) had died many years before.

Ever since I had spoken with the priest of Asclepius at Pergamus, I had been assured in my mind that my mother had not willingly deserted us; yet even now it was joy to know for certain that foul practice, and not our mother's fault, had cast my brother Chrestus and me upon the world; and a great desire seized me to have some speech with my old nurse, Stratonice, concerning my parents before she died. So finding an occasion when I could conveniently leave Colossae, I journeyed to Britain to Philochristus, meaning to return in a short space. But after I had satisfied my heart's desire, learning all the story of the goodness and love and sorrow of my beloved mother from Stratonice (who lived but three months after my coming to Britain) Philochristus persuaded me to tarry with him yet longer, first for a few months, and then for a year; and, in fine, a door being opened to me of the Lord, I laboured with him in the Church of Londinium for the space of seven years, in peace and great joy. For I was drawn toward the old man more than I can describe, because he was wholly given to the Lord Jesus and abhorred vain quarrels and disputations and (which was not so in all the saints) he added to his love of Christ such a love of letters and learning that (next to my beloved master Paulus) he, more than any other, seemed to join together that which is best both in the Jews and in the Greeks.

From the lips of this my beloved teacher I received the tradition of the words and deeds of the Lord pure and uncorrupted; and it was no small strength and refreshment to hear the very sayings of Christ himself from one whose love of truth appeared in this saying of his, a saying often repeated in his doctrine, that "he loved to think of the Lord Jesus as Son of man, and also as Son of God; but he loved no less to think of him as the Eternal Truth, whom no lie could serve nor please." Moreover, because he discerned the divine nature to consist not so much in the performance of fleshly wonders as in the working of spiritual works, for this cause he never was led to magnify (as I had heard some magnify) the mighty acts of Jesus in the healing of the diseases of the body; but he spoke the more of his divine power in casting down mountains of sin, and in the uprooting of error, and in satisfying the hungry soul with bread, and in cleansing the spotted soul from all the defilements of Satan. Therefore in all his discourses, without any straining after new and convenient traditions, and without any fear and avoidance of old traditions as being not convenient, he spoke of the Lord Jesus as being verily a man in all points, sin only excepted; subject, as men are subject, to birth and pain and death; but, none the less, as being the Beginning and the Goal of human life, the Eternal Love of God, spiritually begotten of God before the foundation of the world. In this doctrine I rejoiced, and this doctrine I strove to teach; and it was a great delight that here were no Greek factions nor Jewish factions, nor disputations about traditions, or prophecies, or aught else; but all was peace and harmony, as if in some haven, shut in and sheltered by the hills, wherein the mariner, resting from long tossing on the deeps, can scarce hear the roaring of the sea without.

But after seven years had thus passed away in peace it being now the second year of the Emperor Domitianuss, it came to pass that new troubles fell upon the Church; and, the Bishop of Beroe having borne witness for the Lord with his blood in a tumult in that city, I was called to the charge of the flock there; and the voice of the Lord bade me go. So bidding farewell to the beloved Elder Philochristus with much sorrow, well knowing that I should not again behold him in the flesh, I set forth with his blessing upon my journey, intending first to go to Rome and there to tarry some days, and so to Beroe.

§ 6. OF THE CHURCH IN ROME, AND OF THE NEW GOSPELS

When I came to Rome I was well received of the brethren, and I tarried there two months, observing the manner of their worship, and the teaching of the catechumens and the discourses of the elders to the faithful. But I seemed at first to be listening to a new Gospel; so great a change had fallen on the Church since I had last tarried in the great city, about fifteen years before. This appeared, not only in their worship, but also in the pictures and sculptures wherewith they had begun to adorn the tombs of those that fell asleep in the Lord; for in these I perceived that those very beliefs whereof I had written to Artemidorus as being currently reported among the faithful but not yet added to the Tradition, were now accepted by all. For example, when I entered into one of the places where the congregations commonly assemble themselves for worship these are quarries, after the manner of galleries, hewn out of the rock under the earth beneath the city, commonly called catacombs, and used for entombments by the faithful I perceived there the figure of a certain prophet, with a scroll in his hand, pointing to a Woman which bare a child in her arms, and above the child was a star; and I questioned my companions whether this was the Lord Jesus, the Son of the Virgin Mother, and they said " Yes," but when I went on to speak of the Virgin as the Spiritual Sion, which is the Church of God, then they said, "Nay, but it sheweth the mother of our Lord according to the flesh, according to the saying of the prophet, ' Behold a virgin shall conceive and bear a son, and shall call his name Immanuel.' " Then asking concerning the star, I said that I supposed that it represented the brightness of the Messiah, even as it was written in the Scriptures that "a star should come out of Jacob." To this they assented, "but," added one, "it is also well-known that a star, visible to the eyes of men, did verily shine forth in the days of Herod, being seen of many nations, and especially in the East, insomuch that then was fulfilled the saying of the Psalms that the kings of Arabia and Saba should bring gifts." "Are these things then," said I, "contained in the Tradition of the Acts of the Lord"?" Then he that had spoken replied, "No, not in the Tradition, but in a certain supplement which is now beginning everywhere to be read in all the 'churches, and it is said to have been put forth by the interpreters and disciples of one of the Apostles ": but another, correcting him, said that one of the Apostles himself had written it, not indeed Petrus nor Jacobus who were unlearned men ignorant of letters, but in all likelihood Mattheus, as having been in his earlier days a taxgatherer and therefore ready with his pen.

Going on a little further I saw on the walls another picture of men supping at a table, and the food two fishes and some loaves. When I asked what this meant, they told me that it signified the banquet of the kingdom of God wherein all the faithful partake of the body of the Lord who, said they, is our Bread of Life, and also our true ***ιχθος***; and "of the two fishes," said they, "the one denoteth Baptism, whereby the faithful enter into Christ, and the other the Lord's Supper, whereby they are made partakers of the Lord's body, so that they remain in him and he in them." " And is this also," I asked, in the Tradition?" " Neither in the Tradition," said they, "nor in the Supplement, but it is a symbol." Then I took courage to speak concerning that other parable of a banquet, wherein I had been wont to teach how the Twelve had been bidden by the Lord Jesus to minister both of the Bread of Life and of the Fishes, asking them whether they interpreted this also spiritually and not according to the letter, even as they interpreted that other story of the IXoTC. But hereat their countenances changed, and they said, "Nay, but this story is written according to the letter in the Tradition of the Gospel." Then I told them how Philochristus the Elder had related to me that the Lord Jesus himself, in speaking of these matters, had rebuked his disciples because they understood him not, saying unto them, that when he spoke of leaven, and of bread, he spoke not of earthly bread or leaven, but of spiritual leaven and spiritual bread. But they replied that "it was not so written in the Tradition now, and that Philochristus (albeit to be reverenced as a faithful disciple of the Lord) was not to be too much trusted as a remembrancer of the Tradition, because he had lived now many years apart from the rest of the saints, not having experience of that which had been from year to year newly revealed to the Church, so that he knew naught save what he himself had heard and seen of the Lord Jesus, and this in all likelihood faintly and imperfectly remembered by him, as being wellstricken in years, not much less than fourscore and ten." It came into my mind that to be thus all alone, remembering and teaching the words of Christ which he himself had heard (apart from controversies and colours and glosses of those who were disputing rather than remembering) was perhaps rather a help than a harm to Philochristus. However at that time I said no more,

On the morrow, coming somewhat late into the congregation in the midst of their worship, I heard them singing a psalm which, because there arose hence a question afterwards between myself and the brethren, I will here set down; and as near as I can remember, the words were these:

1.

"Pilot of our bark
What though the night be dark?
What though the tempest rave?
Thou still canst hear and save.

2.

"Tossed by the troubled sea,
Lord, we cry to thee,
And through the murky night
What figure meets our sight?

3.

"Lo, pitying our fear
The Lord himself draws near,
Walking upon the wave
His helpless ones to save.

4.

"In terror of his face
Vanish the clouds apace,
His footsteps on the deep
Lull every wave to sleep.

5.

"The winds obey his will,
The raging storm is still;
Then turn we to adore
And lo, at hand the shore."

Now these words or others like unto them, had been well known to me for a long time, because some such psalm had been brought to us at Colossse from Ephesus (from which city many psalms and hymns had come to divers churches) and it was commonly sung in the churches of Asia; and indeed, even among the ancient poems of the Jews, there is a psalm not much unlike this, wherein the mariners cry unto the Lord in their trouble and he delivereth them out of their distress, for, saith the psalm, "He maketh the storm to cease so that the waves thereof are still "; and another psalm saith, "Thy way is in the sea and thy path on the great waters." But, often as I had sung these words, it had never so much as entered my mind to interpret them according to the letter; for even as the Greeks or Romans compare the state to a ship and the ruler to a pilot, even so had we been wont to speak, in a figure, of the Church as being a ship tossed upon the sea of troubles and persecutions, and of the Lord Jesus as her pilot in the storm; and I had also heard mention made, when I was in Britain, of some new hymn shewing in a figure, how the blessed Apostle Petrus denied his Master, and describing how he adventured to walk, in his own strength, upon the troubled sea of temptation; but his faith failed him so that he began to sink, and he had been drowned in the deep waters of sin, but that the Lord stretched out his hand and saved him; but in this and other such psalms and hymns there was never a thought of any real boat nor of a real storm of wind and waves. Therefore, the worship being now ended, when a certain Philologus, one of the brethren, accosted me asking my judgment of this psalm, as if I should have censured it, I replied (not without some wonder at the strangeness of his question) that the psalm was a good one, and that none could find any fault in it. But Philologus replied, "If therefore, Onesimus, you allow of this miracle of the Lord, why contend you against these other miracles of which the Gospel makes mention?" I said, "Nay, but of what miracle do I allow?" He said, "Even that miracle and no other, which is clearly described in the psalm, how the Lord Jesus walked upon the waters to save the holy Apostles; yea, and one of the new Gospels affirms that the blessed Apostle Petrus adventured himself to walk upon the waves; but his faith failed him so that he began to sink."

Hereat I was speechless; and Philologus, as if he were ill at ease by reason of my silence, bade me follow him and two or three of the other elders into another chamber in the place where they were assembled. Here were depicted divers wonders, first, the sending down of the manna from heaven for Israel, and also the gushing forth of the water from the rock; and said he, if Moses wrought these wonders, must not the Lord Jesus have wrought others still more wonderful? Then said I to them, "Moses not only caused bread but also water to arise for Israel; and again the prophet Elisha, even when dead, had power to raise up a dead man; wherefore, if indeed the Lord. Jesus desired to surpass Moses and Elias in wonders according to the flesh (and not, as I believe, in wonders according to the spirit) he must needs have caused water, as well as bread, to spring up for the multitude, or else perchance honey or wine; and he must needs also have raised up from the dead some one that was on the point to be buried or already buried; but is any such relation as either of these to be found in any tradition concerning the Lord Jesus?" They said there was not; and methought they were somewhat at a stand. But presently Philologus corrected them saying, "Nay, my brethren, say not 'the Tradition containeth not these things' but rather 'These things are not known to us at present,' for although it hath not yet been revealed to the Church in any Tradition that the Lord Jesus hath produced water or wine, or raised up a dead man from the tomb, yet is it possible that he may have wrought these very works, and in time they may be made known to the Church, even as the walking on the waves was not made known in the first Tradition of the Acts of the Lord, nor were other mighty works;" and here he made mention of many unknown to me such as the catching of a mighty draught of fishes, and the finding of a fish with a coin in the mouth of it.

Hereat I ceased from further speech. For I perceived that my questioning had the contrary effect to that which I had intended. For I had hoped to lead Philologus and his companions to see that the spiritual works of the Lord Jesus were greater than those wonders according to the flesh, of which they made so much. But instead thereof, Philologus had been made by my words more greedy than ever of fresh wonders, and was now ready to believe anything if it were only wonderful enough. So I held my peace, and only besought Philologus to lend me copies of the written books of the Gospels such as were now read in the churches.

§ 7. HOW I LABOURED IN BEROEA

Having given myself during many days to the reading and meditating in the three books of the Gospels, I found much less addition of wonders and other doubtful matters than I had expected, and least of all in that book which was said by most to have been written according to the teaching of Marcus; only in rendering the Hebrew into the Greek there had been a few errors; and in some two or three passages, figures of speech appeared to have been interpreted according to the letter. But the other two books, though they contained most excellent traditions, very full and ample, of certain words of the Lord, had added supplements touching the birth of the Lord Jesus and his childhood and youth, and also concerning his manifestations after his rising from the dead, which were not known to me. So, after much debate with myself, I concluded to write to Philochristus, sending to him the three books and asking his judgment concerning them. This done, I bade farewell to the brethren in Rome and betook myself to Beroe where the Lord had prepared for me an abundant work.

Many days I continued labouring in Beroea and hearing naught from Philochristus; yet was I not without some guidance from the Lord. For day by day, ministering to the unlearned among the brethren, I perceived that the presence and the power of the Lord among them were not let or hindered by what I deemed their errors. The three books of the Gospels were beginning at this time to be commonly read among them, and I saw that the multitude willingly believed all things written therein, especially concerning the birth of the Lord Jesus, and concerning his manifesting of himself after death by divers signs and tokens, as by eating in the presence of the disciples, and by giving his body to be touched. Now remembering what the blessed Apostle Paulus had enjoined on me, that I must by all means seek to attain as much of the truth as possible, though there must needs be some error, I was minded at first to restrain the brethren in Beroea from the public reading of these new traditions.' But one of the elders of the Church dissuaded me, saying in the first place that the truth was uncertain; and in the second place, that, if the people believed not these traditions, and especially the tradition concerning the birth of the Lord, they must needs fall into error, not being able to receive the doctrine that the son of Mary and Joseph was verily the Son of God begotten before the worlds and taking flesh as a man for our sakes. "Either therefore," said he, "they will believe that he was merely man and not God; or else that he was not man at all, but a phantom, born of no human father nor mother either; as certain sects in Asia believe." And he added that the Lord seemed to allow this new doctrine, if doctrine might be judged by the fruits thereof; because all that believed it were full of zeal, and patience, and love for the brethren, and all virtue, ready to lay down their lives for the Lord. So I, considering that it was one thing to strive towards certainty, and another thing to restrain others from their opinions, being also myself uncertain, suffered the new gospels to be read in Beroe without hindrance, and the more willingly because the three Gospels now brought in began to drive out many other writings of Gospels which sprang up about this time, or even before, full of wonders and portents, and not preserving the truth of the life of the Lord Jesus. So in a very short time the three Gospels were brought in, and multiplied by transcribers, and were read in all our assemblies, and the catechumens were also instructed in them.

And now, after I had been about one year or more in Beroea, I received from Britain a letter written by Philochristus, which was most welcome; but withal another letter most unwelcome, written by the new Bishop of Londinium, saying that the blessed Elder Philochristus had fallen asleep in the Lord, and that this his letter, written some months before, had only of late been found among his papers, wherefore it had been long delayed in the sending. So, when I opened and read it, I seemed to be receiving his message from beyond the grave, guiding me on the path in which I should go; and these were the words of the letter.

§ 8. THE LAST WORDS OF PHILOCHRISTUS

"PHILOCHRISTUS TO ONESIMUS, GRACE AND PEACE IN THE LORD JESUS CHRIST.

"I received with your letter, my dear Onesimus, the three books of the new Gospels; concerning which having purposed to write to you some months ago, as soon as I had read them, I was hindered by long and grievous sickness.

"They contain relations of certain matters whereof I neither saw nor heard aught, while I followed the Lord Jesus in Galilee; nor have I heard aught of them from the disciples, nor from the Lord's brethren, nor from the mother of the Lord.

"Nevertheless, albeit I heard no such matters, yet is it possible that they may have been revealed to the disciples after my coming to this island in the reign of Caius Caesar. And this, I confess, hath not a little moved me, that during my sickness the three Gospels have been very diligently read by those who are here labouring with me, and by them have been interpreted to the unlearned; and everywhere they meet with great acceptance, and the Church is edified by them, insomuch that they had already begun to be read in the assemblies of certain of the churches when it pleased the Lord to raise me up for a short time from my sickness. Notwithstanding, thou sayest truly that in all things we must not willingly consent to error, though some error be a necessity; and therefore my counsel is that thou take early occasion to go to Ephesus where thou mayst question John the Disciple of the Lord. For if neither he nor I know aught of these new traditions, then it is likely that they are not according to truth; but if he consent unto them, then are they, without doubt, true.

"Not without much prayer and meditation, having striven to put myself in thy place, my dear Onesimus, have I written these words; which do thou take to heart, as my last message, because my mind forebodeth that I shall not write unto thee a second time. I know well thy sincerity and thy unfeigned love of the truth; yet bethink thee that it is the kernel of the truth that thou should st seek and not the shell; and if the kernel be sound, be not thou troubled over much though the shell may shew some blemish. For put this case that John the Disciple of the Lord be no longer in the flesh, or that thou find no occasion to see him, or that in other ways thou be frustrated of thine endeavour to search out the truth. What then? Is it needful or fit that thou shouldst therefore journey from Ephesus to Antioch, or to Nazareth, or to Bethlehem, or to Jerusalem, to inquire of these matters? Nay, but a pastor of the flock should abide with the flock. The exact truth, it may be, thou shalt never find out in this life; but thy duty towards thy brethren thou canst certainly find out. This therefore find out, and do. I say not that thou, in thy doctrine and preaching, shouldst teach or even assent to these new traditions; but what I say is this, that if the worship of the Lord Jesus be enwrapped (among the unlearned) in some integument of doubtful tradition which commendeth itself to the brethren—because they cannot easily believe that he worked mightily in the spirit, except they also believe that he wrought mighty works according to the flesh—then I say it needeth not, nor is it fit, that thou shouldst spend all thy time in rending this integument asunder, but rather that thou shouldst labour to teach the main truth, which is, that our Lord Jesus Christ was verily a man, and verily the Eternal Sen of God, in whom all mankind hath died to sin and is born again to righteousness.

"But thou sayest that 'A time may come when these traditions shall be found to be false; and then as much as they now draw the unlearned to Christ, so much, and more also, shall they then drive the unlearned from Christ. For, being unapt to distinguish, and apt to reject all if they reject a part, the common people, finding a part of the tradition of the Acts of the Lord to be false, will cast aside the whole as a mere fable.' Well and wisely is this said, and providently also according to thy nature, my dear Onesimus; yet have I faith in Truth, according as it is written, that ' Truth is great and shall prevail '; and whensoever the danger whereof thou speakest shall press upon the Church, I doubt not but the Lord, who is also the Truth, shall raise up teachers that shall have skill to sift the true from the false; yea, and if, even now, thou seest this danger, or if thou obtainest certain knowledge that these traditions are false, I deny not but thou shouldst speak openly against them. But until thou shalt obtain such certainty, wait thou patiently upon the Lord, and do with all thy might the works which he hath appointed for thee to do.

"Remember, my son, that thou art called to be a bishop and champion for the souls of men, to deliver them from the mouth of the lion; and the battle presseth sorely against the army of the Lord. Play thou the man therefore, and be no mere pedant nor seeker after the antiquities of small matters. Even in this year, as thou thyself dost write, many of the Saints have borne witness with their lives to the

Captain of our Salvation. Whilst others therefore are fighting among the vanguard and pouring forth their blood for the Lord, be not thou content to lag behind in the rear with the baggage; nor, from being a soldier of the Lord, stoop thou to be a mere campfollower. Lovest thou the Lord? I know thou lovest him with all thine heart. Then be content. The Saints of the Church in Beroe whom God hath committed to thy charge, do they also love the Lord? Thyself hast confessed as much. Then again I say, . Be thou content. 'But,' sayest thou, 'they err in certain traditions concerning the Lord.' Well, then, they err. But which is better, that they should love the Lord and be in some error, or that they should be free from error and void of love"? Better to have wheat with tares than no tares and no wheat. Let both stand till the harvest; and in the day of winnowing of the Master, a separation shall be made. Farewell, Onesimus; and again I say unto thee, as from the Lord, in whose presence I hope to stand when thou shalt read these words, Play thou the man and prevail, in the love and trust of the Lord Jesus Christ; and the Lord shall be with thee and bless thee."

When I had read the letter of the blessed Philochristus, I was confirmed in my purpose not at once to quit the city of Beroe; and the more because at that time the saints began to be sorely persecuted; insomuch that I had no leisure to be absent, no, not so much as for a few days, during the space of two whole years; so busy was I in comforting the afflicted and strengthening the weak, and ministering to the widows of them that bore witness for the Lord. And as I strengthened, or strove to strengthen, others, so also and much more did they strengthen me, when I perceived their constancy and fortitude, and noted how, amidst all their sufferings, even the unlearned (yea, some of those on whom I had been apt to look with some pity for their superstitions), were lifted up with a divine magnanimitv such as no philosopher could surpass. And at this time I began more clearly to understand that which Philochristus had said (and Paulus before him) touching the distinguishing of things great and small. For I now perceived, as never before, that the love of Christ was the main thing, and that whoso could love him and cling to him should be first in the Kingdom of God, and that I myself (though I were bishop in Beroea) should come far behind many of the simple brethren, halting as it were into heaven, while they should come borne upon wings.

But now, two years having passed away and the Church being now at peace, the advice of Philochristus hath come again to my mind that if I crave after certainty concerning the additions to the Tradition, I should go to see John the Disciple of the Lord at Ephesus. For the holy Apostle still lives, although stricken in years and infirm, not having been able for these many years to preach the Gospel. Yet is there a tradition or doctrine at Ephesus (as I have heard say) differing much from the three Gospels, and taught by the disciples of John and especially by one, John the Elder, a man of Alexandria (one that has travelled much, and is well versed in the philosophy of the Alexandrine teachers, but much more in the deep things of the Spirit), whom I met many years ago in Antioch. These lines I now write in the sixth year of the Emperor Domitianus, purposing shortly to set out for Smyrna, and thence to Ephesus, to see John and to obtain concerning the Traditions such certainty as I can. Howbeit the Spirit in me forebodeth that I shall not obtain certainty after this manner, neither shall I come again to Beroe, but the Lord hath some other purpose concerning me.

§ 9. OF MY JOURNEY TO SMYRNA, AND HOW THE LORD HATH HELPED ME EVEN TO THE END

Verily the Spirit deceived me not; for being now about to bear witness for the Lord Jesus with my blood, I add these last words to this history, no longer free, nor amid friends, but in a dungeon, expecting shortly that I shall fight with wild beasts for the Lord in this city of Smyrna, wherein now I write. For coming hither about the time of Passover, I found the people of the city in no small disturbance, because of a great earthquake, and the drying up of the springs, and also incensed against the Proconsul because he had awarded some prize in the games against their judgment. Wherefore the people on the one hand were moved against the Christians, as being causers of the earthquake, and the Proconsul for his part was the more ready to listen to them so as to turn their wrath from himself on us. So when I was, without any disturbance, preaching the Gospel to the Saints on the first day of the week, behold, the Irenarch came suddenly upon us with great violence, and after loading me with fetters he dragged me (with one of the presbyters called Trophimus) before the Proconsul;

who straightway bade me swear by the Fortune of Caesar and reproach Christ. When I refused, he said to me, "I will consume thee with fire, except thou repent." Then Trophimus made answer, somewhat bitterly, "Thou threatenest me with fire which burneth for an hour and, after that, is extinguished; but thou knowest not the fire of the judgment that is to come which is reserved for the ungodly." Hereupon the multitude that were in the Stadium, cried out, "Away with the Atheists." Others bade let loose a lion upon us. But the Proconsul gave orders that we should be taken to the dungeon and there kept for a night and day; and after that, if we would not repent and offer sacrifice saying, "Caesar is Lord," we were to be cast to the wild beasts; for the show was appointed for the day after the morrow. So with many reproaches and blows from the officers, goading me onwards that I might come the quicker out of the multitude—who were gathered round, cursing and threatening, and ready to have torn me in pieces—I was dragged along the streets to the prison, and there my clothes were rent from off me, and I was cast naked, more dead than alive, into the barathrum or pit which is in the centre of the inmost prison, there to abide till the time came that I should fight with wild beasts.

Amid the darkness and mire and stench of that noisome den, it pleased the Lord that I should be tempted of Satan that I might prevail over him with the strength of the Lord. For when I knelt down to call upon the Lord, being always used to make mention of Chrestus and Eucharis in my prayers, behold, I found myself bereft of the tokens of them both, whereon were written TRUST and HOPE; and then a terror fell upon me and a shuddering that was not of the limbs but of the heart (so did my very spirit seem to shiver within me) and a voice of evil whispered in my ear saying, "*Trust* no more," and then again, "Thy *Hope* is dead; " and methought monstrous shapes moved around me, making my flesh to creep; and I was on the brink of a bottomless gulf wherein I must needs fall, and Satan was waiting below, ready to swallow up my soul.

Then fell I upon my face and I called upon the Lord in my sore trouble, and besought him that he would send me help from heaven; and I repeated over and over again his comfortable words, how he bade us not fear them that could slay the body, and how he promised that, though we should be slain, yet not one hair of our heads should perish; and I bethought myself of my beloved teacher Paulus, how he also had lain in just such another dungeon for nine days and nights, and with what a constancy he had held fast to the faith of the Lord Jesus; and I also called to mind the last words of the elder Philochristus, how he had bidden me play the man and fight the good fight for Christ. Now up to this time I had been still wrestling with Satan and trembling lest, coming upon me a second time, he should gain some advantage over me; but now, taking courage, I besought the Lord, as in old times, for Christus and Eucharis, that they also might obtain mercy and be with me in Christ.

Then it pleased the Lord Jesus my Saviour to turn my thoughts wholly upon him. and upon his passion which he endured for men upon the cross; and gazing thereon I was rapt up with him above the stir and tumult of earth; and methought I saw, looking down from above, how all the past had worked together for me for good; and how all my wanderings and gropings, yea, even my sins, being washed away by the blood of him who suffered, had become helps instead of hindrances, helping me to love much because I had been much forgiven. Then also I saw how the Lord in his mercy had taken from me the hope of Eucharis, and the trust of Chrestus, yea, and the love of my dearest mother, that so he might guide me up unto himself, the source and object of all trust and hope and love. So being filled with all certainty of joy I besought the Lord once more for them, and for the mother whom I had never seen in the flesh, that they also as well as Eucharis (who had received the seal of baptism) might attain to the resurrection of the just, and I prayed that, if it were possible, I might receive from him some sign or vision that it was well with them. And so it was that, as soon as I had thus prayed, I was lifted up in the spirit with the cross of Christ yet higher than before, and the Lord showed me a vast sea of death, and beneath the sea of death, a sea of sin; but beneath the sea of sin and of death I saw a great gulf of life and love, which swallowed up the sea of sin and death, so that they vanished away.

How long I remained in the Spirit I know not; but when the Spirit left me I was lying in the courtyard of the prison; and around me were standing some of the elders ministering to me, and bidding me be of stout heart; for, said they, in two hours hence must thou needs fight with wild beasts in the amphitheatre for the Lord Jesus Christ. Then I spoke to them strengthening their hearts, and telling them of all the glories of the vision which the Lord had revealed unto me, and having obtained pen and paper I have written down the vision, and how the Lord helped me; to the intent that others also, in time to come, vile and sinful, and defiled, and faithless, may take courage from this history, perceiving how even the weakest and vilest may be made pure and strong in Christ.

As I write these words, knowing that in the third hour of this same day I shall bear witness for the Lord beneath the jaws of the leopards, how small and petty seem to me now the matters of which I once doubted! Better is it to be a fool (as the world counteth folly) and to love the Lord than to have all knowledge and to be without love. He that loveth his brother hath all things and knoweth all things; and, if he lack aught, behold, all possessions and all knowledge shall be added unto him. Behold, the voice of man calleth me to arise and to go forth unto death. But I obey not his voice but thine. Thou callest me, my Redeemer, and I come.

§ 10. CONCERNING THE PASSION OF THE BLESSED MARTYRS TROPHIMUS AND ONESIMUS

For the edification of the saints it hath seemed good to us, the Elders of the Church in Smyrna, to add to this history a brief relation concerning the passion of the blessed martyrs Trophimus and Onesimus, to the intent that others, taking them as their ensamples, may be encouraged to testify ivith like boldness for the Lord. The manner of their going forth from prison tuas of a strange difference; both rejoicing, but Trophimus threatening the people with the wrath of God, and saying to the Proconsul, "Thou judgest us; but God shall judge thee." Likewise to the Asiarch he said, "Note well our faces that thou mayst remember us in the judgment-day, when we shall laugh, and thou iveep." Hereat the people, being angered, demanded that they should be scourged, passing through two rows of venatores: but the blessed martyr Trophimus rejoiced that he shoidd have received this further torment for the Lord Jesus. Onesimus also showed no less cheerfulness and constancy; but he walked silent and with eyes fixed and uplifted, as if intent on the glory to come.

But before they should make trial of the leopards, Satan had prepared a fierce wild bull to assail the martyrs of the Lord; and first Trophimus was tossed, and fell crushed and, as it seemed, lifeless. Then Onesimus was also tossed; but he arose, as if in a trance; and seeing Trophimus lying crushed, he drew near, and took him by the hand, and lifted him up, himself being all the while in an ecstasy; as was apparent from certain words which he spoke to a young man, one of the catechumens, whose name was Symmachus. For when Onesimus was recalled by the usual gate, while the leopards were making ready, this young man Symmachus received him and ministered to him; and at this time he heard the blessed martyr say, as one in a dream, "marvel when we shall be led out to that wild bull," not knowing what he had already suffered; nor could he believe that he had suffered till he perceived the wounds and bruises on his body. Coming to himself he thanked the young man Symmachus for his kindness and blessed him. Also it pleased the Lord to move the mind of a certain centurion, named Hipponax, who, having before despoiled the blessed martyr of some slight tokens, now came to him restoring them; upon which the blessed martyr, mindful even of the smallest matters, thanked the soldier courteously and placed them around his neck. And by this time also Trophimus was fully recovered, and eager to bear witness for the Lord. So, the Lord having appointed the time for their release, they are led out to the leopards. Then Trophimus, running forward, provoked one of the beasts to attack him; and straightway springing upon him, the beast with one bite drew forth such a stream of blood that all the people, mocking at him (as if he had been baptized in his own blood) cried out saying, "Saved and washed, saved and washed"; and Onesimus also was struck down by another of the leopards, and dragged hither and thither by the beasts. But when the beasts had been taken away, and the blessed martyrs cast on one side to be slaughtered after the usual manner, then the people clamoured that they should be set in the midst of the amphitheatre that their eyes might enjoy the spectacle of the slaughter. So both stood up and moved, of themselves, to the appointed place. Here Trophimus, being very weak with loss of blood, fell on the ground; but Onesimus, standing up, stretched out his hands, looking to heaven as if he saw a vision; and the shouting of the multitude and their scoffing and cursing became less, and at last there was a deep silence, all the people expecting what he should say or do; but the blessed martyr, taking in his hand that which he wore round his neck as if it were some memorial of the Lord, held it up to heaven and cried aloud, "Lord my Hope and my Trust, thou lovest me, yea, and thou shalt love me, for thou art the Eternal Love.^ And having said these words he laid himself down by the side of Trophimus and having embraced him, he bade the gladiator strike his throat; and the sword fell twice, and no more; and so Trophimus and Onesimus, blessed martyrs for the faith, fell asleep in the Lord Jesus, to whom be glory and honour for ever and ever. Amen.

THE END OF THE EIGHTH BOOK

AN ADDITION CONTAINING THE DISCOURSE OF LUCIUS OF CYRENE WHICH WAS OMITTED FROM THE THIRD BOOK OF LUCIUS OF CYRENE"

IT is known unto you all, my brethren, that whensoever we bring forward proofs from the mighty works of our Lord Jesus Christ, desiring thereby to show that he was the Messiah, our adversaries are not thereby persuaded, but the Jews say that he was a magician, and the Greeks that he was an impostor. Wherefore it is meet that we resort to stronger arguments than these, opening the Scriptures and proving from them that Jesus is the very Messiah. For jugglers, say the Greeks, and magicians, say the Jews, can perform mighty works at will; but it is not possible for a juggler, nor even for a magician, so to be born and also to live all his life and to die, so as to fulfil all that is written in the Law and the Prophets. Wherefore it is fit that we should diligently search the Scriptures that we may prove that the Lord Jesus was born and lived, and died, in accordance with the word of prophecy; for thus shall we establish the truth so that it cannot be shaken.

"First therefore concerning his birth, the Prophet saith, 'Who shall declare his generation?' Now of any common mortal this could not be said; but it is predicted concerning him whose generation is a mystery, in that he is the only Son of God. Moreover another prophecy saith, 'A virgin shall conceive and bear a son.' Now if the very heathen assert no less than this about Asclepius, and Heracles, and Romulus, and a hundred others, who were no true sons of God, but only sons of demons, how much more must it be true of our Master and only Saviour that he was veritably born of no human father, but was the Son of God! And it hath been shown to be in accordance with the saying of the Prophet.

"Likewise when the Prophet Daniel speaks of 'one *like* unto the Son of man,' doth he not hint at the very same thing? For, in saying '*like* unto the Son of man,' and not '*the* Son of man,' he declareth thereby that Jesus was man, but not of human seed. And the same thing he doth express in mystery, when he speaketh of 'this stone which was cut out *without hands*,' signifying that it was the work, not of man, but of the Father and God of all things. And again, when Moses saith that 'he will wash his garments in the blood of the grape,' doth not this signify what I have often told you,—albeit enwrapped in obscure terms, after the manner of prophecy—I mean, that he had blood, but not from men: even as God, and not man, hath begotten the blood of the vine?

"Now I know indeed that certain of the Rabbis, interpreting amiss the prophecy of Isaiah concerning him that was to be born of a virgin, affirm the words of the Prophet to have been fulfilled in the time of Hezekiah; for they say that the prophecy was, that 'the riches of Damascus and the spoils of Samaria should be taken away from before the king of Assyria;' and that this was to come to pass before the child, born to the Prophet from the Virgin whom he took to be his wife, had learned to cry 'my father and my mother;' and accordingly they say that the prophet took the prophetess to wife, and that she bore a son, who being yet an infant, Damascus and Samaria were destroyed. But we affirm that the prophecy is not thus written; but it is, 'he, namely the child, shall take away the power of Damascus and the spoils of Samaria.' Now who will dare to assert that, in the days of the King Hezekiah, any infant among the Jews, 'before he had power to cry, my father, or my mother'—for mark this addition—conquered two so great nations?

"Assuredly no one will assert this. But the meaning of the prophecy is as follows. The evil demon who dwelleth in Damascus, and who also may be well termed in parable Samaria, was overcome by Christ as soon as he was born. For I have heard (and it is by all means to be believed, for it is according to the words of Holy Scripture, which needs must be fulfilled) that certain Magi, who dwelt in Arabia—and none of you can deny that Damascus was, and is, in the region of Arabia, although now it belongeth to what is called Syrophoenicia—came from the East to worship Christ at his birth, thereby showing that they had revolted from the dominion of Satan. Now it is said that these Magi came first to Herod, who was the sovereign of the land of the Jews, but who by the Scriptures (on account of his ungodly and sinful character) is called king of Assyria. Nevertheless they gave not their gifts to him, but going forth from his presence, they gave gold, and frankincense, and myrrh,—which were as it were the spoils of Damascus,—to the child Jesus in the manger: and so it came to pass that he who was born of the Virgin, while still a babe, 'took away the power of Damascus and the spoils of Samaria, from the presence of the King of Assyria.'

"Next as to the place of his birth, even the Gentiles do bear testimony that there shall come forth from the East one that shall obtain dominion over the Empire, and this is known throughout the whole world; nor do the prophets write otherwise, saying, 'Behold a Man, the East is his name.' And that our Christ was born in Syria, that is in the East, is confessed of all. But further, touching the city in which he was born, some have been wont to affirm that he was born at Nazareth because he lived there many years from a child. But that he must needs have been born at Bethlehem is clear, because it is written, 'And thou, Bethlehem Ephratah, though thou art the least among the hundreds of thy people, yet out of thee shall come a governor who shall feed my people; 'and that he was to appear first in the south (for Bethlehem is in the south) and not in a northern city, such as Nazareth, is clear also from another Scripture, which saith, 'God cometh from the south.'

"Moreover, which of you knoweth not that the Lord Jesus is the Bread of Life? Therefore, when the Bread of Life was to descend and to find a house and home among men, what city in Israel was more fit for him than that one which is called Bethlehem, which being interpreted, is 'the House of Bread?' Lastly, it is known to all of you that Mary, the mother of Jesus, being of a royal race, was descended from David the king, who was of the city of Bethlehem; wherefore it was the more fitting that the Son of David should be born at the same place. Also I have heard some say that there is a certain cave in Bethlehem wherein he was born; and to this day the cave is shown; and they affirm that it must needs have been so, because it is written, 'he shall dwell in a high cave of the strong rock; 'but because it is commonly reported that he was born in a manger, and because I purpose to speak of none but such things as are certainly believed among us, for this reason I affirm nothing on this matter.

"But (that he might not be inferior to his servant Moses), as Moses was persecuted by the Egyptian king Pharaoh, so was Jesus by Herod, the King of the Jews; and, even as Israel sojourned for a time in Egypt, so must the Redeemer of Israel sojourn in the same country, that it might be fulfilled as it is written, 'Out of Egypt have I called my son.'

His mighty works also, which he wrought on those that believed in him, are they not written in the books of the Prophets? namely, that in that day the ears of the deaf should be unstopped, and the eyes of the blind opened, and the dead should be raised up, and the poor should have the gospel preached unto them: which all are recounted in our tradition, even to the raising of the dead. For as Elisha the prophet raised up the son of the Shunammite, even so did the Son of God raise up the daughter of Jairus; and, whereas our adversaries say that this was but a small matter, doubtless this is but one among a multitude of like marvels. Again, whereas they assert that Moses was superior to Jesus in that he gave unto the people manna in the wilderness, to this I reply that even so did the Lord Jesus prepare a table for his people in the wilderness; yea, and as Moses gave water from the rock, even so did our living Rock grant unto us living water from his own side, yea, wine instead of water, pouring forth his blood to be the drink of many, and affording his body to be the Bread of Life unto all mankind.

"When thou wast born, mighty One—before the Morning Star wast thou begotten—and when the Star of thine uprising was seen, then all the host of heaven worshipped thee and the sun and the moon did thee homage, and the Sons of the Morning sang for joy together at the brightness of thy glory; for thy Star did far outshine all earthly light, appearing as a token of the destruction of the kingdom of Satan, according as it is written, 'A star shall shine out of Jacob, and a sceptre from Israel, and shall destroy the corners of Edom.' Then did Edom tremble, but the poor and simple rejoiced. To thee also the Wisdom of the East did obeisance, the kings of Arabia and Saba brought gifts. Thou also didst feed the hungry, and heal the sick, Satan fled from before thee and thou didst cast his demons into the abyss; thou didst guide thy disciples through the paths of great waters; when they cry unto thee, thou hearest them; thy voice stilleth the wind, and thy path is on the deep. To thee the Law and Prophets do bear witness that thou art the very Christ. Yea, Moses and Elias stand at thy right hand and at thy left, to bear witness unto thee, that in thee must needs be accomplished all things that are written in the Law and the Prophets.

"But concerning the manner of the death of the Lord Jesus, that it is prophesied a hundred times both in the Psalms and in the Prophets, what need is there that I should speak unto you? For ye yourselves know these Scriptures. But as concerning his rising again on the third day, it is written, 'I will lay me down and rest, for thou wilt raise me up;' and again, 'Let us go unto the Lord; he hath smitten and he shall revive us; on the third day he shall raise us up, and we shall live in his sight.' Moreover, brethren, let me also declare unto you, as many as have fathers or mothers according to the flesh who have fallen asleep not having known the Lord Jesus that ye sorrow not for them as if they were lost; for it is written, 'The Lord God remembered his dead people of Israel who lay in the graves; and he descended to preach unto them his own salvation.' And this saying, 'he descended'— what meaneth it except that he went down, even into Hades to break the bonds of Satan, and to preach his Gospel unto the fathers who lived in times past, even unto all the righteous, that they also might have hope of salvation? Wherefore also, when he arose from the dead, a multitude of the saints arose from their graves with him, being delivered from the captivity of death, according to the saying, 'He led captivity captive, and gave gifts for men.' But last of all, after he had risen from the dead, having manifested himself during many days to his disciples, it was necessary that he should ascend into heaven, according as it is written, 'Lift up yourselves, ye gates, and be ye lift up, ye everlasting doors, and the King of glory shall come in.'

"Now therefore, beloved brethren, called of God, heirs of everlasting life, having the Lord Jesus, in his birth and mighty works, and in his death and rising again, thus visibly set forth as it were before your eyes by the Prophets and the Psalms, what remaineth but that ye should watch, and pray, and show forth all patience, esteeming lightly the joys and sorrows of this present world, and making little account of your worldly possessions (for great possessions are great temptations); but be ye possessed with a new Spirit, even with the Spirit of the Lord Jesus Christ, filling your hearts with an insatiable desire of doing good, comforting; the sorrowful, feeding the hungry, healing the sick, and preaching the good news of Christ; and covet no man's wealth, nor slaves, nor apparel; but covet ye every occasion of well-doing. Thus shall ye make yourselves ready for the day of the Lord when, the number of the elect having been at last completed, the Lord your Saviour shall come again from heaven in great glory, and ye shall reign with him in joy unspeakable.

"The Grace of the Lord Jesus Christ and the Love of God and the Fellowship of the Holy Spirit be with you now and always. Go in peace."

THE END

NOTES TO THE DISCOURSE OF LUCIUS OF CYRENE

Page 297.

For the importance attached to prophecy, see Irenaeus (*Against Heresies*, ii. 4): "If, however, they maintain that the Lord performed such works simply in appearance, we shall refer them to the prophetical writings, and prove from these both that all things were thus predicted regarding Him, and did take place undoubtedly." Justin Martyr also takes the same view, I. Apol, 30.

Page 297.

"Who shall declare his generation?" This passage is similarly applied by Justin Martyr, Dialogue, 63.

Page 299.

"He shall take away" etc. So Justin (*Dial*, 77), "But now the prophecy has stated it with this addition: 'Before the child knows how to call father or mother, he shall take the power of Damascus and spoils of Samaria.' And you cannot prove that such a thing ever happened to any one among the Jews. But we are able to prove that it happened in the case of Christ." And he then proceeds to interpret Damascus as referring to the Magi, and Assyria to Herod, as in the text.

Page 300.

"Behold a Man, the East is his name," Zech. vi. 12, according to the Septuagint, quoted by Justin, *Dial*, 106.

Page 301.

"He shall dwell in a cave," etc.: quoted by Justin Martyr from the Septuagint version of Isaiah xxxiii. 16 (*Dial*, 70).

Page 303.

"The Lord God remembered his dead people of Israel," etc. This passage is quoted by Justin Martyr (Dial, 72), who accuses the Jews of cancelling this and other passages of the Scriptures. It is also quoted by Irenaeus (*Against Heresies*, iii. 20) as from Isaiah, and (*ib*. iv. 22) as from Jeremiah. But it is not found in our Scriptures.

NOTES

MANY of the dialogues and some of the descriptions in the preceding pages, are borrowed from ancient authors; who however wrote in most cases after the times of Onesimus. For example, whereas Onesimus lived at Colossae about 60 A.D.; Epictetus probably nourished a generation later; Maximus of Tyre, the defender of polytheism from the social side, who is represented above by the fictitious Nicostratus, wrote under the Antonines; Julius Aristides, the eulogist of Asclepius, who is represented above by Oneirocritus, was born about 117 A.D.; Apuleius, from whom is borrowed (p. 17) the description of the ergastulum, and also (p. 180) the description of the dancers of Cybele, wrote in the second century after Christ; Celsus, the sceptic, who is represented (pp. 122-7) by the sceptical Artemidorus, wrote at the beginning of the second century; and lastly Justin Martyr and Irenaeus, from whom are mainly borrowed the discourse of Lucius of Cyrene, wrote severally about 150 A.D. and 170 A.D.

"A confession of anachronism then?" Yes: anachronism. But if only such sayings have been selected from these authors as express thoughts that were, at least in their germs, contemporaneous with Onesimus, then the life of St. Paul's convert is really far better illustrated by this systematic anachronism than by the most felicitously invented dialogue of modern scholars. Artemidorus, Nicostratus, Philemon and Oneirocritus represent thoughts that must have been in the air throughout Asia as early as 60 A.D., though they did not find expression in extant books till some time later. So also of Justin and Irenaeus; it may safely be asserted that the tendency to see in each of the acts of Jesus the exact fulfilment of some prophecy, and in each prophecy the prediction of some act of Jesus the next step being to believe and then to assert, that that act must consequently have occurred permeated the early Christian church at least as early as the date of the composition of the Introduction to St. Matthew's Gospel, and long before it found expression in the pages of Justin and Irenaeus.

In the following notes on special passages, it has not been thought necessary to give a separate reference for every quotation, but only in those cases where the words of some ancient author seemed in danger of being supposed to be modern.

Book II. § 2. Epictetus was probably a child at this time.

Book II. § 2. The remarks of Nicostratus and Heracleas are taken from Maximus of Tyre.

Book II. § 2. The remark of Heracleas on the ancient transformations is taken from Pausanias.

Book II. § 3. The whole of this description of a festival is from Maximus of Tyre.

Book II. § 4. For the story of the fighting-cock and the rest, see Friedländer's work on the *Religion of the Ancients* (French translation), vol. iv., 180.

Book II. § 4. Oneirocritus, describing his sickness and the favours of Asclepius, here repeats the sentiments of P. Aelius Aristides, born about 117 AD. (see Friedländer, *ib.*, 181-4).

Book II. § 4.Pliny esteemed it right to build temples, etc., of gods in whom he disbelieved.

Book II. § 6. The account of the descent into the cave of Trophonius is borrowed from Pausanias, who himself went down.

Book II. § 6. "I could not restrain myself from laughing ": this detail is borrowed from Pausanias.

Book II. § 7. The whole of this travesty of Socrates is taken from Lucian's *Halcyon.*

Book II. § 7. "Sobriety and incredulity," etc.: see note on iii. 4. iii. 3. Philip is reported to have raised a dead man (Euseb. H. E., iii. 39): but the account given in the text is borrowed from the account of the revivification of the Archbishop of Bordeaux, written out for the Author by one who heard it from the Archbishop himself.

Book III. § 4. "Sober incredulity," etc.—a translation of a Greek proverb.

Book III. § 7. "With whom I do not agree; neither would I," etc.: this statement about the diversity of opinions concerning the nature of Christ, is a quotation from Justin, *Dial.*, 48.

Book III. § 8. The "Tradition" here mentioned by Onesimus in the beginning of this section, is the matter common to the first three Gospels. It may be roughly represented by the Gospel of St. Mark, excluding the verses after Mark xvi. 8, which are recognised by all scholars to be an interpolation. For fuller information on the nature of this "Tradition" the reader may consult the article on Gospels in the new edition of the *Encyclopaedia Britannica.*

Book IV. § 1. The description of the voyage is from Lucian.

Book IV. § 2. Almost the whole of this letter is borrowed from Celsus as represented in Origen's treatise against him.

Book IV. § 6-9. The sayings here put into the mouth of Epictetus are, almost without exception, extracted from his works.

Book IV. § 10. The parable of the ant-hill is from Lucian.

Book IV. § 10. "If you are resolved to deal in such wares," etc. This passage is borrowed from Lucian's *Auction Of The Gods*.

Book IV. § 10. "Though my body dwelleth," etc., "Enjoy the present," etc.; these two inscriptions are still extant on the same tomb of husband and wife. See a paper by Mr. Newton in *The Nineteenth Century*, August, 1878.

Book IV. § 10. "Sleep soundly stretched at ease:" this is the advice of Teiresias in Lucian, 484-5. v. 1. This description of the dancing of the women of the priest of Cybele is from Apuleius.

Book V. § 4. "Heraclitus, the crying philosopher:" this is borrowed from Lucian.

Book VI. § 2. "Whether the true God had nails, and hair, and teeth, and the like." Such are the difficulties suggested by the Manicheans to Augustine, *Confessions*, iii. 7.

Book VIII. § 3. The description of the High-priest is from *Ecclesiasticus*, 50. viii. 3. The description of the miseries of Jerusalem is from Esdras II., iii. 28.

Book VIII. Section 3. "The hand which now had power:" this quotation is from Esdras II., v. 3. "The spoils should be carried back to the cities of the East:" this is from the *Fourth Sibylline Book*.

Book VIII. § 10. The whole of this narrative is borrowed from the account of the Martyrdom of St. Perpetua.

BOOK THREE.
SILANUS THE CHRISTIAN

TO THE MEMORY OF EPICTETUS, NOT A CHRISTIAN BUT AN AWAKENER OF ASPIRATIONS THAT COULD NOT BE SATISFIED EXCEPT IN CHRIST

PREFACE

MANY years have elapsed since the author was constrained (not by *a priori* considerations but by historical and critical evidence) to disbelieve in the miraculous element of the Bible. Yet he retained the belief of his childhood and youth—rooted more firmly than before—in the eternal unity of the Father the Son and the Holy Spirit, in the supernatural but non-miraculous incarnation of the Son as Jesus Christ, and in Christ's supernatural but non-miraculous resurrection after He had offered Himself up as a sacrifice for the sins of the world.

The belief is commonly supposed to be rendered impossible by the disbelief. This book is written to show that there is no such impossibility.

The vast majority of the worshippers of Christ base their worship to a very large extent—as the author did in his early youth, under the cloud of Paley's *Evidences*—on their acceptance of His miracles as historical facts. In the author's opinion this basis is already demonstrably unsafe, and may be at any moment, by some new demonstration, absolutely destroyed.

Nevertheless such worshippers, if their worship is really genuine— that is to say, if it includes love, trust, and awe, carried to their highest limits, and not merely that kind of awe which is inspired by "mighty works"—will do well to avoid this book. If doubt has not attacked them, why should they go to meet it? In pulling up falsehood by the roots there is always a danger of uprooting or loosening a truth that grows beside it. Historical error, if honest, is better (and less misleading) than spiritual darkness. For example, it is much better (and less misleading) to remain in the old-fashioned belief that a good and wise God created the world in six days than to adopt a new belief that a bad or unwise or careless God—or a chance, or a force, or a power—evolved it in sixty times six sextillions of centuries.

To such genuine worshippers of Christ, then, as long as they feel safe and sincere in their convictions, this book is not addressed. They are (in the author's view) substantially right, and had better remain as they are.

But there may be some, calling themselves worshippers of Christ, who cannot honestly say that they love Him. They trust His power, they bow before Him as divine; but they have no affection at all for Him, as man, or as God. What St Paul described as the "constraining" love of Christ has never touched them. And yet they fancy they worship! To them this book may be of use in suggesting the divinity and loveableness of Christ's human nature; and any harm the book might do them can hardly be conceived as equal to the harm of remaining in their present position. One may learn Christ by rote, as one may learn Euclid by rote, so as to be almost ruined for really knowing either. For such learners the best course may be to go back and begin again.

It is, however, to a third class of readers that the author mainly addresses himself. Having in view the experiences of his own early manhood, he regards with a strong fellow feeling those who desire to worship Christ and to be loyal and faithful to Him, if only they can at the same time be loyal and faithful to truth, and who doubt the compatibility of the double allegiance.

These, many of them, cannot even conceive how they can worship Christ at the right hand of God, or the Son in the bosom of the Father in heaven, unless they first believe in Him as miraculously manifested on earth. Not being able to accept Him as miraculous, they reject Him as a Saviour. To them this book specially appeals, endeavouring to show, in a general and popular way—on psychological, historical, and critical grounds—how the rejection of the claim made by most Christians that their Lord is miraculous, may be compatible with a frank and full acceptance of the conclusion that He is, in the highest sense, divine.

Detailed proofs this volume does not offer. These will be given in a separate volume of "Notes," shortly to be published. This will be of a technical nature, forming Part VII of the series called Diatessarica. The present work merely aims at suggesting such conceptions of history, literature, worship, human nature, and divine Being, as point to a fore ordained conformation of man to God, to be fulfilled in the Lord Jesus Christ, of which the fulfilment may be traced in the Christian writings and the Christian churches of the first and second centuries.

It also attempts, in a manner not perhaps very usual, to meet many objections brought against Christianity by those who assert that its records are inadequate, inaccurate, and contradictory.. Instead of denying these defects, the author admits and emphasizes them as being inseparable from earthen vessels containing a spiritual treasure, and as (in some cases) indirectly testifying to the divinity of the Person whom the best efforts of the best and most inspired of the evangelists inadequately, though honestly, portray. Specimens of these defects are freely given, showing the modifications, amplifications, and (in some case) misinterpretations or corruptions, to which Christian tradition was inevitably exposed in passing from the east to the west during a period of about one hundred and thirty years, dating from the Crucifixion.

These objects the author has endeavoured to attain by sketching an autobiography of an imaginary character, by name Quintus Junius Silanus, who in the second year of Hadrian (A.D. 118) becomes a hearer of Epictetus and a Christian convert, and commits his experiences to paper forty-five years afterwards in the second year of Marcus Aurelius Antoninus and Lucius Verus (A.D. 163).

EDWIN A. ABBOTT.

Wellside, Well Walk, Hampstead. 28 Aug, 1906.

SUMMARY

Quintus Junius Silanus born 90 A.D., goes from Rome at the suggestion of his old friend Marcus Aemilius Scaurus to attend the lectures of Epictetus in Nicopolis about 118 A.D.

Scaurus (like Silanus an imaginary character) born about 50 A.D., is a disabled soldiery and has been for many years a student of miscellaneous Greek literature including Christian writings. In reply to a letter from Scaurus extolling his new teacher, Scaurus expresses his belief that Epictetus has passed through a stage of infection with "the Christian superstition" from which he has borrowed some parts of the superstructure while rejecting its foundation.

Silanus in order to defend his teacher Epictetus from what he considers an unjust imputation, procures the epistles of Paul, His interest in these leads him to the "scriptures" from which Paul quotes. Thence he is led on to speculate about the nature of the "gospel" preached by Paul, and about the character and utterances of the "Christ" from whom that "gospel" originated. The epistles convey to him a sense of spiritual strength and "constraining love," He determines to procure the Christian gospels.

During all this time he is occasionally corresponding with Scaurus and attending the lectures of Epictetus, which satisfy him less and less. Contrasted with the spiritual strength in the epistles of Paul the lectures seem to contain only spirited effervescence. And there is an utter absence of "constraining love."

When the three Synoptic gospels reach Silanus from Rome, he receives at the same time a destructive criticism on them from Scaurus, Much of this criticism he is enabled to meet with the aid of the Pauline epistles. But enough remains to shake his faith in their historical accuracy. Nor does he find in them the same presence that he found in the epistles, of "constraining love," The result is, that he is thrown back from Christ.

At this crisis he meets Clemens, an Athenian, who lends him a gospel that has recently appeared, the gospel of John, Clemens frankly admits his doubts about its authorship, and about its complete accuracy, but commends it as conveying the infinite spiritual revelation inherent in Christ less inadequately than it is conveyed by the Synoptists.

A somewhat similar view is expressed by Scaurus though with a large admixture of hostile criticism. He has recently received the fourth gospel, and it forms the subject of his last letter. While rejecting much of it as unhistorical, he expresses great admiration for it, and for what he deems its fundamental principle, namely, that Jesus cannot he understood save through a "disciple whom Jesus loved."

While speculating on what might have happened if he himself had come under the influence of a "disciple whom Jesus loved" Scaurus is struck down by paralysis. Silanus sets sail for Italy in the hope of finding his friend still living. At the moment when he is losing sight of the hills above Nicopolis where Clemens is praying for him, Silanus receives an apprehension of Christ's "constraining love" and becomes a Christian.

No attempt has been made to give the impression of an archaic or Latin style. Hence "Christus" and "Paulus" are mostly avoided except in a few instances where they are mentioned for the first time by persons speaking from a non-Christian point of view. Similar apparent inconsistencies will be found in the use of "He" and "he," denoting Christ. The use varies, partly according to the speaker, partly according to the speaker's mood. It varies also in quotations from scripture according to the extent to which the Revised Version is followed.

The utterances assigned to Epictetus are taken from the records of his sayings by Arrian or others. Some of these have been freely translated, paraphrased, and transposed; but none of them are imaginary. When Silanus says that his friend Arrian "never heard Epictetus say" this or that, the meaning is that the expression does not occur in Epictetus's extant works, so far as can be judged from Schenkl's admirable Index.

The words assigned to Arrian, Silanus' s friend, when speaking in his own person, are entirely imaginary; but the statements made about Arrian's birth-place and official career are based on history.

Any words assigned by Scaurus to his "friend" Pliny, Plutarch, or Josephus, or by Silanus to "the young Irenaeius," or Justin, may be taken to be historical. The references will be given in the volume of Notes.

Scaurus and Silanus occasionally describe themselves as "finding marginal notes" indicating variations in their mss. of the gospels. In all such cases the imaginary "marginal notes" are based on actual various readings or interpolations which will be given in the volume of Notes. Most of these are of an early date, and may be based on much earlier originals; and care has been taken to exclude any that are of late origin. But the reader must bear in mind that we have no mss. of the gospels, and therefore no "marginal notes," of so early a date as 118 A.D.

I. — THE FIRST LECTURE

"I forbid you to go into the senate-house!" "As long as I am a senator, go I must."

TWO voices were speaking from one person—the first, pompous, coarse, despotic; the second, refined, dry, austere.

There was nothing that approached stage-acting—only the suggestion of one man swelling out with authority, and of another straightening up his back in resistance. These were the first words I hear from Epictetus, as I crept late into the lecture-room, tired with a long journey overnight into Nicopolis.

I need not have feared to attract attention. All eyes were fixed on the lecturer as I stole into a place near the door, next to my friend Arrian, who was absorbed in his notes. What was it all about? In answer to my look of inquiry Arrian pushed me his last sheet with the names "Vespasian" and "Helvidius Priscus" scrawled large upon it. Then I knew what it meant. It was a story now forty years old—which I had often heard from my father's old friend, Aemilius Scaurus—illustrating the duty of obeying the voice of the conscience rather than the voice of a king. Epictetus, after his manner, was throwing it into the form of a dialogue:—

"*Vespasian.* I forbid you to go into the senate-house.

"*Priscus.* As long as I am a senator, go I must.

"*Vespasian.* Go, then, but be silent.

"*Priscus.* Do not ask my opinion, and I will be silent.

"*Vespasian.* But I am bound to ask it.

"*Priscus.* And I am bound to answer, and to answer what I think right.

"*Vespasian.* Then I shall kill you.

"*Priscus.* Did I ever say that I could not be killed? It is yours to kill; mine, to die fearless."

I give his words almost as fully as Arrian took them down. But his tone and spirit are past man's power to put on paper. He flashed from Emperor to Senator like the zig-zag of lightning with a straight down flash at the end. This was always his way. He would play a thousand parts, seeming, superficially, a very Proteus; but they were all types of two characters, the philosopher and the worldling, the follower of the Logos and the follower of the flesh. Moreover, he was always in earnest, in hot earnest. On the surface he would jest like Menander or jibe like Aristophanes; but at bottom he was a tragedian. At one moment he would point to his halting leg and flout himself as a lame old grey-beard with a body of clay. In the next, he was "a son of Zeus," or "God's own son," or "carrying about God." Never at rest, he might deceive a stranger into supposing that he was occasionally rippling and sparkling with real mirth like a sea in sunlight. But it was never so. It was a sea of molten metal and there was always a Vesuvius down below.

I suspect that he never knew mirth or genial laughter even as a child. He was born a slave, his master being Epaphroditus, a freedman of Nero's and his favourite, afterwards killed by Domitian. I have heard—but not from Arrian—that this master caused his lameness. He was twisting his leg one day to see how much he could bear. The boy—for he was no more—said with a smile, "If you go on, you will break it," and then, "Did not I tell you, you would break it?" True or false, this story gives the boy as I knew the man. You might break his leg but never his will. I do not know whether Epaphroditus, out of remorse, had him taught philosophy; but taught he was, under one of the best men of the day, and he acquired such fame that he was banished from Rome under Domitian, with other philosophers of note—whether at or before the time when Domitian put Epaphroditus to death I cannot say. In one of his lectures he described how he was summoned before the Prefect of the City with the other philosophers: "Come," said the Prefect, "come, Epictetus, shave off your beard." "If I am a philosopher," he replied, "I am not going to shave it off." "Then I shall take your head off." "If it is for your advantage, take it off."

But now to return to my first lecture. Among our audience were several men of position and one at least of senatorial rank. Some of them seemed a little scandalized at the Teacher's dialogue. It was not likely that the Emperor would take offence, for in the second year of Hadrian we were not in a Neronian or Domitian atmosphere; moreover, our Teacher was known to be on good terms with the new Emperor. But perhaps their official sense of propriety was shocked; and, in the first sentence of what follows, Epictetus may have been expressing their thoughts: "*'So you, philosophers teach people to despise the throne!'* Heaven forbid! Which of us teaches anyone to lay claim to anything over which kings have authority? Take my body, take my goods, take my reputation! Take my friends and relations!

'Yes,' says the ruler, 'but I must also be ruler over your convictions.' Indeed, and who gave you this authority?"

Epictetus went on to say that if indeed his pupils were of the true philosophic stamp, holding themselves detached from the things of the body and with their minds fixed on the freedom of the soul, he would have no need to spur them to boldness, but rather to draw them back from over-hasty rushing to the grave; for, said he, they would come flocking about him, begging and praying to be allowed to teach the tyrant that they were free, by finding freedom at once in self-inflicted death: "Here on earth. Master, these robbers and thieves, these courts of justice and kings, have the upper hand. These creatures fancy that they have some sort of authority over us, simply because they have a hold on our paltry flesh and its possessions! Suffer us. Master, to show them that they have authority over nothing!" If, said he, a pupil of this high spirit were brought before the tribunal of one of the rulers of the earth, he would come back scoffing at such "authority" as a mere scarecrow: "Why all these preparations, to meet no enemy at all? The pomp of his authority, his solemn anteroom, his gentlemen of the chamber, his yeomen of the guard—did they all come to no more than this! These things were nothing, and I was preparing to meet something great!"

On the scholar of the unpractical and cowardly type, anxiously preparing "what to say" in his defence before the magistrate's tribunal, he poured hot scorn. Had not the fellow, he asked, been practising "what to say"—all his life through? "What else," said he, "have you been practising? Syllogisms and convertible propositions!" Then came the reply, in a whine, "Yes, but he has authority to kill me!" To which the Teacher answered, "Then speak the truth, you pitiful creature. Cease your imposture and give up all claim to be a philosopher. In the lords of the earth recognise your own lords and masters. As long as you give them this grip on you, through your flesh, so long must you be at the beck and call of every one that is stronger than you are. Socrates and Diogenes had practised 'what to say' by the practice of their lives. But as for you—get you back to your own proper business, and never again budge from it! Back to your own snug corner, and sit there at your leisure, spinning your syllogisms:

> 'In thee is not the stuff that makes a man
>
> A people's leadcr.'"

Thence he passed to the objection that a judicial condemnation might bring disgrace on a man's good name. "The authorities, you say, have condemned you as guilty of impiety and profanity. What harm is there in that for you? This creature, with authority to condemn you—does he himself know even the meaning of piety or impiety? If a man in authority calls day night or bass treble, do men that know take notice of him? Unless the judge knows what the truth is, his 'authority to judge' is no authority. No man has authority over our convictions, our inmost thoughts, our will. Hence when Zeno the philosopher went into the presence of Antigonus the king, it was the king that was anxious, not the philosopher. The king wished to gain the philosopher's good opinion, but the philosopher cared for nothing that the king could give. When, therefore, you go to the palace of a great ruler, remember that you are in effect going to the shop of a shoemaker or a grocer—on a great scale of course, but still a grocer. He cannot sell you anything real or lasting, though he may sell his groceries at a great price."

At the bottom of all this doctrine about true and false authority, there was, as I afterwards understood, a belief that God had bestowed on all men, if they would but accept and use it, authority over their own wills, so that we might conform our wills to His, as children do with a Father, and might find pleasure, and indeed our only pleasure, in doing this—accepting all bodily pain and evil as not evil but good because it comes from His will, which must be also our will and must be honoured and obeyed. "When," said he, "the ruler says to anyone, 'I will fetter your leg,' the man that is in the habit of honouring his leg cries, 'Don't, for pity's sake!' But the man that honours his will says, 'If it appears advisable to you, fetter it'."

"*Tyrant*. Won't you bend?

"*Cynic*. I will not bend.

"*Tyrant*. I will show you that I am lord.

"*Cynic*. You! impossible! I have been freed by Zeus. Do you really imagine that He would allow His own son to be made a slave? But of my corpse you *are* lord. Take it."

In this particular lecture Epictetus also gave us a glimpse of a wider and more divine authority imparted by God to a few special natures, akin to Himself, whereby, as God is supreme King over men His children, so a chosen few may become subordinate kings over men their brethren. Like Plato, he seemed to look forward to a time when rulers would become philosophers, or else philosophers kings. Nero and Sardanapalus, Agamemnon and Alexander, all came under his lash—all kings and rulers of the old regime. Not that he denied Agamemnon a superiority to Nero, or the right to call himself "shepherd of the people" if he pleased. "Sheep, indeed," he exclaimed, "to submit to be ruled over by you!" and "Shepherd, indeed, for you weep like the shepherds, when a wolf has snatched away a sheep!"

From these old-fashioned rulers he passed to a new and nobler ideal of kingship: "Those kings and tyrants received from their armed guards the power of rebuking and punishing wrongdoing, though they might be rascals themselves. But on the Cynic"—that was the term he used—"this power is bestowed by the conscience." Then he explained to us what he meant by "conscience"—the consciousness of a life of wise, watchful, and unwearied toil for man, with the cooperation of God. "And how," he asked, "could such a man fail to be bold and speak the truth with boldness, speaking, as he does, to his own brethren, to his own children and kinsfolk? So inspired, he is no meddler or busybody. Supervising and inspecting the affairs of mankind, he is not busying himself with other men's matters, but with his own. Else, call a general, too, a busybody, when he is busy inspecting his own soldiers!"

This was, to me, quite a new view of the character of a Cynic But Epictetus insisted on it with reiteration. The Cynic, he said, was Warrior and Physician in one. As a warrior, he was like Hercules, wandering over the world with his club and destroying noxious beasts and monsters. As a physician, he was like Socrates or Diogenes, going about and doing good to those afflicted with sickness of mind, diagnosing each disease, prescribing diet, cautery, or other remedy. In both these capacities, the Cynic received from God authority over men, and men recognised it in him, because they perceived him to be their benefactor and deliverer.

There are, said Epictetus, in each man two characters—the character of the Beast and the character of the Man. By Beast he meant wild or savage beast, as distinct from tame beast, which he preferred to call "sheep." "Sheep" meant the cowardly, passive-greedy passions within us. "The Beast" meant the savage, aggressive-greedy nature, not only stirring us up to external war against our neighbours, but also waging war to the death against our inward better nature, against the "Man." The mark or stamp of the Beast he connected with

Nero. "Cast it away," he said. The opposite mark or stamp he connected with the recently deceased Emperor, Trajan. If we acted like a beast, he warned us that we should become like a beast, and then, according to his customary phrase, "*You will have lost the Man.*" And was this, asked he, nothing to lose? Over and over again he repeated it: "*You have thrown away the Man.*" It was in this light—as a type of the Man—that he regarded Hercules, the first of the Cynics, the Son of God, going on the errands of the Father to destroy the Beast in its various shapes, typifying an armed Missionary, but armed for spiritual not for fleshly warfare, destroying the Beast that would fain dominate the world. But it was for Diogenes that he reserved his chief admiration, placing him (I think) even above Socrates, or at all events praising him more warmly—partly, perhaps, out of fellow-feeling, because Diogenes, too, like himself, had known what it was to be a slave. Never shall I forget the passage in this lecture in which he described Alexander surprising the great Cynic asleep, and waking him up with a line of Homer:—

"To sleep all night suits not a Councillor,"

—to which Diogenes replied at once in the following line, claiming for himself the heavy burden (entrusted to him by Zeus) of caring like a king for all the nations of the earth:—

"Who holds, in trust, the world's vast orb of cares."

Diogenes, according to our Teacher, was much more than an Aesculapius of souls; he was a sovereign with "the sceptre and the kingdom of the Cynic." Some have represented Epictetus as claiming this authority for himself. But in the lecture that I heard, it was not so. Though what he said might have been mistaken as a claim for himself, it was really a claim for "the Cynic," as follows. First he put the question, "How is it possible for one destitute, naked, homeless, hearthless, squalid, with not one slave to attend him, or a country to call his own, to lead a life of equable happiness?" To which he replied, "Behold, God hath sent unto you the man to demonstrate in act this possibility. *'Look on me, and see that I am without country, home possessions, slaves; no bed but the ground, no wife, no children—no palace to make a king or governor out of me—only the earth, and the sky, and one threadbare cloak! And yet what do I want? Am I not fearless? Am I not free? When saw ye me failing to find any good thing that I desired, or failing into any evil that I would fain have avoided? What fault found I ever with God or man? When did I ever accuse anyone? Did anyone ever see me with a gloomy face? How do I confront the great persons before whom you, worldlings, bow abashed and dismayed? Do not I treat them as cringing slaves? Who, that sees me, does not feel that he sees in me his natural Lord and Master?"'*

I confess that up to this point I had myself supposed that he was speaking of himself, standing erect as ruler of the world. But in the next instant he had dropped, as it were, from the pillar upon which he had been setting up the King, and now, like a man at the pedestal pointing up to the statue on the top, he exclaimed, "Behold, these are the genuine Cynic's utterances: this is his stamp and image: this is his aim!"

He passed on to answer the question. What if the Cynic missed his aim, or, at least, missed it so far as exerting the royal authority over others? What if death cut his purpose short? In that case, he said, the will, the purpose, the one essential good, had at all events remained in its purity; and how could man die better than in such actions? "If, while I am thus employed, death should overtake me, it will suffIce me if I can lift up my hands to God and say, 'The helps that I received from thee, to the intent that I might understand and follow thy ordering of the universe, these I have not neglected. I have not disgraced thee, so far as in me lay. See how I have used these faculties which thou hast given me! Have I ever found fault with thee? ever been ill-pleased with anything that has happened or ever wished it to happen otherwise? Thou didst beget me, and I thank thee for all thou gavest me. I have used to the full the gifts that were of thy giving and I am satisfied. Receive them back again and dispose them in such region as may please thee. Thine were they all, and thou hast given them unto me.'" Then, turning to us, he said, "Are you not content to take your exit after this fashion? Than such a life, what can be better, or more full of grace and beauty? Than such an end, what can be more full of blessing?"

There was much more, which I cannot recall. I was no longer in a mood to note and remember exact words and phrases,, and I despair of making my readers understand why. Able philosophers and lecturers I had heard before, but none like this man. Some of those had moved me to esteem and gained my favourable judgement. But this man did more than "move" me. He whirled me away into an upper region of spiritual possibility, at once glad and sad—sad at what I was, glad at what I might be. Alcibiades says in the Symposium of Plato that whereas the orator Pericles had only moved his outer self to admiration, the teaching of Socrates caught hold of his very soul, "whirling it away into a Corybantic dance." I quoted these words to Arrian as we left the lecture-room together, and he replied that they were just to the point. "Epictetus," he said," is by birth a Phrygian. And, like the Phrygian priests of Cybele, with their cymbals and their dances, he has just this power of whirling away his hearers into any region he pleases and making them feel at any moment what he wishes them to feel. But," added he thoughtfully, "it did not last with Alcibiades. Will it last with us?"

I argued—or perhaps I should say protested—at considerable length, that it would last. Arrian walked on for a while without answering. Presently he said, "This is your first lecture. It is not so with me. I, as you know, have heard Epictetus for several months, and I admire him as much as you do, perhaps more. I am sure he is doing me good. But I do not aim at being his ideal Cynic. *'In me is not the stuff'*—I admit his censure—that makes a man into a King, bearing all the cares of all mankind upon his shoulders. My ambition is, some day, to become (as you are by birth) a Roman citizen"—he was not one then, nor was he Flavius Arrianus, but I have called him by the name by which he became known in the world—" and to do good work in the service of the Empire, as an officer of the State and yet an honest man. For that purpose I want to keep myself in order—at all events to some reasonable extent. Epictetus is helping me to do this, by making me ashamed of the foul life of the Beast, and by making me aspire to what he calls 'the Man.' That I feel day by day, and for that I am thankful.

"But if you ask me about the reality of this 'authority,' which our Teacher claims for his Cynic, then, in all honesty, I must confess to doubts. Socrates, certainly, has moved the minds of civilised mankind. But then he had, as you know, a 'daemonic something' in him, a divine voice of some kind. And he believed in the immortality of the soul—a point on which you have not yet heard what Epictetus has to say. As to Diogenes, though I have always faithfully recorded in my notes what our Teacher says about him, yet I do not feel that the philosopher of the tub had the same heaven-sent authority as Socrates, or as Epictetus himself. And, indeed, did you not yourself hear to-day that God gives us authority over nothing but our own hearts and wills? How, then, can the Cynic claim this authority over others, except as an accident? But I forget. Perhaps Epictetus did not mention to-day his usual doctrine about 'good' and 'evil,' about 'peace of mind' and about the 'rule' of our neighbours as being 'no evil' to us. It reappears in almost every lecture. Wait till you have heard this.

"Again, as to the origin of this authority, the Teacher tells us that it is given by God—or by Gods, for he uses both expressions. But by what God or Gods? Is not this a matter of great importance? Wait till you have heard him on this point. Now I must hasten back to my rooms to commit my notes to writing while fresh in my memory. We meet in the lecture-room to-morrow. Meantime, believe me, I most heartily sympathize with you in your admiration of one whom I account the best of all living philosophers. I have all your conviction of his sincerity. Assuredly, whencesoever he derives it, he has in him a marvellous power for good. The Gods grant that it may last!"

II. — EPICTETUS ON THE GODS

ARRIAN was right in thinking that the next lecture would be on the Gods. I had come to Nicopolis at the end of one of the lecture-courses, and had heard its conclusion—the perfecting of the Cynic. The new course began by describing the purpose of God in making man.

But at the outset the subject was, not God, but the Logos—that word so untranslatable into our Latin, including as it does suggestions of our Word, Discourse, Reason, Logic, Understanding, Purpose, Proportion, and Harmony. Starting from this, Epictetus first said that the only faculty that could, as it were, behold itself, and theorize about itself, was the faculty of the Logos, which is also the faculty with which we regard, and, so to speak, mentally handle, all phenomena. From the Logos, or Word, he passed to God, as the Giver of this faculty: "It was therefore right and meet that this highest and best of all gifts should be the only one that the Gods have placed at our disposal. All the rest they have not placed at our disposal. Can it be that the Gods did not wish to place them in our power? For my part, I think that, if they had been able, they would have entrusted us also with the rest. But they were absolutely unable. For, being on earth, and bound up with such a body as this"—and here he made his usual gesture of self-contempt, mocking at his own lame figure—"how was it possible that we should not be prevented by these external fetters from receiving those other gifts? But what says Zeus?"—with that, the halting mortal, turning suddenly round, had become the Olympian Father addressing a child six years old: *"Epictetus, if it had been practicable, I would have made your dear little body quite free, and your pretty little possessions quite free too, and quite at your disposal. But as it is, don't shut your eyes to the truth. This little body is not your very own. It is only a neat arrangement in clay."*

After a pause, the Epictetian Zeus continued as follows, falling from "I" to "we." Some of our fellow-scholars declared to Arrian after lecture that Epictetus could not have meant this change, and they slightly altered the words in their notes. I prefer to give the diffIcult words of Zeus as Arrian took them down and as I heard them: *"But, since I was not able to do this,* WE *gave you a portion of* OURSELVES, *this power"*—and here Epictetus made believe to put a little box into the child's hand, adding that it contained a power of pursuing or avoiding, of liking or disliking—*"Take care of this, and put in it all that belongs to you. As long as you do this, you wilt never be hindered or hampered, never cry, never scold, and never flatter."*

The change from I to WE was certainly curious; and some said that "we gave," *edôkamen,* ought to be regarded as two words, *edôka men,* "I gave on the one hand." But "on the one hand" made no sense. Nor could they themselves deny that Epictetus made Zeus say, first, "I was not able," and then, "a part of ourselves." I think the explanation may be this. Epictetus had many ways of looking at the Divine Nature. Sometimes he regarded it as One, sometimes as Many. When he thought of God as supporting and controlling the harmonious Cosmos, or Universe, then God was One—the Monarch or General to whom we all owed loyal obedience. Often, however, "Gods" were spoken of, as in the expression "Father of Gods and men," and elsewhere. Once he reproached himself (a lower or imaginary self) for repining against the Cosmos because he was lame, almost as if the Cosmos itself were Providence or God: "Wretched creature! For the sake of one paltry leg, to impeach the Cosmos!" But he went on to call the Cosmos "the Whole of Things." And then he called on each man to sacrifice some part of himself (a lame man, for example, sacrificing his lame leg to the Universe: "What! Will you not make a present of it {*i.e.* the leg) to the Whole of Things? Let go this leg of yours! Yield it up gladly to Him that gave it! What! Will you sulk and fret against the ordinances of Zeus, which He—in concert with the Fates present at your birth and spinning the thread for you—decreed and ordained?"

I remember, too, how once, while professing to represent the doctrines of the philosophers in two sections, he spoke, in the first section, of "Him," but in the second, of "Them," thus: "The philosophers say that we must in the first place learn this, the existence of *God*, and that *He* provides for the Universe, and that nothing—whether deed or purpose or thought—can lie hidden from *Him*, In the next place [we must learn] of what nature *They* (i.e. the Gods) are. For, of whatever nature *They* may be found to be, he that would fain please Them and obey [Them] must needs endeavour (to the best of his ability) to be made like unto *Them*"

What did he mean by "THEM"? And why did he use THEM directly after HIM? I believe he did it deliberately. For in the very next sentence he expressed God in a neuter adjective, "If THE DIVINE [BEING] is trustworthy, man also must needs be trustworthy." He seemed to me to pass from masculine singular to masculine plural and from that to neuter singular, as much as to say, "Take notice. I use HIM, THEM, and IT in three consecutive sentences, and all about God, to show you that God is not any one of these, but all."

Similarly, after condemning the attempt of philosophers to please the rulers of the earth, he said, "I know whom I must needs please, and submit to, and obey—God *and those next to Him*." But then he continued in the singular ("*He* made me at one with myself" and so on). And I think I may safely say that I never heard him allow his ideal philosopher or Cynic to address God in the plural with "ye" or "you." It was always " thou," as in the utterance I quoted above—" Thine were they all and thou gavest them to me."

Well, then, whom did he mean by "those next to" God? I think he referred to certain guardian angels—"daemons" he called them, and so will I, spelling it thus, so as to distinguish it from "demon" meaning "devil"—one of whom (he said) was allotted by God to each human being. This, according to Epictetus, did not exclude the general inspection of mankind by God Himself: "To each He has assigned a Guardian, the Daemon of each mortal, to be his guard and keeper, sleepless and undeceivable. Therefore, whenever you shut your doors and make darkness in the house, remember never to say that you are alone. For you are not alone. God is in the house, and your Daemon is in the house. And what need have these of light to see what you are doing?"

This guardian Daemon, or daemonic Guardian, was said by some of our fellow-scholars to be the portion of the divine Logos within us, in virtue of which our Teacher distinguished men from beasts. Notably did he once make this distinction—in answer to some imaginary questioner, who was supposed to class man with irrational animals because he is subject to animal necessities. "Cattle," replied Epictetus, "are works of God, but not preeminent, and certainly not parts of God; but thou"—turning to the supposed opponent—"art a fragment broken off from God; thou hast in thyself a part of Him. Why then ignore thy noble birth? Why dost thou not recognise whence thou hast come? Wilt thou not remember, in the moment of eating, what a Being thou art—thou that eatest—what a Being it is that thou feedest? Wilt thou not recognise what it is that employs thy senses and thy faculties? Knowest thou not that thou art feeding God, yea, taking God with thee to the gymnasium? God, God dost thou carry about, thou miserable creature, and thou knowest it not!"

We were rather startled at this. In what sense could a miserable creature "carry about God"? Epictetus proceeded, "Dost thou fancy that I am speaking of a god of gold or silver, an outside thing? It is within thyself that thou carriest Him. And thou perceivest not that thou art defiling Him with impure purposes and filthy actions! Before the face of a mere statue of the God thou wouldst not dare to do any of the deeds thou art daily doing. Yet in the presence of the God Himself, within thee, looking at all thy acts, listening to all thy words and thoughts, thou art not ashamed to continue thinking the same bad thoughts and doing the same bad deeds—blind to thine own nature and banned by God's wrath!"

From this it appeared that the Daemon in each man was good and veritably God, and turned men towards God and goodness; but that some did not perceive the presence and were deaf to the voice. These were "miserable wretches" and "banned by God's wrath." Thus in some sense, the same God seemed to be the cause of virtue in some but of vice in others. This accorded with a saying of Epictetus on another occasion that God "ordained that there should be summer and winter, fruitfulness and fruitlessness, *virtue and vice*." Then the question arose, To how many did the Logos of God bring virtue and to how many did it result in vice? And again, Did it bring virtue to as many as the Logos of God, or God, desired? Or was He unable to fulfil His desire, as in the case of that imaginary opponent, for example, so that the Supreme would have to say to him, as to Epictetus, "If I could have, I would have. But now, make no mistake. I could not bring virtue unto thee." I was disposed to think that Epictetus would have laid the blame on the opponent, who, he would have said, might have obeyed the Logos in himself, if he had chosen to do so. According to our Teacher's doctrine, God would say to this man nothing more cruel, or less just, than He says to all, "I could not force virtue on thee, nor on any man. If I forced virtue on thee, virtue would cease to be virtue and God would cease to be God." But still the uneasy feeling came to me—not indeed at the time of this lecture (or at least not to any great extent) but afterwards—that the God of Epictetus was hampered by what Epictetus called "the clay," which He "would have liked" to make immortal, if He "had been able." What if each man's "clay" was different? Who made the clay? What if God controlled nothing more than the shaping of the clay, and this, too, only in conjunction with the Fates? What if the Fates alone were responsible for the making of the clay? In that case, must not the Fates be regarded as higher Beings, even above the Maker of the Cosmos—higher in some sense, but bad Beings or weak Beings, spoiling the Maker's work by supplying Him with bad material so that He could not do what He would have liked to have done?

Epictetus, I subsequently found, would never see difficulties of this kind. He represented the Supreme as a great stage manager, allotting to all their appropriate parts: "Thou art the sun; go on thy rounds, minister to all things. Thou art a heifer; when the lion appears, play thy part, or suffer for it. Thou art a bull; fight as champion of the herd. Thou canst lead the host against Ilium; be thou Agamemnon. Thou canst cope with Hector; be thou Achilles." He did not add, "Thou canst spit venom and slander against the good and great; be thou Thersites." But I did not think of that at the time.

For the moment, I was carried away by the fervour of the speaker. "He," I said, "has been a slave, the slave of Nero's freedman; he has seen things at their worst; and yet he believes that virtue, freedom, and peace, are placed by God in the power of all that will obey the Logos, His gift, within their hearts!" So I believed it, or persuaded myself that I believed it. Epictetus insisted, in the strongest terms, that the divine Providence extends to all. "God," he said, "does not neglect a single one, even of the least of His creatures." Stimulating us to *be* good instead of *talking* about being good, he exclaimed, "How grand it is for each of you to be able to say, *The very thing that people are solemnly arguing about in the schools as an impossible ideal, that very thing I am accomplishing. They are, in effect, expatiating on my virtues, investigating me, and singing my praises. Zeus has been pleased that I should receive from my own self a demonstration of the truth of this ideal, while He Himself tests and tries me to see whether I am a worthy soldier of His army, and a worthy citizen of His city. At the same time it has been His pleasure to bring me forward that I may testify concerning the things that lie outside the will, and that I may cry aloud to the world, 'Behold, men, that your fears are idle! Vain, all vain, are your greedy and covetous desires. Seek not the Good in the outside world! Seek it in yourselves! Else, ye will not find it.' Engaging me for such a mission, and for such a testimony as this, God now leads me hither, now sends me thither; exhibits me to mankind in poverty, in disease—ruler in fact but no ruler in the eyes of men—banishes me to the rocks of Gyara, or drags me into prison or into bonds! And all this, not hating me. No, God forbid! Who can hate his own best and most faithful servant? No, nor neglecting me. How could He? For He does not neglect the meanest of His creatures. No, He is training and practising me. He is employing me as His witness to the rest of mankind. And I, being set down by Him for such high service as this—can I possibly find time to entertain anxieties about where I am, or with whom I am living, or what men say about me? How can I fail to be, with my whole might and my whole being, intent on God, and on His commandments and ordinances?*"

I noted with pleasure here the words, "He does not neglect the meanest of His creatures." To the same effect elsewhere, speaking of Zeus, he said, "In very truth, the universal frame of things is badly managed unless Zeus takes care of all His own citizens, in order that they may be blessed like unto Himself" A little before this, he said about Hercules, "He left his children behind him without a groan or regret—not as though he were leaving them orphans, for he knew that no man is an orphan," because Zeus is "Father of men."

In all these passages describing the fatherhood of God and the sonship of man, Epictetus spoke of virtue as being, by itself, a sufficient reward, in respect of the ineffable peace that it brings through the consciousness of being united to God. But how long this union lasted, and whether its durability was proof against death—as

Socrates taught—about this he had hitherto said nothing. The Cynic, he again and again insisted, was God's son; but he did not insist that the son was as immortal as the Father. Sometimes indeed he described the man of temperance and self-control as "banqueting at the table of the Gods." Still more, the man that had passed beyond temperance into contempt of earthly things—a rank to which Arrian and I did not aspire—such a Cynic as this he extolled as being not only fellow-guest with the Gods but also fellow-ruler. These expressions reminded me of what we used to learn by heart in Rome concerning the man described by Horace as "just and firm of purpose." The poet likened him to Hercules transported aloft to the fiery citadel of heaven, and to the Emperor Augustus drinking nectar at the table of the Gods. But this was said about Augustus while he was still alive; and the poem did not seem to me to prove that Horace believed in the immortality of the soul. However, what Epictetus said about that will appear hereafter. For the present, I must explain why the teaching of Epictetus concerning the Gods, although it carried me away for a time, caused me bewilderment in the end, and made me feel the need of something beyond.

III. — ARRIAN ON THE OATH OF THE CHRISTIANS

UP to the time of my coming to Nicopolis, my faith in the Gods had been like that of most official and educated Romans. First I had a literary belief not only in Zeus but also in Apollo, Athene, Demeter, and the rest of the Gods and Goddesses of Homer, tempered by a philosophic feeling that some of the Homeric and other myths about them, and about the less beautiful divinities, were not true, or were true only as allegories. In the next place I had a Roman or official belief in the destiny of the empire, and a recognition that its unity was best maintained by tolerating the worships of any number of national Gods and Goddesses; provided they did not tend to sedition and conspiracy, nor to such vices as were in contravention of the laws. Lastly, I recognised as the belief of many philosophers—and was myself half inclined to believe—that One God, or Zeus, so controlled the whole of things that it would hardly be atheistic if I sometimes regarded even Apollo, and Athene, and others, as personifying God's attributes rather than as being Gods and Goddesses in themselves—although I myself, without scruple and in all willingness, should have offEred them both worship and sacrifice. Personally, apart (I think) from the influences of childhood, I always shrank from definitely believing that the One God ever had been, or ever could be, "alone."

It was with these confused opinions or feelings that I became a pupil of Epictetus. And at first, whatever he asserted about God, or the Gods, he made me believe it—as long as he was speaking. When he said "God," or "Zeus," or "Father," or "HIM," or "THEM," or "Providence," or "The Divine Being," or "The Nature of All Things," or whatever else, he dragged me as it were to the new Name, and made me follow as a captive and do it homage. But afterwards there came a reaction. The limbs of my mind, so to speak, became tired of being dragged. I longed for rest and found none. My homage, too, was dissipated by distraction. When he repeated as he often did—addressing each one of us individually, and therefore (I assumed) me among the rest—"Thou earnest about God," he seemed to say to me, "Look within thyself for Him whom thou must worship." That was not helpful, it was the reverse of helpful—at least, to me. I felt vaguely then (and now as a Christian I know) that men have need not only to look within, but also (and much more) to look up—up to the Father in heaven with the aid of His Spirit on earth. It was due to Epictetus that at this time I—however faintly—began to feel this need.

Epictetus seemed to have no consistent view either of the unity of God or of the possibility of plural Gods. In Rome, we have three altars to the Goddess Febris, or Fever. Epictetus once referred to Febris in the reply of a philosopher to a tyrant. The latter says, "I have power to cut off your head"; the former replies, "You are in the right. I quite forgot that I must pay you homage as people do to Fever and Cholera, and erect an altar to you, *as indeed in Rome there is an altar to Fever*." It was hardly possible to mistake the Master's mockery of this worship. On the other hand, he was bitterly sarcastic against those who denied the existence of Demeter, the Koré her daughter, and Pluto the husband of the Koré. These deities our Master regarded as representing bread. "O, the gratitude," he exclaimed, "o,the reverence of these creatures! Day by day they eat bread; and yet they have the face to say 'We do not know whether there is any such a being as Demeter, or the Koré, or Pluto!' "It never seemed to occur to him that the worshippers of Febris might retort on him, "Day by day scores of people in Rome have the fever, and yet you have the face to say to us Romans, 'I do not know whether there is any such a being as Febris or Cholera!'"

I think he never spoke of Poseidon, Ares, or Aphrodite, and hardly ever of Apollo. Even Athene he mentioned only thrice in Arrian's hearing (so he told me), twice speaking of her statue by Phidias, and once representing Zeus as bemoaning His solitude (according to some notion, which he ridiculed) after a universal conflagration of gods and men and things, "Miserable me! I have neither Hera, nor Athene, nor Apollo!" It was for Zeus alone, as God, that our Teacher reserved his devotion. And for Him he displayed a passionate enthusiasm, the absolute sincerity of which it never entered into my mind to question; nor do I question it now. Under this God he served as a soldier, or lived as a citizen. To this God he testified as a witness that others might believe and worship. In this view of human life—as being a testimony to God—his teaching was most convincing to me, even when I felt, as I always did, that something was wanting in any conception of God that regarded Him as ever being "alone."

Now I pass to another matter, not of great interest to me at the time, but of great importance to me in its results, because it led to my first knowledge—that could be called knowledge—of the followers of the Lord Jesus Christ. It arose from a passage in the lecture I described in my last chapter. Epictetus was speaking about "the whole frame of things" as being a kind of fluid, in which the thrill of one portion affects all the rest, and about God and the Guardian Daemon as feeling our every motion and thought. He concluded by calling on us to take an oath—a military oath, or *sacramentum*, as we call it in Latin—such as soldiers take to the Emperor. "They," he said, "taking on themselves the life of service for pay, swear to prefer above all things the safety of Caesar. You, who have been counted worthy of such vast gifts, will you not likewise swear, and, after taking your oath, abide by it? And what shall the oath be? Never to disobey, never to accuse, never to find fault with any of the gifts that have been given by Him; never to do reluctantly, never to suffer reluctantly, anything that may be necessary. This oath is like theirs—after a fashion. The soldiers of Caesar swear not to prefer another to him; God's soldiers swear to prefer themselves to everything."

On me this came somewhat as bathos. But it was a frequent paradox with him; and of course, in one sense, it was not a paradox but common sense. What he meant by bidding us "prefer *ourselves*" was "prefer*virtue*" which he always described as each man's true "profit." Everyone, he said, must prefer his own "profit" to everything else, even to father, brothers, children, wife. Zeus Himself—so he taught—prefers His own "profit "—which consists in being Father of all. Take away this thin veil of apparent egotism, and the oath might be described as an oath to live and die for righteousness, for the Logos, or Word of God within us, and, thus, for God Himself. But why, I thought, disguise loyalty under the mask of self-seeking? This notion of a military oath taken to God, and at the same time to oneself—and an oath, so to speak, of negative allegiance, not to do this or that—did not inspire me with the same enthusiasm as the more positive doctrine and the picture of the wandering Cynic going about the world and actively doing good and destroying evil.

Arrian, however, was taking down this passage about the military oath with even more than his usual earnestness and rapidity. "Did that impress you?" said I, as we left the lecture-room together. "On me it fell a little flat." He did not answer at once. Presently, as if rousing himself from a reverie, "Forgive me," he said, "I was thinking of something that occurred in our neighbourhood about fifteen years ago. You know I was born in Bithynia. Well, about that time,, there was a great outbreak of that Jewish superstition of which you must often have heard in Rome, practised by the followers of Christus. They are suspected of all sorts of horrible crimes and abominations, as you know, I dare say, better than I do, being familiar with what the common people say about them in Rome. Moreover the new work just published by your Tacitus—a lover of truth if any man is—severely condemns them. I am bound to say our Governor did not think so badly of them as Tacitus does. Perhaps in Rome and in Nero's time they were more savage and vicious than among us in Bithynia recently. However, that matters little. The question was not about their private vices or virtues. Our Governor believed them guilty of treasonable conspiracy. So he determined to stop it.

"Stop it he did; or, at all events, to a very great extent. But the point of interest for me is, that when these fellows were had up before our Governor—it was Caius Plinius Caecilius Secundus, an intimate friend of the Emperor Trajan—he found there was really no mischief at all to be apprehended from them. Secundus had heard something about a sacramentum, or military oath—and this is my point—which these people were in the habit of taking at their secret meetings. Naturally this convinced him at first that there must be something wrong. But, when he came to look into it, the whole thing came to no more than what I will now tell you. I am sure of my facts for I heard them from his secretary, who had a copy of his letter to the Emperor.

It was to this effect, *'They affirm that the sum total of their crime or error is, that they were wont, on an appointed day, to meet together before daybreak and to sing an alternate chant to Christus, as to a God, and to bind themselves by an oath—not, as conspirators do, to commit some crime in common, but to avoid committing theft, robbery, adultery, fraud, breach of faith. This done, they break up. It is true they return to take food in common, but it is a mere harmless repast.'* After the Governor had gone carefully into the matter, putting a few women to the torture to get at the truth, he came to the conclusion that this so-called military oath, or sacramentum, had no harm whatever in it. The thing was merely a perverted superstition run wild. He very sensibly adopted the mild course of giving the poor deluded people a chance of denying their faith as they called it. The Emperor sanctioned his mildness. Most of them recanted. Things settled down, and promised to be very much as they were before. At least so the Governor thought. We, outside the palace, were not quite so sanguine. But anyhow, what struck me to-day was the similarity between the military oath of these Christians and the military oath prescribed by our great Teacher to his Cynics."

"But," said I, "does it not seem to you that our military oath ought to be a positive one, namely, that we Cynics will go anywhere and do anything that the General may command—and not a negative one, that we will abstain from grumbling against His orders?" Arrian replied, "As to that, I think our Master follows Socrates, who expressly says that he had indeed a daemon, or at all events a daemonic voice; but that it told him only what to avoid, not what to do." "Surely," replied I, "what Socrates said on his trial was, 'How could I be fairly described as introducing new daemons when saying that *a voice of God manifestly points out to me what I ought to do?*'" "I do not remember that," said my friend, "but we are near my rooms. Come in and let us look into Plato's Apologia."

So we went in, and Arrian took out of his book-case Plato's account of the Speech of Socrates before the jury that condemned him to death. "There, Silanus," said he, "you see I was right," And he pointed to these words, "There comes to me, as you have often heard me say, a divine and daemonic something, which indeed my prosecutor Meletus mentioned and burlesqued in his written indictment. This thing, in its commencement, dates back (I believe) from my boyhood, a kind of Voice that comes to me from time to time, and, whenever it comes, it always"—"Mark this," said Arrian—*"turns me back from doing that (whatever it may be) which I am purposing to do, but never moves me forward."*

I seemed fairly and fully confuted. But suddenly it occurred to me to ask my friend to let me see Xenophon's version of the same speech. He brought it out. I was not long before I disinterred the very words that I have quoted above—*"a Voice of God that manifestly points out to me what I ought to do."* And the context, too, indicated that the Voice—which he calls *daemonic*, or a *daemonion*—gave positive directions, recognised as such by his friends.

This very important difference between Plato and Xenophon in regard to the daemon of Socrates, as described by Socrates, himself, interested Arrian not a little. "Come back," he said, "in the evening, when I shall have finished reducing my notes, to writing, and let us put the two versions side by side and see how many passages we can find agreeing." So I came back after sunset, and we sat down and went carefully through them.

And, as far as I remember, we could not find these two great biographers of this great man agreeing in so much as a dozen consecutive words in their several records of his Apologia, his only public speech. Presently—Arrian having Xenophon in his hand and I Plato—I read out the well-known words of Socrates about Anytus and Meletus, his accusers, and about their power to kill him but not to hurt him. "What," said I, "is Xenophon's version of this?" "He omits it altogether," replied Arrian; "but I see, reading on, that he puts into the mouth of Socrates an entirely different saying about Anytus, after the condemnation. Let me see the Plato." Taking it from my hand, he observed, "Our Master, Epictetus, who is continually quoting these words of Plato's, never quotes them exactly. 'Anytus and Meletus may kill me but they cannot hurt me'—that is always his condensed version. But you see it is not Plato's, Plato's is much longer."

So the conversation strayed away in a literary direction. We talked a great deal—without much knowledge, at least on my part—about oral tradition. I remarked on the possibilities in it of astonishing divergences and distortions of doctrine—" unless," said I, as I rose up to go, "it happens by good fortune, to be taken down at the time by an honest fellow like you, who loves his teacher, but loves the truth more, so that he just sets down what he hears, as he hears it." "I do my best," said Arrian; "but if it were not nearly midnight, I could show you that even my best is not always good enough. I suspect that such sayings of our Master as become most current will be very variously reported a hundred years hence."

"Good-night," said I, and was opening the door to depart, when it flashed upon me that all this time, although we had been discussing Socrates, and assuming a resemblance between him and our Master, we had said nothing about that great doctrine in the profession of which Socrates breathed his last—prescribing a sacrifice to Aesculapius as though death were the beginning of a higher life—I mean the immortality of the soul. "I will not stay now," said I, "but we have not said a word about Epictetus's doctrine concerning the immortality of the soul; could you lend me some of your notes about it?" "He seldom speaks of it," replied my friend; "when he does, it is not always easy to distinguish between metaphor and not-metaphor. My notes, so far, do not quite satisfy me that I have done him justice. He is likely to touch on it in the next lecture or soon after. I should prefer you to hear for yourself what he says."

"One more question," said I. "Did our Master ever, in your hearing, refer to that last strange saying of Socrates, 'We owe a cock to Aesculapius'? Sometimes it seems to me the finest epigram in all Greek literature." "Never," replied Arrian. "He has never mentioned it either in my hearing, or in the hearing of those whom I have asked about it. And I have asked many."

Departing home I found myself almost at once forgetting our long literary discussion about oral tradition, in the larger and deeper question touched on in the last few minutes. Why should not Arrian have been able to "do justice" to Epictetus in this particular subject? Was it that our Teacher did not quite "do justice" to himself? Then I began to ask what Epictetus had meant precisely by such expressions as that men may become "fellow-banqueters" and even "fellow-rulers" with "the Gods." "If God Himself is immortal, how," said I, "can 'God's own son' fail to be immortal also?"

All through that night, even till near dawn, I was harassed with wild and wearying dreams. I travelled, wandering through wilderness after wilderness in quest of Socrates and nowhere finding him. Wherever I went I seemed to hear a strange monotonous cry that followed close behind me. Presently I heard a flapping of wings, and I knew that the sound was the crowing of the cock that was to be offered for Socrates to Aesculapius. Then it became a mocking, inarticulate, human voice striving to utter articulate speech. At last I heard distinctly, "If Zeus could have, he would have. If he could have, he would have. But he could not."

IV. — SCAURUS ON EPICTETUS AND PAUL

THE cock was still crowing when I started out of my dream. It was not yet dawn but sleep was impossible. When Arrian called to accompany me to lecture, he found me in a fever and sent in a physician, by whose advice I stayed indoors for two or three days. During this enforced inaction, I resolved to write to my old friend Scaurus. Marcus Aemilius Scaurus—for that was his name in full—had been a friend of my father's, years before I was born; and his advice had been largely the cause of my coming to Nicopolis. Scaurus had seen service; but for many years past he had devoted himself wholly to literature, not as a rhetorician, nor as a lover of the poets, but as "a practical historian," so he called it. By this he meant to distinguish himself from what he called "ornamental historians." "History," he used to say, "contains truth in a well; and I like trying to draw it out."

For a man of nearly seventy, Scaurus was remarkably vigorous in mind and thought, with large stores of observation and learning, of a sort not common among Romans of good birth. His favourite motto was, "Quick to perceive, slow to believe." I used to think he erred on the side of believing too little, and his friends used to call him Misomythus or "Myth-hater." But over and over again, when I had ventured to discuss with him a matter of documentary evidence, I had found that his incredulity was justified; so that I had come to admit that there was some force in his protest, that he ought to be called, not "Myth-hater," but "Truth-lover."

In the year after my father's death, when I was wasting my time in Rome, and in danger of doing worse, Scaurus took me to task as befitted my father's dearest friend—a cousin also of my mother, who had died while I was still an infant. He had long desired me to enter the army, and I should have done so but for illness. Now that my health was almost restored, he returned to his previous advice, but suggested that, for the present, I might spend a month or two with advantage in attending the lectures of Epictetus, of whom he knew something while he was in Rome, and about whom he had heard a good deal since. When I demurred, and told him that I had heard a good many philosophers and did not care for them, he replied,

"Epictetus you will not find a common philosopher." He pressed me and I yielded.

Since my coming to Nicopolis, I had written once to tell him of my arrival, and to thank him for advising me to come to so admirable a teacher. But I had been too much absorbed in the teaching to enter into detail. Now, having leisure, and knowing his great interest in such subjects, I wrote to him even more fully than I have done for my readers above, sending him all my lecture notes; and I asked him what he judged to be the secret of Epictetus, which made him so different from other philosophers. Nor did I omit to tell him of my talk with Arrian about the Christians and their sacramentum.

Many days elapsed, and I had been attending lectures again for a long time, before his letter in reply reached Nicopolis; but I will set it down here, as also a second letter from him on the same subject. In the first, Scaurus expressed his satisfaction at my meeting with Arrian (whom he knew and described as an extremely sensible and promising young man, likely to get on). He added a hope that I would take precisely Arrian's view of the advantage to be derived from philosophy. But a large part of his letter—much more than I could have wished—was occupied with our "wonderful discovery" (as he called it) that Plato and Xenophon disagreed in their versions of the Apologia of Socrates. On this he rallied us as mere babes in criticism, but, said he, not much more babyish than many professed critics, who cannot be made to understand that—outside poetry, and traditions learned by rote, and a few "aculeate sayings" (so he called them) of philosophers and great men—no two historians ever agree independently—he laid stress on *"independently"*—for twenty consecutive words, in recording a speech or dialogue. "I will not lay you a wager," said he, "for it would be cheating you. But I will make you an offer. If you and Arrian, between you, can find twenty identical consecutive words of Socrates in the whole of Xenophon's Memorabilia and Plato's Dialogues, I will give you five hundred sesterces apiece.[7] Your failure (for fail you will) ought to strike you as all the more remarkable because both Plato and Xenophon tell us that Socrates used to describe himself as *'always saying the same things about the same subjects.'* That one similar saying they have preserved. For the rest, these two great biographers, writing page

[7] In "Notes on Silanus," 2809a, the author repeats this offer.

upon page of Socratic talk, cannot agree exactly about *'the same things'* for a score of consecutive words!"

He added more, not of great interest to me, about the credulity of those who persuaded themselves that Xenophon's version must be spurious just because it differed from Plato's, whereas, said he, this very difference went to show that it was genuine, and that Xenophon was tacitly correcting Plato. But concerning the secret of Epictetus he said very little—and that, merely in reference to the *sacramentum* of the Christians which I mentioned in my first letter. On this he remarked that Pliny, with whom he had been well acquainted, had never mentioned the matter to him. "But that," he said, "is not surprising. His measures to suppress the Christian superstition did not prove so successful as he had hoped. Moreover he disliked the whole business—having to deal with mendacious informers on one side, and fanatical fools or hysterical women on the other. And I, who knew a good deal more about the Christians than Pliny did, disliked the subject still more. My conviction is, however, that your excellent Epictetus—rationalist though he is now, and even less prone to belief than Socrates—'has not been always unscathed by that same Christian infection (for that is the right name for it).

"Partly, he sympathizes with the Christian hatred or contempt for 'the powers of this world' (to use their phrase) and partly with their allegiance to one God, whom he and they regard as casting down kings and setting up philosophers. But there is this gulf between them. The Christians think of their champion, Christus, as having devoted himself to death for their sake, and then as having been miraculously raised from the dead, and as, even now, present among them whenever they choose to meet together and 'sing hymns to him as to a God.' Epictetus absolutely disbelieves this. Hence, he is at a great disadvantage—I mean, of course, as a preacher, not as a philosopher. The Christians have their God, standing in the midst of their daily assemblies, before whom they can 'corybantize'—to repeat your expression—to their hearts' content. Your teacher has nothing—nay, worse than nothing, for he has a blank and feels it to be a blank.

"What does he do then? He fills the blank with a Hercules or a Diogenes or a Socrates, and he corybantizes before that. But it is a make-believe, though an honest one. I have said more than I intended. You know how I ramble on paper. And the habit is growing on me. Let no casual word of mine make you doubt that Epictetus is thoroughly honest. But honest men may be deceived. Be 'quick in perceiving, slow in believing.' Keep to Arrian's view of a useful and practical life in the world, the world as it is, not as it might be in Plato's Republic—which, by the way, would be a very dull place. Farewell."

This letter did not satisfy me at all. "Honest men," I repeated, "may be deceived." True, and Scaurus, though honest as the day, is no exception. To think that Epictetus, our Epictetus—for so Arrian and I used to call him—had been even for a time under the spell of such a superstition as this! I had always assumed—and my conversation with Arrian about what seemed exceptional experiences in Bithynia had done little to shake my assumption—that the Christians were a vile Jewish sect, morose, debased, given up to monstrous secret vices, hostile to the Empire, and hateful to Gods and men. What was the ground for connecting Epictetus with them? Contempt for rulers? That was no new thing in philosophers. Many of them had despised kings, or affected to despise them, without any intention of rebelling against them. What though Epictetus suggested, in a hyperbolical or metaphorical way, a religious *sacramentum* for philosophers? This was quite different from that of the Christians as mentioned by Arrian. I could not help feeling that, for once, my old friend had "perceived" little and "believed" much.

Perhaps my reply showed traces of this feeling. At all events, Scaurus wrote back, asking whether I had observed in him "a habit of basing conclusions on slight grounds." Then he continued "I told you that I knew a good deal about the Christians. I also know a great deal more about Epictetus than you suppose. When I was a young man, I attended the lectures of that most admirable of philosophers, Musonius Rufus. About the time when I left, Epictetus, then a slave, was brought to the classes by his master, Epaphroditus; and Rufus, whom I shall always regard with respect and affection, spoke to me about his new pupil in the highest terms. Afterwards he often told me how he tried to arm the poor boy with philosophy against what he would have to endure from such a master. Many a time have I thought that the young philosopher must have needed all his Stoic armour, going home from the lecture-room of Rufus to the palace of Nero's freedman.

"But I also remember seeing him long before that, when he came one morning as a mere child not twelve years old, along with

Epaphroditus, to Nero's Palace. I was then about fourteen or fifteen. After we had left the Palace—my father and I—we came upon him again on that same evening, staring at some Christians, smeared with pitch and burning away like so many flaring torches, to light the Imperial Gardens—one of Nero's insane or bestial freaks! I have never been able to forget the sight, and I have often thought that he could never forget it. Somewhere about that time, one of the Christian ringleaders, Paulus by name, was put to death. As happens in such cases, his people began to collect every scrap of his writings that could be found A little volume of them came into my hands some twenty years ago. But long before that date, all through the period when Epictetus was in Rufus's classes, the Christian slaves in Rome had in their hands the letters of this Paulus or Paul. One of them, the longest, written to the Christians in Rome (a few years before Paul was brought to the City as a prisoner) goes back as far as sixty years ago. Some are still earlier. I saw the volume more than once in Caesar's Palace in the days of Vespasian. This Paul was one of the most practical of men, and his letters are steeped in practical experience. Epictetus, besides being a great devourer of literature in general, devoured in particular everything that bore on practical life. The odds are great that he would have come across the book somewhere among his slave or freedman friends.

"But I do not trust to such mere antecedent probabilities. You must know that, ever since Epictetus set up as a philosopher, I have followed his career with interest. Recluse though I am, I have many friends and correspondents. These, from time to time, have furnished me with notes of his lectures. Well, when I came to read Paul's letters, I was prepared to find in them certain general similarities to Stoic doctrine; for Paul was a man of Tarsus and might have picked up these things at the University there. But I found a great deal more. I found particularities, just of the sort that you find in your lectures. Paul's actual experiences had been exactly those of a vagrant Aesculapius or Hercules. Your friend idealizes the wanderings of Hercules; Paul enacted them. Paul journeyed from city to city, from continent to continent, everywhere turning the world upside down—Jerusalem, Damascus, Antioch, Ephesus, Colossae, Philippi, Thessalonica, Corinth, Jerusalem again—last of all, Rome. Everywhere the slaves, the poor, the women, went after him. Everywhere he came into collision with the rulers of the earth. If he did not proclaim a war between them and his God, he at all events implied war.

"Now this is just what Epictetus would have liked to do. Only he could not often get people to take him in the same serious way, because he had not the same serious business in hand. I verily believe he was not altogether displeased when the Prefect of the City banished him with other philosophers of note under Domitian. I know certain philosophers who actually made money by being thus banished. It was an advertisement for their lectures. Don't imagine that your philosopher made, or wished to make, money. No. But he made influence—which he valued above money.

"However, the Emperors and Prefects after Domitian were not such fools. They knew the difference between a real revolution and a revolution on paper. A mere theoretical exaltation of the mind above the body, a mere scholastic laudation of kingship over the minds of men as superior to kingship over their bodies—these things kings tolerate; for they mean nothing but words. But a revolution in the name of a *person*—a person, too, supposed by fanatics to be living and present in all their secret meetings,'wherever two or three are gathered together,' for that is their phrase—this may mean a great deal. A person, regarded in this way, may take hold of men's spirits. Missionaries pretending—or, still worse, believing—that they are speaking in the name of such a person, may lead crowds of silly folk into all sorts of sedition. They may refuse, for example, to adore the Emperor's image and to offer sacrifice to the Gods of the State; or they might even attempt to subvert the foundations of society by withholding taxes, or by encouraging or inculcating some wholesale manumission of slaves. This sort of thing means war, and Paul, fifty years ago, was actually waging this war. Epictetus longs to be waging it now. As he cannot, he takes pleasure in urging his pupils to it, painting an imaginary battle array in which he sees imaginary soldiers waging, or destined to wage, imaginary conflicts with imaginary enemies,

"Hence that picturesque contrast (in the lecture you transcribed for me) between the unmarried and the married Cynic—which, besides the similarity of thought, contains some curious similarities to the actual words of Paul It ran thus, 'The condition of the times being such as it is, opposing forces, as it were, being drawn up in line of battle'—that was his expression. Well, what followed from this nonexistent, hypothetical, imminent conflict? The Philosopher, it seems, must be a soldier, *'undistracted*, wholly devoted to the ministry of God, able to go about and visit men, not bound fast to private personal duties, not*entangled* in conditions of life that he cannot honourably transgress.' And then he describes at great length a married Cynic dragged down from his royal throne by the claims and encumbrances of a nursery. Now this same 'undistractedness' (using the very word) of unmarried life Paul himself has mentioned in a letter to the Corinthians, where he says that 'owing to the pressing necessity' of the times, it was good for a man to be unmarried, and that he wished them to be 'free from anxiety.' He concludes 'But I speak this for your own profit, not that I may cast a noose round you but that you may with all seemliness attend on the Lord*undistractedly*.' Again, he writes to one of his assistants or subalterns, 'Endure hardship with me as a good soldier of Christ Jesus. No one engaged in a campaign is *entangled'*—your friend's word again—'in the affairs of civil life.'

"I lay little stress on the similarity of word, but a great deal on the similarity of thought. There is no such conflict as Epictetus describes. There is no such line of battle '—not at least for us, Romans, or for you, Cynics. *But there is for the Christians*—arrayed as they are against the authorities of the Empire. And that reminds me of your Epictetian antithesis between 'the Beast' and 'the Man.' It is a little like a Christian tradition about 'the Beast.' By 'the Beast' they mean Nero. They have never forgotten his treatment of them after the fire. For a long time after his death they had a notion—I believe some of them have it still—that the Beast may rise from the dead and persecute them again. They also expect—I cannot do more than allude to their fantastic dreams—a sort of 'Son of Man' to appear on the clouds taking vengeance on the armies of the Beast. So, you see, they, too, recognise an opposition between the Man and the Beast. Only, with the Christians it is of a date much earlier than Epictetus. It goes back to a Jewish tradition, which represents a sort of opposition between the empires of Beasts and the empire of the Son of Man, in a prophet named Daniel, some centuries ago.

"Epictetus, of course, does not believe in all this. But still he persuades himself that there is such a line of battle' in the air, and that he and his followers can take part in this aerial conflict by 'going about the world' as spiritually armed warriors, making themselves substantially miserable—or what the world would call such—while championing the cause of unsubstantial good against evil. All that you wrote to me about the missionary life and its hardships—its destitution, homelessness, nakedness, yes, even the extraordinary phrase you added from Arrian's notes about the cudgelled Cynic, how he 'must be cudgelled like a donkey, and, in the act of being cudgelled, must love his cudgellers as being the father of all and brother of all'—all this I could match, in a compressed form, from a passage in my little Pauline volume. Here it is: '*For I think that God has made a show of us Missionaries*'—Missionaries, or Apostles, that is their name for their wandering Aesculapii—'*like condemned criminals in the arena. We have been made a theatre-show to the universe, to angels and men...—up to this very moment, hungering, thirsting, naked, buffeted, driven from place to place, toiling and labouring with our own hands. Reviled, we bless; persecuted, we endure. Men imprecate evil on us, we exhort them to their good. We have been made as the refuse of the universe, the offscouring of all, up to this very moment.*'

"Again, elsewhere, Paul brings in that same Epictetian contrast between the external misery and the internal joy of the Missionary: '*Never needlessly offending to anyone in anything, lest the Service*—which your philosopher calls 'the service of God'—*be reproached, but in everything commending ourselves as the Servants of God, in much endurance, in tribulations, in necessities, in hardships, in scourgings, in prisons, in tumults, in toils, in watchings, in fastings.*' Now comes the contrast, indicating that all these things are superficial trifles, the petty pin-pricks inflicted by the spite of the contemptible world, but underneath lie the solid realities:—'*in parity, in knowledge, in longsuffering, in kindness and goodness, in the holy spirit, in love unfeigned, in the word of truth, in the power of God.*'

"This leads Paul to the thought of the armour of God, and the friends and enemies of God, the good and the evil, which this wandering Christian Hercules has to deal with: '*By the arms of righteousness, on the right hand and on the left; by glory and dishonour; by ill report and good report*— he means, I think, 'glory in the sight of God, dishonour in the sight of men,' and again, 'ill report on earth, good report in heaven.' And so he continues, '*as knaves and true...*'—that is, 'knaves in appearance, in the world's false judgment, but true men in the sight of Him who judges truly.' It is a marvel of compression. And it is kept up in what follows:—'*misunderstood* [*i.e.* by men] *and well understood* [*i.e.* by God); dying, and behold we live; under the headsman's scourge, yet not beheaded; grieving, but always rejoicing; beggars, but making many rich; having nothing, yet having all things for ever!'

"You will be tired of this. But your zeal for your new teacher brought it on you. You admire his 'fervour.' Then what do you think of this man's fervour? He could give points to Epictetus both for fervour and for compression. I admit that Paul has not your master's dramatic flash, irony, and epigrammatic twist. But, as for 'fervour,' here, I contend, is the original Falernian, which your friend Epictetus has watered down. Not that I blame him, either as regards style or in respect of morality. His humorous description of the nursery troubles of the married Stoic was very good—for his purpose, and for a lecture. But it would not have suited Paul. A lecturer must not be too brief. If Epictetus were to pack stuff in his lectures as Paul packs it in his epistles, your lesson would sometimes not last five minutes.

"But I am straying from the question, which is, whether Epictetus borrowed. Let me give you another instance. The Christians are permeated with two notions, the first is, that they have received an 'invitation,' 'summons' or 'calling' (*Klesis* they call it) to a heavenly Feast in a Kingdom of Heaven. The second is, that, if they are to attain to this Feast, they must pass through suffering and persecution, by 'witnessing' or 'testifying' to Christ, as being their King, in opposition to the Gods of the Romans. This 'witness' or*martyria,* is so closely associated in their minds with the notion of persecution that 'martyrdom,' with them, has come to imply, almost always, death. Now, as far as I know, the Greeks do not anywhere use the word 'calling' in this sense. But look at what Epictetus says about a sham philosopher, who, having been 'called' by God to be a beggar, 'disgraces his *calling*': 'How then dost thou mount the stage now? It is in the character of a witness *called* by God, who says "Come thou, and bear witness to me."' Then the sham philosopher whines out, 'I am in a terrible strait, O Lord, and most unfortunate. None take thought for me; none give to me. All blame me. All speak evil of me.' To which Epictetus replies, 'Is this the witness thou wouldst bear, *bringing shame on the calling wherewith He hath called thee*, in that He honoured thee with so great an honour, and counted thee *worthy* to be promoted to the high task of such a witnessing?' Now this phrase, 'worthy of the calling,' is Pauline in thought, and Pauline in word. Here is an instance, from a letter to the Thessalonians, 'That our God would *count you worthy of the calling*.'

And Paul writes to the Ephesians, 'That ye walk *worthily of the calling wherewith ye were called.*'

"Again, you yourself remarked to me on the strangeness and originality of Epictetus's expression about 'eating,' namely, that, in the very act of eating, or going to the gymnasium, or whatever else, the philosopher was to remember that he was 'feeding on God' and 'carrying about God,' and that he must not 'defile' the image of the God within him. Well, I admit it is strange, but I do not admit that it is original. I can match it in the first place with another passage from Epictetus himself, where he bids some of his uppish pupils, who wished to reform the world, first to reform themselves. 'In this way,' he said, 'when eating, help those who eat with you; when drinking, those who drink with you.' In the next place, I can match both out of the letter to the Corinthians, which says, 'Ye are *God's temple*' and 'If anyone destroys *Gods temple*, him will God destroy,' and again,'*Your body is the temple of the Holy Spirit*, which ye have from God.' It adds that people cause shame to others and injury to themselves by greediness at the sacred meals they take in common; and lastly, says Paul, '*Whether therefore ye eat or drink, or whatsoever ye do, do all to the glory of God.*' There are things like this, of course, in Seneca, but none, as far as I know, that come so near as Epictetus does to the language of Paul.

"I could quote more from Paul, and also from other sacred books of the Christians, to show that Epictetus is indebted to them. But I have been already led on by the fascination—to me it is a fascination—of a merely literary discussion, to say more than enough, and a great deal more than I intended. Let me conclude with an extract from a letter I lately rummaged up from my dear old friend Pliny, whom I greatly miss. He was the former Governor of Bithynia about whom you wrote. It refers to a very fine fellow, Artemidorus by name, a military tribune, son-in-law of the excellent Musonius (Epictetus's teacher, whom I mentioned above).'Among the whole multitude of those who in these days call themselves philosophers, you will hardly find one so sincere, genuine, and true, as Artemidorus. I say nothing about his bodily endurance of heat and cold and the most arduous toil, of his indifference to the pleasures of the table, of the strict control with which he keeps his eyes and his passions in order. These are great virtues, but only great in others. In him they are but trifles compared with his other merits.'

"So wrote Pliny. Well, for me at all events,'to keep eyes and passions in order' is not 'a trifle.' Perhaps it is not 'a trifle' for you. I fully believe that Musonius's successor—for as such I regard Epictetus—in spite of some opinions in which I cannot quite follow him, will help you to attain this object. Give yourself wholly to that. I knew Artemidorus. So did your father. We both thought him the model of a soldier and a gentleman. Believe me, my dear Quintus, it would be one of the greatest comforts in my last moments if I could feel assured that—to some slight extent in consequence of advice from me—the son of my old friend Decimus Junius Silanus was following in the footsteps of one whom he so esteemed and admired. Farewell."

This was the end of the letter. But out of it dropped a paper containing a sealed note. On the paper were these words: "To convince you that I had not judged your philosopher unfairly, I transcribed a few passages from other Christian documents, containing words assigned by Christians to Christ himself, which seem to me to have influenced Epictetus. On second thoughts, I have come to think it was waste of my time. That it might not waste yours too, I was on the point of throwing the thing into the fire. But I decided to send it rather than let you suppose me to be a crotchety, suspicious, prejudiced old man, ungenerous towards one whom both you and I respect with all our hearts. I grant that I am slow to believe in new *facts*; but I need hardly assure you, my dearest Quintus, that I am not slow to believe in good *motives*—the motives of good men, tried, tested, and proved, by such severe trials as have befallen your admirable Master. Rather than suspect me thus, break the seal and read it at once. But I hope you will not want to read it. Discussions of this sort must not be allowed to distract your energies as they might do. Better bum it. Or keep it—till you are military tribune."

V. — EPICTETUS ALLUDES TO JEWS

I DID not open the sealed note, though I was not convinced that Epictetus had been a borrower. Paulus the Christian had begun to interest me, because of Scaurus's quotations and remarks on his style. Indeed he interested me so much that I determined at once to procure a copy of his letters. But Christus himself—whom I call Christus here to distinguish the meaning with which I used the name then from that with which I began to use the name of "Christ" soon afterwards—Christus, I say, at that moment, did not interest me at all.

Moreover I was impressed by what Scaurus said about a military career. Though too young to remember much about the shameful days of Domitian, yet I had heard my father describe the anguish he used to feel, when letters from the Emperor to the Senate came announcing a glorious victory (duly honoured with a triumph) after which would come a private letter from Scaurus informing him that the victory was a disgraceful defeat. And even later on, even after the successes of Trajan, my father, in conversations with Scaurus, had often expressed, in my hearing, still lingering apprehensions of a time when the barbarians might break in like a flood upon the northern borders of the empire—if ever the imperial throne were cursed with a second Domitian. Patriotism would be even more needed then, he said, than when Marius beat back the Cimbri. All this gave additional weight to Scaurus's remarks. "Artemidorus," I said, "shall be my model. I will try to be a good soldier and a good Stoic in one." So I locked up the note, still sealed.

Here I may say that afterwards, when I did open it, it did not greatly influence the course of my thoughts. By that time, I had come to think that Scaurus was right, and that Epictetus had really borrowed from the Christians. I opened it, therefore, not because I distrusted the fairness and soundness of his judgment, but because I trusted it and looked to him for information. As a fact, it rather confirmed his hypothesis of borrowing, but did not demonstrate anything. The real influence of that little note in my cabinet amounted, I think, to little more than this. In the period I am now about to describe, while daily studying the works of Paulus the Christian, I was beginning to ask myself "If Paulus the follower of Christus was so great a teacher, must not Christus have been greater?" In those days, when taking out Paul's epistles from my bookcase, I used often to see that packet lying there, with WORDS OF CHRISTUS on it, and the seal unbroken. Then I used to say "If only I could make up my mind to open you, you might tell me wonderful things." This stimulated my curiosity. It was one of many things—some little, some great—that led me toward my goal.

The reader may perhaps think that I, a Roman of equestrian rank, must have been already more prone to the Christian religion than I have admitted, if I attempted to procure a copy of Paul's epistles from a bookseller in Nicopolis frequented by my fellow-students. But I made no such attempt. Possibly our bookseller there would not have had a copy. Probably he would not have confessed it if he had. In any case, I did not ask him. It happened that I needed at this time certain philosophic treatises (of Chrysippus and others). So I wrote to a freedman of my father's in Rome, an enterprising bookseller, who catered for various tastes, giving him the titles of these works and telling him how to prepare and ornament them. Then I added that Aemilius Scaurus had sent me some remarkable extracts from the works of one Paulus, a Christian, and that the volume seemed likely to be interesting as a literary curiosity. This was perhaps a little understating the case. But not much. With Flaccus, my Roman bookseller, I felt quite safe. Rather than buy Paul's epistles from Sosia in Nicopolis, I am sure I should not have bought them at all. Such are the trifles in our lives on which sometimes our course may depend—or may seem to have depended.

Meantime I had been attending lectures regularly and had become familiar with many of Epictetus's frequently recurring expressions of doctrine. They were still almost always interesting, and generally impressive. But his success in forcing me to "feel, for the moment, precisely what he felt "—how often did I recognise the exact truth of this phrase of Arrian's!—made me begin to distrust myself. And from distrust of myself sprang distrust of his teaching, too, when I found the feeling fade away (time after time) upon leaving the lecturer's presence. When I sat down in my rooms to write out my notes, asking myself, "Can I honestly say I hope to be ever able to do this or that?" how often was I obliged to answer, "No!"

I could not trust his judgment about what we should be able to do, because I could not trust his insight into what we were. Two causes seemed to keep him out of sympathy with us. One was his own singular power of bearing physical pain—almost as though he were a stone and not flesh and blood. He thought that we had the same, or ought to have it. Another cause was his absorption in something that was not human, in a conception of God, whom (on some evidence clear to him but not made clear by him to us, or at all events not to me) he *knew* (not trusted or believed, but *knew*) to have bestowed on him, Epictetus, the power of being at once—not in the future, but at once, here on earth, at all times, and in all circumstances—perfectly blessed. Having his eyes fixed on this Supreme Giver of Peace, our Master often seemed to me hardly able to bring himself to look down to us, except when he was chiding our weakness.

Passing over several of the lectures that left me in the condition I have endeavoured to describe, I will now come to the one in which Epictetus alluded to Christians. "Jews" he called them. But he defined them in such a way as to convince Arrian that he meant Christians. Even if he did not, the impression produced on me was the same as if he had actually mentioned them by name. The lecture began with the subject of "steadfastness." "A practical subject, this," I said to myself, "for one in training to be a second Artemidorus." But the "steadfastness" was not of the sort demanded in camps and battlefields. The essence of good, said the lecturer, is right choice, and that of evil a wrong choice. External things are not in our power, internal things are: "This Law God has laid down. *If thou wilt have good, take it from thyself!*" Then followed one of the now familiar dialogues, of which I was beginning to be a little tired, between a tyrant threatening a philosopher, who points out that he cannot possibly be threatened. The tyrant stares and says, "I will put you in chains." The wise man replies, "It is my hands and feet that you threaten." "I will cut off your head," shouts the tyrant. "It is my head that you threaten," replies the philosopher. After a good deal more of this, a pupil is supposed to ask, "Does not the tyrant threaten you then?" To this the lecturer replies, "Yes, if I fear these things. But if I have a feeling and conviction that these things are nothing to me, then I am not threatened." Then he appealed to us, "Of whom do I stand in fear? What things must he be master of to make me afraid? Do you say, 'The master of things that are in your power'? I reply, 'There is no such master.' As for things not in my power, what are they to me?"

Epictetus had a sort of rule or canon for us beginners, by which we were to take the measure of the so-called evils of life: "Make a habit of saying at once to every harsh-looking apparition of this sort, 'You are an apparition and not at all the thing you appear to be. Are you of the number of the things in my power, or are you not? If not, you are nothing to me.'" Applying this to a concrete instance, our Master now dramatized a dialogue between himself and Agamemnon, who is supposed to be passing a sleepless night in anxiety for the Greeks, lest the Trojans should destroy them on the morrow.

"*Epict.* What! Tearing your hair! And you say your heart leaps in terror! And all for what? What is amiss with you? Money-matters?

"*Ag.* No.

"*Epict.* Health?

"*Ag*. No.

"*Epict.* No indeed! You have gold and silver to spare. What then is amiss with you? That part of you has been neglected and utterly corrupted, wherewith we desire etc.. etc."

Here Epictetus—after some customary technicalities—turned to us like a showman, to explain the royal puppet's condition: "'How *neglected*?' you ask. He does not know the essence of the Good for which he has been created by nature, nor the essence of evil. He cries out, 'Woe is me, the Greeks are in peril' because he has not learned to distinguish what is really his own etc. etc." After this apostrophe, which I have condensed, he resumed the dialogue:

"*Ag*. They are all dead men. The Trojans will exterminate them.

"*Epict* And if the Trojans do not kill them, they are never, never to die, I suppose!!

"*Ag*, o, yes, they'll die. But not at one blow, not to a man, like this.

"*Epict.* What difference does it make? If dying is an evil, then, surely, whether they die all together or one by one, it is equally an evil. And do you really think that dying will be anything more than the separating of the paltry body from the soul?

"*Ag*. Nothing more.

"*Epict.* And you, when the Greeks are in the act of perishing, is the door of escape shut for you? Is it not open to you to die?

"*Ag*. It is.

"*Epict.* Why then bewail? Bah! You, a king! And with the sceptre of Zeus, too! A king is never unfortunate, any more than God is unfortunate. What then are you? A shepherd in truth! For you weep, like the shepherds—when a wolf carries off one of their sheep. And these Greeks are fine sheep to submit to being ruled over by you. Why did you ever begin this Trojan business? Was your desire imperilled, etc. etc.?" [Here I omit more technicalities.]

"*Ag*. No, but my brother's darling wife was carried away.

"*Epict.* And was not that a great blessing, to be deprived of a 'darling wife' who was an adulteress?

"*Ag*. Were we then to submit to be trampled on by the Trojans?

"*Epict.* Trojans? What are the Trojans? Wise or foolish? If wise, why make war against them? If foolish, why care for them?"

I doubt whether Epictetus quite carried his class with him on this occasion. He certainly did not carry me, though he went on consistently pouring out various statements of his theory. For the first time in my experience of his lectures, I began to feel that his reiterations were really tedious. My thoughts strayed. I found myself questioning whether my model soldier and philosopher, Artemidorus, could possibly accept this teaching. Would Trajan, I asked, have been so sure of beating Decebalus, if he had considered the disgrace of Rome a matter "independent of choice," and therefore "nothing to him," "neither good nor evil"?

From this reverie I was roused by a sudden transition—to a picture of a well-trained youth going forth to a conflict worthy of his mettle. And now, I thought, we shall have something more like the ideal of my first lecture, a Hercules or Diogenes, going about to help and heal. But perhaps Epictetus drew a distinction between a Diogenes and mere well-trained youths, mere beginners in philosophy. At all events, what followed was only a kind of catechism to prepare us against adversity, and especially against official oppression. "Whenever," said he, "you are in the act of going into the judgment hall of one in authority, remember that there is also Another from above, taking note of what is going on, and that you must please Him rather than the authority on earth." This catechism he threw into the form of a dialogue between the youth and God—whom he called "Another."

"*Another*. Exile, prison, bonds, death, and disgrace—what used you to call these things in the Schools?

"*Pupil*. I? Things indifferent.

"*Another*. Well, then, what do you call them now? Can it be that *they* have changed?

"*Pupil*. They have not.

"*Another*. You, then—have you changed?

"*Pupil*. I have not.

"*Another*. Say, then, what are 'things indifferent?'

"*Pupil*. The things outside choice.

"*Another*. Say also the next words.

"*Pupil*. Things indifferent are nothing to me.

"*Another*. Say also about things good. What things used you to think good?

"*Pupil*. Right choice, right use of phenomena.

"*Another*. And what the end and object?

"*Pupil*. To follow thee.

"*Another*. Do you say the same things still?

"*Pupil*. I say the same things still.

"*Another*. Go your way, then, and be of good cheer, and remember these things, and you will see how a young and well-trained champion towers above the untrained."

I wanted to hear him explain why he spoke of "*Another*" instead of Zeus, or God. It struck me that he meant to suggest to us that in this visible world, whenever we say "*this*" we must also say, in our minds, "*another*" to remind ourselves of the invisible counterpart. "Especially must we say '*Another*'"—this, I thought, was his meaning—"when we speak about rulers. Visible rulers are mostly bad. We must prevent them from encroaching on the place that should be filled in our hearts by the Other, the invisible Ruler."

Instead of this explanation, however, he concluded his lecture by warning us against insincerity, or "speaking from the lips," and against trying to be on both sides, when we ought to choose between two contending sides. This he called "trimming." And here it was—while addressing an imaginary "trimmer"—that he used the word "Jew."

"Why," said he—addressing the sham philosopher—"why do you try to impose on the multitude? Why pretend to be a Jew, being really a Greek? Whenever we see a man trimming, we are accustomed to say,'This fellow is no Jew, he is shamming.' But when a man has taken into himself *the feeling of the dipped and chosen*"—these were his exact words, uttered with a gesture and tone of contempt—"then he is, both in name and in very truth, a Jew. Even so it is with us, having merely a sham baptism; Jews in theory, but something else in fact; far away from any real feeling of our theory, and far away from any intention of putting into practice the professions on which we plume ourselves—as though we knew what they really meant!" I could not quite make out this allusion to Jews. But there was no mistaking his next sentence, and it was the last in the lecture, "So, I repeat, it is with us. We are not equal to the fulfilment of the responsibilities of common humanity, not even up to the standard of Man. Yet we would fain take on ourselves in addition the burden of a philosopher. And what a burden! It is as though a weakling, without power to carry a ten-pound weight, were to aspire to heave the stone of Ajax!"

Thus he dismissed us. I went out, feeling like the "weakling" indeed, but without the slightest "aspiration to heave the stone of Ajax." Perhaps Arrian wished to encourage me. For after we had walked on awhile in silence, he said, "The Master was rather cutting to-day. I remember his once saying that we ought to come away from him, not as from a theatre but as from a surgery. To-day the surgeon used the knife, and we don't like it."

"But what good has the knife done us?" I exclaimed. "If only I could feel that the surgeon had cut out the mischief, a touch of the knife should not make me wince. But the mischief within me seems more mischievous, and my strength for good less strong, for some things that I have heard to-day. Is a Roman to say, when fighting against barbarians for the name and fame of Rome, 'These things are nothing to me'? Is Diogenes, healing mankind, his brethren, to say, 'Your diseases are nothing to me'? And that fine phrase in the Catechism, 'follow thee'—is it not really a disguised form of 'follow myself'? Does it not mean, 'follow the*logos* within me, my own reason, or my own reasonable will,' or 'follow my own peace of mind, on which my mind is bent, to the neglect of everything else'?"

"It does not mean that, for Epictetus himself, I am convinced," said Arrian. "I believe not, for him," said I; "but it has that meaning for me. His teaching does not teach—not me, at least, however it may be with others—the art of being steadfast. And what about others? Did not he himself just now admit that his *logos*was less powerful than the *pathos* of the Jews to produce steadfastness? What, by the way, is this *pathos*? Does it mean passionate and unreasonable conviction? And who on earth are these Jews that are 'dipped and chosen'?"

My friend's face brightened. Perhaps it was a relief to him to pass from theology to matter of literary fact. "I think," he replied, "that he must mean the Jewish followers of Christus—the Christians, about whom we were lately talking." "Then why," said I, "does not he call them Christians?" "I do not know," replied Arrian, "He has never mentioned either Christians or Christus in my hearing; but he has, in one lecture at all events, used the term 'Galilaeans' to mean the

Christians. And I feel sure that he means them here, because the other Jews do not practise baptism, except for proselytes, whereas the Christians are all baptized." "But," said I, "he does not call them 'baptized.' He calls them 'dipped.'" "That is his brief allusive way," said Arrian. "You know that we provincials, and sometimes even Athenians too, speak of *dipping* the hair, or, if I may invent the word, *bapting* it, where the literary people speak of *blacking* or *dyeing* it. That is just what our Master means. These Christians are not merely *baptized*; they are *bapted*. That is to say, they are permanently and unalterably stained, or dyed in grain. They are. We are not. That is his meaning. Afterwards, as you noticed, he dropped into the regular word '*baptism*,' and spoke of us as *sham-baptists*."

"But he also called them chosen" said I, "—that is to say, if he meant *chosen*, and not *caught* or *convicted*." Arrian smiled. "You have hit the mark without knowing it," said he. "I noticed the word and took it down. It is another of his jibes! These Christians actually call themselves '*elect*' or '*chosen*.' I heard all about it in Bithynia. They profess to have been 'called' by Christus. Then, if they obey this 'calling,' and remain steadfast, following Christus, they are said to be '*chosen*' or '*elect*' But our Master believes this '*calling*' and '*choosing*' to be moonshine, and these Christian Jews to be the victims of a mere delusion, caught by error. So he uses a word that might mean '*chosen*' but might mean also '*caught*.' They think themselves the former. He thinks them the latter."

I hardly know why I refrained from telling my friend what Scaurus had told me about the probability that Epictetus had borrowed from the Christians. Partly it was, I think, because it was too long a story to begin just then; and I thought I might shock Arrian and not do Scaurus justice. Partly, I was curious to question Arrian further. So after a short silence, during which my friend seemed lost in thought, I said to him, "You know more about the Christians than I do. Do you think Epictetus knows much about them? And what precisely does he mean by '*feeling*' when he speaks of 'taking up the *feeling* of the dipped'?"

"As for your first question," said Arrian, "I am inclined to think that he knows a great deal about them. How could it be otherwise with a young slave in Rome under Nero, when all the world knew how the Christians were used to light the Emperor's gardens? Moreover his contrast between the Jew and the Greek seemed to me to come forth as though it had been some time in his mind, though it had not broken out till to-day. He spoke with the bitterness of a conviction of long standing. If—contrary to his own rules—he could be 'troubled,' I should say our Master felt a real 'trouble' in being forced to confess that the Jew is above the Greek in steadfastness and constancy. As to your second question, I think he means that, whereas Greeks attain to wisdom through the reason (or *logos*) these Jews follow their God, or Christus, through what we Greeks call emotion or affection (i.e. *pathos*). And I am half disposed to think that this word *pathos* was used by him on the other occasion when he spoke of the Christian Jews as Galilaeans." "Could you quote it?" said I. "No, not accurately," said Arrian, "it is rather long, and has difficulties. I should prefer you to have it exactly. Come into my rooms. I am going out on business, so that we cannot talk about it at present. But you shall copy it down."

So I went in to copy it down. Arrian left me after finding the place for me in his notes. "You will see," he said, "that the Galilaeans are there described as being made intrepid '*by habit*.' Well, that is certainly how I took the words down. But I am inclined to think it might have been 'by *feeling*'—which seems to me to make better sense. But read the whole context and judge for yourself. The two phrases are easily confused. Now I leave you to your copying. *Prosit!* More about this, to-morrow."

VI. — PAUL ON THE LOVE OF CHRIST

THE lecture from which I was transcribing was on "fearlessness." What, it asked, makes a tyrant terrible? The answer was, "his armed guards." A child, or madman, not knowing what guards and weapons mean, would not fear him. Men fear because they love life, and a tyrant can take life. Men also love wealth, wife, children. These things, too, a tyrant can take; so men fear him. But a madman, caring for none of these things, and ready to throw them away as a child might throw a handful of sand—a madman does not fear. Now came the words about "custom" and "Galilaeans" to which Arrian had called my attention: "Well, then, is not this astonishing? Madness can now and then make a man thus fearless! *Custom can make the Galilaeans fearless!* Yet—strange to say—reason and demonstration cannot make anyone understand that God has made all that is in the world, and has made the world itself, in its entirety, absolutely complete in itself and unimpeded in its motions, and has also made its separate parts individually for the use of all the parts collectively!"

The context made me see the force of Arrian's remark. Epictetus appeared to be mentioning three influences under which men might resist the threats and tortures of a tyrant. In the first place was the "madness " of a lunatic. In the third place was the "logic," or demonstration, of philosophy. In the second place, it would make good sense to suppose that Epictetus meant "feeling," or "passionate enthusiasm." This passage would then accord with the one mentioned above. Both passages would then afl&nn that the Christian Jews or Galilaeans can do under the influence of "feeling" what the Greek Philosophers, or "lovers of wisdom," cannot do with all the aid of reason (or "*logos*"). "Custom" would not make good sense unless the "Galilleans," or Christians, had made a "custom" of hardening their bodies by severe asceticism. This (I had gathered from Arrian) was not the fact. In any case, it seemed clear that Epictetus was here again contrasting some kind of Jew with the Greek to the disadvantage of the latter.

Curiosity led me to read on a little further. The text dealt with Man's place in the Cosmos, or Universe, as follows: "All the other parts of the Cosmos except man are far removed from the power of intelligently following its administration. But the living being that is endowed with logoSy or reason, has therein a kind of ladder by which he may reason the way up to all these things. Thus he, and he alone, can understand that he is a part, and what kind of part, and that it is right and fit that the parts should yield to the whole." This reminded me of the saying I have quoted above, "Will you not make a contribution of your leg to the Universe?" I think he meant "Will you not offer up your lameness, as a decreed part of the whole system of things, and as a sacrifice from you to the Supreme?"

This reasonable part of the Cosmos, this "living being that is endowed with *logos*" Epictetus declared to be "*by nature* noble, magnanimous, and free." Consequently, said he, it discerns that, of the things around it, some are at its disposal, while others are not; and that, if it will learn to find its profit and its good in the former class, it will be perfectly free and happy, "being thankful always for all things to God."

This puzzled me not a little. I could not understand how Epictetus explained the means by which these "noble, magnanimous, and free" creatures, created so "*by nature*," had degenerated into the weaklings, fools, profligates, and oppressors, upon whom he was constantly pouring scorn. Was not each man a "part" of the Cosmos? Was not the Cosmos " perfect and exempt from all disorder or impediment in any of its motions"? Did not each "part" in it—and consequently man—partake in this perfection and exemption, being "made for the service of the whole"? What cause did Epictetus find for the folly, vice, and injustice that he so often satirised and condemned as "subject to the wrath of God"? Man was a compound of "clay" and "*logos*." The fault could not lie in the "*logos*." Was it, after all, the mere "clay" that caused all this mischief? And then, lost in thought, turning over the loose sheets of Arrian's notes, one after the other, I came again on the passage I have quoted above from Epictetus, "If I could have, I would have "—laying the fault, as it seemed, upon the "clay." I could not help asking, "If God 'could' not remedy it, how much less 'could' I, being 'clay,' remedy myself, 'clay'?"

Musing on these things I returned to my rooms, and was sitting down to write to Scaurus, when my servant entered with a parcel, from Rome, he said, forwarded by Sosia our bookseller. It contained the books I had ordered from Flaccus, with a letter from him, describing in detail the pains he had taken in having some of the rolls of Chrysippus and Cleanthes transcribed and ornamented, and saying that in addition to the "curious little volume containing the epistles of Paulus," which, as I no doubt anticipated, were "not in the choicest Greek," he had forwarded an epistle to the Hebrews. "This," he said, "does not include in the commencement the usual mention of Paulus's name, and it is not in his style. But I understand that it originated from the school of Paulus."

There was more to the same effect, for Flaccus and I were on very friendly terms; and he was a good deal more than a mere seller of books. But I passed over it, for I was in haste to open the parcel. At the top were the copies of Cleanthes, Chrysippus, and others, in Flaccus's best style. At the bottom of all were two rolls of flimsy papyrus. The larger and shabbier of the two fell to the ground open, and as I took it up, my eye lit on the following passage:—"

Who shall separate us from the love of Christ? Shall tribulation or suffering or persecution or himger or nakedness or peril or the sword? As it is written:

'For thy sake are we done to death all the day long:

We were accounted as sheep of the shambles.'

Nay, in all these things we are more than conquerors through Him that loved us. For I am persuaded that neither death, nor life, nor angels, nor sovereignties, nor things present, nor things to come, nor powers, nor height, nor depth, nor anything in all creation, will be able to separate us from that love of God which is in Christ Jesus our Lord!"

"This, at all events," said I, "Scaurus cannot say that Epictetus has borrowed from Paul. Never have I heard Epictetus mention the word ' love '; and here, in this one short passage. Paul uses it twice!"

My next thought was that Scaurus was quite right in his estimate of Paul's style. It was indeed terse, intense, fervid, strangely stimulating and constraining.

"There is no lack of *pathos*," I said, "Let us now test the *logos*!" So I sat down to study the passage, trying to puzzle out the meaning of the separate words and phrases.

"*The love of Christ!*" Well, Christus was their leader. The Christians still loved him, and clung to his memory. That was intelligible. But "that love of God which was in Christ" perplexed me. I read the whole passage over again. Gradually I began to see that the passage implied the Epictetian ideal—according to Scaurus, not Epictetian but Pauline or Christian— of a Son of God standing fearless and erect in the face of enemies, tyrants, oppression, death. But it also suggested invisible enemies—"angels and sovereignties"—that seemed to be against the sons of God. And still I could not make out the expression, "that love of God which is in Christ Jesus."

So I turned back to the words at the bottom of the preceding column:— "*If God is for us, who is against us? He that spared not His own Son but delivered him up for us all, how shall He not also, with him, freely give us all things? It is God that maketh and calleth us righteous: who is he that shall condemn? It is Christ Jesus that died—or rather that was raised from the dead, who is on the right hand of God, who also "maketh intercession for us.*" And so, coming to the end of the column, I looked on again to the words with which I had begun: "*Who shall separate us from the love of Christ?*" Now I could understand. "This," said I, "is a great battle. There are sovereignties of evil against the good. The Son of the good God is supposed to devote himself to death, fighting against the hosts of evil. Or rather the Father sends him into the battle and he goes willingly. This Christus of the Galiteans is regarded by them as we Romans might think of one of the Decii plunging into the ranks of the enemy and devoting himself to death for the salvation of Rome. Philosophers might ask inconvenient questions about the nature of the God to whom the brave man devotes himself—whether it is Pluto, or Zeus, or Nemesis, or Fate. No philosopher, perhaps, would approve of this theory. But, in practice, the bravery stirs the spirits of those who believe it. Even if the sacrifice is discreditable to the Gods accepting it, it is creditable to the man making it."

Turning back still further, I found that Paul imagined the Cosmos— or "creation" as he called it—to have gone wrong. He did not explain how. Nor did he prove it. He assumed it, looking forward, however, to a time when the wrong would be made right, and even more right than if it had never gone wrong:— "*For I reckon that the sufferings of this present season are not fit to be spoken of in comparison of the glory that is destined to be revealed and to extend to us. For the earnest expectation of the creation waiteth intently for the revealing of the sons of God, For the creation was made subject to change, decay, corruption—not willingly but for the sake of Him that wade it thus subject—in hope, and for hope: because even this very creation, now corrupt, shall be made free from the slavery of corruption and brought into the freedom of the glory of the children of God. For we know that the whole of creation groaneth together and travaileth together—up to this present time.*"

This struck me as a very different message from that of Epictetus about Zeus. Both Paul and Epictetus seemed to agree as regards the past, that certain things had happened that were not pleasing to God, taken by themselves. But whereas the Greek said about God, "He would have, if He could have; but He could not," the Jew seemed to say, "He can, and He will. Only wait and see. It will turn out to have been for the best."

Reading on, I found something corresponding to Epictetus's doctrine of the indwelling Logos, namely, that each of us has in himself a fragment of the Logos of God,—but Paul called it Spirit—in virtue of which we may claim kinship with Him, being indeed God's children. Epictetus, however, never said that we were to pray to our Father for help. He seemed to think that each must derive his help from such portion of the Logos as each possessed. "Keep," he said, "that which is your own," "Take from yourselves your help," "Within each man is ruin and help," "Seek and ye shall find within you," or words to that effect. Paul's doctrine was different, teaching that we do not at present possess salvation and help to their full extent, but that we must look forward in hope: *"And not only so, but we ourselves also, though possessing the firstfruits of the Spirit—we ourselves also, I say, groan within ourselves, waiting earnestly for the adoptimi, namely, the ransoming and deliverance of our body"*—as though a time would come when that very same clay, which (according to Epictetus) the Creator would have wished to make immortal but could not, would be transmuted and transported in some way out of the region of flesh into the region of the spirit.

Moreover, besides looking onward in hope, we must also (Paul said) look upward for help. Epictetus, too, as I have said above, sometimes spoke of looking "upward," and of the Cynic stretching up his hands to God. That, however, was not in prayer but in praise.

Epictetus never used the word "prayer" in my hearing except of foolish, idle, or selfish prayers. But Paul represented the Logos, or rather the Spirit, within us, as an emotional, not a merely reasonable power. "It searcheth all things, yea, even the deep things of God," he said to the Corinthians; and by it (so he told the Romans in the passage I was just now quoting) the children express to the Father, and the Father receives from the children, their wants and aspirations:— *"For by hope were we saved. But hope that is seen is not hope. For who hopeth for that which he seeth? But if we hope for that which we fail to see, then in patient endurance we earnestly wait for it And in the same way tlve Spirit also taketh part with our weakness. For as to what we should pray for, according to our needs, we do not know. But the Spirit itself maJceth representaion in our behalf in sighings beyond speech. Now He that searcheth the hearts knoweth what is the mind and temper of the Spirit, because, being in union and accord with God, it Tnaketh representation in behalf of the saints."*

This passage I only vaguely understood. For I started with the preconception that the spirit or breath or wind, must be only another metaphor—like "word "—to describe a "fragment" of God (as Epictetus called the Logos in man). I did not as yet understand that this Spirit might be regarded as, at one and the same moment, in heaven with God and on earth with men, representing the love and will of God to man below, and the love and prayers of man to God above. Still I perceived that in some way it was connected with the Christian Christ; and that the Father and the Spirit and Christ were in some permanent relation to each other and to man, by which relation man and God were drawn together. And this led me back again to the words, "Who shall separate us from the love of Christ?" and "We are more than conquerors through Him that loved us."

Comparing this "love" with the friendship felt by the Epictetian Diogenes for the whole human race, I found the latter thin and poor. The Greek philosopher, being a "friend" of the Father of Gods and men, seemed to me to be friendly to men in the region (so to speak) of the Logos, "because "—I was disposed to add—" the Logos within him, in a ' logical' way, commanded him to be friendly to them, for consistency's sake, as being'logically' akin to him." Perhaps some reaction against the constant inculcation of loyalty to the Logos during'the last few weeks led me to be a little unfair to the Epictetian ideal. But, fair or unfair, these were my thoughts at the moment while I was turning over the letters addressed by this wandering Jewish Diogenes to some of the principal cities of Greece and Asia, coming every now and then on such sentences as these: *"I have strength for all things in Him that giveth me inward power"*; *"Being made powerful with all power, in accordance with the might of His glory, so that we rejoice in endurance and longsuffering, being thankful to the Father"*; *"Be ye made powerful in the Lord and in the might of His strength."* Here I noted that he did not say (as Epictetus did) "take power from yourselves." Moreover Paul added *"Put on the panoply of God."* Then I turned back again to the Roman and Corinthian letters; and still the same thoughts and phrases met me, about *"power"* in various contexts, such as *"demonstration of Spirit and power,"* and *"abounding in hope through the power of the Holy Spirit." "Love,"* too, was represented as an irresistible power. *"The love of Christ constraineth us,"* he said. And then he added, *"One died for all"* and *"He died for all, that the living should be living no longer to themselves, but to Him that for their sake died and was raised up from death."* There was a great deal in this Roman letter that was almost total darkness to me at first. The references to Abraham—and, still more, those to Adam, coming abruptly in the phrases, "death reigned from Adam," and "the transgression of Adam"—perplexed me a great deal till I perceived that the Jews fixed their hopes on God's promise to their forefather Abraham, just as Romans—if they believed Virgil—might fix theirs on the forefather of the Julian race. As Aeneas was the divine son of Anchises, so Isaac, by promise, was the divinely given son of Abraham. Paul, I thought, might draw a parallel between our Aeneas and his Isaac, as though both were receivers of divine promises of empire extending over all the nations of the earth. At this Jewish fancy (so I called it) I remember smiling at the time, and quoting Virgil from a Jew's point of view:

"Tantae molis erat *Judaeam* condere gentem."

But I soon perceived, not only that Paul was in serious earnest, quite as much as Virgil, but also that his scheme, or dream, of universal empire for the seed of Abraham was compatible with the fact of universal empire for the seed of Anchises. Rome, the new Troy, claimed dominion over nothing but men's bodies. The new Jerusalem claimed it over men's souls.

I did not fully take all this into my mind till I had read the story of Abraham and Isaac in the scriptures, as I shall describe later on. But, with Virgil's help, and Roman traditions, I partially understood it even now; and I remember asking myself, "If Virgil were now alive, would he be as sanguine as this Jew? Is not Rome on the wane? Ever since the Emperor cried to Varus,'Give me back my legions!' have we not had qualms of fear lest we should be beaten back by the barbarians? Do not even the wisest of our rulers say, 'Let us draw the line here. Let us conquer no more'? But this Jew sets no limits to his conquests. His projects may be mad. But at least he has some basis of fact for them. If he has conquered so far, why not further?"

As to "the transgression of Adam," I remained longer in the dark. But I perceived from other passages in the epistles (and from the Jewish scriptures soon afterwards) that the story of Adam and Eve resembled some versions that I had read of the story of Epimetheus and Pandora, who caused sins and pains to come into the world, but "hope" came with them. Adam and Eve did the same. But Paul believed that the "hope" sprang from a promise of a higher and nobler life than would have been possible if Adam and Eve had never gone wrong. I took this for a mere legend, but a legend that might represent the will of Zeus—namely, that man should not stand still, but that he should go on growing, from age to age, in righteousness, which, as Plato says, is the attribute of man that makes him most like God.

Thus I was led on to higher and higher inferences about Paul's "power." First, it was real power, attested by facts—fitcts visible in great cities of Europe and Asia. In the next place, this power was based on faith and hope. Lastly, this faith and this hope—although they extended to everything in heaven and earth (since everything was to be bettered, purified, drawn onward or upward to what Plato might call its idea in God, that is, its perfection)—were themselves based on Christ, as having once died, but now being alive for ever in heaven.

But not only in heaven. For Paul seemed to think of Christ as also still perpetually present with, and in, his disciples on earth. Socrates in the Phsedo says "As soon as I have drunk this poison I shall be no longer remaining among you, but shall be off at once to the isles of the blessed." But Paul spoke of Christ's love, and spirit, and of Christ himself, as still remaining amongst his followers. I knew that the common people think of Hercules as descending from heaven now and then to do a man a good turn; and at this I had always been disposed to laugh. But Paul's view of Christ as being always in heaven, and yet also always on earth, among, or in the hearts of, those who loved him—this seemed to me more noble and more credible; though I did not believe it.

Now I was to be led a step further. For while I was repeating Paul's words "one died for all," and again, "one died," it occurred to me "Yes, but he does not say *how* he died. Is he ashamed to speak of the shamefulness of the death, the slave's death, death upon the cross?" So I looked through the Roman letter, right to the end, and I could find no mention of the "cross" or of "crucifying." But in the very next column, where the first Corinthian letter began, I found this passage:—

"Christ sent me not to baptize but to preach the Gospel, not in wisdom of 'logos' (i.e. word), lest the cross of Christ should he emptied of its power. For as to the 'logos' of the cross, to those indeed who are going the way of destruction, it is folly: but to us, who are going the way of salvation, it is the power of God. For it is written:

'I will destroy the wisdom of the wise

And the subtlety of the subtle will I bring to naught.'

"Where is the 'wise?' Where is the learned writer? Where is the 'subtle' discusser and disputer of this present age?"

Then followed some very difficult words: *"Hath not God made foolish the wisdom of the Cosmos? For since, in the wisdom of God, the Cosmos, through that wisdom, recognised not God, God decreed through the foolishness of the proclamation of the gospel to save them that go the way of belief: for indeed Jews ask for signs and Greeks seek after wisdom, but we proclaim Christ crucified; to the Jews, a stumbling block; to the other nations, a folly; but, to the called and summoned—Christ the power of God and the wisdom of God."*

I have translated this literally so as to leave it as obscure to the reader as it was to me when I first read it. Even when I had read it over two or three times, there was a great deal that I could not understand. But it appeared to me to be ironical. It suggested that the "logos" of God may be different from the "logos" of men, or at all events, the "logos" of Greek philosophers. I had for some time been drawing near to a belief that "logos" might include feeling as well as reason. But this strange contrast between the unwise "wisdom of logos" and the wise "logos of the cross" came upon me as (possibly) a new revelation. As for the saying "the Greeks seek wisdom," it reminded me how Epictetus used to deride the man of mere logic, words without deeds, the futile spinner of syllogisms. "Epictetus," I said to myself, "would agree with this accusation." But then I reflected that Paul would perhaps class Epictetus himself among these futile Greeks; and had not my Master himself confessed that the Jew, by mere force of "pathos," outclassed the Greek in resolution and steadfastness, although the latter was backed by "logos"? The conclusion fell upon me, like a blow, "Here is Paul boasting as a conqueror what my Master confesses as a man conquered! Both agree that the 'feeling' of the Jew is more powerful in producing courage than the 'reasonableness' of the Greek!"

I did not like this turn of things. But I was intensely interested in it; and it quite decided me to continue the investigation. The question turned on "logos" and I quoted to myself Plato's precept, "Follow the *logos*." Epictetus made much of "*logos*." Well, I would "follow the '*logos*,'" in its fullest sense, and would try to find out whether it did, or did not, indicate that "feeling," as well as "reason," may help us towards the knowledge of God. Dawn was appearing when I rolled up the little volume and placed it in my cabinet by the side of Scaurus's sealed note with "WORDS OF CHRISTUS" on it. That reminded me of my old friend. What would he think of all this?

I sat down at once and wrote to him that I had not opened his note. If I ever did, it would be, I said, because I accepted his verdict. Epictetus really did seem to have borrowed from Paul. The subject was very interesting to me from a historical as well as a literary point of view; and I hoped he would not think it waste of time if I investigated it a little further. At the same time, I sent a note to Flaccus. Aemilius Scaurus, I said, had sent me some "words of Christus" extracted from Christian books, and I desired to receive the books themselves. As for the "scriptures" from which Paul so frequently quoted in their Greek form, I knew that I should have no difficulty in procuring copies of all or most of them from Sosia. This I resolved to do on the morrow, or rather in the day that was now dawning. It was not a lecture-day. Even if it had been, in the mood in which I then was, I should have thought a lecture or two might be profitably missed.

VII. — DAVID AND MOSES

THE Greek translation of the Scriptures shown me by Sosia was in several volumes of various sizes and in various conditions. Unrolling the one that showed most signs of use, I found that, although it was in prose, it was a translation of Hebrew poems, mostly very short, and of a lyrical character. One of them had in its title the name of "David," which I had met with in Paul's letter to the Romans. Sosia told me that he was the greatest of the ancient kings of the Jews. Ordering the other volumes to be sent to my rooms, I took this back with me, and began to read it immediately, beginning with the poem on which I had chanced in the shop.

It was a prayer for purification from sin: "Pity me, God, according to thy great pity, and according to the multitude of thy compassions blot out my transgression. Cleanse me still more from my crime, and purify me from my sin." So far, the poem was intelligible to me. I was familiar with the religious rites of cleansing fix)m blood-guiltiness—mentioned in connexion with Orestes and many others by the Greek poets and recognised in various forms all over the world. So I said, "This king has committed homicide. He has been purified with lustral rites and sacrifices. But he needs some further rites: 'Cleanse me still more,' he says. The poem will tell me, I suppose, what more he needs."

After adding some words to the effect that the transgression was against God, against God alone, the king continued, "For behold, in transgressions was I created at birth, and in sins did my mother conceive me. For behold, thou hast ever loved truth; thou hast shown unto me the hidden secrets of thy wisdom. Thou wilt sprinkle me with hyssop and I shall be purified; thou wilt wash me and I shall be whiter than snow." Here I was at a stand. It seemed to me a great and sudden descent to a depth of superstition, to suppose that this particular additional rite of "cleansing with hyssop" could satisfy the king's conscience. Moreover I thought that "wisdom" must mean the wisdom of the Greeks. It was not till afterwards that I discovered how great a gulf separates our syllogistic or rhetorical or logical "wisdom" from that of the Jews—which means "knowledge of the righteousness of the Creator based upon reverence." Thence comes their saying, "Reverence for God is the beginning of *wisdom*."

These two misunderstandings almost led me to put down the book in disgust. But the passionateness of the king's prayer made me read its opening words once again. Then I felt sure I must have done him injustice. So I read on. Presently I came to the words, "Create in me a clean heart, God, and renew a right spirit within me. Cast me not away from thy countenance, and take not thy holy spirit from me." These made me ashamed of having taken "hyssop" literally.

1 saw now that it was just as much metaphorical as "whiter than snow," and that it meant a deep and inward purification—of the heart, not of the body. Still more was I ashamed when I came to the words, “If thou hadst delight in sacrifice I would have given it to thee, but thou wilt take no pleasure in whole burnt-offerings. The sacrifice for God is a broken spirit. A broken and contrite heart God will not despise."

This was all new and strange doctrine to me. The gracefiil lines of Horace about the eflBcacy of the simplest sacrifice—of meal and salt—from the hand of an innocent country girl, and about its superiority to the proffered bribe of a hecatomb from a man of guilt, these I knew by heart; but they did not touch the present question, which was as to how the man of guilt could receive purification, without a hecatomb, without the blood of bulls and goats. And the question went even beyond that. For the king said that he had been "in sins" even from the beginning, even before birth. Did he speak of himself alone, or of himself as the tjrpe of erring mankind? I thought the latter. He seemed to me to say, "Man is from the first an animal, born to follow appetite. In part (no doubt) he is a divine being, born to follow the divine will; but in part he is an animal, born to follow animal propensity." So far this agreed with Epictetus's doctrine about the Beast. The Beast, at the beginning, tyrannizes over the divine Man, so that the human being may be said to be in sin—and indeed is in sin, as soon as he becomes conscious of the tyranny within him. "No lustral rites, no blood of bulls and goats," the king seemed to say, "can purify this human heart of mine now that it has been tainted and corrupted by submitting to the Beast within me. A moment ago, my prayer was 'Purge me with hyssop,' but now it is 'Destroy me and create me anew,' 'Take away my old heart and give me a new heart.'"

These last words were quite contrary to the doctrine of Epictetus, who taught us that we are to receive strength and righteousness from that which is within our own hearts. And, thought I, is not the king's prayer superstitious? The witches in Rome suppose they can draw down the moon by incantations. This king David in Judaea supposes he can draw down "a clean heart" and "a right spirit" by passionate invocation to the God of the Jews! Are not the two superstitions parallel? Would not Epictetus say so? Would not all the Cynics say so? I thought they would: and, as I was rolling up the little book, I said, "It is a fine and passionate poem, but the prayer is not one for a philosopher." Then, however, it occurred to me that there was a true and a deep philosophy—though I knew not of what school—in the doctrine that the true and purifying sacrifice for guilt is a penitent heart. That set me pondering the whole matter again and reflecting on some of the things in my own life of which I was most ashamed, things that I would have given much to forget, and a great deal more to undo. In the end, I found myself thinking—not saying, but thinking of it as a possible prayer—"In me, in me, too, create a clean heart, O thou God of forgiveness!" It might not be a prayer for philosophers, but I could not help feeling that it might be a good prayer for me.

While I was placing my new volume by the side of Paul's epistles it occurred to me that the words I had just been reading might throw some light on a passage in the epistle to the Romans at which I had glanced last night. Then I could make nothing of it. Now I read it again: "I know that in me, that is, in my flesh, there dwelleth no good thing. To will [that which is good] is present with me, but to do is not present. I will to do good and I do it not. I will not to do evil, and I do it." This now seemed to me a truer description of the state of things (within me at all events) than the view mostly presented to us in our lecture-room. Epictetus often talked as though we had merely to will, and then what we willed—at least so far as concerns the mind and the things in the mind's province—would at once come to pass. True, he did not always say this. Sometimes he insisted on the need of training or practice, and then he likened the Cynic to an athlete preparing for the Olympian games. But it seemed to me that he habitually underrated the difficulty of conforming the human to the divine will: and he never—never even once, as far as I know—recognised the need or efficacy of repentant sorrow.

My immediate conclusion was that, although it was not for me to decide between the "feeling" of the Jews and the "reason" of the Greeks in general, yet one thing was certain—I had a good deal to learn from the former. So I welcomed the arrival of Sosia's servant bringing the rest of my new books. A good many of them I unrolled and cursorily inspected at once. Both from their number, and from the variety of their subjects, it was clear that I should only be able to study a few. I resolved to confine myself to such parts as bore on Paurs epistles, and to dispense with lectures for a day or two. Then it occurred to me that Arrian, who had proposed to resume to-day our conversation on the Jews and Galilaeans, might come in at any moment. I put away the Jewish books and went to his lodging, thinking that I could perhaps tell my friend of my new studies in order to explain to him my non-attendance at lecture. Instead of Arrian, however, I found a note informing me that he had been obliged to go suddenly to Corinth (in connexion with some business of his father's) but hoped to return before long.

This saved explanation; and I spent several days (during his prolonged absence) in studying my new volumes. They led me into a maze—or rather, maze after maze—of bewildering novelties. Sosia had told me that my first volume, containing five books, was called by the Jews "the Law." But it included pedigrees, poems, prophecies, histories of nations, and stories of private persons. The legal portion of it was largely devoted to details about feasts and purificatory sacrifices—the very things that David appeared to call needless. However, when I came to look into the Law more closely, I found that its fundamental enactments were humane and gentle—so much so as to give me the impression of being unpractical. It enjoined on the

Jews kindness to strangers as well as to citizens. While retaining capital punishment, it prohibited torture. At least I took that to be a fair inference from the fact that it even forbade the infliction of more than forty blows with the scourge, on the ground that a "brother "—that was the w6rd—must not be so hx degraded as to become "vile" in the eyes of his fellow-citizens. It also placed some limitations on the right of masters to punish slaves, even when the latter were foreigners.

Having been accustomed to regard the Jews as unique for their moroseness and unneighbourliness I was all the more astonished at these things. It occurred to me then, as it does sometimes now, that the Law was almost too humane to have been ever fully obeyed by the greater part of the people. For example, even the slaves, even the beasts of burden, were to have one day in seven as a holiday, on which all labour was forbidden. Periodic remission of debts was enacted by law! This surprised me most of all. To think that the revolutionary measure—so our Roman historians called it—for which our tribunes of the people had contended in vain under the Republic, should here be found legalised by the Law of Moses—and this, too, not as an exceptional and isolated condonation, but as a regular remission after a fixed number of years!

"How," I asked, "could the Lawgiver expect people to lend money to borrowers if the creditor knew that in the course of a few months the obligation to pay the debt would cease?" Was he blind to the most manifest tendencies of human nature? No, I found he was not blind to them. He simply said that they must be resisted: "Beware," said he, "that there be not a base thought in thine heart, saying, The seventh year, the year of release, is at hand."

This notion of forbidding an action, or abstinence from action, in a code of laws as being "base"—not as being "subject to a penalty of such a kind," or "a fine of so much," was quite new to me. I had given some time to the study of Boman law, and had always assumed that when the law says "Do this," it adds a punishment in some form or other, "Do this, or you shall suffer this or that." But here, embedded in the Law of Moses, was a law, or rather a recommendation, without penalty. And presently I found that the last of their Ten Greater Laws—if I may so call them—was of the same kind. It could not possibly be enforced—for it forbade "coveting"! Only a few days ago, before I had bought these books from Sosia, I had read in Paul's epistle to the Eomans "I should not have known covetousness if the law had not said. *Thou shalt not covet*"; and these words had puzzled me a good deal. I had thought that they must refer to some "law" of a spiritual kind, such as we might call "the law of the conscience" or "the law of our higher nature," or the like. Yet I felt that this interpretation did not quite agree with the context. Now I found, to my utter astonishment, that this was the very letter of the first clause of the tenth of the Greater Laws, "Thou shalt not covet."

To crown all, I found that elsewhere the whole of the code was based by the Lawgiver on two fundamental precepts. The first was, "Thou shalt love the Lord thy God," and this love was to call forth all the powers of mind and soul and body. The second was, "Thou shalt love thy neighbour as thyself." How was either of these to be enforced? "Love," say all the poets, "is free." The Law neither prescribed nor suggested any means of enforcing these two Great Commandments of "loving." And how could "love" be at once "free," as poetry protests, and yet a part of the Law, as Moses testified? There seemed no answer to this question, unless some God could make us willing and eager to enforce the two commandments on ourselves, constraining us (so to speak) by love to love both Him and one another. "Truly," said I, "this Law of Moses is very ambitious." It seemed to aim at more than Law could accomplish. It reminded me of a sentence I had found in one of my new volumes, entitled "Proverbs," "The light of the Lord is as the breath of men; He searcheth the storehouses of the soul."

Somewhat similar was a saying imputed to Epictetus—which I had not heard from Arrian but from a fellow-student—reproving one of his disciples in these words, "Man, where are you putting it? See whether the basin is dirty!" The disciple, though an industrious scholar, was of impure life; and Epictetus meant that, if the vessel of his soul was foul, all the knowledge put into that vessel would also become foul. The moral was, "First cleanse the vessel!" So the Jewish Proverb seemed to say, "The light of the Lord must first search the storehouse of the soul: then the food taken out from the storehouse will be pure and wholesome." This brought me back to the words of David, who seemed to think that the searching and cleansing must come from God and not from man alone, "Create in me a clean heart, O God, and renew a right spirit within me!"

Comparing these two fundamental or Greatest Laws of Moses with the fundamental law of Epictetus, "Keep the things that are thine own," I thought at first that the Jew and the Greek were entirely opposed. On second thoughts, however, I perceived that in "the things that are thine own" Epictetus would include justice and kindness, and all social so-called virtues so far as they did not interfere with one's own peace of mind—for he would perhaps exclude pity, and certainly sympathy in the full sense of the term. But Epictetus thought that people could be sufficiently kind and just and virtuous without other aid than that of the "logos" *within* them. David did not, in his own case, unless that which was within him had been cleansed or renewed by a Power regarded as *outside* him, to whom he prayed as God. There seemed to me, in this difiference of "within" and "outside," more than a mere difference of metaphor. But I had no time to think over the matter. For, just as I was regretting that Arrian was not with me to talk over some of these subjects, Glaucus, coming in to borrow a book, informed me that he had met my friend late in the previous night coming from the quay. I had intended to stay at home that morning. But now, finding that Glaucus was on his way to the lecture, I resolved to accompany him, expecting to meet Arrian there.

VIII. — EPICTETUS ON SIN

WHEN we reached the lecture-room, a little late, we found it unusually crowded. My place was taken, and I could not see Arrian in his customary seat. Epictetus was in one of his discursive moods. He began with the assertion—by this time familiar to me, but somewhat distasteful now, fresh as I was from the atmosphere of the Jewish writings—that Gods and men alike seek nothing but "their own profit." As in most of his epigrams, he meant just the opposite of what he seemed to assert. He hated high-flown language as much as he loved high thought and action. Even when he mentioned "the beautiful"—on which most Greeks go off into rhapsodies—he almost always subordinated it to the "logos" or told us that we must look for it in ourselves. So here again. Man, he declared, must give up all things—property, reputation, children, wife, country, if they are incompatible with his true "profit." Then, of course, he showed that man's "profit" is virtue, so that we need not give up these blessings unless their possession is incompatible with virtue.

What he said next was new to me. A father, losing a child in death, must not say "I have lost my child," but "I have given it back." When I say "new," I mean new in his teaching. But I had recently met something like it in my books of Hebrew poems, "The Lord hath given, the Lord hath taken away. Blessed be the name of the Lord." Later on, I heard Epictetus repeat this almost in the same form. This seemed to me not only beautiful and devout but also consistent with reasonable faith.

But I could not follow him when, in reply to the objection, "He that took away this thing from me is a villain," he said, "What does it matter to you by whom the Giver asked back the gifb?" It seemed to me that a recoil from villainy, as well as delight in virtue, ought to find a place even in the calmest of mankind. No philosopher, he said, can have an "enemy," because no one can do him any harm or touch anything that really belongs to him. This was true—in a sense. Its reasonableness contrasted with the passionate poetry of the Jews, which I had found full, too full, of talk about enemies. And yet, the more I meditated on the contrast, the more this "What does it matter to you?" seemed to become a cold-blooded, unnatural and immoral question. Surely it ought to "matter" to us a great deal whether we suffered loss from some neighbour's forgetfulness or from some enemy's premeditated and malignant treachery. He went on in the same chilling style. "Desire," said he, "about that which is happening, that it shall happen. Then you will have a stream of constant peace." I seemed to see Priam "desiring that which was happening" when he saw Troy burned and the women ravished! His son, Polites, was being butchered by Pyrrhus before his eyes, and the old king was standing by, placidly enjoying "a stream of constant peace"!

Then Epictetus said, "An uneducated man blames others for his own evils. A beginner blames himself. An educated man blames neither others nor himself." After this, he introduced what he called the law laid down by God. "Right convictions make the will and purpose good. Crooked and perverse convictions make the will bad. This law," he said, "God has laid down, and He says to each of us, 'If you will have anything that is good, take it from yourself.'" Then came another mention of the law—"the divine law" he now called it. It was connected with "right convictions," as to which he asked "What are these?" His reply was, "They are such as a man ought to meditate on all the day long. We must have such a conviction as will prevent us from attaching our feelings to anything that is other than our own—

whether companion, or place, or bodily exercise, or even the body itself. We must remember the law and have it always before our eyes."

This phrase, "meditate all the day long," reminded me of some words of David, which I had been reading the day before, "Oh how I love thy law! It is my meditation all the day." Other Hebrew expressions also came into my mind concerning the sweetness and fragrance of the Lord's commandment, how the poet "opened his mouth and drew in his breath" to taste its delight. These I could understand, when they applied to a law of love, a law of the emotions, a "feeling." But I wondered what Epictetus could produce for us of a nature to kindle such enthusiasm. He continued, "And what is the divine law? It is this. First, Keep the things that are your own. Secondly, Do not claim things not your own; use them, if given; do not desire them, if not given. Thirdly, When anything is being taken from you, give it up at once in a detached spirit, and with gratitude for the time during which one has used it."

"Keep the things that are your own!"—This he placed first, and on this he laid most emphasis, dwelling on each syllable. I fencied that he knew he was disappointing us and almost took pleasure in it as though he were administering to us a wholesome but bitter medicine. "You find this sour," he seemed to say: "Sour or not, it is the truth, the only solid and safe truth. It is not the dream of a poet, or the scheme of a student. It is the plan of a man of business, practicable for all—for slaves as well as free men, for individuals in a desert as well as for communities in a city. 'Love your neighbour'—that is expecting too much. 'Do not covet what is your neighbour's'—that is expecting too little. 'Keep that which belongs to you!' There you have a rule that makes you independent of all neighbours." I was miserably disappointed; yet I could not help respecting and admiring our Master's unflinching frankness, his determination to force us to face the austere truth, and his contempt for anything that seemed incapable of being put into practice at all times and in all circumstances.

He spoke next of "sin" or "error." Some of his language strangely resembled Paul's, but with great differences. He made mention of a "conflict," but he seemed mostly to mean "a conflicting state of things," "logical contradiction," or inconsistency. It might be called self- contradiction, taken as including actions, and not words alone. He also used the very same phrase as Paul's "that which he willeth he doeth not," but not in the same way, as may be seen from the following extract which I took down exactly: "Every error includes self-contradiction. For since the person erring does not wish to err but to go straight, it is clear that what he wills to do he does not do... Now every soul endowed with 'logos' by nature is disposed to dislike self-contradiction. As long as a man has not followed up the facts and perceived that he is in a state of self-contradiction, he is in no way prevented from doing things that are self-contradictory; but, when he has followed them up, he must necessarily revolt from the self-contradiction... Here then comes in the need of the teacher skilled in 'logos'...but the teacher needs also power to refute what is wrong and to stimulate the pupil to what is right. This teacher will give the erring man a glimpse into the self-contradiction in which he errs, and will make it clear to him that he is not doing that which he mills to do and *that he is doing that which he wills not to do*. As soon as this is made clear to the person in error, he will, of himself and of his own accord, depart from his error."

Then he supposed a case where a man had relapsed from philosophy into a profligate and shameless life. And first he tried to show the offender how much he had lost in losing modesty and decency and true manliness. "There was a time," he said, "when you counted this as the only loss worth mentioning." Next, he showed each of us how to regain what we had lost. "It is you yourself," he exclaimed, "you yourself, no other whom you have to blame. Fight against yourself! Tear yourself away to seemliness, decency, and freedom."

Lastly, he appealed—as I had never heard him do before—to the feelings of loyalty and affiection that we might entertain for himself. I thought he must be recalling his old days in Rome, when he, a boy and a slave, in the house of Epaphroditus, might be exposed to the temptations and coercions to which such slaves were subject; and he asked his pupils to imagine their feelings if someone came to them reporting that their Master, Epictetus, had been forced to succumb.

"If," said he, very slowly and deliberately, with emphasis on each syllable, "if someone were to come and tell you that a certain man was compelling *me*"—here he hurried onward—"to lead the sort of life that you are now leading, to wear the sort of dress that you wear, to perfume mjrself as you perfume yourself, would you not go off straightway and lay violent hands on the man that was thus abusing me? Rescue yourself, then, as you would have rescued me. You need not kill anyone, strike anyone, go anjrwhere. Talk to yourself! Persuade (who else should do it better?)—persuade yourself!"

Never, in my experience, had Epictetus more nearly fulfilled the promise made in his behalf by Arrian—that he would alwajrs make his hearers feel, for the moment, precisely what he wished them to feel. There were two or three in the class notorious for their profligacy; but the appeal went home to others as well, conscious of minor derelictions. "Persuade yourself!" There was no need of it. We were all, to a man, already persuaded. Infants and babies though we were, we could all stand up and walk—for the moment. He proceeded in the same spirit-stirring tone, as though—now that we had all resolved to go on this arduous journey with him as a guide—he would go first and show us how to push our way through the forest.

"First of all," said he, "give sentence against the present state of things." He did not say *"against yourselves."* That would have been too discouraging. We were to condemn *"the present state of things"*; that is, our present self. "In the next place," he continued, "do not give up hope of yoursel£ Do not behave like the poor-spirited creatures who, because of one defeat, give themselves up altogether and let themselves be carried downward by the stream. Take a lesson from the wrestling-ring. That young fellow yonder has had a fall. 'Get up,' says the trainer, 'Wrestle again, and go on till you get your full strength.' Act you in the same spirit. For, mark you, there is nothing more pliable than the human soul. You must will. Then the thing is done, and the crooked is made straight. On the other hand, go to sleep; and then all is ruined. From your own heart comes either your destruction or your help."

He concluded with a word of warning. Perhaps some of us might appeal to his own *dictum* about seeking our own "profit" as being the only right and wise course. He met it as follows: "After this, do you say 'What good shall I get by it?' What greater 'good' do you look for than this? Whereas you once were shameless, you will now have received again the faculty of an honourable shame. From the orgies of vice you will have passed into the ranks of virtue. Formerly faithless and licentious, you will now be faithful and temperate. If you seek any other objects better than these, go on doing still the things you are doing now. Not even a God can any longer save you."

IX. — ARRIAN'S DEPARTURE

WHEN we came out from the crowded room, as Arrian was nowhere to be seen, I went at once to his lodging. To my surprise, he was busy packing, amid books and papers, and a student's other belongings. "Thanks, many thanks," he said, "for this timely visit. This is my last day in Nicopolis. I was just coming round to wish you good-bye. You know I had to go to Corinth. Well, when I got there, I found a letter from my &ther bidding me wait a few days for further news from him; and on the fourth day came a message that I was to conclude my studies at once and return to Bith}aiia, as his health had quite given way and his affairs required all my attention. I had intended to start to-day at the fifth hour; but I have just learned that the vessel will not sail till the eighth. So sit down. Epictetus there is not time to call upon. When I write to you I shall ask you to deliver him a letter from me. Sit down, and begin by telling me about the lecture I have just missed, while it is fresh in your memory."

When I had finished, he said, turning over the papers he was sorting, "I remember another of his lectures in which he warned us against a licentious and effeminate life. Here it is, and these are his exact words: 'Do not, in the name of the Gods, do not you, young man, fall back again! Nay, rather go back to your home and say, now that you have once heard this warning. *It is not Epictetus that has said this. How should he? It is some God wishing well to me and speaking through him. It would never have corns into the mind of Epictetus to say this, for it is never his custom to make personal appeals. Come, then, let its obey the voice of God, lest we fall under God's wrath!*' I have never forgotten these words, and I trust I never shall. I think a God speaks through Epictetus. Do you not agree with me?"

"I do indeed," said I, "but I am not convinced that God speaks all that Epictetus says, and that there is not more to be spoken. For example, he says, 'You have but to will and it is done.' Is that a common experience? Is it yours? He says, 'Take from yourself the help you need.' Do you find in yourself all the help you need? When you fall, he says, 'Get up,' as though we were boys in the wrestling-ring. But what if we have been'stunned? What if one's ankle is sprained or a leg broken? Do you remember what you said to me at the end of my first lecture,'Will itlast?' You also said that Epictetus could make us feel just what he wished us to feel—as long as he was speaking. Well, while I was sitting on the bench in the lecture-room, I felt that getting up from vice was as easy as sitting on that bench. When I walked out, it began to seem less easy. Now that I am quite away from the enchanter, talking the matter quietly over with you, the feeling has almost vanished; and I am obliged to repeat your question about this, and about much more of our Master's doctrine, VWill it last?'"

"Some of it will last," said Arrian, "We must not expect impossibilities. I have heard him admit that it is impossible to be sinless already, but he bade us remember that it is possible to be always intent on not sinning."

"Did he mean," asked I, "by 'already,' that we could not be sinless in this life, but that we might be sinless at what he calls the feast of the Gods, after death?"

Arrian did not at once reply. Presently he said, "I do not think so. I believe he meant that we must not expect to be sinless as soon as we have reached the intermediate stage of what he calls 'the half-educated man.' We must wait till we have reached the further stage, that of complete education, where, as you said just now, a man never blames himself, because he does not find in himself any fault that he could blame."

Here Arrian made a still longer pause. Then he continued, in his usual slow, deliberate way, but with a touch of hesitation that was not usual with him, "I have here a few duplicates of my notes. Among them are some on the subject on which your remarks bear, and about which (I gather) you would like to question me—the immortality of the soul. In my hearing, he has seldom used that precise phrase. And, when he has used the epithet 'immortal,' it has generally applied to life like that of Tithonus—I mean, a deathless life in this present world. To desire such a life, deathless and free from disease, he thinks unreasonable. But I remember his saying once, that he was prepared for death, *'whether it were the death of the whole or of a certain part'*—that was his expression. And I think he may possibly believe that the Logos within us is reabsorbed, after death, into some kind of quintessential or divine fire from which it sprang. But I cannot say that this satisfies me."

Neither did it satisfy me. But I said nothing. Arrian, too, was silent, turning over some of his papers and marking passages for my perusal. But presently, rousing himself, "Did you agree with me," he said, "about the passage you transcribed, when we last met, concerning that sect of the Jews which he called the Galilaeans?" I could see that Arrian wished to divert the conversation to "the Galilaeans," as being a subject of a less serious character than the doctrine of the immortality of the soul. But the subject of the Galilaeans or Jews had become much more serious for me now than it had been when we last conversed together. How much more, I shrank from telling him, in the few minutes at our disposal. He was good, just, a truthful scholar, a gentleman, and a kind friend. Given a few days more—even a few hours—in one another's company, and I should not have kept my secret from him. But how could I hope, in so brief an interval, and amid so many preoccupations, to make him understand what a vast continent of new history, religion, literature—and, above all, "feeling" as opposed to "logic"—had emerged before my mind's eye, during my recent voyages of exploration in the scriptures and in Paul's epistles? So I replied briefly that I agreed with his view.

"Epictetus," I said, "seemed to me to be speaking, not of the [...] 'feeling' (?) as also in the case of the Jews. "And, indeed, I added, "the force of this 'feeling'(?)[...] appears to me most remarkable."

"Well," said he, "I feel we shall hardly meet again in Nicopolis. But I shall always cherish the recollection of the hours we have spent together here, and of our common respect of our common Master whom you already love, and whom, if you were to know him as I do—in his home, and in his kindness to those who need kindness—you will (I trust) love still more." "I do love him," said I, "But tell me, do you Iove a11 his teaching about indifference to what is happening? You know how our Master scoffs as the agony of Priam looking on the ruin of Troy. Well, suppose you were a Roman citizen, as I am sure you will be before long. Or, rather, suppose you were our new Emperor Hadrian, and saw the northern barbarians not only at our gates but inside our walls, and the City in flame, and the Dacians doing in Rome what the Greeks did in Troy to the Trojan men and women, would you, our Elmperor Hadrian, feel it right to say, 'All this is nothing to me'?" "By the immortal Gods," exclaimed Arrian, "I should not." "And if Epictetus were in Hadrian's place, or Priam's place, do you think he could say it?"

I had to wait for an answer. "What I am going to say," he replied at last. "may seem to you monstrous. But I really cannot reply No. I cannot tell what he would say. I am not able to judge him as I should judge others." Then he proceeded, with an animation quite imusual in him, "Of any other Hadrian or Priam I should say that such an utterance stamped him as either liar, or beast, or stone. But Epictetus—absorbed in Zeus, devoted to His will, resolved to believe that His will is good, and seeing no way out of the belief that all things happen in accordance with His will—might not Epictetus conceivably feel, in moments of ecstasy, that all these fires and furies, massacres and outrages, cannot prevent him from believing in Zeus and being one with Zeus, so that he himself, Epictetus, might be, nay, must be, in the bosom of Zeus (so to speak) at the very moment when not only Rome, but all the cities, villages, and hamlets of the world—nay, when the universe itself was being cast into destruction? Well, I am out of my depth. I confess it. But will you not agree with me thus far, that *if* Epictetus said that he felt thus, he would really feel thus?"

"Yes," replied I, "I am sure that he would not say it unless he felt it. But I am not sure that he might not feel it merely because he had forced himself to feel it. However, let us say no more now on such subtle matters. It is no small help to have been lifted up by such a teacher above the mere life of the flesh. We part, do we not, in fiill agreement that Epictetus has been, for both of us, a guide to that which is good? " And thus we did part. I accompanied him to the quay. "May we meet again," were my last words. "May it be soon," were his. But we never met. The death of his father plunged him almost immediately into domestic cares and matters of business. When the pressure of private affairs relaxed, it was soon followed by affairs of state. This was due in part perhaps to his having been a pupil of Epictetus. The new emperor, long before he became emperor, had always admired our Master; whose recommendation (I am inclined to think) had something to do with Arrian s subsequent promotions. At all events, when I was on service in the north, I heard without any surprise, and with a great deal of pleasure, that my former fellow-student—known now to literary circles as Flavianus, a Roman citizen, and author of the Memoirs of Epictetus—had been appointed governor of Cappadocia.

From time to time we corresponded. But it was not upon the topics that used to engross us in old days. He took a great interest in geography. Military service, at one time in the north and then in the east, gave me some knowledge of this subject, which I was glad to place at his disposal. He also studied military affairs with a view to writing on Alexander. Here again I was of use to him. But we never resumed in our letters that subject about which he had once said to me, "More of this to-morrow." Our paths had branched off, leading us far away from each other in everything except mutual good will and respect. He had become a Roman magistrate. Subsequently he was a priest of Demeter. I had become a Roman soldier, but—a Christian. Many of my fiiends knew this and I have little doubt that Arrian guessed it. Privately I feel sure he always loved me. OflScially he must have been forced to disapprove. Hadrian, it is true, discouraged informations against the Christians, and I had been hitherto connived at: but could I condemn my old friend if he shrank from opening up old speculations that might lead him into unofficial, suspected, and dangerous results? Much more might I myself rather feel condemned for keeping silence. Sometimes I have felt thus. But not often. More often I feel that it was better for him not to know what I know, than to know it, in a sense, and to reject it. Presented in mere writing, I felt sure that it would have been rejected. Writings and books brought me on the way to Christ, but something more was needed to make me receive Christ.

Arrian, I think, avoided such opportunities as presented themselves for meeting. I am sure I did. If we had met, surely I should have been constrained to open my mind to him. Once, at least, I touched (in a letter) on our old conversation about "logos" and "pathos." He replied that, in his new career, both "logos" and "pathos" had to give place to pragmata, "business," which, he thought, was likely to take up all his energies during the rest of his life.

Even if I had opened my mind, I cannot help thinking that his would have remained unchanged. One thing, however, I do not think about, but know—namely, that, if we had met, Arrian and I would still have had common ground, as of old, in our love of truth and justice, and that we should still have esteemed, respected, and loved each other. For myself, love him I always shall, not for his own sake alone, but also because he helped me directly and immediately to understand Epictetus, and indirectly and ultimately to perceive the existence of something beyond any truth that Epictetus could teach.

X. — EPICTETUS ON DEATH

RETURNING to my rooms, I sat down to think out my problems alone. Presently, on taking up the lecture-notes Arrian had given me, I found that the title of the first was, "What is meant by being in desolation or deserted? And who can call himself deserted?" The subject suited my mood, and I began to read it, as follows; "Desolation is the condition of a man unhelped. To be alone is not necessarily to be deserted. To be in the midst of a multitude is not always to be undeserted. A man may be in the centre of a crowd of his own slaves. But still, if he has just lost a brother, he may be deserted. We may travel alone, yet never feel deserted till we fall into the midst of a band of robbers. It is not the face of a man that delivers us from desolation; it is the presence of someone faithful and trustworthy, thoughtful and kind, good and helpful."

I liked this. But afterwards the lecture strayed into what seemed to me controversial theology or metaphysics, "If being alone suffices to make you deserted, then say that Zeus Himself is deserted when the final fire comes round in its cycle, consuming the universe. Say that He bewails His loneliness exclaiming 'Alas, me miserable! I have no Hera now! No Athene! No Apollo! Not a single brother, son, or relation! 'Some people actually do assert that Zeus behaves like this in the final fire!" I gathered that he was attacking some philosophic tenet. But it did not interest me any more than his subsequent assertion—or rather assumption—that "Zeus associates with Himself, reposes on Himself, and contemplates the nature of His own administration." I have never felt drawn towards the conception of a self-admiring, or a solitary God.

Arrian's next note bore on the peace of the universe, a peace proclaimed by the Logos, a peace resembling, but far surpassing, the peace proclaimed by the Emperor, such a peace that every man can say, even when he is alone, "Henceforth no evil can befall me. For me, robbers and earthquakes have no existence. All things are full of peace, full of tranquillity. Whether I am travelling on the high road, or living in the city, whether in public assemblies or among private friends and neighbours, nothing can harm me. There is Another, not myself, who makes it His care to supply me with food. He it is that clothes me. He, not myself, gave me the perceptions of my body. He, not myself, bestowed on me the conceptions of my mind."

Then followed a passage about death, which Arrian, during our last conversation, had marked for my special attention: *"But if at any moment He ceases to supply you with the things needful for your existence, then take heed! In that moment He is sounding the bugle for you to cease the conflict. He is saying to you: 'Come!' And whither? Into no land of terrors. Simply into that same region from which you entered into being. Into the company of such eadstences as are friendly and akin to you. Into the elements. Such part as was fire in you will depart into fire; such part of earth as was in you, into earth; such part of air or wind as was in you, into air or wind; of water, into water. No Hades! No Acheron! No Cocytus! No Pyriphlegethon! All things are full of Gods and daemons!"* By this I think he meant "good Gods and guardian angels." He concluded thus, *"Having such thoughts as these in his heart, looking up to the sun, the moon, and the stars, and enjoying the earth and the sea, man has no more right to call himself deserted than to call himself unhelped."*

It was not clear to me how I could continue to call myself "helped" when I was on the point of being dissolved into the four elements. If I were a criminal, successful in escaping punishment on earth, I might deem it "help" (after a fashion) to know that I should be equally successful after quitting the earth, because I need not fear Hades and its three rivers as enemies. But where were the "friends"? The four elements promised but cold friendship! Arrian's comment rose to my mind, and a second time I assented to it, "I cannot say that this satisfies me." Epictetus was so averse from anything like cant or insincerity of expression that I was amazed—as I still am —that he could use, in such a context, the words "friendly and akin." Surely Sappho's cry was truer, when she wandered alone through the woods where she had once been loved by Phaon—

"This place is now dead dust. He was its life."

What would it profit that my "fiery part" should return to fire? It might as well go astray into water, or earth, or into extinction, as far as I cared. To be still loved would have been to be still in some kind of home. But who would love my four elements? I should be "not I," but only four severed portions of what had once been "I," fragments incapable even of mourning, wandering among "dead dust," no better than "dead dust " themselves! How infinitely should I have preferred that Epictetus—if he could not honestly accept the confident hope of

Socrates concerning a life after death,—should have said simply this, "As to what Zeus does with our souls after death, others think they know much. I know nothing, except that He does what is best."

Reviewing passages in which Epictetus had mentioned the "soul," I was more perplexed than ever. For in those he distinctly recognised the *"soul"* as *"better than the flesh"* or *"better than the body"* and as using the body as its instrument. When, therefore, he spoke of God as saying to man, "Come!" he ought to have supposed God to be addressing *the whole man, soul as well as body, or perhaps the soul alone,* (using the body, or the flesh, as its instrument). But if God said to the human soul "Come!" how could He go on to say "Such part as was fire in you" and so on, just as though we knew, without proof, that the soui was composed of nothing but fire, earth, air and water? We knew no such thing. On the contrary, Epictetus continually assumed that we have within ourselves "mind" and "*logos*." He also said that "The being of God" is "mind, knowledge, right *logos*." Now he could hardly suppose that "mind" and "logos" were composed of fire, earth, air, and water. For my part, I did not feel that I knew anything certain about the distinctions between "mind," "soul," "logos" and "I." But those who made distinctions appeared to me under an obligation to say what they meant by them.

It appeared to me that our Master had been inconsistent. As a rule, he dealt with each of us as having a soul that was our real self, and a body that was the tool of the soul. "Tyrants," he would say, "can hurt your *body*but they cannot hurt *you*!" Might not a pupil of his go on consistently to say: "Death can kill your body but it cannot kill you"? This, at all events, was what Socrates meant, when he said, "As for me, Meletus could not hurt me... He might kill, or banish, or degrade," for he certainly meant "kill" the *body*, not "kill" the *soul*.

Subsequently, when I came to read the Christian gospels,, I found two of them making this distinction in the words, "Be not afraid of them that kill the body." One of them added: "but cannot kill the soul," the other added "but cannot do anything more." Then I understood more clearly why Epictetua said nothing about what became of the soul after death. For these two Christian writers spoke of a possibility that the soul might be "destroyed in hell" or "cast into hell." Now this was. just what Epictetus did not himself believe, and wished to make others disbelieve. He preferred to give up the belief of Socrates that the good "go to the islands of the blessed" after death,, rather than believe also that the bad go to a place of the accursed. Hence he dropped all thought of the essential part, or parts, of man, namely, the soul, mind, and *logos*, as soon as he came to speak of man's death.

The consequence was that Epictetus confused us by an ambiguous use of "*you.*" As long as we were alive he said to us, "*You* must regard your body as a mere tool," where by "you" he meant the incorporeal part of man. As soon as we were on the point of death, he said to us, "Do not be alarmed. *You* are going into the four elements," where by "you" he apparently meant our corporeal part. I felt sure then (as I do now) that he did not intend to confuse us. He seemed to me to have been confused by his own intense desire to persuade himself that men must do good without hope of any reward at all except the consciousness of doing good in this present life. I had not at that time read the Christian gospels; but several passages in Paul's epistles occurred to me as contrary to this doctrine of Epictetus, and I thought that our Master might have been biassed in part by Paul (as Scaurus had suggested)—only not, in this instance, imitating Paul, but contradicting him. So I took up the epistle to the Romans intending to read what Paul said there about Christ's death and resurrection.

XI. — ISAIAH ON DEATH

I TOOK up the epistle to the Romans, but I did not read it long. Another subject stepped in to claim immediate attention in the first words on which I lighted. They were these, "Isaiah cries aloud on behalf of Israel, *Though the number of the sons of Israel be as the sand of the sea, the remnant [alone] shall be saved,*" and then, "Even as Isaiah has foretold, *If the Lord of Sabaoth had not left seed to us, we should have become as Sodom and should have been made like unto Gomorrah.*" Previously when I had read these words I could neither understand them nor see the way to understand them, not knowing the meaning of "Sodom" and "Gomorrah," nor even "Isaiah." But now, knowing that Isaiah was one of the principal Hebrew prophets, I began to see that many obscure passages of Paul might become clearer to me if I first studied this prophet. This view was confirmed when I found Paul, later on, quoting him again, "But Isaiah is very bold and says, *I was found by them that sought me not, I became manifest to them that consulted me not*; but with reference to Israel he says, *All the day long, I stretched out my hands to a people disobedient and gainsaying*." The name also occurred toward the close of the epistle thus, "Isaiah says: *There shall be the root of Jesse, and he that is raised up to rule over the nations; on him shall the nations set their hope*." These last words reminded me of the doctrine of Epictetus about Diogenes "to whom are entrusted the peoples of the earth and countless cares in their behalf."

But I did not know what "root of Jesse" meant. The name, "Jesse," I faintly remembered reading in the poems of David; but where it was I could not recall. Hence the phrase was obscure. I determined to put off the further study of Paul for the present, and to glance through the book of Isaiah in the hope of meeting this and other passages quoted above. Accordingly I unrolled the prophecy and began to read it from the beginning.

At first, the language was clear—though the Greek was as bad as in the poems of David. The "children" of God, said the prophet (meaning the ancient Jews or Hebrews, whom he often spoke of as "Israel") had rebelled against their Father and were being punished with fire and sword by hostile nations executing God's vengeance on their impiety. Then came the sentence I quoted above, from Paul, about the "remnant." After this, the prophet introduced "the Lord"—that is the God of the Jews—as saying that He cared no longer for their incense or their offerings because they came from hands stained with blood. This was somewhat like the saying of Horace about Phidyle mentioned above. But what followed was not like anything in Horace: "Wash you, make you clean; cease to do evil, learn to do good; seek judgment, relieve the oppressed, judge the fetherless, plead for the widow." If they would act thus, then, said God, "though your sins be red as scarlet, they shall be as white as snow." As though the nation were molten metal in a crucible, and He Himself were refining them with fire, the Lord said to the whole people of Israel, "I will purge away thy dross... afterwards thou shalt be called the city of righteousness."

I had begun to hope that I should be able to understand this author as easily as Euripides and much more easily than iEschylus. But now came obscurities. First I read of a golden age. People were to "beat their swords into ploughshares," and not to "learn war any more." Then I found a mention of general destruction as by a universal earthquake. Then came, without any chronological or other order apparent to me, the following pictures, or predictions:—a land without a ruler governed by children and women; a picture of luxurious ladies of rank, a list of their dresses, ornaments, jewels and cosmetics; a "branch of the Lord, beautiful and glorious"; a purifying with a "spirit of burning"; "a song of my beloved touching his vineyard"—all confused together (so it seemed to me at the time like the prophecies of the Sibyl.

As far as I could see, most of these prophecies dealt with the internal corruption of the nation. The "vineyard" of the Lord was the people of Israel. When He visited the vineyard, looking for fruit, said the prophet, "He looked for judgment but behold oppression." After this, came a vision of the Lord's glory, and then predictions of external calamities, and invasions of foreign nations. But yet there was a promise of the birth of a Deliverer, a Prince of Peace, to sit "upon the throne of David." Following this, at some interval, were the words for which I was searching, about "the root of Jesse." And now I could understand them, for they were preceded by this prediction, "There shall come forth a shoot out of the stock of Jesse, and a branch out of his roots shall bear fruit." Just before that, 'there had been a description of an invading army, coming as the instrument of the Lord's wrath and "lopping the boughs with terror" and hewing down "the high ones of stature."

Then all was clear to me. I perceived the connexion between the "child" that was to sit on "the throne of David," and the "shoot out of the stock of Jesse." The two together brought back to my mind that passage which I could not before recall from the Psalms, "The prayers of David the son of Jesse are ended." The words of Isaiah were like those of Sophocles where he is speaking of the destruction of the royal house of Laius. Sophocles calls the surviving child the "root," and laments because the axe of Fate was destroying it just when a branch was on the point of "shooting up" from the "stock" so as to produce fruit. So now, but in an opposite mood of hope and joy, Isaiah said that the royal house of David the son of Jesse would not be exterminated, though many of its scions would be cut off. A "branch" would "shoot up" and the succession to the kingdom would be maintained.

In the same way, I perceived, the great Julius, or the Emperor Augustus, being descended from lulus, the son of Aeneas, might be called "the shoot out of the stock of Anchises," transported from Asia to Europe so as to "shoot up" into a new kingdom more glorious than the old. This, too, explained the word "remnant" used by Paul. As the Trojan followers of Aeneas were a "remnant," so too must be the Jewish followers of this " child," a remnant left from defeat, disaster, and captivity, after a great "lopping of the boughs with terror." Virgil sang about the empire of the house of lulus not as a prophet, but as a poet, prophesying, so to speak, after the event. Isaiah appeared merely to predict empire as a prophet, and a false prophet, prophesying what had not been, and never would be, an "event." The tree of the empire of Rome was erect for all the world to look on. The tree of the kingdom of Jesse appeared to me as extinct as the house of Laius. So I thought then.

Yet I knew that Paul looked at the matter differently and regarded these prophecies as having been, or as about to be, fulfilled. And when I looked more closely into the sayings of Isaiah about the future kingdom, I saw that many of them were capable of two meanings. Sometimes the prophet appeared to be contemplating a kingdom established in the ordinary way by force of arms—a conquest achieved, or at all events preceded, by fire, sword, and desolation. But, for the most part, it seemed to be an empire of peace to be brought about by some kind of persuasion, or feeling. A sudden conviction was to take hold of all the nations of the earth, so that they were to exclaim, with one consent, as at the sound of a trumpet, "Come ye and let us go up to the mountain of the Lord," meaning the Temple in Jerusalem.

In this kingdom, however brought about, the Lord was to be King, and there was to be a "covenant" between Him and all the citizens or subjects, a covenant of righteousness. The subjects were to obey the King and the King would give them a righteous spirit. In some respects the covenant of obedience was to resemble that philosophic oath which Epictetus had enjoined on us, namely, to consult our own interests, to be true to ourselves (meaning, to the spirit of righteousness within us).

But the prophet regarded righteousness as loyalty, or truth, not to ourselves, but to our King.

That seemed to me one great difference between the Greeks and the Hebrews in their notions of worship. The Greeks, when they lifted their thoughts above themselves, looked, in the first place, each man to his several city, and in the next place, to the Gods. They did not think in the first place of the Gods. For the Gods were many, while the

City was one. But the ancient Jews, the men of Israel, or at least their prophets, looked to their Lord God as their King—the Father, or sometimes the Husband, of Israel. Although they were many tribes, they had but one God, the Lord God, who had delivered them from the land of Egypt. This Lord God was a God of justice and truth, hating oppression, a defender of the widow and the fiitherless. To be loyal to Him was righteousness.

And herein—as I soon began to perceive—was the great difference between the view of righteousness or justice taken by Isaiah and that taken by our Roman lawyers, or any lawyers bound to a written law. The lawyer's righteousness was legality; the prophet's was loyalty. Epictetus and Isaiah agreed together in aiming at loyalty, not legality. Both disliked obedience paid to mere rules and commandments of men. But the former for the most part inculcated loyalty that seemed like loyalty to oneself; the latter, loyalty to God. This precept of Isaiah agreed with the fundamental law prescribed in the code of Moses that the men of Israel were to "love" the Lord their God.

After searching carefully to see what the prophet said concerning the immortality of the soul (about which Moses seemed to be silent) I could find little of a definite kind. In one passage I read "The dead shall arise and they that are in the tombs shall be roused up." But the preceding lines said "The dead shall assuredly not see life"; so that it was not clear whether the words meant that one nation should be destroyed for ever and another nation should be raised up from destruction to life. The prophet appeared to be thinking of the nation collectively, more often than of separate citizens. The metaphor of the Vine of Israel seemed to be almost always in his thoughts. And his hope seemed to be, not concerning separate branches, that every branch should remain; but that, in spite of being cruelly pruned and cut down almost to the ground, the tree, as a whole, would yet grow up and bear fruit. I noticed also that a certain king ccdled Hezekiah, when praying to be delivered from a disease likely to prove ioXaX, spoke as though there were no life after death.

But there was one passage, of very mysterious import, which seemed to point to a different conclusion. It spoke about a "servant of God," of mean aspect but destined to be a great Deliverer—such as Epictetus had described—"bearing upon him the cares" of multitudes. He was to grow up "as a root in the thirsty ground," which suggested that he was to be "the root of Jesse" above mentioned. But he was not to be like Aeneas, "the root" of Anchises. For Aeneas divided the spoils in Italy as the prize of his sword. But this Deliverer—so the prophet declared—was "despised and reckoned as naught." He was "delivered over" to the enemies of his nation as a ransom to save his fellow-countrymen, and it was by their wickedness that "he was led to death." Yet in the end, said the prophet, "He will inherit many men, and will divide the spoils of the strong, because his soul was delivered over to death, and he was reckoned among criminals, and he carried the sins of many and he was delivered over on account of their crimes."

This was altogether beyond my comprehension at the time. But I saw that I should have to return to this prophecy hereafter; for I recognised its last words as having been quoted by Paul in writing to the Romans. I found afterwards that the passage in Paul spoke about "believing in Him that raised up Jesus our Lord from the dead, who *was delivered over for the sake of our transgressions*, and was raised up for the sake of our being made righteous." For the present, however, the passage in Isaiah about the "servant" of God seemed to me important, for this reason mainly, because it indicated a belief in a life after death. And so did another difficult passage—if Paul had interpreted it rightly. My copy of the prophecy said, "Death by its strength hath swallowed up"; but the margin said: "Death is swallowed up in victory," and these latter words, too, I recognised as being quoted by Paul; and this, or some similar, sense appeared to be required by the context.

It was growing late and I was obliged to break oflF. But I resolved to return to the book next morning before lecture. So far as I had read, it appeared to me that the prophet did not formally recognise the immortality of the soul in general. But in the case of the Suffering Servant he did seem to recognise it. Having the Servant in my mind, I unrolled the book of Isaiah to other passages using the same word, such as, "for my*servant* David's sake," "But thou, Israel, art my *servant*." "My *servant* whom I have chosen." At last I came to "the seed of Abraham my *friend*." In all these passages, God was supposed to be speaking. Then it occurred to me, "Did the prophet make an exception for the Suffering Servant only? Did he not also believe that Abraham's soul was immortal?" It seemed to me impossible that if the God of the Jews were asked, "Where is Abraham thy friend?" He would reply—or that the prophet would regard Him as replying—"Resolved into the four elements." On the whole, I was led to the conclusion that Isaiah implied, though he did not express, some kind of doctrine of human immortality dependent on the relation between man and God.

XII. — ISAIAH ON PROVIDENCE

EVEN when I was in the act of rolling up the book of Isaiah, very late at night, it occurred to me that the question "Is there a life after death?" might be connected with another, "Is there to be hereafter a reign of righteousness?" I tried to give my mind rest by thinking of other things; but this second question came back to me again and again both before and after I retired to rest. Epictetus spoke about "the sceptre and throne of Diogenes ": but I knew he would not assert that the philosopher's "sceptre" implied any present kingdom except over his own mind and the minds of a small band of Cynics—small in comparison with Stoics and Epicureans, and nothing at all in comparison with the non-philosophic myriads. As for a kingdom of righteousness after death in another world, I was now certain that Epictetus did not expect it; and I began to doubt whether he expected such a kingdom at any time in this world. If to believe in Providence means to believe in a God who foresees and prepares that which is best—I could not understand where Epictetus could find a basis for such a belief

With the Jews, it was otherwise. They, I could see, had received a special training, which made them, more than any other nation known to me, begin by expecting a reign of righteousness on earth. Beginning thus, and being largely disappointed, they might be led on to expect a reign of righteousness in heaven. Their history was like a collection of stories for children, teeming with what a child might call surprises, but a prophet judgments—evil, uppermost, suddenly cast down; humble patient goodness, chastened by pains and trials, lifted up to lordship over its past oppressors. Examples occurred to me before I slept, and many more during the night, in my waking moments. I had not noticed them so clearly when reading the Law consecutively. Now, grouped together, they came almost as a new revelation—if not of history, at all events of legend, and of a nation's thoughts, and of the training through which the Jew Paul must have passed in his childhood and youth.

First, there was Abraham—Abraham the homeless, going out from unbelievers to worship the one God, and receiving a promise that he should be the father of blessing, for multitudes in all the nations of the earth; Abraham the childless, rewarded with the child of promise; Abraham the kind and yielding, who gave way to his kinsman Lot, so that the older patriarch was content with the inferior pastures while the younger chose the fertile lands of Sodom and Gomorrah; Abraham the father of the one child that embodied the truth of the one God, offering up that child on the altar, and receiving him back as if from Hades; Abraham the landless, without a foot of ground in the land promised to him, bujdng with money a cave to bury his family. "Surely," I said, "the story of Abraham, in itself, is a compendium of national history not indeed for Rome, but for a nation of peace (if only the nation could live up to it!) most fit for training a child to become a citizen in the City of Righteousness!"

If the life of Abraham was full of surprises or paradoxes, so too were the lives of the other patriarchs and leaders of the nation. Isaac, "laughter," laid himself down to die in appearance, but to "laugh" at death in reality. Esau was the "elder," yet he was to "serve the younger." Jacob was promised lordship over his brother in the future, but he bowed down before him in the present. The same patriarch, a poor man, with nothing but his "staff," became rich and prosperous. Yet, because he had deceived his father, he in turn was deceived by his children and sorely tried by their contentions. Through Samuel, the little child, God rebuked Eli the high priest; and the little one became the prophet and judge of Israel. David, the despised and youngest of many brethren, became the greatest of IsraeFs kings.

Such was the history of the great men of the ancient Jews—tried, but triumphing over trial. On the other hand, the history of the mass of the common people, from the time when they were a family of twelve sons, showed them as going astray, lying, quarrelling and rebelling. For this they were punished by plagues and enemies; then, delivered by judges or prophets; but only, as it seemed, again to fall away, and to be delivered again; so that the reader of the histories, apart from the prophecies, might well suppose that these ebbs and flows were to go on for ever; that Israel was to be always imperfect, always liable to rebellion; and that the promise to Abraham was never to be fulfilled. More especially might a reader of the histories anticipate this when he saw the great empires of the east, Assyria and Babylon, leading the tribes away into captivity and destroying Jerusalem and the Temple.

Such were my thoughts by night concerning the Law and the Histories of Israel. Resuming the study of the prophecy early next morning, I perceived that in the sins and backslidings of the people there was yet another and far deeper illustration of what might be called "the law of paradoxes." Not only came prosperity out of adversity but also righteousness out of sin, and out of punishment promise. Some of Isaiah's most comforting prophecies arose from the invasion of Israel by Assyria. In this connexion there came a promise about a "child" that was to be "born," of whom it was said "the government shall be upon his shoulder." These things reminded me of passages in the poems, where the poet—musing on the chastisements and deliverances that followed the sins of Israel—exclaims "His mercy endureth for ever," or "I remember the days of old, I meditate on all thy doings." In the history of Greece and Rome I could find comparatively few stories of such "doings." How indeed could I reasonably expect them? Romans and Greeks worship many Gods, but only one Father of Gods and men. Athens might claim Athene, and other cities might have their special patrons among the Gods. But how could it be supposed that the Father of Gods and men would make any one nation His peculiar care? Virgil says that Venus was on the side of the future Rome, and that Jupiter favoured Venus; but Juno intervenes for Carthage. Then Jupiter has to compromise between Juno and Venus, or to conciliate Juno by lajdng the blame on fate! "How dififerent," I exclaimed, "all this is from the Hebrew egotism that represents the one God as continually saying to Israel 'Thee have I chosen'!"

Yet I had hardly uttered the word "egotism" before I felt inclined to qualify it, adding, "But it is not 'egotism' from Paul's point of view." For indeed Paul seemed to think that God chose Abraham, not for Abraham's own sake—or at all events not merely for Abraham's own sake—but for the sake of "all the nations of the earth," to bring light and truth to them. Epictetus spoke of Diogenes as "bearing on himself the orb of the world's vast cares." Somewhat similarly—when I took up the Law of the Jews to revise the thoughts that had come to me in the night—I found the Law describing the life of Abraham the friend of God. For I did not find Abraham blessed or happy—as the world would use the terms "blessing" and "happiness."

Abraham begins as a homeless wanderer, going forth from his kindred at the bidding of the one true God; and a homeless wanderer he remains to the end. He is a father of kings but no king himself, not even a landowner ! He has to buy with money land enough to bury his dead! His life is one of intercession as well as concession. Abraham intercedes for the dwellers in Sodom and Gomorrah, feeling it a painful thing that even a few righteous should suffer with the many. Once indeed Abraham becomes a soldier. But it is not for himself. It is for his kinsman and for the rescue of captives. Abraham makes himself a servant, waiting at table upon his guests. Abraham offers to God the life of his only son. If Paul was right, and if the children of Abraham mean the men that do such things as these in such a spirit as this, and if "the seed of Abraham" is the man that incarnates this spirit, then, I thought, there was perhaps no egotism when the prophet of Israel represented God as saying to the descendant of Abraham, "Thou, Israel, my servant, Jacob whom I have chosen, the seed of Abraham my friend." For it may mean "I have not chosen the rich, I have not chosen the great and strong. I have chosen the good and kind and truthful and courageous; him only have I chosen." And soon afterwards God says, "I have chosen thee in the furnace of affiction," that is to say, "I have not chosen thee to make thee selfishly happy and prosperous, but to make thee my servant, like Abraham, for the service of all the world."

The same truth appeared to apply to Moses, who, next to Abraham, might be called the greatest of the "servants of the Lord." Even from the cradle he was in peril of death. He delivered his countrymen, as it were, against their will. The burden of their rebellions pressed on him through his life, and caused him to be cut oflF fix)m the land of promise in the moment of his death. He saw it from afar off but was not allowed to enter it. He was prohibited because of his sin; and his sin fell upon him because his people sinned. "The Lord was wroth with me," said Moses, "for your sakes." That was the greatest burden of all. With the lives of Abraham and Moses before me, it seemed that the greatest servants were also the greatest sufferers.

Having this fresh light, I turned again to the description of the Suffering Servant in Isaiah. Did the prophet mean some particular prince of the house of David who was actually "chosen in the furnace of affliction" in order to deliver Israel? Or did he mean Israel itself, scattered through the world and aiSSicted in order that it might deliver the world? Plato modelled his Republic in the form of a man: had Isaiah any such double meaning? Did he predict a second David delivering sinful Israel, and also a purified Israel delivering a sinful world? Was he carried, so to speak, by the past into the future? That is to say, had he in mind some prince actually tortured and imprisoned, and as good as dead, for the sake of the people, and did the prophet regard this prince as destined to be raised up from the darkness of the prison house and to reign on earth? Or else was the prince, though actually killed, destined to be raised up and to reign after death in his own person, or to reign in the person of his descendants?

About all these questions I felt that it was not for me to judge. I did not know enough about the history of the people and the language of their poets and prophets. But there remained with me this general truth, as being not only at the bottom of this prophecy, but also pervading the history of Israel, namely, that in order to make a great nation, great men must die for its sake. And I began to conceive a possibility that the greatest of all men, some real "son of Abraham "—I mean some spiritual son of Abraham, not necessarily a Jew—might arise in the history of the world, who might be willing to die not for one nation alone but for all the nations of the empire. But how? And against what enemies? As soon as I asked myself these questions, the conception faded away. I thought of Nero enthroned in Rome, and of the Beast enthroned in the heart of man. Against either of these foes I did not understand how the death of any "son of Abraham," or "servant of God," could avail. How could such a Servant "divide the spoils of the strong, because his soul was delivered over to death"? This was beyond me.

For the rest, Isaiah appeared to me to carry on throughout the book of his prophecies that thread of unexpectedness about which I spoke above—I mean, that what prophets (foreseeing them) call judgments, men of the world (not foreseeing) call surprises. Yes, and even prophets and righteous men—not foreseeing enough—often lift up their hands in amazement, exclaiming, "This hath God wrought!" or "The stone that the builders rejected hath become the headstone of the corner!" But there was a dark as well as a bright side in these surprises. The disappointments were often most strange. For example, Isaiah saw a vision of the Lord "high and lifted up." But with what result? The prophet himself was straightway cast down with the thought of being "unclean." Even afterwards, when his lips had been cleansed with the coal from off the altar so that he might deliver God's message, the message was, "Hear ye, indeed, but understand not!"—because his warning was to be rejected. And so it was throughout, paradox on paradox! Israel was "chosen" in one sentence, "backsliding" in the next. The "despised and rejected" servant was to be "lifted up." The transgressions of the world were to be taken away by a deliverer, who was to be "reckoned among transgressors." Sometimes, as if despairing of the noble and learned among his own people, the prophet seemed to appeal to the poor and simple, according to the words of David, "Out of the mouths of babes and sucklings hast thou ordained strength!" Sometimes he even seemed to turn away from Israel itself—at all events from the majority of the nation—to the remnant, and to the pious among other nations, as though they, yes, even foreigners, might receive the fulfilment of the promise made to the seed of Abraham!

Amid all these (to me) perplexing paradoxes, one thing was clear— constituting a great diflference between Isaiah and Epictetus. The former saw God in history. The latter did not. Epictetus said (as I have shown in a previous chapter) that, up to the time of death, man can always find peace by following the "logos" within himself during life; after death he ceases to exist. "Bearing these things in mind," said he, "and seeing the sun and moon and stars, and enjojdng the earth and sea, man is not deserted any more than unhelped." These words now returned to my mind, and I perceived the force of what they did not say. They said that God was to be seen in the sun and moon and stars; but they did not say that He was to be seen where Isaiah saw Him, in the nations of the earth controlled by the Supreme. It is true that Isaiah, too—like Epictetus—bade his readers look up to the stars as witnesses to God. But Isaiah seemed to me to reckon men superior to stars.

David certainly did so. David had "considered" all the glories of the visible heaven. Yet he counted them inferior to "man," who was "made but little lower than God," and inferior to the "son of man," who had received "dominion" over God's works. In the same spirit, Isaiah, as it seemed to me, spoke of the Maker of the heavenly bodies as being adorable, not because He had made them multitudinous and bright, but because He led them like a flock—as though even a star might wander but for the kindness of the divine Shepherd. Moreover God seemed to him to be controlling the mighty powers of the heaven for the service of man, *"Behold, the Lord, the Lord, He Cometh with strength, and His arm with lordship. Behold, His reward is with Him, and His work before Him, As a shepherd shall He shepherd His sheep, and with His arm He shall gather the lambs, and encourage those that are with young. Who measured out the water with His hand, and the heaven with a span, and all the earth with His fingers? Who established the mountains by measure and the valleys with a scale f Who hath known the mind of the Lord and who hath become His fellow counsellor so as to instruct Him?"*

Thus, according to the prophet, there was to be a great advent in which God was to "come" with "reward." He predicted a future "shepherding" of the "sheep" and "gathering" of the "lambs," corresponding to the past "measuring" of the "heaven." According to the philosopher there was to be na such future. All things were to go round and round. Instead of "sheep" or "lambs," bubbles in an eddy seemed a more appropriate metaphor to describe the results of human life in accordance with the general tendency of Epictetian doctrine.

XIII. — EPICTETUS ON PROVIDENCE

IT was now almost the third hour and I was on the point of rolling up the volume, when a fellow-student suddenly entered to borrow some writing materials. Thrusting the book in my garment I supplied him with what he needed, and we hastened together to the lecture-room.

We conversed, about trivial subjects, but my mind was not in them. It was with Isaiah. I could not help marvelling that a native of so small and weak a country should take so wide and imperial a view of the movements of the nations. In a Roman, I could have understood it better; or in a Greek of the days of Alexander. But that a Jew—whose people was as it were the shuttlecock between the great empires surrounding it—that a Jewish prophet should think such thoughts filled me with astonishment. Then I wondered what Epictetus would say on the administration of the world if he ever dealt with it fiilly. "He," I said, "was a Phrygian and a slave. Is it possible that he, too, like Isaiah, could speak in this imperial fashion?" Arriving somewhat late, we found the room almost filled; but my seat was vacant, and I was glad to find Glaucus next to me, in the place vacated by Arrian's departure.

Epictetus was just beginning his first sentence. I will give it as Glaucus took it down, exactly: "Be not surprised if other animals, all except ourselves, have ready at hand the things needful for their bodily wants provided for them, not only food and drink but also bedding, and no need of sandals or blankets or clothes—while we have need of all these additional things." He proceeded to say that the beasts were our servants, and that it would be extremely inconvenient for us if we had " to clothe, shoe, and feed sheep and asses! As if," said he, "a colonel had to shoe and clothe his regiment before they could do the service required of them! And yet men complain, instead of being thankful!" Any single created thing, he said, would suffice to demonstrate Providence to a grateful mind. Then he instanced the production of milk from grass and of cheese from milk. Thence he passed from the "works" of Nature to "by-works," such as the beard, distinguishing man from woman. This (I think) was one of his customary digressions against the fashion of smooth-skinned effeminacy: "How much more beautiful than the comb of cocks! How much more noble than the mane of lions! Therefore it was our duty to preserve God's appointed tokens of manhood: it was our duty not to give them up, not to confuse (so far as lay in us) the classes, male and female, distinguished by Him."

"Are these," he continued, "the only works of Providence in our behalf? What praise can be proportionate to our benefits? Had we understanding, we should be ever hymning the graces He has bestowed on us. Whether digging, or ploughing, or eating, ought we not to sing the appropriate hymn to God, saying 'Great is God, because He hath given us tools wherewith to till the ground,' 'Great is God, who hath given us hands, and the power of swallowing, and a stomach, and a faculty of growing in stature painlessly and insensibly, and of breathing even when we sleep'? Hymns and praises such as these we ought to sing on each occasion. But the greatest and most divine hymn of all should be sung in thanks for that power"—he meant the Logos—"which intelligently recognises all these blessings, and which duly and methodically employs them. But you are silent. What then? Since you, like the common herd, are blind to God's glory, it was but fit that there should be some one herald, though it be but one> to fill the place left empty by your default, and to chant the hymn that goes up to God in behalf of all. What else am I fit to do, a halting old man like me, except to sing the praises of God?"

And so he drew toward the conclusion of the first part of his lecture. Were he a nightingale or a swan, he said, he would do as a nightingale or a swan—that is to say, utter mere sounds, songs without words, songs void of reasonable thoughts, without Logos—

"But as it is, I am endowed with Logos. Accordingly I must sing hymns to God. This is my special work. This I do. Never will I abandon this post of duty, as long as it is given to me. And I invite and urge you also to the same task of song." From this he proceeded to speak of "the things of the Logos," or "the logical things," as being "necessary"; and he spoke of the Logos as that which "articulates"—by which he meant, distinguishes the joints and connexions of all other things—and also as being that which accomplishes all other things. He appeared to mean that this Logos was reason; and he assumed that it is "impossible that anything should be better than reason." But he refused to enter into the question. If the Logos within us goes wrong, what shall set it right? His language at this point was very obscure. The impression left upon me was that Logos, with him, meant two different things and that he did not distinguish them. When he sang hymns to God in accord with the Logos, I thought he must intend to include something more than reason; but when he passed on to say that "the things of the Logos" (or "the logical things") are necessary, he seemed to mean "reason" alone.

Later on, he returned to his first subject: "When you are in the act of blaming Providence for anything, reflect, and you will recognise that it has happened in accordance with Logos." Then, taking the case of some man supposed to have been defrauded of a large sum of money, he placed in his mouth the objection that, if the fraud is "in accordance with Logos," it would seem that injustice is "in accordance with Logos." For, said the objector, "the unjust man has the advantage." "In what respect?" asked Epictetus. "In money," says the objector. To which Epictetus replied, "True, for he is better than you are for this purpose "—he meant, for making money—"because he flatters, he casts away shame, he is always unweariedly working for money. But consider. Does he get the better of you in respect of faithfulness and honour?" Then he rebuked us, would-be philosophers, for being angry with God for bestowing on us His best gifts, namely virtues, and for allowing bad men to take away from us what was not good in itself, namely, our worldly possessions.

This view of Providence and of wealth seemed to differ from the one assumed in Isaiah and often stated by Moses and David. For they had taught me that righteousness, and truth, and obedience to parents, and neighbourly kindness, tend to "length of days" and to peace and prosperity on the earth—for the righteous man himself as well as for the community; and they also distinguished honest wealth, acquired by labour, from dishonest wealth acquired by greediness and injustice. But Epictetus here made no such distinction.

The Jewish poems recognised it as being, at all events on the surface, a strange thing that a righteous man should be subjected to exceptional, crushing, and continuous calamities by the visitations of God. Epictetus appeared to teach us that God had ordained some men to be restless, pushing, shameless, and greedy, that they may take away the wealth acquired honestly by the good and honest and just. God had made these rascals "better" than the virtuous—in rascality! Then he called on us to admire or accept this ordinance or law: "Why fret, then, fellow? You have the better gift. Remember, therefore, all of you always, and have it by heart and on the lips, *This is a Law of Nature that the better should have—in the province in which he is better—the advantage of the inferior*. Then none of you will fret any more."

In his general theory, Epictetus was careful to separate himself from those who maintain that the Gods do not interfere with the affairs of men, or never interfere except on great and public occasions, and he approved of the words of Ulysses to the AUseeing, quoted by Socrates, “Thou seest my every motion." If man, he said, can embrace the world in his thought, and if the air and sun can include all things in their influence, why cannot God? But this seemed to lead to the conclusion that the influence of God is being perpetually and ubiquitously exerted on men in order to produce knaves, slaves, tyrants, and fools: for such our Master appeared to deem the majority of mankind.

In practice, Epictetus avoided such a blasphemy against God, by drawing no inference as to Providence from any of the laws or institutions of men, for he appeared to regard human institutions as radically bad. At all events he allowed his pupils—as I have shown above—to say that the rulers of the world are "thieves and robbers" and that the courts of justice are "courts of injustice." His belief in Providence was—I seemed to see clearly—based on nothing but the consciousness of the Logos within himself. The Logos in the vast majority of mankind appeared to him to have done them no good: so he could not argue from that.

When someone mentioned the fate of the Emperor Galba as disproving a belief in Providence, Epictetus implied a scornful disavowal of any intention to base belief on any such historical event.

Nor did he ever refer to God as controlling the movements of nations. In answer therefore to my silent question, "Does our Master see God in the history of individuals or nations?" his teaching seemed to reply "No, I see it in nothing except Socrates, Diogenes, and a few other philosophers, and also in myself. Beyond this little group of souls, though I feel myself able to infer God in everything, I cannot really infer Him in anything mental or spiritual. Hence I am driven to such physical instances as butter, cheese, stomachs, and beards!"

On leaving the lecture-room I chatted with Glaucus and tried hard to be cheerful. But how I missed Arrian! I felt inclined to turn Epicurean. The "careless" gods of Epicurus seemed at least less unloveable than the Providence of Epictetus. Too much depressed for any kind of study, I did not return to my lodging but walked out into the country by unfrequented paths, resting after mid-day in a little village inn. Coming out, toward the close of the afternoon, I found an acquaintance of mine, Apronius Rufus, standing in the porch and amusing himself by throwing figs and nuts to a crowd of boys just emerging from the doors of a neighbouring school. From scrambling and scuffling the boys had come to fighting—all but two or three, who held aloof with an air of sulky superiority; and one, I think, saw the schoolmaster in the distance. My acquaintance was attending the Epicurean classes in Nicopolis. We Cynics called the followers of Epicurus "swine," and I could not resist the temptation of saying, "Rufus, you are making converts. When they grow up, these little pigs will do you credit." He laughed good-humouredly: "Not all of them, Silanus! A few, as you see yonder, remain of your persuasion, true Cynics, that is to say, puppies or prigs. But we do pretty well. Nature is for us, though you and the schoolmaster are allied against us. By the way, I think I see your ally coming round the corner. I will be off. Two against Hercules are one too many. Farewell!"

"Farewell!" said I, "Your wit is as much stronger than mine as your philosophy is weaker."

"But *is* it weaker?" thought I, as he strode back to Nicopolis, and I in the opposite direction. Was not Apronius right in saying that Nature was on his side? Does not Providence, like Circe, throw down figs and nuts for us human creatures to make us swine? Is she not always saying to us, "Push, and be greedy! Then you will get what you want"? And did not Epictetus acquiesce in this, in effect, saying to the two or three non-pushers, "Be content. The others, the masses of men, are 'better' than you are for pushing and for kicking and for fighting like greedy swine"? But who made them "better"? Was it not Nature? And how could I feel sure that this same Nature or Providence that made "grass" (as Epictetus said) to produce" milk and butter and cheese," did not make man to produce scrambling and scuffling and fighting—a spectacle for some amused God, who watches from the windows of heaven, like Apronius Rufus from the inn-door on earth?

After a long circuit, returning to Nicopolis, I sat down to rest in a copse when the sun was drawing towards the west. Tired out by my walk, I fell asleep. When I awoke, the sun had set and the evening star was shining. As I sat in silence gazing upon it, better thoughts were brought to me. "Five minutes," I said, "with Hesper teach more about Providence than an hour with Epictetus." Then it occurred to me," But, were I Priam, and were this the evening before Troy was taken, would not Hesper shine as brightly before me? What does Hesper prove?" Presently, the lesser stars began to appear, growing each moment in number. Then I remembered how Moses represents the Lord God appearing to Abraham (when he was as yet childless) and sapng to him," Look up to the heaven and number the stars, if thou art able to number them all. So shall thy seed be." And what had come of it all? A nation that was no nation, a race of captives, known to us in Rome chiefly as hating pork and strangers no less than they loved their sabbaths. Then I thought, "Had Hesper any more favour for Abraham than for Priam? Perhaps the stars promised peace and prosperity to both and broke their promise! What Troy is, that Jerusalem is. Nay, worse. Troy has produced a New Troy. Where is the New Jerusalem? And where is the great nation promised to Abraham? A flock (or flocks) of exiles, fanatics, and slaves!"

Just then came into my mind the memory of some words about the stars in Isaiah. I had taken the book with me to lecture. So I unrolled it till I came to them: *"Lift up your eyes on high and see. Who hath appointed all these? He that leadeth forth His host in a numbered array. He will call them all by name. Because of thy great glory, and in the might of thy strength, not one escapeth from thine eye."* Then the prophet declared that, even as the stars of heaven are made visible in the darkness, so the seed of Abraham was not hidden by any darkness from God's eye: *"Say not, Jacob {ah, why didst thou dare to say it, Israel?) 'My way is hidden from God, and my God hath taken away judgment and hath departed from me.' Hast thou not even now found out the truth? Hast thou not clearly heard it? The God eternal, the God that framed and fashioned the earth, even to its furthest corners. He will not faint for hunger, nor is there any fathoming of His wisdom. To them that hunger He giveth strength—but sorrow to them that have no grief. For hunger shall fall on the youths, and weariness on the young men, and the chosen warriors shall utterly lose strength; but they that wait patiently for God shall renew their strength; they shall put forth wings like eagles; they shall run and not be weary; they shall walk erect and shall not faint for hunger."*

I could not believe all this. But neither could I disbelieve it. One voice said to me, "The poet is casting on the God of the stars the mantle that he has borrowed from the God of Abraham, Isaac, and Jacob." But another voice kept saying to me, "Wait patiently for God: He shall renew thy strength." In the afternoon, when I had thrown myself down to rest, I had thought that I would give up the search after truth, get rid of all my books, leave Nicopolis, and go at once into the army. Now I was more hopeful. But I could not give any logical reason for my hope. Isaiah had not convinced me. Far from it! The promise to Abraham seemed still to me to have resulted in failure. I had broken off my study of Paul, almost at its commencement, in order to study Isaiah. And Isaiah, without Paul, presented many difficulties that might perplex wiser minds than mine. "Grant," said I, "that David the son of Jesse was a great poet. Grant that Isaiah was a great prophet. Yet what were their poems and prophecies except so many pillars of vapour, or, if of substance, then substantial failures; pillars with the capital gone and the shaft broken, no longer sustaining anything? Their temple is burned a second time, never to be rebuilt; the rod of Jesse, cut off from the very root, with no life left in it, 'despised indeed and rejected' but with no compensation of being 'exalted' or of 'dividing the spoils of the strong'!"

All these things I said over and over again to myself. But still another voice, deeper than my own, seemed to be repeating "Wait patiently on God and He will renew thy strength! Wait patiently! Wait!" Up to the moment of retiring to rest that night my mind was in a state of oscillation. On the one hand, Scaurus might be right, and my best course might be to give up the study of philosophy, and to prepare myself for a military career. On the other hand, there appeared nothing in these poems or prophecies of Isaiah that would make a man less fit to be a soldier. My last thought was, "I should like to see how the modern Jew, Paul, takes up the teaching of the ancient Jew, Isaiah. I have but glanced at his quotations as yet." So I decided to examine this point on the following day.

XIV. — PAUL'S CONVERSION

HITHERTO my study of Christian or Jewish literature had never followed my intentions. I had intended to read Paul continuously. But first Isaiah, then David, then Moses, and then Isaiah again, had intervened. I was going forward all the while, but by a winding course, like a stream among hills and rocks. Now again I have to describe how—although I sat down with a determination to digress no more but to read through the epistles from the beginning to the end—I was led oflf to another investigation.

The first phrase in the volume did not long occupy me. True, I had greatly disliked it when I first glanced at it, a few days ago—"Paul a *slave* of Jesus Christ." "Slave" was always used by Epictetus in a bad sense, and I had then thought it savoured of servility. But now I knew that the translation of Isaiah often used it to denote a devoted servant of God; and it seemed to me that Paul had perhaps no other word that could so well express how he felt bound to service by Christ's "constraining love."

Nor did the next words now cause me much difficulty:—"*Called* to be an *apostle, set apart* to preach the*good tidings* of God, which He promised beforehand through His prophets in the holy scriptures." Scaurus had told me how Epictetus had borrowed from the Christians this notion of being "called" to bear testimony to God. Whether he was right or wrong, he had prepared me to find "called" in such a passage as this. It was connected here with an "apostle," that is, someone *"sent"* by God. This, too, seemed. natural. Though Epictetus did not use the noun, he often used the verb to describe his ideal Cynic—and especially Diogenes—as being *"sent"* to proclaim the divine law. "Set apart" I understood to mean "set apart" by special endowments of body and mind such as Epictetus frequently attributed to Socrates and Diogenes.

As to the "good tidings," I knew that Epictetus would have considered it to be a message from God to this effect, "Children, I have placed your true happiness in your own control. Take it from yourselves, each of you, from that which is within you." But what was

PauFs" good tidings"? Isaiah had described God's messengers as "proclaiming good tidings," namely, that God was coming to the aid of men: "As a shepherd will He shepherd His jflock and with His arm will He gather the lambs." Epictetus, as I have shown above, scoffed at this metaphor of "shepherd." But I could not help liking it. Homer used it about kings, Isaiah about God. I thought Paul meant, in part, that God would manifest Himself as the righteous King.

But I knew that Paul must also mean more, and that he would not have claimed the attention of the Romans for a mere repetition of an ancient written prophecy. Any child able to read could have repeated that. Paul must have more good news—either about the Shepherd, or about the time, or about the certainty of His coming. At this point, it occurred to me, "Why wait for the gospels that Flaccus is to send me? Why not search through the epistles to find out what Paul's gospel is?" But I checked myself, saying, "No more digressions." The next words were these: "Concerning His Son, who came into being from the seed of David according to the flesh; who was defined Son of God, in power, according to the spirit of holiness, from the resurrection of the dead, Jesus Christ our Lord." These words I have translated literally and obscurely so as to indicate to the reader how exceedingly obscure they seemed to me. "I must pass on," I said, "I can make nothing of this. What follows may make things clearer."

I began to read on, but soon desisted. The words that followed took no hold of my mind. I tried, and tried again, but was irresistibly dragged back to "resurrection of the dead," and "power," and "spirit of holiness," and "defined"—especially to "resurrection." What kind of " resurrection"? During my childhood I had heard my father tell a story or legend how, just before the battle of Philippi, the spirit of the great Julius appeared to Brutus, saying "Thou shalt see me at Philippi." There Brutus slew himself. And Scaurus had remarked that a similar fate had overtaken others of the conspirators; so that some might declare that Julius had power to rise from the grave and turn the swords of his assassins against themselves. That, if true, was an instance of the power of a man, or a man-god, rising from the dead in a spirit of vengeance. But Paul spoke of "resurrection of the dead," and "power," in connexion with a "spirit of holiness." Paul (I knew that already from the epistles) had been an enemy of Christ, as Brutus had been of Caesar. Comparing the two conquests, I asked whether more "power" might not be claimed for Christ's "spirit of holiness" than for Caesar's spirit of vengeance. For Paul, instead of being killed by Christ, had been made a willing and profitable "slave." Brutus had been forced to turn his sword against himself; Paul had been constrained by love to turn his new sword, "the sword of the spirit," against the enemies of his new Master. What light did this passage throw on the causes of PauFs conversion? I read it over again. Christ, he said, "came into being," or was born, "of the seed of David according to the flesh." Well, that might be one cause. A Jew would be more likely to accept as king a descendant of the house of David. And besides, Jews might think that such a birth fulfilled the prophecy above mentioned about "the root of Jesse." But there might be many born "of the seed of David according to the flesh." That which "defined" Christ to be "the Son of God" was "the resurrection of the dead"; and the "defining " was "in power" and "according to the spirit of holiness." By these last words, Paul seemed to separate Christ's resurrection from any such apparition as that of Julius, or other ghosts and phantasms; which may appear to this man or to that, and then vanish, either caused by evil magic, and doing an evil and magical work, or doing no work at all; whereas the rising again of Christ was caused by a holy power and resulted in a work of abiding power and "holiness."

This it was that led me into a new digression. Recalling how the spirit of Caesar was said to have appeared and spoken to Brutus, I desired to know what words the spirit of Christ said to Paul, and when and how Christ appeared to him. I wished also to inquire about the nature of Paul himself, before and after his conversion; and whether he showed signs of restlessness, and of ambition to become a leader in a new sect. Perhaps I should have spared myself this searching if I had known that, along with the gospels, Flaccus was sending me Luke's Acts of the Apostles. But the results of the search were helpful to me. So I will set them down in case they may be helpful to others.

First, then, I found that, before his conversion, Paul had been a Jew of the strictest kind. "Ye have heard," he said to the Galatians, "how that beyond measure I used to persecute the church of God and laid it waste, and I advanced in the Jews' religion beyond many of mine own age among my countrymen, being more exceedingly zealous for the traditions of my fathers." That expression "ye have heard" clearly showed that it was a matter of notoriety. The writer meant (I thought) not only "ye have heard from me," but also "from others," perhaps meaning his enemies, the Judaizers (often mentioned in this epistle), who pointed at him the finger of scorn, saying, "This is the man that changed his mind. This man thought once as we do." To the Philippians also Paul said that he had every claim to be confident "in the flesh," being "A Hebrew of Hebrews; as to the law, a Pharisee; as to zeal, persecuting the church; as to the righteousness that is in the law, blameless." So also he said to one of his assistants, Timothy, that he> Paul, had been "the chief of sinners" because he had persecuted the church.

Elsewhere I found him writing to the Romans that his heart sorrowed for his countrymen and that he could almost have prayed to be "accursed from Christ" for their sake, for they, he said, had the Patriarchs, and to them were made the promises; and he expressed a fervid hope that in the end the nation yould receive the promises, though for a time they were shut out. What he said to the Romans convinced me, in an indirect way, almost as strongly as what he said to the Galatians and Philippians, that Paul had been a genuine patriot, observing the traditions, as well as the written law, of the Jews, and persecuting the Christians with all his might because he thought (as we also were wont to think in Rome) that they were a pestilential sect, destructive of law, order, and morality. So much for what Paul was before his conversion.

Next, as to what happened to him at the moment of his conversion. First I turned to the Corinthian letter describing the appearances of Christ after death, to see whether anything had escaped me in the context—any words uttered by Christ to Paul, for example, at the time. But there was nothing except the bald statements, by this time familiar to me, “He is recorded to have been raised on the third day according to the scriptures; and he appeared to Cephas; then to the twelve; afterwards he appeared to above five hundred brethen, of whom the greater part remain till now, but some are fallen asleep; then he appeared to James; then to all the apostles; and last of all, as unto one born out of due time, he appeared to me also. For I am the least of the apostles, that am not meet to be called an apostle because I persecuted the church of God." All this Paul had previously delivered to the Corinthians—so says the letter—as a "tradition," and as a part of his "gospel."

This gave me no help. All that I could infer from it was that Christ probably "appeared" to his enemy Paul in the same way in which he had "appeared" to his friends and followers, and that the "appearing" must have been of a cogent kind, since it convinced an enemy. Nor did I gain much more from the Galatian account, which was as follows: "But when it was the good pleasure of God—who set me apart for this service even from my mother's womb, and called me by His grace—to reveal His Son in me that I might make it my life's woric to preach the good tidings about him among the nations, immediately I conferred not with flesh and blood, neither did I go up to Jerusalem to those that had been apostles before me, but I went away into Arabia, and turned back again to Damascus."

Here I was in doubt whether "reveal His Son *in me*" meant "reveal *by my means*" or "reveal *in my heart*,' that is, "unveil in my soul the image of the Son, which up to that time I had smothered with self-will and obstinacy"—as though "the Son" had been all the while in Paul's heart, but he had been refusing to acknowledge him. This latter interpretation I preferred. But still there was no mention of any words uttered by Christ to Paul at the moment of his conversion. Only, as Paul implies elsewhere that he had not seen Jesus in the flesh, that is, in person, I presumed that there must have been some such utterance as "I am Jesus," or "I am the crucified":—else, how would Paul have recognised the appearance?

As to the place of conversion, however, some light was afforded by the words "I turned back to Damascus," showing that he had been near Damascus when it happened. And the epistle to the Corinthians said that he had been let down in a basket from Damascus so as to escape the Jews. It appeared that he was persecuting the Christians up to the time of his conversion; that he was doing this in or near Damascus when he was converted; and that the Jews living in that city turned against him after his conversion, so that he had to escape from them.

Hereupon I tried to imagine Paul the persecutor, in his course of "persecuting the church," suddenly stopped by an apparition of Christ. In respect of his acts, Paul—though he could not possibly have been so cruel—might be compared to Nero, who also persecuted the Christians. But in respect of righteousness and truth and fervour, Paul was like Epictetus. Then I recalled the story recently told me by Scaurus, how he and his father had come suddenly upon the young Epictetus, in the Neronian gardens, staring upon the Christians in their torments, and how Scaurus had remarked upon the ineffaceableness of the impression produced on his own mind and (as he believed) on that of my future Teacher. That I could well understand. But Scaurus and Epictetus were merely passive spectators. Paul was a perpetrator. "How much deeper," I said, "and all the more deep and terrible in proportion to his sense of justice and truth, must have been the impression on Paul's mind, when he suddenly woke up to the fact that he had been persecuting the followers of Truth, the disciples of the Sufifering Servant of God, predicted by the prophets!"

Then it appeared to me that perhaps the precise *words* uttered by Christ in that moment of Paul's shock and agony were not of so much importance as the *feeling* of shock and agony itself, followed by a great wrenching away of prejudices and misconceptions, and by a sudden influx of a dazzling light on eyes habituated to darkness. Looking again at the Philippian letter, I perceived how much Paul had to give up, how lightly he regarded the sacrifice of all his prospects of prosperity and promotion among his own people: *"But whatever things were once gains to me, these I have counted as loss for Christ's sake. Nay, more, I count all things as loss for the sake of the preeminence of the knowledge of Christ Jesus my Lord; for whose sake I suffered the loss of all that I had, and I count it all as refuse, in order that I may gain Christ and be found in Him—not having as my own righteousness that which is of the law, but that which is through faith in Christ, the righteousness that is from God based on that faith—that I may know Him, and the power of His resurrection and fellowship with His sufferings, being conformed with His death; if by any means I may attain to the resurrection of the dead! Not that I have already received, or am already perfected. But I pursue the chase, if by any means I may seize as a prize that for which I was also seized as a captive by Christ Jesus!"*

These last words made me understand how Paul might have regarded Christ as manifested in him rather than to him. Isaiah saw God uplifted on high outside him. But Paul felt the Son of God enthroned as sovereign within him. I remembered reading in some drama how the wife of a dethroned and submissive sovereign goads him to rebel against his successor, saying—

"Hath he deposed
Thine intellect? Hath he been *in thy heart*?"

This was just what Paul experienced and exulted in avowing. Christ had "deposed" Paul's former self, and substituted a new self of his own as viceroy, to rule Paul, "in his heart." A soldier might say that

Christ, in the moment of taking Paul prisoner, had (so to speak) given him back his sword, saying "Use it on my side among all the nations of the earth, that they also may receive the good tidings of the forgiveness of sins." But in fact (according to Paul's view) Christ had done much more than this. He had given Paul a new sword, "the sword of the spirit." He had also made his whole nature anew, according to Paul's own saying, "If any man be in Christ, he is a new creature, behold all things are made new."

Not that I was as yet convinced that Christ had actually risen from the dead. For I did not yet feel sure that Paul might not have been deceived by himself and by the Christians. But I did now feel sure that Paul was honest and did not knowingly deceive his readers. And it was becoming more and more difficult to believe that self-deception or Christian deception could have produced effects on multitudes of men so great and permanent as those which were plainly discernible in the epistles.

I remember at this time trying to prevent my growing admiration for Paul's work from blinding me to his defects. Such phrases as "let him be anathema," and "dogs," and "whose belly is their glory," and "I would that those who are thus desolating you would even emasculate themselves"— these and others I marked with red in my volume. I knew Epictetua would have condemned them. But I soon perceived that these fiery flashes of wrath were reserved for those whom Paul j-egarded as proud and greedy ensnarers and oppressors of helpless souls; proud of knowledge that was no knowledge; greedy of money and influence to which they had no right; shutting their eyes against the light, and dragging back poor pilgrims just as they were on the point of entering into the City of Truth. Towards others, even if they might have appeared as rivals, he seemed to me to feel no rivalry, merging all such feeling in allegiance to Christ. Some, he said to the Philippians, preached Christ "thinking to add affliction " to his bonds, out of jealousy and spite. "What then?" he says. "Whatever may be the motive, Christ is preached, and I rejoice. Yea, and I will rejoice." In the same spirit he wrote to the church of Corinth concerning those among them who said, "I am of ApoUos," "I am of Cephas," "I am of Paul "—condemning all partisanship, although he gently reminds them of his singular relation to them, "Even though ye have ten thousand tutors in Christ, yet ye have not many fathers: for in Christ Jesus through the Goiipel I begot you."

Another detail interested me. Paul (I found) differed greatly from Epictetus in physical constitution. Epictetus used to teach us that a C}mic had no business to be "infirm" of body. At all events, he said, no such person can do the work of a Cjniic Missionary. When he extolled "the sceptre of Diogenes," he used to tell a story of the way in which that philosopher, lying by the roadside, sick of a fever, called on the wayfarers to admire him. It was the road to Olympia, and people were on the way to the games: "Villains!" he shouted to them, "Stay! Are you going all that way to Olympia to see athletes fight or perish, and will you not stay to behold a contest between a man and a fever?" But this contest, I think, ended in Diogenes's death. As a rule, both he and Socrates had been perfectly and robustly healthy: and Epictetus seemed somewhat to despise those who were otherwise.

Paul, on the other hand, frequently spoke of his "weakness," meaning physical infirmity or sickness. It was "owing to weakness" he told the Galatians, that he preached the gospel for the first time among them; and he called it a "temptation (or, trial) in the flesh." This I took to mean that he had been delayed in Galatia by some sickness, and had founded the Church there while in that condition. So to the Corinthians he said, "In*weakness* and in fear and in trembling did I come addressing myself to you." But that letter went on to say, "And my word and my preaching were not in the persuasive words of wisdom, but in demonstration of the spirit and *power*"—so that "power" went hand in hand with "weakness." Once at least I found Paul praying to be delivered from "weakness." "I will not boast about myself"—so he writes to the Corinthians—"except in my weaknesses." And then he went on to explain the "boasting" as being quite different from that of Diogenes. For the Cynic cried, in effect, "Come and see how strong I am!" But Paul meant that he would "boast" because, when he felt weakest, then his Master came to his aid and made him strong. This he expressed in a way that perplexed me at first: *"There was given to me a thorn in the flesh, an angel of Satan, to buffet me, that I might not be lifted up above measure. About this, I besought the Lord thrice that it might depart from me. And He said unto me, My grace sufficeth for thee, for in weakness is Power made perfect."*

For some time I could not understand this phrase, "*an angel of Satan*." But afterwards I found Paul writing to his Thessalonian converts that, when he wished to come to help them, "Satan *hindered* him," so that Satan appeared to be a *hinderer* of the gospel. Then it seemed to me that among the Jews and Christians certain diseases might be regarded as demons, or the work of demons—just as, in Rome, "Fever" is worshipped as a divine and has temples. This fact I had heard Epictetus mention; and he also condemned those who pray to be delivered from fever. The right course was, he said, "to have the fever rightly." Paul seemed to say, "first pray to be delivered from fever, if it seems to hinder you from doing the work of the Lord. Then, if it be revealed to you as the will of the Lord that you should bear the fever, be sure that He will make your bodily weakness spiritually strong. Thus the temptation from Satan, the Hinderer and Adversary, shall be turned into a strengthening trial from God, your Helper and Friend."

Summing up the marvellous changes that seemed to have come about for Paul in consequence of Christ's "appearing" to him, I was more than ever disposed to believe that it was of divine origin and a great deal more than a mere "appearing." I thought it must have been an "appearing" to the inner eye, the spirit, as well as to the outer eye.

When we Romans and Greeks use the word "spirit," we mostly think of a shadowy unreal appearance of the dead. We should not call Jupiter, or Zeus, a "spirit." But I perceived that, with Paul, "spirit" was more real—and, if I may so say, more eternally solid—than "body." It was the real "person." The word "person" in Greek, as also in Latin, means a "mask" or "character" There is, with us, no one word to express "real person." Common people think the body real, but the spirit unreal. Paul used the name "spiritual body" to describe a "real person," raised from the dead in Christ. Well, then, it seemed to me that the power of Christ on Paul might be described, not only as an "appearing" but also as the grasp of a "real person," "taking hold of" Paul's spirit with a spiritual hand so as to strengthen and direct him. What else was it that made him so strong?

The strength of Epictetus in bearing trials and sufferings had long excited my admiration. But now the strength of Paul seemed greater. Epictetus bore—or at least professed to bear—only his own burdens. As for those of others, he said, "These are nothing to me." Paul was like a gentle nurse or tender mother with the weaklings among his converts. "Who," he asked, "is made to stumble, and I bum not? Who is weak, and I am not weak?" And yet, in his weakness, he was a very Hercules or Atlas, strong enough to bear "the care of all the churches"! This "weak" man was always fighting, always craving to fight, and always conquering—up to the time of his impending departure, when he exclaimed that he had "fought the good fight "! And through what an extent of the civilised world! "From Jerusalem to Illyricum"—so he wrote to the Romans! In that same letter he announced his intention of carrying the eagles of the New Empire into Rome itself, and of passing onward from Rome to the invasion of Spain! No wonder that he felt able to say, "I take pleasure in weaknesses, in outrages, in straits and necessities, in persecutions and hardships, in Christ's behalf; for in the moment when I am weak, in that moment I am strong."

"I am strong "! Yes. Rolling up the volume as I retired to rest that night, I was constrained to agree with that, at all events. "About some things," said I, "or perhaps about many things in your letters I am doubtful; but assuredly you are strong. I myself am also certain that you are honest. But that you are strong—and that, too, with a strength that comes from faith in the resurrection of your Master—this not even an atheist or Epicurean could deny."

XV. — EPICTETUS'S GOSPEL

I WENT somewhat unwillingly to the next day's lecture. It would probably be interesting, I thought; but I could no longer deny that I was beginning to feel doubtful about that. And certainly I was more interested in PauVs letters. Soon after I was seated, Glaucus came in. He looked worn and haggard, but there was no time to ask him questions. The subject of the lecture was. How are we to struggle with adversity? The answer was, By bearing in mind that death is no evil; that defamation is nothing but the noise of madmen; and that only the rich, the lords and rulers of the earth, are the subjects of tragedies. But the main point was that "the door" is always open: "Do not be more cowardly than children. The moment they are tired, they say, 'I won't play any more.' Say you the same, 'I won't play any more.' And be off. But if you stay, don't keep on complaining." This topic had become familiar. What followed, though not quite novel, interested me more, because it seemed to bear on the Jewish Law.

First came a general descant on the advantages of being absolutely free from fear. Why should a man fear? Had he not power over everything that might cause him fear? Then a pupil was supposed to ask for more rules of life, saying, "But give me commandments." The reply was, "Why am I to give you commandments? Has not Zeus given you commandments? Has He not given and appointed for you what is your own, unhindered and unshackled; but what is not your own, hindered and shackled? Well, then, what is the commandment? Of what nature is the strict injunction with which you have come into the world from Zeus? It is this, 'Keep in all ways the things that are yours, desire not the things that are for others'... Having such suggestions and commands from Zeus, what further commands can you crave from me?" He finished this section of his discourse thus, "Bring these commandments, bring your preconceptions, bring the demonstrations of the philosophers, bring the words you have often heard and have often yourself spoken, read, and pondered."

I could not feel sure whether "bring" meant "bring to bear on each point," or "bring to your aid"; but, in either case, this conclusion, to me at least, was disappointing. "It is all very true," I thought, "and strictly according to reason. We are sure we have 'preconceptions.' We are not sure that we receive strength, in this or that emergency, from any being except ourselves. And yet how tame—and, in emergencies, how flat and unhelpful—such an utterance as this appears in comparison with the oracle that the Christian believed he had heard from his Lord, 'My grace is sufficient for thee. For Power is made perfect in weakness'!"

The rest of the lecture was more lively and expressed with more novelty, but old in substance—addressed to those who wanted to enjoy the best seats in the theatre of life but not to be squeezed by the crowd. His prescription was, "Don't go to see it at all, man, and then you will not be squeezed. Or, if you like, go into the best seats, when the theatre is empty, and enjoy the sun there." Then he added something that made my companion Glaucus shrug his shoulders and cease taking notes, "Remember always, *We squeeze ourselves, we pinch ourselves*. For example, we will suppose you are being reviled. What is the harm in that? Why pinch yourself on that account? Go and revile a stone. What harm will you do the stone? Well then, when you are reviled, listen like a stone. And then what harm does the reviler do you?"

We went out together, Glaucus and I. I think I have said before that Glaucus had some troubles at that time in his home at Corinth, but of what kind I did not exactly know. "Silanus," he said presently to me, with a bitter smile, "I am pinching myself with my shoe." "Then take it off," said I.

"By the immortal Gods," he exclaimed, "I wish I could! But what if my shoe is the universe? What if it is..." He stopped.

I replied at once, like a faithful disciple of Epictetus, "Not the universe, Glaucus, but your opinions about the universe." "Well then," said he, "my 'opinions about the universe.' What if my 'opinions about the universe' include 'opinions about' certain persons and things—home, father, mother, sister, and other such indifferent trifles? To put an imaginary case, could I by 'taking off' my 'opinion about' my father, take my father out of prison, or save him from death, or others from disgrace worse than death? No, Silanus, I am beginning to be a little tired of hearing 'Remember always. *You pinch yourselves!*' Often it is so. But not always. What say you?"

What ought I to have said? I knew exactly what was the correct thing to say." In such cases, give up the game. The door is open. Do you say the universe pinches you? Then take off your shoe by going out of the universe." This would have been the orthodox consistent answer. But I was inconsistent, not indeed in words, but in a heretical glance of sympathy, which Glaucus—I could see—interpreted rightly. We parted. As I walked slowly back to my rooms, I had leisure to reflect that the gospel of Epictetus had no power to strengthen Glaucus, and—I began to fear—no power to strengthen me, except to bear comparative trifles. It was not strong enough—at least in me—to stand up against the great and tragic calamities of human life.

With these thoughts, I sat down once more to study Paul's epistles from the beginning. Once more (but now for the last time) I was led into a digression. It was the word "gospel" that thus dragged me away, coming upon me (in Paul's first sentence) just when I had been deploring the failure of the "gospel" of Epictetus. Reading on, I found that Paul's "gospel" had been "promised beforehand, through God's prophets, in the holy scriptures concerning His son." A little later, the writer said, "I am not ashamed of the gospel. For it is God's power tending to salvation for every one that hath faith, Jew first, and then Greek. For God's righteousness is therein revealed, from faith tending to faith, even as it is written, 'Now the righteous shall live by faith'."

The next words surprised me by mentioning "God's wrath" as a part of the gospel: "For there is revealed therein *God's wrath* from heaven against all ungodliness and unrighteousness of men that hold down the truth in unrighteousness." But I immediately perceived that it might be regarded as "gospel" or "good tidings" to be informed that

God does really feel "wrath" at unrighteousness, or injustice, and that He will sooner or later judge and punish it. Accordingly I was not surprised to find Paul, soon afterwards, connecting "gospel" and "judging" thus: "In the day when God shall judge the secrets of men according to my gospel, through Jesus Christ."

From this I perceived that Paul's gospel promised a righteous judgment as well as immortality. But how could it be proved that there would be this righteous judgment? Paul said that it was "revealed *from faith to faith*." He added, "*as it is written*"; and a note in the margin of my MS. showed me that he was referring to a certain prophet named Habakkuk. I unrolled the passage. It seemed that this Habakkuk was living in times when his nation was grievously oppressed. The oppressors were like fishermen catching the oppressed at their pleasure. The prophet, standing on a tower, said to the people, "Wait and have faith. The righteous shall live by faith." Paul meant that if we would begin by having some faith in a righteous God, in spite of appearances on the surface of things, we should be helped to rise "from faith to more faith," and consequently that we should "live"—that is have *real* life. Faith seemed to Paul needful for life. Life without faith seemed to him no real life but a living death.

As I read on, I saw that this kind of "faith" was regarded by Paul as the foundation of all righteousness. He quoted scripture thus, "Abraham had faith in God, and it was reckoned unto him for righteousness." Then I remembered that he had quoted the same passage in writing to the Galatians, in order to prove to them that the seed of Abraham did not obtain righteousness by doing the works prescribed in the code of Moses, but by following in the faith of their forefather. Now this faith, in the case of Abraham, had seemed to me at first of a narrow and selfish nature:—"God will keep His promise to me. God will give me a child in my old age." But Paul showed that the promise concerned "all the nations of the earth," and that Abraham was not selfish in his faith—any more than in his pleading with God for such righteous people as might be in Sodom and Gomorrah when he said, "Shall not the judge of all the earth do right?" This faith in God's truth and righteous judgments was at the bottom of Paul's gospel, and Paul taught that it was at the bottom of all righteousness both of Jews and Gentiles.

But here came a great difficulty and obstacle in the way of faith, because, when men departed from God's righteousness, God Himself (so Paul taught) departed frm them for a time, allowing them to do the unrighteousness that was in their hearts and to judge unjustly. For this cause (according to Paul) God introduced Law into the world, and especially the Law of Moses. The Law was brought in to represent His righteousness in a poor rough fashion, until the time should come when He would send into the world the real righteousness or justice, the real judge or spirit of judgment. Such a judge (according to Paul's gospel) was Jesus Christ, judging the world already to some extent, but destined to judge it in complete righteousness, "in the day when God shall judge the secrets of men according to my gospel," said Paul, "through Jesus Christ."

At this point came the doctrine of the immortality of the soul, enabling Paul to say, "Wait, and you will see justice done"; whereas Epictetus was forced to say, in effect, "Justice will never be done,"— not at least what a plain man would call justice—"since the justice of this life was, is, and will be, oppression, and no second life is ever to exist."

The only passage in which Epictetus (as far as I could recollect) described a good judge, was one in which the philosopher was supposed to hold a dialogue with the Censor, or Judge, of Nicopolis. The man was an Epicurean; and Epictetus, after representing him as boasting that he was " a judge of the Greeks," and that he could order imprisonment or flogging at his discretion, replied that this was coercing, not judging. "Show us," said he, "the things that are unprofitable for us and we shall avoid them. Make us passionate imitators of yourself, as Socrates made men of himself. He was really a ruler of men. For he, above all others, so framed men that they subordinated to him their inclinations, aversions, and impulses."

This seemed to me, at first, a fine ideal of a spiritual judge. I contrasted it with Pauls picture of the Lord as Judge taking vengeance in fire upon His enemies; and Epictetus seemed to have the advantage. But on consideration it appeared that Epictetus was confusing his hearers by passing suddenly from a judge to a ruler. According to his own account elsewhere, Socrates did not persuade a thousandth part of those to whom he addressed himself. On the other hand Paul distinguished two aspects of Christ. In one, He appeared as constraining His subjects to love Him and to become "passionate imitators" of Him. In the other, He appeared as a judge, making the guilty shrink from their own guilt, and feel pain at their own sin, when the light of judgment reveals them to themselves. Paul spoke of "fire" according to the metaphors of the scriptures. He appeared to be describing the Supreme Judge as destroying the evil while purifying the good—as fire may destroy some things but purify others.

This was not the only occasion when the gospel of Epictetus seemed to me—not at first, but upon full consideration—inferior to the gospel of Paul in recognising facts fairly and fully. For example, Paul, in the epistle I was now reading, adopted the ancient Jewish tradition that death came into the world as a result of the sin of the first man Adam. According to this view, death was a "curse." Now Epictetus appeared to be directly attacking this doctrine when he spoke as follows, "If I knew that disease had been destined to come upon me at this very moment, I would rush towards it—just as my foot, if it had sense, would rush to defile itself in the mire. Why are ears of com created? Is it not that they may be parched and ripened? And are they to be parched and ripened, and yet not reaped? Surely, then, if they had sense, the ears of wheat ought not to pray never to be reaped Nay, this is nothing short of a curse upon wheat—never to be reaped! So you ought to know that *it is nothing short of a curse upon men, not to die*. It is all the same as not being ripened—not to be reaped."

How much finer, thought I at first, is this doctrine of Epictetus than the doctrine of Paul! And how superstitious is that Hebrew story about a serpent, causing death to fall upon man as a curse from God! But coming back to the matter again after I read some way in the epistle, and thinking over what "death" meant to Epictetus and what it meant to Paul, I began to waver. For Epictetus thought that "death" meant being dissolved into the four elements. And how was this like "being ripened and reaped"? When com is reaped, men get good from it. But when I am "reaped," that is to say, distributed into my four elements, who will get any good from that? So, once more, the gospel of Epictetus, as compared with the gospel of Paul, seemed to be deficient not only in power but also in directness and clearness of statement.

It reminded me of the saying of Paul when he said that God sent him to preach the gospel "*not in wisdom of word* lest the cross of Christ should be made of no effect." "Wisdom of word" appeared to mean "calling old facts by new names without revealing any new truth." So far as I could understand the gospel of Epictetus, his language about my being "ripened and reaped" was like that other earlier promise that I should find "friends" in the four elements when I passed into them in the dissolution of death. It was all "wisdom of word."

XVI. — PAUL'S GOSPEL

IN contrasting Epictetus with Paul to the disadvantage of the former, I was far from imagining that the latter had unloosed the knot of the origin of sin. But at all events he recognised the existence of the knot. Epictetus ignored it, or failed to recognise it. He spoke in the same breath of God's ordaining "vice and virtue, winter and summer," as though God's appointing that some men shall be bad caused him no more difficulty than His appointing that some days shall be cold.

Paul, on the other hand, treated death as though it were a curse in the intention of Satan, but a blessing (or step towards blessing) through the controlling will of God. He also spoke of a spiritual body rising out of the dead earthly body, as flower and fruit rise out of the decaying seed. I did not at first feel sure what he meant by this. Flower and fruit resemble seed in that they can be touched. Did Paul mean that the spiritual body resembled the earthly body in being tangible, besides being more beautiful? I thought not. It seemed to me possible that a person in the flesh, dying, might become a person in the spirit, living for ever. A man's actions and sufferings, sown in the transient flesh, might after death become part of the flower of the imperishable spirit, the real man, the spiritual body. That, I thought, was what Paul meant. This belief I found also stimulative to well-doing, according to the saying of Paul himself, "I press on, if by any means I may attain to the resurrection of the dead." Moreover I remembered the "angel of Satan" appointed for Paul to keep him from pride, and how he prayed against it, and received a revelation "My grace is sufficient for thee." If prayer and strength were brought about for Paul by an "adversary" of prayer, might not righteousness be brought about for the human race by the "adversary" of righteousness? I did not myself at that time believe in the existence of such an "adversary;" but Paul's belief seemed to me not unreasonable.

This turned me to other passages in the epistles concerning "Satan," or the "angels of Satan," or "principalities and powers." And I contrasted them with what Epictetus had said, "All things are full of Gods and daemons," meaning good daemons. Once more, the words of Epictetus seemed the nobler. But were they true? What did they amount to in fact? Nothing except "wisdom of word," calling the four elements "friends"! Thus in the end—though very slowly and reluctantly—I was brought, first, to understand, and then to favour, Paul's opinion, namely, that so far as we can see the truth in the "enigma" of the "mirror" of this world, there is being waged a battle of good against evil, order against disorder, light against darkness, life against death.

What Isaiah said concerning the stars and God's "leading them forth" gave me some help, just when I was thinking about the "conflict between light and darkness." For how, I thought, does God bring forth the stars except through the hand of His angel of darkness? Yet we, men, mostly speak of "darkness" as an enemy. And so, in a sense, it often is. Yet it is revealed in the aspect of a servant of God when besides bringing us the blessing of rest and sleep it leads forth the hosts of glories that (except for darkness) would never have been perceived. So, darkness brings God's greatness to light. Paul certainly predicted that the same truth would hereafter be recognised about death and about the apparent disorder of Nature, and her "groanings and travailings"; and it seemed to me that he extended the same doctrine even to sin.

The result was that I found myself content to accept—in a manner, and provisionally—what Paul said about "Satan" and about "principalities" and at the same time what he said to the effect that all things are from God and through God and to God, and, "For them that believe, all things work together for good." In my judgment, it was better—yes, and more reasonable, in Paul's sense of the word "reason"—to feel that I was in the Universe fighting a real fight against evil but looking up to God as my Helper, than to feel that there was no evil or enemy for me anywhere except in myself, and no friend either. So in the end I said, "Better to have been under the curse of death with Paul, if the curse may lead to a supreme blessing of life eternal in the presence of the Father, than to pass out of life with Epictetus, without any experience of curse at all, as so much earth, air, fire and water, into the nominal friendship of Gods and daemons!"

In allowing myself thus to be led away by my new Jewish teacher I was not influenced by his letters alone, but by legends and traditions—to some of which he referred—in the Hebrew histories, visions, and prophecies. Some of these taught, predicted, prefigured, or suggested that, while man and the brute forces of man and nature blindly imagine that they are moving the wheel of the universe, God alone is really moving it, and is using them to move it, towards His own decreed and foreordained purpose.

To the most beautiful of all such visions I was drawn by these words of Paul, "Know ye not what the scripture saith of Elijah?" Here a marginal note in my MS. referred me to the whole story, how Elijah, having slain with the sword the adversaries of God, was himself forced to flee from the sword of King Ahab, to Mount Horeb or Sinai, where the Law had once been given to Israel amid lightnings and thunders. And here the prophet was taught that God is not in the principalities of Nature, not in the tempest or fire or earthquake, but in "the still small voice." This agreed with a passage in Isaiah concerning the Deliverer, "He shall not cry aloud." In comparison with these and other similar poems and prophecies, the best things that the Greeks have written began to appear to me like mere "wisdom of word."

As regards the time when Paul's "good news" or "gospel" of "the righteous judgment" of God was to be fulfilled, I gathered that the judgments of God had been revealed to the apostle as having been working from the beginning of the world—seen, as it were, through openings in a veil—in the deluge, in the destruction of Sodom and Gomorrah, in the punishment of the Egyptians for persecuting Israel, in the punishments of Israel during and after the Exodus, and especially in their captivity and the destruction of their temple. But he seemed to believe that he had received also some special revelation about a judgment to fall upon the Jews, or upon all mankind, as soon as the gospel had been proclaimed to the world, but not before.

His language, however, varied. To the Philippians he spoke as though he were in doubt whether to desire to depart and to be with Christ, or to "remain in the flesh" for the sake of his converts. This showed that he contemplated the possibility of his dying before the Lord's coming. And this was made still clearer in some of his sayings to Timothy, such as "I have fought the good fight," if taken with their contexts. But to the Thessalonians he wrote somewhat differently. It appeared that certain of them were grievously disappointed because some of their brethren had died before the Lord's coming. Paul wrote to console them, saying that they, too—that is the dead brethren—

would be raised up. "We that are alive," he said, "shall in no wise precede them that are fallen asleep "—as though he anticipated that, on the day of the Coming, the greater number of the brethren, and he among them, would be still "alive."

From several of these passages, and from similar words in the prophets, I gathered that, had he lived long enough to witness it, Paul would have considered the destruction of Jerusalem by Titus to have been a "day of the Lord" or "day of judgment." But he was assured that the greatest day of all would not arrive till the sins of mankind had come to a head. Also it appeared to me that Paul did not profess to know when the last "judgment" would come to pass, and that he, like other Christians, at first expected it to come soon, and afterwards changed his mind.

Summing up the results of my study, I found that Paul's gospel appeared to be good news in a double aspect, first outside us, then inside us. First, it said that man was made by a perfectly good God to be, in the end, perfectly good, but was allowed by the Maker to fall into imperfection, through Satan, as a step towards perfection. This could be seen in the history of God's judgments from the beginning, but most of all in the fact that the Son of God, having been sent into the world as a son of David, for the salvation of all the nations of the earth, and having been killed by the Jews, had been raised from the dead to save and judge mankind in righteousness. Secondly, it jsaid that there was in every human being a faculty of faith in the goodness and love and righteous judgments of God, and that this faith, when fixed on the Saviour, enabled men to receive His spirit of righteousness and His love, to await His judgments, and to lead a life of righteousness on earth followed by an immortality of blessedness in heaven.

Comparing this with the gospel of Epictetus I could not but feel that Paul's was far more helpful, but also more diflBcult to believe. Yet it was not incredible. Epictetus himself recognised in Socrates some traces of a power to frame men to his own will. If Socrates the Athenian, and Diogenes the Sinopian, and others, whom God called "His own sons," had this power in some degree, in proportion to their possession of a share of the divine Logos, why might not Jesus the Jew be regarded as possessing this power to the fullest extent, having the fulness of the Logos so that he could succeed where Socrates and Diogenes and Epictetus failed?

I write here "Jesus the Jew," to show that, at that time, I did not know that Jesus was called the Nazarene, nor had I any notion that he was born otherwise than naturally "of the seed of David." But I clearly perceived that Paul placed Jesus far above all patriarchs and prophets. Also I think (but am not quite sure) that I already understood Paul to believe that the Son of God was Son from the beginning of the world, before taking flesh as "the seed of David "—but not in any miraculous way. About this point I did not employ my thoughts. The question for me was, Had this Jesus the power attributed to him by Paul's gospel—to conform men to himself? I was obliged to answer, "Yes, with some men." For the epistles had long ago compelled me to give up the notion that the Christians were a vicious, immoral, and rebellious sect. It was clear to me that they were above the average in morality. And as for Paul himself, I felt sure that Jesus had exerted this, power over him, and, through him, over vast multitudes ia various nations.

Now, too, having a clearer conception of Paul's gospel, I began to understand better something that had perplexed me a good deal on the first reading—I mean Paul's description ta the Galatians of the course he took immediately after his conversion. I had expected that he would have said something to this effect, "You Galatians are revolting from ray gospel. But it is the true gospel. I have told you the truth about all Christ's words and deeds. It is true that I did not know Him—or hear Him, or even see Him—in the flesh. But after I was converted, I took great pains to ascertain as soon as. possible, from those who had known Him in the flesh, all that He did and said. I wrote down these traditions at once, and read them again and again till I knew them by heart. These are the traditions I gave you." This is what I had expected Paul to say. But what I found him actually saying to the Galatians was this: *"I make known unto you brethren, as to the gospel preached by me, that it is not on any human footing, nor did I receive it from any human being, nor was I taught it as teaching, but [it came to me] through revelation of Jesus Christ."*

What he meant by "gospel" was—I now perceived—*not Christ's teaching before the resurrection, but His teaching after the resurrection.* And this included an unfolding of the will of God as revealed in the scriptures and in all the history of Israel. This appeared in what followed. The Galatians all knew (he said) how bitterly he had persecuted the Christians. For he had been a most bigoted and bitter zealot of strict Judaism. But, said he, *"When it pleased God to reveal His Son in me that I might preach His good tidings among the nations, straightway I conferred not with flesh and blood, nor went I up to Jerusalem to those that were apostles before me, but I went away to Arabia."* Afterwards (but not in this context) he spoke of "Mount Sinai in Arabia." Sinai being the place where Moses received the revelation of the old Law, and where Elijah, too, received the revelation of the "still small voice," I had assumed (at the time of reading the epistle) that Paul went to Mount Sinai in Arabia that he also might receive his revelation of the new Law of Christ. Perhaps, however, it merely meant that he wished to be alone. If so, I was wrong. But it does not seem to me, even now, wrong to infer that, all through that sojourn in Arabia, Paul was in communion with that same Jesus Christ, who had recently appeared to him, and who had converted him from an enemy into a friend.

The same Galatian letter described Paul as not going up to Jerusalem till "three years" had elapsed. Even then he remained only "fifteen days" in Jerusalem, and saw (as I gathered) only one or two of the apostles, and did not go up again till "after the space of fourteen years." All these details about time he appeared to add, not out of any jealousy of the older apostles, but to show that he did not attach importance to the things that Christ had said "in the flesh," before death, in comparison with the things that He had said after death, "being raised up according to the spirit of holiness." And who could be surprised at this? The things that Christ said after death, when He had been "defined as Son of God from the resurrection of the dead "—how should not these be more deeply impressed upon the mind of the hearers, and also be most deep and spiritual in themselves, being reserved till the disciples were spiritually prepared to receive them?

So the gospel of Paul resolved itself into this, that God, having decreed from the beginning that men should love Him as Father and one another as brethren, had sent His Son into the world to enable them to do this, by dying for them, and by imparting to them His Spirit. The Son dictated no code of laws to obey. All that He asked was faith in Himself as the Son of God, dying for men, and victorious over sin and death. This seemed simple, but its simplicity did not deceive me into imagining that I believed it. "That is all that is needed," said I, as I closed the volume of the epistles; "but it is more than I possess, or can possess. Paul's gospel is not a message but a person. It is, as he says somewhere, 'Christ, dwelling in the heart through faith.' I feel no such indwelling. In the gospel of Epictetus I am neither able nor willing to believe, I might perhaps be willing, but I am not able, to believe in the gospel of Paul."

XVII. — EPICTETUS CONFESSES FAILURE

FROM such thoughts about my own desires and inabilities it was a relief to turn to some definite matter of fact. I had been spending several hours in attempting to find out what Paul's gospel was. But what was Christ's gospel, so far as it could be gathered from the epistles? This I had made no attempt to discover. "Epictetus," I reflected, "though he does not profess to teach a gospel of Socrates or Diogenes, yet frequently quotes from them. Might I not expect to find at least a few words of Christ—whether uttered before or after the resurrection—quoted here and there in some at least of these numerous letters?" Hitherto I had met with none. But now, on rapidly unrolling the volume and searching onwards from the end of the epistle to the Romans, I came to a quotation that had escaped me. It was in the first of the Corinthian letters, following immediately after some details (not of great interest) about women's head-covering. I had just time to note that the passage contained the words "the Lord Jesus said," and "on the night on which he was delivered over," when my servant announced that Glaucus wished to see me, and I put the book aside.

Ostensibly Glaucus had come to compare some of his lecture notes with mine. But I soon found that his real object was to forget his troubles in the society of a friend. To forget them, not to reveal them. He avoided anything that might lead to personal questions, and I respected his reticence. When, however, he rose to go, he made some remark on the diflBculty of retaining the imperturbability on which Epictetus was always insisting, "under the sword of Damocles." Knowing vaguely that his alarm was not for himself but for others, I suggested that he might return at once to Corinth. "I would do so," he said, "but my father expressly bids me remain at Nicopolis." He said this uneasily, and with a wistful look, as though he suspected that something was amiss and longed for advice. "If action of any kind is possible," said I, "take it. If not..." Then I stopped. "Well," said he, "'if not'—." He waited for me to complete my sentence. I would gladly have left it uncompleted. For the truth was that I had begun the sentence in one mood and was being called on to complete it in another. When I said, "If not," I had a flash of faith coming with a sudden memory of Isaiah's message about God as the Shepherd of the stars and his exhortation to "wait patiently on the Lord."

But it had vanished and left me in the dark. "'If not'," repeated Glaucus for the second time. I ought to have replied, "Then at least keep yourself ready for action." What I did say, or stammer out, was, something about "waiting and trusting."

Glaucus looked hard at me. "'*Wait and trust!*' That is to say, '*Wait and believe.*' That is not like you, Silanus. You don't mean it, I see. It is not like you to say what you don't mean. I would sooner have heard you repeat your old friend Scaurus's advice, which was more like '*Wake and disbelieve.*' 'Wait,' say you, 'and trust.' Trust whom? Wait for what? Wait for the river of time to run dry? I have kept you up too late. Sleep well, and may sleep bring you better counsel for me!" So saying, he departed, but turned at the door to fling a final jibe at me, "Silanus, you are a Roman and I am only a Greek. But you must not think we Greeks are quite ignorant of your Horace. And what says he about waiting? *Rusticus expectat*: 'Hodge sits by the river.' Farewell, and sleep well."

This was bitter medicine; but I had deserved it, and it did me good. My cheeks burned with shame as I recalled his words "It is not like you to say what you don't mean." Had I come to this? Was this the result of my study of these Jewish writings? And yet, did I not "mean" it? Was not the fact rather this, that in my own mind I did to some extent mean and believe it? But it was a dormant belief. And I had no power to communicate it to others. Then I perceived the reason. I had said "Wait and trust." But Isaiah said "Wait thou *upon the Lord.*" In preaching my gospel to Glaucus I had left out *"the Lord"*—the life and soul of the precept! If "the Lord" had been in me, as He was in Isaiah and in Paul, I could not have left Him out. But I left Him out because He was not in me. The truth was that I had no true gospel to preach.

In great dejection I was on the point of retiring to rest when it occurred to me that I had left unfinished, and indeed hardly begun, the study of Christ's words in the Corinthian epistle. Too weary to resume it now, I extinguished the light and flung myself down to forget in sleep all thought of study. But I could not forget. All through the dreams of a restless and troubled night ran threads of tangled imaginations about what those words would prove to be, intertwined with other imaginations about the words of Christ to Paul at his conversion. Along with these came shadows or shapes, with voices or voice-like sounds:—Epictetus gazing on the burning Christians in Rome, Paul listening to the voice of Christ near Damascus, Elijah on Horeb amid the roar of the tempest. Last of all, I myself, Silanus, stood at the door of a chamber in Jerusalem where Christ (I knew) was present with His disciples, and from this chamber there began to steal forth a still small voice, breathing and spreading everjrwhere an unspeakable peace—when a whirlwind scattered everything and hurried me away to the Neronian gardens in Rome.

There, someone, masked, took me by the hand and forced me to look at the Christian martyr whom he was causing to be tortured. I thought it was Nero. But the mask fell off and it was Paul. The martyrs looked down on us and blessed us. Paul trembled but held me fast. I felt that I had become one with him, a persecutor and a murderer. They all looked up to heaven as though they saw something there. At that, Paul vanished, Avith a loud cry, leaving me alone. Fear fell upon me lest, if I looked up, I should see that which the martyrs saw. So I kept my eyes fixed on the ground. But the blessings of those whom I had persecuted seemed to enter into me taking me captive and forcing me to do as they did. Then I too looked up and I saw—that which they saw, Jesus the crucified. I tried to cry out "I see nothing, I see nothing," but my voice would not speak. I struggled to regain control over my tongue, and in the struggle I awoke.

I had dreamed long past my usual hour for rising; and the lecture was already beginning when I took my seat next Glaucus. It was a relief to me to find him there; for his late outbreak of bitterness had made me fear that he might prove a deserter. Epictetus was describing man as being the work of a divine Artist, a wonderful sculpture, he said, superior to the Athene of Phidias. Appealing to us individually, "God," he said, "has not only created you, but has also trusted you to yourself alone, and committed the guardianship of you to yourself, saying 'I had no one more trustworthy than yourself to take charge of yourself. Preserve this person for me, such as he is by nature, modest, faithful, magnanimous'"—and he added many other eulogistic epithets. Here Glaucus passed me his notes with a bitter smile, pointing to the words "preserve me this person such as he is by nature." He had marked them with a query. Nor could I help querying them in my mind. I felt that at all events they were liable to be interpreted in a ridiculous way. My thought was, "Paul bids us trust in God or in the Son of God. Epictetus never does this. But here he says that God trusts us to ourselves. Does He then trust babies to preserve themselves? And if not, when does He begin to trust us—whether as boys or as youths or as men—to preserve ourselves as we are by nature?" And here I may say that, as regards belief, or trust, or faith, Epictetus diflfered altogether from Paul. The former inveighed against babblers, who "trust" their secrets to strangers, and against the Academic philosopher for saying "*Believe* me it is impossible to find anything to be *believed* in." But he never insisted (as Paul does) on the marvellous power possessed by a well-based belief or faith to influence men's lives for good. For the most part Epictetus used the word "belief," like the words "pity" and "prayer," in a bad sense.

But to return to the lecture. In order to illustrate his favourite topic of the necessity of seeking happiness in oneself, Epictetus, as it were, called up Medea on the stage, expostulating with her for her want of self-control: "Do not desire your husband, then none of your desires will feil to be realised." She complained that she was to be banished from Corinth. "Well," said he, "Do not desire to remain in Corinth." He concluded by advising her to desire that which God desires. "And then," said he, "who will hinder or constrain you any more than Zeus is constrained?" To me, even as a dramatic illustration, such advice seemed grotesque. Nor was it a good preparation for what followed, in which he bade us give up desires and passions relating, not only to honour and oflBce, but also to country, friends, children: "Give them all up freely to Zeus and to the other Gods. Make a complete surrender to the Gods. Let the Gods be your pilots. Let your desires be with them. Then how can your voyage be unprosperous? But if you envy, if you pity, if you are jealous, if you are timid, how do you dare to call yourself a philosopher?"

I could perceive that Glaucus was ill pleased at this, and especially at the connexion of "pity" with "envy"—though it was not the first time, nor the last, that I heard Epictetus speak of "pity" in this contemptuous way. Perhaps others were in the same mood as Glaucus, and perhaps our Teacher felt it. If he did, he at all events made no effort to smooth away what he had said. Far from it, he seemed to harden himself in order to reproach us for our slackness and for being philosophers only in name. "Observe and test yourselves," he exclaimed, "and find out what your philosophy really is. You are Epicureans—barring perhaps a few weak-kneed Peripatetics. Stoic reasonings, of course, you have in plenty. But show me a Stoic man! Show me only one! By the Gods, I long, I long to see one Stoic man. But perhaps you have one—only not as yet quite completed? Show him, then, uncompleted! Show him to me a little way towards completion! I am an old man now. Do me this one last kindness! Do not grudge me this boon—a sight that up to this day my eyes have never enjoyed!"

We were all very quiet at this outburst, so unusual in our Teacher. Two or three youths near my seat seemed stimulated rather than depressed. But to me it seemed a sad confession of failure, amounting, in effect, to this, "I have taught from the days of Vespasian to the second year of Hadrian. My business has been to produce Stoics. Up to this day, a real Stoic is"—these were his words—*"a sight that up to this day my eyes have never enjoyed."* What a contrast, thought I, between my Teacher (for "mine" I still called him) and that other, the Jew, Paul, (whom I refused to call "mine") who numbered his pupils by cities, and whose campaigns from Jerusalem to Rome, through Asia and Greece, had been a succession of victories, leading trains of prisoners captive under the banner of the Crucified!

What followed amazed me, forcing me to the conclusion that Epictetus was profoundly ignorant of human nature, at all events of our nature, and perhaps of his own. For instead of saying, "We have been on the wrong road," or "You have not the power to walk, and I have not the power to make you walk," he found fault with himself and us, without attempting to show what the fault was. At first it seemed our lack of noble ambition. "Not one of you," he exclaimed, "desires, from being man, to pass into becoming God. Not one of you is planning how he may pass through the dungeon of this paltry body to fellowship with Zeus!" But then he shifted his ground, saying, in effect, "I am your teacher. You are my pupils. My aim is so to perfect your characters that each of you may live unrestrained, uncoerced, unhindered, unshackled, free, prosperous, blessed, looking to God alone in every matter great or small. You, on your side, come here to learn and to practise these things. Why, then, do you fail to do the work in hand, if you on your side have the right aim, object, and purpose, and *I on my side—in addition to right aim, object, and purpose—have the right preparation?* What is deficient?"

Here was our Master assuming as absolutely certain that he had *"the right preparation"*! But that was just the point on which I had long felt doubtful, and was now beginning to feel absolutely certain in a negative sense. However, he continued with the same perfect confidence in himself and in the practicability of his theory, "I am the carpenter, you the material. If the work is practicable, and yet is not completed, the fault must rest with you or with me. Then he concluded with the following personal appeal; these were his exact words, "Is not this matter "—he meant the art of living as a son of Zeus, free, and in perfect peace—"capable of being taught? It is. Is it not in our own hands? Nay, it is the only thing that is in our own hands. Wealth is not in our own hands, health is not, reputation is not. Nothing is—except the right use of our imaginations. This is the only thing that is by nature ours, unpreventable, unhinderable. Why do you not perform it then? Tell me the reason. Your non-performance is either my fault, or your fault, or the natural and inherent fault of our business. Now our business, in itself, is practicable, and is indeed the only business that is always practicable. It remains, then, that the fault rests either with me, or with you, or, which is nearer the truth, with both of us. What is to be done, then? Are you willing that we should begin together, at last though late, to bring this purpose into effect? Let bygones be bygones. Only let us begin. Believe me, and you will see."

With that, he dismissed us. I was curious to know what Glaucus thought of it, so I waited for him to speak. To my surprise, he said, "It is not often that the Master speaks in this way or suggests that he himself may be in fault. Who knows? He may have something new in store. I felt so angry with him at the beginning of the lecture that I was within an ace of going straight out. But now, as he says, 'Let bygones be bygones.' I shall go on with him a little longer. What say you? For the most part he is too cold for me, always talking about the Logos within us, and the God within us, as though I, Glaucus the son of Adeimantus, who need the help of all the Gods that are, were myself all the God that I needed! He chills me with his Logos. But when he appealed to us in that personal way 'Believe me,' he gave me quite a new sensation. Did it not stir you? I don't think I ever heard him say that before."

"It did stir me," said I, "and I am sure I never heard him say it before. Plato represents Socrates as always persuading his hearers to 'follow the Logos,' not to follow Socrates; and Epictetus, for the most part, uses similar language. For the rest, I am not sure that our Master will do me all the good I had hoped. But I shall do as you do. We shall still sit, I hope, together." So we parted.

I had not said more than the truth. Epictetus had stirred me, but not in the way in which he had stirred Glaucus. "Let bygones be bygones"—the "bygones" of nearly forty years! Why were they to be "bygones"? Had they no lesson to teach? Did they not suggest that for forty years Epictetus had been on the road to failure and that he had consequently failed? Could I believe that during all that time Epictetus himself had been deficient in "purpose"? Not for a day! Not for a moment!

As I sat down to revise the notes of my lecture, it occurred to me that Glaucus—who was of a much less settled temperament than Arrian— must have heard better news from home, and that this helped him to take a brighter view of things in general and of philosophy in particular. "If my old friend were here," said I, "would he not regard Glaucus's change of mood as one more instance of Epictetus's power to 'make his hearers feel precisely what he desired them to feel'? But what if I went on to say that this 'power' was mere rhetoric, not indeed 'wisdom of word' in the sense of hair-splitting logic, but 'wisdom of speech,' the knowledge of the language and imagery best fitted to stir the emotions? What would Arrian say to that?"

I mentally constructed a dialogue between us. "There is something more, Silanus." "But what more?" "That I do not know. Only I know there is something more behind." Then Scaurus's explanation recurred to me of that "something more behind." For Scaurus had asserted that Epictetus had been touched by what he called the Christian superstition, which, although he had shaken it off, had left in his mind a blank, a vacant niche, which he vainly tried to fill with the image of a Hercules or a Diogenes. That brought back to my thoughts Scaurus's first mention of "Christus"; and then it came upon me as a shock that I had spent half-an-hour in my rooms, musing over Epictetus and Glaucus and Arrian, and there, on the table before me, was Paul's first epistle to the Corinthians containing his only quotation of the words of the Lord, and I had taken no notice of it. So I put my notes aside and unrolled the epistle.

XVIII. — PAUL'S ONLY RECORD OF WORDS OF CHRIST

THE first words of the sentence were, "For *I* received from the Lord "—he emphasized "*I*," as though it meant "*I myself*" or "Whatever others may have received, *I* received so and so"—" that which I also delivered over to you, that the Lord Jesus, on the night on which he was to be delivered over... Here I paused and looked back, to see what "for" meant (in "*for* I received") and why Paul was introducing this saying of the Lord. I found that the apostle had been warning the Corinthians thus, "Ye meet together, not for the better, but for the worse." In the first place, he said, there were dissensions among them, and in the next place, "When ye come together it is not possible to eat the Lord's Supper, for each one taketh his own supper, and one is hungry while another is drunken." Then I understood that the Lord's Supper meant that same Christian feast of which Arrian had spoken. This interested me because in Rome, as a boy, I had heard it said that the Christians partook of "a Thyestean meal," that is, they killed children and served up the flesh to the parents. This I do not think I had myself believed, except perhaps in the nursery; but it was commonly taken as truth among the lower classes in Rome.

Now I perceived that the meal was to have been a joint one—like that of the Spartan public meals or syssitia, where all fed alike. But in that luxurious city of Corinth many of the Christians had introduced Corinthian luxury and turned the public meal into a group of private meals, so that some had too little and others too much. Paul tried to bring them back to better things by telling them what Christ said to his disciples on the night of his last meal, "the night on which he was to be delivered over." He implied that their meal ought to have been like Christ's last meal; and now the question for me was, what that, the Lord's Supper, was like.

But first I had to ask myself the meaning of Christ's being "delivered over." About this I had no doubt that it referred to the prophecy in Isaiah concerning the Suffering Servant, who "was *delivered over* on account of our sins." These words Paul had quoted in the epistle to the Romans, and he elsewhere spoke of God, or the Father, as "giving," or "*delivering over*" the Son for the salvation of mankind. Now both Isaiah and Paul had made it quite clear that the Servant, or Son, thus "delivered over" by the Father, goes voluntarily to death, and this I assumed to be the case here. But I did not know by what agency God was said to have "delivered him over." I thought it might be by a warning or daemonic voice, as in the case of Socrates, bidding him surrender himself to the laws of his country. Or Christ's own people, the citizens of Jerusalem, might have delivered him up to Pilate, to procure their own exemption from punishment on account of some rebellion or sedition. Or he might be said to have been delivered over by a decree of Fate, to which he voluntarily submitted.

So much was I in the dark that for a moment I thought of Christ as fighting at the head of an army of his countrymen and giving himself up for their sakes, like Protesilaus or the Decii; and I tried to picture Christ doing this, or something like this. But I failed. Still I was being guided rightly so far as this, that I began faintly to recognise that this "delivering over" might be not a mere propitiation of Nemesis, occurring now and then in battles, but part of the laws of the Cosmopolis, occurring often when a deliverance is to be wrought for any community of men. Of such a propitiation Protesilaus was the symbol, concerning whom Homer says,

"First of the Achaeans leaped he on Troy's shore
Long before all the rest..."

He leaped first, in order to fall first. But his country rose by his fall. His wife sorrowed, "desolate in Thessaly," and his house was left "half built." But in the minds of men he abides among the firstfruits of the noble dead, who have counted it life to lay down life for others. This legend I now began to apply to spiritual things. I was being prepared to believe that the sons of God in all places and times must needs be in various ways and circumstances "delivering themselves over" as sacrifices to the will of God, in proportion to their goodness, wisdom, and strength—the good spending their life-blood for the evil, the wise for the foolish, the strong for the weak.

After this, came a sentence that perplexed me greatly, "This is my body, which is in your behalf Do this to my remembering or reminding." Not being able to make any sense at all of this, I read on, in hope of light: "In the same way also the cup, after supper, sajdng. This cup is the new covenant in my blood." The word "covenant" helped me a little, because I had found Paul speaking elsewhere to the Corinthians in his own person about a "new covenant" and an "old covenant." Also to the Galatians he mentioned "two covenants," one of which, he said, "corresponds to Mount Sinai." So I turned to the scripture that described how God made a "covenant" with Israel that they should obey the Law given to them from Mount Sinai. It had these words: "And Moses, having taken the blood "—that is, the blood from a *"sacrifice of salvation"* consisting of bullocks—"sprinkled it on the people and said, 'Behold the blood of the covenant that the Lord has covenanted with you concerning all these words'." The blood of the old covenant (I perceived) was blood of "sprinkling," purifying the body. David prayed for something more than that, when he said, "Create in me a clean heart, O God, and renew a right spirit within me." So it occurred to me that the "new covenant" was to purify, not the body but the heart and the spirit, entering into man and becoming part of him so as to cleanse him from within.

This seemed to agree with Paul's opinion, and with what I had read in Isaiah, that the sacrifices of bulls and goats cannot make the heart clean. Now, therefore, going back again to the first words "This is my body, which is in your behalf," I inferred that Christ was speaking about Himself as being the *"sacrifice of salvation"* above mentioned, and that He used these words, purposing to devote Himself to death for the people, in order to redeem them from sin by purifying their hearts.

I am writing now in old age. Forty-five years have passed since the night when I first read, "This is my body, which is in your behalf." During that interval I have done my best to ascertain the exact words spoken by the Saviour in His own tongue. And now it is much more clear to me than it was then that the Lord Jesus was herein giving Himself, His very self, both as a legacy to the disciples and also as a ransom for their souls. But even then I perceived that some such meaning must be attached to the words, and that they could not have been invented by any disciple; and they made me marvel more than anything else that I had met with in the Jewish scriptures or Paul's epistles. Such a confidence did they show in the power of His own love, as being stronger than death! I do not say that I believed that the words had been fulfilled. But I felt sure that Christ had uttered them in the belief of their being fulfilled; and, just for a few moments, the notion that He should have been deceived seemed to me so contrary to the fitness of things, and to the existence of any kind of Providence, that I almost believed that they must have had some kind of fulfilment. I did not stay to ask, "How fulfilled?" I merely said, "This is divine, this is like the 'still small voice.' This is past man's invention. This must be from God."

Then I checked myself, doubt rising up within me. "Paul," I said, "was not present on the night of the Last Supper. He says concerning these words, 'I received of the Lord that which I also delivered unto you.' Is it not strange that the oracles or revelations supposed by Paul to have been delivered to him by Jesus after the resurrection should have included matters of historical fact, and historical utterances, which could have been ascertained from the disciples that heard them? I must wait till I receive the Christian gospels from Flaccus."

Then this also occurred to me. "Socrates, too, like Christ, was unjustly condemned. Socrates might have escaped from death, but he refused. The daemonic voice that told him what to do and not to do, bade him remain and die, and he obeyed. In effect, then, this voice from heaven *'delivered over'* Socrates to death. Or he may be said to have *'delivered himself over.'* Now what were the last words of Socrates? Did he leave any such legacy to his disciples? Might I not find some help here? For assuredly Socrates, like Christ, endeavoured to make men better and wiser." I remembered hearing Epictetus say—and I recognised the truth of the saying—"Even now, when Socrates is dead, the memory of the words and deeds of his life is no less profitable to men, perhaps it is more so, than when he lived." So I turned over Arrian's notes and found several remarks of our Master about Socrates and his contempt for death; and with what a humorous appearance of sympathy he accepted the jailer's tears, though he himself felt they were altogether misplaced. At last I came to a passage where Epictetus compared Socrates, on his trial, and in his last moments, to a man playing at ball: "And what was the ball in that case? Life, chains, exile, a draught of poison, to be parted from a wife,, to leave one's children orphans. These were his playthings, but none the less he kept on playing and throwing the ball with grace and dexterity."

This was enough, and more than enough. It was hopeless,. I perceived, to search in Epictetus for what I sought—some last legacy of Socrates to his disciples, implying that he longed to help them after death. Epictetus would have rebuked me, saying, "How could he help them when he was dissolved into the four elements? What could Socrates bequeath to them beyond the memory of his words and deeds?"

Failing Epictetus, I took out from my bookcase such works of Plato and Xenophon as might contain the last thoughts of Socrates. Both of these writers believed in the immortality of the soul. Yet I could not find either of them asserting, or suggesting, that Socrates felt any trouble or anxiety for his friends and for their faith, nor any token of a hope that his soul might help theirs after his death—or rather, to use his phrase,, after he had "transferred his habitation." When I tried to fiind such a hope, I could not feel sure that I was interpreting the words honestly. It seemed to me that I was importing something of the Jewish *pathos*, or feeling, into an utterance of the Greek *logos*. I still retained the conviction that Socrates, in his last moments, had his disciples at heart, and that, in enjoining that last sacrifice to Aesculapius, he wished to stimulate them to something more spiritual and more permanent than that single literal act. But I longed for something more. I thought of Christ s "constraining love," and how a man might be "constrained" in a natural way by the love of the dead—the love of a wife, father, mother, or child. Such a love I said, might be no less powerful, for help and comfort, than the hate of Clytemnestra following Orestes for evil. Aeneas {I remembered) used the word *"image,"* speaking to the spirit of Anchises, "Thy *image*, O my father, constrained me to come hither." But Anchises replies that he himself had been all the while following his son in his perilous wanderings, so that it was not a mere *"image,"* It was a *presence*. "Is it possible," I asked, "that Christ, not in poetry but in fact, thought of bequeathing to His disciples such a presence, to follow and help them after His death?"

Yes. It seemed quite possible, nay, almost certain—that Christ thought this. But who, except a Christian, would believe that the thought was more than a dream?" Scaurus," I said, "who often jests at me as a dreamer, would now jest more than ever. Here am I, pondering poetry, when I ought to be studying history! Yet how can I study history in Paul, when Paul himself tells me that he received these words from one that had died—presumably therefore in a vision? The right course will be to wait till Flaccus sends me the gospels. These may chance to be historical biographies—not records of things seen, or words heard, in visions." And then Scaurus's saying recurred to me, that no two writers agree independently in recording a speech or conversation for twenty consecutive words that are exactly the same. "And this," said I, "I hope to test before many days are over, with regard to these mysterious words of Christ."

But before rolling up the book it came into my mind that Paul said somewhere to the Romans "I beseech you therefore by the compassionate mercies of God to present your bodies a *living sacrifice,* holy, acceptable to God." Having found these words and read them carefully over, I thought that the writer must have had in view some allusion to the sacrifice of Isaac. For that was the only "living sacrifice" that I could find (and indeed it is the only one) mentioned in scripture. Then I turned to the first book of the Law and there I found that God's promise of Isaac to Abraham had been called a covenant, and this, said Paul to the Galatians, was, so to speak, the real *thought* of God. The covenant of Sinai was only an afterthought. The sign of Abraham's covenant by promise was in the blood of circumcision stamped permanently on man's body. The sign of the covenant of Sinai was in the blood of bullocks merely sprinkled on the body. Also there was yet another covenant between God and man, earlier than both of these. This, the earliest covenant of all, was with Noah. Now the sign of this was not on man at all, but on the sky, being the rainbow. And in the covenant with Noah there was no mention of blood (either of man or beast) except this—that man was not to taste the blood of beasts when he ate their flesh, and that he was not to pour out the blood of men, much less to taste of it.

Then it seemed to me that the words and thoughts of Christ, being a Jew, must be studied in the light of the words and thoughts of his countrymen the ancient Jews. The first covenant, that of Noah, said, "The blood is the life, therefore ye shall not taste of blood; and whosoever shall taste of blood, whether of man or beast, shall die; and whosoever shall pour out the blood of man, his blood shall be poured out and he shall die." This was confirmed by the Covenant of Moses the Lawgiver. Then came a second covenant, that of the Son, saying, "I have changed all that. I am the New Covenant. The New Covenant is in my blood, that is, in my life. My blood is truly my life. Ye shall taste of my blood. It shall be poured out for all, as a living sacrifice. Whosoever shall taste of my blood shall not die but shall live for ever, even as I Hve."

Looking back now to that moment, I seem to perceive that I was being led on by the Spirit of God, far beyond my own natural powers of thought and reason, in order that I might have some foretaste of the revelation of the Lord's sacrifice, so as to be strengthened and prepared for the trial that was shortly to fall upon me, when I was to be dragged away from the shore that I had just touched, back again into the tumultuous deep. For a long time I continued musing on this mystery, and turning over passage after passage in Paul's epistles describing how believers are all one "in Christ," and "Christ in them," and how they are made righteous, or brought near to God, "in the blood of Christ."

So passed the greater part of the day, up till the ninth hour. Then came a reaction. The thought of Scaurus returned, and of his criticisms. " He is right," I said, "I am a dreamer. I will go out into the fields." So I went out, taking my Virgil as company. When I came into the woods I sat down in the warmth of the westering sun. There, for a time, listening to the songs of the thrushes and the cooing of the doves, I felt at peace, and opened my Virgil, intending to read about the bees and the fields. But I had brought the Aeneid by mistake, and the first words I met were these:

"Si nunc se nobis ille aureus arbore ramus

Ostendat nemore in tanto!"

Then back again came suggestions of doubt. For I recognised it as a kind of oracle from the Gods, that I must still be seeking for the light of the truth in the dark forest of error, and that I could not find it without divine help. "But," said I, as I started up to return home, "it shall be such help as a Roman may accept without shame. The faith of Junius Silanus shall never be constrained by spells, or incantations, or by anything except reasonable conviction and the force of facts."

Returning home as the sun was sinking I found letters awaiting me. Among these, one was from Flaccus, saying that he had sent me three little Christian books called "gospels," in accordance with my order. After his usual fitshion, addressing me as the son of his old master, but also as a companion in the fellowship of book-lovers, he added some remarks on the contents of the parcel. "The third of these books," he said, "is written by a man of some education, named Lucas, a companion of Paulus (whose works I recently sent you); and he has published a supplementary volume, which I have ventured to add although you did not order it. The supplement is entitled 'The Acts of the Apostles,' that is, of the missionaries sent out by Christus. The 'gospel,' as you probably know, is a record of the acts and words of Christus himself. Also, as you are interested in this sect, I have sent you a book called the Revelation of John. It is written in most extraordinary Greek, without pretensions to grammar, much less to style. But it has some poetic touches in it. Of the eastern style, of course. But that you will understand. This John was himself—(I am told)—one of their 'apostles,' and a man of note among the Christians. He is said to have written it soon after the reign of Domitian."

There was also a letter from Scaurus, or rather a packet of letters. Out of it fell a separate note of the nature of a postscript, and I read that first, as follows: "Two things I forgot to say. First, if you decide to open my sealed note about the similarities of Paul and Epictetus, I shall not now feel hurt. For the reasons I have given in my letter, I hope you will not open it, because I trust you will turn your mind to other matters. But I do not now regard that note as important. By this time, you probably have the books of the Christians. You also know more than you did about Epictetus, so you have been able to judge for yourself whether I have not spoken the truth. But now—I repeat—my advice is to put the whole investigation aside. Go to lUyria and see whether you cannot fimd an opening there for a military philosopher."

As to the sealed note, I have explained above that, when I opened it, I found it was, as Scaurus said, of very little importance to me—knowing what I then knew. Such effect as it had on me was produced before I had opened it, because it provoked my curiosity and stimulated me to study the books of the Christians.

The postscript continued as follows. "The second thing, much more important, concerns a fundamental matter in this Christian superstition. You know, I am sure, from Paul's letters, that the ancient Jews—better called Israelites—have always claimed that God has honoured them above all nations by making a special 'treaty' or 'covenant' with them. Well, Paul admits this for Jews, but claims for Christians that they have a still better 'treaty' or 'covenant,' which he calls 'new,' as distinct from that of the Jews, which he calls 'old.' He represents his leader, Christ, as making or ratifying this 'new covenant' with his blood, on the night on which he was betrayed. Not only this, but he gives the exact words uttered by Christ—and, mark you, *this is the only occasion on which he quotes any words of Christ at all.* Not only this, but he says that he received them from his leader; 'I received from the Lord that which I also delivered over to you.' Now, Silanus, look for yourself. Do not believe me. Look in Paul's first epistle to the Corinthians, some way after the middle, and see whether he does not quote these words, 'This cup is the new covenant in my blood. Do this as often as ye are drinking, to my remembering.'

What the words mean I do not precisely know. But there they are. Next look in the three gospels."

"Now," said I, "I shall get light." I put down the letter and took up the three gospels—the packet from Flaccus. But a glance showed that it would be a long and diflScult business to find the passage in them, and to compare their three versions with the one in Paul's epistle. So I turned to the postscript again, "Next look in the three gospels and prepare to be surprised. You will find the following four facts. First, none of them contain the words 'Do this to my remembering.' Secondly, the latest gospel (that of Lucas) makes no mention of a 'covenant.' Thirdly, the two earliest gospels do not call the covenant 'new.' Fourthly, the Greek word may mean not 'covenant' at all, but 'testament'; and the meaning may be that their leader bequeaths them his blood—whatever that may mean—by his last will and testament.

"Now I put it to you, Silanus, as a reasonable man, whether it is worth while investigating a superstition as to which the earliest documents disagree concerning such a fundamental fact (or rather allegation). These Christians—for I am informed they mostly take Paul's view—assert that their Founder made a *'new covenant'* between them and God on a special night. Three of them give accounts—detailed accounts—of all manner of things that happened on that night. A fourth, Paul, professes to give the very words of the Founder of the Covenant, as he received them from the Founder himself, not alive of course but dead! And he, Paul, *alone of the four, mentions the phrase 'new covenant.'* What do you think of this?"

Indeed I did not know what to think of it. And Scaurus's next words almost decided me to take his view of the whole matter, to put away all my Jewish and Christian books and to have done with every kind of philosophy. "Spare me," so the postscript proceeded, "for the sake of the immortal Gods, my dearest Quintus, spare me the pain—during the few years or months of life that may still remain for me—of seeing the son of my dearest friend ensnared in the net of a beguiling superstition that must lead you away from your duty to your country. Be kind to me and to your father."

Not having read the preceding part of his letter, I was amazed at this outburst of alarm in my behalf But I perceived that, with his usual sympathetic insight, he had read some of my thoughts almost before

I was conscious of them myself, and I was grateful to him. If he had stopped there, I sometimes think things might have happened differently. But he continued, "*Truth*, as Sophocles says, *is always right*. Be true to the truth. Be true to yourself Amid all the shifting fancies and falsehoods around you, esteem the knowledge of yourself the only knowledge that is certain and unchangeable. In that respect the old philosophers were right. 'Know thyself' is the only divine precept. On self-knowledge alone is based the only covenant—if indeed it is fit to imagine any covenant—between God and man."

From these last words I found myself in absolute revolt. During the past few days I had come to think that perhaps the only certain and unchangeable truth was that self-knowledge without other knowledge is impossible, or, if possible, most harmful. Dissenting from these last words I went back to dissent further, or rather to draw a different inference. "Truth is always right." Then could it be right for me to give up the search for truth, lest I should pain myself or Scaurus? From my father, one of the most just and honourable of men, how often had I heard the maxim, *Audi alteram partem!* Why should I not "hear the other side" since that very day had placed at my disposal (thanks to Flaccus) the means of doing this? Scaurus had indirectly challenged me to do it. My father had, in a sense, commanded it. Before I retired to rest that night, I resolved to devote the whole of the next day, and as much time as I could spare afterwards, to the examination of the Christian gospels.

XIX. — HOW SCAURUS STUDIED THE THREE GOSPELS

BEGINNING with the passages that described the Lord's Supper, I soon found that Scaurus was correct in saying that the words of the Lord quoted by Paul were not in any of the gospels. But my copy of Luke—an old one, having been transcribed in the reign of the emperor Nerva as the scribe stated—contained a note in the margin, not in the scribe's handwriting, "After *'my body'* some later copies have these words, *'which is being given in your behalf. Do this to my remembering; and the cup likewise, after supping, saying, This cup is the new testament in my blood which is being shed for you'*." Now these words were very similar to Paul's quotation, and Flaccus had told me that Luke was a companion of Paul. So I reflected that Luke must often have partaken of the Christian Supper with Paul, and must have heard these words from Paul. Why therefore were the words omitted in Luke, except in "some later copies"? Mark, Matthew, and Paul agreed in inserting some mention of "covenant." Why did Luke, Paul's companion, alone omit it?

Looking into the matter more closely, I found that Luke, though he omitted the phrase about "covenant,"*inserted in his context some mention of "covenanting," or "making covenant,"* as follows: "I *covenant* unto you as my Father *covenanted* unto me." The "covenant" was "a kingdom, that ye may eat and drink at my table." Also, in the same context, Jesus said, "The kings of the nations lord it over them, and those who play the despot over them are called"—I think he meant, "called" by their flatterers—"benefactors. But you, not so."

And Jesus went on to say, "He that ruleth must be as he that serveth," and, "I am among you as he that serveth." The words "my Father covenanted unto me" appeared to mean a covenant of sacrifice, namely, that the Son was to sacrifice Himself for the sins of the world, and to pass, through that sacrifice, into the Kingdom at the right hand of the Father. And the other words meant that Jesus "covenanted" with the disciples that they should sacrifice themselves in like manner, taking Him as it were into themselves, by drinking the blood of the sacrifice (that is, His blood) and eating its flesh or body (that is, His body). And thus they, too, being made one with Him, were to pass into the Kingdom.

Such a "covenant" as this, would, I perceived, be so "new" that it might be described as turning the world upside down—all the kings serving their subjects, all the masters waiting on their servants. This was indeed strange. But it was not peculiar to Luke. Mark and Matthew (I found) had a similar doctrine, though not in this passage; only, instead of "I am among you as he that serveth," they had, "to give his soul as a ransom for many." This accorded with what was said above, namely, that the "covenant," or condition, on which the Son came into the world, was, that He should be the "servant," or "sacrifice," or "ransom," for mankind. All three names expressed aspects of one and the same thing. David had said, "The sacrifice of the Lord is a contrite spirit." That meant, contrite for one's own sins. Jesus seemed to go outside a man's self, and to say, "The sacrifice of the Lord is a spirit of service to others" Romans, I reflected, would call this doctrine either an impracticable dream, or—if practicable, and if attempted—a pestilent revolution. But once more the thought recurred that the Jew would say to us, as the Egyptian said to Solon, "You Romans are but children," and that, although Rome had the power (as Virgil said) of "subjecting the proud oppressors in war," it might not have what Epictetus described as the power of the true Ruler (which this Jewish Ruler seemed to claim), namely, to draw the subjects towards the ruler with the chain of "passionate affection."

Scaurus next asserted that some disagreements here between the evangelists arose from translating Hebrew into Greek. Where Mark has "and they drank," Matthew has "drink ye." Scaurus said that the same Hebrew might produce these two Greek translations. "Also," said he, "supposing Jesus to have said in his native tongue, *This is my body for you*, some might take 'for you' to mean 'given *to you* as a gift,' but others 'given*for you* as a sacrifice'." Hence he inferred that it was hardly possible to discover what Jesus actually said, because, besides differences of memory in the witnesses, there might be differences of translation in those who remembered the same words. But on the other side, if Scaurus was right, the facts showed the independence of the witnesses, as well as their honesty and accuracy. If Jesus used one Jewish phrase that might imply two meanings, it seemed natural that his disciples should try to express both meanings in Greek. The nearness of the Passover (at the time when the words were uttered), and the connexion in scripture between "covenant" and "sacrifice," and many things that I had read in Paul's epistles, made me believe that "sacrifice" was implied. Why should not the disciples suppose that their Saviour bequeathed a legacy to them that was also a sacrifice for them? This seemed to me a beautiful and intelligible belief.

The result was that I resolved not to give up the study of these books. Repeating my father's maxim, *Audi alteram partem*, "Scaurus," I said, "shall be on one side, and the three gospels"—which I spread out on the table—"shall be on the other." I soon found, however, that my task was not so simple. There was not merely "the other side," there were often three "sides"—so strangely did the gospels vary. Scaurus made a fourth, or, rather, a commentary on the three. From my youth up (thanks largely to Scaurus) I had some skill in comparing histories. It was necessary first (I perceived) to have the three gospels side by side. For this purpose, the penknife and the pen—the former for transposing, the latter for transcribing—had to be freely used. Mark's gospel I preserved intact. Extracts from

Matthew and Luke—copying or cutting them out—I placed parallel to the corresponding passages in Mark. I also made use of marginal notes in my MS. referring me to parallel passages in the other gospels or in the scriptures. Some days were spent in this labour. After that, I determined to attend lectures regularly, but to devote all my leisure to a close examination of the gospels with the help of Scaurus's comments. Now I must speak of his letter.

It began, as his postscript had ended, with a personal appeal, warning me against a tendency to dreaming, "which," said he, "I think you must have inherited from my Etrurian grandmother, whose blood runs in your veins—through your dear mother—as well as in mine. I myself, at times, have to fight against it." Then he cautioned me against the Jews. "They are all of them," he said, "dangerous people, though in dififerent ways. There are two sorts, plotters and dreamers; the plotters, all for themselves; the dreamers, all for someone else, or something else (the Gods know what!) outside themselves. Now a dreamer in the west, mostly a Greek (for a Roman dreamer is a rare bird) is a harmless creature—dreaming passively. But the Jewish dreamer dreams actively. He is, to use the Greek adjective, *hypnotic*. If I might invent a Greek verb, I would say that he *'hypnotizes'* people. He makes others dream what he dreams. And his dreams are not the dreams of Morpheus, 'golden slumbers' on 'heaped Elysian flowers.' No, they are often dreams like those of Hercules Furens—destroying himself and his friends while he thinks he is destroying 'powers of evil'! I have known several Jews, some very good, more very bad; only one, perhaps, half-and-half. That was Flavins Josephus, whose histories you have read. He could be all things to all men in a very clever way, mostly for his people, sometimes for himself

"Paul was all things to all men in a very different way, and always the same way. Paul, as you know, frankly warns his readers, 'I am become all things to all men that I may by all means save some,' and 'I became to the Jews a Jew that I might gain the Jews'—not for himself, of course, but for his Master, the King of the Jews. I have never told you, before, something that I will tell you now—to warn you against these Jews, especially the Christian Jews. I once saw this Paul, only once. I was but a boy. He was standing, chained, in a corridor in the palace, waiting to be heard. One of the Praetorian guard was talking to him and Paul was replying, while my father and I were passing by; and my father, having something to say to the guardsman, made some courteous remark to Paul about interrupting their talk. Paul stood up. He was rather short, and bent down besides with the weight of his chains; and the guardsman (quite against regulations) had put a stool for him to rest on. He reached up his face to my father's as though he could not see very distinctly: but it was not exactly the eyes, but the look in them, the unearthly look, that I shall never forget. No doubt, he was thankful for the few syllables of kindness. It seemed to me as if he wished to return the kindness in kind. He said something. What it was I don't know. Probably bad Greek or worse Latin. Thanks of some sort, no doubt. But it was the look—the look and the tone, that struck me. Struck! No, rather, bewitched. For days and nights afterwards I saw that man's face, and heard his voice in my dreams. I did not like the dreams. But he made me dream. He was a retiarius. If he had had me alone for a day or two, I feel even now that he would have caught me in his Christian net. I don't want you to be caught."

Then Scaurus went on to speak of himself at some length. I will set down his exact words for two reasons. First, they show what pains he had taken to prepare himself for the work of a critic. Secondly, his letter seemed to me to explain in part why he was so set against what he c>alled the soporific or hypnotic art of Paul. He and I approached the apostle in dififerent circumstances. I came to Paul before coming to the gospels. He read the gospels first, and found it impossible to believe them. Then, with a mind settled and fixed against belief, approaching Paul, he found—this I believe to be the fact—that Paul was drawing him towards Christ. He resisted the constraint, thinking that he was resisting a sort of witchcraft. Yes, and even to the end of his life, he fought against the truth, seeing it masked as falsehood. Yet assuredly he loved the truth and spared no pains to reach it. Let my old friend speak for himself in what I will call—

SCAURUS'S AUTOBIOGRAPHY

"While I am in the mood for telling secrets I may say that, for me, too, this Christian superstition has not been without attractions; and, had there been anything solid in it, I think I should have ascertained it. You must know that in the last year or two of Domitian this sect was brought into notice in Rome among the highest circles by rather painful circumstances—painful, I mean, to me. I had retired from the army. As soon as I had recovered from my wounds, enough to be able to limp about, I looked round me for something to do. I was not in favour with the Emperor. He had lost reputation in the Dacian war; and he was supposed to dislike those officers—there were only a few—who had done creditably in that most discreditable business. I was supposed to be one of the few. At all events, in the 'regrettable incident' of Fuscus, I brought off most of my men safe, and we did not run away. Well, I thought I had better lead a retired life. So under the plea of disablement—which was unfortunately only too true, as I was lamed for life—I kept at home in Tusculum all through the reign of Domitian, giving myself up to literature.

"Even as a boy, I was very fond of Greek, and I liked learning it in my own way and not according to the ways of my masters. My way was to commit to memory—and to keep in memory by constant repetition, a very diflferent thing from mere 'committing'—great masses of such literature as I liked best. Many and many a time have I met and passed a friend or schoolfellow in the Via Sacra, and heard his voice behind me, 'Are you going to cut me, Scaurus?' But I had not been 'Scaurus' when I passed him. I had been Medea frantic, or Demosthenes haranguing the Athenians, or Plato describing Thales on the well's brink, or—for I was an eclectic—Thucydides recording his personal experiences of the plague. I kept this up, even in the army. Many a long night in Dacia has been shortened in the company of my friends, the great Greek authors. The result of all this was, that when I reached consular age, and, instead of going in for consulships, went in for lameness and literature, I was well provided, so far as eoneemed the Greek raw material, for critical studies.

"Well, as time went on, extending the course of my reading, I happened to pick up in Flaccus's shop a Greek translation of the Hebrew book of Job. It was a chaos, with occasional lucidities—some of them magnificent. On my showing it to a learned Jew (whom Josephus had recommended to me) he explained to me that the Greek translators had often been misled by similarities of Hebrew words. Hebrew is a queer language. It has vowels but does not write them. I saw at once what an abundant source of error this might be. Even in Latin, where vowels are written, I have known Greeks go wrong by rendering *amnis* as though it were *omnis*. How much more, if there were no vowels! My rabbi—that is their name for 'teacher'—informed me that even the Greek-speaking Jews were now beginning to be dissatisfied with the Seventy (that is the name they give to their authorised version). Several new translations of some of the books were floating about, he said, and a good and faithful translation of the whole would probably be produced before long. This interested me. Under his guidance I studied the parallelisms in the two books of Esdras and other books of theirs. I learned just enough Hebrew to understand how it would be possible for an expert to go back to a lost Hebrew original from two extant parallel Greek translations. You see what I mean. A very little knowledge of Latin might enable anyone to see, that, in two Greek documents, *'oaks'* and *'flintstones,'* being parallel, point to a Latin *'ilices'* or *'silices'*—the reading being doubtful—from which two Greeks have been translating.

"Now I must pass to the last year or last but one of Domitian. You have heard your father speak of Flavius Clemens (not exactly a strong man, but a good one) who was put to death by his uncle, the Emperor, for 'Judaism' (so it was called) and his poor wife exiled. 'Judaism,' with our people, was only a more respectable name for 'Christianism,' though the two superstitions are poles asunder. Poor Domitilla was a downright Christian. Her husband Clemens was at all events Christian enough for Domitian's purposes. He was put to death and his eflfects confiscated. I bought a few of his books as memorials of my old friend, and among these were certain Christian publications called 'gospels'

"Every Christian missionary is supposed to 'preach the gospel'; so, of course, there might be, theoretically, as many gospels as missionaries, and 'a gospel according to' each missionary, if each chose to write down what he preached. Accordingly I gather from Flaccus that there have been a great number of these 'gospels '; but only three are now in large demand among Christians in Rome—the three he sent you. The earliest of these is 'The Gospel according to Mark.' That it is the earliest you can see thus. Put them (that is, of course, the parallel parts of them) in three columns, Mark in the middle. Then imagine three schoolboys seated together—Sinister, Medius, and Dexter—writing a translation of Homer. Suppose Sinister and Dexter to be cribbing from Medius, who sits between them. The experienced schoolmaster will speedily discover that, whenever Sinister and Dexter closely agree, it is because they cribbed from Medius. Similarly Matthew and Luke largely copied—not 'cribbed,' for they did it honestly enough, no doubt—from Mark. Consequently (subject to certain exceptions, which I will state later on) Matthew and Luke *never agree together—in those parts of the gospel where there are three parallel narratives—without also agreeing with Mark*. Don't trust me for this. Try it yourself."

I did try it. And I found that—subject to the exceptions defined by Scaurus in another letter—his statement was correct. His letter continued, "So I began with Mark. Do not suppose that I began with any prejudice against him. On the contrary, your old friend, whom you are so fond of calling Misomythus, must plead guilty, I fear, to a latent desire of the philomythian kind—that Mark might contain truth and not myth. But hereby hangs another tale, and I must begin another confession.

"Among Domitilla's slaves was one especially dear to her, her librarian, whom she would (no doubt) have manumitted if she had anticipated the blow that was soon to fall on her husband and his household. He was an old man, of Alexandrian extraction, and of some education, simple-minded as a child, perfectly honest, giving an impression of firmness, gentleness, and dignity, quite unusual in a slave. I liked old Hermas—that was his name, you must have seen him, I think, in your childhood—for his own sake, as well as for his love of literature. When I bought the books I bought him at the same time. He was nearly seventy and ailing. The calamities of his mistress helped him to his grave, and he died a few days after he had come to my household. We had very little talk together, and least of all at our last meeting; but what we had then, I never forgot. It happened thus. One afternoon, when he came into the library a little later than usual—slowly, and painfully, and leaning on his staff—I happened to have Domitilla's three gospels rolled out on the table before me. There were some notes in the margin of Matthew. These were in his neat small handwriting and I was looking at them. 'Not Domitilla's hand, I think,' said I, with a smile. He shook his head, opened his lips as if to speak, looked long and wistfully at me, as if he would greatly have liked to talk about something more than mere librarian's business. But all he said was, 'Will my lord give his instructions for the day's work?' I gave them. They were that he should go to bed and keep there till he was fit for business. He bowed, moved slowly toward the door, turned and looked at me a second time with that same expression, only more intense; then left the room without a word. I felt strangely drawn towards the old man, and had almost called him back. But I did not. 'To-morrow,' I said, 'to-morrow.'

"Unexpected business took me from Tusculum late in that afternoon and kept me away for three days. On my return I was told that Hermas was no more. He had earnestly desired to see me, they said; and when he found that I had left Tusculum, and that my return might be delayed, and that his voice was failing, and death perhaps imminent, he had spent his last strength in writing a letter, which, by his request, was to be left by his side until he was carried to the funeral pyre—in case I might come to take it. I went at once to his bedside and read it there. I keep it still. But I will not transcribe it for anyone, not even for you, Silanus. It is a confidence between me and old Hermas, a private confession of a dream of his. A dream fulfilled and to be fulfilled, he says. All a dream, I say. Who shall decide? Though I will not give you the words, you shall have the substance of his letter.

"Well, then, if I might believe this letter, he, old Hermas, lying dead on the couch before my eyes, was not really dead, but only on the way to a beautiful city of justice and truth, to which all the just, honourable, and truthful might attain, Roman, Greek, Jew, Scythian, rich and poor, bond and free, high-born and low-born. No franchise was needed except a patient and laborious pursuit of virtue. In this city no one citizen was greater than another. If anyone could be called greatest, it was the one that made of least account his own pleasures, his own wealth, fame, and reputation, serving the state and his fellow-citizens in all things. Yet it was not a republic, for it had a king. But this king was not a despot like the kings of the east, abhorred by Greeks and Romans. The kingdom was a family at unity with itself, the citizens being closely bound by affection to their king as father and to their fellow-citizens as brethren. 'And if,' said Hermas, 'you desire to be drawn towards that king and to become one with all the fellow-citizens of the City of Truth, I beseech you, my dear lord and benefactor—being, as you are, a lover of truth—to study with all patience those books of my dearest mistress Domitilla, which I saw before you on that day on which you spoke to me your words—your last words to me, so God wills it—words of kindness following deeds of kindness, for which may the Father in heaven be kind to you for ever and ever.'

"A postscript added a further request, that I would search for other papyri, which contained the epistles of Paul, and which, he said, belonged to Domitilla's library, though he had been unable to find them. 'These,' he said, 'give a clue to the meaning of many things that are obscure in the gospels; for in the gospels traditions derived from different documents or witnesses, are sometimes set down without uniform arrangement, and without proportion; so that, in Mark, a whole column of forty lines might be given, for example, to the exorcism of some evil spirit, and only three or four lines to some principal and fundamental saying of Christ. But Paul, though he was neither an eye-witness nor an ear-witness, understood spiritual things, according to his saying, *We have the mind of Christ'.*

"This was written on the day before his death. Another postscript, added on the following day, contained nothing but a hope or prayer that he might meet me in the City of Truth. I should add that I searched at the time in vain for Domitilla's copy of Paul's letters. It was not till three years afterwards that I read them, having procured a copy from another source. Sometimes I regret this and ask myself whether Hermas might have been right in thinking that Paul would have led me to understand the gospels better. But I cannot think that the Gods have decreed that those alone shall find the way to the City of Truth who may happen to have studied four Christian papyri in a particular order. Now I must pass from all this prattle about regrets, hopes, prayers, and preconceptions, to describe my exploration of the gospels and my search for historical fact."

XX. — SCAURUS ON FORGIVENESS

AT this point Scaurus had drawn two lines, thus:

Then the letter continued, "These two lines, my dear Silanus, represent two portions of Mark's *'gospel'*—which word you know, I presume, that the Christians use, as the Greeks do, to mean *'good news,'* Well, the short thin line represents the portion given by Mark to the moral precepts or sayings of Christ. The long thick line represents the portion given to framework—for example, to describing a certain John, called the Baptist, who, so to speak, introduces Christ to the people; to casting out devils; to healing specified diseases, fever, leprosy, paralysis, blindness, deafness, dumbness, lameness; to the raising up of a child apparently dead; to the destruction of a herd of swine by suffering devils to enter into them; to walking on water; to calming a tempest; to a feeding (or rather two feedings) of thousands of men with a few loaves and fishes; to blasting a fig-tree (but that comes later on); to the character of Herod the tetrarch, and his birth-day feasting, ending in the beheading of the above-mentioned John; to the finding of an ass by the disciples in exact accordance with Christ's predictions and precepts; lastly, to very minute details of Christ's trial and crucifixion. There are also a few fables, called parables, likening the good news, or gospel, to seed, which will not grow if sown in wrong places but will grow without man's interference if sown rightly.

But, all this while, about the good news itself, and about its nature, and about the persons to whom the good news is to be brought, and about the good that it will do people—hardly one word! Do not take my word for this. Take your own copy of Mark and look at the first words of Jesus, 'Repent and believe the gospel.' But what gospel? Jesus has not mentioned the word before. This is a specimen of the whole work. It is not a gospel at all. It leaves out essential things. It is only the frame of a gospel."

I did not see at first how to answer this. But on looking into the matter it seemed to me that Scaurus had not noticed Mark's first words, "The beginning of the *gospel of Jesus Christ as it is written in Isaiah the prophet*." Moreover Christ's first words were not "Repent," but *"The time is fulfilled,* and the kingdom of God hath drawn near. Repent and believe in the gospel." Now the first mention of "preaching the gospel" in Isaiah is in a passage that begins thus: "Comfort ye, comfort ye, my people, saith God...because *her humiliation is fulfilled, her sin is loosed...The voice of one crying in the wilderness, Prepare ye the way of the Lord*...and the glory of the Lord shall appear and all flesh shall see *the salvation of God*..."; and soon afterwards come the words, "Unto a high mountain get thee up, O thou *that preachest the gospel* to Sion." A marginal note in my Isaiah said that—instead of *"her humiliation is fulfilled"*—the right translation was *"her time of service is fulfilled,"* which resembled Mark, *"The time is fulfilled"*—words omitted by Matthew and Luke.

Reviewing Mark and Isaiah together, I came to the conclusion that Mark took for granted that his readers would refer to the passage in Isaiah, and that he meant, in effect, this: "*The beginning of the gospel of Jesus Christ was the fulfilment of Isaiah's gospel* (namely, 'Comfort ye my people because *the time is fulfilled and her sin is loosed*')." John the Baptist, according to Mark, fulfilled *Isaiah's prophecy*. He was the voice crying in the wilderness, "Prepare the way," namely, for this gospel of the salvation of God. Then came Jesus saying, in the words *of Isaiah*, "'The time is fulfilled' that is, *for the gospel of the 'loosing of sins'*; believe in this gospel." Looked at in this way, Mark, though brief and obscure, did not seem to me to have *"left out"* what was (as Scaurus said) "essential," but to have referred his readers to Isaiah for what was essential, if they were not already familiar with the passage, so that they might understand the meaning to be, "*Believe in the gospel of the loosing*, or *forgiveness, of sins, predicted by Isaiah, and fulfilled now*."

Scaurus's next objection was this: "Soon after telling us that Jesus called four men away fix)m being fishers of fish to be 'fishers of men' —without explaining the nature or object of this 'fishing,' Mark says, 'Men were amazed at his teaching. For his way of teaching was that of one having authority and not as the way of the scribes.' But what kind of '*authority*'? Listen to the rabble, how they define it (a few lines lower down). 'What is this? A novel teaching! With *authority* does he dictate even to the unclean spirits and they obey him.' Now Flavius Josephus has told me that he himself has known a conjurer or exorcist cast out an unclean spirit or demon—in the presence of Vespasian and his offIcers—and make it knock over a bucket of water in its exit: but he never told me—and you may be sure he would never have supposed—that the conjurer, on the strength of his exorcisms, would claim to preach a gospel!"

This struck me at first as a very forcible objection. And I was not surprised that Matthew omitted the whole of this narrative; for it is liable to be misunderstood. But I found on examination that Jesus did not (as Scaurus said) "claim to preach a gospel" on the strength of such exorcisms. On the contrary, Mark and Luke say soon afterwards, that Jesus "would not allow the demons to speak because they knew him." Moreover I found that the man from whom the demon was said to have been expelled cried out that Jesus was "the Holy One of God." So it appeared possible that Jesus—if he possessed, like Apollo or Aesculapius, some divine power of healing—might heal lunatics or possessed persons among others, and yet might not claim, on the strength of such exorcisms alone, to preach a gospel. From what I had read in Paul's epistles, and also from my recent reading of Isaiah's prediction of the "gospel," it seemed to me more likely that Jesus would connect his gospel—though what the connexion would be I did not yet see—with the forgiveness of sins.

And this indeed I found to be the subject of Scaurus's next objection; "Then Jesus says that he will cure a man of paralysis in order that the spectators 'may know that the Son of man hath authority on earth to forgive sins.' Now this is the first mention of 'the Son of man.' Who, or of what nature, is this Son of man? There is no answer."

Scaurus spoke thus, perhaps, because he had in his mind some passages in the Jewish scriptures where a "son of man" is described as coming on the clouds to judge mankind, and others where a "son of man " means "son of a mere mortal." He may have thought that Mark ought to have explained which of the two was meant.

But Paul's epistles had shown me that, when he regarded Christ as having authority over all things, he, Paul, was in the habit of quoting one of the most beautiful of David's Psalms, which said, "What is man that thou art mindful of him, and the son of man that thou visitest him? For thou hast made him but little lower than the angels." Now here my MS. said, in the margin of the Psalm—as I quoted it above—*"but little lower than God."* Then David continued, "Thou hast *subjected all things under his feet.*" These words "subjecting all things" are frequently applied by Paul to the reign or lordship of Christ over mankind. And "to subject" was precisely the word used by Epictetus concerning the ideal ruler, when he taught us that Socrates had the power "so to frame his hearers" that they would "subject" their wills to his. It seemed to me, then, that if Scaurus had said to Mark "Why did you not explain which son of man Jesus meant?" Mark might have replied, "*Because the Lord Jesus did not recognise two 'sons of men.'* He taught us that the son of man on earth is intended by God to be the son of man in heaven, and that the son of man, even on earth, is superior to the moon and the stars, having 'authority over all things'."

Afterwards I found that Jesus (in Matthew) quotes elsewhere part of another passage in this same psalm of David, namely, "Out of the mouth of babes and sucklings hast thou established strength, because of thine adversaries, that thou mightest still the enemy and the avenger." Paul taught that the "adversaries" of the Lord are the angels of Satan, and the "enemy" is the devil, and these are like wild beasts seeking to devour the soul of man. David, therefore, might be interpreted spiritually as meaning that God has given "authority" to the Son of man, not only over the visible "beasts of the field" but also over the invisible "beasts" that attack the heart of man. "Over these "—Paul might say—"hath the Son of man received authority that he may still the enemy and avenger," that is to say, that he may put Satan to silence by delivering man from the bondage of sin. Some thought of this kind occurred to me at the time. And I was confirmed in it afterwards when I found in the gospels elsewhere mention of "authority" to "trample on, or rule over," wild "beasts" of various kinds. The facts seemed to show that Jesus often meditated on this beautiful poem of David and on the power given by God to "the Son of man" and to "babes and sucklings"—to whom Jesus appears often to refer under the title of "the little ones."

These considerations to some extent met Scaurus's next objection: "Now as to *authority to forgive sins*—what is meant by this? I can forgive you a *debt* of a thousand sesterces. But I cannot forgive you a *theft* of a thousand sesterces—except in the language of the people. Whether you stole them from me or from somebody else, that makes no difference. You remain a thief—a past thief of course—till the end of your days. Jupiter himself, as Horace in effect declares, cannot unthieve you."

This caused me a great deal of thought. It was logical, yet I felt it was not true. It seemed to me, for example, that if two sons had stolen money from two several fathers, one father might so deal with the child that he might feel himself forgiven, even though he had to pay the money back again; while another father, though not exacting the money, might make the boy feel that he was not forgiven, and that he would be a thief all his life long. Even Epictetus, I remembered, said about Diogenes, "He goes about like a physician feeling the pulses of his patients, and saying, 'You have a fever; you, a headache; you, the gout. You must fast; you must eat; you must not bathe; you must have the knife; you must have cautery.'" He was talking of mental or spiritual diseases. Well, to be slavishly afraid of God—was not this a disease? And to one thus diseased, might not a healing Son of God come with a message from the Father, "He loves you, though He may punish. He will punish as a Father that loves. Steal no more; He will not treat you as a thief. Sin no more; He will not treat you as a sinner."

Epictetus once declared that Diogenes had been sent before us as a reconnoitrer into the regions of death and had brought back his report, "There is nothing terrible there." I never could quite understand on what grounds our Teacher based this assertion, unless it was because the Cynic himself had absolutely no fear of death. It was more easy for me to under- stand—I do not say, to prove, but to understand—that a great prophet might bring a similar report from the Father of men, "I come from the House of God to tell you that there is nothing terrible there—except for the cruel and base. There is nothing but kindness and justice and true fatherhood." About the alleged "report" of Diogenes, I had felt that—if I believed it—it would deliver me from bondage to the fear of death. Similarly I felt, about the message or gospel of this Jewish prophet, that—if I believed it—it might raise me above fears into a region of love and trust and loyalty to the righteous Father. This was only theory. I did not believe it. But I felt the possibility of believing and of being strengthened by the belief

Scaurus next objected to the words, "I came not to call the righteous but sinners." This was in Mark and Matthew. "Luke," he said, "adds 'to repentance'; and that of course is meant. Now it is quite right that 'sinners' should be 'called' to 'repentance.' But is that 'good news'? Is that 'gospel'? And, if it is, what about 'the righteous'? They, it seems, are not 'called.' There is no 'gospel' for them!"

Here Scaurus seemed on strong ground. And I felt that he might urge against Mark what Epictetus says about Diogenes, namely, that the ideal physician inspects others, besides those who are manifestly diseased, in order to see who are healthy and who are not. But then I asked myself, "Who are 'the righteous '?" And the answer Paul put into my mouth was, "None are righteous except through faith in God's Son." That is to say, “None are righteous save through the Spirit of Sonship. None are righteous through the Law." Moreover, on examining the context, I found that the words "I came not to call the righteous" were uttered to unrighteous, envious people, the Pharisees, who grudged forgiveness of sins to the sinners. Elsewhere Luke described the Pharisees as "counting themselves to be righteous and despising others." That is, they were "righteous" in their own estimation. In reality, then, Jesus regarded all men as in need of health, that is to say, in need of righteousness. Also, what Jesus called "repenting" was what the prophets call "turning to Jehovah." So the message of the gospel was, "Turn ye to the Lord and He will forgive you and will grant health to your souls." This was addressed to all that needed better health, that is, to all the nation. But some made themselves blind to their own sinful acts and deaf to the sinful utterances of their own hearts. These could not hear the gospel. The "call" of the gospel did not come into their ears. But it was not the gospels fault but theirs.

The more I thought over Scaurus's trenchant criticism, the stronger grew my suspicion that Romans and Greeks might be inferior to the best of the Jews in the knowledge of the depths of human nature. I knew from Paul's epistles that the apostle recognised a certain mysterious power of forgiving sins and infirmities by bearing them. This Paul called "the law of Christ," saying, "Bear ye one another's burdens and so fulfil the law of Christ," and again, "If anyone be overtaken in a fault, do ye, who are spiritual, restore such a one in a spirit of meekness." This word, "restore," came into my mind when Scaurus said, "Once a thief, always a thief." It seemed to me truer to say that a father might "restore" his child, after the theft, so that he might be honest for the rest of his life. This power of "restoring" was (as indeed it still is) a great mystery to me. But it is a mysterious fact, not a mere imagination.

Also Scaurus himself said, "It is very likely that many of the poorer Jews were called 'sinners' by the Pharisees for breaking small and perhaps disputed rules about purification or about the exact observance of the sabbath. This my rabbi admitted, although he did not care to say much about it. I can understand that Christ might deal epigrammatically (so to speak) with poor creatures of this kind by pronouncing them 'forgiven' or 'righteous.' But they would be just as 'righteous' as before; neither more righteous nor less righteous; his 'pronouncing' would make no difference. The Jews closely connect 'pronouncing righteous' and 'making righteous,' as though the sentence of the judge is anything more than the expression of the judge's opinion! But it is a pure delusion."

I did not think Scaurus was right. It did not seem to me that the voice of the true Son of man, saying, "I pronounce you righteous in the name of the Father of men," would be of the same kind or efficacy as the voice of a lawyer, saying, "Having in view sect. 3 of chap. 4 of such and such a Code, I pronounce you not guilty." I had come to feel that the Son of man represented the "authority" of humanity—divine humanity, such humanity as commends itself (without support from statute law) to the consciences of mankind. The Pharisees (I thought) might have *made* some of these poor men really *unrighteous* by making them frightened of God—as though He were an austere lawgiver or hard taskmaster. The Son, delivering them from this servile terror, and raising them into a wholesome fear, that is to say, into a free and loving reverence for a righteous God, might bring the Spirit of the Father into their hearts, thus *making* them*righteous*. If so, Christ's voice, saying "I forgive you," would not be a mere judge's "sentence," or expression of "opinion." It would be a power, causing the guilty to feel, and to be, forgiven.

Scaurus then said, "Now pass on, and you will find nothing worth mentioning except a wilderness of wonders and portents until the twelve apostles are sent out to 'preach the gospel.' And now, say you, Jesus must surely tell his missionaries what this 'gospel' is. But no. Not a word about it. Mark himself says, 'They preached that men should repent.' Wholesome tidings, no doubt, but hardly *good* tidings!" Here, as before, Scaurus (as it seems to me) had failed to see that Jews would understand Mark's meaning to be "They preached that men should turn to God and receive forgiveness "—which would be "good tidings." Moreover he had omitted Christ's doctrine that "the Son of man is lord even of the sabbath," to which Mark alone (I found) prefixed "The sabbath was made for man and not man for the sabbath." According to this doctrine God seemed to say to men, "Priests, temples, sacrifices, fasts, sabbaths, rites and ceremonies, psalms, hymns, and prayers—all these I have given you for your own sake, to draw you nearer to me." This, in a way, was like the doctrine of Epictetus, that each man must take an oath to himself to think of his own interest. But in another way it was different. For Matthew added, "I desire kindness, not sacrifice." That went to the root of the difference between Epictetus and Christ. The former said, "Think of your own virtue"; the latter, "Think how your neighbour needs your kindness." According to the gospel, the rule of God was, "Draw near to me." Then, in answer to men's question, "How draw near?" the reply was, "Draw near to one another. That is the best way. Drawing near to me by sabbaths or sacrifices is a second best way. The second best must not interfere with the first best."

It appeared to me that Scaurus dealt with Mark more severely than he would have dealt with Plato. Plato regards "justice," not as obedience to the written laws, but as "doing that which is best for all." If therefore retribution of good and evil comes on the well-doer and on the evildoer, severally, as being "the best thing" for each and for all, this is "justice." But Scaurus quoted Mark, "In the moment when ye stand praying, forgive, if ye have any charge against anyone, that your Father also in heaven may forgive you your trespasses," and then said, "This is not just. If I forgive my slave for robbing me or for cruelly maiming one of his fellow-slaves, does it follow that Jupiter should forgive me for theft or murder? Not in the least. He ought to punish me twice over, first, for unjustly forgiving crime, and then for being a criminal myself." Here Scaurus was thinking of remitting penalty, whereas Mark meant bearing the burden of sin. And, although the matter was not then as clear to me as it is now, I could see how a man wronged, and prosecuting the wrong-doer, not as offending against society and justice but as offending against himself—a man that does not wish to "do the best thing" for offenders and for the community—creates for himself an image of a God bad and selfish and unforgiving like himself; so that either he trembles before his bad God and is a slave; or else he regards himself as the favourite of a bad God, and becomes confirmed in his own badness.

On the whole, though I was forced to admit the justice of many charges that Scaurus brought against Mark—and especially the charge of disproportion, and of neglecting great doctrines while emphasizing small details of narrative—still I was satisfied that Mark did contain a gospel, namely, the good tidings of the forgiveness of sins. Scaurus called Mark's gospel a mere frame. It seemed to me that it would have been less untrue to call it a picture in which the principal figure was not clearly seen because of intervening objects and inferior figures. Or it might be called a drama in which the leading character is too often absent from the stage; or, when present, he speaks too little, while minor characters are allowed to speak too much.

XXI. — SCAURUS ON THE CROSS

SCAURUS continued, "I pass over a good many columns in Mark before I come to anything of the nature of a precept. Then I find the following, 'There is nothing outside the man, entering into him, that can defile him.' Now you might suppose that this would have been good news, addressed as it is, to the needy multitude. For it would have enabled them (you may say) to eat pork like their Greek neighbours and would have saved them trouble and expense in preparing food.

"But look at the context. Jesus is upholding the written law of Moses against the teachers of unwritten traditions. These teachers told people that if a particle of this or that came off their hands into their mouths while they were eating, they were defiled. These traditions also prescribed minute regulations about preparing meat, and about avoiding meat sold in the markets of Greek cities. Look at Paul's Corinthian letters about this. These regulations must have been very inconvenient for the poor Jews in the Greek cities of Galilee. Jesus stood up for the poor, and for the written law, which said nothing about such details. Long after the crucifixion, Peter was told by 'the Lord' in a vision (you will find it in the Acts) that he might eat anything he liked, pork included. But Jesus said nothing of the kind before his death. Turn to the Acts and you will find it as I have said."

I turned, and found, as usual, that Scaurus was right, though there was no special mention of pork in the Acts, but only of "beasts and creeping things," which Peter calls "unclean." Scaurus continued, "Now look carefully at what follows in Mark and Matthew. Mark represents the disciples—but Matthew represents Peter—as questioning Christ privately about this startling saying. The questioners are said to have called it a 'parable.' There was no 'parable' about it at all. But the fact was that, *after the resurrection, it was revealed to Peter, or to the disciples*, that the meaning of the saying 'Nothing outside defileth' went far beyond its original scope; so that it swept away the whole of the Levitical ordinances about things 'unclean.' If you examine Mark's words carefully you will see that he inserts a comment of his own (which Matthew omits) namely that Jesus uttered these words *'purifying all kinds of food.'* If by 'purifying,' Mark meant 'purifying*in effect*,' or 'purifying, *as the disciples subsequently understood*,' then he was right. If he meant 'purifying*at once*,' or *'purifying in such a way as to abrogate immediately the Levitical prohibitions*,' then he was wrong; for that was not the meaning.

"What indeed do you suppose would have happened, if Jesus and his disciples had sat down to a dinner of pork on that same day? They would have been stoned by the multitude. The meaning was limited as I have said above. Mark has probably mixed together what occurred before, and what occurred after, the crucifixion. It was very natural. How many of the 'dark sayings' or 'parables' of Jesus might remain 'dark' to the disciples, till they reflected on them after his death! Moreover the evangelists believed that Jesus, after his death, rose again and appeared on several occasions to the disciples, apart from the rest of the world—that is, 'in private '—and that he explained to them after death what had been dark sayings during his life. How inevitable for biographers—writing thirty, forty, or fifty years after the events they narrated—sometimes to confuse explanations, or other words of Christ, uttered 'in private' after death, with those uttered before death, whether in private or not! I shall have to mention other instances of such confusion. It is not surprising that Luke omits the narrative."

I could not deny the force of this. But, though it derogated from Mark as a witness, it did not seem to me to derogate from Christ as a prophet. I felt that no wise teacher could have desired, thus by a side-blow, to sweep away the whole of the national code of purifications. So I was ready to accept Scaurus's view, at all events provisionally.

"I pass over," said Scaurus, "the precept, 'Beware of leaven,' which was certainly metaphorical; and two narratives of feeding multitudes with 'loaves,' which in my opinion are metaphorical; and a mention of 'crumbs,' which my reason leads me to interpret in one way, while my desire suggests another. About this I shall say something later on, as also about predictions of being killed and rising again. Now I reach these words, 'If anyone wishes to come after me, let him disown himself, and *take up his cross and follow me*. For whosoever desires to save his life shall lose it, and whosoever will lose his life for the sake of me and the gospel shall save it.' Note that these words are preceded by a prediction that the Son of man must be 'killed.' Also remember that the 'cross' is a punishment sanctioned by Roman but not by Jewish law. Bearing these facts in mind, imagine yourself in the crowd, and tell me what you would think Christ meant, if he turned round to you and said, 'You must take up your cross.' Do not read on to see what I think; for I doubt whether Christ used these words. But, if he did use them, tell me what you think he meant by them."

I was taken aback by this. For I perceived that the sense required a metaphorical rendering, and, at the same time, that such a metaphor was almost impossible among any Jews, *before Christ's crucifixion*. At first I tried to justify it from Paul's epistles, which declared that, in Christ's death, *"all died"*—meaning that all, by sympathy, died to sin and rose again to righteousness. Paul said also "I have been crucified with Christ," and "our old man"—meaning "our old human nature"— "has been crucified with Him," and "the world has been crucified to me and I to the world." But these expressions were all based on the Christian belief that the "cross" was the way to "resurrection." They were quite intelligible after the resurrection, but not before it.

Then I tried to imagine myself in the circle of disciples surrounding Socrates in prison, and the Master, with the bowl of poison in his hands, preparing to drink it, and looking up to us and saying, "If you intend to be disciples worthy of me, you too must be prepared to take up the hemlock bowl." What, I asked, should I have understood by this? It seemed to me that the words could only mean "You, too, must be prepared to be put to death by your countrymen."

Now as the hemlock bowl was the regular penalty among the Athenians, so the cross (as Scaurus had said) was the regular penalty among the Romans *but not among the Jews*. So, when I tried honestly to respond to Scaurus's appeal, and to imagine myself in the crowd following Jesus, and the Master turning round to us, and saying, "Take up your cross," I was obliged to admit, "I should have taken the Master to mean, 'If you are to be worthy followers of mine, you must be prepared *to be put to death as rebels by the Romans*'."

Scaurus took the same view. "Well," he continued, "I will anticipate your answer, for it seems to me you can only come to one conclusion. You, in the crowd, would take the words to mean that you must follow your Master to the death against the Romans. But all intelligent readers of the Christian books ought to know that he could not have said that. He was a visionary, and utterly averse to violence, so averse that he was on one occasion reproached for his inaction by John the Baptist—who once said to him, in effect, 'Why do you leave me in prison? Why do you not stir a hand to release me? 'Moreover, if Jesus had said this, what would the chief priests have needed more than this, to get Pilate to put him to death: 'This man said to the rabble. If you are intending to follow me, you must go with the cross on your shoulders'? 'Can you prove this? ' would have been Pilate's reply. They would have proved it. Then sentence would have followed at once as a matter of course. And who can deny that it would have been just?"

I certainly could not deny it. Then Scaurus pointed out to me how Luke avoided this dangerous interpretation, by inserting "daily," so as to give the words a metaphorical twist, "Let him take up his cross*daily*." But this, he said, was manifestly an addition of Luke's. If Jesus had inserted "daily" why should Mark and Matthew have omitted it? "Daily" would make no sense till a generation had passed away, so that "to be crucified with Christ" had become a metaphorical expression for mortifying the flesh. On this point, at all events, Scaurus seemed to me to be right.

He continued as follows, "I am disposed to think that Mark has misunderstood a Jewish phrase as referring to the cross when it really referred to something else. You know that, in Rome, a rascally slave, regarded as being on the way to crucifixion, is called *'yoke-bearer,'* which means practically *'cross-bearer,'* Mark, who has a good many Latinisms, might regard *'take the yoke' as meaning 'take the cross'—if the former expression could be proved to have been used by Jesus.* Still more easily might *'take the yoke'* be regarded as equivalent to *'take the cross' if it could be proved that the Jews themselves connected 'taking the yoke' with martyrdom.*

"Both these facts can be proved. In the first place, Christ actually said to the disciples, *'Take my yoke* upon you.' It is true that this saying is preserved by Matthew alone; but its omission by others is easily explained, as I will presently show. In my judgment, it is certain that Christ did give this precept, and that it had nothing to do with crucifixion. The context in Matthew declares that the kingdom of heaven is revealed only to 'babes'—whom Christ elsewhere calls 'little ones' or those who make themselves 'least' in the kingdom of God—and soon afterwards come the words, *'Take my yoke upon you* and learn from me, for I am meek and lowly in heart.' This is the fundamental truth of Christ's teaching, that those who make themselves the humblest of servants to one another are greatest in his 'kingdom.' In order to reign, one must serve, or *'take the yoke.'*

"The next fact is that Jews of the present day—so I am credibly informed—would say of a Jewish martyr that he 'took the yoke upon himself,' when he made a formal profession of obedience to the Law just before death. This I must ask you to take for granted. It would be too long to prove and explain." I suppose Scaurus heard this from the teacher he called "his rabbi." It was confirmed, to my own knowledge, by something that happened nearly thirty years ago when one of the most famous Jewish teachers, Akiba by name, was put to death under Hadrian. I heard it said by a credible eye-witness that "they combed his flesh with combs of iron," and another added "Yes, and Akiba, all the while, kept *taking upon himself the yoke of the Kingdom of Heaven,*" by which he meant repeating the profession of faith.

"A third fact," said Scaurus, "is that the Christians, from a very early period, used the word *'yoke'* in a depreciatory sense to mean the 'bondage'—as they called it—of the Law of Moses. Paul calls the latter *'the yoke of bondage.'* The Christians, at their first public council, speak of it as *'a yoke'*; and a Christian writer named Barnabas says that 'the new law' is *'without the yoke of necessity.'* I suspect that among the Greeks and Romans the servile associations of 'yoke' have also tended to the disuse of the term among the Christians of the west. You may object that the associations of 'cross' are still more disgraceful than those of 'yoke.' But I do not think they would be so for Christians, who regarded the disgrace of the cross as a step upward to what they call 'the crown of life.' Indeed I am rather surprised that Matthew's tradition 'Take my yoke upon you' has been retained at all, even by a single evangelist."

Most of this was new to me. But, even if it was true—as seemed to me not unlikely—the same conclusion followed as above. The mistake derogated from Mark, not from Christ. Indeed Scaurus's interpretation seemed to me to exalt Christ. For might not some people, of austere and fanatical minds, find it easier to *"take up the cross,"* that is, to lacerate and torture themselves, than to *"take up the yoke,"* that is, to make their lives subservient to the community in a spirit of willing self-sacrifice? Indeed Scaurus himself said, "If I am right, the Christians have lost by this misunderstanding. When I say 'lost,' I mean 'lost in respect of morality.' For some may *'take up the cross'* like the priests of Cybele, finding a pleasure in gashing themselves—such is human nature. But it is not so exciting a thing to *'take up the yoke'* if it implies making oneself a drudge for life to commonplace people."

This seemed very true. And afterwards I was not surprised to find that the fourth gospel contains no precept to "take up the cross." But it commands Christians to "love one another"—a precept that nowhere occurs in Mark. Also what Scaurus said about "making oneself a drudge " was, in effect, inculcated by the fourth gospel where it commands the disciples to "wash one another's feet." Sometimes I have asked why this gospel did not restore the old tradition about "yoke." Perhaps the writer avoided it as he avoids "faith," and "repentance," and other technical terms that might come between Christians and Christ. Scaurus himself said, "There seems to me more morality in the old rule of Moses, 'Love thy neighbour as thyself than in either 'Take up the cross' or 'Take up the yoke.' If ever this Christian superstition were to overrun the world, I could conceive of a time when half the Christians might fight with the war-cry of 'the yoke,' and the other half with the war-cry of 'the cross,' cutting one another's throats for these emblems. But I could not so easily conceive of a time when men would ever cut one another's throats with the war-cry, 'We love one another'."

These words of Scaurus seemed to me at the time to be quite true. Now, forty-five years afterwards, they seem to me true as to fact, but not quite true as to interpretation. For, since what Scaurus called "the old rule of Moses" included "Love God," as well as "Love thy neighbour," it followed that the Lord Jesus, in saying "Take my yoke," meant "Serve God," as well as "Serve man." And, in order to serve God, must not one be prepared to suffer, as God also is called "longsuffering"? And of such "suffering" can there be any better emblem than Christ's cross?

I cannot honestly deny the force of the evidence adduced by Scaurus to prove that the Saviour did not really utter the precept of "taking up the cross," and that He did utter the precept of "taking up the yoke." But I can honestly accept the former as an interpretation of the latter, an interpretation fit for Greeks and Romans when the gospel was first preached, and likely to be fit for all the races of the world till the time of the coming of the Lord. If Scaurus is right, only the precept of the yoke was inculcated by Christ in word. But all agree that the precept of the cross was inculcated by Christ in act. Both metaphors seem needed, and many more, to help the disciples of the Lord to apprehend the nature of His Kingdom, or Family.

XXII. — SCAURUS ON MARK

SCAURUS continued as follows: "I now come to a passage where Mark represents Christ as saying, 'Whosoever shall be ashamed of me and of my words, the Son of man also shall be ashamed of him.' This suggests to me for the first time (re-perusing these strange books after an interval of more than twenty years) that I may have been blaming Mark for not doing what, as a fact, he had no intention of doing—I mean, for not giving a collection of Christ's utterances in connexion with the 'good news.' If we were to question Mark about the expression 'me and my words,' and to say, 'What words do you refer to?' perhaps he might reply, 'I do not profess to give Christ's words, but only their tenor.' Perhaps Mark has in view a person, or character, rather than any gospel of 'words.' And I think I ought to have explained that, at the very outset of his work, Mark described a divine Voice (a thing frequently mentioned in Jewish traditions of the present day about their rabbis) calling from heaven to Christ, 'Thou art my beloved Son.' It is this perhaps that Mark may consider a 'gospel,' namely, that God, instead of sending prophets to the Jews, as in old days, now sends a Son."

This did not seem to me a complete statement of the fact. "Gospel," as I have said above, seemed to me to have meant, in Mark, the gospel of forgiveness of sins promised by Isaiah. And Scaurus himself was justly dissatisfied with his own explanation, for he proceeded, "Still, this is not satisfactory. For ought not the Son to have a message, as a prophet has?

Nay, ought not the Son to have a much better message? The Voice from heaven is repeated at the stage of the gospel at which we have now arrived. But both before and now, it is apparently heard by no unbelievers. Nor does Christ himself ever repeat it to unbelievers. He never says, 'I am *the Son of God,*' nor even, 'I am *a Son of God.*' He simply goes about, curing diseases, and saying 'The sabbath is made for man,' and, on one occasion, 'Thy sins are forgiven thee,' and, 'The son of man hath authority on earth to forgive sins,' and a few more things of this sort. What is there in all this that would induce Christ to use such an expression as, 'Whosoever shall be ashamed of me and of *my words*'? I could understand his saying 'of me,' but not 'of *my words*,' Surely it would have been better to say, 'Whosoever shall be unjust, or an adulterer, or a murderer, I will be ashamed of him'."

Here it seemed to me that Scaurus had not quite succeeded in his attempt to do justice to Mark by reconsidering his gospel in the light of the words "Thou art my beloved Son." For suppose a Son of God to have come into the world, like an Apollo or Aesculapius of souls. Suppose Him to have had a power, beyond that of Moses and the prophets, of instilling into their hearts a new kind of love of God and a new kind of love of neighbour. Lastly, suppose this Son of God to feel quite contented, and indeed best pleased, to call Himself Son of man, because He regarded man as the image of God, and because He felt, within Himself, God and man made one. Would not such a Son of God say, just as Epictetus might say, "Preserve the Man," "Give up everything for the Man," "Save the Man within you, destroy the Beast"? Only, being a Jew, He would not say "Man," but "Son of man," exhorting His disciples to be loyal to "the Son of man" and never to disown or deny "the Son of man."

I was confirmed in this view by a mention (in this part of Mark) of "angels" with "the Son of man," thus: "The Son of man also shall be ashamed of him when he shall come in the glory of his Father with the holy angels." This seemed to say that the Son of man although, as David said according to one interpretation of the Psalm, *"below the angels"* on earth, will be manifested in the glory of the Father *with the attendant angels* in heaven—thus reconciling the two aspects of the Son of man described by David and Daniel.

I noticed, however, that Matthew, in this passage, does not say (as Mark and Luke do) "the Son of man will be ashamed"; and it occurred to me that, where Christ used the phrase "Son of man," and spoke about "the coming of the Son of man," different evangelists might render these phrases differently so as to make the meaning brief and clear for Greeks. Indeed Scaurus himself suggested something of this kind, saying that some might use "I" or "me" for "Son of man" (in Christ's words). He also added that "the Son of man" might sometimes be paraphrased as "the Rule, or Law, of Humanity"; and, said he, "Matthew has a very instructive parable, in which the Son of man in his glory and with his angels is introduced as seated on his throne, judging the Gentiles at the end of the world. Then those who have been kind and helpful and humane are rewarded because—so says the Son of man—'Ye have been kind to *me*.' 'When have we been kind to*thee*?' they reply. The Son answers, '*Ye have been kind to the least and humblest of my brethren*. Therefore ye have been kind to me.' This goes to the root of Christ's doctrine. The Son of man is humanity and divinity, one with man and one with God, humanity divine."

Scaurus went on to say that Mark's sayings about the Son of man would have been, much clearer if some parable or statement of this kind had been inserted making it clear that Christ as it were identified himself with the empire of the Son of man mentioned by the prophet Daniel, against the empire of the Beasts. "There is always a tendency," said Scaurus, "among men of the world, and perhaps among statesmen quite as much as among soldiers—yes, and it exists among some philosophers, too, spite of their creeds—to deify force. I own I admire Christ for deifying humanity. But his biographers—Mark, in particular—do not make the deification clear. If I were to lend my copy of Mark to a fairly educated Roman gentleman, I really should not be surprised if he were to come to me, after reading it right through from beginning to end, and ask me, 'Who *is* this Son of man?'" These words impressed me at the time; but much more afterwards when I actually met this very question in the fourth gospel, asked by the multitude at the end of Christ's preaching, "Who *is* this Son of man?"

"After this," said Scaurus (not speaking quite accurately, for he omitted, as I will presently show, one short but important saying of Christ) "comes a statement that a certain kind of lunacy cannot be cured by the disciples unless they fast as well as pray. But here, I am convinced, Mark has made some mistake through not understanding 'faith as a grain of mustard-seed,' which the parallel Matthew has. That is a very interesting phrase, which I must go into another time.

"Close on this, occurs a prediction, with part of which I will deal later on. But about part of it I will say at once that I find it quite unintelligible. It is, 'The Son of man is on the point of being betrayed into the hands*of men*,' Why *'of men'*? Surely he could not be betrayed into the hands of anyone else! I observe that Mark and Luke say, 'They were ignorant of this saying,' and I am not surprised. I presume it is simply a repetition of Christ's prediction of his violent death, introduced in order to emphasize his foreknowledge of the treachery of one of his own disciples. But I do not understand 'of men'."

As to this, I have shown above that the word rendered by Scaurus "betrayed," occurs in Isaiah's description of the Suffering Servant, "He was *delivered over* for our transgressions," and that it is quoted from Isaiah by Paul. I had always rendered it "delivered over." And now, too, it appeared to me much more likely that the Lord Jesus used the word in that sense. If so, it would have no reference to treachery, but would mean "delivered over by the Father." This would explain *"of men"* because it would mean that the Father in*heaven* delivers over His Son "into the hands *of men*" *on earth,* I have heard that one of the brethren, a learned man, explains "of men" as being opposed to "of Satan," but "men" seems to me more likely to be in antithesis to "God." I found afterwards that in the gospels the word "deliver over" is regularly used about Judas Iscariot " delivering over "Jesus to the Jews. So Scaurus may be right. But Paul's rendering seems to me to make better sense in Christ's predictions.

I had been prepared by Paul and by Isaiah to recognise that Christ might have had in view the thought that the Son was to be "delivered over" to death by the Father for the salvation of men. Scaurus had not been thus prepared. Otherwise I think he would have been more patient with obscurities in Mark. Mark seemed to me to assume that his readers would know the general drift of "the gospel" as Isaiah predicted it, as Christ fulfilled it, and as the apostles preached it. Hence he was not so careful as the later evangelists to make his meaning clear to those who had no such knowledge. Take, for example, the words "If any one desires to be first he shall be last." "This," said Scaurus, "might mean 'He shall be degraded so as to be last'." Scaurus also attacked the saying that whosoever receives a child in Christ's name receives Christ, and, "Whosoever shall not receive the kingdom of God as a little child shall surely not enter therein." "I suppose," said he, "this means we are to put aside the vices of youth and manhood and to start afresh. But that is more easily said than done. And there is nothing in Mark to show how it can be done."

Here Scaurus seemed to me not to have quite done justice to Mark, because he had not given weight to the precept at the very beginning of his book. It was very short, and might easily have escaped me but for Paul's guidance. Paul, I knew, taught that Abraham was "made righteous " by "having faith" in God's good tidings. Hence I had noted, what Scaurus had not noted, that *Mark, alone of the evangelists, placed the precept "Have faith" in the first sentence uttered by Christ, saying "Have faith in the gospel."* This, then, I perceived—this "faith in the gospel" was supposed by Mark to have power to "make men righteous."

This seemed, from a Christian point of view, to answer Scaurus's objection, "'Start afresh' is more easily said than done." The answer was —not my answer, but such an answer as I thought a Christian might make— "Yes, it is much more easily said than done. But the Son of God has authority both to say it and to give power to do it. He says, in effect, *'Be thou able to start afresh'* and the man is *'able to start afresh'*."

Then, if Scaurus replied, "Prove this," Paul came forward saying, "I at all events have received power to 'start afresh.' Even my enemies will attest what I have been, a persecutor of the Christians. Now I have been 'forgiven' by Him that has authority to forgive. The old things are passed away. Behold, they are become new." And if Scaurus had said, "But have others been enabled to 'start afresh'?" Paul would have answered, "Yes, multitudes, from the Euphrates to the Tiber. Do not trust me. Take a little journey from Tusculum into the poorest alleys of Rome, and judge for yourself." Here I felt Paul would have been on such strong ground that Scaurus would have given way. "Paul"—he might have said—"is superstitious, and under hallucinations, but I must frankly confess he has the power to help people to 'start afresh'." That is just what I, too, felt. It was quite different from the feeling inspired in me by my own Teacher. When Epictetus said "Let bygones be bygones," "Let us start afresh," "Only begin and we shall see," I felt, almost at once, that he was imagining impossibilities. When Paul said "There is a new creation," I felt that he was describing not only a possibility but also a fact—a fact for himself and for multitudes of others; not indeed a fact for me, but, even for me, a possibility.

To return to Scaurus. "At last," said he, "I came upon a definite precept to show how perfection could be obtained. A rich young man asks Jesus how he can inherit eternal life. Jesus replies, 'One thing is lacking to thee. Go, sell thy substance, and give to the poor, and thou shalt have treasure in heaven, and come, follow me.' Definite enough! But is it consistent with morality? Is it not entirely against Paul's protest, 'Though I give all my goods to the poor and have not love, I am nothing'?" Here Scaurus did not seem to me so fair as usual. For, knowing the gospels as well as he did, he was aware that Jesus did not enjoin this rule on all, for example, on Zacchaeus. He laid down no rules. One man He bade go home, another He bade follow Him. Moreover, Scaurus, who accused Epictetus of borrowing from Christ, knew that Epictetus inculcated poverty and unmarried life, not on all his disciples, but on any Cynic wishing to go as a missionary; and therefore he ought not to have inferred that Jesus inculcated poverty on all His disciples because He gave it as a precept in answer to the question, "What lack I yet?" For my part, although I was not at that time a Christian, yet when I read Mark's words, "Jesus, looking upon him, loved (or embraced) him and said. *One thing is lacking to thee*"—I could understand that, for this particular man, the "one thing lacking" really might be that he should "sell all that he had," and that Jesus, knowing this, gave the precept out of His great love. Scaurus called this "a definite precept to show how perfection could be obtained." But I found only Matthew saying "If thou wouldest be perfect." Mark and Luke did not here use the word "perfect."

Scaurus proceeded thus: "Little remains to be added in the way of precepts. There is a repetition of 'whosoever desires to be great, he shall be your servant.' And this is supported by the saying that 'the Son of man came not to be ministered unto but to minister.' Then comes a most startling statement, 'All things that ye pray and ask, believe that ye received them and they shall be unto you,' and, 'In the moment when ye stand praying' but I have spoken of that above. I really do not think that I have omitted anything of importance. Does not this amaze you?"

About the "startling statement" I will speak later on. But here I may say that Scaurus had omitted one short precept: "Have salt in yourselves." And this, to some extent, answered one or two of his objections. For, as I understood it, "Have salt in yourselves" corresponded to a saying of Epictetus, who bade us seek help from "the Logos within us." On one occasion (noted above) Epictetus, rebuking one of our students for saying, "Give me some precepts to guide me," replied, "Have you not the Logos to guide you?" Mark appeared to me to represent Christ as saying, "Take into your hearts the spirit of the Son, which the Son gives you. It will be the salt of life, life for you and life passing from you to others, purifying all your words and actions by imbuing your heart." Elsewhere, also, Mark represented Christ as condemning the Pharisees (in the words of Isaiah) because, though they honoured God with their lips, their heart was far from Him and they "taught as doctrines the commandments of men." Mark seemed to say "Obey the commandments of the Logos," not "of men." Still, I could not but admit that this brief metaphor, overlooked by Scaurus, might easily be overlooked or underrated by hundreds of other readers less careful and candid; and I was forced to sympathize—though not wholly to agree—with the outburst of disappointment which concluded his letter. "O that my old friend Plutarch had had the writing of the life of this Jewish prophet! Or that at least he had been at Mark's elbow, to check him when he began descanting on extraneous matters and to remind him that his readers wanted to hear what he had to say about Christ, not about John the Baptist or Herod Antipas! Many of my friends think but poorly of Plutarch; but he would have been at all events infinitely superior to Mark. I do not wish to be hard upon the latter. The chariot of the gospel, so to speak, was already moving before he was harnessed to it, and he (not being a disciple of special insight or information) had to go the chariot's way. Although his book hardly ever quotes prophecy it is based on prophecy and continually alludes to prophecy. It does not deal with Christ's life as the ancient Jews dealt with the lives of Moses, Samuel, and David. Though it plunges into the midst of things like a book of the prophets—Jeremiah, for example, or Ezekiel—it does not give the words of the prophet in full, but runs off into all sorts of minor matters.

"You remember what Plutarch says about the importance of expression in biography. Mark occasionally attempts to represent a sort of expression —mostly by means of such phrases as 'being moved with compassion,' 'being grieved,' 'looking steadfastly at him,' 'turning round,' and so on. But the deeper sort of 'expression,' the prophet's attitude towards God and man, towards the past and the future, towards the kingdom of God and the kingdoms of men—this he does not represent. Not at least consciously. Perhaps he does, sometimes, unconsciously, when he preserves Christ's darker sayings where the later writers alter or omit them. For this, he deserves thanks. But, in spite of this, Mark's gospel remains, me judice—regard being had to the greatness of the prophet whose life he is writing—the most inadequate of all the biographies I know."

So far Scaurus. But his admission that Mark "sometimes preserves Christ's darker sayings where the later writers alter or omit them" suggested to me that, in summing up, he felt that he might have passed over some of Mark's unique traditions. And, as a fact, he had omitted "every one shall be salted with fire," and three passages declaring that *"all things are possible."* He also omitted the precept "Be at peace with one another." Matthew and Luke omit all these, except that Matthew once has *"all things are possible."*

This last tradition presents manifest difficulty. I have heard unbelievers scoff at it and ask whether "evil things" are "possible" for God. Moreover Scaurus himself urged on one occasion that not even God can undo the past. Later on, when I studied the gospels with more leisure, it seemed to me that, in saying "all things," the Lord Jesus had constantly in view "the things of the invisible world" or "the things pertaining to the redemption of man." So I found "all things" used in Paul's epistle to the Philippians, declaring that the Lord Jesus Christ was to "fashion anew the body of our humiliation that it may be conformed to the body of his glory, according to the working whereby *he is able even to subject all things unto himself.*"

When I came to read the fourth gospel (called John's), finding how often it supports Mark against Luke, I looked about for this word "possible" or "able" (for one and the same Greek adjective represents the two meanings). But John nowhere uses it. So I thought, "This then is an exception." But I soon found that John expressed Mark's saying, though in a different way. It is in a paradox, saying that the Son is *"able to do nothing from himself."* This looks like a confession of *not "being able."* But the sentence proceeds, *"unless he sees the Father doing something"*; and, after this, "The Father loveth the Son and showeth him all things that He Himself is doing." So the meaning really was, *"The Son can do all that the Father is doing and wills the Son to do."* John did not therefore deny the power of the Son. He asserted it. But he disliked speaking of "power." He avoided all words that mean "able," "strong," "powerful"—meaning "might" as distinct from "right." He prefers "authority," as when he says that the Son has "*authority* to lay down his life and to take it again."

My conclusion was that Mark had recorded the actual words of Jesus, "all things are possible," assuming that his readers, being instructed in the teaching of the apostles, would understand that the words had a spiritual meaning, "All things are put by the Father under the feet of the Son of man." But sometimes, as in the Healing of the Lunatic, the meaning might be ambiguous, or the context might not be so given as to make the words clear. Hence Luke always omitted or altered them, as being obscure and likely to be misunderstood. John paraphrased and explained them. If these facts were correct, it followed that a great debt was due to Mark for preserving the difficult truth when there must have been a great temptation to omit it or to alter it into what was easy but not true. Scaurus gave some weight, but hardly weight enough (I thought) to this merit in Mark.

XXIII. — SCAURUS ON SOME OF THE MIRACLES

"AND now," continued Scaurus, "I will tell you how the vision of the City of Truth and Justice, conjured up for me by that dear old dreamer Hermas, vanished into thin air. I intended to have spoken first about some of the miracles; but I will come back to them afterwards. For the present, turn over your Mark till you come nearly to the middle, and you will find a story about an act of healing at a distance. I have heard a Greek doctor tell stories of a man's being influenced by the death of a twin brother at a distance. He invented the word *telepatheia* to express it. Well, I will invent an analogous word for healing at a distance—*teliatreia*. However, it is not from the miraculous point of view that I wish to discuss the story, but simply as a question of morality.

"It contains these words, 'It is not fit to take the children's bread and to cast it unto the dogs.' Who says this? Jesus. To whom? To a poor woman, called 'Greek, Syrophoenician by extraction.' What is her offence? She has been asking Jesus to cast an evil spirit out of her daughter. Now what do you think of that? The Greeks, of old, affected to call all non-Greeks barbarians. But would their philosophers, would Socrates, or gruff Diogenes, or any respectable Greek philosopher, say such a thing to any non-Greek woman? I admit that Jesus ultimately granted this poor creature's request. But that was only because she answered with the tact and patience of a Penelope, acquiescing in the epithet 'dogs' and replying, 'Yea, Lord, yet even the dogs beneath the table eat of the crumbs of the children.' Had it not been for her almost superhuman gentleness, she would have retired rejected, gaining from her petition nothing but the reproach of 'dog.' I write bitterly. I confess I felt bitter when I saw so noble and sublime a character as that of this Jewish prophet apparently degraded and polluted by an indelible taint of national uncharitableness"

I was beginning to investigate the passage, when my eyes fell on a note that Scaurus had appended at the bottom of the column. "Since writing this, I have looked into the passage again, to see whether I could have been misled. And I notice that Luke omits the whole narrative. Also, while Mark represents the *woman* as coming to Jesus and 'asking him' to heal the child, Matthew represents the *disciples* as coming to Jesus and 'asking him' to send her away. I should like to be able to believe that the woman was really a Jewess turned Gentile, that the disciples tried to drive the woman away, calling themselves 'the children' and her 'the dog,' that Jesus replied, as in Matthew, 'It was precisely these lost degraded ones that I was sent to restore.' In order to obtain this meaning, the changes of the text would not be very great. But I fear this cannot be maintained."

I caught at Scaurus's explanation, and was sorry that he himself did not hold to it. For I was more troubled by this objection of his than by anything else that he had said; and I thought long over it. Finally, I came to the conclusion that Scaurus was nearly right; that this woman, though called "a Syrophoenician by extraction," was a Jewess (as Barnabas the Jew is called "a Cyprian by extraction") and that she had fallen away into Greek idolatry and an evil life, so that Jesus—being, like Paul, all things to all men and women—was on this one occasion cruel in word in order to be kind in deed, stimulating her to better things. This agreed with Paul's use of the word "dogs," which assuredly he would not have applied except to "evil-doers." If, however, it should be demonstrated that the woman was not a Jewess, and not leading an impure life, and that Jesus (not the disciples) used these words to her, then I should still believe in the kindness of Jesus, although these words were apparently unkind. No one would suspect cruelty, in a man habitually kind, except on very strong evidence. Here the evidence was not strong. The witnesses were two, not three; and the two narratives disagreed in important details. This was the conclusion to which I then came.

If Scaurus had read the epistles before the gospels, approaching the latter with some feeling of Christ's constraining "love," he could hardly have stumbled (so I thought and so I think still) at this single narrative. Jesus did not call the centurion a "dog." Jesus had also supported the law of kindness against the law of the sabbath. He had said that "that which goes into the mouth" does not defile a man. He had eaten and drunk with publicans and sinners. How was it possible that a prophet of such broad and lofty views as these could call a poor afflicted woman a "dog" simply because she was not a Jewess? I longed to be near my old friend and to appeal to his common sense and justice, and I felt sure that I should have convinced him. Even if Jesus bade the missionaries at first go only to "the lost sheep of the house of Israel," that seemed to me quite consistent with a purpose that in the end the gospel should be proclaimed to all nations.

In another narrative, which had caused me difficulty of the same kind, Scaurus gave me help. It is not in Mark. But I will set it down here because it bears on kindness. Matthew and Luke represented a disciple as asking to be allowed, before following Christ, to "bury" his father, and as not being allowed. "As to this," said Scaurus, "I have no doubt that the man meant, 'Suffer me to wait at home till I have seen my aged father into the grave and have duly buried him.' Similarly Esau says, in effect, 'My father will die before long. I will wait till I have mourned for him before killing Jacob.' So, in Latin, we say 'I have buried them all,' meaning 'I have survived and buried all my relations.' My rabbi confirms me in this view. Christ always defends nature and natural affection against man's conventions, so that it seems to me absurd to suppose that he would enjoin anything really inhuman."

Scaurus next proceeded to attack the miraculous part of Mark's narrative. Mark, he said, considering the smallness of his gospel, describes many more miracles, relatively, than Matthew and Luke. "As to miracles," said he, "I am ready to believe in anything, miraculous or non-miraculous, on sufficient evidence. But the evidence about Mark s miracles leads me to two conclusions. Some of them occurred but were not miraculous. The rest, although they were honestly supposed to have occurred, did not occur.

"Let us take the first class first. Mark calls them 'powers,' i.e. works of power. That is a good name for them. But Mark seems to think that, if a man has 'power' to cast out demons and perform cures without medical means, such a one must be a great prophet or even a Son of God. To that I demur. I remember, when I was in Dacia, one of my men was down with fever, and bad fever, too. But when the bugles sounded out one night, and the enemy came on, beating in our outposts and pouring into our camp on the backs of some of our cowardly rascals, this brave fellow was up and doing, without helmet or armour, in the front with the best of them. Next morning, he was none the worse. Nor was there any relapse. He was quite cured. I think I have told you how Josephus described to me the casting out of a demon in the presence of Vespasian. And I might remind you of Tacitus's story about the cure of a blind man by the same emperor. I suspect, however, that the former was a mere conjuring trick and that the latter was got up by the priests of—Serapis, I think it was. So I lay no stress on either. But I have spoken to many sensible physicians, who tell me that paralysis and some kinds of fever can be cured by what they call an emotional shock. Often the cure does not last. Some of these physicians go a little further and ascribe to certain persons a peculiar power of quieting restless patients and pacifying or even healing the insane. But I entirely refuse to believe that, if a man has such a power, he can consequently claim to be a Son of God."

About the objection thus raised by Scaurus I have said enough already. It seemed to me that the power of permanently healing the paralysed, and permanently pacifying and healing the insane, was quite different from that of startling a paralysed man into a temporary activity. The former appeared to me allied with moral power and with steadfastness of mind, and likely to be an attribute of the Son of God. Still I was sorry that Mark devoted so much space to it. Here I agreed, in part, with Scaurus.

He then passed to the second class of miracles, "those that were honestly supposed to have occurred, but did not occur." "If," said he,

"I assert that Mark turned metaphorical traditions into literal prose, you must not suppose that I accuse him of dishonesty. All the ancient Jews did it. Look at the story of Joshua, describing how he stopped the sun. Perhaps also you have read how God caused a stream to spring up from the Ass's Jawbone (originally a hill of that name, like the headland or peninsula called *Ass's Jawbone* in Laconia, which you and I passed together some five or six years ago). The second (the jawbone miracle) is somewhat different in origin from the first (the sun miracle). There are many shades of verbal misunderstanding capable of converting non-fact into alleged fact. There was all the more excuse for this error in Christian Jews (such as Mark and others) because of two reasons. In the first place, the prophets had predicted that all manner of disease (blindness, deafness, lameness) would be cured in the days of the Messiah (using even such expressions as 'thy dead men shall awake'). In the second place, Christ did actually—as I have admitted—cure some diseases, such as insanity, fever, and paralysis. How, then, could it be other than a difficult task, in such circumstances, to distinguish the literal from the metaphorical traditions about the cures effected by Christ?"

I could all the less deny the force of these remarks because I had been studying the words, "Whatsoever things ye ask, praying, believe that ye have received them and they shall be unto you." These words, if applied literally—to bread, for example, or money—were manifestly not true. Indeed they were absurd. How could a man honestly believe that he had received a thousand sesterces in the act of praying for them? But if applied spiritually, as in Paul's prayer concerning the thorn in the flesh, they might (I felt) be true for one endowed with great faith. Paul prayed that the "thorn" might "depart" from him. In one sense it did not depart. But in another sense, it did depart because God so increased his strength that the "thorn" became as nothing.

Now in this same passage of Mark I found the following: "Whosoever shall say to this mountain, 'Be lifted and thrown into the sea,' and shall not doubt in his heart but believes in that very moment that what he says is happening, it shall be unto him." Luke also elsewhere had, "If ye have faith as a grain of mustard-seed, ye would say to this sycamine-tree, 'Be uprooted and be planted in the sea,' and it would have obeyed you." I took for granted that "mountain," "mustard-seed," and "sycamine-tree," must all have been metaphorically used.

Scaurus confirmed this view, saying that the Jews were in the habit of calling a learned interpreter of the Law an uprooter of mountains, *i.e.* of spiritual obstacles blocking the path of the students of the law. But then he added something that amazed me, "Matthew has, 'If ye have faith, and doubt not, ye shall not only do the deed of the fig-tree, but even if ye say to this mountain, Be lifted and thrown into the sea, it shall come to pass.' Now, 'mountain' being metaphorical, you might naturally anticipate that Matthew intended 'fig-tree' to be metaphorical. But if you look back a little, you will find that *Matthew actually imagines that there was a literal fig-tree in question.* So does Mark. He and Matthew turn the metaphor into a literal miracle, as follows.

"In the first place, Jesus comes to a literal fig-tree, seeking literal fruit. He finds none. Consequently, say Mark and Matthew, a curse of barrenness was pronounced on it by Jesus. What followed? The tree was at once 'dried up,' or (according to Mark) 'dried up from the roots.' Now first note that the Hebrew word that means 'barren' means also *'root up', 'cut off,'* or *'cut down.'* Then pass to Luke. He omits the whole of this *miracle* about a fig-tree. But he has a *parable* about a fig-tree. The Lord of a vineyard comes to a barren fig-tree, and gives orders that it shall be *'cut down.'* The vine-dresser intercedes for it that it may be spared for one year more in case it may bear fruit."

I looked and found that the story in Mark and Matthew was as Scaurus had described it. But another detail astonished me. It was a phrase that followed the words, "While they were passing by early in the morning"—*i.e.* the morning after the curse had been pronounced—"they saw the fig-tree dried up from the roots." Instead of writing that they were all amazed at the speed with which the curse had been fulfilled, Mark wrote, "And *Peter, remembering it,* says to him, 'Rabbi, behold, the fig-tree that thou cursedst is withered up'." Trying to put myself in the place of Peter, I asked, "What should I have done when I approached the spot? How could I fail to be on the alert to note the tree that my Master cursed yesterday? How could any of my companions fail? How was it possible that any of us could forget? How could I possibly talk about *'remembering'* it? How, therefore, could a historian suppose it needful to insert that I, or any of us, *'remembered'*?"

Turning to Matthew, I found that he got rid of "remembering," and of "Peter" too, by making the miracle occur instantaneously, thus, "He said unto it [*i.e.* to the tree], 'Let there be no fruit from thee henceforward for ever.' And immediately the fig-tree withered away. And when the disciples saw it, they marvelled, saying, 'How did the fig-tree immediately wither away '?"

Scaurus explained the whole matter as follows: "Look at Ezekiel's saying, 'I the Lord *have dried up the green tree*' and its context. You will find that *'the green tree'* is Tyre. Elsewhere Luke has a proverb about 'the green tree and the dry,' where 'the dry' refers to the destruction of Jerusalem by the Romans. So here, the fig-tree, green but barren, is Jerusalem. Luke has given the parable correctly. The Lord of the vineyard, he says, comes to a fig-tree, i.e. Jerusalem, in the vineyard, that is, in Judah. He does not say that it is green, but we may imagine that. However, it has no fruit.

'Let it be *cut down*' says the Lord. Well, I have shown you that 'Let it be cut down' might mean, in Hebrew, 'Let it be *barren* so that none may eat fruit from it,' or 'Let it be *dried up*,' As a historical fact, the fig-tree was *cut down*, or *dried up*, when Jerusalem was destroyed by Titus. But that was not immediate. It was long after the resurrection. *When Jerusalem was destroyed,* the disciples *remembered*"—this explained my difficulty above mentioned—"that the Lord had pronounced this curse on Jerusalem. I could show you, if space allowed,, that the name 'Peter' (which would be in Hebrew 'Simon') might be confused (in Hebrew) with our Latin phrase 'qui cum eo erant' meaning 'those that were with him,' *i.e.* Christ's, disciples, and also that Mark's phrase 'passing by *early*' may be an error for 'passing along to *inspect, visit*, or *seek* fruit.' Having regard to the fact that Peter died a year or two before the city was destroyed, I am inclined to think that it was 'the disciples,' not 'Peter,' that 'remembered.' But there is no space for details. It must suffice to have shown you how a *parable* of Jesus, about *cutting down* a fig-tree, *'remembered'* by his disciples long afterwards as referring to Jerusalem, has been converted by Mark and Matthew into a portentous miracle about *withering* a fig-tree instantaneously (according to Matthew) or by the following morning (according to Mark)."

This explanation of *"remembering"* seemed exactly to meet my difficulty. I accepted it at once. Subsequently I found that the fourth gospel twice represents the disciples as "remembering" after Christ's resurrection, things that He had said or done before the resurrection, which things, at the time, they had not fully understood. Moreover that gospel declared that, up to the evening before Christ's crucifixion. His words had been "dark sayings" to them, but that the Spirit would "call them back to their minds," or "remind them" of their meaning. This confirmed me in the conclusion that the Withering of the Fig-Tree was a parable, not a history, and that the disciples *"remembered"* it, and were reminded of its meaning by the Holy Spirit, after the Lord had risen from the dead.

Scaurus added a reference to a lecture of Epictetus, which, he said, I must have heard, and which bore on the story of the fig-tree. I had heard it and remembered it well. The subject was, in effect, "The Precocious Philosopher." Epictetus likened him to a precocious fruit-tree. "You have flowered too soon," he said; "The winter will scorch you up, or rather you are already frostbitten. Let me alone! Why do you wish me, before my season"—he meant, blooming before the seasonable preparation—"to be withered away as you are withered yourself?" This, Scaurus said, was perhaps borrowed from Mark. I examined the text of the lecture, and it seemed to me that his conjecture was by no means improbable.

Scaurus proceeded, "I could go through Mark's other miracles in the same way—those I mean that are not acts of healing—and show you that they are all metaphors misunderstood. But I have given too much space to these unimportant matters. At least I consider them unimportant except so far as they show Mark to be historically untrustworthy. Now I must pass to more important things, merely adding—as an instance of this man's curious want of all sense of proportion—that while giving—how often must I repeat this!—a whole column to Herod Antipas's birthday and its consequences, he does not give one line, or one word, to Christ's resurrection—except in predictions made by Christ himself or in statements made by angels. I am not a Christian, nor a half-way Christian. But I have an immense admiration for Christ and an immense curiosity to know the exact facts about his life, death, and subsequent influence on his disciples. To me therefore, simply as a historian—or as a mere man interested in the affairs of men—this absolute silence about that which should have been most fully stated and supported by the evidence of eyewitnesses, is nothing short of provoking. Will you not agree with me, after this, that Mark is the most inadequate of biographers?"

I could scarcely believe my eyes when I read this. "Scaurus," I said, "must for once have made a mistake, or his copy of Mark must have been defective." But my copy confirmed his. It ended with the words, "For they were afraid." This was too much for me. Perhaps I was overwrought with long and close study and with the strain of attempting to grapple with Scaurus's criticisms. I remember to this day—and not with entire self- condemnation, for it was Mark, not Mark's subject, that disappointed me—that in a sudden storm of passion I threw the gospel down and vowed I would never look at it again.

XXIV. — SCAURUS ON CHRIST'S BIRTH

ON the following morning my indignation against Mark began to seem certainly hasty and possibly unjust. True, his book was apparently without beginning or end, disfigured by superfluities and omissions, and extraordinarily disproportioned. But what if he had no time to revise it? What if it was a collection of notes about Christ's mighty works and short sayings, which he was intending to combine with a collection of Christ's doctrine when he died—died perhaps suddenly, perhaps was put to death? I tried to find excuses for his work. Still, I could not deny that, if Scaurus was right as to the story of the fig-tree, the earliest of the evangelists showed a deplorable inability to distinguish the things that preceded Christ's resurrection from the things that followed it. I resolved, however, that this should not deter me from continuing my study of the other gospels. My disappointment with Mark increased my admiration—it was not then more than admiration—for Christ, whom he seemed to me to have failed to represent. "Perhaps," said I, "Matthew and Luke will do more justice to the subject." So I took up their gospels. The resurrection was what I most wanted to read about. But I decided to begin at the beginning.

"In style, proportion, arrangement, and subject-matter," said Scaurus, "Matthew and Luke are much more satisfactory than Mark, although Mark often preserves the earliest and purest form of Christ's short sayings. When I say 'Matthew,' you must understand that I do not know who he is. I am convinced that Matthew the publican, one of Christ's twelve apostles, is not responsible for the work called by his name. Flaccus—whom I more than suspect of Christian proclivities—knows a good deal about these matters. Well, according to Flaccus, 'Matthew' wrote in Hebrew. 'Everyone agrees about it,' he says. An early Hebrew gospel would naturally be attributed to Matthew. He, being a 'publican,' or tax-collector, would necessarily be able to write. Peter and John are said to have been ignorant of letters. There are more styles than one in Matthew—a fact that suggests compilation. Luke, an educated man, and perhaps identical with a 'beloved physician 'mentioned in one of Paul's epistles, certainly compiled his books from various sources; 'Matthew' almost certainly did the same. Later on, I will speak of their versions of Christ's discourses. Now I must confine myself to their accounts of a very important subject—Christ's supernatural birth."

Up to this point I had been reading with little interest, doubting whether it would not be better to pass on to the accounts of the resurrection. As I have explained above, my study of Paul's epistles had not led me to believe that there would be anything miraculous about the birth of Christ. The phrase "supernatural birth," therefore, came on me quite unexpectedly. What followed, riveted my attention: "Mark, as you know, says nothing about Christ's parentage. First he gives, as title, 'The beginning of the gospel of Jesus Christ'—where, by the way, old Hermas has written, in my margin, 'some add, *Son of God*! Then there is a Voice from heaven, at the moment of Christ's baptism, heard (apparently) only by John the Baptist and Jesus, 'Thou art my beloved Son.' A similar Voice occurs later on. Mark represents a blind man as calling Jesus 'son of David,' and his fellow-townsmen say, 'Is not this the carpenter, the son of Mary? 'This might indicate merely that Joseph the carpenter was dead. But 'Son of Mary' might be used in two other ways. The enemies of Jesus might use it to suggest that he was a bastard. The worshippers of Jesus might use it (later on) to show that he was a Son of God, not born of any human father. Matthew has, 'Is not this the carpenter's son?' This, however, Matthew might write not as his own belief, but as that of Christ's fellow-townsmen. Luke, who has 'Is not this Joseph's son? ', gives the whole of the narrative quite differently. I should add that the first Voice from heaven is differently given in some copies of Luke." I examined this at once. My copy had a marginal note, "Some have, *Thou art my Son, this day have I begotten thee.*"

"You see," said Scaurus, "in these early divergences, traces of early differences as to the time and manner in which Jesus became the Son of God. Paul appears to me to have believed that the sonship pre-existed in heaven. 'God,' he says, 'in the fullness of time, sent forth His son, born of a woman, born under the law, that he might redeem those that were under the law.' In Job, 'born of a woman' implies imperfection, or mortality. In Paul, born of a woman' and 'born under the law' imply two self-humiliations undergone by the Son of God. Paul's view is that the Redeemer must needs make himself one with those whom he redeems. Since the Jews were not only 'born of a woman' but also 'born under the law,' the Son of God came down from heaven and placed himself under both these humiliations. Paul, therefore, seems to have regarded the divine birth as taking place in heaven from the beginning, but the human birth as a self-humbling on earth, wherein the Son of God becomes incarnate in the form of the son of Joseph, of the seed of David, after the flesh."

This had been my inference from Paul's epistles, as I have said above. But what followed was quite new to me: "You are aware from Paul's epistles that Christ is regarded by him as preeminently the Seed of Promise, Isaac being merely the type. Well, listen to what Philo, a Jew, somewhat earlier than Paul, declares about the birth of Isaac. Philo says, ' The Lord begot Isaac' Philo describes Sarah as 'becoming pregnant when alone and visited by God.' It was God also, he says, who 'opened the womb of Leah.' Moses, too, 'having received Zipporah, finds her pregnant by no mortal.' All this is, of course, quite distinct from our popular stories of the love affairs of Jupiter. You may see this from Philo's context: 'It is fitting that God should converse, in an opposite manner to that of men, with a nature undefiled, unpolluted, and pure, the genuine Virgin. For whereas the cohabitation of men makes virgins wives (lit. women), on the other hand when God begins to associate with a soul, what was wife before He now makes Virgin again.' I could quote other instances, but these will suffice. Now I ask you to reflect how such language as this would be interpreted in the west, not only by slaves, but even by people of education, unaccustomed to the language of the east, but familiar with our western stories of the births of Hercules, Castor and Pollux, Bacchus and others."

I saw at once that the language would be liable to be taken literally. But on the other hand it seemed to me that no disciple of Paul could accept anything like our western stories. Scaurus had anticipated an objection of this kind in his next words: "You must not suppose, however, that Hebrew literature contains, or that Jewish or

Christian thought would tolerate, such stories as those in Ovid. Nor will you find anything of this kind in Matthew and Luke, to whose narratives we will now pass. Matthew says, rather abruptly, that Joseph, finding Mary, his betrothed but not yet his wife, to be with child, and intending to put her away secretly, received a vision of an angel and a voice bidding him not to fear to take to himself Mary his wife, for she was with child from the Holy Spirit, and 'she will bring forth a child and thou shalt call his name Jesus.' Luke, after a much longer introduction (about which I shall speak presently), says that a vision and a voice came to Mary—he does not mention one to Joseph—bidding her not to fear, and saying 'Thou shalt conceive and bring forth a child, and shalt call his name Jesus.' In theory, it is of course possible that two similar visions might come, one to Mary and another to Joseph, bidding both 'not to fear.' But Matthew adds something that points to an entirely different explanation: 'Now all this hath come to pass that it might be fulfilled which was spoken by the Lord through the prophet, saying, *Behold the virgin shall be with child and shall bring forth a son and they shall call his name Emmanuel*'."

These words I had myself read in Isaiah and had taken as referring to a promise made in the context, namely, that in a short time—two or three years, just time enough for a child to be conceived and to be born and to grow up to the age when it could say "father" and "mother"—the kings of Syria and Samaria would be destroyed. Accordingly Isaiah says that he himself married a wife immediately afterwards and that the prophecy was fulfilled. Having recently read these words more than once, I was prepared to find that Scaurus interpreted them in the same way. He added that the most learned of the Jews themselves did the same, and that the Hebrew does not mention "virgin," but "young woman." "This," said he, "I heard from a learned rabbi, who added, 'The LXX is full of blunders, but we are hoping for a more faithful rendering, from a very learned scholar named Aquila, which will probably appear soon'." Here I may say that this translation has actually appeared—it came out about ten years ago—in quite unreadable Greek, but very faithful to the Hebrew; and it renders the word, not "virgin," but "young woman," as Scaurus had said.

It was this very rendering that caused a coolness between me and Justin of Samaria. It happened, I am sorry to say, shortly before he suffered for the sake of the Saviour, in this present year in which I am writing. I chanced to meet him coming out of the school of Diodorus, in his philosopher's cloak as usual, but hot and flustered, not looking at all like a philosopher. Some people—Jews, to judge by their faces—were jeering and pointing after him in mockery. Justin—furious with them, but also (as I thought) worried and uncomfortable in himself—appealed to me: "I have been contending for the Lord," said he, "against these dogs. They flout and mock me for demonstrating how fraudulently and profanely they have mutilated the Holy Scriptures, cancelling some parts and altering others, when translating them into Greek." Then he instanced this very passage, in which he said the Jews had vilely corrupted the rendering of the Hebrew from "virgin" to "young woman." I would have kept silence; but, as he pressed me to say whether I did not agree with him, I was obliged to reply that I did not; and I added that not only Aquila rendered it thus, but other good scholars, many of them Christians. Upon this, he flung away from me in disgust, without one word of salutation, and I never saw him again.

The fact was, he had committed himself in writing, about ten years before, to this false charge against the Jews, and to many other baseless accusations. There was no way out of it now, but either to retract or to face it out. He was a brave man and knew how to face death. But he was not brave enough to allow himself to be conquered by facts. Samaritan by birth, he had something of the Samaritan—but not of the Good Samaritan—in his hatred of the Jews. Had he loved the truth as much as he hated those whom he called truth's enemies, he would perhaps have gone on to cease from his hate, and would have become no less faithful as a Christian than as a martyr.

Now I must return to Scaurus. "Luke," said he, "was an educated man, and saw at once that this prophecy about 'the virgin' did not apply. So he omitted it. This he had a right to do. It was only an evangelist's opinion, not a statement of anything that had actually occurred. But there remained the tradition of fact, namely, that an angel had appeared and had announced the future birth of a child begotten from the Holy Spirit. Luke regarded this announcement as made to the mother, like the announcements—not the same of course, but similar—made to Sarah, Rebecca, and the mothers of Samson and Samuel. Moreover in Matthew's account—as I judge from Hermas's marginal notes—there are many variations, some of which leave it open to believe that the utterance to Joseph (like that to Abraham before Isaac's birth) referred merely to God's spiritual generating, so that Jesus, though the Son of God according to the spirit, was yet, according to the flesh, the son of David by descent from Joseph, Luke expresses his disagreement from this view by giving various utterances of Mary and the angel at such length that they may be called hymns or poems. And indeed—if judged liberally and not by the pedantical rules of Atticists or over-strict grammarians—they are poems, by no means without beauty.

"Luke adds another narrative in which he makes the birth of John the Baptist serve as a foil (so to speak) to the birth of Christ. John, like Christ, was born as a child of promise, after a vision of an angel. But there the likeness ceases. The vision is to the father, not to the mother. The father disbelieves and is punished by dumbness. Elizabeth, the mother, was not a virgin. She, like the wife of Abraham, was barren up to old age. There is no vision to Elizabeth, and no mention of divine generation. If a Jew, Philo for example, were to say to Luke, 'Your Messiah may have been a son of God and yet son of Joseph (as Isaac was son of Abraham)' Luke might reply, 'Read my book, and you will see that it was not so. John the Baptist might be called son of God after this fashion, but Jesus was born in quite a different manner.'"

After this, Scaurus went on to treat of Christ's pedigrees, as given by Matthew and Luke, showing Christ's descent, the former from Abraham, the latter from Adam. These details I shall not give in full. Scaurus had something of the mind of a lawyer and something of the eagerness of a hound hunting by scent, and, as he said himself, when once on a trail he could not stop. "Matthew," said he, "omits three consecutive kings of Judah in one place and a fourth in another. I pointed this out to my old rabbi above-mentioned, and he laughed and said, 'My own people do that sort of thing. History is not our strong point. We like facts to fit nicely, and this writer of yours has made them fit. Does he not himself almost tell you that he is squaring matters, when he says that there are fourteen generations from Abraham to David, and fourteen from David to the captivity, and fourteen from the captivity to Christ? This is symmetrical, but it is not what your model Thucydides would call history.' My rabbi went on to say, 'A more serious blunder, from our point of view, is that this Christian has included in the ancestry of his Christ a king called Jeconiah about whom one of our prophets, Jeremiah, says, "Write ye this man childless, for no man of his seed shall prosper, sitting upon the throne of David and ruling any more in Judah ".' Then, seeing the two papyri lying side by side on the table before me, he added, 'I see you have another pedigree there, does that make the same blunder?' 'No,' said I, 'the author was named Luke, a physician, an educated man and a great compiler of documents. He gives quite a different pedigree.' 'I am not surprised,' said my rabbi. 'If he was a sensible man, he could hardly do otherwise.'"

So far Scaurus. He did not anticipate what I have lived to experience. Quite recently I heard some Christians use this very mention of Jeconiah in an opposite direction, namely, as a proof that Matthew believed Jesus to have descended from God, but not from Joseph after the flesh. In particular, I have heard a young but rising teacher, Irenaeus by name, argue as follows, "If indeed He had been the son of Joseph, He could not, according to Jeremiah, be either king or heir, for Joseph is shown to be the son of Joachim and Jeconiah as also Matthew sets forth in his pedigree." Then he went on to quote Jeremiah's prophecy that Jeconiah should be childless and have no successor on the throne of David. And his argument was to this effect, "Christ is the royal son of David. Therefore He could not have descended from Jeconiah, Joseph's ancestor. Matthew knew this. Therefore Matthew, though giving Joseph's pedigree, did not mean to imply that Jesus was the son of Joseph." And this seemed to convince those who heard him! I also heard this same Irenaeus, in the same lecture, say, "If He were the son of Joseph, how could He be greater than Solomon.... or greater than David, when He was generated from the same seed, and was a descendant of these men?"

After we had gone out from Irenaeus's lecture, I asked the friend sitting next to me to explain this argument to me; for it seemed to me to prove that a man could not be greater than his ancestors.

"Ah, but you forget," he replied, "*what* ancestors. They were *royal* ancestors. How could the son of a mere carpenter be greater than David or Solomon?" It seemed to me that the sinless son of "a mere carpenter" might be greater in the eyes of God than a whole world of such royal sinners. But I found it hard to convince him that I was even speaking seriously!

To return to Scaurus. He dealt next with the pedigree in Luke. " You might have supposed in these circumstances," said he, "that Luke would drop the pedigree of Joseph altogether, and give only that of Mary. Well, he has not done this. Another course would have been to state clearly that Jesus was not really, but only putatively, the son of

Joseph (being really the son of God) and to add that he gave the pedigree of Joseph, as Matthew gives it, because Joseph was the putative father. Well, he has not quite done this either; but he has done half of it. He has written 'being the son, as was supposed, of Joseph.' But he has also given a pedigree of Joseph differing from that of Matthew in that portion which extends from Joseph to David. What do you think of this?"

I thought that the whole thing was a cobweb and wished Scaurus would pass to something more interesting. But he continued, "My rabbi suggested that Luke had invented a new genealogy. But when I dissented—for I am convinced that neither Luke nor Matthew invented, and that these early writers generally were very simple honest souls—he asked me whether I knew of any instance in the gospels where the name spelt in Greek *Eli* or *Heli* was misunderstood. I replied that there was one instance where Jesus used it to mean *my God*, but the bystanders took it to mean *Elias*, 'Well then,' said the rabbi, 'I should not be surprised if your honest compiler Luke, a learned man perhaps in Greek, but innocent of Hebrew, had got hold of some tradition saying, *Jesus was supposed to be the son of Joseph, being the son of God,* Though in Hebrew there is a difference between the spelling of *El*, God, and the name *Eli*, there is not much difference in Greek. And Luke, having once started on the scent of a new pedigree supposed to connect Jesus with *Heli*, ransacked various Jewish genealogies till he found one containing the name, and adopted it as a substitute for Matthew's.' This was what my rabbi suggested. All I can say is that it seems to me more probable than that Luke invented the genealogy."

Scaurus entered into further details to vindicate Luke's honesty, concluding as follows, "My own belief is that the parents of John and of Jesus were good, pure, simple, noble-minded people, liable to dreams and to the seeing of visions and to the hearing of voices. As to 'dreams,' by the way, look at the earliest account of the Lord's appearing to Solomon 'In Gibeon, the Lord appeared to Solomon *in a dream... Solomon awoke, and behold it was a dream.*' Then look at the later account in Chronicles, *'In that night did God appear unto Solomon.'* No 'dream' and no 'awaking'! *Verbum sapienti!* The facts above alleged—to which I could add—when combined with the influence of prophecy—seem to me to explain everything in Matthew's and Luke's Introductions as being at once morally truthful and historically untrue."

Later on, Scaurus said, "Luke himself in his story of Christ's childhood, does not seem to me to be so consistent as an educated writer would have been if he had been dishonestly inventing. For he represents Mary as saying to her son, 'Behold, thy father and I seek thee sorrowing.' By 'thy father' she means Joseph. But could she have used this language, or felt this sorrow, if she had realised indeed that her son was not one of the many children of the Father of Gods and men, but that he was unique, God incarnate? This and many other points convince me that Luke (in his account of the birth) is not composing fiction, but only compiling, harmonizing, adapting, and moulding into a historical shape, what should have been preserved as poetic legend."

Scaurus then gave one more detail from Mark, "who," said he, "meagre though he is, often records actual history where later accounts disguise it. Mark says that, when Jesus was preaching the gospel, his own family (literally *'those from him'* that is, *'those of his household'*) 'came to lay hands on him; for they said,*He is beside himself,*' Matthew and Luke omit this. But Matthew and Luke agree with Mark when the latter goes on to describe how the mother of Jesus and his brethren come to the place where he is preaching. Not being able to reach him through the crowd, they send word that they desire to speak to him. Jesus does not go out nor stop his preaching. Those who obeyed the gospel, he said, were his mother and his brethren. I have said that Matthew and Luke omit the attempt of Christ's family to stop him from preaching as being out of his mind. Probably variations in the text enabled them honestly to omit it, believing it to be erroneous. And indeed how could they believe otherwise? How could Matthew and Luke believe that Mary would accompany the brethren of Jesus in an attempt to 'lay hands' on him after recording what they have previously recorded about the supernatural birth? Lay hands on her divine Son, the Son of God, engaged in proclaiming the will of his Father in heaven! The story might well seem to them incredible. But it bears the plain stamp of genuine truth."

Scaurus then pointed out the divergence between Matthew and Luke as to the manner in which Jesus came to be born in Bethlehem. This I omit. But in the course of it he showed me how Matthew has been influenced by prophecies applied by the Christian Jews to Christ, as being their Deliverer from Captivity, and their Comforter in time of trouble. "For example," said he, "since *'Egypt'* in Hebrew poetry is often synonymous with *'bondage'* the Christian Jews might naturally praise God in their songs and hymns for fulfilling, through Christ, the prophecy, 'Out of Egypt have I called my son,' *i.e.* Israel, meaning that God had called them, the new Israel, out of *'bondage'* (as Paul often says) into the liberty of the children of God. But Matthew takes this as meaning that, when Christ was a little child, he was literally *'called out of Egypt.'* Hence he is driven to infer that he must have been taken to Egypt. For such a journey he finds a reason by supposing that it was to escape from the sword of Herod. He fits in this story with another prophecy representing Rachel as weeping for her children, and as being consoled by the Lord. Hence Matthew infers a massacre of children by Herod in Bethlehem, corresponding, on a small scale, to the wholesale destruction from which the infant Moses escaped. But such a massacre is not mentioned by any evangelist, or by Josephus, or by any other historian or writer known to me."

I was depressed by this, and eager to pass on to something more satisfactory. So was Scaurus. "I have no desire," he said, "to dwell on these points. I am interested in the biographies of all great teachers, philosophers, and law-givers, as well as conquerors—*so far as they are true.* Untruth gives me no pleasure, but disappointment—unmixed except for the slight pleasure one may find in tracking an error to its hole and killing it.

"With much greater pleasure shall I turn to Matthew's and Luke's accounts of the words and deeds of Christ. Only I will add that, were I a Christian, I should long for a new gospel that would go back to facts, rejecting these additions of Matthew and Luke. Not that I would go back to Mark. By *'facts,'* I do not mean such facts as John the Baptist's diet of locusts and clothing of camel's hair. But surely a genuine worshipper of Christ—I can conceive such a thing; for after all, what is more worthy of worship on earth, next to God Himself, than 'the man that is as righteous as possible,' concerning whom Socrates says that there is 'nothing more like God'?—I say a genuine Christian, if he were also a philosopher, might surely find it possible to state in a few simple words his conviction that, whereas John the son of Zachariah was sent by the Logos, and contained only a portion of the Logos, Jesus the son of Joseph was actually the Logos incarnate. I wholly reject such a notion myself, partly because I am not sure that I believe that there is any divine Logos at all—having, in fact, given up speculating on these matters. But if I were as sure on that point as your Epictetus is, and if I were a Christian to boot, I am not sure that I should have any great difficulty in believing that some one man might exist—might be 'sent into the world,' I suppose, a Christian would say—as different from ordinary possessors of the Logos as steam is from water—after all, steam is water—superior to Numa the Roman, superior to Lycurgus the Spartan, to Solon the Athenian, yes, superior to Moses the Hebrew.

"You will be disposed to smile at my 'Moses,' as an anticlimax. But let me tell you that this Moses was a very great man. He was a genuine maker of a republic. I don't mention your friend's ideal, Diogenes, for I don't regard him as a maker of anything. I do not even mention my own favourite Socrates. He is not for the man in the street. He is a maker of thinkers. I am speaking of makers of men, and contemplating the possibility of a unique Maker, a Creator of an altogether new social condition. Well, then, suppose I believed in the Logos in heaven and the Logos on earth. Your philosophers would tell me to regard it as a divine flame lighting many human torches without self- diminution. Granted. Then I should believe that every man had his share of the Logos; some, a great share; others, a very great one. Why should I not contemplate the possibility of a unique and complete man, not 'sharing' but containing or being—a man that might be or contain the totality, or, as Paul says, the fullness, of the Logos? I see weak points in this torch-analogy except as an illustration of the belief; yet the belief itself does not appear to me against reason. But enough of this rambling! I have discerned of late many signs that I am growing old, and none more patent than this tendency to expatiate on my cast-off Christian explorations begun in the years when I was vigorous. I pass, and with great relief, to some things that are real possessions—I mean some portions of Matthew's and Luke's versions of Christ's discourses."

For my part, it was not with unmixed "relief" that I turned to the next portion of Scaurus's letter. His conclusions about Christ's birth had merely accorded with my inferences from Paul's epistles; but he had shaken my faith in Matthew and Luke as trustworthy historians; and I looked forward with misgivings to his further criticism, which, I feared, might prove destructive. In this depression, I endeavoured to recall the words of Paul to the Corinthians about having a "treasure in earthen vessels." Mark certainly was an "earthen vessel." Matthew appeared likely to be no better, so far as I could judge from his story of Christ's birth and childhood. Luke, trying to reduce these legends to historic shape, did not seem to me to have succeeded, in spite of all his pains and sincerity. While I was unrolling the Corinthian epistle to refresh my memory, the thought occurred to me, "Is it possible that any God should choose such writers to set forth the life and character of Hip Son! How could the All-wise be guilty of such foolishness?" I had hardly uttered the word *"foolishness"* when my eyes fell on the words, "The *foolishness* of God is wiser than the wisdom of men." Then I became more modest. "God's ways," I said, "are not our ways. Perhaps He desires to force us to think and to feel for ourselves." I felt grateful even to Mark because he alone had preserved some of Christ's deep and difficult sayings. And in the end I recurred to the thought that had been of late growing stronger and stronger within me concerning the possible inferiority of Romans and Greeks to Jews in things of the spirit. "Thucydides," I said, "would have surpassed Isaiah in describing exactly the campaign of Sennacherib against Hezekiah. But in describing visions and judgments of the Lord, Isaiah is, perhaps, the man, and Thucydides the babe. I will continue my exploration, with Scaurus as a guide."

XXV. — SCAURUS ON CHRIST'S DISCOURSES

"MATTHEW and Luke," said Scaurus, "go even beyond Mark in the inculcation of a doctrine, beautiful after a fashion, but unjust, and impracticable. Mark says, 'Love thy neighbour as thyself.' Surely, that is as far as reason can let us go. I should say it is farther. But Matthew and Luke say, 'Love your enemies.' Now I can recall one passage where Epictetus says that the Cynic must love the men that thrash him, but I am sure that his general view is this, 'The man that treats me thus behaves like a beast, or like a mere scourge in the hand of Zeus, whose pleasure it is thus to try me. How can I hate a beast? Or how can I hate a scourge?'"

Then, after reminding me how he had declared that Epictetus borrowed from the Christians, he said, "This, I think, is an instance. The Christian really loves the beast-like man because he believes the man to be made in the image of God and degraded by Satan. The Christian really pities him; he is troubled for the man's sake. Christ says 'Pray for him'; and the Christian honestly prays, 'This man is behaving like a beast. God help him!' The Epictetian does not recognise prayer or pity; he recognises his own peace of mind as God's supreme gift. 'This man,' he says, 'is behaving like a beast. But it is no evil to me. I must see that it does not interfere with my peace of mind. I must beware of pitying him.' Elsewhere Epictetus says that when you are reviled you are to make yourself a 'stone,' whereas Christ says, 'Bless them that curse you.' This exceptional sentence, then, in which Epictetus speaks about 'loving one's cudgellers' appears to me a case where our friend, while cutting away the Christian foundation, has tried to keep the Christian superstructure. Perhaps the view of Epictetus (at all events in word and in appearance) is somewhat selfish. But certainly the Christian precept is contrary to justice and common sense. One ought no more to love the wicked than to admire the ugly."

This seemed at first convincing, or, at all events, overpowering. But he went on to connect it with the doctrine of forgiveness, which Matthew and Luke included in the Lord's Prayer. "This doctrine," said Scaurus, "I have mentioned above, as being in Mark, although he does not give the Lord's Prayer. It is, in fact, intended by Christ to be the very basis of his community. Now of course, Silanus, you and I and all reasonable people are agreed that we ought to be patient, and equable, and to condone faults to our equals, and not to lose our temper with our inferiors, if (as Epictetus says) a slave 'brings us vinegar instead of oil.' And a magnanimous man will put up with much greater offences than these, sometimes with injustice or fraud, sometimes even with insults, if he feels that his honour is not touched by them, or that society does not require a prosecution of the offence. But there is all the world of difference between this—which any gentleman would do, philosopher or no philosopher—and the extraordinary dishonesty—for I can call it by no other name—reduced to a system by the Christians, of 'letting people off' in the hope that God may 'let you off.' I do not want to be 'let off' by God. I should prefer to say (as Epictetus says to the tyrant) 'If it seem advisable, punish me.'"

As soon as Scaurus used this argument, I perceived that he confused the remission of penalty with the forgiveness of sin, that power of "bearing the burdens" of others, and of "restoring" others, which, as I have shown above, Paul recognised as a fact and which Paul made me recognise as a fact, though a very mysterious fact. Hence, reasoning backward, I saw that this faculty of discerning the image of God in the most sinful of sinners, and of pitying the sinner, yes, and even of loving him, might belong to God Himself, and to men in so far as they are like God. If so, the existence of this power of loving one's enemies was a reality, just as the power of forgiving was a reality. "Scaurus himself," I said, "has and uses this power. He often sees good in people where most men would fail to see it. He likes those in whom others see nothing to like. I can conceive that a Son of God might not only possess but impart a power of this kind, increased to such a degree that it might be justly called a new power."

"The curious thing," said Scaurus, "about this doctrine of loving and forgiving is this. Although it appears unpractical and paradoxical, yet the 'kingdom' (to use the Christian word) based on this doctrine is, I must confess, not unpractical at all, but on the contrary a very solid and inconvenient fact in a great number of our largest cities and among the poorest and most squalid of the populace. Note the difference between the kingdom of the Christian and that of the Stoic. The Christian missionary cries aloud like a herald, 'Repent ye; the kingdom of God is at hand,' the Cynic says 'I am a king I or—to quote Epictetus exactly—'Which of you, having seen me, does not recognise in me his natural king and master?' The former prays, and teaches his proselytes to pray, looking up to a God in heaven, 'Thy kingdom come'; the latter neither prays nor enjoins prayer of any kind.

"I suppose no Greek or Roman philosopher would apply the title of king to God quite as freely and naturally as Hebrew and Jewish writers do; for when we Romans say 'king,' we think of 'tyrant.' But apart from that (which is only a superficial difference of word) our philosophers have little or none of that expectation which underlies the words 'Thy kingdom come.' The Christians assert (supported by Matthew and Luke) that Christ himself taught them to pray thus. They anticipate a new kingdom—new family, if you prefer the term—where all the world will be brothers and sisters doing the will of the Father. When they pray 'Thy kingdom come,' they mean 'Thy will be done.' Indeed Matthew has inserted 'Thy will be done' in his version of the Lord's Prayer. Perhaps it was a paraphrase, which Luke has rejected because it was not a part of the original. But in any case, 'Thy will be done' is well adapted to make the meaning of 'kingdom' clear in the churches of the west. If a Christian philosopher were to write a gospel, I should not wonder if he were to go still further and drop the word 'kingdom' altogether, because it is calculated to give a false impression to all that are unacquainted with the Hebrew or Jewish method of speech." Scaurus was nearly right here. When I came to study the fourth gospel, I found that Jesus is represented as never using the word except in explanations to Nicodemus and Pilate.

"Now," said Scaurus, "I do not deny that there are advantages in this scheme of a kingdom over the whole world, where the king is not a despot but a beneficent ruler to whom all may feel heartily and permanently loyal. *As compared with Christ*, such Epictetian 'kings' as Socrates, Diogenes, and Zeno, pass before us like solitary champions, fighting, so to speak, each for his own hand. Or we may liken them to torch-bearers, lighting up the darkness for a time but not succeeding in transmitting the torch to a successor. They depart. There is a momentary wake of light. It disappears. Then we have to wait for a new torch bearer, or a new champion; and the fighting, or the torch-waving, has to begin all over again. Take notice of my qualification—'as compared with Christ.' Even thus qualified, perhaps my remarks about Socrates are too strong. For assuredly his light has not gone out. But to tell the truth, resuming my study of these half-forgotten gospels in the light of Paul's epistles, I find myself sometimes admiring rather to excess that visionary letter-writer and practical church-builder. Our philosophers do not consolidate a kingdom. The Christians do. I am impressed by what Paul calls somewhere their 'solid phalanx.' There is something about it that I cannot quite fathom."

I too was impressed by Scaurus's confession that he had somewhat changed his mind about the gospels in consequence of Paul's epistles. It seemed to me to explain some inconsistencies in his letters. Also I noted that Paul's phrase was "the solid phalanx *of your faith*" and that perhaps *"faith"* explained *"phalanx"*.Scaurus now passed to the doctrine of New Birth. "I call it thus," said he, "for brevity. Mark expresses it ambiguously, saying that no man can enter into the kingdom unless he receives it 'as a little child.' Now this might mean 'as he receives a little child.' And this interpretation is rather favoured by the fact that, somewhat earlier, Mark has a doctrine about 'receiving one of such little children.' I suspect some mystical doctrine is concealed in Mark. But Matthew has, 'unless ye turn and become as little children.' There is no mistaking that. Now I say, in the first place, this is impossible; in the second place, it is wrong. First, it is impossible. The Father of heaven, says Horace, may send fair weather to-day and foul tomorrow. But not even He—

—diffingct infectumque reddet
Quod fugiens simul hora vexit.'

You must agree with me. Jupiter cannot cause what has been done to have been not done. In the next place, it is wrong. A full-grown man has no right to divest himself of full-grown faculties. How much better is the doctrine of Epictetus, 'My friend, you have fallen down. Get up. Try again.' This is possible. This is encouraging. But tell the same man, ' Become a little child,' 'Be born again' I He will think you are playing the fool with him."

I wondered why Scaurus did not see that here again he was inconsistent. He had forgotten the admissions he had made in view of Paul's epistles. In the cities of Asia and Greece, some of the vilest among the vile had been told by Paul, "You must become new creatures in Christ," "You must die to sin and rise again to righteousness." They did not "think he was playing the fool." They had (as Scaurus confessed) been morally "born again." Moreover Paul had met his objection as to "full-grown faculties" by saying, "Be ye babes in respect of malice, but in understanding be full-grown men." Still I was sorry that the gospels had expressed this obscurely. Neither of us had as yet read the fourth gospel. That makes the doctrine quite clear by showing that what is needed is not to be "born over again"—for one might be "born over again" ten times worse than one was before—but to be "born *from above*." This was quite different from "causing what has been done to have been not done." It meant "created anew," or "reshaped" so that the Spirit of Christ, within the Christian, dominated the flesh. Both here and elsewhere, Scaurus's criticisms would have been very different, if he had known the fourth gospel.

"The next point to be considered," said Scaurus, "is the laws for the new kingdom. Matthew has grouped together a collection of precepts as a code. Some of these contrast what 'has been said,' or 'has been said to men of old,' with what Christ now says. Apparently Matthew intended this code of laws (uttered, he says, on a 'mountain') to correspond to the code promulgated on Mount Sinai. But Luke (who by the way omits the 'mountain' and makes the scene 'a place on the plain') while giving many of these precepts, scatters them about his gospel specifying various occasions on which several of them were uttered; and he never inserts the contrasting clause above-mentioned. The conclusion I draw is, that Christ promulgated no law at all. Law deals almost exclusively with actions. Christ dealt almost exclusively with motives, as the last of the Ten Commandments does. When Christ inculcates actions, they are often metaphorical or hyperbolical, as when he says, 'If you are struck on one cheek, turn the other to the striker,' 'Let not your right hand know what your left hand does,' 'If a man takes your cloak, give him your coat too,' and, 'If anyone wants to make you go a mile with him, go two miles,'—to which last precept, by the way, Epictetus would say. No."

I think Scaurus was referring to a passage where Epictetus said, "Diogenes, if you seized any possession of his, would sooner give it up to you than follow you on account of it." Scaurus went on to say, "Matthew's habit of grouping sentences makes it difficult to distinguish sayings uttered before the resurrection from those uttered after it. For example, he speaks of a power of 'binding and loosing' given to Peter, in connexion with a mention of the 'church.' On another occasion, a similar power is given to the other disciples, again in connexion with the 'church.' Now this 'binding and loosing' is not mentioned by any other evangelist. What does it mean? And when was this saying uttered?

"My rabbi tells me that 'binding and loosing' is regularly used by the Jews to indicate that a rabbi 'forbids' or 'sanctions' a certain action—for example, the eating of a particular food. Thus in the Acts of the Apostles, the Lord would be said by the Jews to 'loose' the eating of food that was before unclean, saying to Peter, 'Arise, kill and eat.' And I can conceive that a gospel might describe Jesus as saying to Peter, 'I give thee this power of loosing unclean food, that thou and the rest of my disciples may henceforth eat with the Gentiles, and in their houses, asking no questions concerning the food.' But I do not myself believe that Christ used the phrase 'bind and loose 'in this sense. I think he connected it with that strange doctrine of forgiveness of sins on which he laid so much stress, and that it was uttered after the resurrection, when the term 'church' might be more naturally used." Scaurus was so far right in this that I afterwards found in the fourth gospel a doctrine, not indeed about "binding and loosing," but about "imprisoning and loosing" or "arresting and loosing"; and this was connected with "sins," and Christ gave this power to the disciples after the resurrection.

Scaurus continued, "Look at Matthew's words in one of these passages, 'But if he refuse to hear the church, let him be unto thee as the heathen and the publican,' and then, at some interval, 'Where two or three are gathered together in my name, I am there in the midst of them.' Then look at the last words of Matthew's gospel, uttered after the resurrection, 'Behold I am with you always.' Does not the saying,

'I am there in the midst of you when you are gathered together,' come more appropriately from Christ, appearing after the resurrection, than from Christ before the resurrection? I think so. The context indicates a tradition of some utterance made after the resurrection, conveyed through some apostle in a Jewish form, promising Christ's presence to the disciples. Paul assumes such a presence, writing to the Corinthians 'When ye are gathered together, and my spirit, together with the power of the Lord Jesus Christ, to deliver over such a one to Satan.' These last words about 'Satan' I do not profess to comprehend fully but they seem to me to imply the opposite of 'loosing'—some kind of 'binding' or 'remanding to prison.' And it is to take place in the presence of Christ, with Paul's spirit, when the church of Corinth is 'gathered together'."

I thought Scaurus was probably right as to the date of this promise. But I was much more impressed by what he said concerning the tradition, in Luke, *"Eat those things that are served up to you."* This, in Luke, was almost meaningless to me, but it had been full of meaning in Paul's epistle to the Corinthians, where the apostle spoke about meat sold in Gentile markets: "If an unbeliever invites you, and ye desire to accept, *eat everything that is served up to you, asking no questions*"

Scaurus said, "This tradition about *'eating what is served up'* occurs nowhere in the gospels except in Luke's account of the sending of the Seventy, beginning, 'After these things the Lord appointed other seventy.' Now this word *'appoint'* does not in the least necessitate the conclusion that Christ appointed the. Seventy before the resurrection. Look at the *'appointment'* of the thirteenth apostle in the place of Judas. The Acts says 'Lord, appoint him whom thou hast chosen.' Then Matthias is *'appointed,'* The Lord is supposed to *'appoint'* him in answer to the prayer. Concerning this, Luke might say, *'After these things the Lord appointed Matthias.'* If these words had been inserted in the gospel, they would have given the false impression that Jesus, while living, had appointed Matthias. Well, that is just the impression—a false one—that Luke gives as to the *'appointment'* of the Seventy. The fact is that the Seventy (a number often used by the Jews to denote all the nations or languages of the world) represent the missionaries *'appointed' after the Lord's death to go to the cities of the Gentiles to prepare them for the Coming of the Lord from heaven.*These were to go into the houses of Gentiles. Though Jews, they were to eat of Gentile food—*'everything* *that is served up.'* Without this explanation, the tradition has no meaning—or, if any, an unworthy one, 'Do not be fastidious. If you cannot have pleasant food, eat unpleasant food.' This seems to me absurd. But with this explanation, the precept becomes intelligible and necessary."

This convinced me. Moreover Luke's use of "the Lord," for "Jesus "—since "the Lord" would be more likely to be used than "Jesus" after the resurrection—seemed slightly to favour Scaurus's conclusion. He passed next to a tradition of Matthew's about abstinence from marriage "for the sake of the kingdom of heaven." On this he said, "Looking at Paul's advice to the Corinthians about celibacy and marriage, and at the distinction he draws between 'advice,' and 'allowance' and 'command,' and 'not I but the Lord,' I am convinced that Paul spoke on his own responsibility, except as to Christ's insistence on the old tradition in Genesis, 'The two shall be one flesh.' I mean that Christ upheld monogamy against polygamy and against that modified form of polygamy which -arose from the husband's unrestricted, or scarcely restricted, right of divorce. Soon after the resurrection, in the midst of persecutions, when the Christians expected that Christ might speedily return and carry them up to heaven, it was natural that the Corinthians should apply for advice to Paul, and other churches to other apostles.

"My belief is that Christ's words extended to only the first half of Matthew's tradition. The disciples complain, in effect, 'If a man cannot divorce his wife when he dislikes her, it is best not to marry.' To this Christ replies, as I interpret him, 'Not all grasp the mystery of the true marriage contemplated from the beginning (namely, "the two shall become one") but only those to whom it is given.' This seems to me to have been explained in a wrong sense in the words that follow about 'eunuchs.' At all events, Paul twice quotes the words quoted by Christ (about the 'two' becoming 'one') as though they were the basis of his doctrine about marriage and also a type of the mysterious wedlock between Christ and the church. I do not think, however, that any confident conclusion is deducible. Christ elsewhere indicates—when dealing with an imaginary case where a woman has married seven brothers consecutively—that the marriage tie does not extend to the next life. By the Jews, marriage is, and was, regarded as honourable, and almost as a duty. But a Jewish sect called the Essenes, or some of them, practised celibacy; and you know how Epictetus inculcates celibacy on his Cynics of the first class. These facts, and the pressure of hard times, and Paul's example, may not only have favoured abstinence from marriage among Christians but also have favoured some tampering with tradition in order to enjoin celibacy. A letter to Timothy speaks of certain heretics as 'forbidding to marry.' Perhaps the only safe conclusion about Matthew's tradition is that no conclusion can be deduced from it."

Scaurus next discussed the question whether Christ inculcated poverty on his disciples. He denied it. Not that he denied Luke to be more correct verbally in saying "Blessed are *the poor*" than Matthew in "Blessed are the *poor in spirit.*" But he asserted that Christ meant *"poor in spirit."* Similarly (said Scaurus) Christ meant "hungering *after righteousness*," as Matthew says, though Luke was right verbally in omitting "after righteousness." For, according to Scaurus, "Christ hardly ever used such words as 'bread,' 'leaven,' 'water,' 'hunger,' 'thirst,' ' fire,' 'salt,' 'treasure,' and so on, except metaphorically." Then he quoted the following instance out of Mark's version of Christ's instructions to the twelve apostles, where, he said, Mark's metaphors had been misunderstood literally—and consequently altered—by Matthew and Luke.

"Mark," said he, "has, 'that they should take nothing for the journey, *save a staff only*, no bread, no wallet, no money for the purse.' Matthew and Luke have *'no staff.'* Now turn to Genesis, where Jacob thanks God for helping him on his journey, 'I passed over Jordan with *my staff*,' He *means*, 'with *my staff only*.' Philo explains this *'staff'* metaphorically, as 'training,' *i.e.* the instruction or guidance given by God. David says to God, 'Thy rod and thy staff are my help,' or words to that effect—manifest metaphor. My rabbi showed me a Jewish paraphrase of Jacob's words, 'I had neither gold, nor silver, nor herds, *but simply my staff*.' He also told me that this 'staff' was supposed by the Jews to have been given by God to Adam from whom it descended to the patriarchs in succession. This shows that Jews might find no difficulty in Christ's metaphor, 'Go forth with nothing but a staff! *i.e.* the staff of Jacob, the rod and staff of God. But Greeks and Romans would naturally take the word literally as meaning 'walking-stick.' Then they would find a difficulty, asking, 'Why should Jesus say, *No bread, no wallet— only a walking-stick*?' Hence many, writing largely for Gentiles, might alter it into *'no walking-stick.'* This is what Matthew and Luke have done. Similarly they altered Mark's metaphor *'but shod with sandals,' i.e.* with light shoes fit for the 'beautiful feet' of the preachers of the gospel, into *'no boots'* or words to that effect. The error is the same. Jewish metaphor has been in each case taken literally by Matthew and Luke."

Scaurus added a few remarks on Christ as a historical character, "dimly traceable," he said, "in the combined testimony of Mark, Matthew, and Luke"—where I thought he might have added, "and in the epistles of Paul." His main thought was that, in spite of all the defects of these three writers, it was possible to discern in Christ a successor of Moses and Isaiah. "This man," said Scaurus, "may be regarded in two aspects. As a lawgiver, he took as the basis of his republic a re-enactment, in a stronger form, of the two ancient laws that enjoined love of the Father and love of the brethren. As a prophet, he saw a time when all mankind—recognising in one another (man in man and nation in nation) some glimpse of the divine image, and of the beauty of divine holiness—would beat their swords into ploughshares, and go up to the City of peace, righteousness, and truth, to worship the Father of the spirits of all flesh. Isaiah had foreseen this. But this prophet was also possessed with a belief, beyond Isaiah's, in the unity of God and man. He was persuaded that the true Son of man was the Son of God, higher than the heavens. I think also that he trusted—but on what grounds I do not know, unless it was an ingrained prophetic belief, found in all the great prophets, carried to its highest point in this prophet—that, as light follows on darkness, so does joy on sorrow, righteousness on sin, and life on death. A Stoic would say that these things alternate and that all things go round. But this Jewish prophet believed that all things in the end would go up—up to heaven. That is how I read his expectation. Feeling himself to be one with God, he placed no limits, except God's will, to the mighty works that God might do for him in his attempt to fulfil God's purpose of exalting men from darkness to light and from death to life.

"It is in some of these mysterious aspirations," said Scaurus, "that I cannot follow this prophet of the Jews. At times he seems to me to act and speak (certainly Paul speaks thus) as though God had caused mankind to take (if I may say so) one disease in order to get rid of another. I am speaking of moral disease. God seems to Paul to have allowed man to contract the disease of sin in order to rise to a health of righteousness, higher than would have been possible if he had not sinned. On these and other mystical notions this Jewish prophet may perhaps base views of forgiveness, and of love, and of the efficacy of his own death for his disciples, all of which perplex me. Sometimes I reject them entirely. Sometimes I am in doubt." These last words of Scaurus seemed to me to explain many inconsistencies in his letters. But how could I be surprised? Was I consistent myself? Was not my own mind at that instant fluctuating like a very Euripus? I could understand his doubts only too well.

He concluded by contrasting Christ with John the Baptist. "The one point," said Scaurus, "in which these two prophets or reformers agreed, was that the Lord God would intervene for the people, if only the people would return to Him. But in other respects they appear to me to have altogether differed. John the Baptist seems to have desired to bring about a remission of debts in accordance with the Law of Moses, as insisted on by previous prophets. He also desired an equalisation of property. That is what I gather from the gospels themselves, interpreted in the light of the ancient Law of the Jews. Moreover Josephus told me that Herod the tetrarch put John to death on political grounds, because he seemed likely to stir up the people to sedition, nor did he ever mention the influence of Herodias as contributing to the prophet's execution. Of course the story about the dancing and the oath may be true, and yet the oath may have been a mere excuse for getting rid of an inconvenient person. John was not unwilling (as I gather) to resort to the sword of Gideon or the fire of Elijah if the word of the gospel did not suffice to establish the new kingdom.

"Jesus, on the other hand, was absolutely averse to violence. Jesus was penetrated with the belief in the power of 'little ones' and 'babes' and 'sucklings.' How far he anticipated the future in store for himself I cannot say. Sometimes I am inclined to believe that he thought God would intervene at the last moment and deliver him from the jaws of death. Sometimes he seems to have deliberately faced death with the conviction that he would be swallowed up by it for a short time, emerging from it to victory.

"The Baptist certainly expected to be delivered by Jesus from the prison in which he was being kept by Antipas, and to have been disappointed by his friend's inaction. It must have been a very bitter moment for the latter when John sent to reproach him, as good as saying, 'Are you, too, a false Messiah? Will you leave me to perish in prison? Are you really our Deliverer, or must we, the whole nation, turn from you as a laggard, and wait for another?' In my opinion, this was the very greatest temptation to which Jesus was exposed. In that moment—as I judge when I try to guess the eastern metaphor corresponding to western fact—Jews would say that Satan said to Christ 'Worship me, and I will give you the empire of the world,' or 'Take the risk! Throw yourself down from the pinnacle! See whether God will save you!' In plain words, the temptation was, 'Appeal to the God of battles I Rouse the people to arms, first against Antipas, and then against the Romans!' For a perfectly unselfish and noble nature, believing in divine interventions, this must indeed have been a great, a very great temptation."

Scaurus finished this part of his letter by quoting a passage that I had long had in mind, but I had forgotten its context, "Do you remember, Silanus, how the old Egyptian priest says in the Timaeus, 'Solon, Solon, you Greeks are always boys'? Then comes the reason, *'You have not in your souls any ancient belief based on tradition from the days of old.'* Well, we Romans are in the same position as the poor Greeks. So are the Egyptians for the matter of that. For it is not antiquity alone, but *divine* antiquity, that counts. None of us have this divine antiquity of 'tradition from the days of old' going back to such characters as Abraham, Moses, and the prophets. I think we must put up with our inferiority. These things we had better leave to others. We have, as Virgil says, 'arts' of our own, the arts of war and empire. There, we are men, full-grown men. But as compared with Moses, Isaiah, and above all with this Jesus, or Christ, I must frankly confess I sometimes feel myself a 'boy,' and never so much as now. My conclusion is, *I will keep to the things in which I am not a 'boy.'* Do you the same."

XXVI. — SCAURUS ON CHRIST'S RESURRECTION (I)

PASSING next to the subject of Christ's resurrection, "To deal first," said Scaurus, "with Christ's alleged predictions that he would 'rise again,' what strikes me as the strangest point in them is his frequent mention of being *'betrayed.'* For the rest, if Jesus believed himself to be the Messiah or Christ—as I think he did, if not at first, yet soon—or even if he did not believe himself to be the Christ, but thought that he was to reform the nation, I can well understand that he adopted the language of one of their prophets, Hosea by name, who says, 'Come and let us return unto the Lord... he hath smitten, and he will bind us up. After two days will he revive us. On the third day he will raise us up, and we shall live in his sight.' Using such language as this, a later Jewish prophet, such as Christ, might lead his followers up to Jerusalem at the Passover, not knowing whether he should live or die, but convinced that the Lord would work some deliverance for Israel. And the predictions of 'scourging,' and 'smiting,' and 'spitting,' I could also understand, as coming from the prophets. But 'betrayal' is not mentioned by the prophets, and I cannot understand its insertion here."

With this I have dealt above, and with the double sense of the word meaning "deliver over" and "betray." I now found that the evangelists sometimes apply the word to the act of Judas the betrayer (because by his betrayal Christ was "delivered over" to the Jews); and Scaurus regarded it as meaning "betray" here. I could not however believe that Jesus, when predicting His death, used the word in the sense *"betray."*

It seemed to me that He predicted that His end would be like that of the Suffering Servant in Isaiah, namely, that He would be *"delivered over"* as a ransom for the sins of the people by the will of His Father. Long afterwards, I found that, whereas the Greek in Isaiah has *"delivered over for"* the Hebrew has *"make intercession for."* Then I saw, even more clearly than before, the reason why Christ may have often repeated this prediction, if He foresaw that His death would "make intercession" for the people. The evangelists rendered this so that it might be mistaken for "would be betrayed." But Paul made the matter clear.

Scaurus added that the rising again was predicted as about to occur, sometimes "on the third day," as in Hosea, but sometimes "after three days," corresponding to a period of three days and three nights spent by Jonah (according to a strange Hebrew legend) in a whale's belly. And he also said, "Mark and Matthew represent Jesus as saying, concerning what he would do after death, 'I will go before you to *Galilee*' But Luke omits these words. Later on, after the resurrection, Mark and Matthew again mention this prediction; but there Luke has 'remember that which he said to you *while yet in Galilee,*' My rabbi tells me that the words 'to Galilee' might easily be confused with other expressions having quite a different meaning. This seems to me probable, but into these details I cannot now enter. I take it, however, that Luke knew Mark's tradition *'to Galilee'* and rejected it as erroneous. Matthew also says that certain women, meeting Jesus after death, 'took hold of his feet,' and Jesus sent word by them to the disciples to 'depart *into Galilee.*' Here you see *'Galilee'* again. But this tradition is not in any other gospel. Luke makes no mention of any appearance in *Galilee.*"

These discrepancies about "Galilee" might have interested me at any other time; but *"took hold of his feet"*—this was the assertion that amazed me and carried away my thoughts from everything else. I had approached the subject of the Resurrection through Paul, who mentions Christ merely as having "appeared" to several of the apostles and last of all to himself. I had all along assumed that the "appearances" of the Lord to the other apostles had been of the same kind as the appearance to Paul, that is to say, supernatural, but not material nor tangible. Having read what Paul said about the spiritual body and the earthly body, I had supposed that Christ's earthly body remained in the tomb but that His spiritual body rose from the dead, passed out of the tomb—as a spirit might pass, not being confinable by walls or gates or by the cavernous sides of a tomb—and "appeared" to the disciples, now in this place, now in that. That the "spiritual body" meant the *real spiritual "person"*—and not a mere "shade" or breath-like "spirit" of the departed—this (as I have explained above) I had more or less understood. But I had never supposed that the "body" could be touched. And now, quite unexpectedly, Scaurus thrust before me, so to speak, a tradition that some women *"took hold of Christ's feet"* after He had risen from the dead.

"Of course," said Scaurus, "most critics would say at once that the women lied. But in the first place, even if they did lie, that would not explain why Mark and Luke omitted it. For you may be quite sure the evangelists would not believe that the women told a lie; and, if they believed that the women told the truth, why should they not report it? For the fact, if a fact, is a strong proof of resurrection. In the next place, I am convinced that the Christian belief in Christ's resurrection is far too strong to have been originated by lies. I believe it was originated by visions, and that the stories about these visions were exaggerated in various ways, but never dishonest ways. In this particular case, the explanation probably is, that the women saw a vision of Christ in the air and '*would have held* it fast by the feet,' that is, *desired to do so, but could not.* I could give several instances from the LXX where *'would have'* is thus dropped in translation. The belief of the Christians was, that Christ ascended to heaven. The women are perhaps regarded as *desiring to grasp his feet while he was ascending*, but Christ prevents them, sending them away to carry word to his *'brethren'*—for so he calls them—of his resurrection." I had not, at the time, knowledge enough to judge of Scaurus's explanation; but I afterwards found that *"would have"* might be thus dropped, and that the fourth gospel represents a woman as attempting, or desiring, to "touch" Jesus, but as being prevented (by the words "touch me not") because He had *"not yet ascended"*; and Jesus says to her *"Carry word to my brethren."* Scaurus's explanation was confirmed by these facts.

Scaurus continued as follows, "Mark, the earliest of the evangelists, contains no account of the resurrection, except as an announcement made by angels. He says that the women "were afraid" when they heard this announcement; and there he ends. But in my copy of Mark there is an appendix (not in the handwriting of the same scribe that wrote the gospel) which begins, 'Now having arisen on the first day of the week he became visible at first to Mary of Magdala, out of whom he had cast seven devils.' Then it says that Jesus 'was manifested in a different form' to two of his previous companions, when walking in the country. Then it mentions a third and last manifestation to 'the eleven' seated at a meal." I turned at once to my copy of Mark, but there was no such appendix. It ended with the words "for they were afraid."

Scaurus proceeded, "This appendix is not at all in Mark's style, but it is probably very ancient. Luke mentions no appearance of Christ to women. But he describes an appearance to two disciples walking toward a village near Jerusalem; or rather, not to them while walking, for Jesus did not appear to them at first so as to be recognised; he first walked and talked with them and 'opened their minds to understand the Scriptures.' Then, in the village, during the breaking of bread, he was recognised by them, and vanished. As regards 'walking,' I may mention that the ancient Jews describe God as *'walking with Israel,'* and I have read in a Christian letter, *'The Lord journeyed with me,'* meaning 'enlightened me.' So the word may be used metaphorically. These two disciples expressly mention a 'vision of angels' spoken of by the women, who told them that angels had announced that Christ had risen from the dead; but, according to Luke, the two disciples and their companions disbelieved the women's tale. And not a word is said by Luke, then or afterwards, about any appearance of Christ himself to women.

"You can see for yourself, Silanus, under what a disadvantage this Mark-Appendix placed these poor, simple, ignorant, honest Christians, when it called as their first witness to the resurrection a woman that had been formerly a lunatic. I believe they have been already attacked by their Jewish enemies on this ground. If they have not been, I am sure they will be. Luke, a physician and an educated man, chooses his ground much more sensibly. First, he omits all direct mention, in his own narrative, of manifestations to women. Secondly, he says, in effect—not in narrative but in dialogue—'The women *did* see an apparition, but it was only of angels.' Thirdly, 'the *men*, (and men are not liable to the hysterical delusions of women)—the *men*,' he says, 'treated the women's vision as a mere delusion. The men saw Jesus himself.' Possibly Luke was influenced by Paul, who in his list of the witnesses of manifestations makes no mention of women. The Law of Moses does not expressly exclude women's testimony. But Josephus once told me that his countrymen allowed neither women nor slaves to give public testimony. So it is clear that Jewish tradition has interpreted the Law as excluding women, and that Paul, when controverting Jews, would not appeal to the evidence of women, because Jews would not accept it. Perhaps Luke followed in the same path.

"Luke also makes the following attempt to meet the objections of those who might urge that Christ's apparition was not a rising of the actual body from the grave. He represents Christ as saying to the disciples, 'Handle me '—as a proof that he was not a disembodied spirit. Now I do not believe that Luke invented this, although he, the latest of the three evangelists, is alone in recording it. Curiously enough, I have only recently been reading a letter—very wild and extravagant but manifestly genuine—written some four or five years ago by a Christian named Ignatius, which throws light on these very words in Luke. A few months after writing it, the man suffered as a Christian here in Rome, and his letters naturally had a vogue. Flaccus sent me a copy as a curiosity. Well, this letter says that when Christ came to his disciples—Ignatius says *'to those around Peter'* but the meaning is 'to Peter and his companions' that is, 'to Christ's disciples.' as I have explained above—in the flesh, after his resurrection, he said to them, 'Take, handle me, and see that I am not a bodiless daemon.' Then Ignatius adds—and these are the words I want you to mark—'Straightway they*touched* him and believed, having been *mixed with his flesh and blood.*'

"Do you remember my laughing at you as a boy because you translated Diodorus Siculus literally, 'They *touched* one another because of extreme need,' when it ought to have been, 'They *fed* on one another'? I quoted to you, at the time, the saying of Pythagoras, 'Do not *touch* a white cock,' *i.e.* 'do not *feed on* it.' There are many instances of this meaning. Well, the Christians believed that they *fed on* Christ. His *'flesh and blood was mixed' with theirs*—or they were *'mixed'* with his—when they fed on him in their sacred meal. If there were some Greek traditions saying 'they touched him,' meaning 'they *fed* on him,' there would naturally be other traditions about *'touching'* Jesus meaning that they *'handled'* him. The latter would suggest that they touched the wounds in his body inflicted during the crucifixion."

I remembered my boyish mistake, and I saw clearly that Christians would have had much more excuse for making a similar one. Scaurus added, "This also explains Ignatius's curious use of 'take' (as in Mark and Matthew)." At first I could not understand what Scaurus meant; but on looking at Ignatius's Greek, which Scaurus gave me, I perceived that the words were not *"Take hold of me, handle me,"* but *"Take"*, *i.e.* *"Take me,"* or "*Take* my body (as a whole)." Now *"take"* is similarly used by Mark and Matthew in the sentence "*Take*, eat, this is my body," where Mark omits "eat."

"Moreover," continued Scaurus, "Luke goes on to relate that Jesus said to the disciples, 'Have ye anything to eat?' and that they *gave him* some broiled fish, and that he ate in their presence. Christians in Rome have been in the habit—it would take too long to explain why—of using FISH as the emblem of Christ. The sense requires *'he gave,'* not *'they gave.'* I think Luke has confused *'he gave'* with *'they gave'* The confusion, in Greek, might arise from one erroneous letter."

After giving me several instances of such confusion, he said, "I should not be surprised if some later gospel stated the fact more correctly, namely, that *Christ gave* the disciples 'fish'." This I afterwards found to be the case in the fourth gospel.

Scaurus then proceeded, "I think, however, that Luke's error may have arisen in part from another tradition, which he has preserved in the Acts—somewhat like that of the Christian Ignatius which I have quoted above. Ignatius spoke of *'mixing;'* Luke, in the Acts, speaks of *'incorporating'*—I can think of no better word to give the meaning

—saying that Jesus, *'in the act of being incorporated with'* the disciples, bade them not to depart from Jerusalem till they had received the Holy Spirit. Now this word *'incorporate'*—which is used of men brought into a city, hounds into a pack, soldiers into a squadron, and so on—is adapted to represent that close union which is a mark of almost all the Christians, who say with Paul that they are 'one body in Christ' and 'members one of another.' But this compact union of Christians is also represented by their Eucharist, so that Paul says to the Corinthians, in effect, not only, 'Ye are one body,' but also 'Ye are one loaf.' And I rather think that some Christians at the present time, in their Eucharists, pray that, as the grains of wheat scattered in the field are made into one, so the scattered children of God may be gathered into one. I think you must see how easily errors might spring up from metaphors of this kind used in the various churches of the empire, among people varying in language, customs, and traditions, and for the most part illiterate.

"Even in the letter of Ignatius above-mentioned, a scribe has altered the word 'mixed' into 'constrained' in the margin; and I am not surprised. I do not by any means accuse Luke of dishonesty, nor of carelessness. He did his best. But he was probably a physician—a man of science therefore—and liked to have things definitely and scientifically stated. This word above-mentioned, 'being made into one compact body with them,' might easily be supposed to mean 'partaking of salt with them,' that is, 'sharing a meal with them.' That rendering had the advantage of constituting a definite proof of Christ's resurrection with a body that might be called in some sense material, since it (i.e. the body) was capable of eating. Then, of course, Luke would adapt his other accounts of the resurrection to this tradition, which he would naturally regard as one of central importance. But, though honest and pains-taking, Luke appears to me to have altered and corrupted what was perhaps, in some sense, a real—yes, I will admit, in some sense, a real—manifestation (if indeed any visions are real) into a mere non- existent physical sign or proof.

"Luke represents Jesus as feeding on his own body in order to satisfy his unbelieving disciples that he is really among them. I can easily imagine how very different may have been the feelings of those simple enthusiasts, the early Galilaean disciples, when they used these words—never dreaming that they would be reduced to dry, evidential prose—in psalms and hymns and spiritual songs, praising the Lord for allowing them to 'sit at His table,' and to 'eat and drink with Him,' or for making them 'sharers in the sacred food of His body' and 'partners of His board.' It was only, after a generation or more had passed away, outside the atmosphere of Galilee—it was only to a compiler laboriously tracing back the truth through documents—that all these phrases would suggest the thought of Jesus proving his reality by partaking of food that his disciples give to him.

"It may be said, as though it were to Luke's discredit, 'He represents Peter as positively testifying to this eating.' Of course he does. You know how speeches are written, even in the most accurate histories. No historian, as a rule, professes to record a speech of any length exactly. If Luke first inferred that Christ ate with the apostles after his death, he would also naturally go on to infer that Peter, in attesting Christ's resurrection, must necessarily have included some mention of this fact. I cannot blame him. I think he was perfectly honest, though in error." I agreed. But it seemed to me an error much to be regretted.

On one point, however, Scaurus seemed to me to be not quite accurate, when he said of Luke, "He represents Peter as positively testifying to this eating." For Peter's speech was to this effect, "God raised him up on the third day and granted that he should be manifested—not to all the people but to witnesses previously appointed by God, namely us, who ate with him and drank with him—after he had risen from the dead." Scaurus regarded this as meaning that "the eating and drinking" of Christ's disciples took place "after his death." Even if that had been so, it might be that Jesus was merely present (not eating and drinking) when the disciples ate and drank: and something of this kind I afterwards found in the fourth gospel. But I punctuated the words differently, and interpreted them differently, as meaning that the *"manifestation"* (not the "eating") took place *after the resurrection*) and that the manifestation was limited to those who had been Christ's intimate companions, or as the Greeks say, *"sharers of his table," during his life.*

I remembered also an old remark of Scaurus's about our modern Roman use of "convivo," meaning "I *live with*" and how easily it might be taken to mean the ordinary "convivor," meaning "I *feast with.*" Since that, I have found that, in other ways, *"living with"* and *"eating with"* may be easily confused. For these reasons I concluded that the supposition that Jesus ate with the disciples after His resurrection was not justified.

XXVII. — SCAURUS ON CHRIST'S RESURRECTION (II)

"I NOW come," said Scaurus, "to one of the most interesting of all the traditions of the resurrection—the 'rolling away of the stone' from the tomb. As to the alleged facts, all the evangelists agree. But Mark alone has preserved traces of what I take to be the historical fact, namely, that the narrative, as it now stands, has sprung from Christian songs and hymns based on Hebrew scriptures and Jewish traditions. I showed you above how the precept, 'Go forth with the staff alone,' did not mean 'with a walking-stick' but 'with the staff of God,' a metaphor from the story of Jacob in Genesis. Curiously enough, the same story will help us to explain the rolling away of the stone.

"There Jacob rolls away the stone from the well for Rachel in order that her flocks may obtain water. The Jews have many symbolical explanations of this 'rolling of the stone.' One is, that the stone is the evil nature in man. When worshippers go into the synagogue, the stone (they say) is rolled away. When they come out, it is rolled back again. Philo comments fully on the somewhat similar action of Moses helping the daughters of Jethro, taking it in a mystical sense. The scriptures may be regarded as the 'water of life' or 'living water.' The 'stone' prevents the 'water' from issuing to those that thirst for it. You may perhaps remember that Paul says something of the same kind, but using a different metaphor. To this day, he says, a 'veil' lies on the hearts of the Jews when the scriptures are read.

So Luke says—concerning one of Christ's predictions about his resurrection—' it was veiled from them.' Luke also relates that Christ, after the resurrection, conversed with two disciples, but did not make himself visible to them till he had 'interpreted the scriptures' to them. Then, when he broke bread, 'their eyes were opened and they recognised him.' This 'interpreting,' the two disciples call 'opening the scriptures.' The*'opening of the scriptures'* might be called *'taking the veil from the heart,'* or *'rolling away the stone,'* But the last phrase might still better be used for *'rolling away the burden of unbelief.'*"

All this seemed fanciful to me. But as I knew very little about Jewish tradition I waited to see what traces of this poetic language Scaurus could show in the Greek text of Mark. Before passing to that, however, Scaurus showed me, from Isaiah, that "the stone" might be used in two senses, a good and a bad; a good, for believers, as being "the stone that had become the head of the corner"; but a bad, for unbelievers, as "the stone of stumbling and rock of offence." And he said that the stone rolled away by Jacob was called by some Jews the Shechinah or glory of God. According to Matthew, the "stone" at the door of the tomb was "sealed" by the chief priests, the enemies of Christ. There it stood, as an enemy, saying to the disciples, "Your faith is vain. He will come out no more. He is dead." This was *"a stone of stumbling,"* On the other hand Scaurus said he had read an epistle written by Peter, which bids the disciples come to Christ as *"a living stone."*

"Now," said Scaurus, "taking the accounts literally, we must find it impossible to explain how the women, at about six o'clock in the morning, could expect to find men at the tomb ready and willing to roll the stone away for them; or, if guards were on the spot, how the guards could be induced to allow it. And there are also other difficulties, too many to enumerate, in the differences between the evangelists as to the object of the women's visit. But taking the account as originally a poem, we are able to recognise (I think) two or three historic facts found in Mark alone.

"First, take the statement that the women 'said,' or 'said to themselves.' 'Who *will roll* away the stone for us from the door of the tomb?' I am not surprised that someone has altered this into, 'Who *has rolled* away the stone for us?' Improbable though the latter is, it is at all events conceivable. But it is inconceivable that women, going to the guarded door of a prison, should ask, as a literal question, 'Who will open the door for us?' Taken literally, Mark's text implies something almost as absurd as this. But now take it as a prayer to heaven. Then you may illustrate it by the language of the Psalmist, 'Who will rise up for me against the evil-doers? Who will stand up for me against the workers of iniquity?'—followed by 'Unless the Lord had been my help my soul had soon dwelt in silence.' So the Psalmist says, 'Who will bring me into the fenced city?' and then adds, 'Hast not thou cast us off, O God?' You see in all these cases the question is really a prayer, a passionate and almost desperate prayer, implying 'What man will do this for us? No man. No one but God.' So it is in the Law, 'Who will go up to heaven? Who will go down into the deep?' These last words Paul quotes as the utterance of something approaching to despair. So I take the women's words as having been originally a cry to God, 'Who, if not God, will roll away the stone!'

"Secondly, note that Mark says nothing about any guards at the tomb. According to him, no obstacle was to be anticipated by the women, in their attempt to enter the tomb, except the weight of the stone, which was ' exceeding great.' No other evangelist says this. But I have seen traditions describing the stone as so heavy that twenty men could scarcely roll it, or that it required the efforts of the elders and scribes aided by the centurion and his soldiers. In my opinion the omission of the 'greatness' by Matthew and Luke, and the literalising of it by later traditions, arise from a misunderstanding of its poetical and spiritual character. The 'stone' was 'exceeding great' in this sense, that it could not be moved except by the help of God.

"Thirdly, 'the women *looked up* and saw it (*i.e.* the stone) *rolled upward*,' that is, as I take it, to heaven, in a vision.

The word here used for 'look up' may mean 'regain sight,' as though the women were blind to the fact till they had uttered their aspiration (' who will roll it away? ') and then their eyes were opened. Anyhow, it is more than 'looked.' I think it means 'saw in a vision'." I was certainly astonished at this use of "look up," but much more at the *"rolling up"* of thc stone.

"As to Mark's *'rolling up',"* said Scaurus, "I have looked everywhere, trying to find his word used by others in the sense of 'roll away,' or 'roll back.' But in vain. Its use here is all the more remarkable because, when Jacob rolls away the stone for Rachel, the word *'roll away'* is used. You may say, 'This shows that the term is not borrowed from Jacob's story.' I cannot agree with that. The Christian hymn might contrast Jacob, the type of Christ, rolling the stone merely on one side, with Christ, the fulfilment, rolling it right up to heaven. I should add that a marginal note in Mark inserts an ascension of angels with Jesus at this point."

In attempting to do justice to this narrative and to Scaurus's criticisms of it, I felt at a great disadvantage owing to my ignorance of Jewish literature and thought; and at first I was much more disposed to put by the whole story as an inexplicable legend than to accept Scaurus's explanation. But afterwards, looking at Matthew's narrative, I found that Matthew described an "angel" as "rolling away the stone," and as sa)ring to the women, "Fear not." This seemed decidedly to confirm the conclusion that the women saw "a vision of angels" (a phrase used by Luke) in which vision the stone was seen rolled away—or (as Mark says) "rolled upward"—when the angels went up to heaven. But all this—though it confused and wearied me—did not prevent me from believing that the spirit, or spiritual body, of Christ had really risen from the dead, since I had all along supposed that this alone was what was meant by Christ's resurrection, in accordance, as it appeared to me, with Paul's statements. Nothing that Scaurus had said, so far, seemed to me to shake Paul's testimony to the resurrection.

But Scaurus's next remarks dealt with this matter, and greatly shook my faith. "I had almost forgotten," he said, "to speak of Christ's appearance to Paul. It was clearly a mere image of Paul's thought, called up by his conscience—nothing more. I need write no further about it. Flaccus has sent you Luke's Acts of the Apostles. If you are curious, look there, and you will find enough and more than enough. My belief is, that, if Stephen had not seen Christ, Paul would not have seen Christ. That puts the matter epigrammatically, and therefore (to some extent) falsely; for all epigrams are partly false. But it is mainly true. There may have been other Stephens whom Paul persecuted. But Stephen, I think, summed up the effect of all. Read what Paul says to the Romans about the persecuted and their conquest of persecutors:—'Bless them that persecute you'; that is, instead of resorting to the fire of vengeance against one's enemy, use, he says, the refiner's fire of kindness, 'for in doing this thou shalt heap coals of fire on his head'; finally, 'Be not conquered by evil, but conquer evil with good.' Read this. Then reflect that Paul 'persecuted.' Then read the Acts and see how he persecuted Stephen, and how Stephen interceded for his enemies. I take it that Paul is writing from experience—that the intercession of Stephen 'overcame' Paul (*he* would say 'overcame,' *I* should say 'hypnotized' him) and compelled Paul to see what Stephen saw, namely, Jesus raised from the dead and glorified. Read the Acts and see if I am not right."

It had not occurred to me before, while I was reading what Flaccus's letter said incidentally about the inclusion of the Acts of the Apostles in my parcel, that this book would probably give me Luke's account of the conversion of the apostle Paul, which had been so much in my thoughts, in my conjectures, and even in my dreams. Now, therefore, although barely a dozen lines of Scaurus's letter remained to read, I immediately put them aside and took up the Acts. Here I found that I had been wrong in most of my wild anticipations about the circumstances of Paul's conversion; but I had been right in supposing that the conversion took place near Damascus, and that the utterance of Christ would contain the words, "I am Jesus." Moreover the words, "Saul, Saul, why persecutest thou me?" accorded (not indeed exactly but as to their general sense) with my dream about the Christian martyrs—how they looked at me, as though saying, Why didst thou rack me? Why didst thou torture me?; and how they blessed me, and looked up to heaven; and how they made me fear lest I, too, should be compelled to look up and see what they saw.

Now therefore once more I was seized with a kind of fellow-feeling for Paul as he journeyed to Damascus. I began again to imagine his efforts to prevent himself from thinking of Stephen, and from seeing Stephen's face looking up to heaven, and from hearing Stephen's blessing. It seemed to me that I, too, should have rebelled as Paul rebelled at first, striving against my conscience, like the bullock that kicks against the goad. Then I asked, "Should I have done what Paul did afterwards? Should I, too, have been 'overcome' as Paul was, being brought under the yoke?" I thought I might have been.

But was it seemly or right that a free man should be brought under a " yoke"? That was the question I had now to answer. I seemed to have come to the branching of the paths. All depended on the nature of the "yoke." What was it? On the one hand, Paul said it was "the constraining love of Christ." He had made me feel that there was nothing base in it, nothing to be ashamed of. Nay, under Paul's influence, this "yoke" had begun to seem an ensign of the noblest warfare, a sign of royalty, the emblem of service undertaken by God Himself, the yoke of the risen Saviour, the Son of God, enthroned by the Father's side in heaven, and in the hearts of men on earth. But on the other side stood Scaurus, maintaining that all these Jewish stories were dreams—not falsehoods, but self-deceits more dangerous than falsehoods. He had also convinced me that the gospels contained an unexpected multitude of errors and exaggerations and disproportions. This I could not honestly deny. Thus the gospels flung me back—or at least, as interpreted by Scaurus, seemed to fling me back—from the faith to which I was just on the point of attaining through the epistles. In my bewilderment I was no longer able to say clearly and firmly as before, "Nevertheless the moral power of the gospel is attested by facts that Scaurus and Arrian both admit, facts that Epictetus would be only too glad to allege for himself—by myriads of souls converted from vice to virtue. Does not this moral power rest on reality?"

The Christians themselves seemed to attach so much importance to "Christ in the flesh" that I began to attach importance too. The evangelists appeared to say, in effect, "If we cannot prove that Christ in the flesh arose from the dead, then we admit that He has not arisen." So they—or rather my impression about them—led me away to say the same thing. A few days ago, I had neither desired nor expected that Christ should be demonstrated to have risen in the flesh. Now I said, "I fear it cannot be proved that Christ in the flesh, that Christ's tangible body, rose from the dead. Nay, more, I feel that the belief in what might be called a tangible resurrection arose from some such causes as Scaurus has specified. So I must give up all belief."

I ought to have waited. I ought to have asked, "All belief in *what*?" "Belief in *what kind* of resurrection?" Scaurus himself had casually admitted that visions, though not presenting things tangible, might present things real. If so, then the visions of Israel might be real, the visions to Abraham and the patriarchs, to Moses, to the prophets. These might be a series of lessons given to the teachers in the east to be passed on to the learners in the west. Among the latest of these was a vision of "one like unto a Son of man." He was represented as "coming " with the clouds of heaven. That was a noble vision. Yet how much better and nobler would be a vision of the Son of man "coming" into the hearts of men, taking possession of them, reigning in them, establishing a kingdom of God in them! Such a Son of man had been revealed to Paul, "defined" as "the Son of God ", "from the resurrection of the dead." Being both God and man He brought (so Paul said) God and man into one, imparting to all men the sense of divine sonship, the light of righteousness and spiritual life, triumphant over spiritual darkness and death. This is what I ought to have thought of, but did not.

Such an all-present power of divine sonship Paul seemed also to have in view when he likened belief in the risen Saviour to the faith described by Moses in Deuteronomy. The true believer, said Paul, is not the slave of place, saying, "Who shall go up to heaven?" that is, to bring Christ down to us from the right hand of God. Nor does he say, "Who shall go down to the abyss?" that is, to bring Christ up to us from the dead. The word of faith is "very near." It is "in the heart." It says, "Believe *with the heart* that God raised Christ from the dead." Such belief is not from the "eyes" nor from the "understanding"—as if one saw with one's own eyes the door of the grave burst open by an angel, or heard the facts attested in a law court by a number of honest and competent eye-witnesses incapable of being deceived and of deceiving. To say, "I believe it because Marcus or Gaius believed it," is to avow a belief in Marcus or Gaius, not in Christ, unless the avower can go on to say "and because I have felt the risen Saviour within me."

He alone really and truly believes in the resurrection of Christ whose belief is based on personal experience. If he has that, he can contemplate without alarm the divergences of the gospels in their narratives of this spiritual reality. He will understand the meaning of Paul's words, "It pleased God to *reveal His Son in me*"—not "to me," but "*in me.*" For indeed it is a revelation—not a demonstration from the intellect and senses alone—derived from all our faculties when enlightened by God. God draws back the veil from our fearful and faithless hearts and gives us a convincing sense of Christ at His right hand and in ourselves. This "conviction" is derived from no source but the convincing Spirit of the Saviour, coming to us in various ways, and through many instruments, but mostly through disciples whom the Saviour loves, and who have received not only His Spirit but also the power of imparting it to others.

All these things I knew afterwards, but not at the time I am now describing. I had indeed already some faint conjecture of the truth, but not such as I could put into definite words. I was defeated. In the bitterness of defeat I exclaimed, "There is more beyond, but I cannot reach it. I cannot even suggest it. These evangelists give me no help. They take part with Scaurus against me. I am beaten and must surrender." Yet I felt vaguely that I was not fairly beaten. I was like a baffled suitor retiring from a court of justice, crushed by a hostile verdict, victorious in truth and equity, but beaten and mulcted of all his estate on some point of technical law.

In this mood, sullen and sick at heart, weary of evidence and evidential "proofs" that were no proofs, and irritated rather with the evangelists than with Scaurus—who, after all, was doing no more than his duty in pointing out what appeared to him historical errors—I was greatly moved by an appeal to my love of truth with which my old friend concluded his letter. It was to this effect.

"Well, Silanus, now I have really done. I cannot quite understand what induced me to take up so much of my time, paper, and ink—and your time, too, which is worse—and all to kill a dead illusion. Why do I say 'dead' if it was never alive? Perhaps it was once nearly alive even in my sceptical soul. I think I have mentioned before that I, even I, have had moments when the dream of that phantom City of Truth and Justice had attractions for me. Perhaps I fancied it might be possible to receive this Jewish prophet as a great teacher and philosopher—helpful for the morals of private life at all events, even though useless for politics and imperial affairs—apart from the extravagant claims now raised for him by his disciples. But it is gone—this illusion—if it ever existed. The East and the West cannot mix. If they did, their offspring would be a portent. This Christian superstition is a mere creature of feeling, not of reason. I do not say it has done me harm to study it. Else I would not have sent you this letter. It is perhaps a bracing and healthful exercise to remind ourselves now and then that things are not as we could wish them to be, and that we must not 'feign things like unto our prayers.' A truthful man must see things as they are in truth. The City of Dreams has closed its gates against me, and I am shut out. It is warm in there. I am occasionally cold. So be it! Theirs is the fervour of the fancy, the comfortable warmth of the not-true. I must wrap myself in the cloak of truth—a poor uncomfortable thing, perhaps, but (as Epictetus would say) 'my own.' Truth, my dear Silanus, is your own, too—that is to say, truth to your own reason, truth to your own conscience. Never let wishes or aspirations wrest that from you. '*Keep what is your own!*'"

For the time, this appeal was too strong for me. I wrote to Scaurus briefly confessing that the City of Dreams had had attractions for me, as well as for him, but that I had resolved to put the thought away, though I might, perhaps, continue a little longer the study of the Christian books, which I, too, had found very interesting. When I grew calmer, I added a postscript, asking whether it was not possible that "feeling," as well as "reason," might play a certain lawful part in the search after truths about God. My last words were an assurance that, whereas I had been somewhat irregular of late in my attendance at Epictetus's lectures, I should be quite regular in future. This indeed was my intention. As things turned out, however, the next lecture was my last.

XXVIII. — THE LAST LECTURE

AWAKING early next morning, two or three hours before lecture, I spent the time in examining the gospels, and in particular the accounts of Christ's last words. So few they were in Mark and Matthew that I could not anticipate that Luke would omit a single one of them or fail to give them exactly. They were uttered in public and in a loud voice. According to Mark and Matthew, they were a quotation from a Psalm, of which the Jewish words were given similarly by the two evangelists. They added a Greek interpretation. Luke, to my amazement, omitted both the Jewish words and the Greek interpretation. Afterwards, Mark and Matthew said that Jesus, in the moment of expiring, cried out again in a loud voice. On this occasion they gave no words. But there Luke mentioned words. Luke's words, too, were from a Psalm, but quite different in meaning from the words previously given by Mark and Matthew.

Still more astonished was I to find what kind of words the two earliest evangelists wrote down as the last utterance of Christ—" My God, my God, why hast thou forsaken me?" That Christ said this I could hardly believe. Reading further, I found that some of the men on guard exclaimed "This man calls for Elias"—because the Jewish word "Heli" or "Eli," "my God," resembles the Jewish "Elias." I wished that these men might prove true interpreters. Then I found that, although Luke mentions neither "Eli" nor "Elias," he nevertheless mentions "Elios" or "Helios," which in Greek means "sun." This occurred in the passage parallel to Eli or Heli. What Luke said was that there was an "eclipse" or "failing," of "the sun." I thought then (and I think still) that Luke was glad—as a Christian historian might well be without being at all dishonest—to find that Mark's "Eli" had been taken, at all events by some, not to mean "my God." Perhaps some version gave "Elios," or "Helios," "sun." This Luke might gladly accept. Indeed, in the genitive, which is the form used by Luke, the word "Heliou" may mean either "of the sun" or "of Elias."

But, on reflection, I could not find much comfort from Luke's version. For the difl5cult version seemed more likely to be true. And how could there be an "eclipse" of the sun during Passover, when the moon was at the full? Then I looked at the Psalm from which the words were taken, and I noted that although it began with "Why hast thou forsaken me?" it went on to say that God "hath not hid his face from him, but when he cried unto him he heard him." Also the Psalm ended in a strain of triumph, as though this cry "Why hast thou forsaken me?" would end in comfort and strength for all the meek, so that "all the ends of the earth shall remember and turn unto the Lord." Nevertheless this did not satisfy me. And even the help that I afterwards received from Clemens (about whom I shall speak later on) left me, and still to this day leaves me, with a sense that there is a mystery in this utterance beyond my power to fathom, though not beyond my power to believe.

I was still engaged in these meditations when my servant brought me a letter. It was from Arrian, informing me of the death of his father, which would prevent him from returning to Nicopolis. He also requested me to convey various messages to friends to whom he had not been able to bid farewell owing to his sudden departure. In particular he enclosed a note, which he asked me to give to Epictetus. "Add what you like," he said, "you can hardly add too much, about my gratitude to him. I owe him morally more than I can express. Moreover in the official world, where everybody knows that our Master stands well with the Emperor, it is sometimes a sort of recommendation to have attended his lectures. And perhaps it has helped me. At all events I have recently been placed in a position of responsibility and authority by the Governor of Bithynia. I like the work and hope to do it fairly well. Even the mere negative virtue of not taking bribes goes for something, and that at least I can claim. I am not able, and never shall be able, to be a Diogenes, going about the province and healing the souls of men. But I try to do my duty, and I feel an interest in getting at the truth, and judging justly among the poor, so far as my limited time, energy and intelligence permit.

"In the towns, among the artisans and slaves, I have been surprised to find so many of the Christians. You may remember how we talked about this sect more than once. You thought worse of them than I did. But I don't think you had much more basis than the impressions of your childhood, derived from what you heard among your servants and the common people in Rome. I have seen a great deal of them lately and have been impressed by the high average of their morality, industry, and charity to one another.

"You never see a Christian begging. What is more, they set their faces against the exposing of children. I have often thought that our law is very defective in this respect. We will not let a father strangle his infant son, but we let him kill it by cold, starvation, or wild beasts. Every such death is the loss of a possible soldier to the state. It is a great mistake politically, and I am not sure whether it is right morally. When I first came to Nicopolis I used to hear it said that our Epictetus—one of the kindest of men I verily believe—once adopted a baby that was on the point of being exposed by one of his friends, got a nurse for it, and put himself to a lot of trouble. I sometimes wonder why he did not first give his friend the money to find a nurse and food for the baby, and then give him a good sharp reprimand for his inhumanity. For I call it inhuman. But I never heard Epictetus say a word against this practice. The Jews as well as the Christians condemn it. Perhaps the latter, in this point, merely followed the former; but in most points the Christians seem to me superior to the Jews.

"I am proud to call myself a philosopher, and perhaps I should be prouder than Epictetus would like if I could call myself a Roman citizen; but I am free to confess that there are points in which philosophers and Romans could learn something from these despised followers of Christus. *Fas est et a Christiano doceri.* I have been more impressed than I can easily explain to you on paper by the behaviour of this strangely superstitious sect. There is a strenuous fervour in their goodness—I mean in the Christians, I am not now speaking of the Jews—which I don't find in my own attempts at goodness. I am, at best, only a second-class Cynic, devoid of fervour.

"You may say, like an orthodox scholar of Epictetus, 'Let them keep their fervour and leave me calmness.' But these men have both. They can be seasonably fervid and seasonably calm. I have heard many true stories of their behaviour in the last persecution. Go into one of their synagogues and you may hear their priest—or rather prophet, for priests they have none—thundering and lightening as though he held the thunderbolts of Zeus. Order the fellow off for scourging or execution, and he straightway becomes serenity itself. Not Epictetus could be more serene. Indeed, where an Epictetian would 'make himself a stone' under stripes and say, 'They are nothing to me,' a Christian would rejoice to bear them 'for the sake of Christus.' And even Epictetus, I think, could not reach the warmth, the glow, of their affection for each other. I am devoutly thankful that I did not occupy my present offIce under Pliny. It has never been my fate to scourge, rack, torture, or kill, one of these honest, simple, excellent creatures, whose only fault is what Epictetus would call their *'dogma'* or conviction—surely such a 'dogma' as an emperor might almost think it well to encourage among the uneducated classes, in view of its excellent results. Farewell, and be ever my friend."

The third hour had almost arrived and I had to hasten to the lecture-room taking with me the note addressed to Epictetus. All the way, I could think of nothing but the contrast between what Arrian had said about the Christians, and what Mark and Matthew had said about Christ's last words—the servants tranquil, steadfast, rejoicing in persecution; their Master crying "My God, my God, why hast thou forsaken me?" It perplexed me beyond measure.

In this bewilderment, I took my accustomed place beside Glaucus, who greeted me with even more than his usual warmth. He seemed strangely altered. It was no new thing for him to look worn and haggard. But to-day there was a strange wildness in his eyes. Absorbed though I was in my own thoughts, I could not help noticing this as I sat down, just before Epictetus began.

The lecture was of a discursive kind but might be roughly divided into two parts, one adapted for the first class of Cynics, those who aspired to teach; the other for the second class, those who were content to practise. The first class Epictetus cautioned against expecting too much. No man, he said, not even the best of Cynic teachers, could control the will of another. Socrates himself could not persuade his own son. It was rather with the view of satisfying his own nature, than of moving other men's nature, that Socrates taught. Apollo himself, he said, uttered oracles in the same way. I believe he also repeated—what I have recorded before—that Socrates "did not persuade one in a thousand " of those whom he tried to persuade.

I remembered a similar avowal in Isaiah when the prophet declares that his message is "Hear ye indeed, but understand not"; and this, or something like it, was repeated by Jesus and Paul. But Isaiah says, "Lord, how long?" And the reply is that the failure will not be for ever. In the Jewish utterances, there was more pain but also more hope. I preferred them. Nor could I help recalling Paul's reiterated assertions that everywhere the message of the gospel was a "power,"—sometimes indeed for evil, to those that hardened themselves against it, but more often for good—constraining, taking captive, leading in triumph, and destined in the end to make all things subject to the Son of God. Compared with this, our Master's doctrine seemed very cold.

In the next place, Epictetus addressed himself to the larger and lower class of Cynics, those who were beginning, or who aspired only to the passive life. These he exhorted to set their thoughts on what was their own, on their own advantage or profit—of course interpreting profit in a philosophic sense as being virtue, which is its own reward and is the most profitable thing for every man. It was all, in a sense, very true, but again I felt that it was chilling. It seemed to send me down into myself, groping in the cellars of my own nature, instead of helping me to look up to the sun. Most of it was more or less familiar; and there was one saying that I have quoted above, to the effect that the universe is "badly managed if Zeus does not take care of each one of His own citizens in order that they like Him may be divinely happy." Now I knew that Epictetus did not use the word *eudaemon*, or divinely happy, referring to the next life, for he did not believe that a "citizen of Zeus" would continue to exist, except as parts of the four elements, in a future life. He meant "in this life." And if anyone in this life felt unhappy—more particularly, if he "wept"—that was a sign, according to Epictetus, that he was not a "citizen of Zeus." For he declared that Ulysses, if he wept and bewailed his separation from his home and wife—as Homer says he did—"was not good." So it came to this, that no man must weep or lament in earnest for any cause, either for the sins or sorrows of others, or for his own, on pain of forfeiting his franchise in the City of Zeus. I had read in the Hebrew scriptures how Noah, and Lot, and others of the "citizens of God," lived alone amongst multitudes of sinners; but they, and the prophets too, seemed to be afflicted by the sins around them. Also Jesus said in the gospels, "O sinful and perverse generation! How long shall I be with you and bear you!" as though it were a burden to him. And I had come to feel that every good man must in some sense bear the sins and carry the iniquities of his neighbours—especially those of his own household, and his own flesh and blood. So I flinched from these expressions of Epictetus, although I knew that they were quite consistent with his philosophy.

Glaucus, I could clearly see, resented them even more than I did. He was very liable to sudden emotions, and very quick to show them. Just now he seemed unusually agitated. He was writing at a great pace, but not (I thought) notes of the lecture. When Epictetus proceeded to warn us that we must not expect to attain at once this perfection of happiness and peace, but that we must practise our precepts and wait, Glaucus stopped his writing for a moment to scrawl something on a piece of paper. He pushed it toward me, and I read "*Rusticus expectat.*" I remembered that he had replied to me in this phrase when I had given him some advice about "waiting patiently," saying that all would "come right," or words to that effect. I did not now feel that I could say, "All will come right." Perhaps my glance in answer to Glaucus expressed this. But he said nothing, merely continuing his writing, still in great excitement.

Epictetus proceeded to repeat that "pity" must be rejected as a fault. The philosopher may of course love people, but he must love them as Diogenes did. This ideal did not attract me, though he called Diogenes "mild." The Cynic, he said, is not really to weep for the dead, or with those sorrowing for the dead. That is to say, he is not to weep "*from within.*" This was his phrase. Perhaps he meant that, although in the ante-chamber and even in some inner chambers of the soul there may be tearful grief, and sorrow, and bitterness of heart, yet in the inmost chamber of all there must be peace and trust. But he did not say this. He said just what I have set down above. At the words "*not from within*" Glaucus got up and began to collect his papers, as though intending to leave the room. The next moment, however, he sat down and went on writing.

The lecture now turned to the subject of "distress"—which interested me all the more because I had noticed in the morning that Luke had described Christ as being "in distress" when he prayed fervently in the night before the crucifixion. But it seemed to me that Luke and Epictetus were using the same word for two distinct things. Epictetus meant "distress" about things not in our power, and among these things he included the sins of our friends and neighbours. But Luke seemed to mean "distress" about things in Christ's power, because (according to Luke's belief) Christ had a power of bearing the sins of others. If so, Luke did not mean what Epictetus meant, namely, nervous, faithless, and timid worry or terror, but rather an *agon*, or conflict, of the mind, corresponding to the *agon*, or conflict, of the body when one is wrestling with an enemy, as Jacob was said by the Hebrews to have wrestled with a spirit in Penuel.

At this point, after repeating what I had heard him say before, concerning the grace and dexterity with which Socrates "played at ball" in his last moments—the ball being his life and his family—

Epictetus passed on to emphasize the duty of the philosopher to preserve his peace of mind even at the cost of detaching himself from those nearest and dearest to him. Suppose, for example, you are alarmed by portents of evil, you must say to yourself "These portents threaten my body, or my goods, or my reputation, or my children, or my wife; but they do not threaten me" Then he insisted on the necessity of placing "the supreme good" above all ties of kindred. "I have nothing to do," he exclaimed, “with my father, but only with the supreme good." Scarcely waiting for him to finish his sentence, Glaucus rose from his seat, pressed some folded papers into my hand, and left the room.

I think Epictetus saw him go. At all events, he immediately put himself, as it were, in Glaucus's place, as though uttering just such a remonstrance as Glaucus would have liked to utter, "Are you so hard hearted?" To this Epictetus replied in his own person, "Nay, I have been framed by Nature thus. God has given me this coinage." What our Master really meant was, that God has ordained that men should part with everything at the price of duty and virtue. "Duty" or "virtue" is to be the "*coin*" in exchange for which we must be ready to sell everything, even at the risk of disobeying a father. A father may bid his son betray his country that he, the father, may gain ten thousand sesterces. In such a case the son ought to reply—as Epictetus said—"Am I to neglect my supreme good that you may have it [*i.e.* what you consider your supreme good]? Am I to make way for you? What for?" "I am your father," says the father. "Yes, but you are not my supreme good.". "I am your brother," says the brother. "Yes, but you are not my supreme good."

All this (I thought) was very moral in intention, but might it not have been put differently—"Father, I must needs disobey you for your sake as well as mine," "Brother, you are going the way to dishonour yourself as well as me"? Glaucus could not have taken offence at that. However, this occasional austerity was characteristic of our Teacher. Perhaps it was an ingredient in his honesty. He liked to put things sometimes in their very hardest shape, as though to let his pupils see how very cold, reasonable, definite, and solid his philosophy was, how self-interested, how calculating, always looking at profit! Yet, in reality, he had no thought for what the world calls profit. His eyes were fixed on the glory of God. This alone was *his* profit and*his* gain. But unless we were as God-absorbed as he was—and which of us could boast that?—it was almost certain that we should to some degree misunderstand him. Just now, he was in one of these detached—one might almost call them "non-human"—moods.

A few moments ago, I had been sorry that Glaucus went out. But I ceased to regret it when I heard what followed. It was in a contrast between Socrates and the heroes of tragedy, or rather the victims of calamity. We must learn, he said, to exterminate from life the tragic phrases, "Alas!" "Woe is me!" "Me miserable!" We must learn to say with Socrates, on the point of drinking the hemlock, "My dear Crito, if this way is God's will, this way let it be!" and not, "Miserable me! Aged as I am, to what wretchedness have I brought my grey hairs!" Then he asked, "Who says this? Do you suppose it is someone in a mean or ignoble station? Is it not Priam? Is it not Oedipus? Is it not the whole class of kings? What else is tragedy except the passionate words and acts and sufferings of human beings given up to a stupid and adoring wonder at external things—sufferings set forth in metre!"

This seemed to me gratuitously cruel. If ever human being deserved pity, was it not the poor babe Oedipus, predestined even before birth to evil, cast out to die on Mount Cithaeron, but rescued by the cruel kindness of a stranger—to kill his own father, to marry his own mother, to beget children that were his brothers and sisters, and to die, an exile, in self-inflicted blindness, bequeathing his evil fate to guilty sons and a guiltless daughter! But Epictetus would not let Oedipus alone: " It is among the rich, the kings, and the despots, that tragedies find place. No poor man fills a tragic part except as one of the chorus. But the kings begin with prosperity, commanding their subjects (like Oedipus) to fix garlands on their houses in joy and thankfulness to the Gods. Then, about the third or fourth act, comes 'Alas, Cithaeron, why didst thou receive and shelter me?' Poor, servile wretch, where are your crowns now? Where is your royal diadem? Cannot your guards assist you?"

All this was in stage-play, the agony of the king and the scoffing of the philosopher so life-like as to be quite painful—at least to me. Then Epictetus turned to us in his own person: "Well, then, in the act of approaching one of these great people, remember this, that you are going to a tragedian. By '*tragedian*' I do not mean an*actor*, but a *tragic person*, Oedipus himself But perhaps you say to me 'Yes, but such and such a lord or ruler may be called blessed. For he walks with a multitude ' "—of slaves, he meant—" 'around him.' See, then! I too go and place myself in company with that multitude. Do not I also 'walk with a multitude'? But to sum up. Remember that the door is always open. Do not be more cowardly than the children. When they cease to take pleasure in their game, they cry at once 'I will not play any more.' So you, too, as soon as things appear to you to point to that conclusion, say, 'I will not play any more.' And be off. Or, if you stay, don't keep complaining."

This was the end of the lecture, and I felt gladder than ever that Glaucus had gone; for he seemed to me to have been just in the mood to take to heart that last suggestion, "The door is always open." I hastened to his rooms, but he was not there. I found however that he was expected back soon, for he was making preparations for a journey. Leaving word that I should call again in an hour, I determined to use the interval to leave Arrian's note with Epictetus.

The Master was disengaged and gave me a most kindly welcome, asking with manifest interest about Arrian and his prospects, and giving me to understand that he had heard of me, too, from Arrian and others. His countenance always expressed vigour, but on this occasion it had even more than its usual glow. Perhaps he was a little flushed with the exertion of his lecture. Perhaps he was glad to hear that at least one pupil, likely to do good work in the world, was remembering him gratefully in Bithynia. Possibly he thought another such pupil stood before him. I had never seen him close, face to face. Now I felt strongly drawn towards him, but not quite as pupil to master. From the moment of leaving the lecture-room that day, I had been repeating, "Alas, Cithaeron, why didst thou receive and preserve me?" Poor Oedipus! He seemed to sum up the cry of myriads of mortals predestined to misery. And what gospel had my Master for them? Nothing but mockery, "Poor, servile wretches!"

Yet I had felt almost sure, even from the first utterance of the cruel words, that he had not intended to be cruel. Now, as I stood looking down into his face and he up at mine, some kind of subtle fellowship seemed to spring up between us. At least I felt it in myself and thought I saw it in him. And it grew stronger as we conversed. I rapidly recalled the reproach he had just now addressed to himself in his lecture, as coming from one of his pupils, "Are you so hard hearted?" At the moment I had asked "Could it possibly be true?" Now I knew it was not true. Certainly he had been absorbed in God. His God was not the God of Christ. It was a Being of Goodness of some sort, but impersonal, an Alone, not a real Father. Such as it was, however,

Epictetus had been absorbed in it. He motioned to me to be seated, and began to question me about friends of his in Rome.

I was on the point of replying, when the door burst open and Glaucus suddenly rushed in, beside himself with fury. Striding straight up to Epictetus, he began pouring forth a tale of wrongs, treacheries, outrages and malignities, perpetrated on his family in Corinth. He took no notice of my presence, and I doubt whether he was even aware of it, as he burst out into passionate reproaches on our Master for teaching that a son must witness such sufferings in a father or mother, brother or sister, and say, "These evils are no evils to me."

It would serve no useful purpose, nor should I be able, to set down exactly what Glaucus said. Let it suffice that he had only too much reason for burning indignation against certain miscreants in Corinth. He had only that morning received news—which had been kept back from him by treachery—that cruel and powerful enemies had brought ruin, desolation, and disgrace upon his family. His father had been suddenly imprisoned on false charges, his sister had been shamefully humiliated, and his mother had died of a broken heart. "Epictetus," he cried, "do you hear this? Or do you make yourself a stone to me, as you bid us make ourselves stones when men smite us and revile us? Do you still assert that there are no evils except to the evil-minded? By Zeus in heaven, if there is a Zeus and if there is a heaven, I would sooner torture myself like a Sabazian, or be crucified like a Christian, or writhe with Ixion in hell, that I might at least cry out in the hearing of Gods and men, 'These things are evil, they are, they are' than be transported to the side of the throne above with you, looking down on the things that have befallen my father, mother, and sister, and repeating my Epictetian catechism, *I am in perfect bliss and blessedness; these things are no evils to me!* O man, man, are you a hypocrite, or are you indeed a stone?" So saying, without waiting for a word of reply, he rushed from the room.

I went with him. I was not sure—nor am I now—whether Epictetus wished me to stay or to go. But I thought Glaucus needed me most. My heart went out to him when I heard for the first time how shamefully he had been deceived and how cruelly his family had been outraged, and I did not know what he might do in his despair. Besides, if I had stayed, could Epictetus have helped me to help my friend? What would his helping have been? It could have been nothing more—if he had been consistent—than to repeat for the thousandth time that Glaucus's "trouble," and my "trouble" for Glaucus's sake, were mere *dogmas*, or "convictions," and that our "convictions" were wrong and must be given up. Would he have been consistent? Would he have said these things?

To this day I cannot tell. As I followed Glaucus out of the room, while in the act of turning round to close the door, I had my Master at a disadvantage. I saw him, but he did not see me. His head was drooping. The light was gone from his face; the eyes were lacking their usual lustre; the forehead was drawn as if in pain. It was no longer Epictetus the God- absorbed, but Epictetus the God-abandoned. If I had turned to him with a reproach, "Epictetus, you are breaking your own rule. You are sorrowing, sorrowing in earnest," would he have replied, "No, only in appearance, not *from within*"? I do not think he would. He was too honest. To this day I verily believe that for once, at least for that once, our Master broke his own rule and felt real "*trouble.*" And I love him the better for it. That indeed is how I always like to remember his face—as I saw it for the last time, not knowing that it was the last, through the closing door— clouded with real grief, while I was leaving him for ever without farewell, never trusting so little in his teaching, never loving the teacher so much.

XXIX. — SILANUS MEETS CLEMENS

WE walked on together, both of us silent, till we came to Glaucus's rooms. "Farewell," said he. I replied that I would come in to see whether I could help him to make arrangements for his journey. He said nothing, but suffered me to enter. For some time I busied myself with practical matters. So did Glaucus. But every now and then he stopped, and sat down as though dazed. I questioned him about his journey and time of starting. Finding that only two or three hours remained, I urged him to rouse himself. "It will be of no use," he said, "but you are right." Then he exclaimed bitterly, "Am I not obeying Epictetus? Am I not making myself a stone?" "Not quite," said I, "for a stone feels nothing. You are worse than a stone. For you feel much, yet do nothing to help those for whom you feel." "Thank you for that," said he. Then he roused himself. He did injustice to Epictetus, yet I perceived, as never before, how harmful this "stone-doctrine"—if I may so call it—might prove to many people.

I have no space, nor have I the right, to describe more fally Glaucus's private affairs, the courage, affection, and steadfastness with which he bore the burdens of his family and saved his father and sister from their worst extremity. His course was different from Arrian's. Arrian remained outside the fold. Glaucus found peace as I did. And I know that many a suffering soul in Corinth suffered the less because Glaucus, having experienced such a weight of sorrow himself, had learned the secret of lightening it for others. He died young, thirty years ago, but he lived long enough to "fight the good fight."

Our last words together, as he was in the act of departing, I remember well: "What was that you said to me, Silanus, about waiting and having one's strength renewed?" It was from Isaiah. I repeated it. Then I added, "But I spoke the words, I fear, because I had once felt them to be true. I did not quite feel them to be true at the moment when I repeated them to you. Perhaps I was not quite honest, or at least not quite frank." "Then you don't hold to them now?" said he. "God knows," said I. "Sometimes I do, sometimes I do not. For the most part I think I do. I believe that there is good beneath all the evil, if only we could see it, or at least good in the end, good far off." "Then" replied he, "you believe, perhaps, in a good God?" "I hope I may hereafter believe," said I, "nay, I am almost certain I believe in a good God now. But, if I do, it is in a God that is fighting against evil, a God that may perhaps share in our afflictions and in our troubles." "What?" said he, "you, a pupil of Epictetus, believe that God Himself can be troubled! Then of course you believe that a good man may be troubled?" "Indeed I do," said I. "At least I half believe it about God, and wholly about man." "Then you think I have a right to be troubled. You are a heretic." "We are heretics together," said I. "You have a right to be troubled, and I to be troubled with you." "Thank you, and thank the Gods, for that at least!" said he. "Do you know," said I, "that I am certain that Epictetus felt troubled too, for your sake? I saw him when he did not see me, as I was leaving the room; and I could not be mistaken." "Ah!" said Glaucus, drawing in his breath. Then suddenly, as we were clasping hands in our last farewell, he added "Do not think too much about those scrawls!" And before I had time to ask his meaning, he had ridden away.

Returning to my rooms, I put away my lecture-notes and took out the gospels. But I could not read, and longed to be in the fresh air. As I rose from my seat to go out, my first thought was, "I will take no books with me." But Mark happened to be in my hand, the smallest of the gospels, "This," I said, "will be no weight." But it weighed a great deal in the rest of my life, as the reader will soon see.

Before long, unconsciously seeking familiar solitudes, I found myself on the way to the little coppice where some days ago I had seen Hesperus above the departed sun, and Isaiah had shed on me the influence of his promise of peace. "Now," said I sadly to myself, "I have with me a book that calls itself the fulfilment of that promise. But it fulfils nothing for me." As I spoke, and drew the book from the folds of my garment, several pieces of paper fell on the ground. When I picked them up, I found—what I had completely forgotten—Glaucus's "scrawls." I thought they would contain some requests to perform commissions for him in Nicopolis, or to convey messages to friends, and that he might have written these in the lecture-room when he expected to hear news that might call him suddenly away. But they were something quite different. The first that I opened was entitled "A Postscript," written in verse, rallying me upon my advice about "waiting." It showed me how Glaucus, too, had been affected, not only by the lecture that drove him from the room, but also by that saying of Epictetus concerning Zeus ("He would have if he could have") which had disturbed me so much. It was wildly written as Glaucus himself confessed: but I will give it here, because—besides being a rebuke to me, and to all teachers that preach a gospel they do not feel—it shows how Epictetus himself, the perfection of honesty, stirred up in an honest and truthful pupil questionings and doubts that he could not satisfy or silence:

POSTSCRIPT.

If you, my Silanus
(Who think hopelessness heinous,
And lectured me lately
So sweetly, sedately,
Discussing, dilating,
I will not say "prating,"
On the great use of waiting.
You, whom I respected
But never suspected,
Never, no never,

Of being so clever)
Would but do your endeavour
To find more rhymes for "ever,"
Then cease would I never
But rhyme on forever,
Like that horrible lecture,
Our Master's conjecture,
About Zeus, a kind creature,
Whose principal feature
Was his frankly regretting
That the Fates keep upsetting,
By their cruel preventions,
His noble intentions;
'Tis not that I would not,
But I could not, I could not,
So said Zeus in a lecture
Our Master's conjecture,

P.S. Mad, isn't it? But isn't the lecture madder?

P.P.S. I do hope and trust the Master is mad. I must go out.

The larger "scrawl" touched me more nearly because it condemned those who indulge in "self-deceiving" and "call it believing "—a thing that Scaurus dreaded, and taught me to dread; and I was in special dread of it at that time. I have been in doubt whether to give this in full. But I am sure Glaucus, now in peace, would not take it amiss that his wild words of trouble should be recorded if they may help others who have lost peace for a time. So I give it to the reader just as Glaucus gave it to me. Outside was written, in large letters, "RUSTICUS EXPECTAT." Before the verses came a letter in prose as follows:

Rusticus sends greeting to Silas,

I am scrawling you a little poem, Silanus, to distract myself from this accursed lecture, lest Epictetus should make me absolutely sick with his nauseating stuff about the duty of sons not to be troubled by the troubles of their parents. Some days ago you gave me some edifying advice. Here is the answer to it—a little drama.

Dramatis personae only two:—(1) Rusticus, for shortness called Hodge, i.e. Glaucus the Rustic, or perhaps Glaucus persuaded by Silanus, so that Glauco-Silanus is the true Rustic, unless you like to take the rôle entirely for yourself. Anyhow Hodge is a great fool; (2) The River, i.e. Destiny, alias Fate, alias Zeus, alias the God of Epictetus, alias the Whirlpool of the All, alias Nothing in Particular,

The metre is appropriate to the subject matter, i.e. whirlpooly, eddyish, chaotic. There is no villain. The River would he if it could. But it can't—not being able to help being what it is—like Zeus, you know, who said in our lecture-room recently, "I would if I could but I couldn't." Hodge starves or drowns. This should make a tragedy. But he is such a fool that he turns it into a comedy—for the amusement of the Gods. They are intensely amused—which perhaps should turn the thing back again into a tragedy. Comedy or tragedy? Or tragi-comedy? Or burlesque? I give it up. The one thing certain is—Chaos!

RUSTICUS EXPECTAT

Hodge sits by the river
Awaiting, awaiting.
Across he is going
If it will but stop flowing.
But when? There is no knowing.
He dare not try swimming
In those waves full and brimming.
On foot there's no going.
And there's no chance of rowing.
So there he sits blinking
And calling it "thinking"!
God nor man can deliver
His soul from that river.

But Hodge won't believe it,
His soul can't receive it!
Himself he's deceiving.
But he styles it "believing"!
So this simpleton artless
To a THING that is heartless
Prays!—yes, takes to praying
In the hope of its staying
His soul to deliver:
"Good river, kind river,
Across I'd be going
If you would but stop flowing
Stay! pity my moping!
I'm hoping, I'm hoping .
That you won't flow for ever.
Oh, say, will you never
Cease flowing, cease flowing?
Across I'd be going.
Rest! Flow not for ever!"
Says the river, deep river:
"I care not a stiver
For all your long waiting
And praying and prating
And whining and pining
And hoping and moping.
Wait, if you like waiting,
Prate, if you like prating,
Pray, if you like praying.
But think not I'm staying.
Dream not I'm delaying
For a man and his praying.
For his smiling or frowning.
His swimming or drowning.

Hope, if you're for hoping.
Mope, if you're for moping,
I'm not made for consoling
But for rolling and rolling
For ever. Time's stream none can sever.
Then cease your endeavour
Your soul to deliver
By coaxing the river.
Cease shall I never
But flow on for ever
FOR EVER,"

I was walking slowly onward, with the paper in my hand, my eyes bent on the ground. Suddenly a shadow, and a courteous salutation, made me aware that a stranger had met me and was passing by. Surprised and startled, I recovered myself after a moment and turned round to answer his greeting. He, too, turned, a man past threescore as I guessed, but vigorous, erect, with a dignity of carriage that appeared at the first glance. He bowed and passed on. The face reminded me of someone, but I could not think who it was. I turned again to Glaucus's paper. "Don't think too much of those scrawls" had been his last words. But how could I help thinking of them? How many myriads were in the same case! The myriads did not say what Glaucus said. But how many of them felt it! They had not suffered perhaps as he had, but they had suffered enough—crushed, maimed, forsaken!

Yes, FORSAKEN! As I uttered the word aloud, there came back to me both the face of the stranger and the face like his, the face that I had not been able to recall. I had been thinking of old Hermas, whom I had seen as a child of five or six and had never forgotten. Scaurus's letters had recently brought him back to my memory again and again, depicting him just as I remembered him, and suggesting to me all sorts of new questions as to the mystery that lay behind those quiet eyes and that strong gentle look, which even in my childhood had left on me an indelible impression. I had been asking myself. What was the secret of it? Now I knew. Hermas was not "*forsaken*," And this man, the man I had just met, he too looked not "*forsaken*," "Yet I wonder," said I, "what that stranger would think if Hermas were to invite him to worship a Son of God whose last words to the Father were, 'Why hast thou forsaken me?' Epictetus, I know, would declare that the words expressed an absolute collapse of faith. How would old Hermas explain them? And what would Scaurus say if I confessed that I found no God anywhere in heaven or earth to whom my heart was so drawn as this 'forsaken' Christ? What would the Psalmist say if I used his words thus, 'Whom have I in heaven but thee? And there is none on earth that I should desire in comparison with thee, o, thou FORSAKEN SON OF GOD!'"

By this time I had reached the wood. Pacing up and down, full of distracting thoughts, I came on the place where I had had my first vision of peace. There, tired out in body and mind, I threw myself down to rest. Presently, feeling in the folds of my garment for the gospel of Mark, I could not find it. Yet I had felt it when I first drew out Glaucus's paper. There was nothing for it but to retrace my steps as exactly as possible in the hope of hitting on the place where I must have dropped it. But I had not gone a hundred paces before I heard a rustling in the bushes, and the tall stranger reappeared and a second time saluted me.

I returned his salutation. Then we were both silent.

Nothing was in his hand, yet I felt sure that he had found my book, and I waited for him to speak. But a moment's reflection showed me his diffIculty. Was he, a stranger, to ask a Roman knight whether he had dropped one of the religious books of a proscribed superstition? It was for me, if for either, to begin. I liked the stranger's look even better than before and felt that he could be trusted; so I told him of my loss. He at once placed the volume in my hands saying that he had come back to restore it, believing me to be the owner. I thanked him heartily. He replied that I was welcome, then waited a moment or two, as though to allow me to say more if I pleased. I stood silent, wanting to speak, but as it were tongue-bound—not so much afraid as ashamed. At last, I stammered out something about the wood and its distance from Nicopolis. He smiled as though he understood my embarrassment. Then he repeated that I was welcome and moved away.

I had suffered him to go a dozen paces when a voice said within me, "Why do you let him go? Scaurus let Hermas go and repented it. You said that this man did not look 'forsaken.' Why do you let him 'forsake' you? Why do you make yourself 'forsaken'? Perhaps he can help you." I called him back. "Sir," said I, "pardon me one question. Doubtless you looked at this roll to find some clue to its owner?" "I did," he replied. "I am interested," said I, "in this little book". Then I paused. I had grown into the habit of adding— in writing to Flaccus, to Scaurus, and in speaking to myself too—"from a literary point of view," "as a historical investigation," and so on. But now I could not say such things. In the first place, they would not be true. In the second place, I knew instinctively that the man would know that they were not true. Moreover I had a presentiment that he was to be to me what Hermas had almost been to Scaurus. On the other hand, had I the right to ask a perfect stranger whether he had studied a Christian gospel? He read my thoughts. "You desire," he said, "to ask me something more. Am I acquainted with this book? That, I think, is your question? If so, I say, 'Yes'." "There are," said I, very slowly, and almost as if the words were drawn out of me by force, "some few things that I greatly admire and many things that greatly perplex me, in this little book. I think I might understand some of the latter, had I some guidance." "I am but a poor guide," he replied. "Nevertheless, if it is your will, I am quite willing. I have an hour's leisure. Then I must go on my business. Shall we sit down here?"

So we sat down, and I began to question him about Mark and the other gospels. But before I describe our conversation, I must remind my readers that at that time, forty-five years ago, in the second year of Hadrian, the gospels of Mark, Matthew, and Luke, were not regarded as on the same level as scripture, nor as entirely different from other writings composed by pious Christians such as, for example, the epistle of Clemens Romanus to the Corinthians. No doubt, some Christians, even at that date, were disposed to rank the three gospels by themselves as superior to all others past or future; and some of them may have asserted that the number three was, as it were, predicted in the Law. For Moses said, "Out of the mouth of two witnesses" (that might be Mark and Matthew) "or three witnesses" (that would include Luke) "shall every word be established." But if they spoke thus, I do not know of it.

On the contrary, I have heard, that about the very time of our conversation, that is in the second year of Hadrian, there were traditions about Mark (current in the neighbourhood of Ephesus) placing him on a very much lower level than the Hebrew prophets. Some used to accuse him (as I have confessed above that I was perhaps too prone to do) of being disproportioned and lengthy in unimportant detail. An Elder near Ephesus defended Mark. He laid the blame on the necessities of the case, saying that Mark recorded what he had heard from Peter, and that Peter adapted his teachings to the needs of the moment, so that "Mark committed no error" in writing some things as he did. Whether this Elder was right or wrong, his words showed that neither he, defending Mark, nor his opponents, attacking Mark, regarded the evangelist as perfect. Indeed his gospel was generally underrated, being placed far below that of Matthew and Luke, because people did not perceive that Mark often contained the account that was the truest—although expressed obscurely or in such a way as to cause some to stumble.

At that time it would have been thought profane to put Mark or Luke on the same level with Moses, Samuel, David, Solomon, Isaiah and the prophets, to whom "the word of the Lord" is said to have "come." Luke never says, "The word of the Lord came to me," but, in effect, this: "I have traced things back carefully and accurately, and have thought it well to set them forth in chronological order." Matthew, as being an apostle, might have been placed on a different footing. But as he wrote in Hebrew, and his gospel was circulated in Greek, it was not thought that we had the very words of the apostle. Moreover Matthew's words often differed in such a way from Luke's, that 6ven a child could perceive that two writers were describing the same words of the Lord in two different versions, so that both could not be exactly correct. And, very often, Luke's version appeared better than Matthew's.

Yet even in the reign of Trajan there had perhaps been springing up among a few people the belief that the three gospels above-mentioned were not only superior to others then extant but also to others that might hereafter be written. These men thought that Luke had said the last word on the things that were to be believed, correcting what was obscure in Mark and adding what was wanting. Perhaps it was natural that those who thus favoured Luke's gospel should be for a time averse to a fourth gospel. I believe that my friend Justin of Samaria, who suffered as a martyr in this very year in which I am now writing, always retained a prejudice of this kind, favouring the three gospels, and especially Luke. Even though he could not sometimes avoid using some of the traditions that had found a place in the fourth gospel, he disliked to quote it as a gospel, and, as far as I know, never did quote it verbally in his writings.

On the other hand, some of the younger brethren now go into the opposite extreme, and maintain, not only that the fourth gospel is to be accepted, but also that the number four was, as it were, predestined. This seems to me as unreasonable as it would have been to maintain, in Trajan's time, that the gospels must be three because of the "three witnesses" prescribed by Moses on earth, and the three in 'heaven (the Father, the Son, and the Holy Spirit) and the three angels that visited Abraham, and so on. Yet I have actually heard the teacher Irenaeus—the young man about whom I spoke above—asserting that the gospels must needs be four to correspond with the four quarters of the globe, the four elements, the four living creatures in Ezekiel, and other quadruplicities.

However, I thank God that, when I was a young man, no such stumbling- block as this lay between me and my Saviour. Nor was any such belief in the necessity of four gospels entertained by my new friend Clemens—for that was his name, though he was not a Roman but an Athenian. He had long accepted the three gospels as containing the truth about Christ and about His constraining love. Recently, he had accepted the fourth gospel as also containing the same truth. But he neither believed nor expected me to believe that every word in these four writings was so inspired as to convey the unmixed truth. It was in these circumstances and with these preconceptions—or perhaps I should rather say freedom from preconceptions—that Clemens and I began our conversation.

XXX. — SILANUS CONVERSES WITH CLEMENS

I EXPLAINED to Clemens that I had been attending the lectures of Epictetus. He had taught us, I said, to neglect external things, and to value virtue, as being placed by God in our own power and a possession open to all. "This," said I, "has strengthened me—this and the influence of his character—in the determination to lead a life above the mere pleasures of the flesh. But, on the other hand, Epictetus teaches us that we are never to be troubled, not even by the troubles or misdoings of those nearest and dearest to us. We are to say, 'These things are nothing to us'." I then explained to Clemens how this doctrine had repelled me, and how I had been led by an accident to study the letters of Paul, in which I found a very different doctrine.

"Paul," said I, "counts many external things as evil, and especially the errors and transgressions of his converts. These he feels as evils and pains to himself. Yet he always seems hopeful and helpful, full of strength both for himself and for others. I have felt drawn towards him, and, through him, to the prophet Jesus, or Christ, whom he calls Son of God. Paul speaks of himself as led towards this Jesus by a 'constraining love' filling the heart with joy and peace. I have felt something of this, or at least have felt the possibility of it. In my childhood, 'Christus ' was called one of the vilest of the vile, and I believed it. Now I have come to regard him as—I know not what. Just now I said 'prophet.' But Epictetus calls Diogenes God's 'own son.' Christ, in my judgment, stands far above Diogenes and perhaps even above Socrates. When I say 'above Socrates' I do not mean in reason, but in feeling, and in the power to draw men towards kindness and steadfast welldoing. I think I had come almost to the point of calling this Jesus 'God's own son' in a very real sense, as being above all other men, yes, and more—more than I could understand. And then ."

"And then?" said Clemens. I had paused. He waited an instant longer, questioning, or rather interpreting me, with his eyes. "And then," said he, "something threw you back?" "Yes," said I, "something threw me back. And what do you think it was? Paul drew me on. But the author of this little book, he, and Matthew, and Luke—these threw me back. It happened in many ways. I must tell you the last first. A friend, a fellow-student, has just now left me for Corinth, crushed to the earth by the most shameful outrages on his family. I wished to give him some comfort, to point him towards some hope, to give him what you Christians—for surely you are a Christian?" He assented. "Well, what you Christians call 'good tidings' or 'gospel.'

"Now if I could believe Paul, I should have a 'gospel' For then the spirit of Jesus, having risen from the dead, would be travelling about the world everywhere at hand to strengthen His disciples, and to comfort their hearts, and to assure them that all will be well in the end. 'I have prevailed over death'—so His Spirit would say to us—'I will always help the poor and oppressed. I will never forsake them till I have made them sharers in my eternal kingdom.' This it would say to each one of us, 'You, Gaius, or you, Marcus, I will be with you always. I will never forsake you.' But how can I believe these beautiful assurances, when I find Mark declaring (and Matthew agreeing with him) that Christ's last articulate utterance was, 'My God, my God, why hast thou forsaken me?' How can I assure my friend that God never forsakes the oppressed, if He forsook His own Son? And how can I deny that 'forsaking,' when the Son Himself says, *Why hast thou forsaken?*? Epictetus forbade us to admit that we are ever alone. 'God,' said he, 'is always within you.' Is not that the better and nobler doctrine? If the better and nobler doctrine is not true, does it not follow that the truth is bad and ignoble, and that, in real truth, there is no good and noble power controlling the world? Which of the two is right, Epictetus or Christ?"

"Both, I think," said Clemens. He had been listening with attention and manifest sympathy, but without any change in that steadfast look of peace and trust which his face habitually wore. I seemed to read in his countenance at once pain and faith, pain for my burden, faith that he could help me to bear it or to cast it away. Presently he added, "Do not suppose that by answering so briefly and quickly I wished to cut short your objection or to deny the difficulty. Far from it. You have asked, I think, one of the hardest questions, perhaps the very hardest, that could be put to a worshipper of Christ. Often have I thought of it, and I should not like to answer it hastily. You know perhaps that Luke omits these words, and that he mentions, instead, something about the 'sun'?" "Yes," said I, "but that seemed to me only to show that Luke was willing to accept a version that removed the difficulty in the original." "I agree with you," said Clemens, "and, if so, that indicates that the difficulty was recognised before Luke compiled his gospel. Certainly, certainly, those wonderful words were really uttered."

Then he said, "First let me give you an explanation that is not unreasonable and may have some truth in it. You know, I dare say, that the words are from the Psalms?" "Yes," I replied, "but the Psalmist changes his mood. He goes on to say, 'He hath not hid his face from him, but, when he cried unto him, he heard him,' and afterwards, 'All the ends of the earth shall remember and turn unto the Lord '." "You have mentioned," said Clemens, "the very words that seem to some of our brethren to answer your question; for they say that the Lord had in mind the whole of the Psalm when He quoted the first words, and that He meant this, 'I cry unto thee, Father, in the words of scripture *Why hast thou forsaken me?* knowing that thou hast not indeed hidden thy face from me, but thou art hearing me: and all the ends of the earth shall remember my crying and thy hearing and shall turn unto thee'."

"And are not you content with this explanation?" said I. "Not quite," said Clemens. "For, though this may be true, more may be true. I have read in another gospel, later than these three, that the Son did no work on earth and uttered no word, without looking up to the Father in heaven and listening to the Father's voice, which told Him from time to time what to do and to say. And I have heard one of the brethren, a man full of spiritual understanding, and well read in the scriptures, interpret the question as though it were a real question, not an exclamation—the Son questioning the Father as to His will. If that were so, the Son might be conceived as saying, 'For what reason, O Father, hast thou forsaken me for a while and hidden the light of thy countenance from me? Teach me, O Father, in order that I also may be willing to be forsaken, and may desire to be deprived of the light of thy countenance.' And then the Father replies, 'I forsake thee, O my Son, because thou must needs die, and in my presence is the fullness of life. The time hath come for thee to give up thy life, that is, to lose my presence for a brief space, that all men may gain for ever by thy brief loss and be saved from death by thy sacrifice of life.' And after this, said the brother, the Lord cried out a second time. What He said then, Mark and Matthew have not recorded; but they write that He then expired or sent forth His Spirit. The brother I am speaking of believed that the Son, by crying aloud 'Why hast thou forsaken?' prepared Himself to be willingly forsaken, and to be under the darkness of this momentary forsaking just before He gave up His life as a sacrifice for men."

"But you say," said I, "that Epictetus, too, is right." "Certainly," replied Clemens. "Epictetus says that men, God's children, are never 'alone.' And that is true. Indeed I can show you presently a new Christian gospel—the one I mentioned just now—which represents Christ as saying this very thing, 'Ye shall leave me alone—and yet I am not alone, because the Father is with me.' Look at the matter thus. Do we not know that God may be regarded as being in all places at once, so that to speak of Him as 'here and not there,' is no less a metaphor than to speak of His 'hiding His countenance' or 'bearing us in His arms'? God therefore is, as Epictetus often affirms, 'within us.' But is He not also (as I think Epictetus seldom or never affirms) 'outside us '? Is not the Psalmist's metaphor right when he says that God, being outside us, hides His face sometimes from His children? Sometimes He does this because they have sinned, in order that they may seek His face and cease to sin. But does He not also do this when men have not sinned, in order that the righteous may become more righteous and the pure more pure, by longing more than ever for the sight of His countenance and by thirsting anew for His presence?

"I do not quite like to explain the dealings of God with men by anything that frail human creatures do in sport. And yet there is something so sacred (at least I think so) in the relations between parents and young children, that I have been sometimes led to liken God hiding His face from His children to a mother hiding her face from the babe in her arms. She hides it, but only for a moment, only that the child may be the more joyful afterwards. And the arms never let go their embrace." Then, after a pause, he added, "But perhaps you say, 'Do not you Christians believe that Christ was already perfectly righteous, and perfectly pure, and that He already rejoiced to the utmost in the Father's love? Why then should God forsake such a Son? Why should He hide His face from the Holy One, even for a time? 'That, I think, is the question you would like to ask?"

Reading assent in my face, he proceeded, "Some might reply that this question has been answered by the brother above-mentioned, who says, in effect, 'The Son was forsaken by the Father, not that the Son might be made purer, or freed from sin, but that He might know the Father's will and might prepare Himself for His imminent self-sacrifice.' But is that—I will not say a complete answer, for who will venture to say that he knows completely all the purpose of the Father in causing the Son to feel forsaken?—is it even an answer that ought rightly to satisfy us? Will you be patient with me, my friend—for friends we are already (are we not?) in our joint search after truth" "We are indeed," said I, "and I would gladly hear your fullest thoughts on this matter." " Permit me then," said he, "to put another thought before your mind, namely, that the Son of God, being Son of man, may have been forsaken by the Father in order to learn, as a man, the heights and depths of human nature, and to what an abyss of darkness the purest and most faithful saint may sometimes sink; and how even in that abyss, the saint may feel, through faith, that there are still beneath him the arms of God, not indeed supporting him but ready to support him; and that he is—as the prophets say about Israel—' forsaken' yet 'not forsaken.' No height in saintliness is higher than such a faith as this.

"The scriptures tell us," he continued, "that man is to love God with all his heart and with all his soul and with all his power, and with all his understanding. You know this?" I nodded assent. "Consider then how you and I will feel in the moments or hours before our departure, if God has decreed that we shall pass away by a slow and tedious passage, with a gradual weakening of our mental and spiritual powers, a chill of the heart, a deadening of the understanding, and a fading away of the fire of the soul; so that it is no longer possible for us, no longer permitted to us by God Himself, to love Him with all our human powers, because our powers themselves are becoming powerless. May we not then perhaps feel our grasp on the hand of the heavenly Father loosening, and our souls slipping back from the supporting strength of His presence, downward, and still downward, into the darkness of the infinite abyss? Should that hour of trial come upon us, would it not be a very present help in our trouble to know that the Lord, the Saviour, the Eternal Son of God, in the form of man, was troubled likewise?"

Indeed I thought it would—*if* only I "knew" it. I suppose my face must have shown this, for Clemens, without waiting for an answer, continued with a kindling countenance, "And now, dearest brother, be still more patient with me while I put one more thought before you. You have been talking to me about 'trouble' and about your friend's 'trouble ': and you said that it made you, as well as your friend, feel 'forsaken'." I assented. "And you were not ashamed," he continued, "of feeling his 'trouble' to some extent as yours, nor was your friend ashamed of feeling the 'trouble' of his family? Well, then, believe me, the Lord Jesus Christ felt the troubles of all His disciples, friends, followers, yes, all the troubles of all the sinful children of men, as though they were His own troubles. And in feeling 'troubled' along with others I venture to think that He also felt 'forsaken' along with others.

"This is sacred ground. I fear even to kneel, much less to tread upon it. But I think the Lord Jesus meant this also, amidst a multitude of meanings, 'O Father, why hast thou forsaken me, making me feel one with the sinners whom thou forsakest? Is it that thou art breaking for a time the sensible bond between me and thee in order to bind me to them? Is it that I may be made one with them, so as to make them one with me? Wouldst thou make me to be sin that the world may be made to be righteousness? ' "

I remembered the words of Paul, "Him that knew not sin God made sin in our behalf": but I had never understood them before. Nor did I now, but I thought I caught a glimpse of their meaning. It was only a glimpse, and I sat silent, afraid as it were to move lest I should lose it. I seemed in a new world, or rather, in a mixed world, in which the old and the new were contending. I could neither see clearly nor move freely as yet. I felt that light and freedom were around and very near, forcing their way towards me, if I would but reach out my hand to them. But I could not do it.

"I feel," said I, "as though, in time, these hard words might become intelligible, or rather, I should say, beautiful and full of comfort to me. But how different they are from the last words of Socrates!" "Most different," replied Clemens. "Often have I pondered on the difference. I was born in Athens, and I admire the literature and language of my native city. But my mother was of Jewish extraction; and when I worship, and pray, and feel sorrow, and seek consolation, it is in the thought and phrase (though not in the language) of my mother's people. And again and again have I reflected on the strange contrast between the two 'last words,' the Jewish and the Greek. These 'last words' represent last thoughts.

Socrates felt righteous, and happy, and not 'forsaken,' and not at all anxious about his friends nor about his doctrine. The Lord Jesus felt forsaken—doubly forsaken. First He sorrowed for His disciples because He knew that they would forsake Him; and He prayed for them that they might not utterly fail. Afterwards He Himself felt forsaken by the Father.

"Perhaps, so far, Socrates may seem to have the advantage. But what has followed? Socrates is enshrined in books, a companion and dear friend of students for ever, but in books. He is not for the crowd in the street, nor for the ploughman in the field, nor for the poor, the simple, and the unlettered. And though he may fortify some of us against the fear of death, he does not bring the deepest consolation to those who are suffering under a perpetual burden of pains or sorrows. But the Spirit of the Lord Jesus moves among all sorts and conditions of life in all the races of mankind, bringing joy to them that rejoice righteously, and wholesome sorrow to those that sin, and strength to the heavy laden, and comfort to all that mourn, and freedom from all servile fear. Yes, He brings freedom, even to those enemies against whom He makes war, turning their consciences against themselves and making them His willing captives to lead others captive in turn. For indeed this captivity is no captivity but an embracing with the arms of a Father revealed in the Son according to the words of Hosea 'I taught Ephraim to walk. I took him in my arms. He knew not that I healed him. I drew him with cords, with bands of love.' Dear friend, it is my firm conviction that those only can relieve pain of the heart who have felt pain of the heart. Those only can save the forsaken who have felt forsaken. It was in fact because Christ had been forsaken that He was enabled to draw Paul towards Him with the cords of His constraining love."

"But," said I, "if love was the foundation of Christ's doctrine, how is it that Mark hardly ever mentions it? Should I be wrong in saying that Mark never mentions 'love' at all except in one place where Jesus, being asked what is the greatest commandment, quotes from the scripture the ancient commandment to love God and one's neighbour?" "Alas," replied Clemens, "you would be only too right! Yet believe me, Christ's doctrine of doctrines was 'love'—and that, too, not the old commandment, but a new commandment, because Christ introduced into the world a new kind of love, a more powerful love, a constraining love. This He imparted through His blood to His disciples, as is made clear in this new gospel "—and here he took a roll out of his garment—" about which I spoke to you lately, and in a letter, by the same author, which is an appendix to the gospel." And then he read to me, from John's gospel, the words, "A new commandment give I unto you that ye love one another," and " By this shall all men know that ye are my disciples if ye have love one to another"; and he pointed out the newness and greatness of the love, reading the words, "Greater love hath no man than this that a man lay down his life for his friends." Lastly, he added, from the epistle, "God is love."

All this astonished me not a little, and I replied, "Here at last, it seems to me, we have the only true gospel, Paul's gospel, the gospel of the constraining love of Christ. But how came it to pass that, whereas this was the true gospel, such a gospel as Mark's, full of marvels, and portents, and exorcisms, should be the first published to the world—so I have been told on good authority—a gospel that gives a whole column to the dancing of the daughter of Herodias and not one line to 'love one another'?"

"Often and often," replied Clemens, "have I asked myself the same question. I think, though I am not sure, that the reason is this. After the resurrection of the Lord, the apostles went forth to the world to attest the resurrection, and to preach the gospel, saying, in effect, what we find Peter and Paul actually saying in their epistles. But perhaps you have not read Peter's epistle?" I had not. "If you had, you would have found that Peter, like Paul, teaches this commandment of love. Doubtless all the apostles did the same. Consequently, before any gospels were written, all the churches were familiar with this doctrine of love, and with the doctrine of the resurrection. These were the important things. These had been handed down by the apostles to the elders, and by the first generation of the elders to the second. These, therefore, the churches knew. But the unimportant things, as Paul deemed them, the things that concerned Christ in the flesh, and His works of healing and of casting out spirits, and His sayings in the flesh to the disciples, and His discussions and controversies with the Pharisees, and how He was delivered over to Pilate, and how He suffered this and that particular humiliation (such as 'spitting' and 'smiting ') in exact accordance with the scriptures—these things the churches had not committed to memory in any kind of detail. These therefore the earliest evangelist wrote down. Hence it came to pass that he recorded, in large measure, not the most important but the least important things."

"I understand now," said I, "but is it not to be regretted?" "For all reasons but one," replied Clemens, "I think it is to be regretted. I am often sorry that Mark does not give us the Lord's Prayer. I suppose he omitted it, as being known to everybody. But, as it is, we have two versions, and Matthew's is very different from Luke's. A version by Mark might have taught us whether the two versions are from one original, or whether the Lord gave His disciples two prayers at two different times—perhaps one before the resurrection, one after it. Again, Mark does not give us any account of the Lord's resurrection. Some think that a page of the manuscript of his gospel was lost. I, too, once thought so; but now I am disposed to think that he stopped short here, saying, 'Here begins the testimony of the apostles. It is their part to testify to the Lord's resurrection.' In any case it is to be regretted."

"But," said I, "your expression, just now, was, 'to be regretted *for all reasons but one.*' What did you mean by that?" "I meant," said Clemens, "that if all the evangelists had agreed exactly in their reports of all Christ's words, there might have been, amidst many advantages, this one disadvantage, the danger that the letter of the words of the Lord might have become a second law, like the law of Moses, to be interpreted by lawyers. In that case, what the Lord said about divorce, and marriage, and about the manner of life of the evangelists, and their sustenance, and about giving up or retaining one's possessions—all these things might have been collected into a small code. On this code might have been written a large commentary; on that, perhaps, another commentary, still larger. Thus the Church of Christ might have drifted into the legalities of men far away from the one true law of Christ, as it is defined in Paul's epistles 'Bear ye one another's burdens,' and (in the new gospel that I showed you just now) 'Love one another with the love with which I have loved you '."

"Tell me more about that new gospel," said I. "I would gladly do so," said Clemens, "if time permitted. But the shadows are lengthening and the hour we were to spend together is past. Most willingly would I stay with you, but my work calls me away. Tomorrow, however, if you would like to come to my lodging in the house of Justus, at the corner of the market-place, soon after sunset, I shall have returned to Nicopolis, and you shall have a sight of the new gospel and such aid as I can give you in explaining it." So we parted for the time, after I had eagerly accepted his invitation.

XXXI. – CLEMENS ON THE FOURTH GOSPEL

"HOW many things I should have asked him if he could only have stayed!" was my first thought, as Clemens disappeared behind the bushes. My next thought was, "How many new things I already have to think about!" Mechanically I turned homewards and took a few steps on the way to the city. Then I sat down to reflect.

Not many minutes had elapsed before I heard footsteps behind me. Presently, a little on my left, Clemens, without noticing me, passed striding hastily onwards in the direction of Nicopolis. I called to him. He turned and came up to me with an exclamation of joy, "I am thankful to have found you so soon. It has been on my mind that I ought to have at least explained to you why I did not offer to lend you this new gospel." " I would not have lent it to anyone had I been in your place," said I. "Yes," said Clemens, "you would have. Trust me, dear friend, if you believed this gospel, as I do, you would long to lend it to those who did not as yet believe it. But the truth is, I did not wish to lend it to you without a few words of introduction, for which I feared there would be no time. I forgot that the moonlight would suffIce to guide me to the end of my journey. Have you leisure and desire for a little more conversation? Without it, I fear this little book might make you stumble, might even repel you. It is entirely different from the other three gospels both in its style and in its language. Whether reporting Christ's sayings or relating His actions, it almost always differs from the earlier accounts. It is also largely different in the facts related. What say you?"

"I say 'Thanks' with all my heart," replied I; then, as we sat down together, "May I ask first, who wrote it?" "You not only may, but ought," he replied. "It is just the question I expected from you, and, alas! just one of the questions that I cannot answer in the usual way by saying 'A the son of B.' It seems to hint the authorship in dark expressions. At the end of the book it says, 'This is the disciple that beareth witness of these things and he that wrote these things'; but the texts vary and it is not quite clear whether the 'writer' and the 'bearer of witness' are one and the same. Nor does it give any name to the witness or the writer, nor any means of ascertaining the name or names, except that it describes him, a little before, as being 'the disciple whom Jesus loved, who also leaned on His breast,' *i.e.* at the last supper. Also, going back further, I find it written concerning a certain flow of blood and water from the side of the Saviour on the cross, 'He that hath seen hath borne witness and his witness is true, and he knoweth that he saith true, that ye may believe.' Going back further still, and comparing the beginning with the end of the gospel, the reader is led indirectly to the conclusion that the disciple that 'hath borne witness' is John the son of Zebedee.

"This John is often referred to as one of the chief apostles, in the three gospels; but his name is not so much as once mentioned in the fourth. Whenever 'John' occurs in this gospel, it is always John the Baptist, even though 'Baptist' is not added. Not till the last chapter does it become clear that the author is one of the 'sons of Zebedee.'" "But might it not be James?" said I. "It might," replied Clemens, "but for the following fact. The gospel goes on to say, in effect, that, whereas Peter was to be crucified hereafter, this disciple was to live so long that a report sprang up in the church that he would never die. Now this could not apply to James, as he was beheaded quite early in the history of the church. It follows therefore that the author was John, who, though he became a martyr, or witness, for the Saviour, survived his martyrdom and lived to a great age."

This seemed to me an unsatisfactory way of writing history, and not quite fair to readers. For ought they not to be partly guided, in their judgment of the historian's statements, by their knowledge of his character, and of his opportunities for obtaining information?" How much more satisfactory," said I, "is the honest straightforwardness of the Greek writer, 'This is the third year of the history that Thucydides compiled.'" "You are right," replied Clemens, "I cannot deny it. It would have been more satisfactory—if it could have been written with truth—that we should read at the end of this little roll, 'I John, the son of Zebedee, wrote this work.' But what if he did not write it yet had a great part in originating it? What if there was some kind of joint production, revision, or correction, of the work, so that it would not have been true to say, 'I John wrote it'?"

"Is there any evidence of this?" I asked. "A little," he replied. "It is the only one of the four gospels that contains 'we' in its conclusion, thus, 'We know that his testimony is true.' I have also heard a tradition that it was revealed to Andrew that John was to write the gospel and that his fellow-disciples and bishops should revise it. But the following is more important evidence: John the son of Zebedee wrote a book called the Apocalypse—have you seen it?" I said that I had glanced at it. "It was written when he was a very old man, after he had been sent to the mines in Patmos by Domitian, and it is written in, I will not say bad Greek, but a dialect of Greek entirely different from that of any of the gospels or epistles. Now the fourth gospel is written in very fair Greek and in a style as different as possible from that of the Apocalypse. It is quite impossible that John, after writing the Apocalypse when he was eighty or ninety, should then write a gospel in a style so absolutely different."

"Then why," said I, "should the gospel be called by his name?" "I explain it thus," said Clemens. "When John returned from Patmos a very old man, saved from the fiery trial of the sufferings he had undergone—both before his condemnation and also afterwards in the mines—it was natural that every word uttered by him should be treasured up. I have heard it said that he could hardly be carried into the church, and that, when there, he repeated nothing but 'Little children, love one another.' In time, the brethren grew weary of this and remonstrated with him. This seems to have gone on for a long while. For (as I have said above) a report was current about him that he would 'never die' but would wait for the Lord's coming. There is no record (known to me) of any time, place, or manner, of his departure.

I infer that, during the period of his decrepitude, the brethren at Ephesus would collect traditions from him and preach his gospel for him as far as they could. Afterwards, when it was clear that he would die, the gospel would be reduced to writing." "But this," said I, "greatly lowers the value of the gospel as history." "It does," said he, "and its historical value may also be lowered by the fact that, even before the gospel was written, the apostle was a great seer of visions. A seer is not the best kind of historian. He is liable to mix vision with fact. Especially might this be done by a seer that had seen Christ both before and after Christ's death. But still I greatly value this gospel because, like the epistles of Paul, it seems to me to go to the root of the matter. I told you just now that the old man, when he could say nothing else, repeated over and over again the words 'Little children, love one another.' When they asked him to say something else, he said 'that was enough.' And the old man was right. It is 'enough '—if we can receive strength to do it."

"This greatly attracts me," said I. "But, if your explanation is true, a great deal depends upon the apostle's friend, or friends, who wrote down the substance of his traditions and arranged them as a gospel." "A great deal, as you say," replied Clemens. "I have been informed that there was a great teacher near Ephesus, who was called preeminently '*the Elder*'—a name given, I believe, by students to their teacher, even in some of the schools of the Stoics. Has that ever fallen within your experience?" "Something of the kind," I replied. "I remember that Epictetus lately spoke of himself as '*the Elder*.' It seemed to me a modest way of saying 'I whom you call your Teacher, or your Master, but I merely call myself your Elder.' He said we ought to be so superior to the fear of death that his great business ought to be to keep us from dying too soon, not to make us fearless of death. 'This,' he said, 'ought to engage the attention of *the Elder* sitting in this chair.' And then he added, 'This ought to be the great struggle of *your Teacher* and *Trainer*, if indeed you had such a one'—as though Elder and Teacher were much the same thing."

"That," said Clemens, "is exactly to the point. Well then, you must know that John the son of Zebedee is commonly supposed to have written not only a gospel but also an epistle, or perhaps three epistles. The first epistle is quite in the style of the gospel, but it mentions not 'John,' nor even 'I,' at the beginning, but 'we,' 'That which we have heard.' The two other letters, which are very short, begin, '*The Elder* to so-and-so.' These two letters are in style similar to that of the first, but some doubt exists as to their authorship, and I have seen it written, in connexion with them, that the Wisdom of Solomon was not written by Solomon but 'by his friends to do him honour.' Whoever wrote that, seems to have believed that '*the Elder*' mentioned in the two epistles was not John the son of Zebedee but one of his 'friends'."

"What was the Elder's name?" said I. "The two epistles do not mention it," replied Clemens. "But the Elder near Ephesus of whom I spoke above, was called by the same name as the son of Zebedee, 'John'; and the tradition that mentions him (along with another teacher named Aristion) appears to distinguish the two Johns, mentioning both in the same sentence. I ought to add that I mentioned this same Elder above as defending Mark on the ground that he was the mere interpreter of Peter. 'Mark,' said the Elder, 'made it his single object to leave out nothing of the things that he heard and to say nothing that was false therein.' Now you will find—I think I have already mentioned the fact—that this new gospel frequently intervenes, where Luke omits, or alters, anything that is in Mark, so as to explain Mark's obscurity or set forth Mark's tradition in different language. This points to the conclusion that the writer of the fourth gospel agreed with the Elder called John in his verdict on Mark, which is, in effect, 'Not erroneous in fact though imperfect in expression.' My own belief is that this tradition about two persons of the same name is accurate; and that, besides John the Apostle, there was also the Elder John, residing in or near Ephesus about the same time."

"But," I asked, "might not 'John the elder' naturally be taken to mean 'older in age' as opposed to 'John the younger'? And is it not strange that, in view of the great age of John the Apostle, such a distinctive appellation should be given to his namesake?" "Perhaps it would be," replied Clemens. "But it is not given. Have you not noticed that I did not speak of '*John the Elder*' but of '*the Elder, John*'? The two are quite different. The former (at least among Christians) would simply mean 'John the Presbyter or Elder' as distinct from 'John the Deacon,' 'John the Bishop,' and so on. But 'the Elder, John'—a phrase twice repeated in my tradition—may imply that the teacher was known during his life among his pupils as '*the Elder*,' and that, after his death, 'John' was added for the sake of clearness. I believe it was the custom to describe the elders near Ephesus in this indefinite way."

The view here taken by Clemens has been somewhat confirmed of late years by a practice that I have noticed—a bad practice, I think—in the young Irenaeus. In the course of his lectures, when referring to his authority—instead of mentioning an elder by name, Polycarp, Aristion, Papias, John, as the case may be—he used such expressions as "He that is greater than we are," "The divine old man and herald of the truth," "He that is superior to us," and all these, as far as I could gather, about elders in the province of Ephesus. Concerning this indefiniteness I am in the same mind now as I was when I replied to Clemens, "It is very unfortunate."

"It is," said he, "but I believe it is fact. Well then, according to my view, one particular elder of these Johannine elders—I mean the elders in the region of Ephesus collected round the aged apostle, John the son of Zebedee—was so much superior to the rest that he was called preeminently '*the* Elder.' If 'the Elder' preached and wrote for John the Apostle, and if the Elder's name was John, there would be an additional reason why the writer of the gospel would avoid the name John (except in connexion with John the Baptist) throughout the gospel.

"But my conviction is that the aged apostle, besides preferring oral tradition to books (as you will see from the last lines of his work), shrank from putting himself forward as the author by the name of 'John,' and insisted that, if he was to be mentioned at all, it was to be only by the title, 'the disciple whom Jesus loved.' John the Elder may have accepted this condition because he felt it to express a deep truth—namely, that the Lord Jesus is best known through some one whom He has loved.

"You know how carefully the Greeks distinguish 'voice' or 'sound' from 'word.' Well, this new gospel introduces John the Baptist as testifying to Christ and saying that he was a mere voice, 'I am the *voice* of one crying in the wilderness. *Make straight the way of the Lord!'* To the inferior and preparatory witness is given a distinctive name 'John' The superior and perfected witness was also called 'John' after the flesh; but the writer of the gospel preferred that the name after the flesh should be dropped, yes, and even his distinctive personality merged, as it were, in the title, 'the disciple whom Jesus loved.'"

"But you spoke, above, about 'brethren' as perhaps preaching John's gospel for him during his decrepitude. Now you seem to incline to think that only one man wrote it?" "Yes," replied Clemens, "I used ' brethren 'first, to leave the question open. Then I endeavoured to give reasons for thinking it was one brother; and this conclusion is supported by the style. There are some slight differences in this gospel between the words of the Lord and the words of the evangelist, in respect of style. That is natural; indeed, one would expect many more. But, taken as a whole, the gospel does not show many styles, as Luke's does, but only one style—extending to the words of all characters introduced in the book, so that it is sometimes hard to say where a speaker ceases to speak and the evangelist begins to comment."

"But this is surely astonishing," said I, "that the author should have so little regard for the words of the Lord as not to make it absolutely and always clear where they end, and where his own comments, or the words of someone else, begin."

"It is astonishing," said Clemens, "but I am disposed to think that John the Apostle himself may in some cases have left his friends in doubt; and the Elder—or whoever it was that wrote the gospel—may have thought it best to leave the ambiguity as he found it. I pointed out to you above how the differences between the three gospels had this advantage that they forced the reader to think of the spirit rather than the letter of the words of the Lord. But they also had a danger, namely, that men might be puzzling their brains as to the differences of scribes and reporters instead of refreshing their hearts with the Spirit of Christ. Now if the Elder had, so to speak, simply added a fourth parallel column to the three existing parallel columns of the sayings of the Lord, the result might have been to increase that danger.

"You may say that if the Elder felt sure that he had received the exactly correct form of the Lord s words from John the Apostle, he ought to have set them down thus, whatever might be the consequences. But I do not believe that he did feel sure. More probably he knew that it was impossible, from the old man's reminiscences, to restore the words exactly, as uttered by Jesus, and that it was best not to attempt a restoration, but to prefer paraphrase, giving their spiritual essence. Or else, in cases where the three evangelists differed seriously among themselves, the Elder might think it best to substitute an entirely new tradition on the same subject."

"Is it not possible," said I, "that some part of the gospel may have been written at an earlier date? Are there for example any expressions that show the Temple to have been still standing at the time of writing?" "I have looked through the volume, searching for such evidence," replied Clemens, "and can find absolutely nothing except a phrase in a rather obscure and corrupt passage about the existence of a pool, an intermittent pool, near Jerusalem. Now of course a pool is not destroyed even when a neighbouring city is utterly destroyed; and parts of Jerusalem continued to be inhabited, after its capture by Titus, although the walls, and a large part of the city, were razed to the ground. The gospel says, 'There is in Jerusalem a pool... having five porches.' I have not ascertained whether this pool is still used (as the narrative says it was then) for medicinal purposes, and whether the 'porches' still exist. I must also confess my belief that this is one of several narratives in which perhaps allegory may have modified history. But in any case the phrase 'there is a pool' seems to me to afford no basis, worth calling such, for a hypothesis of date. It seems to me of little more importance than if a writer said 'There *is* a mountain called the Mount of Olives' or 'There *is* a brook called Kedron.' I could, if you liked, discuss the passage with you more fully."

"Let me rather ask you," said I, "about a matter that greatly interests me. The words of Christ at the last supper—does John give them as Mark and Matthew do, or as Luke, or as Paul?" "That is a case," said Clemens, "where John does not correct but substitutes. He does not give these words at all. But he inserts a narrative about Christ's washing the feet of the disciples, and a precept that the disciples are to do the same. The 'washing of feet,' as I could show you if time allowed, is connected with sacrifice, in Leviticus. As to the partaking of the bread and wine, he says expressly that the Saviour gave some of it to Judas—meaning (I think) to show that there was no efficacy for good in the food, apart from faith and love."

"And what," I asked, "as to the words about 'forsaking' uttered on the cross, where Luke again differs from Mark and Matthew?" "Here," replied Clemens, "I do not feel sure whether John introduces a new saying altogether, or gives the substance of the old saying in Mark. Certainly he does not agree with Luke. And let me add that I have examined a great number of passages where words of Mark, being obscure or difficult, are altered or omitted by Luke, and I find that in almost every case John intervenes to support Mark—only expressing Mark's meaning more clearly and spiritually.

"Concerning the 'forsaking,' I suggested to you before that it is a metaphor. If so, the reality may be expressed by other metaphors in the scriptures, such as 'I have lost the light of thy countenance,' 'I am cast away from the joy of thy presence,' 'My soul is deprived of the fountain of thy light.' The Psalms say, 'God, my God... my soul is athirst for thee,' and again, 'My soul thirsteth for God... when shall I come and appear before God?' The 'thirst' implies absence from God. It will be satisfied by 'coming' to God. Well, John represents Jesus as saying, 'I thirst,' in accomplishment of 'the scriptures.' Then (as I take it) the soldiers misunderstand this thirst as meaning simply literal thirst. They offer Christ vinegar. Christ 'took it,' says the gospel. Then He said, 'It is finished' and 'rested His head'—that is to say, on the bosom of the Father, and 'delivered over His spirit '."

"'Rested His head' is a strange expression," said I. "It is," said Clemens, "but it occurs in Matthew and Luke as follows, 'The Son of man hath not where to rest His head,' meaning 'He hath no home, no resting-place, on earth, but only with the Father above.' One of the ablest Greek scholars among the brethren assures me that John also uses the phrase to mean this; and I believe it is not used in Greek in any other sense. So, too, 'delivered over His spirit' signifies that in the supreme moment the 'delivering over' of the Suffering Servant was not passive but active. He delivered Himself over. But I ought to add that, in Aramaic, the same verb means (in different forms) 'finish,' 'deliver over,' and—the word used here by Mark and Luke—' expire '."

Scaurus had said something of this kind concerning the three gospels, and had argued that it increased the difficulty of ascertaining what Christ actually said. But I had supposed that it would not extend to a gospel written in a Greek city like Ephesus and so long after the other gospels, when Greek traditions might be expected to predominate. I was depressed by this frank avowal on the part of Clemens, and remained in silence for a moment or two weighing its consequences.

XXXII. — CLEMENS LENDS SILANUS THE FOURTH GOSPEL

CLEMENS waited patiently for me to resume our conversation. Soon it occurred to me that I had been unreasonable in my expectations if the circumstances were as he had described them. Suppose this new gospel to have originated from the reminiscences of John the son of Zebedee, a fisherman of Galilee, and the aged author of such a book as the Apocalypse. How could such traditions, if set down exactly as they came from the old man's lips, fail to abound in Jewish phrases and thoughts such as I had met with in the apocalyptic work? But these would have made the gospel very unsuitable for Greeks and Romans and indeed for almost all except Jews. It was therefore natural, and indeed almost necessary, that the old man's recollections, after being imparted to his friends, who would probably be the elders of Ephesus, should be freely interpreted, or perhaps paraphrased, in a form fit for all readers. Such interpreters, or such an interpreter, might not always be perfectly successful.

It was foolish of me not to have foreseen this. But still I was disappointed. "This," said I, "adds a new element of uncertainty, if John has sometimes preserved traditions of Christ's words translated from the Jewish tongue." "It does," said Clemens, "and so does another fact that applies both to Greek and to Hebrew or Aramaic. You know that, in Greek, 'he *said*' or '*used to say*' or 'it *says*,' often signifies 'he *meant*' or 'it*means*.' The same is true in Hebrew. Hence if an evangelist or scribe, after giving Christ's actual words, for example, '*Do righteousness*,' were to add 'But he meant, *Do alms*'—because, in Hebrew, 'righteousness' often means 'alms'—it would be possible to misinterpret the addition as meaning 'But he [also] *said* (or,*used to say*) *Do alms*,' thus erroneously creating a second precept. For these and other reasons I cannot feel sure that the saying 'I thirst,' about which we were just now conversing, may not be a paraphrase of the Lord's words about being ' forsaken.' John the son of Zebedee may have known that the latter words were misunderstood from the first by the soldiers, and also that they were misinterpreted by some Christians. Hence I think the aged apostle may have prayed for a revelation as to the true meaning of the words, and it may have been revealed to him, 'The Lord said—that is. He really said. His real meaning was—that He "*thirsted*". This indeed would be a surprise or paradox compared with what the gospel says elsewhere. But the scriptures are full of such paradoxes."

"But how 'elsewhere'?" said I. "Do you mean that here Christ feels thirst whereas 'elsewhere' He quenches thirst? I do not remember that." "I forgot," replied Clemens, "that you had not read the new gospel. That gospel represents Christ as saying to a sinful woman, 'Give me to drink,' and afterwards, to the same woman, 'He that believeth on me shall never thirst,' and, after that, to the Jews, 'If any one be athirst, let him come unto me and drink.' This same gospel says that the 'food' of the Son is to do the will of the Father. This, then, may be described as His meat and drink. If, therefore, He 'thirsts,' He is athirst to do the Father's will, so that He hungers and thirsts for righteousness in the souls of sinful men and women, thirsting to free them from thirst by giving them the water of life. All through His life He has not thirsted because the living water has been passing freely from the Father to Him and from Him to others. But now, on the point of death, the Giver of the water of life is Himself caused to thirst for it! The Father, in His infinite love, causes the Son Himself to thirst for that love! Instead of helping others, the Son is constrained to ask as it were to be helped—in order that He may help others better. This is perhaps the deepest and most wonderful of all the Lord's deep sayings—

'I thirst for the righteousness and love of God, that I and mine may be in the Father, and that the Father may be in me and mine.' In the end, this will be one of the Lord's words that will never pass away. But what was its effect at the time? When Socrates uttered his last wishes, Crito was at hand to say, 'This shall be done' But when Christ cried 'I thirst,' no friend was at hand to satisfy that thirst, and the cry was taken by the soldiers as meaning, 'I thirst for a little of your sour wine'!"

"It seems to me," said I, "that you regard this gospel, not exactly as history, but as history mingled with poetry or with vision?" "Not quite so," said Clemens. "I should prefer to say, 'as history *interpreted* through spiritual insight or poetic vision.' I take the historical fact to be that there came into the world, as man, a divine Being, endowed with a power of drawing man and God into one, by drawing the hearts of men towards Himself, and, through Himself, to the Father. Making men one with Himself, He also made them one with each other in Himself. This is the great historical fact, the fact of facts, foreordained before the foundation of the world. This, then, is the fact that needs to be brought out clearly in the history of Christ—not the facts (though they are facts) that the Pharisees often washed their hands and that the daughter of Herodias danced before John the Baptist was beheaded. Well, then, put yourself in the position of—whoever it was that wrote this fourth gospel, say, 'the Elder.' Imagine him returning fresh from an interview with the old man John, the son of Zebedee, who will not allow himself to be called a 'son of thunder'—."

"But why," said I, "should he not have allowed himself to be called John the son of Zebedee? And why should he object to be called one of the sons of thunder, if Jesus called him so?" "As to the latter name," replied Clemens, "I very much doubt whether Mark has translated the term correctly; I will tell you why, another time: but assuredly he was not a noisy 'son of thunder' as we should understand the phrase in the west.

"As to the former name, you will find in this gospel that 'Simon son of John' is thrice mentioned as Peter's name, in a passage where Peter is rebuked for having denied his Master. It is, so to speak, his name after the flesh, his unregenerate name. 'Peter,' or 'stone,' is his regenerate name. So, '*John son of Zebedee*' would be this disciple's unregenerate name. The fourth gospel never uses that name except once, in the phrase 'the sons of Zebedee,' on the same occasion on which Peter is rebuked as '*Simon son of John*,' For the most part John the son of Zebedee is described (in this gospel) as 'the other disciple'—that is, the one as yet unheard, the one whose testimony is still to be given. Or else, the name is connected with Christ's love—' the disciple that Jesus loved.' He feels that he owes all that he has, his very being, to the fact that Jesus loved him, that Jesus made him what he now is. Moreover Jesus gave him, by perpetual visions after His death, an insight into the meanings of His words uttered before death. Hence he might feel that Christ's words, once dark sayings, have now become clear. From being old, they have become quite new, so as to require an altogether new record."

"I am not sure," said I, "that I understand your meaning. Do you hold that the fourth gospel differs from the three because of the special character of John the son of Zebedee, or because of the special interpretation of 'the Elder'?" "Because of both," said Clemens. " Then," said I, "you think that John the son of Zebedee, far from being a 'son of thunder' in the sense in which Pericles might be so called by Aristophanes, was a man of a retiring and vision-seeing nature, who merged himself in Christ; and that his namesake, the Elder, believed that the aged apostle was as it were a mirror, in whom, and in whose traditions, it was possible to discern more of Christ's real expression than in the ancient document of Mark."

"That comes near the truth, I think," replied Clemens. "And yet I should be very far from denying that Mark, and the other early gospels, are right in several features apparently omitted by John—for example, Christ's love of 'the little ones,' and His anxiety lest they should be caused to stumble, and His insistence on the necessity of receiving the Kingdom of God as little children. But it seems to me that some of these precepts about 'little ones' may have been misunderstood so that the brethren needed Paul's warning, 'Be *not little children* in your minds,' and again, 'In malice be babes, but *in understanding be men*,' The root of all these precepts was the divine feeling of 'littleness,' or 'childhood,' or 'sonship.' This is realised in the Son of God doing the will of the Father. In order to do that will on earth. He must be always keeping His eyes on the Father in heaven. The earlier gospels represent Christ with His eyes fixed on the 'little ones' on earth, the sick, the sorrowful, the ignorant, the sinful. That also is true. The new gospel appears to me to attempt to show how the two truths are combined."

"But you surely do not mean to say," I exclaimed, "that Jesus, in the new gospel, never makes mention of the 'little ones' or the 'little children,' so frequently mentioned by the earlier evangelists!" "I do indeed," replied Clemens. "He does not make mention of either term once, except that, after the resurrection, seeing the disciples engaged in labour that has lasted through the night and effected nothing, He calls to them and says 'Little children!' But yet, although He does not elsewhere use the word 'children,' He has the thought constantly before Him. At the beginning of the gospel. He teaches that men must be '*born from above*' that is, become little children in the eyes of God. Towards the end, He uses a mother's word to them ('*teknia*' 'darlings'). He also says, 'I will not leave you *orphans*' and declares that His disciples are to be in Himself, the Son. Now to be in the Son, means to be made 'a little child' in the perfect sense of Christ's meaning."

"Perhaps," said I, "this explains why Paul seldom mentions the word 'little children'." "'Seldom'," said Clemens, "is not the right word. Paul *never* mentions it, except in the warning I mentioned above. Moreover John, in his epistle, says, 'I have written unto you little children, *because ye have known the Father*,' That word 'known' goes to the root of the matter. The essence of 'little childhood,' in Christ's sense, is *not ignorance but knowledge*—'knowing the Father.' And 'knowing the Father' implies loving the Father, or desiring the Father.

There are cases where 'desire' may perhaps be well substituted for 'love' so as to indicate that kind of love which leads one onwards to the object desired. This gospel seems to me to attempt to express—if I may so speak in accordance with the prophets of Israel—a desire of God for man, producing a desire of man for God. The work of the Son of God is to unite these two desires. This is a great mystery, a mystery past mere logic, that God, the Creator, should 'desire.' Yet I accept it—as it has been expressed by a certain holy woman of Athens, whom I verily believe to have been inspired by God, 'The Son of God chose to be lifted up upon the tree of the Cross that we might receive the food of angels. And what is this food of angels? It is the desire of God, which draws to itself the desire that is in the depths of the soul and they make one thing together'."

This saying was beyond me at the time. But I felt that it contained truth, and that I should grow into some apprehension of it. And what Clemens had said, though very strange at first, had been gradually growing to seem possible and even reasonable, if one may use the word concerning that which accords with the spiritual Logos—namely, that the Son of God, being human, was caused to feel forsaken by God, and to desire God, and to ask why this strange feeling of forsakenness, this unwonted, unsatisfied desire, was brought upon Him by the Father. Then, according to the saying of this holy woman of Athens, the answer of the Father was, "In receiving this forsakenness and this desire for my presence, thou art receiving from me my desire, which draws up to me thy desire, and they two make one together."

But to return to Clemens, whom I began to trust all the more because I felt that he was keeping back nothing from me. "What I am attempting," said he, "to express, but expressing very feebly, is this. I am trying to put myself in the position of the Elder, preaching the gospel for John the son of Zebedee in Ephesus, some time after the aged apostle returned from his martyrdom in Patmos, when he was quite decrepit and no longer able to be carried into the midst of the congregation, to utter even a few words. If I came into that old man's presence and heard from him traditions about the Master, whom he loved and who loved him, I might say, 'Here indeed is a revelation of Christ. Here I feel Christ Himself' Nevertheless, on going out, I might find it very hard to make a chronological and consecutive history out of his utterances. Sometimes he might be describing past fact; sometimes he might be prophesying the future; sometimes he might speak of the past as if still present—as though he were even now with his Master in Cana or Jerusalem; sometimes he might be rapt in a present ecstasy; sometimes he might be describing ecstatic visions of the past; sometimes he might speak in poetic metaphor, sometimes in literal prose; but always he would be penetrated and imbued with the love of Christ. The result—for me, I confess it—would be that I should go out, thinking, 'This is not history in the common sense of the term. But it is something, I will not say better, but more needed by the church, than a mere history of facts such as a writer like Mark could have given with fuller information. It gives glimpses into a divine and human personality that includes in itself a real history—a history of a great invisible war of good against evil, a great invisible redemption, God coming down to earth to lift man up to heaven '."

"But," said I, "do not Matthew and Luke give these glimpses in their description of the incarnation?" "I should rather have said," replied Clemens, "that, instead of giving glimpses, they attempt to describe a spiritual fact in the language of material history. John, you will find, does not make this attempt. He simply says that 'the Logos became flesh.' Then he introduces disciples believing in their Master as Messiah, undeterred by their supposition that He is 'the son of Joseph' and 'from Nazareth.' John assumes all through his gospel that Jesus came down from heaven and is to go up thither again. He refuses to recognise that this coming down and this going up are impossible for the Son of God incarnate as the son of Joseph. All this appears to me true. And in many respects I admire this little book more than I can find time or words to express. Yet I must deal frankly with you and confess that this new gospel, like the rest, appears to me inadequate. What gospel would be othenvise? All the written records of Christ's words and acts seem to me to have, as their main use, the awakening in us of a want of something more, a sense of something insufficient and imperfect and unjust to the reality, so that we cry vehemently to God for the reality, the living truth, the spiritual light—such light as no words or books can give us. The Spirit alone can bestow it, crying within us Abba, Father. Some interpreters, however, seem in a special degree to have 'the mind of Christ.' Among the foremost of these seems to me to stand 'the disciple whom Jesus loved'."

"I understand," said I, "at least I think I do, a little. You mean that the written biographies must first make the reader feel that they are dead in comparison with the living person. Then the reader is to feel drawn towards his ideal of the living person, and more and more drawn, so that in the end ." "In the end," said Clemens, "assuredly the living Person will come to him, or draw him to Himself, if he will but be patient in waiting, walking according to the light he already has." On this he rose to depart. "One word more," said I. "You told me that John gives nearly a quarter of his gospel to the doctrine of the Lord on the night on which He was delivered over. Does he give much space to the period after the resurrection? And what does he say about that? Does he agree with Matthew and Luke?"

"No," said Clemens, "he differs greatly, and, as it appears to me, deliberately, intending to correct them. For example, Matthew represents certain women as taking hold of Christ's feet, before He sends them to carry word to His 'brethren.' John says that Jesus said to Mary Magdalene, 'Touch me not for I am not yet ascended to my Father,' and then sends her to His 'brethren.' Luke says that Christ said to all the disciples, 'Handle me,' to show that He was not a bodiless spirit. John says that an offer of this nature was made to Thomas, but mentions no such offer to any other disciple. Luke says that the disciples gave Jesus food and He ate. John says that Jesus gave food to the disciples. In all these points John appears to me to be nearer than Matthew and Luke to the truth. And sometimes I think that the touching of Christ's body by the disciples in the Eucharist, that is to say, the touching of the bread and tasting of the wine in our sacred meal, has been taken by Luke (if not by Matthew) in a literal sense "—here Clemens agreed with Scaurus—" whereas John understood the meaning correctly. But at the same time I think that the Saviour may have been visibly present at the Eucharist, showing the wounds in His body, though it was not a body that could be touched."

"Does it not seem to you," I asked, "that this agrees better with Paul's descriptions of the manifestations of Jesus after death?" "Yes," said Clemens, "and in other respects John seems to me to be nearer the truth. For he apparently represents Christ as having ascended to the Father before He could be 'touched,' that is to say, before His spiritual body and blood could be imparted to the disciples. Moreover, whereas Matthew places before the Resurrection a tradition relating how Christ imparts to the disciples authority to bind and to loose *i.e.* to forgive sins, John places it afterwards. And John also describes Peter as plunging into the water and coming to Jesus after the Resurrection,—which seems to me a symbol of Peter passing through the waters of temptation to the Saviour whom he had denied. But Matthew places it before the Resurrection and takes it literally, as though Peter tried to walk on literal water and was nearly drowned, but for the Lord's help."

"Then," said I, after a long pause—for I was not prepared to find Clemens so far in agreement with Scaurus, an unbeliever, concerning the facts of the Christian histories—"you are very far indeed from saying, 'I believe in every word of the gospels of Mark, Matthew, and Luke, as being historically accurate.' Nay, I can hardly think you would say that, even about the gospel of John?" "Assuredly," he replied, "I would not say that about any of the gospels. Indeed, dear friend, do you yourself think you would venture to say as much as that, even about the history of your favourite Thucydides? And does it not seem to you that, in any book that describes the life of a man, the greater the man, and the more living the life, the greater must be the failure of the book, and the deadness of the book, as compared with the inexpressible spirit, not to be expressed in any book, no, not in a universe of books?"

Then, rising, and pointing seaward, "Look!" he said, "the moon is up already! Now indeed I must stay with you no longer. I have done my best to deal fairly with you, even to the point perhaps of being not quite fair to this little book, which I now hold in my hand, and am about to place in yours, if you desire it. But are you sure that you do still desire it? If you do indeed, I shall most gladly lend it, and you can return it to me, this time to-morrow, at the house of Justus. But be honest with me as I have tried to be with you. Do not take it as yet if you are not prepared to read it as a book that comes from the east through a western medium; a book that mingles, so as not always to be clearly distinguished, words of the Lord with words of the evangelist, facts and visions, histories and prophecies, metaphors that may be misunderstood, and poems that may be taken as literal prose. It will make you feel perhaps irritated, certainly unsatisfied. Perhaps you may end in saying, 'I want much more, I want to see the person to whom this book points, but whom no book can make me feel.' Then it will have done you good. But perhaps you will put it aside and say, 'I want no more'."

He paused, and looked anxiously at me. "In that case," continued he, "I shall have done you harm. But what say you? After this warning, do you—a Roman with Greek training, a reader of Homer and Thucydides—do you still desire to see this little volume that is neither a true poem nor a true history, a biography that hardly professes to draw the life of Jesus as He was, but only to make us feel that it must be felt, if at all, through 'a disciple whom Jesus loved'?" I assured him that I greatly desired to read it and thanked him with all my heart for the loan, and for the frankness of his warning. "Farewell," said he, placing the book in my hand, "my friend, my brother—brother in the search after truth, farewell!" "Your help," said I, as he turned away from me, "has been more like that of a father." He stopped and looked round at me for a moment. "Would indeed," said he, "that it might prove so! Farewell!"

XXXIII. — SCAURUS ON THE FOURTH GOSPEL

THE sun had set, and the moon was well above the sea, when, after parting from Clemens, I turned towards Nicopolis, with the new gospel in my hand. Unrolling it, I found twilight enough to read the first few lines while I walked slowly for some two or three hundred paces. Then I stood still to read better in the fading light. When it had quite faded, I sat down repeating what I had read.

"In the beginning was the Logos." Never shall I forget the unexpectedness of those words. I had supposed that the Christians altogether rejected the Logos except as meaning "utterance" or "doctrine." "In the beginning" was, in some senses, familiar. I had read in Mark, "The *beginning* of the gospel of Jesus Christ." Luke, too, had spoken of "those who were from the *beginning* eyewitnesses and ministers of the Logos." But how different was Luke's "logos" and Luke's "beginning" from this!

I read on: "In the beginning was the Logos and the Logos was with God." What did "with" mean? Was the Logos "at home with God"? Or "conversing with God"? Or "in union with God"? Or did "with" include all these meanings? And what was this Logos? The next words gave the answer: "The Logos was God."

These words alone, contrasted with Luke's preface, sufficed to indicate a difference between Luke and John, just such as Clemens had suggested. Luke began with a reference to many inadequate "attempts" to draw up a relation about what he called "the *facts*"—meaning "*facts*" as distinct from *fancies*—"consummated among us." Then, like a careful compiler, he distinguished his authorities, giving the first place to "*eye-witnesses*" the second to accessories, or "*ministers.*" These were eyewitnesses, he said, "from the beginning"; and he declared that he had followed and traced their evidence from the fountain head. John, like a prophet, went back to a "beginning" of which there could be no "eyewitnesses." He did not say, as Luke did, "*it seemed good to me*" to write. He said—as though he had himself been with Him who was from the beginning—" The Logos was God"

Glancing down the column before folding up the scroll, I could barely read in the fast expiring twilight the words, "And the Logos became flesh and tabernacled among us, and we beheld his glory, glory as of the only begotten from the Father." Clemens had prepared me for such words. As I understood them, the "glory" did not mean any splendour of material light or fire, such as is mentioned sometimes in the theophanies of Greek, Roman, and Hebrew writers, but the glory of God's constraining love. But I greatly desired to study the words in their context. Repeating them over and over again, as I rolled up the book, I hurried homeward. Star after star came out in the darkness; and with each new star a new suggestion of invisible "glory" shone on me more clearly. "This gospel," I said, "will grow on me like these visible glories. Night by night, and day by day, its words will become less strange and more wonderful."

On my arrival, I lit my lamp, and sat down at once, preparing to continue my reading, when my servant entered with a letter. Not recognising the superscription, I put it on one side. The boy waited about in the room, doing nothing that needed doing. I was on the point of dismissing him, when he said, "Sir, I think it is from Tusculum; but the superscription is not in my lord's handwriting." Looking again, I saw that it was in the handwriting of Marullus,

Scaurus's secretary. Scaurus usually superscribed his letters to me with his own hand. In alarm about his health, I tore the letter open, and throwing the cover hastily aside, glanced at the beginning. This reassured me. It was from Scaurus, and in his handwriting.

My apprehensions were soon banished. He had been ill, he said, but had now recovered after a somewhat severe attack. Then the old war-horse passed on to his favourite battle-field—criticism of Christian gospels. I was in the act of putting the letter down—for I had had enough, for the present, of criticizing the old gospels, and was longing to study the new one—when I caught sight of the words "fourth gospel," and discovered that he had recently procured the very book I was beginning to read, and that his letter contained a discussion of it. This was not quite welcome—not, at least, at the moment. I wished to read the gospel first, for myself, before looking at Scaurus s criticism, which (I felt sure) would be destructive. "Yet," thought I, "I have heard Clemens on the one side; ought I not to hear Scaurus on the other? If Scaurus goes wrong, ought I not to be able to find it out?" Scaurus was always fair and honest, and had helped me hitherto, even when I had not agreed with him. These considerations made me finally decide to read the letter and the gospel together, comparing each criticism with the passage or subject criticized, as I went on.

"Let me begin," wrote Scaurus, "with the point that will most interest you. I have accused Epictetus of borrowing from the Christians. I now assert that this writer—Flaccus tells me that the Christians say it was John the son of Zebedee y I am sure they are wrong, but for convenience I will call him John—this man John deliberately contradicts Epictetus, using our friend's language but in a different or opposite sense, or with opposite conclusions.

"For example, Epictetus mocks at Agamemnon for calling himself a shepherd of the people. He dislikes the Homeric language and says 'Shepherd you are in truth; for you weep, *as the shepherds do, when a wolf snatches away one of their sheep.*' John makes Christ distinguish between the good shepherd and the hireling. It is only the hireling that *flees and lets the wolf snatch away the sheep*. In John, Christ says: 'I am the good shepherd,' and '*The good shepherd lays down his life for the sheep.*'

"Again, Epictetus declares that a good man never weeps. He blames Ulysses in particular for weeping at his separation from

Penelope. John represents Christ as shedding tears in sympathy with a woman weeping for her dead brother.

"Epictetus constantly says that self-knowledge is everything—herein (I must admit) going with other philosophers. John represents Christ as saying, 'This is eternal life, to know thee, the only true God and Jesus Christ whom thou hast sent.' It is impossible that Christ could have uttered the last part of this sentence exactly as it stands. But that does not weaken my argument, which is, that John (alone of the evangelists) insists on other-knowledge, not on self-knowledge, as being the essential thing. And this he does throughout his. gospel."

Then Scaurus came to that cardinal doctrine of Epictetus which had caused Glaucus and me so many searchings of heart. "You know," he said, "that Epictetus teaches that no good man is ever troubled. It is not John's custom to contradict what he deems errors in a formal and direct way. But if he had resorted for once to direct methods, he could hardly have contradicted this Epictetian doctrine more effectively than he does in his indirect dramatic fashion. He represents Christ as thrice 'troubled.' First—on the same occasion on which he lets fall tears in sympathy with the woman above mentioned—he is said to have 'troubled himself.' Secondly, on an occasion when he is (as I take it) preparing for some act of self-sacrifice, he says, 'Now is my soul troubled.' On a third occasion, when announcing that he is to be betrayed by one of the Twelve, he is said to have been 'troubled in spirit.' I cannot doubt that this description of threefold 'trouble' is intended to attack the Stoic doctrine that the wise and good man is to shrink from 'trouble'." This convinced me, and it convinces me still.

Scaurus proceeded to say, "Some innocent readers of this gospel might say, 'Well at all events John agrees with Epictetus in his .use of the term Logos.' And (no doubt) the first three lines of the gospel might suggest this. But read on, and you will find the two are in absolute opposition. The Logos, in John, instead of being the philosophic Logos or reason, is really an unreasonable and hyperbolical sort of love, regarded by him as born from God, and as part of God's personality, and as constituting unity in God's nature. This Logos he regards as incarnate as a man for the purpose of uniting mankind to God! This doctrine Epictetus would absolutely reject.

"Later on, in this gospel, you will find Christ saying to the disciples, 'Ye are clean on account of the Logos that I have spoken to you.' Now Epictetus also connects cleanness with the Logos. 'It is impossible,' he says, 'that man's nature should be altogether clean, but the Logos being received into it, as far as possible attempts to make it cleanly.' Verbally, there is an appearance of agreement. Read the two contexts, however, and you will find that, whereas Epictetus makes 'cleanness' consist in right convictions, John makes it consist in a mystical doctrine of sacrifice, or service, typified by the Master's washing the feet of the disciples.

"I could give you other instances of the way in which John uses other language of philosophers in a non-philosophic sense. But his use of Logos suffices for my purpose. It gives the clue to the whole gospel. This writer adds one more to my list of Christian *retiarii*. The innocent reader, unrolling the book and reading its first words, prepares himself for a Platonic treatise in which he is to 'follow the Logos' in accordance with Socratic precept. Then, step by step, he is lured on into regions of non-logic and sentiment, till the net suddenly descends on him, and he finds himself repeating, 'the Logos became flesh'."

What Scaurus said interested me but did not convince me as to John's motive. Nor did Scaurus himself adhere to it. He did not always use the epithet "retiarian" in a bad sense. As I have said above, I had come to believe that right "feeling," rather than right "reason," may be regarded as revealing the nature of God. So I did not feel that John was beguiling his readers. But Scaurus's criticism helped me to recognise the extreme skill and tact—as well as the terseness, beauty, and solemnity—with which the evangelist introduces the doctrine of the incarnation. And I could not help agreeing with my friend's next remark, "The man that wrote the Apocalypse—though he, too, was a prophet and a poet in his line— could no more have written this prologue than Ennius could have written the Aeneid,"

After some more observations on the difference of style in the Apocalypse and the Gospel, he returned to the criticism of the latter. "Compare," he said, "the prologue and the conclusion with the rest of this book, and you will see that there is some mystery about its authorship. Under one style it conveys two currents of thought. Sometimes it repeats itself like an old man. Sometimes it is as brief and dark as an oracle. Moreover, some events—such as the expulsion of the tradespeople from the temple—which ought to come at the end—this writer places at the beginning. It has occurred to me that he must have started with the intention of describing nothing but Christ's acts in Judaea and then changed his mind. Or is it possible that documents arranged Hebrew-fashion—last, first—have been interpreted Greek- fashion and consequently reversed? Allegory is most strangely mixed with fact. There is a wedding in which water is changed into wine. This is allegory. The Bride is the Church. The water of the law is changed into the wine of the gospel. After that, comes a statement that Christ spoke about destroying the temple and building it in three days. This is, according to Mark and Matthew, history. Luke took it as not history and left it out. John took it as history and allegory and put it in. But how differently from Mark and Matthew! Look at the passages. John often does this. I mean, that where Luke differs from Mark, John (who prefers Mark) intervenes to support the latter."

This general remark (about John's "preferring Mark") agreed with what Clemens had said. As for the particular instance, I found that Scaurus was right. Mark and Matthew had mentioned a project to "destroy the temple" as having been imputed to Christ by false witnesses. Luke omitted it. John declared that Christ said to the Jews, "Destroy this temple!" and that Christ "spoke about the temple of his body."

"If I could believe," continued Scaurus, "that John the son of Zebedee, the author of the Apocalypse, had any part in the production of this gospel, I should be disposed to say that he must have contributed to it, not as a scribe, but as a prophet or seer. Take, for example, the description, recorded in this gospel alone, of a flow of blood and water from the side of Christ on the cross. I do not believe for a moment that this was invented, any more than Luke's description of the sweat of blood on the night before the crucifixion. But I should explain the two as resulting from two quite different causes, differing as the authors differ. Luke was not a seer, but a man of literature, a student of documents. He found some narrative based on the expression that it was 'a night of watching and sweat'—which you know very well means in Greek 'watching and anxious toil.' The narrator took this literally. This literal interpretation commended itself to Luke, who desired to connect the death of Christ with the Jewish sacrificial 'blood of sprinkling'." I had not noticed in Luke any tradition about "sweat." But on referring to my copy I found that, though not in the text, words of this kind were written in the margin.

Scaurus went on to show in detail that John's tradition was quite different in origin. It was supported by an asseveration, "He that hath seen hath borne witness, and his witness is true; and he *knoweth* that he saith true that ye also may believe." As to this, Scaurus said, "Only a little child, a baby Gaius, would use such an asseveration as '*Gaius knows* that Gaius is telling the truth.' 'He knoweth' means 'HE knoweth,' *i.e.* 'The Lord knoweth.' HE is often thus used in the epistle that forms a sort of epilogue to this gospel. The prophet, or seer, is appealing to his Lord about the truth of the vision of blood and water, which the Lord has revealed to him. In the Bible 'he that seeth' is a common phrase for < the seer,' a man habitually seeing visions. When John came back from Patmos and wrote the Apocalypse, he might naturally be called by preeminence, 'he that hath seen.' Or the phrase might apply to this special vision: 'The seer (he that hath seen) hath borne witness to the vision of the stream of blood and water, and HE (*i.e.* the Lord) knoweth that his witness is true.'

"I do not deny that the vision is a fulfilment of a prophecy—which you may have read in the book of Zechariah—concerning a certain 'fountain to cleanse sin and defilement.' But still I say that it is an honest, genuine, vision, not an invention. That it is not a fact could be proved, if needful. According to the other evangelists, some women were present near the cross, but no men are mentioned. It is extremely doubtful whether two streams of water and blood could issue from the side. If they had issued, and if John had been present, the soldiers would not have let him stand near enough to distinguish them. My copy of Matthew, in a marginal note, has a similar tradition, but *before the death*, and without any order from Pilate to kill the crucified criminals—as if a soldier would dare to do this at his own pleasure! A book called Acts of John (only recently circulated, Flaccus tells me) contains other visions of John, and, among them, some revealed during the crucifixion. The Acts is not written by the author of this new gospel, and it is very wild and fanciful; but it suggests that visions may have been falsely ascribed to John because he was known to have really seen visions (like laws falsely assigned to Numa because he was supposed to have really made laws). I take it that John the son of Zebedee may have had a vision of this kind about a 'fountain' of blood and water. This may have been current among the Christians for some time. My annotator in Matthew seems to have found it in a wildly improbable form. The new gospel gives it less improbably."

Scaurus then commented on the contrast between what he called the "soaring" thought of the book and its occasionally "pedestrian" or vernacular language, as when John preserves the old traditional "crib" for "bed"—a word abominated by Atticists and avoided by Luke. He also commented on his ambiguities, his subtle plays on words, his variations in the forms of words, and his veiled allusions—utterly unlike anything that might be expected from a fisherman of Galilee—declaring that the writer must have been conversant with the works of Philo as well as with the teaching of the Cynics.

Then he pointed out how Christ in this gospel never uses the word "cross" but always speaks of being "lifted up"—a phrase, he said, current among Jews as well as Roman slaves, to mean "hanged" or "crucified": and he gave it as an instance of the writer's irony—and of his recognition that things low in man's eyes are high in God's eyes—that a criminal's death is called by this writer "being exalted," or "being glorified." "Have you not"—he said—" heard your servants ever say that Geta has been 'lifted up,' or that Syrus has been a rich man and has 'fed multitudes'—meaning that the poor wretch has been crucified and has fed multitudes of crows with his flesh on the cross?" I had often heard it; and I was astonished that such a phrase could be used in this gospel. Scaurus continued, "He uses this vernacular talk, this unfeeling slavish jest, to represent the very highest truth of Christian doctrine, that the Redeemer is to be 'exalted' by suffering on the cross so as to give his flesh and blood to be the food of all the world!"

According to Scaurus, although the style was very different indeed from that of Philo, and although the writer knew (what Philo did not) that the Septuagint was often erroneous, yet there was a great likeness between John and Philo in respect of their symbolism. Of this he gave a great number of instances. And he also quoted allusions to Jewish proverbs or sayings, one of which I will set down here, because it has given rise to an error among some of the brethren at the present day.

John represents the Jews as saying to Jesus, "Thou art not yet fifty years old." Now, according to Scaurus, this referred to an enactment in the Law that the Levites must serve with laborious service "up to fifty years of age," after which they are exempt, so that the saying, "Thou art not yet fifty "meant, "Thou art but a junior Levite," used as a term of reproach. "This enactment," said Scaurus, "was applied by Philo to inferior spiritual attainment, and, I have no doubt, was used allusively by John. But it might easily give the impression that Christ was about fifty years old and that the Jews meant the saying literally."

I mention this because I have myself heard the young Irenaeus maintain that Christ was actually about fifty years of age. And he not only quoted John in support of this assertion but declared that it was also the opinion of the elders conversant with John. When I heard him, I remembered what Scaurus had said. I have never had any doubt that Scaurus was right. At the same time it seems to me that a Jewish allusion of this kind was extremely liable to be misunderstood, and that the writer of this gospel would not perhaps have set it down if he had not received it from the originator, John the son of Zebedee. This, however, is only my conjecture. The error of Irenaeus is a fact. And I could mention another of the brethren, who wrote a commentary on John, and actually altered "fifty" to "forty"—I suppose, to make sense! Both these errors arose from not understanding John's allusion.

Then Scaurus passed to the structure of the work which, he said, under appearance of great simplicity, and of an iteration that might sometimes seem almost garrulous or senile, conformed to certain Jewish rules of twofold and threefold attestation. He showed how the book—describing a new creation of the world—begins and ends with six days. He also showed how the author takes pleasure in refrains of words, and cycles or repetitions of events. For example, he describes Christ as being baptized at the beginning in one Bethany and anointed at the end in another Bethany. "I could give you," he said, "other instances of this sort of thing. The book is a poem, not a history."

About this I was not yet able to judge; but I felt that by "poem " he did not mean "mere fiction." For he had already admitted that the book contained historical as well as spiritual truth. And knowing his deep love of goodness, I was not altogether surprised at what came next: "O my dear Quintus, while reading this extraordinary book I have been more than once tempted to say, 'Along with a great deal that I do not want, this man almost gives me what I do want—what I have been long desiring.' I have told you how, years ago, I craved for a city of truth and justice. Well, I knew the Jews were a narrow, bigoted, and uncharitable race. No Jewish philosopher or prophet was likely to be my guide to such a city. But Isaiah was an exception. And somehow I fancied that this Jesus might be a developed Isaiah, and that his new city would have over its gates, 'Entrance free. Not even Roman patricians excluded.' But what did I find in some of the earliest gospels? In effect, this, 'None but the lost sheep of the House of Israel admitted here!'

"Now comes this latest of all the evangelists and says, 'We have changed all that. The old inscription is taken down. See the new inscription, ROOM FOR ALL! We welcome the universe. Read me, and see what I say about *other sheep,* and *about one flock, one shepherd.*' To all which I reply, 'Alas, my unknown but well-intentioned friend, I see, too clearly, that your friendliness exceeds your judgment. You honestly think that your gospel is so good that it must be true. You are not, I feel sure, decoying me—not consciously at least. You are the decoy bird. You have been decoyed yourself to decoy others. But Scaurus is too old a bird to be caught in such a manifest net. Whence this new doctrine? Why was it not in the earliest gospels?' I think John would find it hard to answer that question! If I had come to Jesus the Nazarene and said to him, 'What shall I do to inherit eternal life? 'I doubt not that he would have replied to me, 'Marcus Aemilius Scaurus, you doubtless think yourself a great person, as much superior to the low born Pontius Pilate as Pilate thinks himself superior to me. Understand, then, that I have no message for you. You know what name I gave to the Syrophoenician woman. I give the same to you'."

This passage was written in very large irregular characters, especially towards the close, quite unlike my old friend's usual hand. Then followed these words, in his own neat regular writing—as though he had been interrupted and resumed his pen in a cooler mood—"Let me try to be honest. I may have said rather more than I meant. I meant this fifteen years ago. Perhaps I mean it still. But after reading this new gospel, I feel somewhat less certain. Still, I fear that the truth may be as I have said."

XXXIV. — THE LAST WORDS OF SCAURUS

HAD I read to the end of Scaurus's letter I should not have been so startled by this sudden outburst. As it was, I had but a feint perception of the cause. I did not give weight enough to the indications—slight to others but they ought to have been clear to me—that the old man was writing under a great mental strain. Striving to be fair to the evangelists, he desired also to do justice to himself, half repenting that he had rejected the Saviour, half vindicating the rejection on the ground that truth constrained it. The whole tone of his letter—the handwriting itself, if I had only noted it more closely—should have made me perceive that he was passing rapidly through many transient phases, and that this outburst of passionate indignation—not with Christ but with what he supposed to be Mark's Christ—was but one of them. I did not notice these things. I was too much wrapped up in my own thoughts, and in imaginations of what I could have said, and how I could have pleaded with him for Christ.

It was now late, and I could read no more. I retired to rest—but not at first to peaceful rest. Thoughts and dreams, fancies and phantoms, passed indistinguishably before me: Scaurus and Clemens opposing one another, Hermas mediating, while Epictetus looked on; Troy, Rome, Jerusalem, and the City of Truth and Justice coming down from heaven; sunset and sunrise ushered by Hesper and Phosphor—with snatches of familiar utterances about "perceiving," "believing," and "deceiving," and mocking repetitions of "logos," "logos"—a confused, shifting, and multitudinous medley that resolved itself at last into one vast and dizzying whirlpool, in which all existence seemed endlessly revolving round a central abyss, when suddenly I heard "In the beginning was the Logos." Then the whirlpool was drawn up to the sky as though it had been a painted curtain; and we were standing below, Scaurus and I, and Clemens, and Epictetus, and Hermas—all of us gazing upwards to an unspeakable glory ascending and descending between heaven and earth. Then I fell into a peaceful sleep.

Next morning I continued reading the letter. "About the marvels or miracles in this gospel," said Scaurus, "it is worth noting that the author mentions only seven, that is to say, seven before the resurrection. This, I believe, is the number assigned to Elijah, whereas Elisha has fourteen—having 'a double portion' of Elijah's spirit. This selection of seven is one among many indications that the work uses Jewish symbolism. I have shown above that the Jewish genealogies are sometimes adapted in that way, as with Matthew's 'fourteen generations.' A more important fact is that this writer calls the miracles 'signs '—not 'mighty works,' which is the term in the three gospels. This is very interesting and I like him for it. He hates the words 'strong,' and 'mighty,' and 'mighty work.' For the matter of that, so does Epictetus. Both would agree that it is only slaves that obey 'the stronger.'}

"He also dislikes arithmetical 'greatness' and discussions about 'who is the greatest?' He prefers to lay stress on unity. Christians, he thinks, are 'one with the Son,' or they are 'in' the Son, or the Son is 'in' them. They are also to be 'one,' as the Father and the Son are 'one.' When men are regarded in this way, arithmetical standards of greatness—based on one's income, or on the amount of one's alms, or the amount of one's prayers, or one's sufferings, or one's converts—become ridiculous. He is quite right.

"He makes no mention of 'repentance.' That, I think, is because he prefers such expressions as 'coming to God' or 'coming to the light,' rather than mere 'change of mind.' He never uses the noun 'faith' or 'belief.' Probably he found it in use as a technical term among some foolish Christians— speaking of 'faith that moves mountains'—who forgot to ask 'faith in *what*?' For the same reason, no doubt, he preferred the word 'signs' to 'mighty works,' because the former—at all events while it was a novel term—might make men ask 'signs of what?' The phrase 'mighty work' makes us ask nothing. Nor does a 'mighty' work prove anything, except that the doer is 'mighty '—perhaps a giant, perhaps a magician, perhaps a God. Who is to decide? Epictetus says that Ceres and Pluto are proved to be Gods because they produce 'bread.' So this John represents Christ as producing bread and wine and healing disease and raising the dead; and these are 'signs' that he is a Giver of divine gifts and a Healer, like Apollo.

"In the case of one miracle, omitted by Luke, John intervenes and gives the sign a different aspect—I mean the one in which Mark and Matthew represent Christ as walking over the water to the disciples in a storm and as coming into their boat. John represents Christ as standing on the edge of the sea and as drawing the disciples safely to himself as soon as they cry out to him. I have no doubt that the story is an allegory. But John seems to me to give it in the nobler, and perhaps the earlier, form.

"There were probably multitudes of exorcisms performed by Jesus, as I have said to you before. But John does not mention a single instance. Perhaps he thought that more than enough had been said about these things by the earlier evangelists. On the other hand, he describes the healing of a man born blind, and the raising of a man named Lazarus from the dead, after he had lain in the tomb three days.

"The nearest approach to this is a story in Luke about raising from the coffin a young man, the son of a widow. I was long ago inclined to think Luke's story allegorical, and a curious book, which recently came into my hands, confirms this view. It is assigned to Ezra, but was really written, at least in its present form, about five and twenty years ago. I think it mixes Jewish and Christian thought. Ezra sees a vision of a woman sorrowing for her only child. She has had no son till after 'thirty years ' of wedlock. The son grew up and was to be married. When he 'entered into his wedding chamber, he fell down and died.' Presently it is explained, 'The woman is Sion.' For 'thirty years' there was 'no offering.' After 'thirty years,' Solomon 'builded the city and offered offerings.' Then Jerusalem was destroyed. But Ezra sees a new city builded, 'a large place.' It is a strange mixture. David, -says the scripture, was a 'son of thirty years' when he began to reign, and he may be supposed to have died about the time when the Temple began to be built. On the other hand Christ also was a 'son of thirty years' when he began to preach the gospel, and Christ might be said to have died at the time when he entered the Temple to purify it (that is, as Jews might say, 'entered the wedding chamber').

"I don't profess to explain all this Ezra-allegory. The only point worth noting is that it describes events that befell *the City and the Temple* of the Jews as though they befell *persons*—a 'woman' and a deceased 'son.' Luke omits the charge brought against Christ that he threatened to destroy '*the temple*' and build another. But there can be no doubt that there was some basis of fact for the charge. John gives that basis, by saying that Christ had in view a *'body,'* meaning himself. This indicates that Luke was misled through not understanding Jewish metaphor. So here Luke may have been misled again. He found a tradition describing the 'raising up' of the 'widow's son,' and he took it literally." The explanation thus suggested by Scaurus seemed to me probable. It explained why Luke omitted "the raising up of the temple." It also explained why Mark and Matthew omitted "the raising up of the widow's son."

Scaurus proceeded to the account of the raising of Lazarus. "This narrative," he said, "is extremely beautiful and may perhaps have had some basis of historical fact. Luke speaks of a Lazarus, who dies, and is carried after death into Abraham's bosom. Some Christians might take this Lazarus for a historical character. But I do not think any confusion arising from that story can have had very much to do with the story in John. The latter seems to me to have been thrown into allegorical form, so that Lazarus may represent humanity, first, corrupt, mere '*flesh and blood*'; secondly, raised up by '*the help of God.*' 'My God helps' is the meaning of Eliezer or Lazarus. Philo sees in the name these two associations. Also a Christian writer named Barnabas has some curious traditions that may bear on this name; and so have the Jews. Possibly John may mean—over and above the man Lazarus—the human race, raised up to life by the Messiah at the intercession of two sisters, representing the Jewish and the Gentile Churches of the Christians. Similarly I am told that Christians describe the two sisters Leah and Rachel as representing the Synagogue and the Church.

"For my part, having spoken to many physicians, and having investigated some instances of revivification, I have come to the conclusion that Jesus possessed a remarkable power of healing the sick and even perhaps of restoring life to those from whom (to all appearance) life had recently departed. Nay, I am dreamer enough to go beyond anything that physicians would allow, and to suppose that Christ may have had a certain power of what I called above *teliatreia*, 'healing at a distance,' producing a corresponding*telepatheia*, or 'being healed at a distance.' But there is against this particular narrative the objection—not to be overcome except by very strong evidence indeed—that the other evangelists say nothing about this stupendous miracle. Having in view Christ's precept to the disciples, 'Raise the dead,' I see how easily honest Christians might be led to take metaphor for fact. It is much more easy to explain how the narratives of the widow's son and of Lazarus may have arisen from misunderstanding in the two latest gospels, than to explain how, though true, they were omitted in the two earliest."

Upon this, I read the story of the raising of Lazarus two or three times over. It appeared to me certain that the writer of the gospel must have taken the story as literally true. But I saw how easy it was to mistake metaphor for literal meaning in stories of this kind. I was also impressed by what Scaurus said concerning the precept, "Raise the dead," which is recorded by Matthew. No other writer mentions this; and I had assumed, at the time of which I am now speaking, that it was meant spiritually, and that Luke omitted it because he thought that it might be misunderstood as having a literal meaning. And here I may say, writing forty-five years afterwards, that I have lately spoken to several of the brethren about this precept. Some leave it out of their text of Matthew. Some refuse to say anything about it. But I have not as yet found a single brother ready to admit that Jesus must have used it, or even probably used it, metaphorically.

All this I did not know at the time when I was reading Scaurus's letter; but I recognised the force of his arguments and was constrained to sympathize with his disappointment when he proceeded as follows: "O, my dearest Quintus, what earthen vessels, what mere potsherds, these gospel writers are, even the best of them, in comparison with the man whom they fail to set before us! Yes, even this John, whom I regard as by far the greatest of them all, even he is a failure—but in his case, perhaps, from want of knowledge, not from want of insight. As for the others, why do they not trust to the greatness of their subject, the man Jesus Christ? Why can they not believe that the Logos might become incarnate as a man, that is to say, a real man—what Jesus himself calls 'son of man '? Why do they lay so much stress on mere 'mighty works,' some of which, even if they could be proved to have happened, would give us little insight into the real greatness of their Master, whom they wish us to worship?

"For my part, I take such stories as those of the destruction of the swine and the withering of the fig-tree, to be allegories misinterpreted as facts. But even if I were shown to be wrong, they would not prove to me that I was right in worshipping the doer of such wonders. If I can judge myself aright, I, Marcus Aemilius Scaurus, am quite prone enough already to worship the God of the Thunderbolts and the God of War, These Jews might have taught me better. They have, to some extent—especially this fourth writer. But how much more from the first might have been effected if, from the first, they had recognised the truth taught in the legend of Elijah—that the Lord is 'not in the earthquake' but 'in the still small voice' I..."

At this point, Scaurus's handwriting became irregular and sometimes not easy to read. "I have been interrupted again," he said. "This time, it was Flaccus. Now I take up my pen positively for the last time, wondering why I take it up, and why I ramble on in this maundering fashion. I think it is because I feel as though you and I were dreaming together, and I am loth to leave off. There is no one else in the world with whom I can thus dream in partnership. This shall really be my last dreaming.

"Do not be vexed with me, Quintus, for charging Flaccus not to send you a copy of this littlc book. Hc told mc that for some time past you had been interested in these subjects, and that, if he could find another copy, he intended to forward it to you. The rascal added something about 'mere literary interest.' I suspect him of Christian tendencies. Your recent letters have reassured me. But I cannot help feeling that there have been moments with you, as with me, when the 'interest' was more than 'merely literary.' I had half thought of sending you my copy. But I shall not. The subject is too fascinating—like chess; and, like chess, it leads to nothing. I was glad to hear—in your last letter, I think—that you were now giving your mind to practical affairs. If you decide on the army at once, there is likely to be work soon in Illyria.

"Things also look cloudy, not black yet but cloudy, in Syria. In spite of the thrashing they got from the late Emperor, these Jews have not yet learned their lesson. They are as stubborn and obstinate as Hannibal made us out to be:—

'Gens quae cremato fortis ab Ilio
Jactata Tuscis aequoribus sacra
Natosque maturosque patres
Pertulit Ausonias ad urbes,
Duris ut ilex tonsa bipennibus
Nigrae feraci frondis in Algido
Per damna, per caedes, ab ipso
Ducit opes animumque ferro.'

"How every word of this would suit the Jews! I mean in their past history. According to my news (from a friend of Rufus the new Governor) it may suit their future, too; and we may have to take Jerusalem again. Then—to quote Isaiah and Horace in one—there will be another 'lopping of the boughs' in the future. But I mean their past. I wonder whether you understand what I am dreaming of Probably not, and it is not worth explaining. Nor indeed am I well enough to explain clearly and briefly. I have been going in too much for books of late, and feel at this moment (to quote an old friend) 'dead from the waist down.' However—as I am not going to write about these Jews again—I will scribble my last thoughts to the end.

"How strange it would have been, then, my dearest Quintus, if these Jews—I mean the Jewish Jews not the Christian Jews—how strange, I say, it would have been, looked at as a poem, if these fellows had fulfilled Hannibal's prophecy. They went some way towards it. Though their Ilium has been twice burned they are still alive, numerous, and active. Their 'ilex' has had 'pruning' enough, heaven knows, from the Roman axe of late, and from the Assyrian and Babylonian axes in days gone by. But they want pruning still. Witness a score of eastern cities, where they have lately been massacring myriads of Greeks—not, I own, without having seen myriads of their countrymen massacred first.

"Their disadvantage has been that they have never made a new start as Aeneas did, so as to turn old Troy into new Rome. Aeneas could take his gods with him. The Jews could not. The only place where they have done anything of the kind is Alexandria. There they have an imitation temple—not a rival temple of course, but an imitation—and there they are at their best. But elsewhere the stubborn creatures—from Gaul to Euphrates—recognise no home or sacred ground except in a little corner of Syria. Providence has done its best to detach them from this servitude by using Titus to destroy their temple a second time, and by leaving their sacred utensils no existence except upon Titus's arch. But still they are servants of the *genius loci*, so to speak. As they cannot serve the temple, they serve the ground on which it stands and the traditions that have collected round it.

"The Christian Jews have immense advantages. They are like the Trojan Romans. The Christians have left their Troy (that is to say, carnal Jerusalem) in order to dwell in Rome (that is to say, heavenly Jerusalem) the city of truth, the city of justice, the city of freedom and universal brotherhood. Their sacred fire is the Holy Spirit. Their sacred vessels are human beings. Every great city in Asia contains their 'holy things.' To celebrate their feast on the body and blood of their Saviour, a table of pine wood, a platter, and a mug, supply them with all they need! A little bread, and wine mingled with water, have taken the place of Solomon's hecatombs! Surely this is the very perfection of religious simplicity—an ambassador in a plain Roman toga amid the courtiers of a Ptolemy!

"Again, when we Romans call on Jupiter, offering our costliest white oxen, who supposes that Jupiter descends? But when these Christians meet, without a denarius in their pockets, three in a room, they tell you that Christ is with them. What is more, many of them believe it! What is most, some of them act as though they believed it! I have called their city a city of dreams, and I repeat it. But, mark you, a city of dreams has one great advantage over a city of bricks or stone.

You can smash the latter. But neither Nero, nor Trajan, has been able to smash the former; and I begin to doubt whether it could be smashed by Hadrian, if he tried. At the present rate, I should not be surprised if, in the next hundred years, the empire from the Euphrates to Britain were dotted with colonies of Christ.

"'Let arms of war. give place to the gown of peace!' So sang the lawyer of Arpinum when he tried his hand at poetry. He was better advised, in his lawyer's gown, when he confessed 'Laws are silent among arms.' But there is a third power more powerful than either laws or arms. You won't believe me when I tell you its name. It is 'dreams.' Yes, 'Among dreams,' says Scaurus—and he knows, having been himself a dreamer, in his day, besides being a bit of a soldier and a good deal of a looker on—'Among dreams, arms are *vain*.' I don't say they are '*silent*.' That is their contemptible feature—they are *not* 'silent.' But they are impotent. Mars against dreams may make what fuss and bustle he pleases, clash, clang, thunder, like the brazen wheels of Salmoneus. But his thundering will effect nothing. Nor will his steel. '*Frustra diverberet umbras*.'

"When I say 'dreams,' do not take me to mean that the personality of a great prophet is a 'dream.' But the notion that an empire can be spun out of it, or built on it, seems to me a dream. Yet there is something attractive in it—I mean in the conception of a soul like a vast magnet, attracting and magnetizing a group of souls, of which each in turn becomes a new magnet, magnetizing a group of its own, and so on, and so on, till the whole empire (or family) of souls is bound together by this magnetic law. Yes, 'law' one may call it, not a magical incantation, but a natural law, the law of the spiritual magnet. It is all very strange. Yet, given the personality, it is possible.

"For it all comes to this, a personality—nothing more. There is nothing new in what the Christians call their Testament or Covenant—nothing new at all, from the Jewish point of view, except that the new Jews have cast aside a great deal of the Covenant of the old Jews. I sometimes think the Christian leader was really what Socrates calls himself, a 'cosmian' or 'cosmopolite,' going back, behind the law of Moses, to a beginning of things before unclean food was Levitically forbidden and before free divorce was Levitically sanctioned. His two fundamental rules are the same, both for Jews and for Christians, 'Love God,' 'Love man.'

"The difference is, that to the Christians (so they assert) Christ has introduced a new kind of love, a new power of love. He has not only breathed it into his disciples but also given them (they say) the power of breathing it into others. The question is. Have they this power? I am obliged to admit—from what I hear—that a good many of them appear to me to have it. This is the real miracle. This, if true, is sunlight. All the so-called miracles of their books, even if true, are the merest, palest moonlight compared with this.

"This dreamer seems to me to have planned an imperial peace throughout his cosmopolis, to be brought about, not by threats based on the power of inflicting death, not by edicts on stone backed by punishments with steel, but by means of a spirit that is to creep into our hearts, dethrone our intellects, drag us in triumph behind his chariot wheels, making us fanatically happy when we are in love with him—and with all the weak, the foolish, the suffering, and the oppressed—and making us unreasonably unhappy, foolishly sad and sick at heart, when we resist a blind affection for others and when we consult our own interests and our own pleasures, following the path of prudent wisdom.

"In one respect, this work of John's has proved me a false prophet. I prophesied that East and West could not unite in one religion. They *have* united—on paper, and in theory—in this little book. But I also said that, if they did unite, their offspring would be a portent. To that I adhere. If John's form of the Christian superstition were to overspread the world, do you seriously suppose that it would remain in his form? No, it is impossible but that the spiritual will be despiritualised. The superstition of pure spirit will probably become a superstition of unmixed matter. The life will be narrowed to the Body and the Blood. The Body and the Blood will be narrowed down still further to the Bread and the Wine. Then their hyperbolical self-sacrifice will give way to hyperbolical malignity. How these Christians will, in due time, hate one another! How they will wall in, and imprison, the Spirit that bloweth whither it listeth! How they will war against one another for their Prince of Peace! How they will philosophize and hair-split about the Father and the Son, tearing one another in pieces for the unity of the one God! And yet, and yet, even if all my prophecies of the worst come to pass, might not a Christian philosopher of those far-off days say that the 'worst is often the corruption of the best,' and that his Prophet had discovered a 'best,' buried for a time beneath all this rubbish and litter, but destined to emerge and grow into the tree of a great spiritual empire? It may be so. I do not deny that there may be such a 'best.' But it is not for me.

"I give it up. The problem of the Sphinx is too hard for my brains. Perhaps Destiny knows its own mind, and it may be a good mind—not my mind, but perhaps an infinitely better and wiser. Perhaps this Christian superstition is intended to found an empire after the Spirit, an empire of 'the Son of man,' like, but unlike, the empires of Egypt, Babylon, Greece, Rome. Daniel dreamed this for Jewish Jews. It may come true for Christian Jews. If it should come, what a tyranny it will be—for those, at least, who are tyrants at heart! The yoke of the Imperium Romanum will be nothing to the yoke of the Imperium Romanochristianum. We Romans despotize over bodies: the Roman Christians will despotize over souls. 'Debellare superbos' is only one of our arts. 'Pacis imponere mores' is a second. 'Parcere subjectis' is a third. These Roman Christians will know how to crush, but not how to spare. What saints it will create—for the spiritual! What devils—for the carnal! And which will win in the end, saint or devil? I incline, with oscillation, to the saint. But I am sick and tired of inclinations and oscillations; I want to *know*, I *know* that the sun shines. I want to *know*—just at this moment I feel very near knowing, nearer than I ever have been in my whole life—that the world has been made all of a piece, and is being shaped by the Maker to one end, and that, the best.

"O, my dear Silanus, I am weary of these books. I must go out into the fresh air and see the sun. Books, books, books! I agree with Epictetus, who thinks that Chrysippus wrote some two hundred too many. I agree with John, too, who says, in effect, that not all the pens and paper in the world could draw the portrait of his master—or rather his friend, for 'friend,' not 'servant,' is the title at the end of the book. That reminds me, by the way, of a beautiful thought in this gospel—I mean that the author is 'the disciple whom Jesus loved'! As much as to say, 'Do you want to know Jesus? Then get a *friend* of his—some one *whom Jesus loved*—to introduce you. There is no other way. Not an impartial biographer—he is of no use—but a *friend*! And I think he means to hint, at the close of his little book, that there always will be, 'tarrying,' till Jesus comes again, a 'disciple whom Jesus loved,' to represent him to the world.

"That is most true. That is real insight, the insight of an artist and a prophet in. one. I can forgive John almost all his faults—

ambiguities, artificialities, statements of non-fact as fact, I can condone them all as orientalisms or Alexandrian Judaisms—for the sake of this one truth, that we cannot know the greatest of the departed great, save through a human being that has loved him and has been loved by him. This is the thought with which John ends and with which I will end. I wish to part friends with him. Indeed at this moment, for his sake, I could almost call myself an amateur Christian. But then I pull myself together and recognise that it only proves what I have said to you a score of times, and now repeat for the last time, that whereas we Romans are only coarse, clumsy, brutal Samnites, these Christians are the wiliest, kindest, and gentlest of retiarii.

"And that makes me think of old Hermas. You remember I told you of our last interview. It comes back to me while I am finishing this last dream. I always felt there was more in his face than I could understand. Now, after reading this gospel, I seem, just at this moment, to understand his face for the first time, quite well. The old man had in him the love of 'the disciple whom Jesus loved.' It had been breathed into his being. This it was that half fascinated me, shining out of his eyes as he silently left the room on that afternoon—to me unforgettable—when I dismissed him. What if I had not dismissed him? What if ."

These words were the last of a column. They were the last that Scaurus was ever to write. The next column was blank. At first I thought he had been again interrupted and had forgotten to finish the letter. But then I recollected with alarm that, quite contrary to custom, the cover had not been directed in his handwriting. I had thrown it hastily aside on the previous evening. Now I searched for it and my alarm was speedily justified. Inside was a short and hurried note from Marullus saying that my dear old friend had been struck suddenly with paralysis in the act of writing to me. A messenger (said Marullus) who happened to be at that moment waiting to carry Scaurus's letter, would carry at the same time Marullus's note. On the following day, whatever might happen, he would send a second letter by a special messenger.

It was now drawing towards evening. I hastened out to ascertain how soon a vessel, available for my purpose, would be leaving Nicopolis. Finding that I could start on the following day at noon, I determined not to wait for Marullus's second letter but to make preparations for an immediate return.

XXXV. — CLEMENS ON THE SACRIFICE OF CHRIST

SCAURUS, and not the fourth gospel, nor any other book, person, or thing, was uppermost in my mind, when, late in the evening, I hurried to the house of Justus to keep my engagement with Clemens. Two or three hours ago, I had been longing for this interview. Now I would willingly have avoided it. I seemed to see my old friend speechless on his bed in Tusculum, saying to me with his eyes, "Do not desert me. Do not go over to the enemy." Not till later did I feel that Scaurus could not have called Clemens "enemy."

"I am tired of books"—so Scaurus had written. So was I, quite tired. I wanted to think, not talk; or, if to talk, to talk about Scaurus, not about gospels or books of any sort. "How glad should I be to exchange this interview for five minutes' chat with old Marullus!"—that was my thought when I found myself, more than an hour after sunset, sitting face to face with Clemens.

I returned him the book—so precious to me yesterday—with some words of formal thanks. What should I say next? About the one subject that filled all my thoughts I felt no desire to talk to a stranger—"yes" (I said to myself) "a stranger to Scaurus, though a friend, a real friend, to me." Yet something had to be said. I began by excusing myself, at an absurd length, for being late. Clemens acknowledged the excuse with a slight inclination of the head. His face was questioning me, and his eyes were reading me. But he left it to me to speak, and to open our interview if I desired one.

Then I blundered out some absurd stuff—in the way of humour !—about the possibility that he might suppose me to have forgotten my engagement.

Clemens did not seem in the least ruffled or even surprised. After a pause, in which the questioning look gave place to one of sympathy, he said, very slowly and gently, "No, my dear friend, I could not suppose that. Nor could you think that I could suppose that. Some trouble, I perceive, has befallen you. You felt bound to keep your engagement with me, and you have done so. You did right. But you will not do right if you stay longer, put of courtesy to me, when your conscience tells you that it would be better for you to be alone."

When I entered the room, I had distinctly preferred to be alone. Even now, I so far desired solitude that I murmured some words of thanks for his consideration, and rose to go. But something kept me standing irresolute. I do not know what it was at first. Certainly it was not any thought about the new gospel. Perhaps it was my new friend's directness, truthfulness and insight, in discerning and brushing aside my pretence, and his kind and courteous way of forgiving it, that made me suddenly feel, "This is a man that Scaurus would have liked to know. This is a man that Scaurus would like me to know. He tells me to go if I feel that it will be 'better' for me to be alone. But will it be 'better '?"

It may have been this that checked my going. I do not know for certain. But I do know what decided me to stay. I suddenly saw Scaurus. He was in the library at Tusculum, with his back to me, at his writing-table, but not writing, half risen from his seat, and looking towards the door, which was slowly closing. As it closed, he turned and looked round at me, with such a sadness as I had never seen on his face except once or twice, when I had gone wrong and he was striving to lead me right. I knew what he meant, as well as if he had said the words aloud, "Hermas is gone, and I shall repent it through my life. Do not let your Hermas go!" I resumed my seat and tried to collect my thoughts.

It seemed to me now only right and natural that I should tell Clemens of Scaurus's illness and of my intention to leave Nicopolis on the morrow. He took my departure as a matter of course. Could he be of service, he asked, in making arrangements for my sailing? I assured him that everything had been done that was needful for that day. Then I told him how Scaurus had urged me to join Epictetus's classes, and that he wished me afterwards to join the army. Finding him interested and sympathetic, I gave him an account of my old friend's life, his affection for me, his love of research, his literary pursuits, and his study of Jewish as well as Greek literature, not omitting his early reading of the gospels, nor forgetting to tell him about old Hermas the Christian, his librarian. He listened with more and more attention. "I am not surprised," he said, "that you love so good a friend and so honest a man."

Presently I said, "I wonder whether it would be still possible and right for me to join the army, if" and there I stopped. "Dear friend," said he, "if that unmentioned thing were to come to pass, trust me that nothing would be possible or right for you against which your conscience cried out, and nothing wrong that your conscience permitted. Some might condemn your decision—whether to join the army or not to join. But you would not be bound by their condemnation. Your conscience would receive guidance. Those who follow on that unmentioned path do not follow with an 'if' Should that path be taken, it would be, not on conditions, but because of a friendly constraint. Let us not speak of that now. Tell me more about your friend." " I have his letter here," said I, "and would read it if you cared to hear it. But it deals freely, very freely, with the gospels. Once, at least, I think my old friend is unfair to them. It would perhaps pain you." "It would not pain but please me," said he. "I always like to hear honest, able, and educated men speak their minds freely about our Christian writings. The pity of it is, that we have hitherto had few such critics. If we had had them when the gospels were first written, perhaps they would have contained fewer things that may in after times cause some of the faithful to stumble."

So I began to read Scaurus's letter to him. At first I omitted portions here and there, either because they were personal, or because they might hurt the feelings of a Christian. Presently, halting in the middle of a bitter saying, I finished the sentence in my own way—somewhat awkwardly. Clemens smiled. "Pardon me," said he, "for interrupting you. I am not a master of styles. Yet, if I mistake not, those last words did not come from Aemilius Scaurus. If I am wrong, forgive me. But if I am right in thinking that you altered something to spare my feelings, then let me assure you again that it would trouble me that you should do this, even though the criticism came from the bitterest enemy of the Christians. As it is, I have learned already to esteem your friend as a genuine lover of truth, and one from whom I have even now learned some things and hope to learn more. The more you will allow me to learn (without giving pain to yourself) the better shall I be pleased." "Well then," said I, "we will talk about the letter afterwards. For the present, I will read on steadily without omitting a single word, unless you stop me." And so I did. Clemens listened intently, without stopping me, only he now and then, especially towards the end, expressed assent or interest, or sympathy, by a slight movement or inarticulate murmur; till we came to the last words, the uncompleted sentence, suggesting what might have happened on one memorable afternoon, if he had not dismissed a "disciple whom Jesus loved." This I did not read, but I placed the letter before him. "These," said I, "were his last words, the very last."

He read them, and turned away his face. I thought, and rightly, that he was feeling with me. But I am sure now that he was also praying for me, and for Scaurus too. For a time we sat in silence. I was the first to break it, expressing my sorrow that the story of the Syrophoenician woman should have led Scaurus to form what seemed to me a wrong conception of Christ. "But you see," replied Clemens, "he revolted from that wrong conception, or was ready to revolt from it, at the last moment of all. And I agree with you that, if he had approached that story with the preparation that Paul gave you, he would have regarded it as you did. I am sure Christ was never cruel to anyone. If He really uttered those seemingly cruel words to that sorrowful woman, He was cruel in word, only that He might be the more kind and the more helpful in deed. He intended this gospel to be preached to all the world, though He waited for the Father to teach Him the time and the manner of the preaching to the Gentiles."

"Is there anything in John's gospel," said I, "that resembles this story?" "There is a dialogue," he replied, "between Christ and a Samaritan woman, who is described as living in sin, just as you have suggested concerning the Syrophoenician. And Christ chides her, but with great gentleness, and finally reveals Himself to her as Messiah. It has occurred to me that this is one of the many instances where John steps in to remove a misunderstanding liable to be caused by some passage in Mark, which Luke omits."

Then he added, "I will talk with you, if you please, about the letter or the gospel or anything else, if you really desire it. But if you would wish to be alone with your own thoughts (as you well might wish), do not, I beseech you, stay longer. You have laid me under a debt by introducing me to a genuine lover of truth on whom the Light of the World has dawned, even though it may not be given to him to see the full day. May he find peace!"

I was quite willing to stay now. "Do you agree with Scaurus," said I, "that John alludes in parts of his gospel to the teaching of Epictetus?" "I feel sure," replied Clemens, "that John alludes to the doctrine of the Stoics and Cynics. Now Epictetus has been, for some years past, most widely known among all classes, rich, poor—yes, and slaves, too—as the representative of the Cynic doctrine. So that your friend seems to me likely to be right." "Scaurus," said I, "mentions self knowledge and God-knowledge as if the former were inculcated by Epictetus, the latter by John, in opposition. Is that so, in your opinion?" "Not quite," said he, "but nearly so. All the Stoics lay stress, as you know, on self-knowledge. Epictetus, perhaps more than most, teaches men to look for God within themselves. Luke also—alone of the evangelists—has one tradition of this kind, 'The kingdom of God is within you.' John, feeling that many were prevented thereby from looking for God out of themselves, laid stress on the latter. That is to say, John paraphrased Christ's teaching about 'the Father in heaven' in such a form that it should be more familiar to the Greeks, urging them to 'know God.' So Paul is said by Luke to have taken as his text on the Areopagus an inscription TO THE UNKNOWN GOD; and he tried to teach the philosophers that God could be 'known.' But neither Paul nor John would deny that self-knowledge, and the consciousness of our own sins, and the sense of our own burdens, are necessary if we are to have our burdens lightened, our sins forgiven, and our souls brought into the light of the glory of the knowledge of God."

" And as to the 'troubling' of Christ'," said I, "mentioned thrice in the fourth gospel, do you agree with Scaurus that there, too, the author is alluding to Epictetus?" "I do indeed," said he. "I did so from the first moment when I read the new gospel. Man is born to trouble as the sparks fly upward. We are born to be lifted up to heaven by troubles. But trouble of soul does not mean confusion or turbidness of soul. Trouble is on the surface, peace is beneath, peace that is deeper than the deepest of depths. In the world, says the Saviour, we shall have tribulation, and tribulation brings trouble with it. But He bids us be of good cheer amidst and beneath all our trouble, because He has overcome the world. Perhaps, however, John emphasizes this doctrine of 'trouble,' not out of hostility to the Cynic philosophy, but rather out of a friendly feeling to it, as much as to say, 'This notion of yours, that you must avoid "trouble," is the weak point in your teaching. It tends to lower you to the level of the Epicureans. And it gives you a false and unworthy notion of God, who is our Father, and who bears the troubles of His children'."

From that we passed to other matters, most of which I shall omit—details about the fourth gospel, about its authorship and about Scaurus's view, that it blended history with allegory. On some of these he thought that Scaurus might be correct. But he was doubtful as to the possibility of explaining, as Scaurus had suggested, the different order in which the evangelists place the purification of the Temple. "For," said he, "it seems to me scarcely possible that, within the time from Tiberius to Trajan, an evangelist should be led to change the order of such an event simply because of its order in some one book—because it was placed at what Gentiles might take to be the beginning (being really the end) of a Hebrew gospel." At the same time Clemens admitted that there was an astonishing difference of opinion among Christians as to the period of Christ's preaching, "and," said he, "instead of quoting statements or referring to historical facts, they often quote prophecies, or argue from the fitness of things. It is all very unsatisfactory."

Of this I afterwards had experience. For, after I had become a Christian, I found that some, even though they received the gospel of John, argued that Christ could only have preached for one year—because Isaiah contains the words, "to preach the acceptable year of the Lord "! On the other hand, the young Irenaeus, bitterly attacking this view, maintained that Christ must have preached till His fortieth or fiftieth year! As I have said above, I have actually heard him supporting this extraordinary supposition by appealing to the authority of the elders that had seen John!

Clemens therefore admitted that he could not feel certain as to the order of events in John's gospel. It might be, he said, that two events, mentioned in different parts of the gospel as taking place at, or before, a feast, and apparently at, or before, different feasts, might really have taken place at, or before, the same feast. Among several details in which he agreed with Scaurus, one was the narrative of the Walking on the Water. Concerning this he said that, according to John, the walking was not really on the water, any more than a city is really "*on* a sea" when it is said to lie "*on* the Aegean" or "*on* the Hadriatic." He also agreed with Scaurus as to the story about Peter plunging into the water to come to Christ, which might (he thought) explain Matthew's story, according to which Christ first walked on the water, and then Peter attempted to walk on it towards the Lord, but failed. Both these, he thought, might be metaphorical.

As regards what Scaurus had said concerning the ambiguity of many words and phrases in the fourth gospel, Clemens admitted it. "But," said he, "my conviction is that the writer did not use them thus for the mere purpose of being ambiguous, like the oracle 'Aio te, Aeacida.' I do not deny that he plays upon words, but so does Isaiah. He also repeats and varies phrases, but so do all the prophecies and the Psalms. Similarly he is often dark and obscure. But are there not obscurities also in Aeschylus, and Pindar, and in the deepest thoughts of Plato? And whence do these arise? Not surely from a desire to be ambiguous, but from the lawful feeling of a great poet, prompted to use strange language, and sometimes dark language, that is put into his mind to express strange and dark thoughts. So it is with John, at least in my judgment. And as to other parts, which seem artificial—as, for example, when he repeats things twice or thrice in a kind of refrain—I should plead in the same way that a poet, even when most inspired, follows rules. Aeschylus and Pindar do not break the laws of Greek metre. Well, Jewish tradition also has rules of its own, quite different from ours, and I believe John observes them."

Then he referred to Johns use of the word "*logos*." Scaurus had described John as leading on his readers from *logos* to *pathos*. Clemens admitted that this was true if *pathos* meant the affections and included that one affection in particular which we call "love." And he justified John's course. "For," said he, "if the Logos is related to God as word is to thought, must we not say that 'word' should include every expression of thought, and that the perfect Logos must be the expression of the perfect thought? And what thought can be more perfect than that which Scaurus himself suggests, in his similitude of a magnet attracting all things to itself and causing each attracted object to attract others, so that the multitudinous world is made one harmony? And in the region of the affections, what is this but the highest kind of love, as your friend himself testifies, binding men together in families, cities, nations, and destined, in the end, to unite all as citizens of the city of the universe, or children in the family of God?"

Then Clemens added, without any questioning from me, that he entirely concurred with Scaurus in his feeling that the miracles or signs of Christ, however far they might be literally true, would not be so convincing a proof of His greatness as the power of His Spirit to infuse peace and power, yes, and wisdom, and harmony of thought, into the minds of those who received Him. "I do not mean to assert," said he, "that all who receive Christ remain steadfast in Him. Many have fallen away through subtle temptations of the world and the flesh; some few, under persecution and the open cruelty of the devil. But as to these last I have noted this. Strong men have fallen while boasting 'We can endure every torture.' Weak women have stood fast confessing 'We can do nothing. Our strength is in the Lord. Our Saviour will stand fast for us.' Yes, that has been the great miracle, to see slaves changed to nobles, peasants and clowns to orators, fools become wise, and human beasts, not worthy to be called men—ape-like and wolf-like creatures—transmuted into citizens of the kingdom of God.

"And that reminds me of what I specially admired in your friend—the sagacity with which he penetrated to the root of the matter, declaring that our religion is, in reality, no religion at all (not at least what augurs or priests would call a religion) but only union with a personality, a Lord and Saviour and Friend, who is in us and in whom we are, 'a very present help in trouble.' We have no system of sacrifices. For He is our sacrifice offered up once visibly on the cross, and offering Himself up invisibly and continually in the hearts of His faithful disciples. We have no code of laws. For He is our law, uttered by Himself once to the ears of the disciples in the two commandments 'Love God' and 'Love thy neighbour,' when He showed them how to make all men 'neighbours'; and now He utters the same law to our hearts, every moment of our lives, giving us a strong desire to do that which is best for our 'neighbours,' and helping us to see what is best, and, seeing it, to do it."

When Clemens said, "He is our sacrifice," I thought of Paul's words, "Christ our Passover is sacrificed for us," and of "the blood of sprinkling" about which Scaurus had written.

And this led me to ask concerning that other tradition which (Scaurus had told me) was written in the fourth gospel alone, about blood and water issuing from Christ's side.

"That," said Clemens, "was the only passage in your friend's letter where I was strongly moved to ask you to stop reading that we might talk of it at once. His view was new to me. Yet I confess I had always found it difficult to explain how the writer could call on himself to testify to what he himself had asserted. If Aemilius Scaurus should prove right, that difficulty of mine would be removed. Moreover I cannot but admit that John, or any other disciple, would probably have been prevented by the soldiers from approaching to the cross close enough to distinguish the water from the blood flowing from His side. Yet it came on me as a shock to believe that this particular narrative—to which I attach great importance—was based on a vision. Now the shock is somewhat softened. I have been thinking over your friend's arguments. He is quite right in saying that in John's epistle, which may be called an epilogue to his gospel, the words 'He knoweth,' as expressed in this particular emphatic phrase, would mean 'Jesus knoweth.' The meaning may be the same here. Nevertheless, even if it is so, and even if the narrative describes a vision, I should still feel as certain as ever that this vision expressed the real eternal truth."

"What do you mean," I said, "by eternal truth?" "I mean this," replied Clemens, "that the sacrifice of Christ on the cross appears to me foreordained from eternity and destined to last to eternity, as the symbol of the fundamental law of the universe, what Scaurus calls the Law of the Magnet. Call it a dream, if you please. Then such is my dream. But I act on it, or try to act on it, as a reality. The Father gives His life to men in giving His Son to them. The life, says the scripture, is the blood. Some of our brethren would not scruple to say 'God gives His blood to men.' I would rather say God has been giving of His life to men from the time when man was first created—not only as a Father and a Mother, but also as a Servant, serving His servants, nursing His children, 'washing their feet' (so to speak) as a nurse does, and as Christ did. There are two spiritual realities, or, if you like, two metaphors, to express this spiritual reality. One is, that life or blood is to be infused, like new blood, into our veins. The other is, that in this life, or life-blood, we are also to bathe ourselves, that we may be born again. I know that this will seem to you and to many others an exaggerated, or (as I have heard it called) an 'unsavoury and distasteful similitude.' But these protests are outweighed, in my mind, by the faith and feeling of multitudes of simple devout Christians of the deepest and purest insight. One of these, a woman—the most inspired of all women known to me with holy wisdom—continually speaks of bathing herself in the blood of Christ crucified; and so do some of our most inspired poets. You have spoken to me of 'the constraining love of Christ.' One of our poets—a man experienced in troubles and knowing only too well what it is to feel forsaken of God—describes it thus in the person of Christ:—

'Mine is an unchanging love:
Higher than the heights above,
Deeper than the depths beneath,
Free and faithful, strong as death,'

Do not these words seem to you to come from the heart? Are they not heart-realities? Yet they are metaphors. Well, this same poet speaks of 'seeing by faith' the 'stream' supplied by Christ's flowing wounds.' Are such visions, or metaphors, or heart-realities, lightly to be discarded? Speaking for myself, I cannot give up this heart-fact—if I may so call it—for fact it is to me, whether seen by the material or by the spiritual eye. Some may think it to be spiritually false. For them it must be (in efficacy) false, even if it were historically true. For me it is true."

He checked himself, and then continued, "Do not suppose, dear brother and fellow-seeker after truth, that I expect all others to see the truth in the same form in which I see it. Only I should hope to induce them to see the same truth in *some* form. See here these words"—and he took up a scroll and showed them to me—"'Every wise man is a ransom for the bad.' Do they remind you of anything?" "Yes," said I, "they are like the saying in Mark and Matthew, 'The Son of man came to give his soul a ransom for many.' Luke omits those words." "He does," said Clemens. "Luke has 'I am among you as one that serveth.' John combines the two views. For first he represents Jesus as girt with a napkin like a servant pouring forth water in a basin and washing the feet of the disciples; and then he represents Him as pouring forth His blood and water for their souls."

Then Clemens told me that the words "Every wise man is a ransom for the bad" were written by Philo of Alexandria, who, though a Jew, was also a philosopher, and he showed me a similar passage in the same writer, to the effect that the good and worthy and wise are both the physicians and the ransoms of every community in which they exist. Then he took up Ezekiel and read to me the vision of the dry bones in the valley, and how they come together into living bodies, being quickened by the breath of the Lord. Next he turned to Greek literature, touching on the old allegory of Amphion,. whose music was so sweet that the very stones were constrained by it to come together in unity building up the walls of a great city.

"Should we be wrong," said Clemens, "in saying that all these metaphors (to which others might be added) from various nations and literatures—about 'harmony,' and 'service,' and 'ransom,' and 'blood,' and 'breath'—point to one deep truth, not exaggerated by Philo, that the less are purified by the greater, and that the greater are intended to sacrifice their independence and to come together with the less, in order to create cities and nations, which are the larger families that lead men towards the Fatherhood of God? No doubt, the greater are also purified by the less. Every community is built up and bound together by the self-sacrifice of all. And this binding together implies a purification of all, a cutting away of excessive protuberances, a purging away of selfish, isolating, schism-making qualities, so that each soul may take its place in the wall of the City of Concord. But still, as a rule, the less are purified by the greater; the most selfish by the least selfish; families by the father and the mother; peoples by their true princes, priests, and prophets. Prince, priest, prophet, each according to his several gift, washes the feet of his inferiors, and spends his life to increase and ennoble theirs. Looking back to our childhood, do we not recognise this, as a matter of our own experience? How then can we call God Father, and yet refuse to believe that He may be as loving as a human father, and that God's children may be purified by God Himself, giving His own blood in the blood of His Son as a ransom for the sinful souls of men?"

As he said these words, he stood up, extending his hand; "I have allowed myself," he said, "to keep you too long, when you have many things to do. Once or twice, intending to check myself, I have broken loose again. I will not a third time. Only this word, this one additional word. Believe me, Aemilius Scaurus was right, in saying 'The religion of the Christians is a person.' But your friend went on to say '*and nothing more*,' I should prefer to say the same thing differently. 'Our religion is a person—*and nothing less*'."

XXXVI. – SILANUS BECOMES A CHRISTIAN

IT was very late, but I was unwilling to say farewell. During the last two or three hours, Clemens had in some strange way so associated himself with my thoughts of Scaurus that I now began to feel as though, in parting from my new friend, I should be parting from the old one—whose living self I should perhaps not see again in Tusculum and whose likeness I was leaving in Nicopolis. But Clemens would not resume his seat. Quoting Scaurus's words with a kindly smile, "It takes a great deal," he said, "to make you 'tired of books '." "Perhaps my old friend would not have been tired," I replied, "if he had had you as his interpreter. I wish he could have been present with us to-night." "I shall always think of him as a friend," said Clemens, "for your sake, for his own sake, and for truth's sake."

Then he asked me at what hour I was to set sail, to-morrow, "or rather," said he, "to-day, for it is long past midnight." "About noon," I replied. "Long before noon," said he, "I must be at some distance from Nicopolis on a visit to some sick folk. But I expect to be returning, by way of the wood where we first conversed together, just in time to catch sight of your vessel before it disappears round the cape. So you must think of me then as wishing you over again from a distance the good things that I now wish you face to face." "When we last parted," said I, as we clasped hands at the open door, "you wished me peace. Wish it me again." "May peace," he said, "be multiplied to you!" Then, drawing me gently towards himself, after standing for a moment as though unable to speak, "that peace," he said, "which passes understanding!"

When I returned to my lodging I found a messenger awaiting me with a note from Marullus. Scaurus was still living, though unconscious. The doctors thought it possible, though not probable, that be might recover for a short time. "I fear," said Marullus, "that, by the time you receive these lines, my dear patron will be no more. If you wish to come, in the slight hope of seeing him, you will do well to come at once." I was prepared for this, so that it made no difference in my arrangements. These were nearly completed except for writing letters of farewell to friends in Nicopolis.

The sun was well above the horizon before I began the letter that I had reserved for the last—my farewell to Epictetus. To several acquaintances I had been scribbling away, fluently enough. Nor had I been at a loss for what to say to the one or two more intimate friends to whose kindness I was indebted. But, all the time, there had been in my mind an undercurrent of anxious questioning as to what I should say to the man to whom I owed most. Should I explain? Should I confess? Should I distinguish between what I had received from him for which I was his debtor, and what I had not been able to receive so that I could not call myself indebted? To what end? Whatever might happen in the future, I could never cease to be grateful to him for having raised me to a higher sense of a life above the level of the Beast, and for stimulating me to follow and revere the Man. What though a new ideal of the Man had been presented to me? Did that make me less Epictetus's debtor? Nay, did it not possibly increase my debt, because, but for him, I might not have taken—if ever I should be proved to have taken—the path that led towards a, higher and nobler goal?

I wrote, tore up, re-wrote, corrected, re-corrected, and again rewrote. There was a want of directness in all my attempts, and they all ended in tearing up. At last I said, "I will try to write as my Master himself would have written." That made my letter of the briefest. After explaining my sudden departure, and thanking him for his teaching, "I am your debtor," I wrote, "and always shall be." I was on the point of adding, "If ever I possess myself, I shall owe myself to you." But the words struck me as familiar. Then I remembered something like them in the Epistle to Philemon: "I say not unto thee how that thou owest to me even thine own self." "Could I say with strict Epictetian truth that I owed to Epictetus as much as Philemon owed to Paul? I re-wrote it thus: "If ever I possess myself I shall in large measure owe myself to you." That had the disadvantage of being a little longer, but the advantage of being quite true. Sealing the letter that I might not be tempted to alter it again, I threw myself down for two or three hours of rest.

A little before noon my servant roused me. All was ready,, and we went down at once to the quay. Besides the usual bustle—sailors, fishermen, merchants, passengers mostly in a hurry—there was some dispute (I know not what, but I think it was among the fishermen). This added to the confusion. Not many blows were interchanged, but there was no lack of threats, imprecations, scurrilous jests, and obscene abuse. As I was making my way through the crowd, some one touched me on the shoulder. It was my Epicurean friend, Apronius Rufus, whom I had last seen in the little village of Lycus, scattering nuts and figs to make the schoolboys scramble. I had caught sight of him, a minute or two before, lounging in a corner and looking on at the quarrelsome crowd; but being in no mood for his jests I had turned aside in the vain hope that he would not see me. As soon as he overtook me, he began in his usual fashion, "What brings you here at this hour, most serious Cynic? A truant humour, I fear. For it is lecture time, or at all events not much past: and Epictetus gives long lessons. Yet no. You are no truant. Truants don't look so serious. You have come here as a philosopher, to see life as it is, and to set up as a heretic. You come from books to things; from ideals to facts. Good! Now begin to learn! Look at these bipeds! Look, and listen! Up above, in your schoolroom, they were 'sons of God,' were they not! Look, then, at that son of God hitting his brother son of God in the eye! Listen to those two daughters of God and their harmonious antiphon!"

I was vexed, but let him talk on, as being the best means of getting myself free from him without explanation; and he, following close behind me, kept pouring his jests into my ear, till, I suppose, he got a clearer view of my face. For he suddenly checked himself, saying, "But, my dear Silanus, pardon me if something is really wrong. You would not, I am sure, let my idle talk pain you. Your servant is here with baggage. I fear some bad news is taking you from Nicopolis." Then I briefly explained.

He had some slight acquaintance with Scaurus and was instantly and sincerely apologetic. "I was a fool," said he, "not to have noticed that something was amiss. Really I am grieved. And Scaurus, too! That fine old soldier! Often have I heard my father speak of his splendid service in Moesia. Well, Silanus, there are humanities as well as philosophies. Believe me, I feel with you. Farewell! Forgive me as sincerely as I condemn myself" He pressed my hand, and I his. He was a good fellow at heart and died in Syria, a soldier's death—such as Scaurus would have approved and no Cynic could have censured.

In a few minutes, we were outside the port, seeing from a distance (without hearing) the bustle on the quay. It was not an unpleasing scene —now. A few minutes more, and the whole of the city stood out as a bright picture in a framework of fields. Presently Nicopolis was receding and lessening. Hills rose up behind. The frame was becoming the picture and Nicopolis a small part in it. I paced the deck, this way and that, turning in my mind all that had befallen me since I had gazed on these same scenes in reversed order, arriving from Italy. How few days ago in time! How many ages ago in thought and experience!" What strange things," I exclaimed, "what marvellous things have happened to me! Am I not a changed man?" Then a sense of unreality began to creep over me. "Am I not, after all, the same Silanus, recovering from a dream? Have these 'strange things' been real things? Have they not been mere pictures—pictures of the mind, phantasms, dreams, from which I, the old Silanus, am now awaking to find myself just what I was in old days when I was wasting my time in Rome?"

I looked back on Nicopolis and it was now little more than a hamlet, and the quay was a dot. But it still loomed large on my mind. I had spoken of "phantasms" and "dreams." But I could not think of the human scene in the harbour as a "dream." Only too life-like were those bipeds—noisy, scurrilous, vile, obscene! How unworthy of the bright and glorious sunlight in which all things were bathed at that moment of full noon—all things in heaven and earth! How glorious was everything except man! Yes, everything except man! Rufus spoke in jest, but did he not speak the truth? What were those "sons of God" on the quay? Surely, surely, they were "sons of clay," mere puppets to play with and break! To this day I cannot tell why just at this moment so strong a temptation should have so suddenly seized me. But seize me it did. I write it as it happened, that others may take heart if the same thing should happen to them. It was God's way of dealing with me, suffering me to be almost cast down by evil that He might lift me up for good.

Feeling the evil coming, I tried at first to strengthen myself with the sayings of my Master, Epictetus, "See then that thou do nothing as a beast. Else thou hast lost the Man. Thou hast not fulfilled the promise of the Man," and again, "Man is a being that has nothing more sovereign than his will. He has all other things in subjection to this." Then I thought of Man as the Psalmist describes him, saying to God, "Thou hast put all things under his feet... yea, and the beasts of the field," and how the Christians regarded this as meaning that Man was to triumph over sin.

But, against these hopeful thoughts, there rose up, first, the confessions of Epictetus that he had never succeeded in producing a Man of this kind, nor anything approaching to it; and then the words of the other Psalm, "Man being in honour hath no understanding, but is like unto the beasts that perish." I longed to believe the good Voices, but truth seemed to compel me to believe the bad Voices. Worst and strongest of all, there rose up recollections of my own evil deeds, words, and thoughts, from childhood upwards, and they strengthened the Voices of evil. I could not at that moment recall the brighter and better side of my own life. I could not remind myself how different a man in a crowd may be for a moment from the same man in his home and at his work during his daily life. It seemed to me that I ought to be on my guard against hoping contrary to facts. Was not Glaucus right in taunting me with "self-deceiving," which I called "believing"? Was it not the plain and manifest fact that the Beast was Lord over the Man?

Again and again this question put itself before me, as though from the mouth of the Beast, saying, "Am I not your Lord? Can you honestly deny it?" And at that instant I could not deny it. Never had I felt so weak, so forsaken—abandoned by all the hopes that had been lately gathering round me, more hopeless than if I had never entertained them.

But just when I seemed to be touching the bottom of the lowest depth, I received a sense of the nearness of 'help. If I could not trust in the Good, at least I could rebel against the Evil. What though the Beast be Lord of mankind? "At least," I exclaimed, "there are those who will not be his slaves—Epictetus, Scaurus, my father, others known to me, multitudes unknown. Rather than submit to the Beast, it is better to be on the conquered side—along with the good, and worthy and noble. It is better, yes much better, to be on the side of the Man crushed down, trampled on, destroyed!" Then a great longing fell on me that the Man thus crushed down and destroyed by the Beast might prove to be not destroyed in the end, for such a Man, if only He existed, seemed the only fit object of worship for mankind. Yes, victorious or defeated, He alone was to be worshipped. "Whom have I in heaven but thee? And there is none upon earth that I desire in comparison with thee, thou FORSAKEN SON OF GOD!"

As I uttered these words I remembered where I had first uttered them—on the hills yonder, while I was thinking of Glaucus's troubles just before I met my new friend Clemens. That made me think of him and of his promise to wait on the hill, and look on my vessel as it vanished, and "wish me well." I glanced back over the stern just in time to see our little coppice disappearing. "Clemens," I said, "is there. Clemens is praying for me." With that, there came back to me all he had said about the power of the FORSAKEN to help those who felt "forsaken"; and about the "cross," as the real throne whereon the Son of man reigns as the real king and subjects all things to Himself. In that moment I understood how both the Psalms were true: "Man being in honour—*as the world counts honour*—is like unto the beasts that perish." But "man being in honour—*as God counts honour*—is uplifted on the throne of suffering and reigns over those for whom He suffers and whom He redeems." A sudden conviction fell upon me that here at last I had the light that makes all things clear, and I cried from the deepest depth of my being, "Whom have I in heaven but thee, O thou forsaken one that art NOT FORSAKEN? And there is none upon earth that I desire in comparison with thee. Make no long tarrying, O my Helper and my Redeemer!"

All this, which takes time to describe, passed in the twinkling of an eye, and then something befell me that I cannot exactly describe. Only I know that it was no act of reason. Nor was it vision. It was more like feeling. The arm of the Lord seemed to lift me up and carry me to something that I felt to be the Cross. Then the thought of the Cross sent down upon me the thought of an overwhelming flood of the mighty love and pity of God, the Father of the fatherless and Servant of the meanest of His servants, descending on my soul from the side of the Saviour and bathing me in His purifying blood, creating me anew in the eternal Son. And thus, at last, after so many delays, refusals, and resistances, willingly led captive out of the dominion of darkness and fear and sin, I was carried as a little child into the joy of the family of God.

When I reached Tusculum, Scaurus was in his grave. He had died on the day when I left Nicopolis, and about noon. I could not discover among his papers any last instructions, or indications of any wishes connected with the subject of his last letter. Only I found a paper with "For Hermas's tomb" on it. Below was written in large characters IN PEACE. I asked Marullus whether he understood this. He said that on the morning of the last day of his active and conscious life the old man had gone (with Marullus's aid, for he was very feeble) to see the tomb he had erected for Hermas in years gone by. After standing for some time silent he repeated aloud the last words of the inscription, "For memory's sake." "That," said he, "is not enough." Then, as they walked home, he said, "Hermas would have liked IN PEACE. There is room. See that those words are added." I saw that they were added. I also placed them on Scaurus's own tomb.

For the rest, in the years that followed—forty-five in number—nothing has befallen me that would greatly interest my readers. I became a soldier. Many of the brethren condemned me for it. But when the war broke out in Illyria I felt that, although a Christian, I had no right to cease to become a Roman, or to spare my blood, if need arose, in defence of the peace of the Empire. In doing this, I was glad to think that I had fulfilled Scaurus's last wish. Clemens also supported me.

From him I received several letters before I went to Illyria. Soon afterwards, he passed away in Corinth, but not before he had done for Glaucus the same service that he did for me. His first letter told me that he had seen my vessel at noontide from the hills above Nicopolis, and that he had kept his promise of "wishing me well." He always called me brother; and no brother could have been more brotherly. But assuredly he was more than that. Paul sowed the seed of the gospel in my heart, but it was the spirit of Clemens that helped to quicken and to foster it. He was my father in the faith.

Yet Scaurus, too, was a helper—helper in deed even when opposing in word—guiding me indirectly towards the City of Truth. I have read Apologies for the Christian faith written by worthy men—Justin for example and others. But they have not helped me towards Christ as Scaurus did. They have been special pleaders for their religion, and sometimes great manipulators of words and arguments. But what Scaurus said, even in dispraise of the gospels, was often so qualified by praise, admiration, yes, and love, of the character of the Saviour, that it had much more effect with me than the arguments of Justin afterwards had, when I came to know them. Moreover Scaurus was such a lover of truth, and so quick and keen to detect an untruth, that in meeting his attacks upon the gospels I felt I had met the worst. I doubt not that he has found peace in one of the "many mansions." If I may not call him my father in the faith, yet certainly he was the kindest of stepfathers, helping me to the living Truth by causing me to love all truth, and indirectly strengthening my feet in the path towards the Saviour by not suffering me to walk too soon.

And you, too, good Epictetus, truth-loving, keen Epictetus—I will not say "kind Epictetus," not at least always kind in word, though always good at heart even when most bitter in word—always fervid against falsehood, always zealous with a fiery zeal for that strange cold aspect of a "Father of all" in which you placed your trust and strove to make us place ours: what shall I say of you and how thank you for the help you gave me ! How often in Rome and Tusculum, how often on night watches in Illyria, Moesia, and the East, have I seen your face, dear Master, as I saw it for the last time in Nicopolis, leaving you without bidding you farewell, spying on you unfairly through the open door, and detecting you in the act of breaking the rules of your own philosophy by feeling trouble, real trouble, for a sorely troubled disciple ! Epictetus in trouble, yes, Epictetus in trouble, that is how I shall remember you to my dying day, as seen in the moment when I trusted your teaching least and loved you most, when you dropped the veil of your philosophy to show me your real human heart—my "tutor" to bring me to Christ.

THE END

Made in the USA
Columbia, SC
03 October 2022